'Good fun . . . vivid action-thriller moments'
Metro

'Admirably informed . . . riveting . . . an engaging summer
read . . . except that after reading *The Swarm* you
may want to avoid beaches forever'
Globe and Mail

'An effervescent cocktail of adventure'
Der Spiegel

'A massively good read. A gripping marine biodiversity thriller
the like of which I have not seen since *Jaws*'
Dr James Mallet, Professor of Biological Diversity,
University College London

'A gripping thriller starring nature unleashed'
Stern

'Frank Schätzing competes with the likes of Michael Crichton'
Brigitte

About the author

Frank Schätzing has enjoyed a highly successful career in marketing as
well as writing several bestselling historical crime novels. *The Swarm*
(*Der Schwarm*) topped Germany's bestseller charts for over two years,
selling over two million copies in its original German.

THE SWARM

A Novel of the Deep

Frank Schätzing

Translated by Sally-Ann Spencer

HODDER

Copyright © 2004 by Verlag Kiepenheuer & Witsch, Köln
English Language Translation Copyright © 2006 by Sally-Ann Spencer

Originally published in German in 2004 as *Der Schwarm* by Verlag Kiepenheuer & Witsch
First published in Great Britain in 2006 by Hodder & Stoughton
A division of Hodder Headline

The publication of this work was supported by a grant from the Goethe-Institut.

The right of Frank Schätzing to be identified as the Author
of the Work has been asserted by him in accordance with
the Copyright, Designs and Patents Act 1988.

A Hodder & Stoughton Book

6

A CIP catalogue record for this title is available from the British Library

ISBN 978-0-340-92075-6
ISBN 0-340-92075-0

Typeset in Monotype Janson by Hewer Text UK Ltd, Edinburgh
Printed and bound by Mackays of Chatham Ltd, Chatham, Kent

Hodder Headline's policy is to use papers that are natural, renewable
and recyclable products and made from wood grown in sustainable
forests. The logging and manufacturing processes are expected to
conform to the environmental regulations of the country of origin.

Hodder & Stoughton Ltd
A division of Hodder Headline
338 Euston Road
London NW1 3BH

Love, deeper than the ocean.
For Sabina

ACKNOWLEDGEMENTS

Most books numbering over 800 pages, crammed full of scientific fact and learning, draw on the wisdom of a host of clever people, and this book is no exception. I would especially like to thank:

Prof Uwe A. O. Heinlein, Miltenyi Biotec for lessons about the yrr and thinking genes, and for drops of enlightenment found at the bottom of a good glass of wine.

Dr Manfred Reitz, Institute for Molecular Biotechnology, Jena, for insights into extraterrestrial life and for inspirational yrr-sense.

Hans-Jürgen Wischnewski, former cabinet minister, for packing half a century of experience into three hours, and for a thoroughly sociable meeting with poppy-seed cake.

Clive Roberts, Managing Director, Seaboard Shipping Co. Vancouver, for the advice of an expert/father-in-law and simply for being himself!

Bruce Webster, Seaboard, for his time and patience and for painstakingly answering twenty-six rambling questions.

Prof Gerhard Bohrmann, GEOMAR Kiel and the University of Bremen, for adding his own special fizz to the hydrates and for playing a leading role in methane fact and fiction.

Dr Heiko Sahling, University of Bremen, for providing dissected, fixed and all other manner of worms, and for taking part.

Prof Erwin Suess, GEOMAR, for a sun-lit lunch in the depths of the ocean and for his literary presence.

Prof Christopher Bridges, University of Düsseldorf, for assorted moments of illumination in the lightless depths.

Prof Wolfgang Fricke, Technical University of Hamburg-Harburg, for two incredibly constructive days spent working on destruction.

Prof Stefan Krüger, Technical University of Hamburg-Harburg, for tirelessly filtering out the errors on board the sinking ships.

Dr. Bernhard Richter, Germanischer Lloyd, for contributing via telephone to the productive disaster-based summit with Dr Fricke.

Prof Giselher Gust, Technical University of Hamburg-Harburg, for her incisive thoughts and for a veritable Circumpolar Current of ideas.

Tobias Haack, Technical University of Hamburg-Harburg, for labouring intellectually inside the various boats.

Stefan Endres for whale-watching, real Indians and large mammals leaping over small planes.

Torsten Fischer, Alfred-Wegener-Institute Bremerhaven, for authorizing a last-minute research trip to a research vessel.

Holger Fallei for a dry-dock *Polarstern* expedition that was anything but dry.

Dr Dieter Fiege, Senckenberg Research Institute, Frankfurt, for a day in which the worm turned – in the most constructive possible way.

Björn Weyer, defender of the fleet, for his readiness to collaborate with the enemy – on a purely fictional level.

Peter Nasse for providing invaluable contacts, for always being willing to help, and for the pleasure of one day seeing him on screen.

Ingo Haberkorn, Federal Criminal Police Office Berlin, for his in-depth crisis management of non-human atrocities and crimes.

Uwe Steen, PR division of the Cologne police force, for his help in answering the question as to who and what would respond when and how in the time of the yrr.

Dieter Pittermann for opening up the route to oil platforms and to the scientific side of Trondheim, and generally for *håper det er til hjelp*.

Tina Pittermann for establishing the line of communication to her father, for her grandma's books, and for waiting patiently for the return of said books.

Tina's grandma for the books.

Paul Schmitz for photos, beard transplants, two years of doing without music and the faultless recommendation: *never get old!*

Jürgen Muthmann for his insights into Peruvian fishing, for being patient with writers who don't like to fly, and for always being close in spite of the distance.

Olaf Petersenn, my trusty editor at Kiepenheuer & Witsch, for finally adding the word *cut* to my vocabulary.

Helge Malchow, publisher, for engaging in a leap of faith and for publishing the longest book in the history of Kiepenheuer & Witsch.

Yvonne Eiserfey, who cast her expert eye over the original German edition for splling mstakes and typos.

Jürgen Milz, my friend and business partner, for all his understanding and for his ability to keep a small ship afloat despite the hefty swell.

My gratitude as well to everyone at Hodder & Stoughton, especially my editor Nick Sayers, his assistant Anne Clarke and my publicist Henry Jeffreys. An extra thank you is due to Sally-Ann Spencer, who did more than 'just' translating *The Swarm* fabulously, to Loma Slater, for proofreading, and to Hazel Orme, for copyediting.

My sincere thanks also to Cologne's long-serving mayor Norbert Burger for putting me in touch with Hans-Jürgen Wischnewski, to Hans-Peter Buschheuer for writing to Ben Wisch, to Claudia Dambowy for medical advice, to Jürgen Streich for supplying reading material on Greenpeace, to Hejo Emons for the loan of thrilling and informative deep-sea films, for Jochen Cerhak for more of the same, and especially to Wahida Hammond for all the many kindnesses – it was about time that was said!

A special thank-you is due to my parents Brigitte and Rolf Schätzing, who can take the credit for any good points I may have, and who are always there for me, and have steered me through calm and troubled waters, always choosing the right course, even in the fog.

In the great cycle of life on Earth the end is always also the beginning. And following the same neat logic, my biggest thank-you is saved until last. In the same way as I start and end each day of my life with the most wonderful thing I could wish for, I end and begin these acknowledgements with the love of my life. According to some people, Sabina is my secret editor; others see her as my great good fortune. Both interpretations are right. This book, my love, was written for you.

hishuk ish ts'awalk
Nuu-chah-nulth tribe, Vancouver Island

PROLOGUE

14 January

Juan Narciso Ucañan went to his fate that Wednesday, and no one even noticed.

A few weeks later the circumstances surrounding his sudden disappearance sent shockwaves around the globe, but Ucañan's name wasn't mentioned. He was one of many. Too many. What he'd experienced in the early hours of that morning had been going on elsewhere all over the world. The parallels were striking – once you knew what had happened, and only Ucañan did. Maybe the fisherman, with his simple way of seeing things, had even sensed the more complex connections, but in the absence of his evidence, the mystery went unsolved. Neither he nor the Pacific Ocean on the Huanchaco coast in the north of Peru gave anything away. Like the fish he caught in his lifetime, Juan Narciso Ucañan stayed silent. When he next showed up, he was just a statistic. No one had time to wonder about his whereabouts: events had entered a new and graver phase.

Not that anyone had ever shown much interest in him anyway, even before 14 January.

At least, that was how Ucañan saw it. He'd never been able to reconcile himself with his village's reincarnation as an international beach resort. For the tourists, Huanchaco was a time-forgotten paradise where locals went fishing in old-fashioned boats. But what use was that to him? To own a fishing-boat at all was old-fashioned. These days, most of his countrymen earned their living on factory trawlers or in the fishmeal and fish-oil industries. Peru's fish stock was dwindling, but its fishing industry was still one of the largest in the world, on a par with Chile, Russia, the US and parts of Asia. Even the threat of El Niño hadn't stopped the coastal city of Huanchaco sprawling out in every direction, the last preserves of nature sacrificed to make way for row after row of hotels. In the end nearly everyone had profited one way or another. Only

Ucañan was left with nothing, just his boat, a *caballito de totora*, or 'reed pony', as the admiring conquistadors had called the distinctive craft. But the way things were going, the pretty little vessels would soon be gone too.

The new millennium had decided to pick on Ucañan.

His emotions were already starting to get the better of him. At times he felt as though he was being punished – by El Niño, which had plagued Peru since the beginning of history and that he was helpless to prevent, and by the environmentalists, whose talk of overfishing had set the politicians searching for a culprit, until in the end they realised they were looking for themselves. So they'd shifted their focus from the fisheries to Ucañan, who couldn't be held responsible for the environmental mess. He hadn't asked for the floating factories, or for the Japanese and Korean trawlers lurking on the 200-mile boundary, waiting to tow away the fish. None of this was Ucañan's fault, but even he no longer believed it. That was the other thing he couldn't help feeling – guilty. As though he was the one who'd pulled millions of tonnes of mackerel and tuna from the sea.

He was twenty-eight years old and one of the last of his kind.

His five elder brothers all worked in Lima, and thought he was a fool because he clung to a boat no better than a surfboard, waiting doggedly in deserted waters for the mackerel and bonito to return. 'You won't find life among the dead,' they told him. But it was his father who worried Ucañan. The old man was nearly seventy and had set sail every day, right up until a few weeks previously. Now Ucañan the elder no longer went fishing. Bedridden, his face covered with blotches, he had a nasty cough and seemed to be losing his mind. Juan Narciso clung to the hope that by continuing the family tradition he could keep the old man alive.

For over a thousand years Ucañan's people, the Yunga and the Moche, had been fishing in reed boats. Long before the Spanish arrived, they had settled along the Peruvian coast from the northern reaches to modern-day Pisco, supplying the immense metropolis of Chan Chan with fish. Back then the area had been rich in *wachaques*, coastal marshes fed by fresh water from underground springs. Vast quantities of reed grass had grown there – the *totora* that Ucañan and the other remaining fishermen still used to make their *caballitos*, in the manner of their forebears. It required skill and inner calm. There were no other boats quite like them. Measuring three to four metres long, with an upward-curving prow and

4

light as a feather, they were practically unsinkable. In days gone by thousands of *caballitos* had cut through the waves of the 'Golden Fish' coast, named at a time when even the worst catches brought more fish than Ucañan could ever dream of.

Eventually the marshes had vanished and so, too, the reeds.

At least you could count on El Niño. Every few years around Christmas time the trade winds would slacken and the cool Humboldt Current would warm up, destroying the feed and scattering the hungry mackerel, bonito and sardines. Ucañan's forefathers had called it El Niño – the Christ-child. Sometimes it was content just to shake things up, but every fourth or fifth year it would wreak God's vengeance on the people as though it was trying to wipe them from the Earth. Whirlwinds, thirty times the normal rainfall and murderous mudslides – on each occasion hundreds were killed. El Niño came and went, as it always had done. No one welcomed it, but they managed to get by. These days, though, even prayers couldn't help them: the nets that robbed the Pacific of its riches were wide enough to capture twelve jumbo jets at once.

Maybe, thought Ucañan, as his *caballito* bobbed up and down on the swell, maybe I am a fool. Foolish and guilty. Guilty like the rest of them for trusting in a patron saint who'd never done anything about El Niño, the fisheries or international law.

In the old days, he thought, we had shamans in Peru. Ucañan knew the stories about what the archaeologists had discovered in the pre-Columbian temples near the city of Trujillo, behind the Pyramid of the Moon. Ninety skeletons had been found there, men, women and children, killed with a blow to the head or stabbed with a spear. In a desperate attempt to stop the flood waters of AD 560 the high priests had sacrificed the lives of ninety to their gods, and El Niño had gone.

Whom would they have to sacrifice to stop the overfishing?

Ucañan shivered. He was a good Christian: he loved Christ and St Peter, the patron saint of fishermen. He always put his heart and soul into the festival of San Pedro, when a wooden effigy of the saint was paddled by boat from village to village. And yet . . . In the morning the churches were full, but the real fires burned at night. Shamanism was as strong as ever – but how could any god help them when even the Christ-child refused to intervene? Trying to control the forces of nature was exhausting enough, apparently, without attempting to cure the fishermen's latest woes. That was a matter for the politicians and lobbyists.

Ucañan squinted up at the sky.

It was going to be a beautiful day.

At moments like this, north-western Peru looked picture-perfect. There hadn't been a cloud for days. The surfers weren't up yet. Ucañan and a dozen or so other fishermen had set off some thirty minutes earlier, paddling their *caballitos* in the darkness over the undulating waves. The sun was slowly starting to peep out from behind the mist-shrouded mountains, bathing the sea in its pastel yellow light. Only moments before the vast expanse of water had looked silver; now it turned a delicate blue. In the distance you could just make out the silhouettes of mighty cargo ships as they headed for Lima.

Untouched by the beauty of first light, Ucañan reached behind him and felt for his *calcal*, the traditional red net used by *caballito* fishermen. It was a few metres long and tipped with hooks of varying sizes. He inspected the closely woven mesh, squatting upright on his little reed boat. There were no seats inside a *caballito* – you had to straddle the boat or crouch on top – but there was plenty of space at the stern for stowing nets and other equipment. Ucañan balanced his paddle diagonally in front of him. Traditional paddles made of split guayaquil cane had fallen out of use elsewhere in Peru. His belonged to his father, and Juan Narciso had brought it with him so the old man would sense the energy with which he thrust it through the water. Every evening since his father had fallen ill he had laid the paddle alongside him, placing his right hand over it, so that the old man could feel it was still there – the ancient tradition and the core of his life.

He hoped his father knew what he was holding: he no longer recognised his son.

Ucañan finished inspecting the *calcal*. He had already looked it over on dry land, but nets were precious and worth the extra attention. Its loss would mean the end for him. He might have been defeated in the bidding war for the Pacific's remaining riches, but he had no intention of jeopardising what was left to him with sloppiness or by turning to drink. He couldn't bear the crushed look on the faces of those fishermen who had left their boats and nets to rot. Ucañan knew it would kill him if he were to glimpse it on himself.

He glanced around. The flotilla that had set sail with him that morning had spread out in both directions, now more than a kilometre from the shore. For once the little ponies weren't bobbing up and down:

6

the water was almost perfectly still. Over the next few hours the fishermen would sit and wait, some patiently, others with resignation. In time they were joined by a few other boats – larger craft made of wood – while a trawler motored past, heading out to sea.

Ucañan watched as the men and women lowered their nets into the water, securing them to their boats with rope. He hesitated. The round red buoys drifted on the surface, shining brightly in the sunshine. He knew he should get started, but instead he thought of the last few days' fishing.

A few sardines were all he'd caught.

He watched the trawler disappear into the distance. El Niño had paid them a visit this winter too, but it had been harmless by comparison. There was another side to El Niño when it was like that – a brighter, friendlier one. Normally the Humboldt Current was too cold for the yellowfin tuna and hammerhead sharks, but warmer water would lure them in, guaranteeing a Christmas feast. Of course, the smaller fish all ended up in the bellies of the big ones rather than in the fishermen's nets, but you couldn't have it all. Anyone who ventured out a bit further on a day like today stood a good chance of bringing home a nice fat specimen.

Idle thoughts. *Caballitos* couldn't go that far. As a group they some-times ventured ten kilometres from shore – there was safety in numbers. The little reed ponies had no trouble coping with the swell: they rode on the crest of the waves. The real problem was the current. In rough conditions, when the wind was blowing out to sea, you needed good muscles to get your vessel back to shore.

Some fishermen didn't make it.

Ucañan crouched stock-still on the woven reed of his boat. His back was straight. They'd begun their vigil at daybreak, but the shoals wouldn't come today either. He scanned the horizon for the trawler. At one time it would have been easy for him to get work on a big ship or in one of the fishmeal factories, but not any more. After the catastrophic El Niños at the end of the 1990s, even the factory workers had lost their jobs. The big shoals of sardines had never returned.

And he couldn't afford to go another day without catching anything.

You could teach the señoritas how to surf.

That was the alternative. A job in one of the numerous hotels that loomed above Huanchaco, making the old town cower beneath their shadows. He could go fishing for tourists. Wear a ridiculous cropped jacket. Mix cocktails. Entertain spoilt American women on surfboards or waterskis . . . and later in bed.

But the day that Juan Narciso cut his ties with the past would be his father's last. The old man had lost his reason, but he would still know if his youngest son broke the faith.

Ucañan's fists were clenched so tightly that his knuckles blanched. He seized his paddle and started to follow in the wake of the trawler, paddling with all his strength, his movements violent and jerky. With every stroke of the paddle he moved further away from his comrades. He was making rapid progress. He knew that today he had nothing to worry about – no vast breakers would appear from nowhere, no treacherous currents, no powerful north-westerlies to hinder his return. If he didn't risk it now, he never would. There were plenty of tuna, bonito and mackerel in the deeper waters, and they weren't there just for the trawlers.

After a while he stopped. Huanchaco, with its rows of tightly packed houses, looked smaller, and all around him there was nothing but water. He'd left the flotilla far behind.

'There was a desert here once,' his father had told him, 'the desert plains. Now we've got two deserts – the plains and the ocean beside them. We're desert-dwellers threatened by rain.'

He was still too close to shore.

As he powered through the water some of his old confidence returned. It was an almost exhilarating sensation. He imagined riding his little pony right out to sea, paddling on and on until he saw glints of silver darting through the water, catching the sunshine in shimmering cascades. The grey humps of whales would appear above the surface and swordfish would leap through the air. His paddle splashed rhythmically, taking him further and further from the stench of corruption in the town. His arms moved almost of their own accord now, and when he finally set down his paddle and looked back at the fishing village, it was just a squat silhouette surrounded by white specks, the curse of modern Peru: the hotels.

Ucañan started to feel anxious. He'd never been so far out on a *caballito*. It was hard to tell in the early morning haze, but he was at least twelve kilometres from Huanchaco.

He was on his own.

For a moment he was still. Silently he petitioned St Peter to bring him home safely with a boat full of fish. Then he filled his lungs with the salty air, pulled out his *calcal* and let it slip into the water. Gradually the web of net and hooks disappeared into the glassy depths until only the little red buoy was visible, floating alongside the boat.

What had he been worrying about? It was a fine day and, besides, Ucañan knew exactly where he was. Not far from here a jagged range of fossilised white lava rose up from the seabed, almost to the surface. Sea anemones, mussels and crabs had made it their home, while countless little fish inhabited its chasms and hollows. Some of the bigger fish came there to hunt, but it was too dangerous for the trawlers: they might rupture their hulls on the sharp peaks of rock. In any case, they were after bigger catches. But for a daring fisherman astride his *caballito* there was more than enough.

For the first time that morning Ucañan smiled. His boat swayed back and forth on the swell. Out here, far from the coast, the waves were bigger, but he was comfortable on his raft of reeds. He stretched out his arms and squinted at the sun as it cast its pale yellow light over the mountains. Then he picked up his paddle and, with a few quick strokes, steered the *caballito* into the current. He squatted and prepared to spend the next few hours watching the buoy as it bobbed up and down not far from the boat.

In just over an hour he had caught three bonitos. Their plump bodies were piled up in the stern, glistening in the sun.

Ucanan felt jubilant. That was more than he'd caught during the past four weeks. There was no real need for him to stay any longer, but now that he was here he might as well wait. The day had got off to an excellent start: perhaps it would end even better.

In any case, he had all the time in the world.

The *caballito* was drifting leisurely along the edge of the underwater rocks. He let the rope slacken and watched as the buoy skittered away. Every now and then he scanned the water for the lighter patches where the lava reached the surface. He needed to keep the net out of danger. He yawned.

He felt a gentle tug on the rope.

A split second later the buoy disappeared in a flurry of motion. Then it shot up, danced wildly on the surface and was wrenched under again.

Ucañan seized the rope. It strained in his hands, tearing his palms. He

9

cursed. Within seconds the boat was tilting dangerously. He wobbled and let go. Deep beneath the surface of the water, the buoy flashed red. The rope hung vertically below it, taut as a wire, dragging the *caballito* down by its stern.

Something must have swum into the net. Something big and heavy. A swordfish, perhaps. But swordfish were faster than that. A swordfish would have sped off, taking the *caballito* with it. Whatever was trapped in the net seemed determined to dive to the seabed.

Ucañan made a grab for the rope. The boat jolted again, pitching him into the waves. Spluttering, he rose to the surface – in time to see the *caballito* disappear underwater, its bow pointing upright into the air. The bonitos drifted into the sea. He seethed with rage – he couldn't even dive after them. He had to save himself and his boat.

The morning's catch, all wasted.

The paddle was floating a short distance away from him, but Ucañan didn't have time to go after it now – he could fetch it later. He flung himself over the prow but the boat was being pulled inexorably into the depths. In a frenzy he hauled himself towards the stern. With his right hand he fumbled for what he needed. Blessed St Peter – his knife hadn't been washed away and neither had his diving mask, his most precious possession, apart from the *calcal*.

He sliced through the rope, and the *caballito* shot to the surface, spinning giddily. Ucañan saw the sky circle above him and his head plunged back into the water. Then he lay coughing on the little reed craft. The boat rocked gently in the waves as though nothing had happened.

He sat up in confusion. The buoy was nowhere to be seen, but the paddle was drifting nearby. With his hands he steered the *caballito* towards it, hauled it on board and laid it in front of him. Then he looked around him.

There they were: light patches of lava in the crystal water.

He'd drifted too close to the underwater rocks, and his *calcal* had snagged. No wonder he'd gone under – he shouldn't have been day-dreaming. Now he knew where the net and the buoy were: they were tied together, so if the net was caught on the lava, the buoy couldn't rise to the surface. Yes, that was what had happened. Still, Ucañan was shocked by how violently he'd been pulled underwater – he was lucky to have survived. But he'd lost his net.

Paddling swiftly, he steered the *caballito* to the site of his accident. He peered into the depths, straining to see the net through the clear blue water. There was no sign of it or the buoy.

Was this really the right spot?

Ucañan had the sea in his bones – he'd spent all his life on the ocean – and even without technical equipment he knew that this was the place. This was where he'd cut the rope to save his boat from being ripped apart. His net was down there somewhere.

He had to go after it.

The thought of diving filled him with trepidation. He was an excellent swimmer but, like most fishermen, he had a deep-seated fear of the water. Few fishermen loved the sea, even though they took to it every morning. Some had fished all their lives and couldn't live without it – yet they had trouble living with it too. The sea sapped their strength – making them pay with their lifeblood for every catch they brought home – and leaving them washed up in the ports, withered figures hunched silently at bars, with nothing left to hope for.

But Ucañan had his mask. It had been a present from a tourist he'd taken out on his *caballito* last year. He leaned back and pulled it out, spat on the lens and rubbed it carefully so that it wouldn't cloud over. Then he dipped it into the water, pressed it over his face and pulled the strap round the back of his head. It must have cost a lot of money: the fittings were made of soft latex that moulded to his face. He didn't have any breathing equipment but he wouldn't need it. He could hold his breath for long enough to dive down and untangle the net from the rocks.

The sharks in these waters weren't usually a threat. Hammerheads, shortfin makos and porbeagles occasionally plundered fishing nets, but that was much further out. It was almost unheard of to sight a great white. Besides, he wouldn't be swimming in the open: he'd be near the rocks and the reef, which offered some protection. In any case, whatever had ruined his net, it hadn't been a shark, he thought.

It was his own fault for not being more careful.

He filled his lungs, dived into the water and sped away from the surface, body vertical, arms pressed to his sides. From the boat the water had looked forbidding, but now a welcoming bright world opened up around him. He had a clear view of the volcanic reef, which stretched into the distance, dappled with sun. There were few fish, but he wasn't looking for them. He scanned the reef for the *calcal*. He couldn't stay down too long or his *caballito* might drift away. He'd give himself a few more seconds, then go up and try again.

He'd make ten trips if he had to. He didn't mind if it took all day. He wasn't going back without his net.

Then he spotted the buoy.

It was hanging ten to fifteen metres below the surface, suspended over a tip of jagged rock, the net directly below it. It seemed to be caught in several places. Tiny reef fish were swarming around the mesh, but they dispersed as he swam over. He straightened up, treading water as he tried to free it, his shirt billowing in the current.

The net was in tatters and he stared at it in disbelief. It had taken more than the rocks to do that. Something had been on the rampage. What, in God's name, had been here?

And where was it now?

Ucañan felt uneasy as he fumbled with the net. It would take days to repair. Now he needed to breathe. He would go back up, check on the *caballito*, then dive again.

Before he could move, a change took place around him. At first he thought the sun had disappeared behind a cloud. The light stopped dancing over the rocks; the reef and weeds no longer cast a shadow . . .

His hands, the net, everything around him was losing its colour and turning a murky grey. He dropped the *calcal* and looked up.

Gathered just beneath the surface of the water was a shoal of shimmering fish, each as long as his arm, stretching as far as he could see. The shock made him gasp and bubbles rose from his mouth. Where had a shoal of that size come from? He'd never seen anything like it. It seemed almost stationary, but now and then he saw the flick of a tail-fin or a flash of silver as a fish darted forward. Then, as a unit, the shoal changed course by a few degrees. The gaps between the bodies closed.

It was normal shoaling behaviour, but something wasn't right. It wasn't so much what they were doing that unnerved Ucañan: it was the fish themselves.

There were too many of them.

Ucañan swivelled round. Wherever he looked there were fish. He craned his neck. Through a chink in the mass of bodies he saw the outline of his *caballito*, a dark shadow on the rippling waves. The darkness thickened and his lungs began to burn.

Dorado! he thought in astonishment.

Everyone had given up hoping that they'd ever return. He should have been pleased to see them. They fetched a good price in the market, and a net packed full of dorado would feed a fisherman and his family for a long time.

But fear surged through Ucañan.

A shoal of that size was unreal. It filled his view. Had they destroyed his net? But how?

You've got to get out of here, he told himself.

He pushed off from the rocks. Trying to keep calm he ascended slowly and carefully, exhaling continuously. He was rising straight towards the expanse of fish that separated him from the sunlight and his boat. The shoal was motionless. A wall of indifference stared back at him through bulbous eyes. It was as though he'd conjured them out of nowhere. As though they'd been waiting for him.

They want to trap me. They're trying to cut me off from my boat.

Terror swept through him. His heart was racing. He forgot about controlling his speed, about the ruined net and the little red buoy. He even forgot his *caballito*. All he could think of was breaking through the dense mass of fish and reaching the surface, seeing the light, going back to where he belonged, finding safety.

The shoal parted.

From its midst something writhed towards Ucañan.

After a while the wind got up.

It was still a beautiful day, not a cloud in the sky. The swell had risen, but it was nothing a man in a boat couldn't handle.

But there was no one for miles.

Only the *caballito*, one of the last of its kind, drifted on the open sea.

PART ONE

ANOMALIES

And the second angel poured out his vial upon the sea; and it became as the blood of a dead man: and every living soul died in the sea. And the third angel poured out his vial upon the rivers and fountains of waters; and they became blood. And I heard the angel of the waters say, Thou art righteous . . .

Revelation 16:2–5

Last week a huge unidentified carcass washed up on the coast of Chile. According to statements made by the Chilean Coast Guard, the shapeless blob, which decomposed rapidly on land, was only a small part of a much larger mass of flesh previously seen floating on the water. Chilean scientists have found no trace of a skeleton, ruling out the possibility that the remains could be those of a mammal. The mound was too big to be whale skin and is said to have a different smell. Test results so far reveal astonishing parallels to the so-called 'globsters' – gelatinous blobs that wash up periodically on coastlines around the world. Speculation continues as to what type of creature these corpses belong to.

CNN, 17th April 2003

4 March

On the face of it, the city was too cosy for a university or a research institute. In districts like Bakklandet or Møllenberg it seemed almost inconceivable that Trondheim could be a capital of technology. Its old timber houses, parks, rustic churches, colourful water warehouses on stilts, picturesque gardens and courtyards belied the advance of time and knowledge, but the NTNU, Norway's principal university for the sciences, was just round the corner.

Few cities combined past and future as harmoniously as Trondheim, which was why Sigur Johanson felt privileged to live there. His apartment was in old-fashioned Møllenberg, in Kirkegata Street, on the ground floor of an ochre-coloured house whose pitched roof, white steps and lintel would have captured the heart of any Hollywood director. Johanson was a marine biologist and a thoroughly modern scientist, but nothing could persuade him of the merits of his times. He was a visionary and, like most visionaries, he combined his love for the radically new with an attachment to the ideals of the past. His life was defined by the spirit of Jules Verne, whom he admired for his old-fashioned chivalry, his passion for the seemingly impossible and his celebration of technology. But as for the present . . . the present was a snail, its shell piled high with practical problems and the vulgar business of everyday life. There was no real place for it in Sigur Johanson's universe. He served it, knew what it expected from him, enriched its store of knowledge, and despised it for the uses that it put it to.

It was late morning by the time he steered his jeep along the wintry Bakklandet road, past the shimmering waters of the Nid towards the university campus. He was on his way back from a weekend spent deep within the forest, visiting isolated villages where time had stood still. In summer he would have taken the Jaguar, with a picnic hamper in the boot: freshly baked bread, goose-liver pâté wrapped in silver foil from the deli, and a bottle of Gewürztraminer – a 1985, if he could find one. Since he had moved from Oslo to Trondheim, Johanson had hunted out the quiet spots, far from the hordes of tourists and day-trippers. Two years ago he'd come across a secluded lake, and beside it, to his delight, a country house in need of renovation. It had taken a while to track down the owner – he worked in a managerial capacity for Statoil, Norway's state-run oil company, and had moved to Stavanger – but when Johanson finally found him, the deal was quickly done. Pleased to be rid of the place, the owner had sold it for a fraction of its value. A few weeks later a team of Russian immigrants had restored the dilapidated house. They didn't charge much, but transformed it into Johanson's ideal of a proper country residence – a nineteenth-century *bon vivant*'s retreat.

During long summer evenings he sat on the veranda, which looked out over the lake, reading visionary writers like Thomas More, Jonathan Swift or H. G. Wells, and daydreaming to Mahler or Sibelius. The house had a well-stocked library. He owned nearly all of his favourite books and CDs in duplicate – he wanted them with him wherever he was.

Johanson drove on to the NTNU campus. The main university building lay straight ahead, covered with a dusting of snow. It was an imposing, castle-style edifice, dating to the turn of the twentieth century, and behind it lay lecture halls and laboratories. With ten thousand students, the campus was almost a town in itself. It hummed with activity. Johanson sighed in contentment. He had enjoyed his time at the lake. Last summer he'd spent a few weekends there with a research assistant from the cardiology department, an old acquaintance from various conferences. Things had moved swiftly, but he'd ended the relationship. He hadn't been in it for the long term – and anyway, he had to face facts: he was fifty-six, and she was thirty years younger. Great for a few weeks, but unthinkable for a lifetime. In any case, Johanson didn't allow many to get close to him. He never had.

He left the jeep in its bay and headed for the Faculty of Natural Sciences. As he entered his office, Tina Lund was standing by the window. She turned as he walked in. 'You're late,' she teased him. 'Let me guess – too much red wine last night, or was someone reluctant to let you go?'

Johanson grinned. Lund worked for Statoil and seemed to have spent most of her time lately at one or other of the SINTEF institutes. The

SINTEF Group was one of the biggest independent research organisations in Europe, and the Norwegian oil industry in particular had benefited from its groundbreaking innovations. The close links between SINTEF and the NTNU had helped to establish Trondheim as a centre of technological excellence, and SINTEF centres were dotted throughout the region. Lund had risen swiftly through the Statoil ranks and was now deputy director of exploration and production. She had recently set up camp at Marintek, the SINTEF centre for marine technology.

Johanson surveyed her tall slim figure as he took off his coat. He liked Tina Lund. A few years ago they'd nearly got together, but instead they'd decided to stay friends. Now they just picked each other's brains and went out for the occasional meal. 'An old man like me needs his sleep,' he said. 'Coffee?'

'Sure.'

He popped into the adjoining office, where he found a fresh pot. His secretary was nowhere to be seen.

'Milk, no sugar,' Lund called.

'I know.' Johanson poured the coffee into two mugs, added a splash of milk to one, and returned to his office. 'I know all about you, remember?'

'You didn't get that far.'

'Heaven forbid! Now, take a seat. What brings you here?'

Lund picked up her mug, but remained standing. 'A worm, I think.'

Johanson raised his eyebrows and took a gulp of his coffee. 'What do you mean, you *think*?'

She picked up a small steel container from the windowsill and placed it in front of him on the desk. 'See for yourself.'

Johanson opened it. The container was half filled with water. Something long and hairy was writhing inside. He examined it carefully.

'Any idea what it is?' she asked.

He shrugged. 'Worms. Two big ones.'

'We'd worked that out, but what species?'

'Ah! So that's why you need a biologist. They're polychaetes – bristleworms.'

'I'm familiar with polychaetes . . .' she hesitated 'but could you take a proper look and classify them?'

'Hmmm.' Johanson peered into the container. 'As I said, they're bristleworms. Nice ones too. The ocean floor is covered with creatures like them. No idea what species, though. What's the problem with them?'

'If only we knew.'

'What *do* you know?'

'We found them on the continental slope, seven hundred metres down.'

Johanson scratched his chin. They must be hungry, he thought. He was surprised they were still alive: most organisms didn't take kindly to being hauled up from the depths.

He glanced up. 'There's no harm in taking a look at them. I'll be in touch tomorrow.'

'Great.' She paused. 'You've noticed something odd about them, haven't you? I can tell by the way you're looking at them.'

'Perhaps.'

'What is it?'

'I can't say for sure. Taxonomy isn't my speciality. Bristleworms come in all shapes and colours and I'm not familiar with them all, but these . . .'

Lund flashed him a smile. 'Why don't you look at them now? You could tell me your findings over lunch.'

'I do have a job to get on with, you know.'

'Well, you can't be too pushed at the moment – judging by the time you rolled up this morning.'

How irritating; she was right.

'OK.' He sighed. 'We'll meet at one in the cafeteria. Were you planning on a long-term friendship with them, or can I cut them up?'

'Do whatever it takes, Sigur. I'll see you later.'

She hurried out. Johanson watched her go. Perhaps the two of them could have made a go of it, he thought. But Tina Lund lived life at a sprint. She was much too hectic for someone like him.

He sorted his post and caught up on some phone calls. Then he picked up the container and carried it into the lab. There was no doubt that they were polychaetes, members of the *Annelida* phylum. Segmented worms, like the common earthworm. They weren't complex, as far as organisms went, but they fascinated zoologists: polychaetes were among the oldest known organisms. Fossil records showed that they'd survived, practically unchanged, since the Middle Cambrian era, more than 500 million years ago. A few species were found in fresh water or on marshy ground, but the seas and oceans teemed with them. They aerated the sediment and provided fish and crabs with a rich source of nutrition. Most people found them repellent, but Johanson saw them as the survivors of a lost world: he found them exceptionally beautiful.

He took a few moments to examine the pinkish bodies, with their tentacle-like growths and clumps of fine white bristle. Then he dripped magnesium chloride solution into the container to anaesthetise them. There were a number of ways to kill a worm, but the most common was to immerse them in alcohol, usually vodka or aquavit. For humans that would mean death by intoxication – not a bad way to go. But worms felt things differently and screwed themselves into a ball to die, unless you relaxed them first. The magnesium chloride slackened their muscles, so that you could do what you liked with them.

He decided to freeze one worm: it was always good to have a specimen in reserve, in case you decided to examine its DNA or do a stable isotope analysis. He fixed the other worm in alcohol, then laid it out for measuring. Nearly seventeen centimetres, he noted. Then he cut it open lengthways and gave a low whistle. 'Well, well, well,' he murmured.

The specimen had all the classic features of an annelid worm. Its proboscis was tucked within its body, ready to unfurl and seize its prey. It was tipped with chitinous jaws and rows of minuscule teeth. Over the years Johanson had examined plenty of polychaetes, inside and out, but those were the biggest jaws he'd ever seen. As he gazed at the worm he couldn't help wondering if it was a new species. Few had the luck to discover a species, he thought. His name would be immortal . . .

He turned on his computer to consult the Intranet, then wandered through the maze of data. The outcome was baffling. In one sense the worm was there, but in another it wasn't.

By the time he was rushing through the glass-covered walkways towards the cafeteria, he was already a quarter of an hour late. He burst into the room, spotted Lund at a corner table and went over to her. She was sitting under a palm tree, and gave him a little wave.

'Sorry,' he said. 'Have you been here long?'

'Ages. I'm starving.'

'Let's have the shredded chicken stew,' said Johanson. 'It was good last week.'

Lund nodded: she knew she could trust his recommendation. She ordered Coke, while he had a glass of wine. When the waiter brought their drinks, she was shifting impatiently on her chair. 'Well?'

Johanson sipped his wine. 'Not bad. Fresh and full-bodied.'

Lund rolled her eyes.

'OK, OK.' Amused, he put down his glass, settled back and crossed his legs. Anyone who lay in wait for him on a Monday morning deserved to be kept in suspense, he thought. 'We'd already established that they're annelid worms, polychaetes. I'm hoping you don't need a full report because that would take weeks, if not months. For the moment I'd treat the two specimens as a mutation or a new species – or both, to be precise.'

'That doesn't sound precise.'

'Sorry, but that's the way it is. Where did you find them?'

Lund described the site. It was a considerable distance from the coast, on the continental slope, where the Norwegian shelf descended towards the deep ocean floor.

'Dare I ask what Statoil was doing down there?' Johanson asked.

'Looking at cod.'

'Cod? Now, that *is* good news – I thought they'd died out.'

'It's not funny, Sigur. You know how many obstacles have to be cleared before we can even think about drilling. We don't want to be accused of not doing our homework.'

'You mean you're building a platform? But oil yields are dropping.'

'That's not my problem,' Lund said tersely. 'What I'm worried about is whether we can build there in the first place. It's the furthest out to sea we've ever drilled. We've got to get on top of the technological challenges *and* prove that we're respecting the environment. Which is why we're trying to find out what's swimming around down there and how the site functions ecologically – so that people like you don't complain.'

Johanson nodded. Lund was contending with the fallout from the recent North Sea Conference, at which the Norwegian Ministry of Fisheries had castigated the oil industry for expelling millions of tonnes of contaminated water into the sea every day. It had lain undisturbed in sub-seabed petroleum reserves for millions of years but was now being pumped to the surface by the hundreds of offshore North Sea platforms that lined the Norwegian coast. The oil was separated from it by mechanical means, and the chemical-saturated water discharged back into the sea. No one had questioned the practice until, after decades, the Norwegian government had asked the Institute of Marine Research to undertake a study. The findings dealt a blow to the oil industry and environmentalists alike. Substances in the water were interfering with the reproductive cycle of cod. They worked like female hormones, causing the male fish to become infertile or even to change sex. Other species were affected too. The oil companies were ordered to stop dumping the water and had no choice but to look for an alternative.

'They're right to keep an eye on you,' Johanson said. 'The closer the better.'

'You're a great help.' Lund sighed. 'Anyway, our recce of the slope took us pretty deep into the ocean. We did the usual seismic survey, then sent a dive robot down seven hundred metres to take a few shots. We weren't expecting to find worms so deep.'

'They're everywhere. How about above seven hundred metres? Did you find them there too?'

'No. So what are we going to do about them?'

Johanson rested his chin on his hands. 'The trouble with your worm,' he said, 'is that it's really two separate worms.'

She looked at him blankly. 'Well, I know that. I gave you two.'

'That's not what I meant. I'm talking about its taxonomy. If I'm not mistaken, your worm belongs to a new species that has only just come to light. It was found on the seabed in the Gulf of Mexico availing itself of the bacteria that live off methane.'

'Really?'

'And that's where it starts to get interesting. Your worms are too big. Sure, some types of bristleworm grow to over two metres and live to a ripe old age. But they're nothing like yours, and you wouldn't find them around here. If yours are the same as the Mexican ones, they've done a fair bit of growing since we found them. The worms in the Mexican Gulf measure five centimetres at most, but yours are three times as long. And there's no record of them ever being found on the Norwegian shelf.'

'How do you account for that?'

'I can't. Right now I can only think that you've stumbled on a brand new species. Congratulations to Statoil. Your worm *looks* like a Mexican ice worm but, as far as its length and other features are concerned, it's a completely different fellow. In fact, it's more like a prehistoric worm, a tiny Cambrian monster that we thought was extinct. But I still don't see how . . .'

He paused. The Norwegian shelf had been picked over with a fine-tooth comb. Surely the oil companies would have noticed a worm of that size before now.

'What?' Lund pressed him.

'Well, either we're all blind or your worms have only just got there. They may have originated even further down.'

'So why did we find them where we did?' Lund asked. 'And how soon can you let me have a report?'

'You're not going to start hassling me, are you?'

'Well, I can't wait a month, if that's what you mean.'

'Whoa.' Johanson held up his hands. 'I'll have to send the worms on a trip round the world. Give me two weeks – and don't argue. There's no way I can do it any faster.'

Lund sat in silence. The chicken stew had arrived, but she hadn't touched hers. 'They feed on methane, you say?'

'On the bacteria that feed on methane,' Johanson corrected her. 'It's a complex symbiotic system. And, remember, we're talking about a worm that *may* or *may not* be related to yours. Nothing's proven yet.'

'If these worms are bigger than the ones in Mexico, they're probably hungrier too,' Lund mused.

'Hungrier than you, at least,' said Johanson, with a pointed glance at her plate. 'Incidentally, I need a few more of those monsters, if you have any.'

'We're not about to run out.'

'You've got more in reserve?'

'A dozen or so,' she said, 'but there are plenty more where those came from.'

'How many?'

'Well, it's only a guess . . . but I'd say several million.'

12 March

Vancouver Island, Canada

The days came and went, but the rain kept falling. Leon Anawak couldn't remember the last time it had poured for so long. It must have been years ago. He gazed out across the perfectly still surface of the ocean. In the far distance a thin silvery line divided the water from the low, thick cloud, promising a break in the rain, the first one for days. You couldn't count on it though; the fog could always roll in instead. The Pacific Ocean did as it pleased, usually without a moment's notice.

Keeping his eyes fixed on the chink of light, Anawak opened the *Blue Shark's* throttle and headed further out to sea. The Zodiac, a big rubber dinghy with powerful outboard motors, was full to capacity. Its twelve passengers, covered from head to toe with waterproof clothing and armed with binoculars and cameras, were rapidly losing interest. They'd been waiting patiently for over an hour and a half to catch a glimpse of the grey whales and humpbacks that had left the lagoons of Baja California, and the warm waters of Hawaii in February on their way to their summer feeding grounds in the Arctic. The round trip would take them sixteen thousand kilometres, from the Pacific Ocean through the Bering Sea to their frozen pool of plenty, the Chukchi Sea, where they'd swim to the edge of the pack ice to feast on amphipods and krill. When the days shortened, they'd set off on their long journey home towards Mexico to give birth out of reach of their deadliest enemy, the orca. Twice a year vast herds of the enormous mammals passed through British Columbia and the waters off Vancouver Island, and during those months the whale-watching tours in coastal towns like Tofino, Ucluelet and Victoria would be fully booked.

Not this year, though.

So far not a flipper or fluke had been captured on film. The chances of spotting one or other species were usually so good at this time of year that Davie's Whaling Station offered free repeat trips if you didn't see a whale. To go a few hours without a sighting was not unheard of, but to see nothing all day was seriously bad luck. A whole week would be cause for concern, but that had never happened.

This year, though, the whales seemed to have gone astray and today's adventure was over before it had begun. Everyone put away their cameras. All they'd glimpsed from the boat was the hint of a rocky coastline, and they hadn't even been able to see that properly because of the rain.

Anawak would accompany each sighting with explanations and comments, but now his mouth dried. For an hour and a half he'd held forth on the history of the region, trying to lift the group's spirits with anecdotes. Now everyone had heard enough about whales and black bears. He'd run out of ideas as to how to divert them and, besides, he was worried about the whales' whereabouts. As skipper, he should probably have been more worried about the tourists, but that wasn't his way.

'Time to go home,' he announced.

There was a disappointed silence. The journey through Clayoquot Sound would take at least three-quarters of an hour. He decided to cut short the afternoon with a burst of excitement. The Zodiac's twin outboard motor would give them an adrenaline-pumping ride. Speed was all he had left to offer.

Tofino's waterfront, with its houses on stilts and the Whaling Station on the wharf, was just coming into view when the rain stopped abruptly. From a distance the hills and mountains looked like grey cardboard cut-outs. Their tips were enveloped in a haze of mist and cloud. Anawak helped the passengers out of the boat, then moored it to the side. The steps leading up to the wharf were slippery, and the next bunch of adventurers had gathered on the patio in front of the station. There wouldn't be any thrills for them either.

'If things don't pick up soon we'll all be out of a job,' said Susan Stringer, as he walked into the ticket office. She was standing behind the counter, restocking the plastic leaflet-holders. 'Maybe we should offer squirrel-watching instead. What do you think?'

Davie's Whaling Station was a cosy place, crammed with a mishmash of handmade objects, tacky souvenirs, clothing and books. Stringer was the office manager. She'd taken the job to finance her studies – which was why Anawak had started there too. But four years after completing his doctorate he still worked for Davie. He'd used the past few summers to write a groundbreaking book about intelligence and social bonding among marine mammals. His pioneering research had earned him the respect of experts and established his reputation as a rising star of science. Now letters were trickling in with offers of highly paid jobs that made his comfortable life in the wilds of Vancouver Island seem to lack definition. Anawak knew it was only a matter of time before he moved away. He was thirty-one years old. Soon he would take up a lectureship or become a research fellow in one of the big institutes. He would publish articles in specialist journals, travel to conferences and live on the top floor of a desirable condo, whose foundations would shake in the throb of rush-hour traffic.

He started to peel off his waterproofs.

'If only we could do something,' he muttered.

'Like what?'

'Go looking for them.'

'Didn't you want to talk to Rod Palm about the feedback from the telemetric tracking?'

'I have already.'

'And?'

'From what he said, there's not much to tell. They tagged a few bottlenose dolphins and sea-lions back in January, but the trail goes dead at the beginning of migration. All the tags stopped transmitting, and it's been quiet ever since.'

Stringer shrugged. 'Don't worry, they'll turn up. Thousands of whales can't just disappear.'

'Well, obviously they can.'

She grinned. 'I guess they must be stuck in traffic near Seattle.'

'Very funny.'

'Hey, loosen up a bit. It wouldn't be the first time they've been late. Anyway, why don't you join us later at Schooners?'

'Uh . . . sorry. I'm still setting up that trial with the belugas.'

'You work too hard,' she said sternly.

'I've got to, Susan. It really matters to me. And at least I understand it, unlike stocks and shares.'

The dig was aimed at Roddy Walker, Stringer's boyfriend. He was a broker in Vancouver and was staying in Tofino for a few days. His idea of a holiday entailed talking at top volume into his mobile, offering unwanted financial advice and generally getting on everyone's nerves. It hadn't taken Stringer long to grasp that the two men wouldn't become friends, especially after Walker had pestered Anawak for one long painful evening with questions about his roots.

'You probably won't believe me,' she said, 'but that's not all he ever talks about.'

'Seriously?'

'You only have to ask him nicely,' she said pointedly.

'OK,' said Anawak, 'I'll join you later.'

'No, you won't. You've no intention of coming.'

Anawak grinned. 'Well, if you ask me nicely . . .'

He wouldn't go, of course. He knew that and so did Stringer, but she repeated the invitation all the same. 'We're meeting at eight, in case you change your mind. Think about it: maybe you *should* drag your mussel-covered butt down there. Tom's sister's coming, and she's got a thing about you.'

It was almost enough to persuade him. But Tom Shoemaker was the manager of Davie's, and Anawak wasn't keen to tie himself to a place he was trying to leave. 'I'll think it over.'

Stringer laughed, and left.

Anawak stayed to deal with the customers until Shoemaker took over. Eventually he left the office and headed on to the main road. Davie's Whaling Station was one of the first buildings on the way into Tofino. It was a pretty place, made of timber just like everywhere else in town, with a red roof, a sheltered terrace and a front lawn on which its trademark totem towered into the air – a seven-metre-high whale fluke made of cedar. It was set on the edge of a thick forest of pines. The area was exactly how most Europeans imagined Canada, and the locals did their best to reinforce this impression: sitting by the light of their lanterns, they would tell stories about meeting bears in their front gardens or riding on a whale's back. And most of it was true. The gently sloping beaches, rugged scenery, marshes, rivers and deserted coves, with the ancient pines and cedars that lined the west coast from Tofino to Port Renfrew, drew in hordes of tourists every year. On a good day you could look out to sea and spot a grey whale or watch the otters and sea-lions sunning themselves. And even when rain lashed the island, many people still thought it was heaven on earth.

That wasn't how Anawak saw it.

He walked a little way into town, then turned off towards one of the wharfs. A dilapidated twelve-metre-long sailing-boat was anchored there. Davie owned it, but he had been reluctant to pay for it to be repaired, so Anawak lived there for a peppercorn rent. His real home was a tiny apartment in Vancouver city but he only used it if he had business in town.

He went below deck, picked up a bundle of papers and walked back to the station. In Vancouver he owned a rusty old Ford, but on the island he made do with Shoemaker's ancient Land Cruiser. He got in, started the engine and drove to the Wickaninnish Inn, a top-class hotel a few kilometres out of town on a rocky promontory with breathtaking views of the ocean. The cloud was breaking up, revealing patches of blue. A well-maintained road led through the dense forest and he drove for ten minutes. When he came to a little car park he left his vehicle and continued on foot, past enormous dead tree-trunks that lay rotting on the ground. The path climbed upwards through trees that glowed green in the evening sunshine. He could smell damp soil and hear water dripping. The pine branches were covered with ferns and moss. Everything seemed vibrantly alive.

By the time he reached the Wick he was feeling better for his walk. Now that the sky was clearing he could sit on the beach and work in peace. It wouldn't get dark for a while yet. Maybe, he thought, as he descended the wooden steps that zigzagged down from the hotel, I should treat myself to dinner. The food at the Wick was always excellent.

Armed with his notebook and laptop he made himself comfortable on an upturned tree-trunk, but he'd been there barely ten minutes when someone came down the steps and wandered along the beach. It was low tide and the evening sunshine lit the driftwood-strewn shore. The figure kept close to the silvery-blue water. Whoever it was didn't seem to be in any hurry; but all the same it was obvious that their meandering path would eventually lead to Anawak's tree. He frowned and tried to look as busy as possible. After a while he heard the soft, gravelly crunch of approaching footsteps.

'Hello.'

Anawak glanced up.

A woman in her late fifties was standing in front of him, cigarette in hand. Her face was tanned, and criss-crossed with lines. Barefoot, she wore jeans and a dark windcheater.

'Hello.' He sounded less brusque than he'd intended – as soon as he'd looked up, his irritation at the interruption had dissipated. Her deep-blue eyes sparkled with curiosity. She must have been stunning in her youth.

'What are you doing here?' she asked.

Under normal circumstances he would have given a non-committal answer, but instead he heard himself say. 'I'm working on a paper about beluga whales. You?'

The woman sat down beside him. He looked at her profile, the delicate nose and high cheekbones – and knew, suddenly, that he'd seen her somewhere before.

'I'm working on a paper too,' she said, 'but I don't expect anyone will read it when it's published.' She paused. 'I was on your boat today.'

The small woman wearing sunglasses and a hood, he remembered.

'What's up with the whales?' she asked.

'There aren't any.'

'How come?'

'That's what I keep asking myself.'

The woman nodded. 'My lot haven't shown up either, but at least I know why. Maybe you should stop waiting and start searching.'

'But we are.' He put down his notebook. 'We've got satellite tags – telemetry. And sonar. We can track down pods.'

'But they've slipped the net.'

'There were some sightings in early March off the coast of Los Angeles, but since then, nothing.'

'So they've all just vanished?'

'Not all of them.' Anawak sighed. 'It's complicated. Are you sure you want to hear it?'

'Sure.'

'You can see twenty-three different types of whale from Vancouver Island. Some are just passing through – grey whales, humpbacks, minke and so on – but others live here. We've got three different types of orca, for example.'

'Killer whales?'

'I guess,' Anawak said irritably. 'But orcas have never been known to attack humans in the wild. Pliny set them up, though, in his *Natural History*. He called them, "*A mightie masse and lumpe of flesh without all*

30

fashion, armed with most terrible, sharpe, and cutting teeth." And Cousteau described them as our number-one enemy. What nonsense!'

'OK, point taken . . . so what does *orca* actually mean?'

'*Orcinus orca*, their full scientific name, means *from the realm of the dead*. I've no idea where it came from.'

'You said there were three types of orca here.'

Anawak pointed out to sea. 'Offshore orcas. We don't know much about them but they come and go, mostly in big groups, and tend to live a long way out. Transient orcas are nomadic and live in smaller pods. They come closest to your idea of a killer whale. They'll eat anything they can get their teeth into – seals, sea-lions, dolphins and birds. They'll even attack blue whales. In areas like this, where the coast is rocky, they stay in the water, but in South America they'll haul themselves on to the beach to hunt seals and other animals. It's amazing to watch.'

He paused, but she didn't speak so he went on: 'The third type lives in the waters around the island in large family groups. How well do you know the island?'

'A little.'

'To the east there's the Johnstone Strait, a channel of water separating it from the mainland. Resident orcas live there all year round. They only eat salmon. We've been monitoring their social behaviour since the 1970s—' He stopped. 'Why am I telling you all this?'

She laughed. 'I'm sorry, I got you sidetracked. And I'm curious. You were trying to explain which whales have vanished and which are still here.'

'That's right. But—'

'You're busy.'

Anawak glanced at his notebook and laptop. His paper had to be finished by tomorrow but . . . 'Are you staying at the Wickaninnish Inn?' he asked.

'Yes.'

'Do you have plans for the evening?'

'Oh!' She grinned. 'The last time anyone asked me that was ten years ago.'

He grinned back. 'I was thinking of my belly. I thought we could talk more over dinner.'

'Good plan.' She slid off the tree-trunk, stubbed out her cigarette and dropped the butt into her pocket. 'I warn you, I always talk with my mouth full. By the way,' she held out her hand, 'I'm Samantha Crowe. Call me Sam.'

'Leon Anawak.'

Situated on a rocky promontory at the front of the hotel, the restaurant commanded an impressive view of Clayoquot Sound and the islands, with the bay and the temperate rainforest behind it. Anawak and Crowe sat at a table by the window – which would have been perfect for whale-watching, if there'd been anything to see.

'The problem,' Anawak said, 'is that the transients and the offshore orcas haven't shown up. There are still large numbers of residents, but they don't like the west of the island, even though living in the Johnstone Strait is starting to get uncomfortable for them.'

'Why?'

'How would you feel if you had to share your home with ferries, cargo ships, liners and sport-fishing vessels? Besides, the region lives off the timber industry and entire forests are being transported to Asia. Once the trees are gone, the rivers fill with silt, the salmon lose their spawning grounds and the resident orcas have nothing to eat.'

'It's not just the orcas you're worried about, though, is it?'

'The grey whales and humpbacks are a major headache. They usually reach Vancouver at the beginning of March by which stage they won't have eaten for months. During the winter, in Baja California, they live off their blubber, but they can't do that for ever. It's only when they get here that they eat again.'

'Maybe they've gone further out to sea.'

'There's not enough for them to eat out there either. Here in Wickaninnish Bay, for instance, the grey whales find a key source of nutrition that they can't get in the ocean. *Onuphis elegans*.'

'*Elegans*? Sounds lovely.'

Anawak smiled.

'It's a long, thin worm. The bay is nice and sandy, which suits the worms, and the grey whales love them. Without little snacks like that they'd never make it to the Arctic.' He took a sip of his water. 'In the mid-1980s things were so bad that the whales didn't stop here. But that was because hardly any were left – they'd been hunted almost to extinction. Since then we've managed to raise their numbers but there are only about twenty thousand grey whales in the world, and you should find most of them here.'

'But this year they haven't come?'

'The residents are here, but they're just a minority.'

'And the humpbacks?'

'Same story.'

'You said you were writing a paper on beluga whales?'

'Isn't it time you told me something about yourself?' Anawak asked.

'You already know the most important stuff – that I'm an old busybody who asks too many questions,' she said.

The waiter appeared with their main course: grilled king prawns on saffron risotto.

'OK, but what *kind* of questions, to whom and why?'

Crowe started peeling a garlicky prawn. 'It's simple, really. I ask, "Is anybody out there?"'

'And what's the response?'

'I've never had one.'

'Maybe you should ask a bit louder,' said Anawak.

'I'd love to,' said Crowe, between mouthfuls, 'but right now our technological capacity limits me to a period of about two hundred light years. It didn't stop us analysing sixty billion signals during the mid-1990s. We narrowed them down to just thirty-seven that couldn't be matched with any natural phenomenon. Thirty-seven signals that might have been someone saying hello.'

Anawak stared at her. 'You work for SETI,' he said.

'Yep. *The Search for Extra-terrestrial Intelligence.* Project Phoenix, to be exact.'

'And you're listening to signals from space?'

'We target stars similar to our sun – a thousand of them, each more than three billion years old. There are other projects like it, but ours is the crucial one.'

'Well, I'll be damned.'

'It's not that amazing. You analyse whalesong and try to figure out what they're telling each other. We listen to noises from space because we're convinced that the universe is packed with civilizations. I expect you're having more luck with your whales.'

'I'm dealing with a few oceans. You've got the universe.'

'It's on a different scale, but I'm always being told that we know less about the oceans than we do about space.'

'And you've intercepted signals that indicate the presence of intelligent life?'

She shook her head. 'No. We've found signals we can't place. The chance of making contact is remote, almost beyond all probability. So, I should really throw myself off the next bridge in frustration. But the signals are my obsession. Like you and your whales.'

'At least I know they exist.'

'Not right now you don't.' Crowe smiled.

Anawak had always been interested in SETI. The institute's research had begun in the early 1990s when NASA had funded a targeted search for extra-terrestrial life on nearby stars – timed to coincide with the five-hundredth anniversary of Columbus's arrival in the New World. As a result, the world's largest radio telescope, in the Puerto Rican town of Arecibo, had embarked on a new kind of observation programme. Thanks to generous private sponsorship, SETI had since been able to set up other projects across the globe, but Phoenix was probably the best known.

'Are you the woman Jodie Foster plays in *Contact*?'

'I'm the woman who'd like to take a ride in her spaceship and meet the aliens. You know what, Leon? I don't usually tell this stuff to anyone – I want to run away screaming when people ask me what I do. I can't bear having to explain myself.'

'I know the feeling.'

'Anyway, you told me what you do, so now it's my turn. What do you want to know?'

Anawak didn't take long to consider. 'Why hasn't it worked?'

The question seemed to amuse her. 'What makes you think it hasn't? The Milky Way is made up of roughly a hundred billion stars. Trying to establish whether any of them is anything like the Earth is tricky because they don't emit enough light. We can only find out about them by using scientific tricks. Theoretically they're everywhere. But you try listening for signals from a hundred billion stars!'

'I get the picture.' Anawak grinned. 'Tracking twenty thousand whales is easy by comparison.'

'Do you see now how a job like mine can make you old and grey? It's like trying to prove the existence of a teeny-weeny fish by straining the ocean litre by litre. And, remember, fish don't keep still. There's a good chance that you'll strain for ever and decide in the end that the fish was never there. Yet all the while it was swimming along with thousands of others – just always somewhere else. Phoenix can strain several litres at once, but it's still limited to, say, the Georgia Strait. Do you see what I'm getting at? There *are* civilizations out there, but I can't prove it. The universe is big, maybe infinite – the observatory's drinks dispenser can brew coffee stronger than our chances.'

Anawak thought for a moment. 'Didn't NASA send a message into space?'

'Oh, that.' Her eyes flashed. 'You mean, why don't we get off our butts and start making some noise of our own? Well, you're right. In 1974 NASA sent a binary message from Arecibo to M13, a globular star cluster a mere twenty-one thousand light years away. But the essential problem remains the same: whether a signal comes from us or from somebody else, all it can do is wander through interstellar space. It would take an amazing coincidence for someone to intercept it. Besides, it's cheaper for us to listen than transmit.'

'Even so, it would improve your chances.'

'Maybe we don't want that.'

'Why not?' Anawak was bewildered.

'Well, at SETI *we* want to, but plenty of folk would rather we didn't draw attention to ourselves. If other civilizations knew we were here, they might rob us of our planet. God help us, they might even eat us for breakfast.'

'But that's ridiculous.'

'Is it? If they're clever enough to manage interstellar travel, they're probably not interested in fisticuffs. On the other hand, it's not something we can rule out. In my view, we'd be better off thinking about how we could be drawing attention to ourselves unintentionally, otherwise we could make the wrong impression.'

Anawak was silent. Eventually he said, 'Don't you ever feel like giving up?'

'Who doesn't?'

'And what if you achieve your goal?'

'Good question.' Briefly Crowe was lost in thought. 'For years now I've been wondering what our goal really is. I think if I knew the answer I'd probably quit – an answer is always the end of a search. Maybe we're tortured by the loneliness of our existence, by the idea that we're just a freak of nature, the only ones of our kind. Or maybe we want to prove that there's no one else out there so we have the right to occupy a privileged position. I don't know. Why do you study whales and dolphins?'

'I'm just . . . interested.' But that's not quite true, he thought. It's more than an interest . . . So what am I looking for?

Crowe was right. They were doing much the same thing, listening for signals and hoping for answers. They both had a deep-seated longing for the company of intelligent beings other than humans.

She seemed to know what he was thinking. 'Let's not con ourselves,' she said. 'We're not really interested in other forms of intelligent life. We want to know what their existence might mean for us.' She leaned back and smiled. 'I guess we're just looking for meaning.'

It was nearly half past ten when they said goodbye after a drink in the lounge – bourbon for Crowe and water for Anawak. Outside, the clouds had dispersed and the sky was scattered with myriad twinkling stars. For a while they gazed up at it.

'I hope you find your whales,' she said at last.

'I'll let you know, Sam.'

'They're lucky to have you as a friend. You've a good heart.'

'You can't know that!'

'In my line of work, knowing and believing share a wavelength.'

They shook hands.

'Maybe we'll meet again as orcas,' Anawak joked.

'Why?'

'The Kwakiutl Indians believe that if you lead a good life you'll return as an orca.'

'I like the sound of that.' Crowe grinned. 'Do you believe it?'

'Of course not.'

'But I thought . . .'

'You thought?' he said, although he knew without asking.

'That you were Indian.'

Anawak felt himself stiffen. Then he saw himself through her eyes: a man of medium height and stocky build, with wide cheekbones, copper skin, almond eyes and thick, shiny black hair that fell across his forehead. 'Something like that,' he said awkwardly.

Crowe glanced at him. Then she pulled out a packet of cigarettes, lit one and took a long drag. 'Another of my obsessions,' she remarked, blowing smoke. 'Look after yourself, Leon.'

13 March

Norwegian Coast and North Sea

Sigur Johanson heard nothing from Tina Lund for a week, during which he stood in for another professor, who'd been taken ill, and wrote an article for *National Geographic*. He also contacted an acquaintance who worked for the distinguished wine producers Hugel & Fils in Riquewihr, Alsace, and arranged to be sent a few vintage bottles. In the meantime, he tracked down a 1959 vinyl recording of the *Ring Cycle*, conducted by Sir Georg Solti, which, with the wine, pushed his study of Lund's worms to the back of his mind.

It was nine days after their meeting when Lund finally called. She was in good spirits.

'You sound laid-back,' said Johanson. 'I hope that's not affecting your scientific judgement.'

'Highly likely,' she said.

'Explain.'

'All in good time. Now, listen: the *Thorvaldson* sets sail for the continental slope tomorrow. We'll be sending down a dive robot. Do you want to come?'

Johanson ran through a mental checklist of his commitments. 'In the morning I have to familiarise students with the sex appeal of sulphur bacteria.'

'That's no good. The boat leaves at the crack of dawn.'

'From where?'

'Kristiansund.'

It was a good hour away by car on a wind-blown, wave-battered stretch of rocky coast to the south-west of Trondheim. There was an airport nearby, from which helicopters flew out to the many oil rigs crammed along the North Sea continental shelf and the Norwegian Trench.

'Can I join you later?' he asked.

'Maybe,' Lund said. 'In fact, that's not a bad idea – and there's no reason why I shouldn't go later too. What are you doing the day after?'

'Nothing that can't be postponed.'

'Well, that's settled. If we stay on board overnight, we'll have plenty of time for observations and evaluating the results. We can get the helicopter to Gullfaks and take the transfer launch from there.'

'Where shall we meet?' asked Johanson.

'Sveggesundet, at the Fiskehuset. Do you know it?'

'The restaurant on the seafront, next to the timber church?'

'Exactly.'

'Shall we say three?'

'Perfect. I'll get the helicopter to pick us up from there.' She paused. 'Any news on the worms?'

'Not yet, but I may have something tomorrow.'

He put down the phone and frowned. It was puzzling to see a new species within an ecosystem as well researched as this one. But it makes sense for them to be there, thought Johanson. If they're related to the ice worm, they must depend indirectly on methane. And methane deposits were present on every continental slope, the Norwegian slope included.

But it was odd all the same.

The taxonomic and biochemical findings would resolve the matter. Until then there was no reason why he shouldn't continue to research Hugel's Gewürztraminers. Unlike worms, they couldn't be found everywhere – not in that particular vintage, at least.

When he got to work the next morning he found two envelopes bearing his name. He glanced at the taxonomic reports, stuffed them into his briefcase and set off for his lecture.

Two hours later he was driving over the hilly terrain of Norway's fjord landscape towards Kristiansund. The temperature had risen, melting large sections of snow to expose the earth beneath. In weather like this it was hard to know what to wear, so Johanson had packed as much as the weight restrictions on the helicopter allowed. He had no intention of catching cold on the *Thorvaldson*. Lund would tease him when she saw the size of his suitcase, but Johanson didn't mind. In any case, he had put in a few things that two people might enjoy together. He and Lund were only friends, of course, but that didn't mean they couldn't share a cosy glass of wine.

Johanson drove slowly. He could have reached Kristiansund within an hour, but he didn't believe in rushing. At Halsa he took the car ferry over the fjord and continued towards Kristiansund, driving over bridge after bridge across slate-grey water. Several little islands made up the town, which he drove through, then crossed to the island of Averoy, one of the first places to have been settled after the last ice age. Sveggesundet, a picturesque fishing village, lay at its furthest tip. In high season it was packed with tourists, and boats streamed out of the harbour, heading for the neighbouring islands. At this time of year, though, there were few visitors, and scarcely a soul was in sight as Johanson's Jeep crunched over the gravel of the Fiskehuset's car park. The restaurant had an outdoor seating area, overlooking the sea. It was closed, but Lund was sitting outside at one of the wooden tables, next to a young man Johanson didn't know. He walked up to them. 'Am I early?'

She looked up, eyes shining, and glanced at the man next to her. He was in his late twenties, with light brown hair, an athletic build and chiselled features.

'Do you want me to come back later?' Johanson asked.

'Kare Sverdrup,' she introduced them, 'this is Sigur Johanson.'

The young man grinned and stretched out his hand. 'Tina's told me about you.'

'Nothing too awful, I hope.'

Sverdrup laughed. 'Actually, yes. She said you were an unusually attractive scientist.'

'Attractive – and ancient,' said Lund.

Johanson sat down opposite them, pulling up the collar of his parka. His briefcase lay beside him on the bench. 'The taxonomic section's arrived. It's very detailed, but I can summarise it for you, if you like.' He looked at Sverdrup. 'I don't want to bore you, Kare. Has Tina told you what this is about?'

'Not really,' he said.

Johanson opened the case and pulled out the envelopes. 'I sent one of your worms to the Senckenberg Museum in Frankfurt and another to the Smithsonian Institute. The best taxonomists I know are attached to them. I also sent one to Kiel to be examined under the scanning electron microscope. I'm still waiting to hear the results on that and the isotope ratio mass spectrometry, but I can tell you now what the experts agree on.'

'Go on then.'

Johanson settled back and crossed one leg over the other. 'That there's nothing to agree on. In essence, they've confirmed what I suspected – that we're almost certainly dealing with the species *Hesiocaeca methanicola*, also known as the ice worm.'

'The methane-eater.'

'Wrong, but never mind. Anyway, that's the first point. The second is that we're baffled by its highly developed jaws and teeth, which usually indicate that the worm is a predator or that it gets its food by burrowing or grinding. Ice worms don't need teeth like that, so their jaws are significantly smaller. They live symbiotically, grazing off the bacteria that live on gas hydrates . . .'

'Hydrates? asked Sverdrup.

Johanson glanced at Lund. 'You explain it,' she said.

'It's quite simple, really,' said Johanson. 'You've probably heard that the sea is full of methane.'

'So the papers keep telling us.'

'Well, methane is a gas. It's stored in vast quantities beneath the ocean floor and in the continental slopes. Some of it freezes on the surface of the seabed – it combines with water to form ice. It only happens in conditions of high pressure and low temperature, so you have to go pretty deep before you find it. The ice is called methane hydrate. Does that make sense?'

Sverdrup nodded.

'Hordes of bacteria inhabit the oceans, and some live off methane. They take it in and give out hydrogen sulphide. They're microscopically small, but they congregate in such large numbers that they cover the seabed like a vast mat – a "bacterial mat". They're often found in places where there are big deposits of methane hydrate.'

'So far, so good,' said Sverdrup. 'I expect this is where the worm comes in.'

'Precisely. Certain species of worm live off the chemicals expelled by bacteria. In some cases, they swallow the bacteria and carry them around inside them; in others, the bacteria live on their outer casing. Either way, that's how the worms get their food. And it explains why they're attracted to gas hydrates. They make themselves comfortable, help themselves to the bacteria, and relax. They don't have to burrow because they're not eating the ice, just the bacteria on it. The only effect they have on the ice is through their movement, which melts it, leaving a shallow depression, and that's where they stay.'

'I see,' said Sverdrup, slowly. 'So there's no need for them to dig, whereas other worms have to?'

'Some species eat sediment, or substances present in it, and others eat any detritus that sinks to the seabed – corpses, particles, remains of any kind. Worms that *don't* live symbiotically with bacteria have powerful jaws for catching prey or burrowing.'

'So ice worms don't need jaws.'

'Well, they might need them for grinding tiny quantities of hydrate or filtering out bacteria – and, like I said, they've got jaws. But not like the ones on Tina's worms.'

Sverdrup seemed to be getting into the discussion. 'But if Tina's worms live symbiotically with bacteria . . .'

'We need to figure out why they have such killer teeth and jaws.' Johanson nodded. 'And that's where it gets interesting. The taxonomists have found a second worm with that jaw structure. It's called *Nereis* and it's a predator found in ocean depths all over the world. Tina's worms have Nereis's teeth and jaws but in other respects they resemble its prehistoric forebears – a kind of *Tyran-nereis rex*.'

'Sounds ominous.'

'I'd say it sounds like a hybrid. We'll have to wait for the results of the microscopy and the DNA analysis.'

'There's no end of methane hydrate on the continental slope . . .' said Lund, playing with her lip '. . . so that would fit.'

'Let's wait and see.' Johanson cleared his throat. 'What do you do, Kare? Are you in oil too?'

Sverdrup shook his head. 'No,' he said. 'I'm a chef.'

'He's an amazing cook,' said Lund.

That's probably not the only thing he's good at, thought Johanson ruefully. Sometimes he found Tina Lund hard to resist, but deep down, he knew she would be too demanding. Now she was off-limits.

'How did you two meet?' he asked, not that he cared.

'I took over the Fiskehuset last year,' said Sverdrup. 'Tina was here a few times, but we only ever said hello.' He put his arm round her shoulders. 'Until last week, that is.'

'A real coup de foudre,' said Lund.

'Yes,' said Johanson, looking up at the sky. The helicopter was approaching. 'I can tell.'

Half an hour later they were sitting in the aircraft with a dozen oil workers. The dull grey surface of the choppy sea stretched out beneath them, littered with gas and oil tankers, freighters and ferries as far as the eye could see. Then the platforms came into view. One stormy winter's night in 1969 an American company had found oil in the North Sea, and since then the area had taken on the appearance of an industrial landscape. Factories on stilts extended all the way from Holland to Haltenbank off the coast of Trondheim.

Fierce gusts buffeted the helicopter, and Johanson straightened his headphones. They were all wearing ear-protectors and heavy clothing, and were packed in so tightly that their knees touched. The noise made talk impossible. Lund had closed her eyes.

The helicopter wheeled and proceeded south-west. They were heading for Gullfaks, a group of production platforms belonging to Statoil. Gullfaks C was one of the largest structures in the northern reaches of the North Sea. With 280 workers, it was practically a community in its own right and Johanson shouldn't have been allowed to disembark there. It was years since he'd taken the compulsory safety course for visitors to the platforms. Since then, the regulations had been tightened, but Lund's contacts had cleared the way. In any case, they were only landing in order to board the *Thorvaldson*, which was anchored off Gullfaks.

A sudden gust caused the helicopter to drop. Johanson clutched his armrests but nobody else stirred: the passengers were used to stronger gales than this. Lund opened her eyes and winked at him.

Kare Sverdrup was a lucky man, thought Johanson, but he'd need more than luck to keep up with Tina Lund.

After a while the helicopter dipped and started to bank. The sea tilted up towards Johanson, then a white building came into view. The pilot prepared to land. For a moment the helicopter's side window showed the whole of Gullfaks C, a colossus supported by four steel-reinforced pillars, weighing 1.5 million tonnes altogether, and with a total height of nearly four hundred metres. Over half of the construction lay under water, its pillars extending from the seabed surrounded by a forest of storage tanks. The white tower block where the workers slept was only a small section of the platform. Bundles of pipes, each a metre or more in diameter, connected the layers of decks, which were flanked by cranes and crowned with the derrick – the cathedral of the oil world. A flame shot over the sea from the tip of an enormous steel boom, burning natural gas that had separated from the oil.

Touch-down was surprisingly gentle. Lund yawned and stretched as far as she could. 'Well, that was pleasant,' she said, and someone laughed.

The hatch opened and they clambered out. Johanson walked to the edge of the helipad and looked down. A hundred and fifty metres below, the waves rose and fell. A biting wind cut through his overalls. 'Is anything capable of knocking this thing over?'

'There's nothing on earth that can't be toppled. Get a move on, will you? We don't have time to hang about.' Lund grabbed him by the arm and pulled him after the other passengers, who were disappearing over the side of the helipad. A small, stocky man with a white moustache was standing at the top of the steel steps, waving at them.

'Tina!' he shouted. 'Have you been missing the oil?'

'That's Lars Jörensen,' said Lund. 'He's responsible for monitoring the helicopter and seagoing traffic on Gullfaks C. He's an excellent chess player too.'

Jörensen was wearing a Statoil T-shirt and reminded Johanson of a petrol-pump attendant. He clasped Lund to his chest, then shook hands with Johanson. 'You've picked an inhospitable day,' he said. 'In good weather you can see the full pride of the Norwegian oil industry from here, every last platform.'

'Are you busy at the moment?' asked Johanson, as they climbed down the spiral steps.

'No more so than usual. Your first time on a platform, is it?'

'It's been a while. How much are you producing these days?'

'Less and less. Production on Gullfaks has been stable for a while now, with two hundred thousand barrels coming from twenty-one wellheads. We should be pleased with that, but we're not.' He pointed to a tanker moored to a loading buoy a few hundred metres away. 'We're filling her up. There'll be another along later, and that's it for today. Soon we'll start running out.'

The wellheads weren't directly below the platform but were scattered a fair distance away. The oil was extracted, separated from the natural gas and water, then stored in the tanks on the seabed. From there it was pumped to the loading buoys. A safety zone stretched five hundred metres around the platform and only its maintenance vessels were allowed to cross it.

Johanson peered over the iron railings. 'Hasn't the *Thorvaldson* arrived?' he asked.

'She's at the other loading buoy, just out of sight.'

'So, you don't even let research vessels come close?'

'The *Thorvaldson* doesn't belong to Gullfaks and she's too big for our liking. It's enough trouble trying to persuade the fishermen to steer clear.'

'Do you have much trouble with them?'

'Last week we had to chase away a couple of guys after they'd followed a shoal right under the platform, and at Gullfaks A recently a tanker drifted loose – engine problems. We sent a few people to help, but the crew got it sorted just in time.'

Jörensen spoke casually, but he had described the catastrophe that everyone prayed would never happen: a loaded tanker heading straight for a platform. The impact would send shudders through some of the smaller structures, but, worse still, the tanker might explode. Every platform was equipped with sprinklers that would release several tonnes of water at the least sign of fire, but an exploding tanker could tear a platform to pieces. Such accidents were rare, and usually happened in South America where safety regulations weren't as strictly observed.

'You're looking slim,' said Lund, as Jörensen held the door open for her. They went into the accommodation module and walked down a corridor lined with identical doors that led into the living quarters. 'Don't they feed you well enough?'

'Too well,' laughed Jörensen. 'The chef's amazing. You should see our dining room,' he added quickly to Johanson. 'It makes the Ritz look like a roadside café. No, the platform boss doesn't like North Sea bellies. He's told us to get rid of any extra kilos, or else he'll ban us from the platform.'

'Seriously?'

'Directive from Statoil. I don't know if they'd really go that far. In any case the threat was effective. No one wants to lose their job.'

They reached a narrow staircase and walked down, passing a group of oil workers whom Jörensen greeted. Their footsteps echoed in the steel stairwell.

'Right, this is the end of the line. You've got a choice. Either we go left, grab a coffee and chat for half an hour, or right, to the boat.'

'Coffee sounds good,' said Johanson.

'We haven't time.' Lund told him.

'The *Thorvaldson* won't leave without you,' said Jörensen. 'You could easily—'

'I don't want to have to race there. Next time I'll stay longer, I promise. And I'll bring Sigur too. It's about time someone played you into a corner.'

Jörensen laughed, and Lund and Johanson followed him outside. Wind blasted their faces. They were at the bottom edge of the accommodation module, standing on a thick steel grating, through which they caught glimpses of billowing waves. A constant hissing and droning filled the air. Jörensen led them towards another short gangway. An orange launch was suspended from a crane. 'What are you doing on the *Thorvaldson?*' he asked casually. 'I heard Statoil might be building further out.'

'It's possible,' said Lund.

'A new platform?'

'Not necessarily. Maybe a SWOP.'

Single Well Offshore Production Systems were enormous vessels similar to tankers with their own oil-recovery facility, used in depths of more than three hundred and fifty metres. A flexible flowline kept the vessel in position over the well while the oil was pumped into the hold, which served as a temporary storage tank.

They got into the launch. It was spacious inside, with several rows of benches. Apart from the helmsman they were the only ones on board. The boat jerked as the crane lowered them into the sea. Cracked grey concrete flashed past the side windows, then they were bobbing on the waves. The crane detached itself from the boat and they motored away from the platform.

The *Thorvaldson* was now in view, recognizable, like most research vessels, by its boom, used for manoeuvring submersibles and other equipment into the water. The launch drew up alongside it and docked. Johanson and Lund climbed up a steel ladder, fixed securely to the vessel. As he struggled with his suitcase, it occurred to Johanson that maybe it hadn't been such a good idea to pack half of his wardrobe. Lund, who was ahead, glanced round. 'You thought you were here for a holiday, did you?' she asked.

Johanson sighed. 'I was beginning to think you hadn't noticed.'

Every large landmass in the world was bounded by a relatively shallow strip of water, no more than two hundred metres deep, known as the continental shelf. Technically, it was the underwater continuation of the continental plate. In some parts of the world it extended only a short way into the sea, but in others it continued for hundreds of kilometres until it dipped towards the ocean's floor, either falling away sharply or inclining gently in a terraced slope. The depths beyond the shelf were an unknown universe, more mysterious to science than outer space.

The shelf regions, however, had long been conquered by mankind. Humans were land animals, but needed water to survive, which was why two-thirds of the world's population could be found within sixty kilometres of the shore.

While oceanographic charts showed the shelf around Portugal and northern Spain as a narrow strip of seabed, the perimeter of the British Isles and Scandinavia extended into the water for some distance, so that the two regions merged together to form the North Sea, a relatively shallow expanse of water that averaged between twenty and 150 metres in depth. In its present form it dated back barely ten thousand years, and at first glance there was nothing remarkable about it, with its complex currents and fluctuating water temperatures. In the world economy, though, it played a central role. The North Sea was one of the busiest areas in the world, lined by industrial nations, and home to Rotterdam, the biggest port in history. Although the English Channel was only thirty kilometres wide at its narrowest point, it was one of the world's most travelled waterways: freighters, tankers, ferries and smaller craft jostled for space within its narrow confines.

Three hundred million years ago, vast swamps connected Britain to the continent in an unbroken chain of land. From time to time the area flooded as the waters advanced, then retreated. Gradually, mighty rivers swept into the basin, laying down mud, plant and animal remains that built up into a deposit many hundreds of metres thick. Seams of coal formed, while the land continued to sink. New deposits accumulated, compacting the sediment into sandstone and lime, and trapping organic debris underground. At the same time the temperature in the rock rose. Exposed to the combined effects of heat and pressure, the organic matter underwent complex chemical changes, eventually forming oil and gas, some of which leached out of the porous rock and permeated upwards into the water. The rest remained buried.

For millions of years the shelf had lain untouched.

Then oil was discovered, and Norway joined Britain, Holland and Denmark in a race to exploit the underwater riches. In thirty years, it had become the world's second largest exporter of petroleum. The Norwegian continental shelf contained the bulk of the deposits – roughly half of Europe's oil reserves – and its store of natural gas was equally impressive. The drilling extended ever deeper, and simple scaffold constructions gave way to oil platforms the size of the Empire State Building. It wasn't long before plans to build autonomous subsea processors became reality. It seemed as though the party would last for ever.

However, as fishing yields declined, so did the supply of petroleum. Many subsea oil fields had already been drained, and Europe was faced with the spectre of an enormous scrapyard full of disused platforms. There was only one way out of the plight that the oil nations had brought upon themselves. On the other side of the continental shelf untapped reserves of petroleum were stored beneath the surface of the deep-sea basins and in the continental slopes. Conventional platforms were useless in such conditions, so Lund and her team were developing a different kind of technology. The continental slope wasn't uniformly steep, and in places it sloped down to form terraces – the ideal terrain for a subsea facility. The risks involved in working at depth meant that human labour had to be avoided. With the fall in oil production, the oil workers' fortunes had waned. In the 1970s and 1980s they had been well paid and in demand, but now there were plans to reduce the workforce on Gullfaks C to two dozen. Even an enormous construction like the Troll A platform practically ran itself.

The fact of the matter was that the North Sea oil industry was no longer profitable. But closing it down would be even more costly.

Johanson emerged from his cabin. The atmosphere on board the *Thorvaldson* was one of quiet routine. The boat wasn't especially big. Some of the giant research vessels, like the *Polarstern* from Bremerhaven, had space for helicopters to land on board, but the *Thorvaldson* needed every spare metre for equipment. He strolled over to the railings and gazed out to sea. They had been sailing for almost two hours, passing through conurbations of platforms and oil rigs. Now they were north of the Shetland Islands, beyond the continental shelf, and the view had opened out. Nearly seven hundred metres of water lay between the seabed and the ship's keel. The continental slope had been charted and surveyed, but the zone of eternal darkness still retained its mystery. Powerful floodlights enabled scientists to illuminate small sections, but it was like exploring an entire country by night with a streetlamp.

Johanson remembered the bottle of Bordeaux and the French and Italian cheeses in his suitcase. He went to look for Lund and found her conducting a pre-dive check on the robot. The three-metre-high open-sided box was suspended from the hydraulic boom. The outer casing of its lid bore the name 'Victor'. Cameras and an articulated arm were mounted on the front.

Lund beamed at him. 'Impressed?'

Johanson dutifully looped back around Victor.

'It's a great big yellow vacuum cleaner,' he said.

'Spoilsport.'

'How much does it weigh?'

'Four tonnes. Hey, Jean!' A thin man with red hair peered out from behind a cable drum. Lund beckoned him over. 'Jean-Jacques Alban is first officer. He keeps the *Thorvaldson* afloat,' said Lund. 'Jean, I've got stuff to get on with. You'll look after Sigur for me, won't you?' She hurried off. The two men watched her go.

'I expect you've got more important things to do than explain Victor to me,' said Johanson.

'Oh, it's no problem. You're from the NTNU, right? I gather you've been examining the worms.'

'Why's Statoil so interested in them?'

Alban made a dismissive gesture. 'It's the characteristics of the slope that we care about, really. We found the worms by accident. I reckon the problem's all in Tina's mind.'

'But isn't that why you're here? I mean because of the worms,' said Johanson, surprised.

'Is that what she told you?' Alban shook his head. 'No, that's only part of the mission. We'll follow it up, of course, as we always do, but our

48

main task is to clear the way for an underwater monitoring station. The idea is to build it on top of the oilfield, so if the site seems safe, we can install a subsea unit.'

'Tina mentioned something about a SWOP.'

Alban looked at him uneasily. 'Er, no. As far as I'm aware, the subsea processor is a done deal. I don't think there's been a change of plan.'

So, no floating platforms, then. Johanson decided to quiz him about the robot.

'It's a Victor 6000, a remotely operated vehicle, or ROV,' Alban explained. 'It's got a working depth of six thousand metres and can stay under water for days at a time. We guide its movements from the boat – a cable leading up to the control room delivers its data simultaneously. The next trip is a forty-eight-hour recce. We'll get it to fetch you a handful of worms – Statoil prides itself on preserving biodiversity.' He paused. 'What do you make of the creatures?'

'It's too early to say,' said Johanson.

There was a clunk and Johanson watched as the boom hoisted Victor off the deck.

'Follow me,' said Alban. They headed amidships towards five shed-sized containers. 'Most vessels aren't equipped for using Victor, but since we could accommodate it, we borrowed it from the *Polarstern*.'

'What's in the containers?'

'The hydraulic unit for the winch, plus some other bits of machinery. The one at the front is home to the ROV control room. Mind your head.'

They stepped through a low door. Inside, over half of the space was taken up by the control panel and twin banks of screens. Some were switched off, but the rest showed navigational data and operational feedback from the ROV. A group of men sat with Lund at the consoles.

'The guy in the middle is the pilot,' Alban murmured. 'To his right, the co-pilot operates the articulated arm. Victor's very sensitive and precise, but the operator has to be equally skilled in telling it what to do. The next seat along belongs to the co-ordinator. He maintains contact with the watch officer on the bridge to ensure that the vessel and the robot work together. The scientists are over there, with Tina. She'll operate the cameras and record the footage.

'Are we ready?' he asked her.

'Prepare to lower,' said Lund.

One after another the blank screens lit up. Johanson could make out sections of the stern, the boom, the sky and the sea.

'From now on we can see what Victor sees,' said Alban. 'There are eight separate cameras, one main camera with zoom, two piloting cameras and five others. The picture quality's amazing – sharp images and luminous colours even several thousand metres below the surface.'

The robot descended and the sea loomed closer. Water sloshed over the camera lens and Victor continued downwards. The monitors showed a blue-green world that gradually dimmed.

The control room was filling with people, men and women who'd been working on the boom.

'Floodlights on,' said the co-ordinator.

The area around Victor brightened, but the light remained diffuse. The blue-green paled, and was replaced by artifically lit darkness. Small fish darted into the picture, then the screen filled with bubbles. Plankton, thought Johanson. Red-helmet and transparent comb jellyfish drifted past.

After a while the swarm of particles thinned. The depth sensor recorded five hundred metres.

'What's Victor going to do down there?' asked Johanson.

'Test the seawater and sediment, and collect a few organisms,' said Lund, focusing on the screen, 'but the real boon is the video footage.'

A jagged shape came into view. Victor was descending along a steep wall. Red and orange crayfish waved delicate antennae. It was pitch black in the depths, but the floodlights and cameras brought out the creatures' natural colours vividly. Victor continued past sponges and sea cucumbers, then the terrain levelled off.

'We made it,' said Lund. 'Six hundred and eighty metres.'

'OK.' The pilot leaned forwards. 'Let's bank a little.'

The slope disappeared from the screens. For a while they saw nothing but water until the seabed emerged from the blue-black depths.

'Victor can navigate to an accuracy of within less than a millimetre,' said Alban.

'So where are we now?' asked Johanson.

'Hovering over a plateau. The seabed beneath us contains vast stores of oil.'

'Any hydrates?'

Alban looked at him thoughtfully. 'Sure. Why do you ask?'

'Just interested. So it's here that Statoil wants to build the unit?'

'It's our preferred site, assuming there aren't any problems.'

'Like worms?'

Alban shrugged.

The Frenchman seemed to have an aversion to the topic, thought Johanson. Together they watched as the robot swept over the alien world, overtaking spindly legged sea spiders and fish half buried in the sediment. Its cameras picked up colonies of sponges, translucent jellyfish and miniature cephalopods. At that depth the water wasn't densely populated, but the seabed was home to all kinds of different creatures. After a while the terrain became pockmarked, coarse and covered with what appeared to be vast whip marks.

'Sediment slides,' said Lund. 'The Norwegian slope has seen a bit of movement in its time.'

'What are the rippled lines here?' asked Johanson. Already the terrain had changed again.

'They're from the currents. Let's steer round to the edge of the plateau.' She paused. 'We're pretty close to where we found the worms.'

They stared at the screens. The lights had caught some large whitish areas.

'Bacterial mats,' said Johanson.

'A sure sign of hydrates.'

'Over there,' said the pilot.

The screen showed a sheet of fissured whiteness – deposits of frozen methane. And something else. The room fell silent.

A writhing pink mass obscured the hydrate. For a brief moment they saw individual bodies, then the writhing tubes were too numerous to count. Pink flesh and white bristles curled under and over each other.

There was a sound of disgust from the men at the front. Conditioning, thought Johanson. Most humans disliked crawling, wriggling, sliding creatures, even though they were everywhere. He pictured the hordes of bugs swarming over his skin, and the billions of bacteria in his belly.

But, despite himself, Johanson was unsettled by the worms. The pictures from the Mexican Gulf had shown similarly large colonies, but with smaller worms sitting calmly in their holes. These worms never stopped slithering over the ice, a vast heaving mass that obliterated the surface.

'Let's zigzag round,' said Lund.

The ROV cut through the water in a sweeping slalom movement, the worms ever-present.

Suddenly the ground fell away. The pilot steered the robot to the edge of the plateau. Even with the combined power of eight strong floodlights, visibility was limited to just a few metres, but it was easy to imagine that the worms covered the length of the slope. To Johanson they seemed even bigger than the specimens Lund had brought into the lab.

The screens went dark. Victor had launched itself over the edge. There was a hundred-metre vertical drop to the bottom. The robot raced on at full speed.

'Turn,' said Lund. 'Let's take a look at the wall.'

Particles danced in the beam of the floodlights. Then something big and bright billowed into the frame, filling it for an instant, then retreating at lightning speed.

'What was that?' Lund called.

'Turn back!'

The ROV retraced its steps.

'It's gone.'

'Circle!'

Victor stopped and started to spin, but there was nothing to see, apart from impenetrable darkness and showers of plankton glittering in the light.

'There was something out there,' said the co-ordinator. 'A fish maybe.'

'Bloody big one,' growled the pilot.

Lund turned to Johanson, who shook his head. 'No idea.'

'OK. Let's go a bit deeper.'

The ROV headed towards the slope. A few seconds later a steep wall of seabed loomed into view. A few raised areas of sediment were visible, but the rest was covered with the now-familiar pink masses.

'They're everywhere,' said Lund.

Johanson joined her. 'Have you got a chart of the hydrate deposits here?'

'The area is full of methane – hydrates, pockets in the rock, gas seeping through the seabed . . .'

'I mean the ice on top.'

Lund typed something. A map of the seabed appeared on her screen. 'See the light patches? Those are the deposits.'

'Can you point out Victor's current position?'

'About here.' She indicated an area of the map covered with light patches.

'OK. Steer it this way, along and then up.'

The floodlights found a section of seabed devoid of worms. After a while the ground sloped upwards and then the steep wall appeared.

'Take us higher,' said Lund. 'Nice and slowly.'

Within a few moments they were back to the same picture as before. Pink tubular bodies with white bristles.

'Just as you'd expect,' muttered Johanson. 'Assuming your map is right, this is the site of the main belt of hydrates. The bacteria will be grazing the methane here . . . and being gobbled by the worms.'

'How about the numbers? Would you have expected to see millions?'

'No.'

Lund leaned back in her chair. 'All right,' she said, to the man controlling the articulated arm. 'Let's set Victor down for a moment. We'll pick up a batch of worms and take a look at the area.'

It was gone ten when Johanson heard a knock at his door. Lund came in and flopped into the little armchair, which, together with a tiny table, was the only comfort the cabin offered.

'My eyes ache,' she said. 'Alban's taken over for a while.'

Her gaze wandered over to the cheese and the open bottle of Bordeaux. 'I should have guessed.' She laughed. 'So that's why you rushed off.'

Johanson had left the control room thirty minutes earlier.

'Brie de Meaux, Taleggio, Munster, a mature goat's cheese and some Fontina from the mountains in Piedmont,' he said. 'Plus a baguette and some butter. Would you like a glass of wine?'

'Do you need to ask? What is it?'

'A Pauillac. You'll have to forgive me for not decanting it. The *Thorvaldson* doesn't have any respectable crystal. Did you see anything interesting?'

He handed her a glass, and she took a gulp. 'The bloody things have set up camp on the hydrates. They're everywhere.'

Johanson sat down opposite her on the edge of the bed and buttered a piece of baguette. 'Remarkable.'

Lund helped herself to some cheese. 'The others are starting to think we should be worried. Especially Alban.'

'So there weren't as many last time?'

'No. I mean, more than enough for my liking – but that put me in a minority of one.'

Johanson smiled at her. 'People with good taste are always out-numbered.'

'Tomorrow morning Victor will be back on board with some specimens. You're welcome to have a look at them.' She stood up, chewing, and peered out of the porthole. The sky had cleared. A ray of moonlight shone on the water, illuminating the rolling waves. 'I've looked at the video sequence hundreds of times, trying to work out what we saw. Alban's convinced it was a fish . . . and if it was, it must have been a manta or something even bigger. But it didn't seem to have a shape.'

'Maybe it was a reflection,' Johanson suggested.

'It can't have been – it was just a few metres away, right on the edge of the beam, and it disappeared in a flash, as though it couldn't stand the light or was afraid.'

'A shoal can twitch away like that. When fish swim close together they can look like a—'

'It wasn't a shoal, Sigur. It was practically flat. It was a wide two-dimensional thing, sort of . . . glassy. Like a giant jellyfish.'

'There you are, then.'

'But it wasn't a jellyfish.'

They ate in silence for a while.

'You lied to Jörensen,' Johanson said suddenly. 'You're not going to build a SWOP. Whatever it is you're developing, you won't need any workers.'

Lund lifted her glass, took a sip and put it down carefully. 'True.'

'So why lie to him? Were you worried it would break his heart?'

'Maybe.'

'You'll do that anyway. You've no use for oil workers, have you?'

'Listen, Sigur, I don't like lying to him but, hell, this whole industry is having to adapt and jobs will be lost. Jörensen knows that the workforce on Gullfaks C will be cut by nine-tenths. It costs less to

54

refit an entire platform than it does to pay so many people. Statoil is toying with the idea of getting rid of all the workers on Gullfaks B. We could operate it from another platform, but it's scarcely worthwhile.'

'Surely you're not trying to tell me that your business isn't worth running?'

'The offshore business was only really worth running at the beginning of the seventies when OPEC sent oil prices soaring. Since the mideighties the yield has fallen. Things'll get tough for northern Europe when the North Sea wells run dry, so that's why we're drilling further out, using ROV's like Victor, and AUVs.'

The Autonomous Underwater Vehicle functioned in much the same way as Victor, but without an umbilical cord of cable to connect it to the ship. It was like a planetary scout, able to venture into the most inhospitable regions. Highly flexible and mobile, it could also make a limited range of decisions. With its invention, oil companies were suddenly a step closer to building and maintaining subsea stations at depths of up to five or six thousand metres.

'You don't have to apologise,' said Johanson, as he topped up their glasses. 'It's not your fault.'

'I'm not apologising,' Lund snapped. 'Anyway, it's everyone's fault. If we didn't waste so much energy, we wouldn't have these problems.'

'We would – just not right now. But your environmental concern is touching.'

'What of it?' She bristled at the jibe. 'Oil companies *are* capable of learning from their mistakes.'

'But which ones?'

'Over the next few decades we'll be grappling with the problem of dismantling over six hundred uneconomic, out-of-date platforms. Do you have any idea what that costs? Billions! And by then the shelf will be out of oil. So don't make out that we're irresponsible.'

'OK, OK!'

'Unmanned subsea processors are the only way forward. Without them, Europe will be dependent on the pipelines in the Near East and South America.'

'I don't doubt it. I just wonder if you know what you're up against.'

'Meaning?'

'Well, massive technological challenges for a start.'

'We're aware of that.'

'You're planning to process huge quantities of oil and corrosive chemicals under extreme pressure, with little provision for human intervention . . .' Johanson hesitated '. . . you don't really know what it's like in the depths.'

'That's why we're finding out.'

'Like today? It's not enough. It's like Granny coming home from holiday with some snapshots and saying she *knows* about the places that she's been. Basically, you're interfering with a system you simply don't understand.'

'Not that again,' groaned Lund.

'You think I'm wrong?'

'I can spell ecosystem backwards. I can even do it in my sleep. Is this some kind of anti-oil vendetta?'

'No. I'm just in favour of getting to know the world around us, and I'm pretty certain you're repeating your mistakes. At the end of the sixties you filled the North Sea with platforms – and now they're in the way. You need to make sure you're not so hasty in the deep sea.'

'If we're being so hasty, why did I send you the worms?'

'You're right. *Ego te absolvo.*'

Johanson decided to change the subject. 'Kare Sverdrup seems a nice guy.'

'Do you think so?'

'Absolutely.'

Lund swirled the wine in her glass. 'It's all very new,' she said. Neither said anything for a while.

'In love?' asked Johanson, eventually.

'Me or him?'

'You.'

'Hmm.' She smiled. 'I think so.'

'You think so?'

'I work in exploration. I guess I'm still feeling my way.'

It was midnight when she left. At the door she looked back at the empty glasses. 'A few weeks ago I'd have been yours,' she said, sounding almost regretful.

Johanson propelled her into the corridor. 'At my age you get over it,' he said.

She came back, leaned forward and kissed his cheek. 'Thanks for the wine.'

Life consists of compromises and missed opportunities, thought Johanson, as he shut the door. Then he grinned. He'd seized too many opportunities to be entitled to complain.

18 March

Leon Anawak waited with bated breath. Go on, he thought. You can do it.

For the sixth time the beluga turned and swam towards the mirror. Inside the underwater viewing area at Vancouver Aquarium, a small group of students and journalists waited expectantly. Through the glass wall in front of them they could see right across the inside of the pool. Rays of sunshine slanted into the water, dancing on the bottom and the sides. In the darkened viewing area, sunlight and shadow flickered across the watching faces.

Anawak had marked the whale with temporary dye, and a coloured dot now graced its lower jaw. The position had been chosen carefully so that the only way the whale could see it was by looking into the mirror. The beluga swam steadily towards one of two large mirrors that had been mounted on the reflective glass walls of the tank. The single-mindedness of its approach left Anawak in no doubt as to the outcome of the trial. As the beluga passed the viewing area it twisted its white body as if to show them the dot on its chin. When it got to the wall it sank through the water until it was level with the mirror. Then, pausing for a moment, it manoeuvred itself into a vertical position, turning its head from side to side, trying to find the best angle at which to view the dot. It paddled its flippers to keep itself upright, pointing its bulbous forehead first this way, then that.

In general, whales looked nothing like people, but at that moment the beluga seemed almost human. Briefly it seemed to smile. Indeed, unlike dolphins, the entire species could make their mouths smile or droop, even purse their lips, but it had nothing to do with their mood: the change in facial expression enabled them to vocalise.

At that moment, inspection complete, the beluga lost interest in the dot. Banking through the water in an elegant curve, it swam away from the wall.

'Well, that's that,' said Anawak, softly.

'Which means what?' asked a female journalist, when the whale showed no sign of returning.

'It knows who it is. Come on, let's go upstairs.'

They emerged into the daylight, with the pool on their left. Swimming close to the rippled surface, the two belugas glided past. Anawak had deliberately refrained from explaining the experiment in advance. He was cautious about reading too much into a whale's behaviour, in case wishful thinking gained the upper hand, so he let the others share their conclusions first.

They confirmed his findings.

'Congratulations,' he said. 'You've just witnessed an experiment that went down in the history of behavioural science as the "mark-test" or "mirror-test". Does everyone know what that means?'

The students did, but the journalists were less sure.

'Not to worry,' said Anawak. 'We'll whiz through it now. The mark-test dates back to the seventies. Some of you may have heard of Gordon Gallup . . .' Half of his listeners nodded; the others shook their heads. 'He's a professor of psychology at the State University of New York. One day he hit on the crazy idea of exposing primates to their reflections. Most of them ignored the mirror, some assumed it was a rival and went on the attack, but the chimpanzees recognised themselves and used the mirror to look at themselves. Now, that was significant, since most animals can't identify their mirror image. Most animals feel, act and react – but they're not *aware* of themselves. They don't perceive themselves as independent individuals, distinct from other members of their species.'

Anawak went on to explain how Gallup had used a coloured dye to mark the foreheads of the apes before he exposed them to the mirror. The chimpanzees were quick to realise who they were looking at. They inspected the dye, raised their hands to touch it, then sniffed at their fingers. Gallup carried out the same experiment with parrots, elephants and other primates. The only animals consistently to pass the test were chimpanzees and orang-utans, leading him to the conclusion that they were capable of self-recognition and were therefore self-aware.

'But Gallup went further than that,' said Anawak. 'For years he'd rejected the idea that animals could understand the state of mind of other beings, but the results of the mark-test changed all that. These days, he not only believes that chimpanzees and orang-utans are aware of their identity but that their self-awareness allows them to attribute intent and emotion to other beings and so empathise with them. In other words, it enables them to infer the mental states of others. That's the essence of Gallup's theory, and it's got a big following.'

He'd have to rein in the journalists later, he thought. He didn't want to open a paper in a few days' time and see headlines about belugas as psychiatrists, dolphins setting up rescue missions and chimpanzees playing chess.

'Until the early nineties the mark-test was conducted almost exclusively on land animals. There'd been plenty of speculation about IQ in whales and dolphins, but proving their intelligence was never going to be popular with certain sectors of industry. Monkey meat appeals to only a small percentage of the world's population but whales and dolphins are sought after, and it never looks good for hunters when their prey turns out to be smart. When we started conducting mark-tests on dolphins we upset a lot of people. In the run-up to the experiments we lined the pool with reflective glass and added some mirrors, then marked the dolphins with a spot of black ink. They searched the walls until they located the mirrors – they had obviously realised that they'd be able to see the spot more clearly in the mirror than the clear glass. To make the test more rigorous, we didn't always use a real pen. Sometimes we used a water-filled marker. That way we could test whether or not the dolphins were just reacting to the sensation of the mark being made. The test results showed that the dolphins looked longer and harder at their reflections whenever the mark was visible.'

'Did you reward them for their behaviour?' asked a student.

'No, and we didn't train them. In fact, we even kept changing the location of the mark to make sure the results weren't skewed by learning or by habit-forming behaviours. A few weeks ago we began the trials again, this time with belugas. So far we've marked them six times, including twice with the placebo pen. You've seen for yourselves what happens. The whale approached the mirror and looked for the mark. When the mark wasn't there, it swam away. To me, that proves that belugas possess a degree of self-awareness on a par with chimpanzees. In some respects whales and humans may have more in common than we think.'

A student raised her hand. 'Can we tell from the experiment that dolphins and whales have minds then?'

'That's right.'

'Then where's the proof?'

Anawak was taken aback. 'I thought I'd explained that. Didn't you see what happened in the pool?'

'Sure. I saw a whale inspecting its mirror-image. The beluga knows who it is – but does that necessarily mean it's self-aware?'

'You've just answered the question. It knows who it is. It's *aware* of itself.'

'That's not what I meant.' She took a step forward. She had red hair, a small pointy nose and incisors that seemed too big for her mouth. 'The experiment looks for observational faculties and the ability of the whale to recognise its body. From what we've just seen, the beluga passed on both counts. But you still haven't proven that whales have any *permanent* sense of identity, and you can't jump to conclusions about their attitude to other living things.'

'I didn't.'

'You did. You cited Gallup's theory about certain animals being able to infer the mental state of others.'

'I said primates.'

'Well, that's pretty controversial in itself. In any case, I didn't hear you qualify your statement in relation to dolphins or whales – or maybe I misheard you.'

'There's no need for me to qualify anything,' Anawak said peevishly. 'We've just proven that whales can recognise themselves.'

'That seems to be what the experiment indicates, yes.'

'Then what are you trying to say?'

Her eyes widened. 'It's obvious, isn't it? I mean, you can see how a beluga *responds*, but there's no way of knowing what it's *thinking*. I've read Gallup's stuff too. He thinks he can prove that animals are sensitive to each other's mental states, but he relies on the assumption that animals think and feel as we do. You're trying to humanise whales.'

So that was her objection. Unbelievable. It was exactly what Anawak had always argued. 'Is that how it seemed to you?'

'Well you said so yourself. "Whales have more in common with humans than we think."'

'You should have paid more attention, Miss. . .'

'Delaware. Alicia Delaware.'

'Miss Delaware.' Anawak was back in control. 'I said, "Humans and whales may have more in common than we think."'

'And the difference is?'

'In the perspective. It's not a question of finding parallels to prove that whales are like humans, or of using mankind as the template by which to judge whales. It's about finding fundamental similarities that—'

'But I don't think you *can* compare an animal's self-awareness with a human's. Even the basic stuff is so different. I mean, first of all humans have a permanent sense of identity, which allows them to—'

'Wrong,' Anawak interrupted her. 'Humans only develop a stable sense of self-awareness under specific sets of circumstances. Research shows that infants first start to recognise themselves in a mirror between the ages of eighteen and twenty-four months. Until then they're unable to conceptualise the self. In fact, they're even less self-aware than the whale we just observed. And stop referring back to Gallup. My aim is to try to understand the whales. What's yours?'

'I was only trying to—'

'Well, before you try anything else, may be you should imagine how a beluga might judge you. I mean, what's a whale going to think if it sees you looking in the mirror painting your face? Oh, it'll realise you've identified the person in the mirror, sure, but it won't find much evidence of intelligent behaviour. Come to think of it, if it doesn't like your makeup, it might even wonder if you're really self-aware. It's bound to question your IQ.'

Alicia Delaware went red. She started to answer, but Anawak cut her off. 'Needless to say, these tests are just a start,' he said. 'In any case, no one seriously involved in studying whales and dolphins wants to bring back the old myth of man's aquatic friend with the winning smile. I don't suppose whales and dolphins are especially interested in humans, particularly since they inhabit a different environment. They've got different needs from us and they've evolved differently. But if our research can persuade people to respect and protect them, it's worth the effort.'

He answered a few more questions, and finally said goodbye to the group. He waited until they were out of sight, then reviewed the trial with his research team and arranged the dates and procedures for the remaining tests. When everyone had gone, he walked to the edge of the pool, took a deep breath and tried to relax.

PR wasn't one of his strengths, but he had to learn to deal with it. His career was on track, and he'd made his reputation as a brilliant young scientist. No doubt he'd be dragged into countless more arguments with the Alicia Delawares of this world, kids fresh out of university who were so immersed in their textbooks that they'd never even touched the sea.

He crouched and dabbled his fingers in the cool water of the belugas' pool. It was still early. They always tried to conduct tests or demonstrations either before the aquarium opened or when it was closed in the evening. After the long stretch of rain, March was redeeming itself, and the morning sunshine felt pleasantly warm on his skin.

She'd said he treated whales like humans. The accusation had hit home. Anawak prided himself on his sober approach to science. In fact, he led his whole life soberly. He didn't drink and he never went to parties. His research was based on rigour, not attention-seeking theories. He was an atheist, who detested new-age spirituality and avoided projecting human values on animals. Dolphins in particular had become the focus of a romantic way of thinking that was almost as dangerous as hatred or contempt. People tended to view them as a superior species, clinging to them as though their supposed goodness would somehow rub off. The ignorance that exposed dolphins to horrendous cruelty also led to their unqualified idealisation. Humans either tortured or loved them to death.

And Alicia Delaware had had the nerve to use his own arguments against him.

Anawak patted the surface of the water. After a while the beluga with the dot on its chin swam over, poked up her head and allowed herself to be stroked. She gave a series of low whistles. Anawak wondered if she felt or could understand any of the emotions that humans experienced. There was no evidence to prove it – in that respect Alicia Delaware had been right. But no one had proven that they *didn't* have feelings.

The beluga warbled and disappeared underwater. A shadow fell over Anawak. He turned, and found himself looking at a pair of hand-stitched cowboy boots. Oh, great, he thought. That's all I need.

'Good morning, Leon,' said the man standing beside him. 'Who've you guys been mistreating today?'

Anawak stood up to greet the intruder. Jack Greywolf looked like something out of a modern-day Western. His colossal muscular frame was clad entirely in grease-speckled suede. Chains of traditional Indian jewellery dangled over his barrel-like chest. Long silky black hair streamed down his back from beneath his feathered cap. It was well groomed, but in all other respects he looked as though he'd spent weeks living wild on the prairie, deprived of soap and water. Anawak responded to the mocking grin with a thin smile. 'Who let you in, Jack? No, don't tell me. The Great Spirit Manitou, I bet.'

The grin widened. 'I got special permission.'

'Oh, yeah?'

'From the Pope in person. For Christ's sake, Leon, I came through the gate with the rest of them. The aquarium's open.'

Anawak realised he had lost track of the time. 'This better be a coincidence.'

Greywolf pursed his lips. 'Not exactly.'

'Uh-huh. So you were looking for me.' Anawak started to walk away, forcing Greywolf to follow. The first visitors were already strolling past. 'What can I do for you?'

'You know exactly what you can do.'

'Oh, don't start that again.'

'Join us.'

'Forget it.'

'Come on, Leon, you're one of us. Those hordes of rich assholes are filming the whales to death. That's not what you want, is it?'

'Nope.'

'People listen to you, Leon. If only you'd speak out against whale-watching, they'd take it seriously. We could use a guy like you.'

Anawak stopped in his tracks. 'That's just it. You think I could be useful. But I don't want to be useful to anyone except those who really need me.'

'Look!' Greywolf pointed in the direction of the beluga pool. 'They need you. It makes me sick to see you here, getting cosy with a pair of *captives*. If you're not keeping them locked up, you're hounding them down. Every time you people take the tourists out in your boats you're hastening their death.'

'Tell me, Jack, are you a vegetarian?'

'What?' Greywolf squinted at him.

'I was wondering whom they'd skinned to make your jacket.' He walked on.

Greywolf hurried after him. 'That's different. Indians have

always lived in harmony with nature. They used the skins of the animals to—'

'Spare me the details.'

'But that's how it is.'

'Do you know your problem, Jack? Actually, you've got two. In the first place you pretend to be a devoted environmentalist, when all you're doing is fighting a war on behalf of the Indians who sorted out their problems years ago. And, second, you're not an Indian.'

Greywolf bristled. Anawak knew that Greywolf had been charged several times with assault, and wondered how far he could push him. One blow from the giant would finish the argument for once and for all.

'Why do you talk such shit, Leon?'

'You're only half Indian,' said Anawak. He paused by the sea otters' pool to watch them dart through the water like torpedoes. Their fur glistened in the morning sun. 'In fact, you're not even that. You're about as Indian as a Siberian polar bear. You don't know where you belong, you never make a go of anything, and you use your environmental crap to piss all over other people. Now, let me out of here.'

Greywolf squinted up at the sun. 'I can't hear you, Leon,' he said. 'It looks like you're talking but I can't hear the words. All I hear is a meaningless din, like gravel pouring on a roof.'

'Ouch!'

'Come on, it's not like I want much from you, just a little support.'

'I can't support you.'

'I've even gone to the trouble of coming here to tell you what we're planning next. I didn't have to.'

Anawak stiffened. 'What is it?'

'Tourist-watching.' Greywolf burst out laughing. His white teeth glinted like ivory. 'We'll be joining you in our boats to photograph the tourists. We'll stare at them, pull up alongside them, try to grab hold of them. Then they'll know what it feels like to be gawped at and pawed.'

'I'll have you stopped.'

'You can't. This is a free country, and no one can tell us when and where to sail. We've laid our plans and we're ready for action – although maybe if you were a bit more accommodating I'd think about calling it off.'

Anawak stared at him. 'There aren't any whales around anyway,' he said.

'Because you've driven them away.'

'It's nothing to do with us.'

'Yeah, right. We're never the ones at fault. It's always the animals. They're forever swimming into harpoons or posing for photos In any case, I heard humpbacks had been sighted.'

'A few.'

'I guess your business must be suffering. You don't want us to dent your profits even more.'

'Get lost, Jack.'

'That was my final offer.'

'Thank God.'

'Leon, you could at least put in a good word for us. We need money. We rely on donations. It's for a good cause. Can't you see that? We're both working for the same thing.'

'I don't think so. Take care, Jack.'

Anawak quickened his pace. The eco-warrior didn't follow. Instead he shouted, 'Stubborn bastard!'

Anawak walked determinedly past the dolphinarium and headed for the exit.

'Leon, you know what *your* problem is? Maybe I'm not a proper Indian, but *you are*.'

'I'm not an Indian,' murmured Anawak.

'Oh, sorry!' yelled Greywolf, as if he'd heard him. 'You think you're special, don't you? Well, how come you've abandoned your people? Why aren't you there for them, where you're needed?'

'Asshole,' hissed Anawak. The beluga test had gone so well – it might have been a really good day. Now he felt worn down and miserable.

His people . . .

Who did Greywolf think he was?

Where he was needed!

'I'm needed here.' He snorted.

A woman walked past, looking at him strangely. Anawak glanced round. He was on the street outside the aquarium. Shaking with fury, he got into his car, drove to the terminal at Tsawwassen, and took the ferry back to Vancouver Island.

The next day he rose early and decided to walk to the whaling station. Wisps of pink cloud trailed on the horizon, but the mountains, houses and boats still cast dark shadows on the perfectly still water. Within a few hours the tourists would arrive. Anawak walked the length of the jetty to where the Zodiacs were moored and leaned over the wooden railings.

Two small cutters sailed past. Anawak wondered whether to call Susan Stringer and talk her into going out with him to look for whales. As Greywolf had said, the first humpbacks had been sighted, which was reassuring, but it didn't explain where they'd been hiding. Maybe together he and Stringer could identify a few. She had sharp eyes, and he enjoyed her company. She was one of the few people who never pestered him with questions about his background.

Even Samantha Crowe had asked about it. Oddly, he might have told her a bit about himself, but by now she would be on her way home.

Anawak decided to let Stringer sleep and set off on his own. He went in to the station where he stowed a laptop, camera, binoculars, tape-recorder, hydrophone and headphones in a waterproof bag. He placed a cereal bar and two cans of iced tea on top, then headed for the *Blue Shark*. He let the boat chug leisurely through the lagoon, waiting until the town was behind him before he opened the throttle. The prow rose up in the waves and wind swept into his face, driving the gloomy thoughts from his mind.

Twenty minutes later he was steering through a group of tiny islands and out on to the silvery-black open sea. The waves rolled in sluggishly, separated by long intervals. He eased off the throttle, and as the coast disappeared, he gazed into the morning light, trying not to succumb to the pessimism that had lately become a habit. Whales had been sighted, and not just residents: the humpbacks were migrants, on their way from California or Hawaii.

Once the boat was far enough out he turned off the engine, opened a can of iced tea, drank it, and sat down with the binoculars.

It was an age before he spotted anything. Then a dark shape caught his eye, but vanished in a trice. 'Go on, show yourself,' he whispered. 'I know you're out there.'

He scanned the ocean intently. The minutes ticked by and nothing happened. Then, one after the other, two dark silhouettes rose above the waves at some distance from the boat. A sound like gunfire rang out across the water as two clouds of white spray shot into the air, like breath on a winter's morning.

Humpback whales.

Anawak was laughing with joy. Like any competent cetologist, he could identify a whale by its blow – a large one could fill several cubic metres. The air in the lungs would compress, then shoot out at high speed through the narrow holes, expanding and cooling in the atmosphere to form a spray of misty droplets. The shape and size of the blow varied, even within a single species. It depended on the whale's size, the duration of a dive and even the wind. But this time there was no doubt: those bushy clouds of spray were characteristic of the humpback.

Anawak flipped open the laptop and booted it up. The hard drive contained a database with descriptions of hundreds of whales which regularly passed that way. To the untrained eye the little of the whale visible above the water was scarcely enough to identify the species, let alone the individual, and to make matters worse, the view was often obscured by rough seas, mist, rain or blinding sunshine. But each whale had its own identifying features. The easiest way to tell them apart was by looking at the flukes. When a whale dived, its tail often flicked right out of the water and the underside of each fluke was unique to that animal, differing in pattern, structure and form. Anawak could identify many flukes from memory, but the photos on the laptop helped.

He was willing to bet that the two whales out there were old friends.

After a while the black humps resurfaced. First to appear were the blowholes, little raised bumps on top of the head, barely visible among the waves. Then came the firing noise again, followed by two puffs of air, rising in synchrony. This time the whales didn't sink back into the water, but raised their humps high above the waves. Their stumpy dorsal fins came into view, arching slowly through the air, then slicing back into the water. Anawak had a clear view of the whales' backs with their prominent vertebrae. Then they dived again, their flukes rising leisurely out of the water.

Hurriedly Anawak raised the binoculars for a glimpse of the undersides, but failed. Not to worry. The first commandment of whale-watching was patience, and there was plenty of time before the tourists arrived. He opened the second can of iced tea, unwrapped the cereal bar and took a bite.

He didn't have long to wait before his faith was rewarded, and five humps ploughed through the water not far from the boat. Anawak's heart quickened. The whales were close now. Full of anticipation he waited for the flukes. He was so engrossed in the spectacle that he didn't notice the enormous black shadow by the boat. It was only when the creature loomed vertically out of the water, towering above him, that he turned and jumped.

Instantly he forgot the other humps.

The whale's head had risen almost silently. Now it was almost touching the boat's rubber hull. Three and a half metres of whale extended upright out of the water, the drooping mouth covered with barnacles and knotty bulges. An eye as big as a human fist stared at him.

It wasn't the first time Anawak had seen a whale at such close-quarters. On dive trips he'd swum alongside them, stroking and clutching on to them. He'd ridden on them. It wasn't unusual for grey whales, humpbacks or orcas to poke their heads out of the water right next to the Zodiac to look for landmarks or examine the boat.

But this was different.

Anawak wasn't sure if he was watching the whale or if it was watching him. The enormous mammal didn't seem interested in the boat. Looking out from under its elephantine lid, the humpback's eye was fixed on him. Beneath the surface, whales had acute vision, but outside their natural element they were damned to short-sightedness by their globular eyes. Close up like that, though, the humpback must be able to see him as clearly as he could see it.

Slowly, so that he did not frighten it, Anawak stretched out an arm and stroked the smooth, damp skin. The whale showed no sign of wanting to dive. Its eye shifted focus slightly, but returned to him. There was something almost intimate about the scene. As pleased as he was to see the animal, Anawak wondered what it stood to gain from such a lengthy observation. Under normal circumstances a spyhop lasted seconds. It cost a lot of energy to stay vertical like that.

'Where've you been all this time?' he asked.

A barely audible splash sounded from the other side of the boat. Anawak swivelled just in time to see another head rising from the water. The second was smaller than the first, but just as close. It, too, fixed Anawak with a black eye.

What did they want from him?

Uneasiness crept over him. It wasn't normal for whales to stare fixedly like that. He'd never seen anything like it. All the same he couldn't resist bending down to his bag and fishing out his digital camera. He held it up in the air. 'Now, keep nice and still . . .'

Maybe the camera was a mistake. If so, it was the first time in the history of whale-watching that humpbacks had objected to having their picture taken. As if on command, the two enormous heads vanished, like a pair of islands sinking beneath the waves. There were a few quiet gurgling noises, a slurp and some bubbles, then Anawak was alone again on the shimmering sea.

The sun was rising over the nearby coast. Mist hung over the mountains. The grey water was turning blue.

Not a whale in sight.

Anawak released the air from his lungs and stuffed the camera back into the open bag. He was about to pick up the binoculars when he thought better of it. His two new friends couldn't have gone far yet. He pulled out the cassette-recorder, put on the headphones and lowered the hydrophone slowly into the water. The headphones crackled, plunked and droned, but there was nothing to indicate the presence of a whale. Anawak waited, expecting to hear the distinctive call of a humpback, but everything was quiet.

In the end he hauled the hydrophone back on board.

Some time later he spotted clouds of spray in the distance, but that was the last he saw of them.

On the way back to Tofino, he thought about how tourists would have reacted to the spectacle – and how they'd react if it happened again. The news would travel fast. Davie's and their tame whales – they'd be inundated with bookings.

Fantastic!

As the Zodiac forged ahead through the still waters of the bay, Anawak stared out at the nearby forest. It was almost too fantastic.

23 March

Sigur Johanson woke with a start, groped for his alarm-clock, then realised his phone was ringing. Rubbing his eyes and swearing, he hauled himself upright, but his sense of balance eluded him and he fell back on to his pillow. His head was spinning.

He tried to remember the previous night. They'd stayed out late drinking, he, some colleagues and a few students. They'd only meant to have dinner at Havfruen, a restaurant in a converted wharf warehouse not far from Gamle Bybro, the old town bridge. It served great seafood and some very good wine. Some truly excellent wine, he recalled. From their table next to the window they'd looked out at the Nid, with its jetties pointing upstream and the little boats, and watched the river flow leisurely towards the nearby Trondheim fjord. Someone had started to tell jokes, then Johanson had gone with the owner into the restaurant's dank wine-cellar to inspect the precious vintage bottles . . .

He sighed. I'm fifty-six, he told himself, as he pulled himself up again. I shouldn't do this any more.

The telephone was still ringing. He got to his feet and stumbled into the living room. Was he supposed to be lecturing that morning? He imagined himself standing in front of his students, looking every minute of his age, barely able to stop his chin sagging on to his chest. His tongue felt heavy and furred, disinclined to do anything involving speech.

When he reached the phone it dawned on him that it was Saturday. His mood improved dramatically. 'Johanson,' he answered, sounding unexpectedly lucid.

'You took your time,' said Tina Lund.

Johanson rolled his eyes and lowered himself into an armchair. 'What time is it?'

'Half past six.'

'It's Saturday.'

'I know it is. Is something wrong? You don't sound too good.'

'I'm not feeling too good. Why the hell are you phoning me at this uncivilised hour?'

Lund giggled. 'I was hoping to talk you into coming over to Tyholt.'

'To the institute? For Christ's sake, Tina, why?'

'I thought we could have breakfast together. It'll be fun. Kare's in Trondheim for a few days, and I know he'd love to see you.' She paused. 'Besides, there's something I want your opinion on.'

'What?'

'Not on the phone. So, are you coming or not?'

'All right, give me an hour,' said Johanson. He yawned expansively, then stopped in case he strained his jaw. 'In fact, give me two. I'll call in at the lab on the way. There might be news on the worms.'

'Let's hope so. Weird, isn't it? First I was the one making all the fuss, and now it's the other way round. OK, take your time – but don't be too long!'

'At your service,' Johanson mumbled. Still dizzy, he dragged himself off to the shower.

Thirty minutes later, he was feeling more alive. Outside, it was sunny and Kirkegata Street was all but deserted. The last piles of snow had melted and as Johanson drove out towards the Gloshaugen campus he was whistling Vivaldi. The university was supposed to be closed at the weekend, but no one paid any attention to the rules: it was the best time to sort your mail and work undisturbed.

Johanson went to the post-room, rummaged in his pigeon-hole and pulled out a thick envelope. It had been sent from Kiel and almost certainly contained the lab results that Lund was so desperate to see. He stowed it away, unopened, went back to his car and resumed his journey to Tyholt.

The Institute for Marine Technology, or Marintek, as it was known, had close links with the NTNU, SINTEF and the Statoil research centre. In addition to its collection of simulation tanks and wave tunnels, it also housed the world's biggest artificial ocean-research basin, offering scientists scale-model testing in simulated wind and waves. The Norwegian shelf was covered with floating production systems that had been tested in the eighty-metre-long by ten-metre-deep pool. Two wave machines created miniature currents and storms that seemed terrifyingly powerful. Johanson was pretty sure that Lund would use it to test the underwater unit that she was planning for the slope.

As he had expected, he found her at the poolside, talking to some scientists. There was something droll about the scene. Divers were weaving through the blue-green water past Toytown platforms, while miniature tankers floated past lab staff in rowing-boats. It resembled a cross between a toy-shop and a boating party, but it had a serious purpose: the offshore industry needed Marintek's blessing before any new structure could be built.

Lund spotted him, broke off her conversation and headed over. It meant walking all the way round the pool, which she did at her usual canter.

'Why not take a boat?' asked Johanson.

'This isn't the village pond, you know,' she said. 'Everything has to be co-ordinated. If I ploughed willy-nilly through the basin, hundreds of oil workers would die in the tidal wave.'

She gave him a peck on the cheek. 'You're all scratchy.'

'All men with beards are scratchy,' said Johanson. 'It's lucky for you Kare hasn't got one, or you'd have no excuse for picking him instead of me. So, what are you working on? The subsea problem?'

'As best we can – the basin only lets us simulate realistic conditions for depths of up to a thousand metres.'

'You don't need to go deeper.'

'Theoretically, no. But we still like to run through the scenarios on the computer. Sometimes its predictions don't fit the results from the basin, so we keep adjusting the parameters until we get a match.'

'Shell's looking into building a unit two thousand metres down. It was in the papers yesterday. You've got competition.'

'I know. Marintek's doing the research for them too. It'll be an even harder nut to crack. Come on, let's get some breakfast.'

Once they were out in the corridor Johanson said; 'I still don't understand why you can't use a SWOP. Isn't it easier to work on a floating platform and connect it via flexible flowlines?'

She shook her head. 'Too risky. Floating structures still have to be anchored.'

'I know that.'

'And they can always come adrift.'

'But the shelf's full of them!'

'Granted, but only where it's shallower. In deeper water, the waves and currents are different. Besides, it's not just a question of anchoring

73

the units. The longer the riser, the less stable it becomes. The last thing we need is an environmental disaster. And, anyway, who'd want to work on a floating platform on the other side of the shelf? Even the hardiest would spew their guts out. This way.'

They went up some stairs.

'I thought we were going for breakfast,' said Johanson in surprise.

'We are, but there's something I want to show you first.'

Lund pushed open a door and they went into an office on the floor immediately above the ocean basin. The large glass windows looked down on neat rows of sunlit gardens and gabled houses that stretched out in the direction of Trondheim fjord.

She walked over to a desk, pulled up two Formica chairs and flipped open the widescreen laptop. Her fingers drummed impatiently while the program loaded. The screen filled with photos that seemed strangely familiar. They showed a milky-white patch dissolving into darkness at the edges. All of a sudden Johanson realised what he was looking at. 'The footage from Victor,' he said. 'It's that thing we saw on the slope.'

'The thing I was worried about.' Lund nodded.

'Do you know what it is yet?'

'No, but I can tell you what it isn't. It's not a jellyfish, and it's definitely not a shoal. We've tried putting the image through countless different filters, but this is the best we could do.' She enlarged the first photo. 'The thing was caught in Victor's floodlights. We saw a part of it, but not as it would have looked without the artificial lighting.'

'Without the lighting you wouldn't have seen anything. It was far too deep.'

'You reckon?'

'Unless, of course, the thing was bioluminescent, in which case—' He broke off.

Lund appeared pleased with herself. Her fingers danced over the keyboard and the picture changed again. This time they were looking at a section from the top right-hand corner. At the edge of the image, the bright patch dimmed into darkness, and faint marks could be seen. It was a different kind of light, a deep-blue glow streaked with pale lines.

'When light is directed at a luminescent object you can't see its natural glow. Victor's floodlights are so powerful they illuminate everything, except at the very edge of the picture where they're no longer so bright.

But there's definitely something there. That proves to me we're dealing with a luminescent creature – a pretty big one.'

Many deep-sea creatures could luminesce. Their light was the result of symbioses with bacteria. Some organisms on the surface of the ocean could emit light too – algae, for instance, and some small species of squid – but the real sea of lights only started where darkness began, beyond the reach of the sun.

Johanson stared at the screen. There was only a hint of blue, barely visible, and most people would have missed it. Still, the robot was known for the high resolution of its pictures. Perhaps Lund was right. He scratched his beard. 'How big is it, do you think?'

'It's difficult to say because it disappeared so quickly, but in that time it must have swum to the edge of the beam. If you look here, though, it still almost covers the frame, which suggests . . .'

'That the part we're looking at measures ten to twelve square metres.'

'Exactly. The *part*.' She paused. 'Judging by the light at the edge of the picture, I'd say we saw just a fraction of it.'

A different explanation occurred to Johanson. 'It could be planktonic organisms,' he said. 'Micro-organisms of some kind. Plenty of species glow.'

'How do you explain the markings?'

'You mean the paler streaks? Coincidence. We're only assuming that they're markings. We used to think that the channels on Mars were markings too.'

'I'm certain they're not plankton.'

'We can't see well enough to tell.'

'Oh, but we can. Take a look at this.'

Lund called up the next images. The milky patch retreated further into the darkness. It had been visible for less than a second. The pale area of luminescence was still apparent in the second and third frames, but the streaks seemed to shift. By the fourth frame everything had vanished.

'It turned off its light,' Johanson said, amazed. Certain species of squid could communicate with bioluminescence, and it wasn't unusual for them to flip the switch and disappear into darkness when they felt threatened. But this creature was bigger than any known species of squid.

There was an obvious conclusion, but he was reluctant to draw it. It had no business on the Norwegian continental slope. '*Architeuthis*,' he said.

'Giant squid.' Lund nodded. 'It makes you wonder, doesn't it? But it'd be the first time anything like that showed up in these waters.'

'More like the first time it showed up anywhere.'

That wasn't strictly true. For a long time stories about *Architheuthis* had been dismissed as sailors' yarns. Then some enormous corpses had washed ashore, which seemed to prove its existence – or would have done, if it weren't for the fact that normal squid flesh was amazingly elastic and could be stretched to almost any size, even when it was decaying. Then a few years ago a team of scientists working off the coast of New Zealand had caught some juvenile specimens whose genetic profile demonstrated conclusively that in less than eighteen months they would grow into twenty-metre squid, weighing a tonne each. But no one had ever seen such a monstrous creature. *Architheuthis* lived in the ocean depths, and there was no reason to believe it might be luminescent.

Johanson's brow furrowed. 'No.'

'What do you mean, "no"?'

'Think of all the evidence against it. For a start, it's the wrong place for giant squid.'

'That's all very well,' Lund waved her hands in the air, 'but we don't know where they live. We know nothing about them at all.'

'They definitely don't belong here, though.'

'Nor do those worms.'

They fell silent.

'OK, suppose you're right,' Johanson said eventually. '*Architheuthi* are shy creatures. No one's ever been attacked by one, so what have you got to worry about?'

'That's not what people who've seen them say.'

'For heaven's sake, Tina, maybe they've capsized the odd boat, but you can't seriously be suggesting that they're a danger to the oil industry.'

Lund closed down the screen. 'All right. So, what have you got for me? Any new test results?'

Johanson brandished the envelope at her and opened it. Inside was a fat parcel of closely typed documents.

'God!' she exclaimed.

'Don't worry, there'll be a summary . . . and here it is!'

'Let me see!'

'Just a moment.' He glanced over the sheet of paper. Lund got up and walked over to the window. Then she started pacing round the room.

Johanson frowned and leafed through the bundle of documents. 'Interesting.'

'Spit it out!'

'They say the worms are polychaetes. This isn't a taxonomical report, but they mention similarities with *Hesiocaeca methanicola*. They're puzzled by the size of the jaws. They also found . . . hmm, details, details . . . OK, here we go. They examined the jaws. Powerful mandibles, designed for boring or burrowing.'

'We knew that already,' Lund said impatiently.

'That's not all. Next come the results from the isotope ratio mass spectrometry and the scanning electron microscope. Our friend is minus ninety parts per thousand.'

'Would you care to translate?'

'It's as we thought. The worm is methanotrophic. It lives symbiotically with bacteria that break down methane. It . . . I'm not sure how to explain this . . . You see, depending on the isotope – you do know what an isotope is, don't you?'

'Any two or more atoms of a chemical element with the same atomic number but with differing atomic mass.'

'Ten out of ten! So, take carbon. It doesn't always have the same atomic mass. You can have carbon-12 or carbon-13. If you eat something with more of the lighter form of carbon in it – that is, with more of the lighter carbon isotope – your isotopic ratio will decrease too. Do you see?'

'No problem.'

'Now, take methane. Methane contains both isotopes of carbon, so when worms live symbiotically with bacteria that feed on the lighter form, the bacteria start to get lighter and so do the worms. Our worm is very light indeed.'

'You're an odd lot, you biologists. What the hell do you have to do to a worm to figure that out?'

'It's a most unsavoury process. It means grinding it into powder, then measuring its mass. Now, the results from the scanning electron microscope . . . They dyed the DNA . . . All very rigorous . . .'

Lund strode over to him and tugged at the documents. 'I don't need a lecture. All I want to know is if it's safe for us to drill.'

'There's no—' Johanson snatched back the summary and reread the final lines. 'Fantastic.'

'What is it?'

'They're coated with bacteria, inside and out. Endosymbiotic and exosymbiotic bacteria. It seems your worms are transporting bacteria by the busload.'

'And what does that mean?'

'Well, it doesn't add up. The worm lives on gas hydrates and is bursting with bacteria, so it doesn't hunt and it doesn't bore. It just lies there on its fat belly, lazing around on the ice. Yet it's equipped with enormous jaws that are perfect for boring. And the worms on the shelf looked anything but fat and lazy. I'd say they were distinctly agile.'

Neither said anything for a while. In the end Lund asked, 'What are they doing down there, Sigur?'

Johanson shrugged. 'I don't know. Maybe they really have crawled straight up from the Middle Cambrian. But I've no idea what they're up to.' He passed to consider. 'And I'm not sure if it matters. I mean, what's the worst they can do down there? They'll wriggle all over the place, sure, but they're hardly going to chew through a pipeline.'

'Well, what *are* they chewing, then?'

Johanson stared at the summary. 'There's one more place that might help us,' he said, 'and if they can't, we'll have to wait for a revelation.'

'I'd rather it didn't come to that.'

'I'll send off a few specimens.' Johanson yawned. 'You know what would be ideal? If they sent out their research vessel to take a proper look. At any rate, you're going to have to be patient. There's nothing we can do for the moment so, if you don't mind, I'd like some breakfast. Besides, I need to give Kare a piece of advice.'

Lund smiled, but it was clear from her expression that she wasn't satisfied.

5 April

Business was picking up again. Under any other circumstances Anawak would have shared wholeheartedly in Shoemaker's rejoicings. The whales were returning. The manager of Davie's could talk of nothing else. Slowly but surely they were all coming back: grey whales, humpbacks, orcas and even some minkes. Of course Anawak was pleased to see them – it was what he'd been hoping for – but he would have liked them to show up with a few answers to his questions, such as how they'd eluded the satellites and probes. He kept thinking back to his encounter with the humpbacks. He'd felt like a rat in a laboratory: the two whales had examined him as coolly and thoroughly as though he'd been laid out for dissection.

Were they spies? And, if so, what were they looking for?

It was a ridiculous idea.

He closed the ticket desk and went outside. The tourists were waiting at the end of the jetty. They looked like a Special Forces unit in their orange overalls. Anawak made his way over to them.

Someone was running after him. 'Dr Anawak!'

He stopped. Alicia Delaware was beside him, red hair scraped into a ponytail and wearing trendy blue sunglasses.

'Can I come too?'

Anawak glanced at the hull of the *Blue Shark*.

'We're full.'

'But I ran all the way to get here.'

'Sorry. The *Lady Wexham*'s got a tour in half an hour. She's more luxurious, with heated indoor seating and a snack-bar. . .'

'I don't need a snack-bar. Come on, there must be room for me somewhere. How about at the back?'

'There are two of us in the cabin already – Susan and me.'

'I can stand.' Alicia smiled at him. Her large front teeth made her look

79

like a freckled rabbit. 'Please, Dr Anawak. You're not still mad at me, are you? Your tour is the only one I want to go on.'

Anawak frowned.

'Don't look at me like that!' Delaware rolled her eyes. 'I've read your books and I like your work.'

'That's not the impression I got.'

'At the aquarium?' She made a dismissive gesture. 'Forget it. Dr Anawak, I'm only here for one more day. It really means a lot to me.'

'It's against the regulations.' The excuse was lame and made him sound petty.

'God, you're stubborn,' she said. 'I'm warning you it doesn't take much to make me cry. If I can't come along, I'll be sobbing on the plane all the way to Chicago. You wouldn't want to be responsible for that.'

Anawak couldn't help laughing. 'All right. If it means that much to you, you can come.'

'Really?'

'Really. But don't get on my nerves. And try to keep your abstruse theories to yourself.'

'It wasn't my theory. It's from—'

'On second thoughts, don't say anything at all.'

She opened her mouth, then thought better of it.

'Wait here a moment,' said Anawak. 'I'll fetch you some water-proofs.'

For a full ten minutes Alicia Delaware stuck to her promise. Then, when the skyline of Tofino had disappeared behind the first of the tree-covered mountains, she sidled up to Anawak and held out her hand. 'Call me Licia,' she said.

'Licia?'

'From Alicia. You're Leon, right?'

He shook her hand.

'OK. Now, there's something we need to settle.'

Anawak looked at Stringer for help, but she was steering the Zodiac. 'Such as?' he asked cautiously.

'The other day at the aquarium I was acting like a stupid know-it-all and I'm sorry.'

'No problem.'

'Now it's your turn to apologise.'

'What for?'

She glanced away. 'I didn't mind you criticising my arguments in front of other people – but you shouldn't have mentioned my appearance.'

'Your appearance? I didn't . . . Oh God.'

'You said that if a beluga saw me doing my makeup, it would have to question my intelligence.'

'I didn't mean it like that.'

Anawak ran his hand over his thick black hair. He'd been annoyed with the girl for turning up, as he saw it, with preconceived ideas, then drawing attention to herself through her ignorance, but his angry words had hurt her. 'All right. I'm sorry.'

'Apology accepted.'

'You were citing Povinelli,' he said.

She smiled. It was proof that he was taking her seriously. In the debate about intelligence and self-awareness in primates and other animals, Daniel Povinelli was Gallup's principal critic. He supported Gallup's theory that chimpanzees who recognised themselves in the mirror must have some idea of who they were, but he rejected the claim that this meant they understood their own mental state and therefore that of others. In fact, Povinelli was far from being convinced that any animal was endowed with the psychological understanding common to humans.

'It takes guts to say what he's saying,' said Delaware. 'Povinelli's ideas seem so old-fashioned, while things are easier for Gallup – everyone likes to claim that chimpanzees and dolphins are on a par with humans.'

'Which they are,' said Anawak.

'Ethically speaking, yes.'

'That's got nothing to do with it. Ethics are a human invention.'

'No one would contest that. Least of all Povinelli.'

Anawak looked out over the bay. Some of the smaller islets were coming into view. After a while he said, 'I know what you're trying to say. You think it shouldn't be necessary to prove that animals are like humans to treat them humanely.'

'It's arrogant,' Delaware said fiercely.

'You're right. It doesn't solve anything. And yet most people would be lost without the idea that life increases in value the more it resembles our own. We still find it easier to kill animals than people. It gets tricky when you start seeing animals as relatives of mankind. Most people are aware that humans and animals are related, but they like to think of themselves as the pinnacle of creation. Few will admit that other forms of life might be as precious as their own. And that creates a dilemma: how can they treat animals or plants with the same respect as other humans when they think that the life of an ant, an ape or a dolphin is worth less than their own?'

'Hey!' She clapped her hands. 'You think the same as I do after all.'

'Almost. I think you're a bit, er, dogmatic in your approach. I believe that chimpanzees and belugas *do* have a certain amount in common with us psychologically.' Anawak held up his hand before she could protest. 'OK, let me put it another way. I'd say that humanity rises in the estimation of belugas the more *they* discover that humanity has in common with *them*. Assuming whales care about such things.' He grinned. 'Who knows? Some belugas might even think we're intelligent. Does that sound better?'

Delaware wrinkled her nose. 'I don't know.'

'Sea-lions!' Stringer called out. 'Over there!'

Anawak shielded his eyes with his hand and squinted in the direction she was pointing. They were coming up to a tree-lined island. A group of Stellar sea-lions were sunning themselves on the rocks.

'This isn't about Gallup or Povinelli, is it?' said Anawak, picking up his camera. He zoomed in and took a few shots of the sea-lions. 'So why not change the terms of the debate? There's no hierarchy of life-forms in nature: it's a human concept, and it needn't concern us now. We both agree that it's wrong to treat animals like humans. That said, I think it's within our power to gain a limited insight into the psychology of animals – to understand them intellectually, if you like. What's more, I'm convinced that certain animals have more in common with us than others and that one day we'll find a way of communicating with them. You, on the other hand, take the view that non-human forms of life will always be a mystery to us. We can't get inside the head of an animal, *ergo*, we can't communicate. Which leaves us with the fact of our difference. So you're saying we should hurry up and get used to the idea, and leave the poor creatures in peace.'

The Zodiac slowed to pass the sea-lions. Stringer imparted some information about them, while the tourists got out their cameras.

'I'll have to think about it,' said Delaware, finally. She said scarcely another word until they reached the open water.

Anawak was content. It was good to start the trip with some sea-lions: it had put the tourists in a good mood.

Soon a herd of grey whales had appeared. Greys were slightly smaller than humpbacks, but still imposingly large. Some swam within a short distance of the boat and peeped briefly out of the water – to the delight of everyone on board. They looked like enormous moving pebbles, with their mottled grey skin and powerful jaws covered with barnacles, copepods and whale lice. Most of the tourists were filming frenetically or taking photos. The others looked on in silence, visibly moved. Anawak had seen grown men cry at the sight of a whale rising out of the water.

Three other Zodiacs and a bigger boat with a solid hull waited nearby, engines switched off. Stringer radioed the details of the sighting. They were all committed to responsible whale-watching – but that wasn't enough for the likes of Jack Greywolf.

Greywolf was a dangerous jerk. Anawak didn't like the sound of tourist-watching. If it came to the crunch, the media would side with Greywolf – initially, at least. He and the others at the station could be as conscientious and careful as they liked, but a protest from an animal-rights group, however disreputable, would reinforce people's prejudices against whale-watching. No one bothered to distinguish between serious organisations and fanatics like Greywolf and his Seaguards. That only happened later, when the press got hold of the true facts and the damage had been done.

Anawak scanned the ocean intently, camera at the ready. Maybe he'd succumbed to paranoia after his meeting with the humpbacks. Had he been imagining things or were those whales behaving oddly?

'Over there, on the right!' Stringer shouted.

Inside the Zodiac all heads turned. Not far from the boat some grey whales were diving in glorious close-up. They looked as though they were waving with their flukes. Anawak was busy taking pictures for the archive. Shoemaker would have jumped for joy at the sight of it. It was a picture-perfect trip – as though the whales had decided to make up for their absence by putting on a real performance. Further out to sea three large ones stuck their heads out of the water.

'Those aren't grey whales, are they?' said Delaware, chewing gum.
'Humpbacks.'

'That's what I thought. I don't see any humps, though.'

'There aren't any. They make a hump when they dive, arching their backs in the water.'

'I thought it was because of the lumps on their mouths. Those bumpy things.'

Anawak sighed. 'You're not trying to start another argument, are you?'

'Sorry.' She gesticulated excitedly. 'Hey! Look over there! What are they up to?'

The heads of the three humpbacks had shot up through the surface. Their enormous mouths were wide open, revealing their tongues hanging down from their narrow upper jaws. The baleen plates were clearly visible and the throat grooves looked as if they were straining. A column of water rose up between them, with glints of something that sparkled in the light. Tiny fish, twitching frantically in the air. From out of nowhere flocks of gulls and loons appeared, circled, then plunged down to share the feast.

'They're feeding,' said Anawak, while he photographed the scene.

'Unbelievable! They look like they could eat us.'

'Licia! Try not to make yourself sound dumber than you seem.'

Delaware pushed her gum from one side of her mouth to the other. 'I was joking,' she said. 'I know perfectly well that humpbacks eat krill and other little fish, but this is the first time I've seen them feeding. I thought they just swam with their mouths open.'

'That's how *Eubalaena* feed – right whales,' said Stringer, turning. 'Humpbacks swim under shoals of fish or copepods and surround them with a net of bubbles. Small organisms don't like turbulent water, so they swim away from the bubbles and cluster together. Then the whales lunge out of the water, expand their throat grooves and start to gulp.'

'Don't try to explain it to her,' said Anawak. 'She knows it all already.'

'To gulp?' echoed Delaware.

'Rorqual whales gulp-feed. They expand their throat grooves, which is why they look as though they've been puffed up. As the grooves open up, the throat turns into an enormous pouch, which the whale fills with food. In one huge mouthful the krill and fish are sucked in. The seawater drains out, but the prey is stuck in the baleen.'

Anawak squeezed in next to Stringer. Delaware must have sensed he wanted to talk to her privately because she made her way unsteadily out of the cabin towards the passengers in the front and started to explain gulp-feeding.

After a few moments Anawak asked softly, 'How do they seem to you?'

'Weird question.' Stringer thought about it. 'Same as always, I suppose. How do they seem to *you*?'

'You think they look normal?'

'Sure. They're putting on a great show, though. In fact, I'd say they're having the time of their lives.'

'So you don't think they've changed?'

She squinted across at them. The sunshine glistened on the water. A mottled grey body rose to the surface, then disappeared again. 'Changed?' she said slowly. 'How do you mean?'

'You know I told you about the *megapterae* that suddenly appeared either side of the boat?' At the last second he chose to use the humpbacks' scientific name. What he was thinking was mad, but at least when he put it like that it sounded half-way serious.

'So what?'

'It was weird.'

'That's what you told me. Humpbacks on either side of you. Some people have all the luck – an experience like that, and I missed it.'

'It was like they were checking me out . . . They looked like they were up to something.'

'I don't follow.'

'It wasn't nice.'

'Wasn't nice?' Stringer shook her head in disbelief. 'Are you feeling OK? I'd give anything to be so close to them. If only it had been me!'

'You wouldn't say that if you'd been there. You wouldn't have liked it at all. I'm still trying to figure out which of us was watching whom. And why . . .'

'Leon, they're whales, not spies.'

He passed his hand over his eyes. 'Forget it. I must have been mistaken.'

There was a crackle from Stringer's walkie-talkie. Tom Shoemaker's voice screeched through. 'Susan? Tune into ninety-nine.'

They were currently on ninety-eight, the frequency used by various whale-watching stations to send and receive messages. It was a practical arrangement that allowed them to keep up with all the different sightings. Tofino Air and the coastguards also used the channel, as, regrettably, did various sport fishermen, whose idea of whale-watching was considerly less sophisticated. Each station had its own frequency for private conversations. Stringer switched over.

'Is Leon with you?'

'Yes.'

She passed the walkie-talkie to Anawak, who took it and spoke to Shoemaker for a while. Then he said, 'All right, I'll do it. No, it doesn't matter that it's short notice. Tell them I'll fly over as soon as we're back. Catch you later.'

'What was all that about?' asked Stringer, as he handed her the radio.

'A request from Inglewood.'

'The shipping line?'

'Tom had a call from the directorate. They didn't say much except they needed my help and it was urgent. He had the impression they would have liked to beam me over.'

Inglewood had sent a helicopter. Less than two hours after his radio conversation with Shoemaker, Anawak was in the air watching the spectacular landscape of Vancouver Island unfold beneath him. Hills covered with fir trees gave way to rocky mountain peaks connected by shimmering rivers and turquoise lakes. But even the island's beauty couldn't disguise the ravages of logging. The deforestation of vast swathes of land was all too evident.

They left Vancouver Island and flew over the bustling Strait of Georgia. The Rockies, peaks dotted with snow, ran along the horizon, while towers of pink and blue glass lined the sweeping bay, where seaplanes soared and dipped in the air like colourful birds.

The pilot radioed ground control. The helicopter dropped down, banked and headed for the docks. Minutes later they landed. Stacks of cedar towered on either side of them, while mounds of coal and sulphur rose in cubist-style arrangements from the wharf. A colossal cargo vessel was moored nearby. A man detached himself from a group of people and headed over. The wind from the helicopter's rotor ruffled his hair. He was wearing a long coat, and hunched his shoulders against the blast. Anawak unbuckled his seatbelt and made ready to disembark.

The man opened the door for him. He was in his early sixties, tall and well-built, with a round, friendly face and intelligent eyes. He smiled at Anawak and held out his hand. 'Clive Roberts,' he said, 'managing director.'

Anawak followed him to the others, who were inspecting a freighter. They seemed to be a mixture of crew members and people in suits.

They were walking along the starboard side of the boat, staring up at it, pausing, then setting off again.

'It's very good of you to come at such short notice,' said Roberts. 'We wouldn't normally call and expect you to come running, but it was urgent.'

'No problem,' said Anawak. 'What are we looking at?'

'An accident. We think.'

'Involving that freighter?'

'Yes, the *Barrier Queen*. Although it's more to do with the tugboats that were supposed to be bringing her home.'

'You know I'm a cetologist, right? An expert in animal behaviour? Whales and dolphins.'

'That's exactly what we need.'

Roberts introduced him to the others. Three were from the shipping line's management team; the rest were representatives from the technical contractors. A short distance away two men were unloading dive equipment from a truck. Anawak looked into the circle of worried faces, then Roberts took him to one side.

'Unfortunately we can't speak to the crew right now,' he said, 'but I'll forward a confidential copy of the report as soon as it's available. We don't want to involve any more people than are absolutely necessary. Can I count on your discretion?'

'Of course.'

'Good. I'll give you a rundown on what's happened, and when I'm done, you can make up your own mind whether you want to stick around or fly home. Either way we'll reimburse you for your trouble and expense.'

'It's no trouble.'

Roberts looked at him gratefully. 'The *Barrier Queen* is fairly new. When she sailed, everything was in A-1 condition and it's all been properly certified. She's a sixty-thousand-tonne freighter that we've been using to transport HGVs, mostly to Japan and back. We've had no trouble with her until now. We put a lot of money into making sure our boats are safe – more than strictly necessary. Anyway, the *Barrier Queen* was on her way home, fully laden.'

Anawak nodded.

'Six days ago she reached the edge of the two-hundred-mile zone on her way into Vancouver. It was three in the morning. The helmsman changed course by five degrees – a routine correction. He didn't bother checking the display: he could see the lights on a vessel ahead, which gave him perfect visual reference. He waited for the lights to shift right, but they stayed where they were. The *Barrier Queen* was heading straight on. He tried moving the rudder again, but there was no noticeable change in direction, so he went for full rudder, and suddenly it worked. The trouble was, it worked too well.'

'She hit the other vessel?'

'No, she was too far away for that. But the rudder blade seemed to have jammed. Nothing could budge it. Just imagine: a speed of twenty knots and you're stuck on full rudder . . . A ship of that size isn't simply going to stop. She heeled with her cargo. A ten-degree heel – do you know what that means?'

'I can guess.'

'The drainage system for the vehicle deck is located just above the waterline. In rough conditions the water floods in, then pours straight back out, but at an angle like that the drainage holes would be submerged. It wouldn't take a second for the ship to fill with water. Luckily for us, the sea was calm that day, but the situation was still critical. The rudder had stuck.'

'So what was wrong with it?'

'We can't be sure . . . but one thing's certain: that was when the trouble really started. The *Barrier Queen* stopped her engines, radioed a mayday and waited for help. It was clear she wasn't seaworthy. Several ships in the vicinity changed course to head over in case they were needed. In the meantime two salvage boats set out from Vancouver. They arrived two and a half days later, in the early afternoon. One sixty-metre deep-sea tug and one twenty-five-metre craft. The trickiest part of any rescue operation is to get the rope from the tug to land safely on the vessel. In bad weather it can take hours: first a thin line, then a slightly thicker one, then a heavy-duty cable. It's an interminable procedure. But in this case, well, there should have been no problem. Conditions were good and the water was calm. But the tug was obstructed.'

'By what?'

'The thing is . . .' Roberts grimaced. 'Have you ever heard of an attack by whales?'

It was the last thing Anawak had expected. 'An attack? On a ship, you mean?'

'Yes. A big ship.'

'It's almost unheard-of.'

'Almost?' Roberts was listening carefully. 'So this wouldn't be the first time?'

'There's one recorded incident from the nineteenth century. Melville wrote a novel about it.'

'You mean *Moby Dick*?'

'The novel was inspired by the story of the *Essex*, a whaling ship sunk by a sperm whale. The vessel was forty-two metres long, made of wood and probably rotten, but that's not the point. The whale rammed the boat and it sank within minutes. Its crew are supposed to have drifted for weeks in their lifeboats . . . Oh, and there were two further cases last year off the coast of Australia. In both incidents a whale was reported to have sunk a fishing-boat.'

'What happened?'

'It smashed them to pieces with its tail. A man died. He had a heart-attack after plunging into the water.'

'What kind of whales were they?'

'No one knows. They disappeared too quickly.' Anawak looked across at the *Barrier Queen*'s hull: there was no sign of any damage. 'I can't imagine a whale attacking *her*.'

Roberts followed his gaze. 'It was the tugs they were attacking,' he said, 'not the *Barrier Queen*. They came at them from the side. It was obvious they were trying to capsize them, but they didn't succeed. So they tried to prevent them attaching the tow line, which was when—'

'They launched their attack.'

'Yes.'

'Impossible,' Anawak asserted. 'Whales can overturn objects as big as or smaller than themselves. Certainly nothing any bigger. And they wouldn't attack a larger object unless they had no choice.'

'The crew swears blind that that was what happened. The whales attacked and—'

'What kind of whales?'

'God knows.'

Anawak frowned thoughtfully. 'Let's imagine the scenario. Suppose the tugs were attacked by blue whales, the largest species. *Balaenoptera musculus* can grow to thirty-three metres long and weigh over 120 tonnes. They're the largest animals to have lived on this planet. Now, supposing a creature like that tried to sink a boat of the same or similar length. It would have to be as fast as the boat, if not faster. Still, over short distances a blue whale can manage fifty or sixty kilometres per hour without too much hassle: its body is streamlined and there's almost no resistance. But how much momentum would it have? And what would be the counter-momentum of the boat? To put it simply, in the event of a collision, who would be knocked off course?'

'A hundred and twenty tonnes is pretty heavy.'

Anawak nodded at the truck. 'Do you think you can pick that up?'

'Of course not.'

'You see? The ground's supporting you and you still can't lift it. In the water you don't have that luxury. When you're swimming, you can't lift more than your weight. It doesn't matter if you're a whale or a human. It's all a question of relative mass. Besides, you've still got the problem of the displaced water. How much does it weigh in relation to the whale? It doesn't leave you with much, just the propulsion from the flukes. With a bit of luck the whale might nudge the ship off course. On the other hand it might deflect at an angle from the hull. It's a bit like billiards, if you see what I mean.'

Roberts scratched his chin. 'Some say they were humpbacks. Others talk about fin whales. And the crew on board the *Barrier Queen* think they saw sperm whales.'

'Three species that couldn't be more different.'

'Dr Anawak, I'm a reasonable man,' Roberts said. 'It seems to me that the tugs could have found themselves in the middle of a herd by accident. Maybe the boats weren't rammed by whales but the other way round. Maybe the crews did something stupid. But one thing is certain, the smaller craft was sunk by whales.'

Anawak could hardly believe what he was hearing.

'The crew had just connected the cable,' continued Roberts. 'It was a taut steel one reaching from the *Barrier Queen*'s bow to the stern of the tug. The whales rose out of the water and crashed down on top of it – so, you see, in this instance there was no displaced water to slow the momentum. And they were pretty big specimens, according to the crew.' He paused. 'The tug whipped round and sank. It lifted up and over in the air.'

'And the men?'

'Two missing. The others were rescued. Tell me, Dr Anawak, is there any explanation for their behaviour?'

Good question, thought Anawak. Dolphins and belugas recognised themselves in the mirror. So, could they think? Could they plan? Could they plan in a way that we could understand? What motivated them? Did whales have a future and a past? What possible reason could they have for ramming or sinking a tug?

Unless the tug had threatened them or their young.

'It just doesn't fit with whales,' he said.

'That's what I thought,' Roberts said helplessly. 'But the crews see it differently. In any case, the bigger tug was also rammed. In the end they managed to attach the cable. This time it didn't come under attack.'

Anawak stared at his feet, searching for an answer. 'Coincidence,' he said. 'A horrible coincidence.'

'Do you really think so?'

'We'd have more chance of working it out if we knew what had happened to the rudder.'

'That's why we've called in the divers,' Roberts told him. 'In a few moments they'll be ready to go down.'

'Did they bring a spare set of equipment?'

'I expect so.'

Anawak nodded. 'I'm going too.'

The water was revolting, but it always was in docks. The thick dark liquid contained at least as much dirt as it did water. The bottom was covered with a metre-thick coating of mud, over which swirled a permanent cloud of organic matter and silt. As the waves closed over Anawak's head he asked himself how he was supposed to see anything. He could just about make out the hazy outlines of the two divers in front of him and beyond them a dark, misty patch – the *Barrier Queen*'s hull.

The divers gave him the OK sign. Anawak made a circle with his forefinger and thumb in return. He released the latent air in his dive vest and dropped slowly down the side of the boat. They had only gone a few metres when they switched on their head-torches. Exhaled air bubbled and thundered in Anawak's ears. Little by little the rudder emerged in the half-light. Notched and stained, its plate was bent at an angle. Anawak felt for his depth gauge. Eight metres. Ahead of him, the divers disappeared behind the rudder, leaving two stray beams of light flitting through the darkness.

Anawak approached the rudder from the other side.

At first he could see only raised edges and irregular hollows. Then it hit him. The rudder was encrusted with black-and-white mussels. He swam closer for a better look. At the bottom of the rudder, where the plate swept the shaft, the mussels had been ground to pieces. A thick gritty paste filled the cracks and grooves. No wonder it wouldn't respond. It was clogged.

He swam further down the hull. The mussels continued. He reached out gingerly to touch the shells. They were glued to each other in layers, small molluscs no more than three centimetres long. Very carefully, to avoid cutting himself on the edges, he pulled at the mussels until some came loose. They were half open. The fibres that had anchored them in position now poked out of the shells, like tendrils. Anawak stowed them in one of his collection bags, and racked his brains.

His knowledge of molluscs was sketchy. A number of species had a similar-looking byssus, composed of adhesive fibres secreted by the foot. The best known and most feared were the zebra mussels that had been brought over from Asia. In recent years they had colonised the eco-systems of Europe and America, destroying native fauna. If the mussels that had infested the *Barrier Queen* were zebras, it would explain why there were so many of them. They could establish themselves in no time, spreading at an alarming rate.

Anawak prodded the creatures with his finger. So, the rudder had been invaded by zebra mussels. It seemed the only explanation. But how? They usually preferred a fresh-water habitat. They could survive and reproduce in salt water, but that didn't explain how they could overrun a moving vessel miles from the seabed in the middle of nowhere. Had they latched on to it before it set sail?

The freighter had been *en route* from Japan. Did Japan have a problem with zebra mussels?

Further down the stern, two curved blades loomed up like ghostly apparitions from the murk below. Anawak swam towards them, kicking his fins until he could grip the edge of one. The propeller measured four and a half metres in diameter. Eight tonnes of solid steel. For a moment he imagined what it would be like when it was turning at full speed. It seemed impossible that anything could so much as scratch it without being shredded.

Yet the propeller was covered with mussels.

An unpleasant possibility occurred to Anawak. Hanging off the edge of the blade, he swung himself hand over hand towards the middle of the propeller. His fingers touched something slippery. Gobbets of a light-coloured substance slid off and floated towards him. He snatched at them, caught one and peered at it.

It was jelly-like, rubbery, and looked like animal tissue.

He stashed it in a collection jar, and felt his way forward. One of the divers appeared on the far side, lamp shining on his mask, making him look oddly alien. He signalled for Anawak to follow. Anawak glided between the rudder shaft and the propeller. He stopped and let himself sink through the water until his fins touched the propeller shaft. A film of slime coated it. The divers were trying to tear it off and Anawak joined in, but they were wasting their energy. It had wrapped itself round the propeller and, without proper tools, they couldn't pull it off.

Anawak thought back to what Roberts had told him. The whales had tried to get rid of the tugs. It was absurd. Why would they sabotage a tow line? So that the freighter would sink? In rougher conditions she might easily have gone under – after all, she was effectively disabled. The sea wouldn't have stayed calm for ever. Had the whales been trying to stop her reaching safe water before the weather changed?

He glanced at his gauge. Still plenty of oxygen. He signalled to the divers that he wanted to inspect the hull, and the three left the propeller, fanning out along the side of the vessel, with Anawak at the bottom, where the hull curved round to the keel. The beam of his head-torch explored the steel casing. The paint looked relatively new, with few scratches and little discoloration. He dropped down towards the seabed, further into the gloom. His eyes darted back to the surface: two hazy spots of light marked the position of the divers inspecting the hull. There was nothing to worry about. He knew where he was. All the same he had a heavy feeling in his chest. He kicked his fins a few times and drifted along the hull. No sign of any damage.

All of a sudden his head-torch dimmed. Anawak's hand flew up to check it – but the problem wasn't the lamp: it was where the lamp was shining. Further up, the beam had reflected evenly. Now it was swallowed by a bed of jagged mussels, whose dark outline obscured the painted stern.

How had they got there?

For a moment Anawak considered swimming back to the others, then decided against it and continued down the hull. As he neared the keel the layer of mussels thickened. If the rest of the underside was covered to

93

that extent, a significant weight had accumulated. But someone must have noticed the state the ship was in. On the high seas a load like that would slow a freighter noticeably.

He reached the point where he was obliged to swim on his back. A few metres beneath him lay the muddy wasteland of the harbour floor. He could barely see anything, the water was so murky – just the huge mound of mussels above him. Kicking rapidly with his fins he swam towards the bow. Suddenly the bed of mussels stopped as abruptly as it had begun. For the first time he realised the true size of the outcrop. The mussels had formed a layer two metres thick along the bottom of the *Barrier Queen*.

There was a chink at the edge of the outcrop. Anawak hovered in front of it. Then he reached down to his ankle, where his knife was in its sheath. He pulled it out and plunged it into the shells.

The outer crust split open and something shot out towards him, twitching frantically. It collided with his face, almost pulling off his breathing apparatus. Anawak jerked backwards. His head hit the bottom of the boat. A harsh light exploded in his eyes. He wanted to get out of the water straight away, but the keel was above him. Kicking desperately, he swivelled round and was confronted by another mound of shells. Their edges seemed to be stuck to the hull with a jelly-like substance. Forcing himself to calm down, he set about hunting among the floating particles for traces of the thing that had attacked him.

It was gone. All he could see were strange formations of mussels.

Suddenly he realised he was clutching something. It was his knife. A scrap of something dangled from the blade – a blob of milky-coloured, semi-transparent material. Anawak stowed it in the collection jar with the tissue. He couldn't wait to get out of there. His heart was pounding, so he ascended slowly, with small, controlled movements, following the hull upwards until the lights of the two divers appeared in the distance. He headed towards them. They'd found the mussels too. One was using his knife to prise individual shells away from the crust. Anawak tensed, steeling himself for something to hurtle towards them, but nothing happened.

The second diver motioned upwards with his thumb and they ascended slowly to the surface. Gradually the light grew stronger, but the water remained murky.

At last Anawak found himself blinking in the sunshine. He pulled off his mask, and breathed in gratefully.

Roberts and the others were waiting on the jetty.

'So, what does it look like down there?' Roberts asked. 'Did you find anything?'

Anawak coughed and spat out a mouthful of harbour water. 'You could say that.'

They were standing around the tailgate of the truck. Anawak had been nominated as spokesman.

'The rudder was blocked with *mussels?*' asked Roberts, incredulously.

'That's right – zebra mussels by the look of them.'

'How the hell did that happen?'

'Good question.' Anawak got out his collection jar, opened it and carefully emptied the blobs of jelly into a larger container filled with seawater. He was anxious about the tissue: it looked as though decomposition had already set in. 'There's no way of knowing, of course, but I'd picture it like this. First, the helmsman tries to apply five degrees rudder. The rudder doesn't move. As it turns out, it's blocked by countless mussels that have settled all over the shaft. Now, you guys know more about boats than I do, but a rudder is pretty easy to disable – although in practice it rarely happens. Consequently it never occurs to the helmsman that the rudder might be blocked. He still thinks he hasn't shifted it far enough, so he tries to shift it further. Again, nothing seems to happen. Then the helmsman goes all out, and the rudder breaks free. As it swings across the shaft, it crushes the mussels in its path, but they don't fall off. A paste of ground molluscs clogs the rudder. The blade is wedged tight and can't move back across the shaft.' Anawak pushed strands of wet hair out of his eyes. 'But that's not what really bothers me.'

'What then?'

'The sea-chests are clear of mussels, but the propeller is covered with them. It's completely infested. I don't know how they managed to latch on to the boat, but one thing is certain: a rotating propeller would be too big a challenge for even the most determined mussels. Either the molluscs climbed aboard in Japan – which seems unlikely, since the rudder was in fine working order right up to the two-hundred-mile zone, or they clung to the propeller when the engine cut out.'

'The ship was invaded by mussels in the middle of the ocean?'

95

'Right, although "appropriated" might be a better term. I'm trying to picture how it happened. A gigantic swarm of mussels settles on the rudder. When the rudder jams, the ship heels. Within minutes the engines are turned off. The propeller stops rotating. More and more mussels descend on the rudder, reinforcing the blockade. In no time they extend across the propeller and along the hull.'

'But the ship was out to sea,' said Roberts, confused. 'Where would tonnes of adult mussels come from?'

'Why would whales scare off tugs and jump on a tow line? You're the one who started telling stories, not me.'

'I know, but . . .' Roberts bit his lip. 'It all happened simultaneously. It almost makes you think there's a link. But it doesn't make sense. I mean, whales and mussels?'

Anawak hesitated. 'When was the last time you inspected the *Barrier Queen*'s keel?'

'There are constant inspections. Besides, she's coated with a special paint. Before you ask it's environmentally friendly. But there aren't many things that can latch on to it. At most, a few barnacles.'

'You've got more than a few barnacles down there.' Anawak stared at Roberts. 'But that's just it . . . By all rights, they shouldn't be there. The *Barrier Queen* looks as though she's been exposed for weeks to hordes of mussel larvae. And in any case . . . there was something else down there . . .' Anawak described how something had shot out towards him from inside the crust of mussels. While he was talking, it all came back to him. First the shock, then hitting his head on the boat – he had seen stars.

No, not stars – flashes of light.

A single flash of light.

Then it struck him: the creature had flashed.

For a moment he was speechless. The flow of words dried up as it dawned on him that the creature had luminesced. But if it had luminesced, it must have come from the depths. It could scarcely have found its way on to the *Barrier Queen* while the ship was in dock. It must have latched on at the same time as the mussels. Maybe it had been drawn there by them. Perhaps they were a food source. Or a shield. The creature could have been a squid . . .

'Dr Anawak?'

He stopped staring into space and turned to Roberts. Yes, he thought.

It must have been a squid. It had been too quick for a jellyfish and too strong. Like a single elastic muscle, it had burst through the shells. Then he remembered something else: the creature had appeared as soon as he reached into the chink. He must have cut it with his knife. Had he hurt it? Either way the thrust of the knife had triggered a reflex.

No need to get carried away, he told himself. It was too murky to see down there.

'I recommend you have the dock checked over,' he said to Roberts, 'but first you need to send these samples' – he pointed to the sealed containers – 'to the laboratory in Nanaimo. Have them taken by helicopter. I'll come too – I know exactly who should look at them.'

Roberts drew Anawak aside.

'Leon, what do you *really* make of all this?' he asked quietly. 'There's no way that tonnes of mussels could have accumulated in such a short time. It's not as though the ship had been neglected for weeks.'

'Those mussels are a pest, Mr Roberts.'

'Call me Clive.'

'Well . . . Clive . . . zebra mussels don't show up in small groups. When they find somewhere new to settle, they march in like an army. That much is known.'

'But not as fast as that, surely?'

'Every single one of those damned things can produce a thousand young every year. The larvae drift with the currents or stow away on the fins of fish or feathers of birds. In some lakes in America there are nine hundred thousand of them in a single square metre. And they appeared there overnight. They colonise waterworks and irrigation plants, and get into the cooling systems of factories built near rivers. Entire pipes are blocked and ruined by them. And from what we see here, salt water suits them just as well as fresh.'

'I get the picture – but you're talking about larvae.'

'Millions of larvae.'

'There could be billions of them, all over Osaka harbour and across the ocean seabed, but you can't seriously be suggesting that in just a few days they all turned into adult mussels, complete with shells? Can you even be sure that they're zebra mussels?'

Anawak glanced back at the truck. The divers were packing their equipment. The containers, sealed as well as he could manage it, were on the ground in front of them in a plastic crate.

'We're looking at an equation with several unknowns,' he said. 'Suppose the whales were trying to ward off the tugboats. Why? Because something was happening to the freighter and they didn't want it interrupted? Because it was supposed to sink once the mussels had immobilised it? Then there's the matter of the mysterious thing that took flight when I intruded on its den. How does that sound?'

'Like the sequel to *Independence Day* but without the aliens. Do you seriously think—'

'Hang on. Let's look at it again. A herd of jumpy grey whales or humpbacks feels threatened by the *Barrier Queen*. To make matters worse, two tugs turn up and ram them by accident. They retaliate. Coincidentally, the freighter is simultaneously afflicted by a biological plague it picked up abroad. Then, while it was at sea, a squid strayed into the mussels.'

Roberts stared at him.

'I don't believe in science fiction,' Anawak continued. 'It's all a question of interpretation. Send a few of your people down there. Have them scrape off the mussels and keep an eye open for other surprise guests. If they see any, they should catch them.'

'How soon will we hear from the lab in Nanaimo?'

'Within a few days, I guess. It would help if I could have a copy of Inglewood's report.'

'A confidential copy,' Roberts reminded him.

'Naturally. And I'd like to have a word with the crew – confidentially, of course.'

Roberts nodded. 'It's not up to me, but I'll see what I can do.'

They walked over to the truck and Anawak pulled on his jacket. 'Do you normally call in scientists in cases like this?' he asked.

'There's nothing normal about this business,' Roberts said. 'It was my idea. I'd read your book and I knew you were based on the island. The board of inquiry wasn't too happy about it, but I think it was the right thing to do. Whales aren't our strong point.'

'Well, I'll do my best. Let's get the samples into the helicopter. The sooner we get to Nanaimo the better. I'll hand them straight to Sue Oliviera. She's head of the lab, a molecular biologist.'

Anawak's mobile rang. It was Stringer. 'We need you back here,' she said.

'What's wrong?'

'The *Blue Shark* radioed to say there's trouble.'

Anawak had a sense of foreboding. 'With the whales?'

'Of course not! Why would whales cause trouble? No, it's that asshole Jack Greywolf again. He's such a jerk.'

6 April

Two weeks after he'd given Tina Lund the final reports on the worms, Sigur Johanson was sitting in a taxi on his way to the Geomar Centre, Europe's leading research centre for marine geosciences. For anyone interested in the structure, development or history of the seabed, it was the first port of call. James Cameron, no less, had made regular trips there to get its seal of approval for films like *Titanic* and *The Abyss*. But trying to convince the public of the value of its research was more difficult. On the face of it, poking about in sediment or measuring seawater salinity was unlikely to solve the world's problems. Besides, few had any understanding of what the seabed was like. After all, it had taken scientists until the early 1990s to discover the truth. Although it was cut off from the warmth and light of the sun, the bottom of the ocean was not a barren wasteland. Rather, it teemed with life.

It was no secret that deep-sea hydrothermal vents were occupied by numerous exotic species, but when geochemist Erwin Suess arrived at the Geomar Centre from Oregon State University in 1989, he told of stranger things – cold seeps surrounded by oases of life, mysterious sources of chemical energy rising from inside the Earth, and vast deposits of a substance that until then had been dismissed as an intriguing but insignificant by-product of natural processes: methane hydrate.

It was time for the geosciences to break out of the seclusion in which they, like most other scientific disciplines, had worked. Now they tried to make themselves heard. They hoped to develop methods for pre-dicting and averting natural disasters and long-term changes to the environment and climate. Methane seemed the answer to the energy problem of the future. The media sensed a story, and the geoscientists learned gradually how to make use of the new-found interest in their work.

None of this seemed to have come to the attention of the man steering Johanson's taxi towards the Firth of Kiel. For the past twenty minutes he had been venting his frustration at the idea of a research centre that had cost millions of euros being entrusted to a team of scientists who took off on cruises round the world while he could barely make ends meet. Johanson spoke excellent German, but felt no desire to set the record straight. Besides, he couldn't get a word in edgeways – the driver was talking and gesticulating wildly as the taxi veered from side to side. 'God knows what they get up to in there,' he grumbled. 'Are you a reporter?' he asked, when Johanson failed to respond.

'A biologist.'

The driver took that as a signal to launch into a tirade about food-safety scandals, for which he seemed to hold Johanson personally responsible.

'A biologist? So what, in your expert opinion, is safe for us to eat? Because I'm damned if I know! We must be mad to eat the stuff they sell us.'

'You'd starve if you didn't,' said Johanson.

'If I don't eat, I'll starve, and if I do, the food'll finish me off.'

'If you don't mind me saying so, I'd rather die from a toxic steak than be crushed to death on the bonnet of that tanker.'

Without a flicker of concern the driver spun the wheel and crossed three lanes to take the next exit. The tanker thundered past. Now they were speeding along the eastern shore of the firth. On the opposite bank, giant cranes reached into the sky.

The driver had evidently taken offence at Johanson's last comment: he didn't say another word. They drove in silence along suburban streets past tall, gabled houses until a long row of linked buildings appeared ahead. The complex of steel, brick and glass looked out of place in its domestic surroundings. The driver took a sharp right and screeched to a halt in front of the Geomar Centre. The engine juddered and stopped. Johanson took a deep breath, paid, and got out. The ride in the Statoil helicopter had been a breeze compared to the last fifteen minutes.

'God knows what they're doing in there,' said the driver, apparently to his steering-wheel.

Johanson bent down to the open passenger door. 'Do you really want to know?'

'Sure.'

'They're trying to save the taxi-driving industry.'

The driver gazed at him blankly. 'It's not as though we get many fares out here,' he said doubtfully.

'No, but when you do, you need your vehicle. Which means that when the world runs out of petrol, you'll either have to scrap it – or use another fuel. And that fuel, methane, is at the bottom of the ocean. They're looking for a way to convert it.'

The driver frowned. Then he said, 'You know what the problem is? They never bother to tell you.'

'It's all over the papers.'

'Not the ones I read, mate.'

Johanson nodded and closed the door.

'Dr Johanson.' A tanned young man had emerged from a round glass building and was heading towards him.

Johanson shook his outstretched hand. 'Gerhard Bohrmann?'

'Heiko Sahling, marine biologist. Dr Bohrmann's giving a lecture. We could listen, if you like, or grab a coffee in the canteen.'

'Which would you rather?'

'Entirely up to you. Interesting worms you sent us, by the way.'

'You've been working on them?'

'We've *all* been working on them. Tell you what, why don't you come this way? We'll save the coffee for later. Gerhard will be finished in a moment, and he won't mind if we eavesdrop.'

They entered a spacious foyer with an air of sophisticated function-ality about it. Sahling led him up some stairs and across a steel suspension bridge. For a serious research institute, thought Johanson, the Geomar Centre was suspiciously trendy.

'We usually use the auditorium for lectures,' explained Sahling, 'but today we've got a class of schoolkids.'

'How terribly worthy.'

Sahling grinned. 'To a bunch of fifteen-year-olds, an auditorium is just another classroom, which is why we do a tour with them instead. They can look at whatever they want – and touch nearly everything too. We saved the *lithothek* until last. It's where we keep our samples. Now Gerhard is telling them their bedtime story.'

'About what?'

'Methane hydrates.'

Sahling slid open the metal door. The raised platform continued on the other side. They took a few steps along it. The storeroom was at least as big as a medium-sized aircraft hangar and led out on to the quay, where Johanson caught a glimpse of a relatively large boat. Crates and equipment were piled against the walls.

'We mostly collect sediment cores and pore-water,' explained Sahling. 'It's an archive of geological history and we're proud of it.'

He raised his hand briefly. Below, a tall man returned the greeting, then focused on the group of teenagers clustered around him.

'It was one of the most exciting things we've ever seen,' Gerhard Bohrmann was saying. 'The grab sampler returned from a depth of nearly eight hundred metres, carrying several hundred pounds of sediment, interspersed with white lumps. We watched as it emptied them on to the deck. Not all of the substance survived the journey.'

'That was in the Pacific,' murmured Sahling, 'in 1996 on the RV *Sonne*, a hundred or so kilometres off the coast of Oregon.'

'There wasn't a moment to lose. Methane hydrate is highly unstable,' continued Bohrmann. 'I don't suppose any of you will have heard much about it, so I'll try to explain without boring you senseless. Let's imagine the ocean seabed. There's a lot going on down there, but we're going to focus on gas. Biogenic methane, for example, forms over millions of years when plants and animals decay. Large amounts of carbon are released as algae, fish and plankton decompose. Bacteria play a central role in that. One of the key things to remember, though, is that the temperature on the ocean floor is very low, but the pressure's very high. For every ten metres you descend through the water, you gain another bar of pressure. With breathing apparatus you can get to fifty metres, or maybe even seventy, but that's about the limit. The record is a hundred and forty, but I wouldn't recommend it – almost everyone who tries it ends up dead. In any case, we're talking about depths in excess of five hundred metres, and that changes the physics completely. So, when high concentrations of methane seep through the seabed something extraordinary happens: the gas combines with cold water and forms ice. They call it "methane ice" in the papers, but that's not entirely accurate. It's not the methane that freezes, but the seawater around it. Groups of water molecules solidify, forming cage-like structures around each methane molecule. Vast amounts of gas are compressed within the tiniest spaces.'

A schoolkid stuck up his hand. 'Five hundred metres isn't exactly deep, is it?' he said. 'Jacques Piccard went down eleven thousand metres in his bathyscaphe. Now, that's really deep. Why didn't he see ice down there?'

'So you know the story of the deepest manned dive. Very good. But how would *you* explain it?'

The teenager thought for a moment, then shrugged.

'Well, it's obvious, really,' said one of the girls. 'There's not enough life down there. Once you get below a thousand metres not much decays, so there's hardly any methane.'

'I knew it,' muttered Johanson from his vantage-point on the bridge. 'Women are simply more intelligent.'

Bohrmann smiled at her. 'That's right. Although, as always, there are exceptions. Methane hydrates can also be found in deeper water, even at depths of three thousand metres, if enough sediment containing organic matter is washed down there. It sometimes happens in marginal seas. As a matter of fact, we've also found methane hydrates in very shallow water, where there isn't much pressure. But as long as the temperature is low enough, hydrates will form – on the polar shelf, for example.' He turned back to the rest of the group. 'The main deposits of methane hydrates – compressed methane – are on the continental slopes at depths of between five hundred and a thousand metres. One of our recent expeditions took us to an underwater ridge just off the American coast. It was five hundred metres high and twenty-five kilometres long, and made mainly of hydrates. Some was buried deep within the rock, but the rest lay exposed on the seabed. Since then we've found out that the oceans are full of it, but another important discovery's been made: methane hydrates are the only thing holding the continental slopes together. They act like cement. If you took away the hydrates, the slopes would look like Swiss cheese. Without the hydrates, there'd be landslides.' Bohrmann paused to let his words sink in. 'But there's more to it than that. Like I said, methane hydrates are only stable in conditions of low temperature and high pressure. So, you see, not all the gas compresses, just the top layer. Under the Earth's crust the temperature increases, leaving pockets of methane deep in the sediment that never freeze. The methane stays in a gaseous state, with the frozen layer of hydrate acting like a lid to trap it.'

'I read about that,' said the girl. 'Aren't the Japanese trying to extract the methane?'

Johanson smiled. There was always one kid in every class who was exceptionally well prepared and knew most of the lesson before it had begun. He guessed she wasn't too popular with her peers.

'Oh, it's not just the Japanese,' said Bohrmann. 'The whole world would like to extract it. But it's not that simple. When we were collecting our samples from a depth of eight hundred metres, the hydrates started to dissociate when they were half-way to the surface. By the time we had them on board, there was only a fraction of what we'd extracted. Methane hydrates are incredibly unstable. A temperature increase of just one degree at a depth of five hundred metres might be enough to destabilise the entire stock stored at that level. We knew we had to act quickly. We grabbed the lumps of hydrate and plunged them into liquid nitrogen to stop them dissociating. Come and have a look over here.'

'He's got a knack for this,' said Johanson, as Bohrmann led the class to a shelving unit made of stainless-steel frames. Containers of various sizes were stacked inside, with four tank-like, silvery barrels at the bottom. Bohrmann dragged one out, slipped on a pair of gloves and opened the lid. There was a hissing noise and vapour rose from inside. A few kids shrank away.

'It's only nitrogen.' Bohrmann reached down into the container and pulled out a fist-sized lump of something that looked like muddy ice. Within a few seconds it was fizzing and cracking. He beckoned to the girl, then broke off a chunk and held it out to her. 'It's pretty cold, but it won't hurt you,' he said.

'It stinks,' she exclaimed.

Some of the others laughed.

'Yep, like rotten eggs. It's the smell of gas dispersing.' He broke off more chunks and handed them round. 'The dark threads in the ice are seams of sediment. In a few seconds there'll be nothing left but a few specks of dirt and a puddle of water. The ice melts and the molecules of methane are released from their cages to escape into the air. Or, to put that in context, an apparently stable piece of seabed disintegrates, leaving almost nothing behind. That was what I wanted to show you.'

The kids' attention was on the fizzing ice. Bohrmann waited until it had melted, then continued: 'Now, while you were watching, something else happened invisibly. It's why we respect hydrates as much as we do. Remember I said that the methane was compressed by the ice crystals? Well, from every cubic centimetre of the hydrate that you were clutching, a hundred and sixty-four cubic centimetres of methane escaped into the air. During dissociation, the volume of methane increases by a factor of a hundred and sixty-four in the blink of an eye – leaving you with just a puddle in your hand. Taste it, if you like,' he said to the girl, 'and tell us what you think.'

She gazed at him in horror. 'But it smells!'

'Not any more. The gas has dispersed. But if you're worried about it, I'll do it.'

The girl lowered her head towards her hand and licked. 'Normal water!'

'That's right. When seawater freezes, the salt separates out. On that basis, the Antarctic is the largest reservoir of fresh water on the planet. Icebergs are made of fresh water.' Bohrmann closed the tank of liquid nitrogen and pushed it back into the unit.

'The idea of exploiting methane hydrates is hugely controversial, and you've just seen why. Suppose we were to destabilise the hydrates? We might set off a chain reaction. Imagine what would happen if the substance cementing the seabed suddenly evaporated. Think how it would affect our climate if methane from the deep sea escaped into the air. Methane is a greenhouse gas. It could heat up the atmosphere, which in turn would warm the seas, which would trigger the breakdown of hydrates, and so on. That's the kind of problem that keeps me and the other scientists here busy.'

'Why bother to extract it in the first place?' asked one of the boys. 'Why not leave it down there?'

'Because it could solve all our energy problems,' the girl chimed in. She pushed to the front of the group. 'That's what it said in the stuff about the Japanese. They don't have natural fuels of their own so they're forced to import them. Methane would solve the problem.'

'That's stupid,' said the other kid. 'If something causes more problems than it solves, it doesn't solve anything.'

Johanson grinned.

'You both have a point.' Bohrmann raised his hands in a conciliatory gesture. 'Methane hydrates *could* solve our energy problems, and that alone is enough to ensure that it's not a purely scientific question. The energy industry has a big interest in hydrates research. According to our estimates, marine gas hydrates contain twice as much burnable methane as all the other known deposits of gas, oil and coal combined. Just take the hydrate ridge off the coast of America. OK, so it extends over twenty-six thousand square kilometres, but there are thirty-five *gigatons* of hydrate in there. That's equivalent to one hundred times the amount of natural gas used in the whole of America in a year.'

'Sounds impressive,' Johanson whispered to Sahling. 'I'd no idea there was so much.'

'There's far more than that. I can never remember the figures, but Gerhard could tell you exactly.'

Bohrmann continued as if on cue: 'We can't know for sure, but we think over ten thousand gigatons of methane may be trapped in marine gas hydrates. And then you've got the onshore hydrates under the permafrost in Alaska and Siberia. To give you an idea of the quantities in question, all the available reserves of coal, oil and gas come to barely five thousand gigatons – less than half the amount of methane stored within the hydrates. No wonder the energy industry would give anything to know how to extract it. Just one per cent of that methane would double the United States' fuel reserves in an instant – and fuel consumption there is far higher than anywhere else in the world. Unfortunately it's the usual story. From the perspective of the energy industry, hydrates are an enormous reserve of untapped fuel; but scientists see them as a time bomb. The only option is for both sides to work together – in the interest of mankind, of course. Well, that brings us to the end of our tour. Thanks for coming.' He smiled to himself. 'And for listening, of course.'

'Not to mention understanding,' Johanson murmured.

'Well,' said Sahling, 'we hope so.'

'I pictured you differently,' said Johanson. He and Bohrmann shook hands. 'On your web page you've got a moustache.'

'I shaved it off.' Bohrmann fingered his upper lip. 'Your fault.'

'How come?'

'It happened this morning. I was shaving and thinking about your worm, when suddenly I could picture it clearly, wriggling across the mirror in front of me, swinging its tail in a loop. Too bad that my hand and the razor followed. I chopped off a corner and had to sacrifice the rest to science.'

'So now I've got a moustache on my conscience.' Johanson was amused.

'Oh, don't worry – it'll grow back in no time when the next trip starts. On the RV we all sprout beards. The lab's this way. Or would you like some coffee first?'

'No, thanks. I'm dying to see what you've got. So, you're off on another expedition?'

'In the autumn.' Bohrmann led them along glass corridors. 'We'll be heading for the cold seeps in the Aleutian subduction zone. You were lucky to catch me in Kiel. I got back from the Antarctic two weeks ago, after nearly eight months at sea. The day after we docked, I got your call.'

'What kept you there for so long?'

'Delivering over-winterers.'

'Over-winterers?'

Bohrmann laughed.

'Over-winter scientists and technicians. They started work at the station in December. They're extracting ice cores from a depth of four hundred and fifty metres. Unbelievable, isn't it? Ice as old as that can tell us the history of our climate over the last seven thousand years.'

Johanson was reminded of the taxi driver. 'Most people wouldn't be impressed,' he said. 'As far as they're concerned, climate history won't help eliminate world poverty or win the next world cup.'

'We're partly to blame for that, though. Science tends to keep itself to itself.'

'That wasn't the impression I got from your lecture just now.'

'I sometimes ask myself whether all this PR business does any good,' said Bohrmann, as he set off down a flight of stairs. 'Open days are all very well, but they don't change the general mindset. We had one recently and it was packed; but I bet if you'd asked afterwards whether we deserved an extra ten million in funding . . .'

Johanson thought for a moment. Then he said, 'maybe the real problem is the gulf between the different branches of science, don't you think?'

'You mean we don't communicate enough?'

'Exactly. The same applies to science and industry, and science and the military.'

'While between science and the *oil industry* . . .' Bohrmann said pointedly.

Johanson smiled. 'I'm here because someone needs an answer,' he said, 'not to force one out of you.'

'Big business and the military depend on science, whether they like it or not,' said Sahling. 'And we do communicate, you know. If you ask me, it's more a question of each party not being able to convey its point of view.'

'Or not wanting to.'

'Right. Research into ice cores *can* help prevent people starving – but also to build weapons. We're all looking at the same thing, but everyone sees something different.'

'And they don't see the rest.' Bohrmann nodded. 'The specimens you sent us, Dr Johanson, are the perfect example. Now I don't know whether the presence of worms should affect plans for building on the slope but, without more evidence, I'd be inclined to assume so. In the interests of safety, I'd advise against construction. Maybe that's the fundamental difference between science and industry. The way we scientists see it, we don't know enough about the role of the worms so we can't recommend drilling on the slope. The oil companies will start from exactly the same premise but reach the opposite conclusion.'

'In short, unless someone proves that the worms are affecting the slope, they won't change the plans.' Johanson looked at him. 'What do you think? How important are the worms?'

'I can't say for sure. The specimens you sent us are unusual, to say the least. I don't want to get your hopes up – I could have explained our findings on the telephone, but I thought you might like to see a bit more. And there's plenty we can show you here.'

They came to a steel door. Bohrmann pressed a switch on the wall and it slid open noiselessly. Through the doorway was a hall, and in the middle of the hall an enormous metal container, as big as a two-storey house. It was studded with portholes at regular intervals. Steel ladders led up to walkways and past pieces of machinery that were connected to its sides with pipes.

Johanson had seen photos of the lab on the web, but nothing had prepared him for its dimensions. The water in the container was kept at such high pressure that the idea of it made him feel queasy. It would kill a human in less than a minute. The deep-sea simulation chamber was the reason he'd sent the worms here. It contained an artificial world complete with seabed, continental shelf and slope.

Bohrmann flipped a switch to close the door behind them. 'Not everyone is convinced of the benefits of the pressure lab,' he said. 'Even the simulator can only give us a rough picture of what really happens on the seabed, but it saves having to launch an expedition every time there's something we need to investigate. The trouble with marine geoscience is that we never see more than a tiny fraction of the whole. At least with the simulator we can try out general hypotheses. It allows us to study the dynamics of methane hydrates under changing conditions.'

'You've got methane hydrates in there?'

'A couple of hundred kilos. We recently managed to produce some ourselves, but we don't advertise it. The oil companies would like us to use the simulator entirely for their purposes and, of course, we wouldn't mind their cash, but not at the expense of our scientific autonomy.'

Johanson craned his neck to look at the top of the tank. High above him a group of scientists were gathered on the uppermost walkway. The whole thing looked strangely unreal – like a *Bond* scene from the 1980s.

'We can regulate the temperature and pressure with absolute precision,' Bohrmann continued. 'At the moment they correspond to a depth of eight hundred metres. At the bottom of the chamber we've got a layer of stable hydrates two metres deep. In the ocean it would be twenty or thirty times that. Underneath that layer we've simulated heat from the Earth's core to create a pocket of gaseous methane. It's a fully functional miniature seabed.'

'Amazing,' said Johanson. 'But what are you doing with it? I mean, you can observe the hydrates, of course, but . . .' He tailed off.

Sahling came to his aid. 'You want to know what we do apart from observe?'

'Yes.'

'At the moment we're trying to re-create a geological situation dating back fifty-five million years. At some point in the late Paleocene epoch, just prior to the Eocene, there seems to have been a global-warming event of massive proportions. The ocean emptied. Seventy per cent of all life on the seabed died, including the majority of single-cell organisms. Large sections of the deep sea became uninhabitable, while on land there was a biological revolution. Crocodiles appeared in the Arctic and primates and modern mammals migrated from subtropical climates to North America. All in all, an almighty mess.'

'How can you tell?'

'Sediment cores. Everything we know about global warming in that period is due to a single core of sediment taken from a depth of two thousand metres.'

'And does the sediment tell us what caused it?'

'Methane,' said Bohrmann. 'The sea temperature seems to have risen, causing large quantities of hydrates to become unstable. The continental slopes collapsed, resulting in underwater landslides that exposed further deposits of methane. Over a period of only thousands – or maybe hundreds – of years, billions of tonnes of gas were released into the ocean, and dispersed into the atmosphere. It was a vicious circle. Methane has thirty times the global-warming potential of carbon dioxide. The temperature rose all over the planet, including in the oceans, prompting the hydrates to dissociate, and setting the whole thing in motion all over again. The Earth became a gigantic oven.' Bohrmann turned to Johanson. 'The temperature in the depths reached fifteen degrees. Nowadays it's between two and four. That's a pretty major shift.'

'Disastrous for some species, but as for the rest . . . I guess they got off to a warm start. I see what you're saying. Next up is the extinction of mankind, I suppose?'

Sahling smiled. 'Things aren't that drastic yet. But you're right. There's reason to believe that we're currently in a phase of climatic fluctuation. The hydrate reserves in the oceans are highly volatile. That's why we're paying so much attention to your worm.'

'But what's a worm got to do with the stability of hydrates?'

'In theory, nothing. The layers of hydrate are hundreds of metres thick. The worms stay on the top layer, melt a centimetre or two of ice, and sit there contentedly with their bacteria.'

'But our worm's got vast jaws.'

'Our worm makes no sense at all. Come and see for yourself.'

They walked over towards a semi-circular control panel at the back of the room. It reminded Johanson of the control desk for Victor, but this one was significantly bigger. Most of the two dozen or so monitors had been switched on and were transmitting pictures from inside the tank. The technician on duty greeted them.

'We keep tabs on what's happening with the help of twenty-two cameras. In addition to that, we're constantly taking readings from every cubic centimetre,' explained Bohrmann. 'See those white patches on the upper row of monitors? They're hydrates. We set down two of your polychaetes just on the left here. That was yesterday morning.'

Johanson squinted up at the screens. 'I see ice, but no worms,' he said.

'Take a closer look.'

Johanson scrutinized every detail of the pictures. Suddenly he noticed two dark patches. He pointed to them. 'What are those? Indentations in the ice?'

Sahling said something to the technician. The picture changed. All of a sudden the worms came into view.

'The dark spots are holes,' said Sahling. 'Let's look at the sequence in time-lapse.'

Johanson watched the worms wriggle over the ice. They crawled around for a bit, as though they were on the scent of something. Speeded up, their movements were alien and disturbing. On either side of their pink bodies, their bristles quivered as though they were charged.

'Now, watch carefully.'

One of the worms had stopped crawling. Wave-like movements pulsed through its body. Then it disappeared into the ice.

Johanson gave a low whistle. 'My God! It's burrowed in.'

The second worm was still on the surface, a little further to one side. Its head moved and suddenly its proboscis shot forward, revealing its jaws.

'They're eating their way into the ice!' exclaimed Johanson.

He stood, paralysed, in front of the screens. There's no reason to be shocked, he told himself. The worms live symbiotically with bacteria that break down hydrates, but they're equipped with jaws for burrowing.

The solution was obvious. The worms were trying to reach the bacteria buried deeper in the ice. He watched them, fascinated, as they dug into the hydrates, their rear ends wiggling. Then they were gone. Only the holes remained, two dark patches in the ice.

It's nothing to get worked up about, he thought. Some worm species spend their whole lives burrowing. But why would they burrow into hydrates? 'Where are they now?' he asked.

Sahling glanced at the monitor. 'They're dead.'

'Dead?' Johanson echoed.

'They suffocated. Worms need oxygen.'

'I know – that's the whole point of the symbiosis. The bacteria produce nutrients for the worm, and the worm provides oxygen for the bacteria. What went wrong?'

'They dug themselves to death. They chomped their way through the ice, fell into the pocket of methane and died.'

'Kamikaze worms,' muttered Johanson.

'It does look like suicide.'

Johanson thought for a moment. 'Unless they were thrown off-course by something.'

'Maybe. But what? There's nothing in the hydrates that could explain such behaviour.'

'Maybe the gas pocket.'

Bohrmann scratched his chin. 'We wondered about that, but it doesn't explain why they'd dig their way to death.'

Johanson pictured the mass of wriggling worms at the bottom of the ocean. He was feeling increasingly uneasy. What would happen if millions of worms burrowed into the ice?

Bohrmann seemed to hear his thoughts. 'The worms can't destabilise the ice,' he said. 'On the seabed the hydrate layers are infinitely thicker than they are here. Even crazy creatures like these would only dent the surface. They'd manage a tenth at most before death reeled them in.'

'So, what's the next step? Will you test some more specimens?'

'We can use the worms we kept in reserve. Ideally, though, we'd like to examine them *in situ*. That should please Statoil. In a few weeks' time the RV *Sonne* will be leaving for Greenland. If we set sail a little earlier, we could stop off at the place where they first showed up and take a look.' Bohrmann shrugged. 'It's not up to me, though. We'll have to wait for a decision. It was just an idea I developed with Heiko.'

Johanson glanced back at the tank and thought of the dead worms. 'It's an excellent idea,' he said.

After a while Johanson went back to the hotel to get changed. He tried to reach Lund, but she wasn't picking up. He imagined her lying in Sverdrup's arms and hung up.

Bohrmann had invited him to dinner that evening in one of Kiel's best restaurants. He went into the bathroom and inspected himself in the mirror. His beard needed trimming, he thought. It was at least two millimetres too long. Everything else was just right, though. His once-brown hair was thick and shiny, despite the strands of grey, and his eyes still twinkled beneath heavy brows. At times he found it hard to resist his own charisma. One of his female students had told him that he looked like the actor Maximilian Schell. Johanson had felt flattered – until he found out Schell was over seventy.

He rummaged through his suitcase, pulled out a zip-neck sweater and put it on, then struggled to force his suit jacket over the top. He wrapped a scarf round his neck. He didn't look well dressed, but that was how he liked it. He cultivated a scruffy look. It took him longer to achieve his dishevelled hairstyle than most people would spend on a respectable coiffure.

He flashed himself a smile in the mirror, left the hotel, and took a taxi to the restaurant.

Bohrmann was waiting for him. They had a few glasses of wine with their dinner, but eventually the conversation drifted back to the ocean. Over dessert Bohrmann asked casually, 'How much do you know about Statoil's plans?'

'Only the basic details,' said Johanson. 'I'm not especially well informed about oil.'

'What *are* they planning? It can't be a platform – it's too far out to sea.'

'It's not a platform.'

'I don't want to pressure you and I've no idea how confidential these things are . . .'

'I shouldn't worry about that. If *I*'ve been told, it can't be very secret.' Bohrmann laughed. 'So, what *are* they building out there?'

'They've got plans for a subsea plant. A fully automated one.'

'Like SUBSIS?'

'What's that?'

'Subsea Separation and Injection System – a unit off the coast of Norway in the Troll field. It's been active for a number of years now.'

'Never heard of it.'

'You should ask the guys who sent you here. SUBSIS is a processing plant that operates three hundred and fifty metres down. It separates the water from the oil and gas at seabed level. In conventional plants, the process takes place on the platforms and the water is discharged into the sea.'

'Oh, I remember!' Lund had said something about it. 'The water makes fish infertile.'

'SUBSIS can get round that. The water is injected back into the reservoir, pushing the oil upwards, so more oil pumps out. In the meantime, the water is removed, re-injected, and so it goes on. The oil and gas are carried through pipelines to the coast. It's pretty neat, as far as it goes.'

'But?'

'I'm not sure there is a but. SUBSIS is supposed to work perfectly in depths of up to fifteen hundred metres. Its manufacturer thinks it can do two thousand, and the oil companies are aiming for five thousand.'

'Is that feasible?'

'In the not too distant future, yes. Anything that works on a small scale will probably work on a larger one, and the advantages are obvious. It won't be long before remote-controlled plants replace all of the platforms.'

'You don't sound enthusiastic,' said Johanson.

There was a pause. Bohrmann seemed unsure how to respond. 'What bothers me isn't the subsea plant as such. It's the naïvety of it all.'

'It's a remote-controlled unit?'

'Fully automated. It's operated from the shore.'

'Which means repairs and maintenance work are carried out by robots.'

Bohrmann nodded.

'I see,' said Johanson.

'There are pros and cons,' said Bohrmann. 'It's always risky when you enter unknown territory. And, let's face it, the slopes are certainly that, so it makes sense to automate the system. There's nothing wrong with sending down a robot to do a bit of monitoring or to take a few samples. But a subsea station is a different proposition. Suppose oil spurts out of a well five thousand metres down. How are you going to fix it? You don't know the terrain. All you've got is piles of data. We're as good as blind down there. OK, we can use satellites, digital sonar and seismic profiling to create a map of seabed morphology that's accurate to within half a metre. OK, we've got bottom-simulating reflectors to detect oil and gas deposits, so we can tell where we should drill, where we'll find oil, where the hydrates are stored, and where best to avoid . . . But as for what's down there, no one really knows.'

'That's my refrain,' murmured Johanson.

'Don't get me wrong, I'm not against fossil fuels *per se*, but I object to making the same mistake twice. When the oil industry took off, we erected our junk in the sea, without anyone thinking about how we could dispose of it. We emptied wastewater and chemicals into rivers and seas, as though they'd simply disperse. Radioactive material was dumped in the oceans. Natural resources and life-forms were exploited and destroyed. No one stopped to consider how complex the connections might be.'

'But subsea plants are here to stay?'

'Almost certainly. They're more economic, and they can tap oil reserves that humans can't reach. After that, the stampede will start for methane. It burns more cleanly than fossil fuels and it will slow down the greenhouse effect. All the arguments in favour are perfectly valid – providing everything goes to plan. People in these companies often confuse what should happen in an ideal scenario with what could happen in reality. It makes their lives easier. Whenever they're presented with a range of possible outcomes, they pick the most favourable so they can start work straight away – even if they know nothing about the world they're intruding on.'

'But how will they exploit the methane?' asked Johanson. 'Won't the hydrates dissociate on the way to the surface?'

'That's where remote-controlled processors enter the equation. If you get the hydrates to dissociate while they're down there, by heating them, for example, all you've got to do is trap the gas and channel it to the surface. It sounds great, but who's to say that an operation like that won't start a chain reaction and trigger a heatwave like the one in the Paleocene?'

'Do you think that's possible?'

Bohrmann spread his hands. 'Every time we tamper with our environment without knowing what we're doing, we're dicing with death. But it's started already. The gas hydrate programmes in India, Japan and China are already quite advanced.' He gave a bleak smile. 'But they don't know what's down there either.'

'Worms,' murmured Johanson. He thought of the video images that Victor had taken of the seething mass on the seabed. And of the ominous creature that had disappeared into the dark.

Worms. Monsters. Methane. Natural disasters.

It was time for a drink.

11 April

The sight of it made Anawak angry. From head to fluke it measured over ten metres, an enormous male orca, one of the biggest transients he had ever seen. Its half-open jaws revealed tightly packed rows of glistening conical teeth. The whale was past its prime, but still immensely powerful. It wasn't until Anawak examined it more closely that he noticed the dull, worn patches that flecked its shiny black skin. One of its eyes was closed and the other was hidden from view.

Anawak had recognised it straight away. On the database it was listed as J-19, but its distinctive dorsal fin, curved in the shape of a scimitar, had earned it its nickname: Genghis. He walked to the other side of the body and spotted John Ford, director of Vancouver Aquarium's marine-mammal research programme, talking to Sue Oliviera, head of the lab in Nanaimo, and another man. They were gathered under the line of trees that fringed the beach. Ford beckoned Anawak over. 'Dr Ray Fenwick from the Canadian Institute of Ocean Sciences and Fisheries,' he said.

Fenwick was there for the autopsy. As soon as they'd heard that Genghis was dead, Ford had suggested that the dissection should be conducted on the beach, where the carcass had been found, rather than behind closed doors. He wanted to drum up a large group of students and journalists and give them an insight into the orca's anatomy. 'Besides,' he'd said, 'the autopsy will look different in the open – less clinical and distant. We'll be staring at the corpse of an orca close to the sea – in its own world. People will be more involved, more compassionate. It's a gimmick, of course, but it'll work.'

They'd thrashed it out between them: Ford, Fenwick, Anawak and Rod Palm, a naturalist from the marine research station on Strawberry Isle, off the coast of Tofino. Palm and the Strawberry Isle team monitored the ecosystem in Clayoquot Sound, and Palm had made a name for himself by studying the orcas there.

'The external evidence suggests that it succumbed to a bacteriological infection,' said Fenwick, when Anawak pressed him, 'but I don't want to rush to any hasty conclusions.'

'You don't have to,' said Anawak grimly. 'Remember 1999? Seven dead orcas, and all of them infected.'

'"The Torture Never Stops",' murmured Oliviera, recalling an old Frank Zappa song. She nodded conspiratorially at Anawak. 'Come with me a second.'

Anawak followed her over to the carcass. Two large metallic cases and a container had been placed beside it, full of tools for the autopsy. Dissecting an orca was a different matter from dissecting a human. It meant hard work, vast quantities of blood and one hell of a stench.

'The press will be here in a moment, with the students,' she said, glancing at her watch, 'but since we're together, we should have a word about those samples.'

'Made any headway?'

'Some.'

'And you're keeping Inglewood in the picture?'

'I thought you and I should talk first.'

'Sounds like you haven't reached any firm conclusions.'

'Put it this way, we're amazed on one count and stumped on the other,' said Oliviera. 'For one thing, the mussels aren't described in any of the existing research.'

'I could have sworn they were zebras.'

'On the one hand, yes, but on the other, no.'

'Fill me in.'

'There are two ways of looking at it. We're either dealing with a species related to the zebra mussel or with a mutation. They look like zebra mussels and they form colonies like zebra mussels, but there's something odd about the byssus. The fibres extending from the foot are unusually thick and long. We've nicknamed them "jet mussels".' She pulled a face. 'We couldn't come up with anything better. We've observed a number of living specimens, and they're able to . . . Well, they don't just drift like normal zebra mussels. They set their course by sucking in water and expelling it. The force drives them forwards, and they use their fibres to steer. Does that remind you of something?'

'Squid use jet propulsion.'

'Well, some species do, but there's something else. I was thinking of dinoflagellates, unicellular organisms. In certain species, the cells have a pair of flagella extending outwards from the cell wall. They use one flagellum to steer, while the other rotates, moving them forward.'

'But apart from that they've got nothing in common.'

'I'm treating it as convergent evolution in a very broad sense. At this stage, I need every lead I can get. As far as I know, no other species of mussel moves around like that. These swim like shoaling fish, and they can keep up their momentum, in spite of the weight of their shells.'

'Well, that would explain how they settled on the *Barrier Queen*'s hull in the middle of the ocean,' mused Anawak. 'Is that the amazing part?'

'Right.'

'What's stumped you?'

Oliviera stepped closer to the dead whale and stroked its skin. 'The fragments of tissue you found down there. We don't know what to do with them – and there's not much we can do. For the most part it had already decomposed. The small amount that we were able to analyse seemed to indicate that the substance on the propeller and the substance on your knife were identical. Apart from that, it bore no resemblance to anything we've ever come across before. The tissue is unusually well developed in terms of its contractibility. It's incredibly strong, but also extremely elastic. We don't know what it is.'

'Could that be an indication of bioluminescence?'

'Possibly. Why?'

'Because it flashed at me.'

'You're talking about the thing that knocked you over?'

'Yeah. It shot out while I was poking around in the mussel bed.'

'Maybe because you'd cut a lump out of it. Although I can't believe this tissue contains nerve fibres or anything else that might make it feel pain. It's really just . . . cell mass.'

They heard voices approaching. Across the sand, a group of people were heading towards them, some with cameras, others with notepads.

'We're on,' said Anawak.

'OK.' Oliviera looked at him helplessly. 'But what do you want me to do? Should I forward the results to Inglewood? I can't imagine they'll be of any use. I'd rather look at a few more samples – especially of that tissue.'

'I'll get in touch with Roberts.' Anawak stared at the orca, depressed.

First the whales had disappeared for weeks, and now there was another corpse. 'Why did this have to happen? It's such a mess.'

Oliviera shrugged. 'Save your lamentations for the press,' she said.

The autopsy took more than an hour, during which Fenwick, assisted by Ford, cut open the whale and explained its anatomical structure, exposing its intestines, heart, liver and lungs. Its stomach revealed a half-digested seal. Unlike the resident orcas, transient and offshore orcas ate sealions, porpoises and dolphins – even baleen whales could fall prey to a pod of orcas.

Specialist science journalists were in the minority among the spectators, but reporters from the broadsheets, magazines and TV networks were out in force – exactly the sort of people the team had hoped to attract.

Fenwick started by explaining the distinguishing features of an orca's anatomy. 'As you can see, its shape resembles that of a fish, but that's because nature adopted this body form for sea creatures that have evolved from land animals. It happens a lot. We call it convergent evolution: in order to cope with similar environmental pressures, two totally different species develop convergent structures – that is, structures designed to solve the same problem.'

He removed sections of the thick outer skin to expose the layer of fat. 'Fish, amphibians and reptiles are ectotherms, which means they're cold-blooded, so their body temperature corresponds to that of their surroundings. Mackerel, for example, are present in the Arctic Ocean and in the Mediterranean. In the Arctic their body temperature is four degrees Celsius, but in the Med it's twenty-four. The same doesn't apply to whales: they're warm-blooded, like us.'

Fenwick had uttered two little words that never failed to hit their mark. As soon as the spectators heard them, they sat up and paid attention.

Fenwick continued, 'They could be swimming in the Arctic or in the Baja California, it makes no difference. Wherever they are, whales have a constant body temperature of thirty-seven degrees, and to maintain it they accumulate the layer of fat we call blubber. See this white, fatty mass? Water normally draws heat away from the body, but this layer of fat prevents it happening.'

His gloves were red and slimy with the orca's blood and fat.

'But blubber can also be fatal to a whale. The reason they die when they get stranded is because of their weight, due in part to their magnificent fat layers. A blue whale measuring thirty-three metres and weighing a hundred and thirty tonnes is four times heavier then the biggest dinosaur that ever walked the Earth. Even an orca can weigh up to nine tonnes. Creatures of that size can only survive in water. It all comes down to Archimedes' principle, which states that the weight of a body immersed in fluid will decrease by an amount equal to the weight of the fluid it displaces. On land, whales are crushed to death by the pressure of their own weight – if they haven't already been killed by the insulating effect of their blubber, which absorbs the heat of the environment. Beached whales often die of overheating.'

'Is that what happened to this one?' asked a journalist.

'No. Over the past few years we've come across an increasing number of whales whose immune systems have collapsed. They all died of bacterial infections. J-19 was twenty-two, not exactly a youngster but most healthy orcas live to thirty. So, he died early and there are no external signs of a struggle. My guess is that an infection killed him.'

Anawak took a step forward. 'We can tell you why that happens, if you're interested,' he said, in as neutral a tone as he could muster. 'There's been extensive toxicological research into the problem, and the results show that the orcas off the coast of British Columbia are badly contaminated with PCBs and other environmental pollutants. This year we've found orcas with PCB levels of a hundred and fifty parts per million: A human immune system wouldn't stand a chance against that level of toxin.'

He saw a mixture of compassion and excitement in the listeners' upturned faces. The journalists had their story.

'The worst thing about toxins,' he continued, 'is that they're fat-soluble, which means they're passed to the calves in the mothers' milk. When human babies come into the world with AIDS, it's all over the media and everyone is appalled. Write about what you've seen here and make people angry about this. Hardly any other species on the planet is as packed with toxins as the orcas.'

'Dr Anawak.' The journalist cleared his throat. 'What happens when humans eat the flesh of these whales?'

'They absorb some of the toxin.'

'Does it kill them?'

'It might in the long-term.'

'In that case, aren't businesses that dump their chemicals in the water – like the timber industry – indirectly responsible for death and disease among humans?'

Anawak hesitated. The reporter was right, of course, but Vancouver Aquarium was keen to avoid direct confrontations with local businesses, preferring to try for a diplomatic solution. Painting British Columbia's economic and political élite as a bunch of near-murderers would increase the existing tensions. 'There's no doubt that eating contaminated meat would pose a risk to human health,' he said evasively.

'Meat that our businesses have knowingly contaminated.'

'That's something we're working on with those responsible.'

'I get it.' The reporter made a note of something. 'I was thinking in particular of the people where you come from, Dr . . .'

'I come from round here,' said Anawak curtly.

The journalist stared at him in surprise.

No wonder, thought Anawak. The poor guy had been snapped at for doing his homework.

'That's not what I meant,' the man responded. 'I meant where you came from originally—'

'Very little whale or seal flesh is consumed in British Columbia,' Anawak interrupted. 'By contrast, relatively high levels of toxins have been recorded among inhabitants of the Arctic Circle, in Greenland, Iceland, Alaska and further north in Nunavut, but also in Siberia, the Kamchatka peninsula and the Aleutian Islands. In other words, everywhere that marine mammals are part of the staple diet. It doesn't matter where the mammals pick up the toxins because they migrate.'

'Do you think the whales know they're being poisoned?' asked a student.

'No.'

'But in your books you say that they're intelligent. If only they realised there was a problem with their food . . .'

'Humans carry on smoking until they need an amputation or die of lung cancer. They're aware of the problem but it doesn't stop them. And humans are a good deal smarter than whales.'

'How can you be sure? It might be the other way round.'

Anawak made an effort to answer politely. 'You have to see whales as whales. They're highly specialised, but specialisation brings with it certain limitations. An orca is a streamlined living torpedo, but that comes at the expense of legs, hands, facial expressions and stereoscopic vision. They're not like humans. Orcas are probably cleverer than dogs. Belugas are intelligent enough to know who they are, and dolphins certainly have a unique brain. But take a moment to think about what they achieve with all that. Whales and dolphins share a habitat with fish and have a similar way of life, but fish get by with only a few neurons.'

Anawak was almost relieved to hear his mobile buzz. He signalled to Fenwick to carry on with the autopsy and took a few paces away from the group.

'Leon,' said Shoemaker, 'Can you prise yourself away?'

'Maybe. What's wrong?'

'He's back.'

This time Anawak was so angry he could barely contain himself. A few days ago, when he'd been called back to Vancouver Island in a hurry, Jack Greywolf and his Seaguards had disappeared, leaving two boatfuls of disgruntled tourists in their wake. Shoemaker had been besieged by people complaining at being filmed and stared at like animals, and had only just succeeded in calming them down, in some cases by handing out free tickets. After that, things had seemed to return to normal. But Jack Greywolf had caused an upset, exactly as he'd hoped.

Back at the station they'd gone over all the options. Was it better to ignore the protesters or take action against them? If they made an official complaint they would give Greywolf a forum. People like him were as much of an irritation to serious environmental organisations as they were to the whale-watching business, but in the media uproar, an unsuspecting public would receive distorted information. Many would sympathise with Greywolf, without knowing the facts.

They'd decided to ignore him.

Perhaps, thought Anawak, as he steered the motorboat along the coast through Clayoquot Sound, that was a mistake. Maybe a simple letter of complaint would have satisfied Greywolf's need for acknowledgement. Anything to show he'd made an impact.

He scanned the surface of the ocean. The Zodiac was racing through the water and he didn't want to risk scaring or hurting a whale. Several times he spotted flukes in the distance, and once he saw glistening black fins cutting through the water not far from the boat. He kept in radio-contact with Susan Stringer on the *Blue Shark*. 'What are they doing?' he asked. 'They're not getting physical, are they?'

The walkie-talkie crackled. 'No,' came Stringer's voice. 'They're taking photos like last time, and yelling at us.'

'How many?'

'Two boatfuls – Greywolf and another guy in one boat, and three in the second. Oh, God, they've started to sing.'

Anawak heard a faint rhythmic sound above the radio interference.

'They're drumming,' Stringer bellowed. 'Greywolf's beating a rhythm and the others are chanting Indian songs.'

'Keep calm. Don't let yourself be provoked. I'll be with you in a moment.'

'Leon? What kind of Indian is this asshole?'

'He's a con artist,' said Anawak, 'not an Indian.'

'But I thought—'

'His mother's half Indian, but that's as far as it goes. His real name is Jack O'Bannon.'

Anawak sped on towards the boats. The noise of the drum floated over the water.

'Jack O'Bannon,' said Stringer slowly. 'I've got a good mind to—'

'You'll do no such thing. Can you see me now?'

'Yes.'

'Sit tight.'

Anawak stowed his radio and turned the boat towards the open water. At last he could see what was happening. The *Blue Shark* and the *Lady Wexham* were in the middle of a group of humpbacks that had spread out across the sea. From time to time flukes disappeared under the waves or a cloud of droplets rose into the air. The *Lady Wexham*'s white hull shimmered in the sunlight. Two small, dilapidated sport-fishing boats with red-painted hulls were circling the *Blue Shark* tightly.

If Greywolf had noticed Anawak approaching, he didn't let on. He was standing in the boat, banging a drum and chanting. The people on the other boat, two men and a woman, were shouting insults and curses. Every now and then they took pictures of the *Blue Shark*'s passengers and pelted them with something that sparkled. Fish scraps, Anawak realised The people on the *Blue Shark* ducked. Anawak felt like ramming Greywolf's boat and watching as the man toppled overboard, but he restrained himself.

He pulled up close to the boats and shouted, 'Quit drumming, Jack. Let's talk.'

Greywolf ignored him.

A male voice came over the radio: 'Hello, Leon. Good to see you.'

It was the *Lady Wexham*'s skipper. The boat was about a hundred metres away. The people on the top deck were leaning over the rails, staring at the beleaguered Zodiac. Some were taking photos.

'Everything OK at your end?' asked Anawak.

'Fine. What are we going to do about the bastards?'

'I'll try the peaceful approach.'

'If you want me to run them down for you, just say the word.'

The *Blue Shark* was being jostled by the Seaguards' motorboats. Greywolf swayed as his boat hit the inflatable, but he carried on drumming. The feathers on his hat quivered in the wind. Behind the boats a fluke rose into the air and disappeared again, but no one had eyes for the whales.

'Hey, Leon! Leon!' One of the *Blue Shark*'s passengers was waving at him – Alicia Delaware. She was bouncing up and down. 'Who are those guys? What are they doing here?'

Anawak did a double-take. The other day she had told him she was about to leave the island. But right now it didn't matter.

He manoeuvred his Zodiac towards Greywolf's boat and drew up at right angles to it. He clapped his hands loudly. 'All right, Jack, you can stop now. Tell us what you want.'

Greywolf increased the volume. His monotonous chant rose and fell like an aggressive dirge.

'For God's sake, Jack!'

The noise stopped. Greywolf faced Anawak. 'Do you want something?'

'Tell your people to back off. Then we can talk about whatever you like, so long as you tell them to stop.'

Greywolf's face contorted with rage. 'We're not backing off.'

'What's your point, Greywolf? Why all the fuss?'

'I tried to tell you at the aquarium but you wouldn't listen.'

'I didn't have time.'

'And I don't have time to talk to you now.' His supporters laughed and jeered.

Anawak nearly lost his temper. 'I'm going to make you an offer, Jack,' he said, as calmly as he could. 'You call this off, and we'll meet tonight at Davie's. Then you can tell us what you'd like us to do.'

'Just keep away from here.'

'But why? What harm are we doing?'

Two dark islands surfaced next to the boat, textured and mottled like weathered stone. Grey whales. It would have made an amazing photo, but Greywolf had ruined the day.

'Turn back,' shouted Greywolf. He stared at the *Blue Shark*'s passengers and lifted his arms imploringly. 'Turn back and leave the whales in peace. Live in harmony with nature. Your boats are polluting the air and the ocean. Whales are being hounded so you can take photos. This place belongs to them. Go home. You don't belong here!'

What a load of garbage, thought Anawak. Surely even Greywolf didn't believe it. But his supporters cheered.

'Come on, Jack! We're here to *protect* the whales, remember? Whale-watching helps us to understand them. It lets people see them in new light. It's not in their interest for you to disrupt our work.'

'Their interest? You'd know all about that, wouldn't you?' Greywolf jeered. 'Can you read their minds, Mr Scientist?'

'Jack, drop all the Indian crap. *What do you want?*'

'Publicity,' Greywolf said.

'And how are you going to get that here?' Anawak waved his hand at the ocean. 'There's just a couple of boats and a few people. Let's talk about this properly and get some real publicity. Both sides can put forward their arguments, and may the best side win.'

'Pathetic,' said Greywolf. 'Listen to the voice of the white man.'

Anawak lost his patience. 'That's crap and you know it. You're more of a white man than I am, O'Bannon. Get real.'

For a moment Greywolf stared at him. Then a grin spread across his face. He pointed to the *Lady Wexham*. 'Why do you think the people on your boat are so interested in filming us?'

'Because of you and your mumbo-jumbo.'

'Exactly,' laughed Greywolf. 'You got it in one.'

Then it dawned on Anawak. The people on the *Lady Wexham* weren't tourists: they were reporters whom Greywolf had invited for the show.

The son-of-a-bitch.

He was about to make a suitably cutting response, when he noticed that Greywolf was still staring at the *Lady Wexham*. Anawak followed his gaze, and gasped.

A humpback had catapulted itself out of the water just in front of the boat. For a moment it looked as though it was balancing on its flukes. Only the tip of its tail was still submerged as it towered above the *Lady Wexham*'s bridge. The throat grooves on its lower jaw and underbelly were clearly visible. Its long pectoral fins stuck out like wings, two shiny white appendages with dark markings and knobbly edges. A loud *ooh!* went up as the gigantic body tipped slowly to one side and hit the water in an explosion of spray.

The people on the top deck shrank back. Part of the *Lady Wexham* disappeared behind a wall of foam. But the jet of water had cloaked another dark shape. In a mantle of mist and water a second whale surged up from the waves. This time it was even closer to the vessel. Even before the cry of horror went up, Anawak knew that the leap had gone wrong.

The whale hit the *Lady Wexham* with such force that the vessel rocked violently. There was a cracking, splintering sound. The whale dived down, and people on the top deck were thrown to the floor. The sea around the craft foamed and boiled, then several humpbacks rose to the surface. Two dark bodies launched themselves into the air and hurled themselves at the hull.

'Vengeance!' shrieked Greywolf. There was a hysterical edge to his voice.

The *Lady Wexham* was twenty-two metres long, far longer than any humpback whale. She had a permit from the Ministry of Transport and conformed to the Canadian Coast Guard's safety standards, which required passenger vessels to be able to withstand rough seas, metre-high breakers and the occasional collision with a lethargic whale. The *Lady Wexham* had been designed to cope with all such misfortunes. But she hadn't been designed to contend with an attack.

From across the water Anawak heard her engines start. Pandemonium broke out on the two viewing decks, and screams of terror echoed over the waves. People were pushing past each other in blind panic. The *Lady Wexham* started to move, but a whale rose out of the water, catapulting itself against the bridge. Even this assault wasn't enough to capsize her, but now she was pitching dangerously, as debris rained into the water.

Anawak knew he had to do something. Maybe he could distract the whales. His hand reached for the throttle.

At that moment another scream pierced the air, but this time it was coming from behind him. Anawak spun round.

He was just in time to see the body of an enormous humpback surge vertically out of the water, looking almost weightless. It rose, ten, twelve metres into the air and for a heartbeat it hung above the little red motorboat with the three protestors.

Anawak had never seen anything so terrifying, and yet so beautiful at such close range.

'Oh dear God no,' he whispered.

As if in slow motion the body gently tipped and started falling. A shadow descended on the little red motorboat, then swallowed the *Blue Shark's* bow. It grew longer and longer as the enormous body plummeted downwards, travelling faster by the second . . .

Anawak jammed down the throttle. Greywolf's boat was also quick off the mark – heading straight for Anawak. The two boats collided and Greywolf's driver disappeared overboard but Anawak didn't stop. Before his eyes, thirty tonnes of humpback crashed on to the motorboat, burying it and its crew in the water, and hitting the front of the *Blue Shark*. The Zodiac's stern flipped up at right-angles to the water, sending its load of orange-clad passengers spinning through the spray.

It was a chilling sight. The campaigners' boat had been reduced to splinters and the *Blue Shark* was drifting upside-down. The water was full of people, shouting and paddling wildly. Their orange suits had inflated automatically to keep them afloat but some lay still on the water, killed by the weight of the whale. Across the waves, the *Lady Wexham* was surrounded by flukes and fins. He watched as she picked up speed, listing severely.

Anawak picked his way slowly through the drifting bodies, trying to avoid causing more injuries. He flipped on to channel 98 and reported his position. 'We're in trouble,' he barked. 'Casualties and maybe fatalities.' Every boat in the area would pick up his distress signal. He didn't have time to say more or to explain what had happened – there'd been a dozen or so passengers on the *Blue Shark*, plus Stringer and her deputy, then the three protestors in the motorboat, seventeen in all.

'Leon!' Stringer was swimming towards him. Anawak grabbed her hand and pulled her aboard, then spotted dorsal fins in the water not far from his boat. The orcas' black heads and backs poked out of the water as they sped towards the carnage.

They were moving with a single-mindedness that made his stomach lurch.

Alicia Delaware was floating nearby. She was holding the head of a young man whose orange suit hadn't inflated. Anawak steered the boat towards her, then he and Stringer hauled the unconscious man and the girl on board. Others were swimming towards them now, stretching out their arms to be pulled out of the water. The boat was filling rapidly. It was much smaller than the *Blue Shark* and already overloaded. Frantically they kept pulling people in, while Anawak scanned the sea for bodies.

'There's one!' shouted Stringer.

A man was floating motionless in the water, face down, no suit – a protester from the motorboat.

Anawak and Stringer grabbed him by the arms and lifted him.

He wasn't especially heavy.

Not nearly heavy enough.

His head lolled back and his eyes stared blankly. His body ended at the waist, torn flesh, arteries and intestines dangled from the torso, blood dripping over the waves.

Stringer gasped and let go, then Anawak lost his grip and the corpse splashed back into the water.

All around the boat, sword-like fins swirled through the waves. There were at least ten of them, maybe more. A blow sent the boat spinning. Anawak leaped to the wheel, opened the throttle and sped off. Three vast backs rose out of the water before him. He swerved and the whales dived. Two more appeared on the other side, heading straight for the boat. Anawak swerved again. He heard screaming and crying and panic took hold of him, but somehow he steered the Zodiac past the black-and-white bodies blocking their escape.

There was a crunching sound. He swung round in time to see the *Lady Wexham* shudder and heel in a cloud of spray. In that split second of inattentiveness, the Zodiac's fate was sealed. A giant tail was already hurtling towards the boat.

The Zodiac flew into the air and flipped over.

Anawak soared up, past a cloud of spray, then plummeted down into the ocean. It was bitingly cold. He kicked with all his might, and fought his way up to the surface. Gasping, he was pushed back down. Seized by panic he thrashed about, paddling madly until, spluttering, he surfaced again.

There was no sign of the boat or any of its passengers. The coastline bobbed into view. He was lifted by a wave and at last he saw some of the others – half a dozen at most. Then gleaming black blades cut through the surf and dived down. A head jerked under and didn't resurface.

An elderly woman saw the man vanish. 'The boat! Where is it?' she shrieked.

Where was the boat? It was too far for them to swim ashore. The woman's screams became more desperate.

Anawak swam over to her. She saw him coming and stretched out her arms. 'Please! You've got to help me.'

'I'm going to,' called Anawak. 'Just try to stay calm.'

'I can't keep my head up. I'm sinking.'

'You won't sink.' He took deep long strokes to reach her. 'The suit won't let you.'

The woman didn't seem to hear him: 'You've got to help me. Oh, God, don't let me drown! I don't want to drown.'

'Don't worry, I'll—'

Suddenly her eyes widened and she vanished under water. Something brushed against Anawak's leg.

Fear coursed through him. He pushed his upper body clear of the water and looked around. The Zodiac was drifting upside-down. All that separated him and the others from it was a few metres – and three black torpedoes.

As the whales powered towards them, something in Anawak protested. Not once had an orca attacked a human in the wild: they treated humans with curiosity, amity or indifference. And whales didn't attack boats – they just *didn't*. Suddenly he was hit by a rush of water and a flash of red came between him and the whales. Hands reached down to grab him. Then Greywolf steered towards the rest of the swimmers. He pulled Alicia Delaware out of the water and set her down on a bench while Anawak hauled up a wheezing man. He scanned the surface for others. Where was Stringer?

He caught a glimpse of her head between two waves. A second woman was with her. The orcas had surrounded the upturned Zodiac and were closing in from both sides. Their shiny black heads cut through the waves, jaws parted to reveal rows of ivory teeth. In a few seconds they would be upon the women. But Greywolf was at the wheel, steering purposefully towards them.

Anawak held out a hand to Stringer.

'Take her first,' she shouted.

Greywolf helped him drag the other woman to safety. Then Stringer tried to climb on board. She slid back into the water and the whales dived down behind her.

Suddenly she was alone. 'Leon?' She stretched out her arms, eyes wide with fear. Anawak caught her right hand.

The blue-green water parted as something shot up at incredible speed. Its jaws were open, exposing white teeth. Then they snapped shut and Stringer screamed. Her fist hammered on the snout that held her prisoner. 'Get off!' she yelled.

Anawak's fingers dug into her jacket. Their eyes met. 'Susan! Give me your other hand!' He held on to her, determined not to let go, but the orca's jaws were clamped round her. Her mouth opened in a dull cry that become a piercing scream. With a sickening jolt, she was wrenched from Anawak's grip. Her head disappeared underwater, then her arms and her twitching fingers. For a second her orange suit shone in the water, a scattered kaleidoscope of colour that paled, faded and vanished.

Anawak stared at the water. Something glittered in the depths. A column of bubbles. As they reached the surface they popped and foamed.

Then the water turned red.

'No,' he whispered.

Greywolf pulled him away from the railings. 'There's no one here,' he said. 'Let's go.'

As the motorboat roared off, Anawak tripped and steadied himself. The woman whom Stringer had saved was lying on a bench, whimpering softly. Delaware was soothing her, voice shaking. The man stared fixedly ahead.

From across the water Anawak heard another commotion. He whirled round and saw that the *Lady Wexham* was surrounded by blades and humps. She was barely moving and listed dangerously to one side.

'We have to turn back!' he shouted. 'They're not going to make it!'

Greywolf was powering towards the coast. 'Forget it.'

Anawak reached over and snatched up the walkie-talkie. He tried to call the *Lady Wexham*. The radio crackled and hissed. 'We've got to help them, Jack! Turn back, damn it!'

'With this boat it's hopeless. We'll be lucky if we make it ourselves.'
The worst thing was, he was right.

'Victoria?' Shoemaker yelled into the phone. 'What the hell are they doing in Victoria? . . . Why? Doesn't Victoria have its own Coast Guard? There are people drowning in Clayoquot Sound! We've got one skipper dead and a boat going down and you're telling me to be patient?'

He strode up and down in the office, waiting for a reply. He stopped in his tracks. 'As soon as they can? Sorry, but I'm not interested in your damn excuses. Send someone else . . . What? Now, just you listen to me . . .'

The voice at the other end of the line was so loud that, metres away, Anawak heard it. The station was in turmoil. Davie and Shoemaker had been talking non-stop into radios and phones. Shoemaker dropped the receiver and shook his head.

'What's going on?' asked Anawak. Greywolf's decrepit old boat had fought its way back to Tofino fifteen minutes earlier, and since then the office had been swamped with people. The news of the attack had spread like wildfire through the town. All the skippers who worked for the station had come in and the frequencies were jammed. At first nearby sport fishermen had called in, ridiculing the inexperienced idiots 'too dumb to dodge a bunch of whales', and bragging about how they would save them. Then the calls had dried up. Anyone who tried to help had become the target of a fresh attack. All hell had broken loose – and no one knew for sure what was going on.

'The Coast Guard's run out of people to send us,' said Shoemaker angrily. 'They've all been dispatched to Victoria or Ucluelet. Apparently the Lady isn't the only boat in trouble.'

'More attacks?'

'And deaths, by the sound of it.'

'News from Ucluelet,' Davie called. He reached behind the counter and twiddled the dials on his shortwave radio. 'A signal from a trawler. She picked up a distress call from a Zodiac and went to help, but she was attacked. She's turning round.'

'What kind of attack?'

'Signal's gone. I've lost her.'

'And the Lady Wexham?'

'No news. Tofino Air has sent two planes – I got hold of them just now.'

'And?' asked Shoemaker impatiently. 'Can they see the *Lady*?'

'Tom, they only just took off.'

'Why aren't we with them?'

'Don't be a jerk. You know perfectly well why—'

'They're our boats, for Christ's sake! We should be in those darned planes.' Shoemaker was pacing wildly. 'What's happened to the *Lady*?'

'We'll have to wait and see.'

'Wait? We can't wait! I'm going out there.'

'Tom—'

'We've got another Zodiac, haven't we? We'll take the *Devilfish* and see for ourselves.'

'Are you nuts?' said a skipper. 'Haven't you been listening to a word Leon's said? We need to leave this to the Coast Guard.'

'There *is* no Coast Guard!' yelled Shoemaker.

'Maybe the *Lady Wexham* will make it back without us. Leon said—'

'Maybe isn't good enough. I'm going out there!'

'That's enough now!' Davie held up a hand to silence them. He shot Shoemaker a warning glare. 'Enough lives have been lost, Tom. I don't want anyone taking needless risks. We'll wait for the pilots to report back, then we'll decide what to do.'

'Doing nothing never solved anything!'

Davie didn't answer. He was tuning his radio, trying to make contact with the seaplanes. In the meantime Anawak did his best to persuade the crowd to leave the office. His knees trembled and he felt dizzy. He was probably in shock, he thought. He would have given anything to lie down and close his eyes – but if he did, he knew he would see Stringer in the jaws of an orca.

The woman she had saved was lying semi-conscious on a bench near the door. If it hadn't been for her, Stringer would still be alive. The man they'd rescued was sitting next to her, crying softly: he'd lost his daughter, who'd been with him on the boat. Alicia Delaware was looking after him. For someone who'd only narrowly escaped death, she seemed remarkably composed. A helicopter was supposed to be on its way to take them to hospital, but right now they couldn't count on anyone or anything.

'Hey, Leon!' said Shoemaker. 'Will you come with me? You'll be able to tell me what to look out for.'

'Tom, you're not going,' snapped Davie.

'None of you idiots should go out there,' said a deep voice. 'Not ever again. I'll go.'

Anawak swivelled round. Greywolf had walked into the station. He pushed his way through the milling crowd, brushing the hair out of his eyes. The room fell silent and everyone stared at the long-haired giant dressed in suede.

'What are you talking about?' said Anawak. 'Go where?'

'I'm going back to *your* boat, to rescue *your* people. I'm not afraid of the whales. They won't hurt me.'

'That's very noble of you, Jack, it really is. But from now on maybe you should keep out of it.'

'Leon,' Greywolf snarled, 'if I'd kept out of it earlier, you'd be dead by now. You should keep out. In fact, you should've kept out in the first place.'

'Out of what?' said Shoemaker, with a dangerous edge.

'Nature, Shoemaker. You're the ones to blame for the whole damn disaster – you and your boats and your cameras. You're responsible for the deaths of my people and your own people and the people whose money you pocketed. It was always going to happen. It was only a matter of time.'

'Asshole!' Shoemaker screamed at him.

Delaware got to her feet. 'He's not an asshole,' she said firmly. 'He saved us. And he's right. If it hadn't been for him, we'd be dead.'

Anawak was well aware that they were indebted to Greywolf – he more than anyone else – but he couldn't forget all the trouble that the man had caused them in the past. He said nothing. For a few seconds there was an uncomfortable silence.

'Jack,' said Anawak, 'if you go out there, someone's going to have to fish *you* out of the water. The only place you should take your boat is a museum. It won't survive another trip.'

'You're going to let them die out there, then?'

'I don't want anyone to die – not even you.'

'Oh, so it's me you're worried about, is it? But I wasn't planning on using my boat. It took a few knocks out there. I'll take yours.'

'The *Devilfish*?'

'Sure.'

'I can't just hand it over to anyone,' he said, 'least of all you.'

'Then you'll have to come with me.'

'Jack, I—'

'You can tell that loser Shoemaker he can come too. We'll be in need of some bait, now the orcas are eating their enemies.'

'You've lost it, Jack.'

Greywolf bent down to him. 'Leon,' he hissed. 'My friends died out there too. Do you think I don't care?'

'Well, if you hadn't brought them along . . .'

'Arguing won't get us anywhere. We're talking about your people, and I'm not the one who needs to go out there. You owe me a bit of gratitude, Leon.'

Anawak swore. He glanced at the others. Shoemaker was on the telephone. Davie was speaking into his walkie-talkie and beckoned to him. 'What do you think of Tom's idea?' he said, in a low voice. 'Would we be able to help or would it be suicide?'

Anawak chewed his lip. 'What did the pilots say?'

'The *Lady* has capsized. She's on her side, taking in water.'

'Oh, God.'

'The Victoria Coast Guard says it can scramble a helicopter in a rescue operation, but I doubt they'll make it in time. They're busy enough already, and the calls keep coming in.'

The idea of re-entering the hell that they'd just left was a terrifying prospect, but Anawak knew he would never forgive himself if he didn't do everything in his power to help the *Lady Wexham*. 'Greywolf wants to come too,' he said quietly.

'In the same boat as Tom? You've got to be joking. I thought we were trying to solve a problem, not create one.'

'Greywolf could be useful. God knows what's going on in his head, but we could do with having him around – he's strong and completely fearless.'

Davie nodded gloomily. 'Keep the two of them apart, OK? And if it looks hopeless, come straight back here. I don't want anyone playing the hero.'

Anawak headed over to Shoemaker, waited for him to put down the phone, then told him of Davie's decision.

'You want to take that phoney Indian with us?' Shoemaker said indignantly. 'Are you crazy?'

'I think it's more a case of him taking us.'

'In *our* boat.'

'Look, you and Davie are in charge around here, but I've seen what we're up against and I'm telling you now: we'll be glad to have him with us.'

The *Devilfish* was the same size as the *Blue Shark* and had the same horsepower, so it was small and easy to turn. Anawak prayed it would give them enough of an advantage. The creatures still had the element of surprise on their side. No one could tell' when or where they might attack next.

As the Zodiac sped across the lagoon, Anawak wrestled with the question of why. He had thought he knew about whales, but now he was at a loss. He couldn't begin to work out what was happening. The attack on the *Barrier Queen* was his only obvious lead. It must be some kind of infection, he thought. A strain of rabies, perhaps.

But what kind of disease would affect different species? The attacks had been carried out by humpbacks, orcas and grey whales. The more he thought about it, the more certain he was that a grey had overturned his Zodiac.

Could the high levels of PCBs in the sea and the toxins in their food have played havoc with their instincts? But orcas ingested toxins through contaminated salmon and other creatures. Grey whales and humpbacks ate plankton. Their metabolism was different from that of toothed whales.

Disease didn't explain it.

He stared at the glistening water. He'd made this trip hundreds of times before, and each time he'd been full of anticipation at the thought of seeing a whale. He'd always known about the dangers: fog might come down; the wind might change and send treacherous waves pounding into the cliffs – in 1998 a skipper and a tourist had died like that in Clayoquot Sound. And then there were the whales: placid, friendly, but unpredictable animals of enormous size and power. They were a mighty force of nature, as any experienced whale-watcher could testify. Yet if you sought out storms, monstrous breakers and wild animals, they no longer seemed so terrifying. Fear gave way to respect – and Anawak had immense respect for nature.

But now, for the first time, he was afraid.

Seaplanes cut through the sky above the *Devilfish* as she sped across the waves. Anawak was at the wheel with Shoemaker, who had insisted on steering, and Greywolf was at the bow, scanning the water for trouble.

The tree-covered shores of tiny islets flashed past on their left. On the rocks, sea-lions sunned themselves, as if nothing could disturb their tranquillity. The Zodiac roared past them. The open sea lay ahead – a uniform expanse of endless water, at once familiar and forbidding.

Beyond the sheltered waters of the lagoon, the swell was higher. The Zodiac bounced noisily over the waves. During the past half-hour the sea had grown rougher and dark clouds gathered on the horizon. There was still no sign of a storm, but conditions were deteriorating rapidly – as was often the case in these waters. A rain front was probably heading their way. Anawak strained his eyes to glimpse the *Lady Wexham*. What if she had sunk? In the distance he saw another vessel, one of many cruise ships passing the Canadian coast at this time of year, heading north to Alaska.

'What brings them here?' shouted Shoemaker.

'I expect they heard the mayday.' Anawak peered through the binoculars. 'MS *Arctic*. She's from Seattle. I've seen her before – she's sailed this way regularly over the past few years.'

'Leon!'

A small, pointed outline had appeared in the distance, barely visible above the swell. Only the *Lady Wexham*'s superstructure was still above water. People had gathered on the bridge and on the viewing platform in the bow. Orcas circled menacingly, biding their time until the vessel slid into the water.

'Oh, God,' said Shoemaker. 'It doesn't seem possible . . .'

Greywolf turned to them, making signs for them to slow down. Shoemaker backed off the throttle. A grey, grooved hump surfaced in front of them, followed by two others. The whales lingered on the surface for a few seconds, expelled their bushy, V-shaped blow, then dived without showing their flukes.

Anawak could sense their approach underwater. He could practically feel the impending attack.

'Go, go, go!' yelled Greywolf.

Shoemaker slammed down the throttle. The *Devilfish* pitched forward and shot away. Behind them, the huge dark bodies of the whales surged out of the water and fell backwards. Travelling full-speed ahead the Zodiac shot towards the sinking *Lady Wexham*. At last they could make out individuals, waving at them from the platform and the bridge. Shouts carried over the water. To Anawak's relief the skipper was among the survivors. One by one the gleaming black blades disappeared under-water.

'We'll be next,' said Anawak.

'You mean they're coming for us?' Shoemaker was panic-stricken. For the first time he seemed to take in what was going on. 'What will they do? Capsize us?'

'They might. The grey whales and humpbacks seem to be in charge of demolition, while the orcas take care of the rest.'

Shoemaker's face drained of colour.

Greywolf pointed to the cruise ship. 'They're sending reinforce-ments,' he shouted.

Two small motorboats left the side of MS *Arctic* and moved leisurely towards them.

'Tell them to hurry or get out of here, Leon,' Greywolf yelled. 'At that speed they'll be easy pickings.'

Anawak grabbed the radio. 'MS *Arctic*. This is *Devilfish*. You're in danger of attack.'

For a few seconds there was silence. The *Devilfish* was almost level with the *Lady*.

'This is MS *Arctic*. What kind of attack, *Devilfish*?'

'The whales will try to sink your boats.'

'Whales? Is this a joke, *Devilfish*?'

'For your own safety I advise you to turn back.'

'We received a mayday from a sinking vessel.'

Anawak lurched forward as the Zodiac careered over a wave. He steadied himself and shouted into the radio, 'We don't have time to talk, but you can take my word for it – you need to move faster.'

'Are you kidding? We intend to assist that vessel. Out.'

Greywolf was signalling frantically from the bow. 'They've got to get away from here!' he yelled.

The orcas had changed course. They were no longer bearing down on the *Devilfish* but swimming out towards the open sea, in the direction of MS *Arctic*.

'Shit,' cursed Anawak.

A humpback soared out of the water directly in front of the motor-boats, a corona of droplets shimmering round it. For a moment it was suspended in the air, then it dropped to one side. Anawak gasped. The motorboats continued unharmed through the cloud of falling droplets.

'MS *Arctic!* Pull back your boats! Clear the water! We'll take care of this.'

Shoemaker cut the engine. The *Lady Wexham*'s bridge jutted through the surface at an angle and the *Devilfish* halted in front of it, where a dozen men and women were huddled. The swell crashed against the bridge, spilling over the side. Anawak saw more people on the viewing platform in the stern. As the waves battered the boat, they hung on to the railings, like monkeys in a cage.

The *Devilfish* chugged forward between the bridge and the platform. Beneath the Zodiac, the *Lady*'s main deck shimmered green and white. Shoemaker manoeuvred the boat towards the bridge. A powerful wave seized the *Devilfish* and raised it into the air. The boat rose like an elevator till they were level with the bridge. For a moment Anawak was in touching distance of the outstretched hands. He looked into the frightened faces, seeing hope mixed with horror in their eyes. Then the *Devilfish* plummeted.

'This isn't going to be easy,' said Shoemaker, through gritted teeth.

Anawak glanced round nervously. The whales had lost interest in the *Lady Wexham*. They had regrouped further out and were targeting the two motorboats, which were trying feebly to evade them.

Anawak knew they had little time. The whales could return at any moment and, in any case, the *Lady* was sinking fast. Greywolf crouched. A steep wave took the *Devilfish* and lifted her. The peeling paint of the bridge flashed past. Greywolf launched himself into the air and grabbed hold of a ladder on the side of the boat. The water rose to his armpits, then the wave fell away and he was left in mid-air, holding on by one hand, a living link between the people above him and the Zodiac below. He lifted his other hand towards the bridge.

'Climb on to my shoulders,' he shouted, 'one at a time. Cling to me and wait till the boat comes, then jump.'

The group hesitated. Greywolf yelled his instructions again. A woman grabbed his arm. In no time she was on his back, hugging his shoulders. The Zodiac rose. Anawak grabbed her and pulled her in.

'Next!'

At last the rescue operation had gained momentum. One after another the passengers dropped into the boat. Anawak wondered how much longer Greywolf could hold on. He was bearing his own weight, plus that of each passenger and dangling from only one hand while waves surged over him. The bridge groaned piteously as the metal warped and cracked. Now the skipper was the only one left. A sudden screech filled the air – the bridge had taken a hit. Greywolf's body smashed against the side of the ship and the skipper lost his balance and skidded off the deck. A grey whale raised its head above the waves. Greywolf let go of the ladder and dropped into the water. Coughing, the skipper surfaced a few metres ahead of him and reached the Zodiac in a couple of powerful strokes. Hands stretched down and pulled him in. Greywolf made a grab for the side, but was knocked back by a wave.

Behind him, a few metres away, a blade rose through the water.

'Jack!' Anawak rushed to the stern. Greywolf surfaced and swam rapidly towards the boat. The dark blade pivoted, and followed. Greywolf reached up and clutched the side. The orca was ready to lunge. Anawak snatched Greywolf and, helped by others, heaved him into the boat. The orca looped round and swam off. Swearing, Greywolf broke free of the solicitous hands and slicked back his long, dark hair.

Why didn't the orca attack? wondered Anawak.

I'm not afraid of the whales. They won't hurt me.

But that was all talk . . .

Then it dawned on him. The orca couldn't have attacked. The flooded deck beneath the Zodiac meant the water wasn't deep enough for it to launch itself. Unless, of course, it had learned from its South American cousins how to hunt in the shallows or on dry land.

The Zodiac's period of grace would last until the bigger vessel sank. It was crucial that they used it.

Anawak heard screaming.

A grey whale had smashed into one of MS *Arctic*'s boats. Debris flew into the air. An engine howled as the other boat spun round to make its escape. Anawak stared at the spot where the whale had pulled the boat under, and saw a line of grey humps heading their way.

Now it's our turn, he thought.

Shoemaker seemed incapable of movement. His eyes bulged.

'Tom!' yelled Anawak. 'We've got to fetch the others from the viewing platform.'

'Shoemaker!' Greywolf snarled. 'Can't you handle it?'

Trembling, Shoemaker seized the wheel and steered the Zodiac towards the platform. A wave surged beneath them and the bow struck the railings where the passengers were stranded. He was breathing heavily, trying to jockey the boat closer so that people could jump in.

The grey whales bore down on them, set on a collision course with the *Lady Wexham*. The wreck shook with the force of the impact. A woman was thrown off and landed screaming in the water.

'Shoemaker, you moron!' shouted Greywolf.

Some of the passengers on the Zodiac rushed to pull the woman on board. Anawak looked at the *Lady*. How long could she withstand a fresh wave of attacks? We're not going to make it, he thought in despair.

Then something incredible happened.

Two mighty bodies rose up on each side of the boat. One was instantly familiar to Anawak: its backbone was covered with a pale criss-cross of scars so they'd nicknamed it Scarback. The elderly grey had already outlived most others of its kind. Both animals lay still in the water, rising and falling on the swell. Then one of the whales discharged its blow, followed by the other. Clouds of tiny droplets wafted over the water.

The real surprise wasn't so much the appearance of the two greys, but the effect they had on the others, who promptly vanished underwater. When they resurfaced, they'd travelled a considerable distance from the boat. Orcas continued to circle the wreck, but they, too, had backed off.

Somehow Anawak knew they had nothing to fear from the new arrivals. In fact, the two greys had scared off their attackers. There was no telling how long the peace would last, but the unexpected turn of events gave them some breathing space. Even Shoemaker had stopped panicking. He guided the Zodiac confidently under the railings. An enormous wave surged towards them and they shot upwards.

'Jump!' Anawak shouted. 'Now!'

The *Devilfish* rose on the swell and sank back down. The people on the railings leaped after it, crashing one on top of another, amid screams of pain. Some landed in the water, but were soon fished out. Eventually everyone was aboard.

It was time to make their getaway.

But not everyone had jumped. Crouched behind the railings a boy was crying, face buried in his hands.

'Jump!' shouted Anawak. He held out his arms. 'There's no need to be afraid.'

Greywolf joined him. 'When the next wave comes, I'll fetch him.'

Anawak glanced over his shoulder. An enormous wall of water was heading straight for them. 'That might be sooner than you think,' he said.

The two grey whales sank below the surface. The sea around the *Lady* gurgled and foamed, then the bridge disappeared in a whirlpool of water. Her stern rose into the air and the *Lady Wexham* slid bow first into the depths.

'Get closer!' shouted Greywolf.

Somehow Shoemaker obliged. The *Devilfish*'s bow struck the *Lady*'s deck as she sank, with the boy still clutching the railings. Greywolf shoved his way to the stern, but a wave hit the Zodiac and a veil of frothy water billowed over the rails. As Greywolf leaned out to grab the boy, the *Devilfish* tipped, he lost his balance and crashed to the deck, but he didn't let go. His arms supported the boy like two firm tree-trunks. His bear-like hands were locked around his waist. Then the *Lady Wexham* vanished into the depths.

Shoemaker thrust the throttle forward. The waves rolling in from the Pacific were long and regular. They wouldn't pose a risk to the overcrowded Zodiac, providing that her skipper was careful. But Shoemaker had recovered his cool. The Zodiac shot over the crest of a wave, sank down the other side and headed for the coast.

Anawak glanced back at MS *Arctic*. The second motorboat was nowhere to be seen. A fluke plunged into the water, waving in what seemed to be a mocking farewell. A humpback . . . He would never see another whale's tail without a sense of foreboding.

A few minutes later they passed the narrow strip of land that separated the open water from the lagoon.

The boat pulled up at the jetty, crammed with people. In the moments following their return, the sight of the unscathed *Devilfish* was Davie's only comfort. They read out the names of the missing. People collapsed in shock. Then the crowd dispersed. The Zodiac's passengers nearly all had hypothermia. Most were taken away by friends or family to be treated at the nearest clinic. Some had sustained more serious injuries, but no one could say when the helicopter would arrive to take them to Victoria. The radio was still jammed with reports of new horrors.

Davie had been forced to endure hostile questioning, accusations and defamation. Physical violence was threatened if the passengers didn't return. Roddy Walker, Stringer's boyfriend, had put in an appearance, telling everyone in earshot that they'd be hearing from his lawyer. Yet no one was trying to establish who was really to blame. The idea that whales might attack unprovoked was rejected out of hand. They were placid creatures – like people, but nicer. The surviving tourists rounded on Davie and his skippers, as though they were responsible for first-degree murder. According to their accusers, they were irresponsible, took unnecessary risks and went to sea in battered old boats. It was true that the *Lady* had seen several seasons, but she didn't deserve to be posthumously maligned. No one was prepared to listen.

At least her crew and the majority of the passengers were escorted home safely. Most remembered to thank Shoemaker and Anawak, but Greywolf was hailed as the hero of the hour. He was everywhere at once, talking, listening, organising and offering to take people to the clinic. He was trying so hard to be a Samaritan that Anawak felt sick.

Greywolf had risked his life; there was no doubt about it. And, of course, they were right to thank him – on their knees, if he insisted. But Anawak didn't feel like it. This sudden burst of altruism seemed deeply suspect. He was sure that Greywolf's efforts to help the *Lady Wexham* hadn't been as selfless as they seemed. It had been a hugely successful day for Jack O'Bannon. He was the one they'd listened to and trusted. He'd always said that whale-watching would end in a disaster – well, if only they'd listened . . . And now this! Soon people would attest to his clear-sighted prescience. He couldn't have hoped for a better platform.

Furiously, Anawak paced up and down the empty office. They *had* to find out why the whales had behaved like that. Suddenly he remembered the *Barrier Queen*. Roberts had been going to send him that report. Now he needed it urgently. He went to the phone, dialled the operator and asked to be connected to the shipping line.

Roberts's secretary answered. Her boss was in a meeting and couldn't be disturbed. Anawak mentioned his involvement with the *Barrier Queen*, and intimated to her that his business was urgent. The meeting was even more so, she assured him. Yes, she'd heard about the catastrophic events of the past few hours. Full of motherly concern for his welfare, she commiserated sympathetically – but refused point-blank to put Roberts on the line. Would he like to leave a message?

Anawak hesitated. Roberts had said the report was confidential. He didn't want to get the MD into trouble. Maybe he shouldn't mention it. Then he had an idea. 'It's about the infestation on the *Barrier Queen*'s bow,' he said. 'There were mussels and some other organic material stuck there. We sent some to the institute in Nanaimo. They need fresh stock.'

'Fresh stock?'

'Fresh samples. I suppose you've checked every inch of the vessel by now?'

'Of course,' she said, a strange undercurrent in her voice.

'And where is she now?'

'Still docked.' She paused. 'I'll tell Mr Roberts it's urgent. Where should we send the samples?'

'To the institute in Nanaimo for the attention of Dr Sue Oliviera. Thanks for your help.'

'Mr Roberts will be in touch directly.' The line went dead. He'd been fobbed off.

What was going on?

His knees started to tremble. He felt exhausted and despondent. He leaned against the counter and closed his eyes. When he opened them, Alicia Delaware was in front of him.

'What are you doing here?' he asked tersely.

She shrugged. 'I'm fine. There's no need for me to see a doctor.'

'Oh, yes, there is. You were in that water, and the water here is darned cold. Now, run along to the clinic before anyone decides to blame us for your frozen intestines too.'

'Hey!' She glared at him. 'None of this is my fault, OK?'

Anawak straightened up from the counter and walked to the window at the rear of the office. The *Devilfish* was moored outside as though nothing had happened. It was drizzling lightly.

'What was all that rubbish you told me about leaving the island?' he said. 'I broke the rules to take you with me. I only did it because you gave me that sob story.'

'I. . .' She faltered. 'I. . . Well, I really wanted to go. Are you mad at me?'

Anawak turned to her. 'I can't stand being lied to.'

'I'm sorry.'

'Well, why don't you go away and let me get on with my work, then? Run along to Greywolf. He'll take care of you.'

'For God's sake, Leon.' She took a step forward, and he drew back. 'I wanted to go on your tour, that's all. I'm sorry I lied to you. The truth is, I'm here for another few weeks, and I don't come from Chicago. I'm at the University of British Columbia, studying biology. What's the big deal? I thought you'd find it funny—'

'So that's your idea of a joke? What's so funny about someone taking advantage of me?' He was losing control, but he couldn't stop shouting, even though he knew she was right. None of it was her fault.

Delaware flinched. 'Leon—'

'Why can't you just leave me alone, Licia?'

He expected her to go, but she didn't. She just stood in front of him. Suddenly Anawak felt dazed. The office was spinning, and he thought briefly that his legs were about to buckle. Then his mind cleared and he saw that she was holding something.

'What's that?' he growled.

'A camcorder.' She handed it to him.

It was a top-of-the-range Sony handycam, encased in underwater housing to protect it from splashes.

'Well?' he said.

Delaware made a despairing gesture. 'I thought you wanted to find out why it happened.'

'And you'd know all about that, I suppose.'

'There's no need to take your anger out on me, Leon!' she retorted. 'A few hours ago I nearly died out there. I could be sitting in a clinic, crying, but I'm not. I'm here and I'm trying to help. So, are you going to listen to me or not?'

Anawak took a deep breath. 'OK.'

'Did you get a good look at the whales that rammed the *Lady Wexham*?'

'Sure. They were greys and hump—'

'No.' Delaware shook her head impatiently. 'Not the species. The actual whales. Were you able to identify them?'

'It happened too fast.'

She smiled. It wasn't a happy smile, but it was a smile all the same. 'Remember the woman we pulled out of the water? I knew her from the *Blue Shark*. She's in shock. She doesn't know what's happening. But when I want something, I don't give up.'

'Don't I know it.'

'I saw the camera hanging round her neck. It was strapped on tightly, which was why she hadn't lost it in the water. Anyway, when you went out the second time, I talked to her and she'd filmed the whole thing. She was filming when Greywolf arrived. And as far as I remember, from where we were positioned, the *Lady Wexham* was behind Greywolf's boat.'

Suddenly Anawak saw what she was getting at.

'She filmed the attack,' he said.

'She filmed the *individual whales*. I don't know how expert you really are at identifying them but you live around here and you know them. And with a camcorder you can take as long as you like.'

'I suppose you forgot to ask her whether you could keep the camera?' asked Anawak.

She stuck out her chin defiantly. 'What of it?'

He twisted the camera in his hands. 'All right. I'll take a look.'

'*We*'ll take a look,' said Delaware. 'I don't want to be left out. And don't even think of asking me why. It's the least I'm entitled to, all right?'

Anawak was dumbstruck.

'And besides,' she said, 'it's about time you started being nice to me.'

He exhaled slowly, pursing his lips. He had to admit that Delaware's idea was the best lead they had. 'I'll give it a go,' he murmured.

12 April

Trondheim, Norway

The summons came as Johanson was preparing to drive out to the lake. On his return from Kiel he'd contacted Tina Lund to tell her about the experiment in the deep-sea simulation chamber. They hadn't talked for long: Lund was up to her ears in work, and spent every spare second with Kare Sverdrup. Johanson had had the impression that her mind was elsewhere, but whatever was bothering her didn't seem to relate to her job, so he didn't ask questions.

A few days later Bohrmann called with the latest on the worms. The scientists in Kiel had been running more tests. Johanson had already packed his suitcase and was about to leave the house when he decided to call Lund and tell her the news. She seemed more focused now and jumped in before he could begin. 'Why don't you pay us a visit?' she suggested.

'At Marintek?'

'No, at the Statoil research centre. The project-management team is here from Stavanger.'

'Do you want me to regale them with stories of sinister creepy-crawlies?'

'I've already done that. Now they want details so I said I'd ask you.'

'Why me?'

'Why not?'

'Because you've got all the documentation,' said Johanson. 'Reams of it. All I can do is pass on what other people have told me.'

'You can do more than that,' said Lund. 'You can give them your personal opinion.'

Johanson was too surprised to answer.

'They know you're not an expert on wellheads or even worms, for that matter,' she said, 'but you've got a fantastic reputation at the NTNU and you can judge things impartially. At Statoil we're coming at this business from a different perspective.'

'You mean you're only interested in whether it's viable.'

'There are other factors! Look, the trouble is, we've got a bunch of people here, all acknowledged experts in something but—'

'They don't have the first clue about anything else.'

'That's not true!' She sounded put out. 'They're all extremely capable – they wouldn't be here otherwise. But we're too involved in it all, too bogged down. Christ, how else do you want me to put it? We just need some outside opinions, that's all.'

'But I hardly know anything about oil.'

'No one's forcing you.' Lund sounded annoyed now. 'If you're not interested, forget it.'

Johanson rolled his eyes. 'OK, OK. I don't want to leave you in the lurch – and in any case, there's some new data from Kiel and—'

'Can I take that as a yes, then?'

'Jesus, Tina! So, when is this meeting?'

'There's a whole row of them coming up. Every day is just one long meeting.'

'Fine. It's Friday today. I'll be away at the weekend, but Monday would be—'

'That's . . .' She checked herself. 'That would actually be . . .'

'What?' Johanson prompted her. He had a nasty feeling about this.

'Got something nice planned for the weekend?' she asked conversationally. 'Another trip to the lake?'

'Well guessed. Do you want to come too?'

She laughed. 'Why not?'

'I see. And what would Kare have to say about that?'

'Who cares? It's none of his business.' She paused. 'Oh, hell.'

'If only you were as good at everything else as you are at your job,' said Johanson, so softly that he wasn't sure she'd heard.

'Please, Sigur. Can't you set off a bit later? We're meeting in two hours, and I thought . . . Well, it's not far for you to come and it won't take long. We'll be finished in no time. You can go to the lake this evening.'

'I—'

'We really need to make progress. We've got a schedule to stick to, and you know how much these things cost. Now we're slipping behind and all because . . .'

'I said I'd do it, all right?'

'You're a honey.'

'Do you want me to pick you up on the way?'

'I'll be there already. You've made my day, Sigur. Thank you.' She hung up.

Johanson looked at his suitcase wistfully.

As Johanson was ushered into the conference hall at the Statoil research centre, the tension was almost tangible. Lund was sitting with three men at a huge table. Late-afternoon sunshine seeped into the room, lending warmth to the glass, chrome and dark-wood furnishings. The walls were lined with blow-ups of diagrams and technical drawings.

'Here he is,' said the woman who had brought Johanson from reception, and a man rose to greet him. He had close-cut dark hair and was wearing designer glasses.

'Thor Hvistendahl, deputy director of the Statoil research centre,' he introduced himself. 'I apologise for encroaching on your time at such late notice. Tina assures us that we're not disrupting your plans.'

Johanson shot Lund an eloquent look, then shook Hvistendahl's hand. 'No problem,' he said. 'I was free this afternoon.'

Lund suppressed a smile. She introduced him to the other men. One was from the Statoil headquarters in Stavanger – a burly man with red hair and friendly blue eyes. He was a member of the executive committee, and was there to represent the management board. 'Finn Skaugen,' he boomed.

The third, a bald man with heavy jowls and the only one wearing a tie, turned out to be Lund's immediate superior, Clifford Stone. He came from Scotland, and was head of the exploration and production unit in charge of the new project. He gave Johanson a distant nod. He didn't seem overjoyed at the biologist's arrival but, then, nothing about him suggested that he ever smiled.

Johanson exchanged a few pleasantries, declined the offer of coffee and took a seat.

Hvistendahl picked up a stack of papers. 'Let's get straight to business. You're familiar with the situation. We're having difficulty gauging whether the whole thing spells trouble or whether we're overreacting. I imagine you're aware of some of the regulations governing the oil industry?'

'The North Sea Conference,' Johanson said, guessing.

Hvistendahl nodded. 'That's one side of it. But we're also subject to other pressures – laws for the protection of the environment, technological limitations and, of course, public opinion, which sets the tone on many of the unregulated issues. When it comes down to it, we have to take account of anything and everything. We've got Greenpeace and a host of other organisations breathing down our necks – and we don't have a problem with that. We know the risks involved in drilling new boreholes, and what to expect when we're planning a new project, so we factor in plenty of time.'

'In other words, we're pretty good at handling things ourselves,' Stone interjected.

'Generally speaking, yes,' said Hvistendahl. 'Not every project makes it to completion, though. There are all the usual reasons – like finding out that the sediment is unstable, that we're in danger of drilling through a gas pocket or even that the water depth and current don't lend themselves to certain types of platform, you know the sort of thing. But in most cases we realise fairly early on what we can and can't do. Tina tests the technology at Marintek, we analyse lots of different samples, check out the conditions down there, get an expert opinion, then start building.'

Johanson crossed one leg over the other. 'But this time there's a worm in the system,' he said.

Hvistendahl laughed uneasily. 'You could say that.'

'Assuming they're relevant,' said Stone, 'which, in my opinion, they're not.'

'What makes you so sure?'

'Worms are nothing unusual. We find them everywhere.'

'Not this species.'

'What makes them so special? Sure, they eat hydrates,' he glared at Johanson, 'but if I remember rightly, your friends in Kiel said that wasn't anything to get worked up about. Or have I missed something?'

'That's not quite what they said. They said—'

'The worms can't destabilise the ice.'

'They're eroding it.'

'Yes, but they can't destabilise it!'

Skaugen cleared his throat. It sounded like a minor explosion. 'We called in Dr Johanson so that we could listen to what he has to say,' he said, glancing at Stone, 'not to tell him what we think.'

Stone bit his lip and stared at the table.

'You mentioned some new data, didn't you, Sigur?' said Lund. She smiled encouragingly at the others.

'I'll run you through it now,' he offered.

'Bloody worms,' grumbled Stone.

'Well, that's one way of describing them. Anyway, the scientists at Geomar introduced six further specimens into the simulation chamber. Each burrowed head-first into the ice. Next they placed two fresh specimens on a layer of sediment without any hydrates. They didn't react – didn't eat, didn't burrow. Finally they put two specimens on a layer of hydrate-free sediment above a pocket of gas. The worms didn't burrow, but they became agitated.'

'What happened to the worms that burrowed?'

'They're dead.'

'How far did they get?'

'All except one made it through to the gas,' Johanson glanced at Stone, 'but that doesn't mean we can draw any hard and fast conclusions about their behaviour in the wild. The gas on the continental slopes is covered by layers of hydrates measuring tens or even hundreds of metres thick. The layers in the simulator are barely two metres. According to Bohrmann, it's unlikely that the worms could go deeper than three or four metres, but in the chamber there's no way of knowing.'

'What kills them?' asked Hvistendahl.

'They need oxygen and can't get enough in the narrow hole they make.'

'But other worms burrow,' objected Skaugen. He grinned. 'You can tell we did our homework before you got here. We didn't want to look completely stupid.'

Johanson smiled back. He knew he could get on with Skaugen. 'Other species burrow in sediments,' he said, 'in loose ones, where there's plenty of oxygen – and most worms don't dig very deep. But burrowing in hydrates is like moving through concrete. Before long, there's no air, which leads to suffocation.'

'Do you know of other creatures that behave like that?'

'You mean creatures with a death wish?'

'Is that what it is?'

Johanson shrugged. 'That would assume intent, which doesn't fit with worms. They're conditioned to behave as they do.'

'Do animals commit suicide?'

'Of course they do,' said Stone. 'What about lemmings? They throw themselves off cliffs.'

'No, they don't,' said Lund.

'They do!'

Lund placed her hand on his arm. 'Clifford, you're comparing apples and oranges. People liked the idea of lemmings committing suicide so they took it for granted that they did. But when someone looked into it properly, they found out that lemmings are just stupid.'

'Stupid?' Stone turned to Johanson. 'Tell me, Dr Johanson, is it normal scientific practice to call an animal stupid?'

'They are,' Lund continued, unabashed. 'When you get enough of them together, people can be stupid too. The lemmings at the front know that there's a cliff ahead, but the mob behind them surges on, pushing them forward – it's like fans at a rock concert. They carry on shoving each other into the sea until the procession eventually halts.'

Hvistendahl said, 'Some animals are known to sacrifice themselves, though. I guess you'd call it altruism.'

'Yes, but animal altruism always serves a purpose,' replied Johanson. 'Bees are prepared to die after losing their sting because warding off an intruder is good for the colony – or, at any rate, for the queen.'

'So there's no species-related motive for the worms' behaviour?'

'No.'

'Biology lessons aren't going to help.' Stone sighed. 'Just listen to you all! Soon we won't be able to build the unit because you'll have turned the worms into monsters.'

'And another thing,' said Johanson, ignoring him, 'Geomar would like to take a look at the area you've marked for exploration. With Statoil's backing, of course.'

'That's interesting.' Skaugen leaned forward. 'Are they proposing to send someone over?'

'A research vessel. The RV *Sonne*.'

'That's kind, but they can do all their research on the *Thorvaldson*.'

'They'll be stopping off on their way to another site. And, in any case, the *Sonne* has all the latest equipment. They're mainly interested in testing some of the data they got from the simulator.'

'What kind of data?'

'It relates to an increase in methane levels. By burrowing into the ice, the worms set free small quantities of methane, which disperse into the water. The Geomar scientists would like to excavate a couple of loads of sediment with some worms. They want to look at things in their true proportions.'

Skaugen laced his fingers together. 'So far we've only talked about the worms,' he said, 'but have you seen the ominous video footage?'

'Of the thing in the sea?'

Skaugen smiled wanly. 'You make it sound like a horror movie. What do you think it might be?'

'I'm not sure whether we should bracket the worms and this . . . this creature together.'

'But you know what it is?'

'No idea.'

'You're a biologist. Isn't there anything you can think of?'

'The images Tina extracted from the footage would suggest that the creature is bioluminescent, but there aren't any big creatures that would fit that description. And it rules out mammals *per se*.'

'Tina mentioned the possibility that we might be dealing with a giant squid.'

'Yes,' said Johanson, 'but it's unlikely. The size and structure of the body don't look right. And, anyway, *Architeuthis* has always been thought to inhabit entirely different waters.'

There was silence. Stone played with his pen.

'May I ask,' said Johanson, 'what kind of unit you'll be building out there?'

Skaugen glanced at Lund.

'I told Sigur we were thinking of building a subsea unit and that nothing had been decided,' she said.

'How much do you know about subsea units?' Skaugen asked Johanson.

'Well, I've heard about SUBSIS,' he said.

Hvistendahl raised his eyebrows. 'Not bad. You'll soon be an expert. If you join us for another few meetings, you'll—'

'SUBSIS is old hat,' snapped Stone. 'We've come a long way since then. Our units can go much deeper and, safety-wise, they're far superior.'

'The system comes from FMC Technologies in Kongsberg. They specialise in developing subsea solutions,' explained Skaugen. 'It's a more advanced version of SUBSIS. In fact, we've already decided to use the technology. The only question is whether to link the unit to one of the existing platforms or run the pipelines to the shore. They'd have to cover a vast distance and be able to cope with varying depths.'

'Couldn't you build a floating processing plant above the unit?' asked Johanson.

'Sure, but either way the main unit will still be on the seabed,' said Hvistendahl.

'In any case, we know how to evaluate the risks,' continued Skaugen, 'so long as they're defined risks. But the presence of the worms is a factor we can't identify or explain. Maybe – like Clifford says – we're blowing it out of proportion and there's no need to jeopardise our schedule because of a strange glowing creature and some mysterious worms. But where there's doubt, we need to do everything in our power to eliminate it. I don't expect you to take this decision for us, Dr Johanson, but what do you think we should do?'

Johanson felt uncomfortable. Stone was staring at him with open hostility. Hvistendahl and Skaugen were waiting expectantly, and Lund's expression gave nothing away. If only I'd talked to her first, he thought. But she hadn't pressured him. Maybe she'd be glad if he called time on the project. Then again, maybe she wouldn't.

Johanson placed his hands on the table. 'If it were up to me, I'd go ahead and build the thing,' he said.

Skaugen and Lund stared at him in bewilderment. Hvistendahl frowned, and Stone leaned back with a triumphant smile.

Johanson waited for a moment. Then he said, 'I'd build it – but I'd wait until Geomar had carried out its tests and given the green light. I don't think we'll find out any more about the creature on the video – it's probably a distant relative of the Loch Ness Monster and I'm not even sure it's worth worrying about. The real question is what effect untold numbers of mysterious hydrate-eating worms will have on the stability of the slope and on future boreholes. Until you know the answer to that, I'd recommend you put the project on hold.'

Stone pursed his lips and Lund smiled. Skaugen exchanged a glance with Hvistendahl, then said, 'Thank you, Dr Johanson, and thank you for sparing your time.'

*　　*　　*

That evening, when he'd put his suitcase into the car and was doing a last check before leaving the house, there was a ring at the door.

He opened it. Lund was standing outside. It had started to rain and her hair clung to her face. 'You did well,' she said.

'Did I?' Johanson stepped aside to let her in. She walked past him, wiping the raindrops from her eyes.

'The decision was as good as made before you arrived. Skaugen just wanted your approval.'

'Who am I to approve or disapprove of Statoil's projects?'

'Like I said, you've got an excellent reputation. But that's not all Skaugen's interested in. He's the one who'll have to take responsibility for the project. He knows that anyone with any connection to Statoil will be biased. He wanted to talk to someone who had nothing riding on the project. Also, you know a bit about worms and you don't give a damn about subsea units.'

'So he put the project on hold?'

'Until Geomar can clarify the situation. Statoil's lucky to have people like him at the top.' She was standing in the hallway, arms hanging at her sides. For someone who was usually so energetic and determined, she seemed oddly at a loss. 'So, where are your bags?'

'What do you mean?'

'Aren't you going to the lake?'

'My case is in the car. You were lucky to catch me – I was about to leave.' He gave her a look. 'Is there anything else you want me to do before I abandon myself to peaceful isolation? Because now I'm going to do just that. No more delays.'

'I won't keep you long. I just wanted to tell you what Skaugen had decided . . .'

'Yes?'

'. . . and to ask if your offer still holds.'

'What offer?' he said, although he knew what she meant.

'To take me with you.'

Johanson leaned against the wall next to the coat rack. He sensed that things were about to get tricky. 'And I asked you what Kare would have to say about it.'

'I don't need his permission, if that's what you mean.'

'I don't want to be responsible for any misunderstandings.'

'You won't be responsible for anything,' she said. 'If I want to go to the lake with you, it's my decision.'

'You're dodging the issue.'

Water from her hair was trickling down her face. 'Then why did you invite me?'

Yes, why?, thought Johanson.

Because he'd wanted to. But only if it didn't screw things up. Something bothered him about Lund's sudden decision to join him. A few weeks ago he would have thought nothing of it. Sporadic trips together, dinner dates – all that was part of their long flirtation, which had never gone further. But this was different.

Suddenly he knew what was wrong. 'If you two have fallen out,' he said, 'don't drag me into it. You're welcome to come with me, but not if it's just to put pressure on Kare.'

'You're reading way too much into this.' Lund shrugged. 'OK, maybe you're right. Forget it.'

'No problem.'

They hovered in the hallway.

'Well, I'll be off, then.' He gave her a peck on the cheek and pushed her gently out of the house, then locked the door behind him. It was nearly dusk, and the rain was still falling. He'd have to drive most of the way in the dark, but the prospect was almost appealing. He'd listen to Sibelius. *Finlandia*, at night – not a bad combination.

'So you'll be back on Monday?' asked Lund, as she walked him to the car.

'Sunday afternoon, more likely.'

'I'll give you a ring some time.'

'Sure. What have you got planned then?'

'There's always work.' She paused. 'Kare's gone away for the weekend. He's with his parents.'

Johanson opened the car door. 'You don't always have to work, you know.'

She smiled. 'Of course not.'

'Besides . . . you couldn't come anyway – you're not equipped for a weekend in the country.'

'What would I need?'

'Sturdy shoes, for one thing.'

Lund glanced at her feet. She was wearing heavy lace-up boots. 'Anything else?'.

'A jumper . . .' Johanson ran his hand over his beard. 'I suppose I've got some spares . . .'

'Uh-huh. For all eventualities, I suppose.'

'That's right. Best to be prepared.' He couldn't help laughing. 'All right, Miss Complicated. This is your last chance.'

'Me? Complicated?' Lund opened the passenger door. 'We can thrash that out on the way.'

Gravel crunched under the tyres as they turned on to the track leading to the house, and wound their way past the dark shapes of trees. The lake lay ahead, like a second sky embedded in the forest; its surface studded with stars. In Trondheim it was probably still raining.

Johanson parked the car and carried his case into the house, then joined Lund on the veranda. The floorboards creaked. The stillness of the place had always filled him with awe, and it seemed more intense for all the sounds he could hear – rustlings, the faraway call of a bird, twigs cracking, a scurrying in the undergrowth, and others he couldn't distinguish. A few steps led down from the veranda to a sloping meadow that separated the house from the lake. A crooked landing-stage jutted into it. At the far end, the boat he used for fishing lay motionless on the water.

Lund was gazing into the night 'And you've got all this to yourself?'

'Mostly.'

'I guess you're happy in your own company, then,' she said.

Johanson laughed. 'What makes you say that?'

'Well, if there's no one else, you'd have to be'.

'When I'm out here, I can do exactly as I please – like or loathe myself, whatever . . . Come on, let's go inside. I'll make us a risotto.'

A few minutes later Johanson was frying onions, adding rice, stirring then pouring in hot chicken stock. He sliced a few porcini mushrooms and left them to sizzle gently over a low heat.

Lund was watching him. She couldn't cook, Johanson knew. He opened a bottle of red wine, decanted it and poured two glasses. The usual routine. They ate, drank, talked and got closer in a secluded romantic setting. An ageing Bohemian and a younger woman. He knew how it would end.

If only she hadn't insisted on coming.

He was tempted to let things take their course. Lund was sitting at the kitchen table in one of his jumpers, more relaxed than she'd seemed in a long time. There was an unexpected softness about her features that perturbed him. He'd tried to persuade himself that she wasn't his type, too hyperactive and too Nordic, with her straight white-blonde hair and eyebrows. Now he was forced to admit it wasn't true.

You could have had a quiet weekend, he told himself, but you had to go and complicate things.

They ate in the kitchen, drank their wine, chatted easily and laughed. Soon they had started on another bottle.

At midnight Johanson said, 'Fancy a boat trip? It isn't too cold.'

She propped her chin in her hands and grinned at him. 'How about a dip?'

'I'd give that a miss. In a month or two, maybe, when the water's warmer. No, I thought we could motor to the middle of the lake, take the wine with us and . . .'

'And what?'

'Gaze up at the stars.'

Their eyes met, and Johanson felt his defences crumble. He heard himself saying things he hadn't meant to say, setting things in motion, leading her on. He edged closer to her until he could feel her breath on his face. 'OK, let's go.'

The wind had dropped. They walked along the landing-stage and hopped down into the boat. It rocked in the water and Johanson caught her arm. He nearly laughed. It was like a film, he thought – a corny romantic comedy, with Meg Ryan as the lead.

He'd purchased the little wooden boat with the house. At the bow end, planks had been nailed together to create storage space. Lund sat cross-legged on top, and Johanson started the outboard engine.

They didn't speak while the boat was moving. and soon Johanson released the throttle and let the engine die. They were some distance from the house but the veranda lights reflected in the water as a rippling band of brightness. The silence was punctuated by soft splashes as fish darted up to seize insects. Johanson picked his way carefully across to Lund, with the half-empty wine bottle in one hand. 'If you lie back and look at the sky,' he said, 'the universe and everything in it will be yours.'

She looked at him, eyes glinting in the dark. 'Ever seen a shooting star from here?'

'Plenty.'

'Did you make a wish?'

'I'm not enough of a romantic,' he said, and squeezed in beside her. 'I just enjoyed the view.'

Lund giggled. 'You don't believe in such things, then?'

'Do you?'

'Of course not!'

'You're not the type for flowers either. Kare will have his work cut out with you. A stability analysis for subsea construction would be the most romantic present anyone could give you.'

Lund gazed at him. Then she lay down, and her jumper rode up to reveal a taut abdomen. 'Do you mean that?'

Johanson propped himself up on his elbow. 'No, not really.'

'You think I'm unromantic.'

'I think you've never stopped to think what romance is about.'

Their eyes met.

And lingered.

His fingers were already in her hair, combing through the long blonde strands.

'Maybe you could show me,' she murmured. She wrapped an arm round his neck, eyes closed.

Kiss her. Now.

Neither of them moved. They were locked in position, as if they were waiting for a sign.

What's wrong? thought Johanson. Why isn't it working? He could feel the warmth of Lund's body and he breathed in her scent – but he felt like an intruder.

'It's not happening,' said Lund.

Johanson felt as though he'd been thrown into the lake's cold water. Something had been extinguished. His ardour dispersed, giving way to relief. 'You're right,' he said.

They disentangled themselves reluctantly. Johanson saw a question in her eyes that was probably mirrored in his: have we spoilt what we had? 'Are you all right?' he asked.

Lund didn't reply. He sat down in front of her, with his back against the side of the boat, and offered her the bottle. 'Good friends like us,' he said, 'should never be lovers.'

It was a cliché, but it had the right effect. She giggled, grabbed the bottle and took a swig. Then she laughed. She put her hand to her mouth to stifle it, but noisy laughter spilled between her fingers, and Johanson joined in.

'Phew,' she said. 'Are you angry with me?'

'No. What about you?'

'No – it's just . . .' She hesitated. 'I don't get it. On the *Thorvaldson* that night in your cabin, if I'd stayed a moment longer something could have happened, but now . . .'

He took the bottle from her and drank some wine. 'No,' he said. 'It would have been like tonight.'

'But why?'

'Because you love him.'

Lund wrapped her arms around her knees. 'Kare?'

'Who else?'

For a long time she stared silently into space. 'I thought I could get away from him.' She paused, then went on, 'You and I were always on the verge of something happening. Neither of us wanted anything serious so we were perfectly suited . . . But I never thought, it has to happen now. I wasn't in love with you. I didn't *want* to be in love. And then I met Kare and I knew I was . . .'

'In love.'

'I couldn't focus on my job, my mind was always elsewhere – and that's just not me.'

'So you thought you'd cash in your chips before things got out of hand.'

'Then you *are* angry with me!'

'I'm not angry. I was never in love with you either.' He thought for a moment. 'I wanted you – but only really since you started seeing Kare. It dented my pride . . .' He laughed. 'There's a wonderful film, *Moonstruck*, with Cher and Nicolas Cage. Someone asks, "Why do men chase women?" And the answer comes, "Maybe it's because they fear death." Why am I telling you this?'

'Because it's all about fear – fear of being alone, fear of never being asked and, worst of all, the fear of having a choice and making the wrong one. You and I could have an affair, but with Kare . . . With Kare, it would be much more than that. I knew it from the start. When you find yourself wanting someone you don't even know, whatever the price. But their life is part of the deal, and you have to take that too – so you get nervous.'

'It might be a mistake.'

She nodded.

'Have you ever been in a serious relationship?' he asked.

'Once,' she said, 'a long time ago.'

'What happened?'

'He finished with me, and I was a snivelling wreck.'

'And then?'

She rested her chin on her hands. Sitting there in the moonlight, brow furrowed, she was utterly beautiful, but Johanson didn't feel a hint of regret about the way things had worked out. 'I was always the one who ended it,' she said.

'An avenging angel, then.'

'Don't be ridiculous. Mostly they got on my nerves – too slow, too sweet, too stupid. Sometimes I ran away to make sure I escaped before I. . .'

'So you're afraid of building a house in case a storm destroys it.'

'Maybe.' She frowned. 'But there's another way of looking at it. You build the house, then knock it down before anyone else can.'

Somewhere a cricket was chirping and another answered from the other side of the lake.

'Well, you almost succeeded,' said Johanson. 'If we'd slept together, you could have dumped him. Did you really think you could fool yourself like that?'

'I told myself I'd be better off having an affair with you than throwing myself into a relationship that might stifle me. Sleeping with you would have confirmed it.'

'So, you'd have screwed your way to safety?'

'No.' She glared at him. 'I was attracted to you, believe it or not. You weren't just there to help me escape. I didn't just—'

'It's OK.' Johanson made a dismissive gesture. 'You're in love.'

'Yes,' she said sullenly.

'Don't sound so grudging. Say it again.'

'Yes!'

'That's better.' He grinned. 'And now that we've turned you inside out and upside-down, let's drink to Kare.'

She gave him a lopsided grin.

'Still not sure?'

'Yes and no.'

Johanson passed the bottle from one hand to the other. 'I tore a house down once, a long time ago. The people were still inside. They both got hurt, but eventually it passed – for one of them, at least. I still haven't decided whether it was right.'

'Who was the other?' asked Lund.

'My wife.'

'You were married?'

'Yes.'

'You never said.'

'We're divorced.'

'Why?'

'That's just it. There was no real reason. No major dramas, no crockery throwing. Just the feeling that things were closing in. I was scared . . . of becoming dependent. I could see us starting a family. Soon there'd be children in the house and a dog in the yard, and I'd have to take responsibility.'

'And now?'

'There are times when I see it as the only real mistake I've made.' He stared into the water. Eventually he straightened and raised the bottle. 'Now for a toast! Whatever you want to do, go ahead and do it.'

'But I still don't know,' she whispered.

To Johanson's astonishment they spent the whole weekend together by the lake. After their failed attempt at romance, he'd imagined she'd want to leave first thing in the morning, but in fact the air had cleared. Their flirtation was over. So, they went for walks, talked, laughed and forgot about the outside world with its universities, oil rigs and worms – and Johanson cooked the best Bolognese of his life.

On Sunday evening they drove home. Johanson dropped Lund at her place, then went on to his own. As he stepped into his house in Kirkegata Street, he was struck by the difference beween solitude and loneliness, but the feeling soon passed. He left it in the hallway: anxieties and melancholy were allowed that far but no further.

He took his case into the bedroom and turned on the TV. Zapping through the channels, he came across a concert from the Royal Albert Hall. Arias from *La Traviata*, sung by Kiri Te Kanawa. He started to unpack, humming with the music and wondering what he might like as a nightcap.

The music stopped, but he was folding a shirt and didn't register that the concert had ended. In the background, the news took over.

'. . . in Chile. It is not yet known whether the disappearance of the Norwegian family can be linked to similar incidents that are said to have occurred around the same time off the coasts of Peru and Argentina. In all three countries fishing-boats have disappeared or been found abandoned at sea. None of those involved have been traced. The conditions were calm and sunny when the family of five boarded the trawler on a deep-sea fishing expedition.'

He smoothed a sleeve and folded it to the middle.

'Costa Rica is currently experiencing a jellyfish invasion of unprecedented proportions. The so-called Portuguese man-of-war, or "bluebottle," has descended on the area, swamping coastal waters. Local media reports say that fourteen people have been killed by the highly poisonous creatures, while many others have been injured, including two British citizens and a German. The number of missing is still to be confirmed. The Costa Rican Foreign Office has called an emergency session of Parliament, but firmly rejects the suggestion that beaches should be closed, insisting that there is no real threat to swimmers.'

Johanson stopped what he was doing. 'Those assholes,' he muttered. 'Fourteen dead! They should have closed the beaches long ago.'

'Swarms of jellyfish are also causing concern off the coast of Australia. This time the culprits are thought to be box jellyfish, another highly venomous species. The local authorities are urging people to stay out of the water. Over the past hundred years, box jellyfish have caused seventy deaths, making them more dangerous to man than sharks.

In another story of marine tragedy, fatalities have been reported off the coast of western Canada. The exact cause of the accidents, which resulted in the sinking of several tourist vessels, is not yet known. Reports suggest that navigational errors may have caused them to collide.'

Johanson was gazing at the screen now. The newsreader had put down a piece of paper and was smiling emptily into the camera. 'And now for a round-up of today's other stories . . .'

Johanson thought of the woman he'd seen in Bali, who'd flailed in the sand, shaken by convulsions. He hadn't touched the creature and neither had she. She'd been walking along the beach when she noticed something floating in the shallows and had fished it out with a stick. Cautious by nature, she'd kept it at arm's length, turning it this way and that. Then she'd made a mistake.

The Portuguese man-of-war belonged to the genus *Physalia*, a type of hydrozoa that scientists still found baffling. Strictly speaking, it wasn't a jellyfish but a floating colony of tiny organisms, hundreds of thousands of polyps, grouped according to function. The main body, a jelly-like float tinted violet or blue, had a gas-filled crest that rose above the water, allowing the colony to sail across the surface. You couldn't see what hung beneath it.

But you knew as soon as it touched you.

A net of tentacles up to fifty metres long and covered with miniscule stinging cells swept beneath each Portuguese man-of-war. The structure and purpose of the cells was a masterstroke of evolution. Each consisted of a hollow sphere that curled in on itself to form a coiled tube tipped with a harpoon-like barb. At the slightest touch the tube would unfurl, bursting forth at a pressure equivalent to seventy exploding tyres. Thousands of barbed harpoons would penetrate the victim's flesh, injecting a mixture of phenols and proteins that attacked the blood and nerve cells. The victim's muscles would contract and pain would sear the skin. Shock would follow, then breathing difficulties and heart failure. Those fortunate enough to be close to the shore usually survived, but divers and swimmers further out stood little chance against the trailing tentacles.

The woman on the beach in Bali had dropped the hydrozoan but the stick had brushed her toe. It must have left a trace of venom – enough to ensure that she never forgot it.

But the Portuguese man-of-war was harmless compared to the box jellyfish – *Chironex fleckeri*, the deadly Australian sea wasp.

In the course of evolution, nature had developed an impressive array of toxins. *Chironex fleckeri* was the *pièce de résistance*. A single box jellyfish contained enough poison to kill 250 people. Its highly potent venom paralysed the nervous system, causing immediate loss of consciousness. Within minutes, or sometimes seconds, most of its victims suffered heart failure and drowned.

All this ran through Johanson's mind as he stared at the screen.

Fourteen dead and countless others injured in a matter of weeks. Had the death-count ever been so high on a single stretch of coastline from just a single species? And what about the disappearing ships?

Portuguese men-of-war in South America. Box jellyfish in Australia. Bristleworms in Norway.

It's probably coincidence, he thought. Swarms of jellyfish appeared all over the world. The holiday season wouldn't be the same without them. They had nothing in common with worms.

He tidied away the last few items of clothing, switched off the television and went into the living room to listen to music or read. But he didn't put on a CD or pick up a book. For a while he paced up and down, eventually stopping at the window. The streetlamps lit the street outside.

The lake had been so peaceful . . .

It was peaceful here too . . .

When things were so peaceful, there was usually something wrong.

Don't be ridiculous, Johanson told himself.

He poured himself some grappa, took a sip, and tried to forget about the news.

Then he remembered Knut Olsen, a fellow biologist at the NTNU. He knew a lot about jellyfish, coral and sea anemones.

Olsen picked up on the third ring.

'Were you asleep?' asked Johanson.

'Not with the kids still up,' said Olsen. 'It's Marie's fifth birthday today. How was the lake?'

Olsen was a perpetually cheerful family man whose cosy domestic life seemed like a nightmare to Johanson. They never saw each other socially, unless you counted lunch breaks, but Olsen was a nice guy with a decent sense of humour. With four children he needed it, thought Johanson. 'One of these days, you should come with me,' he said, although they both knew it wouldn't happen. 'Have you seen the news?'

There was a short pause. 'The jellyfish, you mean?'

'Right first time. What's going on?'

'It's obvious, isn't it? Biological invasions happen all the time. Frogs, locusts, jellyfish . . .'

'But Portuguese men-of-war and box jellyfish?'

'It's unusual . . .'

'In what way?'

'They're two of the world's deadliest sea creatures. And there's something peculiar about what they're saying on the news.'

'Seventy fatalities in a hundred years?' said Johanson.

'Oh, that's rubbish.' Olsen gave a derisive snort.

'Too many?'

'Too few! The real death toll's much higher – ninety at least, if you count the Gulf of Bengal and the Philippines, not to mention all the unreported and unexplained cases. Australia has always had a problem with box jellies. They spawn in the river mouths north of Rockhampton. Almost all the accidents happen in the shallows – they can kill you in less than three minutes.'

'Is it jellyfish season?'

'In Australia, yes – October to May. In Europe they only really bother you when it's too hot to stay out of the water. We were in Menorca last summer and the kids were going crazy. The whole place was inundated with *Velella*.'

'Sorry?'

'*Velella velella*. By-the-wind sailors. Quite pretty, really, providing they're not rotting on the beach. Little violet-coloured jellies – the sand was covered with them. Everyone knows I'm a big fan of jellyfish, but there were too many even for me. The Australian story is seriously odd, though.'

'In what sense?'

'You find box jellies on the coastline, where the water's nice and shallow, not out to sea, and definitely not on the Barrier Reef – but they're saying they've been found there too. It's the opposite with *Velella*. They're an offshore species, and no one understands why they sometimes turn up on the beach.'

'I thought the beaches were protected by nets.'

Olsen roared with laughter. 'They're useless. The mesh stops the jellies, but the tentacles break off and carry on drifting. No one can see them.' He stopped. 'But why are you so interested? You must know a bit about jellyfish yourself.'

'Not nearly as much as you do. Is this a scientific anomaly?'

'You can pretty much bet on it,' said Olsen, balefully. 'Jellyfish distribution is linked to rising water temperatures and high levels of plankton. Plankton thrive in nice warm water, and jellyfish eat plankton, so you can guess what happens next. It's why they turn up in their hordes towards the end of summer and disappear a few weeks later. It's their natural cycle. Hang on a moment.'

Johanson heard shrieks in the background. He wondered what time the Olsen children went to bed – whenever he called, some kind of riot was going on. Olsen yelled at them to quieten down. Then he was back. 'Anyway, I reckon we get these invasions because the sea is being over-fertilised. Sewage encourages plankton levels to rise, and it all takes off from there. You only need a strong westerly or north-westerly, and the jellyfish are on your doorstep.'

'Yes, but those are normal jellyfish plagues. I want to know—'

'You want to know if it's an anomaly – and I think it probably is. But it's precisely the kind that's difficult to spot. Tell me, have you got any pot plants?'

'Yes.'

'A yucca?'

'Two.'

'There you go – an anomaly. The yucca isn't native.'

Johanson rolled his eyes. 'Don't tell me we're being threatened by a yucca invasion. Mine are fairly placid.'

'That's not what I meant. I'm saying that we've forgotten what's natural and what's not. Back in 2000 I was called out to the Gulf of Mexico to investigate a plague of jellies that was threatening the local fish stock. They invaded the spawning grounds in Louisiana, Mississippi and Alabama, devouring fish eggs and larvae, plus the plankton that the fish would normally eat. The damage was caused by an Australian jellyfish from the Pacific that shouldn't have been there at all.'

'An invasive species.'

'Exactly. The jellies were destroying the food chain and slashing the fish yield. It was catastrophic. A few years before that, the Black Sea was on the brink of an ecological disaster because during the eighties a cargo vessel had shipped in some comb jellies with its ballast water. They didn't belong there. The Black Sea countries kicked up a fuss, but before anyone could do anything about it, the region was screwed. Eight thousand jellies per square metre of sea. Do you know what that means?'

Olsen was talking himself into a fury.

'Then this other business. Portuguese men-of-war off the coast of Argentina. That's not their territory. Central America, Peru and Chile, maybe. But further south? Impossible. Fourteen deaths, just like that. A biological invasion. You can bet the locals weren't expecting it. And now box jellies on the Barrier Reef. It's as if someone had magicked them there.'

'What I find peculiar,' said Johanson, 'is that it's the two most venomous species.'

'Absolutely,' Olsen said slowly. 'But I hope you're not about to give me some kind of conspiracy theory. This is Norway, not America. There are plenty of possible explanations for the rise in jellyfish plagues. Some scientists say it's El Niño and others blame global warming. In Malibu the plagues are the worst they've had in years, and Tel Aviv's seeing some gigantic specimens. Global warming, invasive species – it all makes sense.'

Johanson wasn't listening. Olsen had said something that stuck in his mind.

As if someone had magicked them there.

It was the same for the worms.

As if someone had magicked them there.

'. . . breeding in the shallows,' Olsen was saying. 'And another thing. When they say "unusually large numbers", they don't mean thousands, they mean millions. And the government says it's under control! There have been far more than fourteen deaths, believe me.'

'Uh-huh.'

'Are you listening?'

'Of course. More than fourteen deaths. What were you saying about conspiracy theories?'

Olsen laughed. 'Very good. But seriously, though, I think it's definitely an anomaly. It might look like a cyclical phenomenon, but I think it's something else.'

'Interesting.' Should he tell Oslen about the worms? But it was none of his business, and Statoil wouldn't be happy if the story hit the headlines – Olsen talked too much.

'How about lunch tomorrow?' asked Olsen.

'Sure.'

'I'll see if I can find out more. Fish for some information.' He chortled.

'Great,' said Johanson. 'See you tomorrow.' He hung up. Then he remembered that he'd meant to ask Olsen about the missing boats. Never mind – he'd mention it tomorrow.

He wondered whether the jellyfish story would have made such an impression on him if he hadn't known about the worms. Probably not, because the jellies weren't what interested him. He wanted to know about the connections – if there were any.

The following morning, on the way to the NTNU, Johanson listened to the news, but there was nothing he hadn't heard already. People and boats were going missing in different parts of the world, giving rise to endless speculation but no satisfactory explanation.

His lecture was scheduled for ten. Enough time to read his emails and glance at the post. It was pouring with rain, and the grey sky hung heavy over Trondheim. He'd scarcely turned on the lights and sat down at his desk with his coffee when Olsen poked his head round the door. 'It's never-ending,' he said, 'all this bad news.'

'You mean the missing boats? I was going to ask you about that yesterday, but I forgot.'

Olsen came into the room. 'Are you going to offer me some coffee?' he said, looking around intently. Curiosity was one of Olsen's useful but slightly wearisome traits.

'It's all next door,' Johanson told him.

Olsen leaned into the adjoining office and asked for a coffee at the top of his voice. Then he sat down and let his eyes rove round the room. Johanson's secretary marched in, slammed a mug in front of Olsen and stalked back to her desk.

'What's wrong with her?' said Olsen, surprised.

'I pour my own coffee,' said Johanson. 'It's all laid out. Flask, milk, sugar, cups . . .'

Olsen took a noisy gulp. 'So you didn't listen to the news?'

'I heard it in the car.'

'Ten minutes ago there was an emergency newsflash on CNN. I've got a telly in my office – I keep it on all day.' The overhead lighting shone on Olsen's emerging bald patch. 'A gas tanker's exploded off the coast of Japan, then two container ships and a frigate collided in the Strait of Malacca. One of the ships sank, the other isn't seaworthy, and the frigate's gone up in flames. It belonged to the military. There was an explosion.'

'Christ.' Johanson warmed his hands on his mug. 'As far as the Malacca Strait is concerned,' he said, 'I can't say I'm surprised. It's astonishing there aren't more accidents.'

'Sure, but it's quite a coincidence.'

Three stretches of water competed for the title of busiest waterway in the world: the English Channel, the Strait of Gibraltar and the Strait of Malacca, which formed part of the main route between Europe, South East Asia and Japan. Six hundred tankers and freighters passed through the strait each day, and sometimes the channel between Malaysia and Sumatra carried as many as two thousand vessels. The strait was eight hundred kilometres long, but its narrowest point was only 2.7 kilometres wide. India and Malaysia had urged the tankers to use the Lombok Strait further south, but their pleas had fallen on deaf ears. Taking a detour would decrease the profit margin, so fifteen per cent of international shipping continued to stream through the Malacca Strait.

'Does anyone know what happened?'

'Not yet.'

'How awful.' Johanson sipped his coffee. 'So, what's all this stuff about disappearing boats, then?'

'Oh, that. You haven't heard?'

'Well, if I had, I wouldn't ask,' said Johanson. His temper was starting to fray.

Olsen lowered his voice. 'It turns out that swimmers and small fishing-boats have been going missing for some time in South America, but the media didn't report it – or not in Europe, at least. They say it started in Peru. The first person to disappear was a fisherman. His boat was found a few days later, a little reed craft, drifting out to sea. At first they thought a wave had caught him, but the weather's been perfect for weeks. Since then, people have been vanishing left, right and centre. The latest victim was a trawler.'

'Why hasn't anyone mentioned it?'

Olsen spread his hands in a gesture of resignation. 'Because no one likes to advertise this kind of thing. Tourism's crucial to the region. And, anyway, it was happening on the other side of the world.'

'But the jellies made the news.'

'Oh, come on, Sigur, that's totally different. *American* citizens have died. Plus a German, and God knows who else. And now a Norwegian family has vanished off the coast of Chile. One of the local companies organised a deep-sea angling trip – one minute they were all on the trawler and the next they were gone. Norwegians, for God's sake! That kind of thing's always reported.'

'OK, I take your point.' Johanson leaned back in his chair. 'Did no one radio for help?'

'There were a few distress signals, nothing more – the boats that went missing weren't exactly high-tech.'

'And no sign of a squall?'

'For Christ's sake, Sigur, no. At least, nothing that could sink a vessel.'

'And western Canada? What's going on there?'

'You mean those boats that were in collision? No idea. According to one witness, they got into a fight with a bad-tempered whale. Who knows? The world's a cruel place . . . Now how about another coffee? Actually, I think I'll get it myself.'

Dry rot was easier to get rid of than Olsen, but eventually he left. Johanson checked his watch. Nearly time for his lecture. He rang Lund.

'Skaugen has contacted other teams working in exploration,' she said, 'oil companies all over the world. He wants to know if anyone's found anything similar.'

'Like the worms?'

'Exactly. He thinks the Asians know at least as much as we do.'

'Why?'

'You said it yourself. Asia is trying to exploit gas hydrates. I thought that's what they told you in Kiel. Skaugen wants to sound them out.'

It wasn't a bad idea, thought Johanson. If the worms were crazy about hydrates, the companies that wanted the hydrates would have come across them too. The trouble was . . . 'I can't imagine the Asians will be open with him,' he said. 'They'll be as cagey as he is.'

'So you don't think Skaugen'll mention it?'

'Certainly not the whole story. And especially not now.'

'But what else can he do?'

'Well . . .' Johanson scrabbled for words '. . . I don't mean to insinuate anything, but suppose someone decided to build a unit regardless of the worms.'

'Impossible!'

'Just supposing.'

'But I told you, didn't I? Skaugen's taking your advice.'

'All credit to him. But this is money we're talking about. Some people would decide it's OK to pretend not to know about the worms.'

'You mean they'd go ahead and build the unit?'

'You never know, it might go smoothly. And if it didn't . . . Well, a firm can be liable for technical incompetence, but not for methane-eating worms. Sure, they knew about them beforehand, but who could prove it?'

'Statoil wouldn't hush up a thing like that.'

'Forget Statoil. Take the Japanese. Selling methane would be equivalent to an oil boom, if not better. They'd be unbelievably rich. You can't honestly think they'd want to show their hand.'

'I guess not.'

'Would Statoil?'

'Look, this is getting us nowhere,' said Lund. 'We need to find out the truth before anyone else does. If only we had some independent observers who couldn't be traced back to Statoil. Like . . .' She made thinking noises. 'Couldn't you ask around a bit?'

'In the oil industry?'

'At universities, institutes – people like your friends in Kiel. Aren't hydrates being studied all over the world?'

'Yes, but—'

'And how about marine biologists? Deep-sea divers?' She was sounding excited now. 'Maybe you should take over the entire thing! We could set up a new division for you. I'll call Skaugen right away and ask him for funding. Then we can—'

'Whoa! Not so fast, Tina!'

'I'm sure it would be well paid, and it wouldn't mean much work.'

'It'd be bloody awful. And there's no reason why you lot shouldn't do it.'

'You'd do it better. You're neutral.'

'Come off it, Tina.'

'Instead of arguing with me, you could've rung the Smithsonian three times already. Please, Sigur, it'd be easy . . . You've got to see it our way. We're a big multinational with vested interests. The minute we start asking questions, hundreds of environmental groups will pounce. They're waiting for something like this.'

'I see. So sweeping it under the carpet would be in your interest?'

'You can be bloody annoying at times, Sigur.'

'So people keep telling me.'

Lund sighed. 'What do you think we should do, then? As soon as

172

people know about it, they'll think the worst. And you can take my word for it, Statoil isn't going to build this unit until we've found out more. But if we start making official enquiries, the news will get out and we'll be in the spotlight. Our hands will be tied.'

Johanson rubbed his eyes and glanced at his watch again. It was gone ten. 'Tina, I have to go. I'll ring you later.'

'Can I tell Skaugen you'll do it?'

'No.'

There was silence. 'OK,' she said finally, in a small voice.

Johanson took a deep breath. 'Will you at least give me time to consider it?'

'You're a sweetheart.'

'I know. That's my problem.'

He gathered up his papers and hurried to the lecture-hall.

Roanne, France

Jean Jérôme was looking critically at twelve Brittany lobsters. He looked critically at most things. He owed his scepticism to the establishment for which he worked. Troisgros prided itself on being the only French restaurant to have kept its three Michelin stars for over thirty consecutive years. Jérôme had no desire to go down in history as the man who broke that tradition. He was responsible for seafood, Troisgros's lord of the fish, so to speak, and he'd been on his feet since dawn.

His wholesaler had been up even longer – his day began at three in the morning in Rungis, an otherwise unremarkable suburban town fourteen kilometres outside Paris that had transformed itself almost overnight into a mecca of *haute cuisine*. Spread over four square kilometres and fully lit, it was the place for wholesalers, restaurateurs and anyone else who spent their life in a kitchen to purchase their ingredients. Produce from all over France could be found there: milk, cream, butter and cheese from Normandy, high-quality vegetables from Brittany, and aromatic fruits from the south. Oyster farmers from Belon, Marennes, the Arcachon basin, and tuna fishermen from St Jean-de-Luz would thunder down the *autoroutes* to deliver their freight on time. Refrigerated lorries laden with shellfish jostled with vans and cars on the roads. Top-quality produce was on sale in Rungis before anywhere else in France.

But not all top-quality produce was the same. The lobsters, like the vegetables, came from Brittany, but some specimens were more enticing than the rest. Jean Jérôme picked them up one by one and studied them from every angle. There were six in each of the large polystyrene crates lined with seaweed. They were alive, of course, but barely moving, which was only natural, since their pincers had been tied.

'They're good,' said Jérôme.

That was praise indeed, coming from his lips. In fact he was exceptionally pleased with the lobsters. They were on the small side, but fairly heavy to make up for it, and their shells were a shiny dark blue.

Then he came to the last pair. 'Too light,' he said.

The wholesaler frowned. With one hand he picked up a lobster that had met with Jérôme's approval, and in the other he held one of the rejects. He weighed them against each other.

'You're right, Monsieur,' he said, in consternation. 'I do apologise. But there's not much in it.'

'True,' said Jérôme. 'A little difference like that wouldn't be noticed in a seaside café – but this is Troisgros.'

'Please accept my apologies. I can go back and—'

'That won't be necessary. We'll see which of our guests has the smallest appetite.'

The wholesaler apologised again.

A short while later Jérôme was in Troisgros's magnificent kitchens, getting to grips with the evening menu. He had put the lobsters in a tub.

When it was time to blanch them, he asked for a large pan of water to be heated. Speed was of the essence when dealing with lobster – as soon as it was caught, its flesh began to lose flavour. Blanching killed the lobster and stabilised the taste. Later, when it was almost time to serve them, they would be cooked through. Jérôme waited until the water reached boiling point, then dropped a lobster head-first into the pan. The air inside its body cavity escaped in a high-pitched scream. Then he drew it out and put it aside. One by one he repeated the process . . . nine, ten . . . He reached for the eleventh, lighter than the others, and lowered it into the steaming water.

He pulled it out, and swore under his breath.

What on earth had happened to the creature? Its shell had been ripped open and a claw had fallen off. Jérôme snorted with rage. He put it down on the work surface and nudged it gently on to its back. The underside was damaged, and a slimy white substance filled the shell where the meat should have been. He turned to the pan and stared into it. Blobs of something that bore no resemblance to lobster flesh were floating in the water.

There was nothing he could do about it, and besides he only needed ten. Jérôme never risked buying too little – he had a reputation for getting the balance just right. It was important to know precisely how much of everything would be needed – in the interests of economy, of course, but also to have sufficient in reserve. Once again, the strategy had paid off.

But it was annoying all the same.

The tub caught his eye. There was one lobster left, the second of the pair he hadn't liked. But there was no time to worry about that now – into the pan with it.

Wait! He hadn't cleaned the water.

A thought struck him. The diseased lobster had been lighter than the others. This live lobster felt lighter too. Maybe it was infected with a virus or a parasite. Jérôme took the twelfth lobster out of the tub and laid it on the work surface. Its long antennae slanted back along its body twitching constantly, while its bound claws moved feebly. When lobsters were removed from their natural habitat, they tended towards lethargy. Jérôme prodded it gently and bent down to it. A transparent substance was oozing from the joint where the carapace met the segmented tail.

What the hell was that?

Jérôme crouched close to it.

The lobster raised its upper body and its black eyes seemed to fix on him.

Then it burst.

The apprentice whom Jérôme had put to work scaling fish was only three metres away from the scene, but a narrow wall unit stacked with utensils obscured his view of the stove. The first he heard was a bloodcurdling scream. Then Jérôme staggered backwards, clutching his face. The apprentice darted towards him, and both men lurched into the cupboard behind them. Saucepans jangled and something crashed to the floor, shattering.

'What is it?' the apprentice asked, panicking. 'What happened?'

The other chefs came running. The kitchen was like a well-organised factory in which each worker carried out a particular task. One was responsible for game, another for sauces, a third for pâtés, a fourth for salads, a fifth for pâtisserie and so on. For a moment everything was thrown into confusion. Then Jérôme lowered his hands and pointed a trembling finger towards the work surface next to the stove. A thick transparent substance was dripping from his hair. Blobs covered his face and a stream ran down his neck. 'It – it exploded at me,' he gasped.

His apprentice took a step forward and looked with revulsion at the lobster fragments. Only the legs were still intact. A claw lay on the floor and the jagged edges of the shell gaped open. 'What did you do to it?' he whispered.

Jérôme's face was distorted with disgust. 'I didn't do anything!' he yelled. 'It just burst!'

They fetched towels for him to wipe himself clean. The apprentice touched the substance with his fingertips. It felt taut and rubbery, but it disintegrated easily, dispersing over the worktop. Without stopping to think, he took a jar from the shelf and spooned in clumps of the jelly. Then he swept some of the liquid over the top and twisted on the lid tightly.

Pacifying Jérôme posed more of a problem. In the end someone poured him a glass of champagne, and eventually he recovered some of his poise. 'Clean up that mess,' he commanded. 'I'm going to wash.'

Immediately the kitchen staff started putting his workplace back to rights. They scrubbed the stove and the surrounding area, disposed of the lobster remnants, cleaned the pan and threw away the water in which the lobsters had spent the last hour of their lives. It went the way of all waste water – down the drain and into the sewers where it mingled with the other fluids that the town had flushed away.

The apprentice took charge of the jar with the jelly. He hadn't thought what to do with it so he asked Jérôme, who had returned to the kitchens in clean chef's whites.

'Good idea to save some,' Jérôme said. 'God knows what it could be. Send it somewhere where they test that kind of thing. But don't mention the incident. It never happened. Not at Troisgros.'

The story never left the kitchens, which was just as well as it would have shown the restaurant in an unjustly negative light. Troisgros wasn't to blame, but nothing was worse for a top-class restaurant than whisperings about its hygiene.

The apprentice kept a close eye on the substance in the jar. When it started to disintegrate, he added more water because it seemed the right thing to do.

It looked like pieces of jellyfish, he thought, and jellyfish needed water – in fact that was pretty much all they were made of. In any case it seemed to do the trick. For the time being the substance remained stable. Troisgros made some discreet telephone enquiries, and the jar was immediately sent for analysis at the nearby university in Lyons.

Two hours later, it landed on the desk of Bernard Roche, a professor of molecular biology. Even with the extra water in the jar, the jelly was disintegrating again. Only a few small clumps remained. Roche began to test it straight away, but the last blob dispersed before he could examine it in detail. He'd seen enough, though, to identify some molecular compounds, whose presence surprised and bewildered him. One was a highly potent neurotoxin, but he couldn't be certain whether it came from the jelly or the water in the jar.

The liquid, he discovered, was saturated with organic matter and all kinds of chemicals. Since he didn't have time to analyse it immediately, he decided to return to it in a few days' time. He put the jar in the fridge.

That evening Jérôme fell ill. At first he felt nauseous. The restaurant was full, so he tried to forget about it and carried on as usual. The ten intact lobsters were exquisite, and there was no call for any more. In spite of the unpleasant incident that morning, everything went smoothly – as was expected at Troisgros.

It was getting on for ten o'clock when the nausea worsened and was coupled with a headache. Then Jérôme noticed he was losing concentration. He had omitted to put the finishing touches to one of the dishes, and had forgotten to tell his apprentice what to do next.

Jean Jérôme was enough of a professional to know when to pull the plug. He was feeling truly awful. He handed responsibility to his deputy, an ambitious and talented chef who'd learned her trade in Paris under Ducasse. He was just popping outside, he told her. The kitchens backed on to the garden: when the weather was good, diners were taken there on arrival and served their apéritif with canapés. Later they were led into the restaurant through the kitchens, catching a glimpse of the proceedings and sometimes a demonstration by a chef. Right now the discreetly lit garden was deserted.

For a few minutes Jérôme paced up and down. Through the large windows he could still see the bustle of the kitchens, but he was having trouble focusing for more than a few seconds at a time. He couldn't get enough air, and there was a weight on his chest. His legs felt like jelly. He sat down at one of the wooden tables. His thoughts returned to the events of that morning. His hair and face had been splattered with the lobster's insides. He was sure he must have inhaled a bit or swallowed some fluid. He'd probably caught a drop on his tongue when he licked his lips.

Perhaps it was the thought of the lobster, but before he knew it, he was vomiting violently over the plants. As he sat there, bent double, retching and choking, he thought it was probably for the best. At least he'd got rid of it. Now all he needed was a glass of water, and he'd feel much better.

He dragged himself to his feet. His head spun. His forehead was burning and he was gazing into a spiral. He sat down again. You've got to get up, he told himself. You need to check that things are all right in the kitchen. It was vital that nothing went wrong. This was Troisgros, after all.

He managed to stand up and take a few dragging steps, then darkness overwhelmed him.

18 April

Vancouver Island, Canada

Anawak could feel his eyes reddening and swelling, while the skin round them creased. Struggling to keep his head upright, he stared at the monitor. Ever since Canada's west coast had been plunged into chaos, his eyes had barely left the screen, yet he'd sifted only a fraction of the data – electronic evidence that owed its existence to one of the most ground-breaking inventions in animal behavioural science. Telemetry.

In the late 1970s, scientists had come up with a revolutionary new method for monitoring animals. Until then there had been no accurate means of collecting data on a species' distribution or its patterns of migration. How animals lived, hunted and mated, what they needed or wanted were all matters of speculation. Of course, thousands of animals were being watched around the clock – but almost always under circumstances that made it impossible to predict how they would normally behave. Monitoring an animal in captivity was like observing a man behind bars: there was no way of telling how it lived when it was free.

But attempts to observe animals in their natural habitat were similarly unsuccessful. The creatures either took flight or failed to show up in the first place. Animals tended to see more of the scientists than the scientists did of them. Some of the less timid species – chimpanzees or dolphins, for example – put on shows for their observers, displaying aggression or curiosity, and sometimes even flirting or striking a pose, making objective conclusions all but impossible to reach. Once they'd tired of performing, they'd disappear into the jungle, take off into the sky or dive into the depths, where they'd resume their natural behaviour – except no one could see them.

It was the mystery that biologists from Darwin onwards had been longing to solve. How could we understand the ability of fish and seals to survive in the cold dark waters of the Antarctic? How could humans see inside a biotope that was sealed with layers of ice? What would the Earth look like from the sky, if we crossed the Mediterranean on the back of a goose? How did it feel to be a bee? How could we measure the speed of an insect's wings and its heartbeat, or monitor its blood pressure and eating patterns? What was the impact of human activities, like shipping noise or subsea explosions, on mammals in the depths? How could we follow animals to places where no human could venture?

The answer came in the form of a technology that allowed haulage companies to locate each of their lorries, and helped drivers to pinpoint streets in towns they'd never seen. It was a modern invention that everyone knew and used, without realising that it would revolutionise zoology: telemetry.

In the late 1950s, US scientists had already started to develop ways of electronically tagging animals. Not long afterwards the US Navy was using the technology on trained dolphins, but the experiment failed because the tags were too heavy: it was no good hoping to gain accurate information on dolphins' natural behaviour from tags that affected their movements. The initiative ground to a halt, but the invention of the microchip heralded a breakthrough. In no time ultra-light cameras and tags the size of chocolate bars were being used to transmit relevant data from the wild. The animals carried on as normal, roaming through the rainforests or swimming through the pack-ice in McMurdo Sound, unaware of the fifteen grams of equipment they were carrying. At long last grizzly bears, dingoes, foxes and caribous were divulging their secrets. Scientists were initiated into their ways of life, mating rituals, hunting habits and migration patterns. They could even fly across the world in the company of white-tailed eagles, albatrosses, swans, geese and crows. At the cutting edge of technology, insects were fitted with miniature devices that weighed a thousandth of a gram and were powered by radar waves. They could send back their signal at double the frequency, allowing the data to be received from distances of more than seven hundred metres.

Most of the tracking was done by satellite. The system was as simple as it was ingenious. The signal from the transmitter was sent into space, where it was received by ARGOS, a satellite-based system run by the French space agency CNES. From there it was transmitted to head-quarters in Toulouse and on to a terrestrial station in Fairbanks, USA, for forwarding to other institutions worldwide. The data reached the end-user in less than ninety minutes.

Research into whales, seals, penguins and turtles soon developed into a distinct field of telemetry. The planet's least-known and most fascinating habitat was opened up to view. Data could be recorded at considerable depth on ultra-light transmitters, which registered temperature, length of dive, distance from the surface, location, direction of travel and speed. Frustratingly the signals could only be received from the water's surface, which meant that ARGOS was blind where the depths were concerned. Humpbacks spent a good deal of their lives within a few kilometres of the Californian coast, but surfaced for an hour a day at most. While ornithologists could see and monitor a stork in flight, marine scientists were cut off from their subjects while they were under water. For a complete understanding of marine mammals, they needed cameras that kept rolling at all times – but the Pacific was too deep for any diver, and submersibles lacked the necessary agility and speed.

Eventually the solution came from scientists at the University of California in Santa Cruz, who invented a tiny, pressure-resistant underwater camera. They tried the device on an elephant seal and some Weddell seals and finally a dolphin. In no time they came across the most amazing phenomena. Within a few weeks their understanding of marine mammals was transformed. If only whales and dolphins had proven as easy to tag as other animals, everything would have been perfect. Instead it was virtually impossible. So Anawak was left with far less data than he would have liked – yet at the same time he had more than he could handle. Since no one knew what was important, every piece of information was significant – and that meant evaluating thousands of hours of images, audio recordings, readings, analyses and stats.

'Project Sisyphus' was what Ford had called it.

But at least Anawak had plenty of time to devote to it. The station's reputation had been restored, and yet Davie's was closed. The waters off the west coast of Canada and North America were restricted to large vessels only. The disaster that had hit Vancouver Island had been repeated along the coast from San Francisco to Alaska. During the first wave of attacks, over a hundred smaller craft had been sunk or severely damaged. The number of casualties had fallen over the weekend, but only because no one was prepared to set sail unless they owned a freighter or a ferry. The media was awash with conflicting reports. Even the death toll was uncertain. Various government-appointed emergency-response teams had been brought in to deal with the situation, which meant that the skies were filled with helicopters whirring up and down the coast, laden with soldiers, scientists and politicians peering down at the ocean, each more helpless and bewildered than the next.

It was standard procedure for emergency committees to draw on outside advisers, and that was what the Canadian authorities had done. Vancouver Aquarium was co-opted as the hub of all science-based operations under the leadership of John Ford. Almost every marine-science or research institute was placed under his control. For Ford it was a weighty burden: he was leading a mission without knowing what it was. There was a protocol for everything from catastrophic earthquakes to terrorist nuclear attacks, but no one had prepared a brief for *this*. Ford lost no time in proposing Anawak as an additional adviser. If anyone in North America or Canada could understand what was going on inside a whale's head, it was him. And surely that was where they'd find their explanation. Whales were supposed to be intelligent, so had the creatures all gone mad? Or was something else affecting their behaviour?

Yet even Anawak, of whom so much was expected, was unable to help. He'd begun by assembling all of that year's telemetric data from the Pacific coast. Twenty-four hours ago he and Alicia Delaware had started to analyse the material, helped by staff at the aquarium. They'd pored over positioning data and listened intently to hydrophone recordings but they still had nothing to show for it. None of the whales had been carrying tags when they set out from Hawaii and Baja California towards the Arctic – with the sole exception of two humpbacks, who'd lost their transmitters almost as soon as they'd started migrating. The video shot by the woman on the *Blue Shark* seemed to be their only piece of evidence. They'd studied it at the Station with the help of some skippers who were adept at recognising flukes. After replaying the footage and magnifying the images, they'd identified some of the attackers: two humpbacks, a grey and several orcas.

Delaware had been right: the video was a valuable clue.

Anawak's aversion to her had soon evaporated. Delaware had a big mouth and seldom stopped to think before she spoke, but beneath her brash manner was an intelligent, analytical mind. Besides, she had time to help. Her parents lived in the British Properties, an exclusive district for Vancouver's élite. They gave her anything she wanted, but were hardly ever there. Anawak suspected that their financial generosity was an attempt to make up for their lack of interest, but their daughter didn't seem to care – she could spend their fortune and do as she pleased. Things had worked out perfectly: Delaware saw working with Anawak as an opportunity to back up her studies with practical experience, and he needed an assistant now that Stringer was dead.

Susan Stringer . . .

Every time he thought of her he was overcome with guilt for having failed to save her. He had told himself that nothing he or anyone else could have done would have freed her from the orca's jaws, but the uncertainty remained. What good were all his papers and articles about intelligence in marine mammals if he couldn't understand a whale's thought processes? Was it possible to convince an orca to let go of its prey?

He reminded himself continually that orcas were animals – highly intelligent ones, but animals all the same. And prey was prey.

But orcas didn't prey on humans. Had the whales eaten the people drifting in the water or just killed them?

Anawak sighed. He wasn't making any progress. The burning in his eyes was getting worse. Half-heartedly he picked up another disk of digital images, then put it back. He couldn't concentrate. He'd spent the whole day at the aquarium, discussing findings or calling people, and now he felt drained. Wearily he switched off his computer. It was gone seven. He got up and went in search of John Ford. The director was in a meeting, so he called in on Delaware, who was studying satellite data.

'Fancy a juicy whale steak?' he asked glumly.

She looked up with a smile in her eyes. She'd swapped her blue glasses for contact lenses, but her irises were still suspiciously violet. Apart from the buck teeth, she was actually very attractive. 'Sure. Where do you want to go?'

'The snack bar on the corner's not bad.'

'Snack bar?' she said in amusement. 'I don't think so. Come on, I'll treat you.'

'There's no need.'

'Let's go to Cardero's.'

'Christ!'

'They do great food.'

'I know, but firstly, I can pay for myself, and secondly, Cardero's is . . . well, it's . . .'

'It's *fabulous!*'

Cardero's was situated amid the yachts of Vancouver's Coal Harbour. It was a big place with large windows and high ceilings – one of the trendiest outfits in town. The restaurant offered stunning views and good west-coast cuisine, while the adjoining bar was filled with the young and chic, laughing and sipping drinks. In his frayed jeans and faded sweater Anawak could hardly have been less appropriately dressed, but he always felt uncomfortable and out of place in smart restaurants. He couldn't deny that Delaware belonged there, though.

So, Cardero's it was.

They took his old car and drove to the harbour. They were in luck. It was usually necessary to book at Cardero's, but one table was empty. It was a little removed from the bustle of the main restaurant, which was perfect for Anawak. They ordered the house speciality – salmon baked with soy, brown sugar and lemon on a cedar plank.

'OK,' said Anawak, once their order had been taken. 'What have we got?'

'Nothing,' said Delaware. 'I'm baffled.'

Anawak rubbed his chin. 'Well, maybe I've found something. The video footage put me on to it.'

'*My* video footage, you mean.'

'Yes,' he admitted, and added ironically, 'We're all very grateful.'

'Well, you should be, if it's given you a lead.'

'It's the whales we identified. Only transient orcas were involved in the attacks, not a single resident.'

'You're right.' She wrinkled her nose. 'We haven't heard anything bad about residents.'

'The Johnstone Strait was clear of attacks – even though it was full of kayaks at the time.'

'So the threat's being posed by the newcomers.'

'By transients, and maybe offshore orcas too. The grey and the two humpbacks on the video were all transients. All three whales spent the winter in Baja California – we've got it all on file. We emailed pictures of their flukes to the institute in Seattle, who confirmed that the whales have been seen there several times in recent years.'

'So what's the big deal? Everyone knows that greys and humpbacks migrate.'

'Not all of them.'

'I thought . . .'

'Something weird happened the second time we went out that day. I'd practically forgotten about it after everything else. We were desperate to get the people off the *Lady Wexham*, but the boat was sinking and a group of greys was trying to ram us. I couldn't see any of us getting out of there alive, let alone saving anyone. Then two more greys appeared alongside us, and lay there in the water until the others backed off.'

'Were they residents?'

'Yes. A dozen or so greys stay on the west coast all year round – they're too old for the gruelling journey. When the herds arrive from the south, they make a big show of welcoming the old guard back into the fold. One of the two whales was an elderly grey that lives here. He definitely didn't want to hurt us – far from it. In fact, I think we owe those whales our lives.'

'Unbelievable. To think they *protected* you!'

'Tut, tut, Licia.' Anawak raised an eyebrow. 'You of all people projecting human intentions on a whale.'

'After what I saw three days ago I'm ready to believe anything.'

'I wouldn't say they actually *protected* us, but it seemed as though they kept the other whales at bay. They weren't keen on our attackers. All in all, we could reasonably infer that only migrants are affected. No matter which species we're dealing with, the residents appear harmless. They seem to know that the others are deranged.'

Delaware scratched her nose. 'It would fit. A large number of whales went missing in the middle of the Pacific on their way here from California. The aggressive orcas live in the middle of the ocean too.'

'Precisely. So whatever has caused the change in their behaviour, we'll find it in the deep blue sea, miles away from anywhere.'

'The question is, what?'

'We'll work it out,' said John Ford, who had materialised beside them. He pulled up a chair and sat down. 'The sooner the better – before the politicians and their perpetual phone calls drive me nuts.'

'I noticed something too,' said Delaware, as they were eating their dessert. 'I can see how the orcas might have enjoyed themselves, but it can't have been fun for the others.'

'What makes you say that?' asked Anawak.

'Well,' she said, through a mouthful of chocolate mousse, 'imagine how you'd feel if you kept running into something and trying to knock it over. Or flinging yourself on top of something with lots of hard edges and corners. The chances are, you'd hurt yourself.'

'She's right,' said Ford. 'Animals only hurt themselves for the survival of the species or to protect their young.' He removed his glasses and polished them. 'How about we let our imaginations run wild for a minute? What if the whole thing was a protest?'

'A protest against what?'

'Whaling.'

'Whales protesting against whaling?' exclaimed Delaware.

'Whalers have come under attack in the past,' said Ford, 'usually because they were hunting calves.'

Anawak shook his head. 'You can't seriously believe that.'

'It was just an idea.'

'Not a plausible one, though – it's not even proven that whales know what whaling's about.'

'You mean they don't know they're being hunted?' said Delaware. 'Crap!'

'I meant that they may not see a pattern,' Anawak retorted. 'Pilot whales always strand themselves on the same stretch of coastline. In the Faroe Islands whole herds are rounded up by fishermen and killed with metal gaffs. It's a bloodbath every time. Then there's Futo in Japan, where countless dolphins and porpoises are slaughtered each year. It's been going on for generations, so they must know what awaits them. But why go back for more?'

'It doesn't seem very smart,' agreed Ford. 'But we're still pumping greenhouse gases into the air and chopping down rainforests, even though we know we shouldn't. And that's not very clever either.'

Delaware frowned and scraped up the last of her chocolate mousse.

'It's true, though,' said Anawak.

'What?'

'Licia's point about the whales getting hurt when they launched themselves at the boats. I mean, if you decided to take out some humans, you'd find yourself a cosy niche with a good view, then point the gun and fire, making sure you didn't shoot yourself in the process.'

'Unless something affected your judgement.'

'Hypnosis?'

'Perhaps they were ill – or just confused. That's it! They're confused.'

'Or maybe they've been brainwashed.'

'Come on, guys, cut it out.'

They all fell silent, immersed in their thoughts. The background noise grew louder and snatches of conversation drifted over from neighbouring tables. The situation at sea still dominated the media and a strident voice was linking the attacks along the went coast to accidents in Asia. Some of the worst shipping disasters in decades had just occurred in the Malacca Strait and Japan. Everyone in the restaurant was speculating and hypothesising, their appetites undiminished.

'Suppose toxins are responsible,' said Anawak at last. 'PCBs and so on. What if something's driving them mad?'

'Mad with rage more likely.' Ford was fooling around again. 'They're up in arms about the Icelanders who want new whaling quotas, the Japanese who can't stop eating them, and the Norwegians who don't give a damn about the IWC. Christ, even the Makah want to hunt them again. Hey, there's our answer!' He grinned. 'They must have read it in the paper.'

'For someone who's head of a scientific think-tank,' said Anawak, 'you don't seem to be taking this seriously. You've got an academic reputation to keep up, remember.'

'The Makah?' echoed Delaware.

'The Makah are part of the Nuu-chah-nulth people,' said Ford. 'Indians from the west coast of Vancouver Island. They want to start whaling again. They've been campaigning for years for legal recognition.'

'No way! Are they crazy?'

'Your civilised outrage is all very commendable, Licia, but the Makah haven't hunted whales since 1928.' Anawak yawned. He could barely keep his eyes open. 'In any case, it wasn't them who pushed grey whales, blue whales and humpbacks to the brink of extinction. For the Makah it's a question of preserving their culture. They say that the art of traditional whaling will soon be forgotten.'

'They could always try shopping like everyone else.'

'I hope you're not spoiling Leon's noble plea for tolerance,' said Ford, refilling his glass.

Delaware stared at Anawak. Oh, no, he thought. He looked like an Indian, anyone could see that, but she was about to draw the wrong conclusions. He could hear her question gather steam. He'd be forced to explain himself and he hated doing that. If only Ford hadn't mentioned the Makah . . .

He caught the other man's eye.

'Let's talk about it some other time,' Ford said hastily. Before Delaware could argue, he went on, 'The toxins theory is something we should talk about with Oliviera, Fenwick or Rod Palm, but I don't buy it. The pollution stems from oil spills and chlorinated hydrocarbons. We know what that leads to: damaged immune systems, infection and premature death – but not madness.'

'I thought all the orcas on the west coast were supposed to be dead in thirty years?' Delaware piped up.

'Thirty to a hundred and twenty, if we don't do something about it. But it's not just the chemicals. The orcas are being deprived of their main prey, so they either die of poisoning or they're forced to find new waters. And because they're hunting in areas they're not familiar with, they get caught in nets. The odds are stacked against them.'

'Actually, forget the toxins theory,' said Ford. 'If it were just the orcas, I'd say you were on to something – but when orcas and humpbacks join forces like that . . . I don't think so, Leon.'

Anawak thought for a moment. 'You know my stance on whales,' he said softly. 'I'm usually the last person to read intentions into animal behaviour or to talk up a creature's intelligence. But . . . don't you have the feeling they wanted to get rid of us?'

He'd expected vehement protests, but Delaware nodded. 'Yes. Except the residents.'

'Because the residents haven't gone wherever the others have been or experienced whatever it is that has changed them. Those whales that sank the freighter . . . We'll find the answer out to sea.'

'Christ, Leon.' Ford gulped some wine. 'It's like a horror movie. Go forth and kill humanity.'

Anawak didn't reply.

That night, as he was lying awake in his Vancouver apartment, Anawak played with the idea of tagging a whale. The creatures were still in the grip of whatever had possessed them, so if he could fit one with a transmitter and a camera, maybe it would provide them with the answers they so desperately needed.

But how could he tag a rampaging humpback, when even the calmest of whales seldom stayed still?

And there was the problem of the skin.

Tagging a whale and tagging a seal were two entirely different propositions. Seals could be caught on land while they were resting. The tag's biologically degradable adhesive would stick to the fur and dry quickly. After a set period of time it was designed to fall off. Later in the year, when the animal moulted, the last traces of glue would disappear.

But whales and dolphins didn't have coats. It was hard to imagine anything smoother than the skin of an orca or a dolphin. It felt like a freshly peeled boiled egg, and was covered with a thin layer of gel that decreased water resistance and kept out bacteria. The top layer was continually being replaced. When the animal breached, it shed its skin in long thin strips, ridding itself of parasites and tags in the process. The skin of grey whales and humpbacks was scarcely any easier to deal with.

Anawak got out of bed and felt his way to the window. His apartment was in an old block with a view of Granville Island. He gazed out at the cityscape, glittering in the night, and started to tick off the options. There were tricks he could use, of course. American scientists had taken to attaching tags and depth-time recorders with suction cups. With the help of a long pole, they could affix them to nearby whales or bow-riding dolphins without leaving the boat. But even suction cups only withstood the force of the water for a few hours at most. Other scientists had tried bolting the tags to the dorsal fins. Either way, he'd still have to approach the whale without being sunk.

Maybe he could stun it . . .

No, that was far too complicated. In any case, they'd need more than just a tag. They'd need pictures as well. Satellite telemetry plus video footage.

Then he had an idea. It would require a good marksman . . .

Anawak rushed to his desk, logged on to the web and started calling up sites. Another possibility had occurred to him, a technique he'd read about. He rummaged through a drawer, sifting through piles of notes, until he found the web address of the Underwater Robotics and Application Laboratory in Tokyo.

They'd have to cobble two methods together. The emergency committee would have to come up with the money, but right now it was prepared to do anything that might solve the problem.

He didn't fall asleep until the early hours of the morning. His last thoughts were devoted to the *Barrier Queen* and Clive Roberts. That was another mystery. The MD had never called back, although Anawak had chased him several times. He hoped Inglewood had at least sent the samples to Nanaimo.

Where was that report?

He wouldn't let them fob him off.

There was so much to do.

I'll have to get up and make myself a list, he thought.

Then he dozed off, utterly exhausted.

20 April

Lyons, France

Bernard Roche felt a pang of guilt for not having dealt sooner with the water samples. But how was he to know that a lobster could kill a man – and that it might kill more?

Jean Jérôme, the *chef-poissonnier* at Troisgros in Roanne, had failed to emerge from his coma and had died twenty-four hours after the contaminated Brittany lobster had exploded in his face. It was still impossible to say what had caused his death, but one thing was clear: his body had never recovered from a severe toxic shock. There was no real proof that the lobster – or, indeed, the substance found inside it – was to blame, but it certainly looked that way. Other members of the kitchen staff had been taken ill, but the worst affected was the apprentice who had put the mysterious substance in the jar. They were all suffering from dizziness, nausea and migraines, and had difficulty concentrating. It was no laughing matter, especially for Troisgros, which was in danger of closing its doors. But what really worried Roche was the number of people who had consulted their doctors with similar symptoms since Jérôme had died. Their cases weren't nearly as critical, but Roche feared the worst, especially now he knew what had happened to the water in which the lobsters had been stored.

For the sake of the restaurant, the press had tried to play down the story, but the incident was reported, and Roche was hearing rumours from elsewhere in the country. Troisgros was not the only establishment to have been affected. In Paris several people had died, allegedly from shellfish poisoning – but Roche suspected there was more to it than that. He'd heard similar news from Le Havre, Cherbourg, Caen, Rennes and Brest. One of his assistants had agreed to look into it and a story emerged in which the Brittany lobster played an unsavoury role. In the end Roche put aside his other work and devoted himself to analysing the water samples.

In no time he found yet more unusual chemicals, whose presence he couldn't explain. He needed fresh samples urgently, so he made enquiries in all the relevant cities. Regrettably no one had thought to preserve the substance. The lobster in Roanne was the only one to have exploded, but elsewhere people talked about unpalatable lobsters that they'd been forced to throw away or lobsters that had been leaking before they were cooked. If only everyone had had the presence of mind demonstrated by the apprentice at Troisgros, but Roche knew that fishermen, wholesalers and kitchen staff couldn't be expected to respond like scientists. For the time being he had to rely on speculation. In his opinion the lobster had been inhabited by two separate organisms. First there was the jelly, which had disintegrated, leaving nothing behind.

Then there was the other organism, which was very much alive and in plentiful supply. Something about it seemed ominously familiar.

He stared into his microscope.

Thousands of transparent spheres were rolling around like fast-moving tennis balls. If he was right in his assumption, inside each sphere was a coiled pedunculus – a kind of feeding tube.

Were these the organisms that had killed Jean Jérôme?

Roche reached for a sterilised needle and jabbed it into the tip of his thumb, producing a tiny droplet of blood. With great care he injected it on to the sample on the slide and looked through the lens. Magnified to seven hundred times their normal size, Roche's blood cells looked like ruby-red petals, each one packed with haemoglobin. They mingled with the water. The transparent spheres sprang into action, unfurling their tubes and falling on the human protoplasm. The peduncles entered the cells like miniature cannulae and the sinister micro-organisms took on a reddish hue as they sucked the blood cells dry. The assault on Roche's blood intensified: as soon as one cell was empty, the micro-organisms turned to the next, swelling all the time, as Roche had expected. Each could hold the content of ten cells. In less than forty-five minutes their work would be done. He watched, fascinated: the process was much faster than he'd believed.

Fifteen minutes later the frenzy was over.

Roche sat motionless next to his microscope. Then he noted, 'Query *Pfiesteria piscicida.*'

'Query' stood for any lingering doubt, but Roche was sure that the agent responsible for the sickness and death had been identified. What truly unnerved him was that it seemed more monstrous than *Pfiesteria piscicida*, which made it a double superlative, since *Pfiesteria* was already thought to be a monster – albeit of just one hundredth of a millimetre in diameter. It was one of the smallest predators on Earth – and one of the deadliest.

Pfiesteria piscicida was a vampire.

He'd read a lot about it. Scientists' acquaintance with it was relatively new. It had started in the 1980s with the death of fifty fish in a laboratory at North Carolina State University. At first there was no apparent problem with the water in which they were swimming: the aquarium was swarming with tiny unicellular organisms, but that was nothing new. So the water was changed and new fish brought in. They didn't last a day. Something was exterminating them with incredible efficiency. It killed goldfish, striped bass and Nile tilapia in hours, sometimes minutes. Time and again the researchers watched as the fish twitched, then died an agonising death. Again and again the mysterious micro-organisms appeared out of nowhere, then vanished just as fast.

Slowly they pieced things together. A botanist identified the sinister organism as a new species of dinoflagellate. Numerous types had been categorised, some of which were harmless, but others had been exposed as living sacs of poison. They were known to have contaminated mussel farms, and certain species were responsible for the feared 'red tides' that turned the water red or brown. Shellfish were affected too. But these dinoflagellates were nothing compared to the newly discovered organisms.

Pfiesteria piscicida was different from other members of its order. It actively attacked. In some ways it resembled a tick – not for its appearance, but for its extraordinary patience. It lurked in the sediment of riverbeds or seas, seemingly lifeless. Each individual was encased in a protective cyst, and survived for years without food. All it took was a shower of secretions from a passing shoal of fish to trigger its appetite.

A lightning attack ensued. The algae cast aside their cysts, rising through the water in billions. Each cell was driven by a pair of flagella, one of which rotated like a propeller while the other steered. As they settled on a fish, the cells released their toxins, paralysing the creature's nervous system and burning coin-sized holes in its skin. The peduncles shot into the wounds and sucked the lifeblood from the victim. Then they sank back to the seabed and retreated into their casing.

By and large, toxic algae were seen as normal, like poisonous toadstools in a wood. People had known of the phenomenon since Biblical times. Exodus contained a description that seemed to fit perfectly with the red tides: 'And all the water in the Nile turned into blood. And the fish in the Nile died, and the Nile stank, so that the Egyptians could not drink water from the Nile . . .' For a fish to be killed by a single-cell organism was clearly nothing new. But the method and the degree of brutality were. It seemed as though the planet's water had been seized by a terrible sickness and, for the moment, the most spectacular symptoms bore the name *Pfiesteria piscicida*. Toxins were killing marine life, coral was succumbing to new forms of disease, and beds of algae had become infected. But all of this was merely a reflection of the true state of the seas, which were suffering the consequences of overfishing, chemical dumping, the urbanisation of coastal regions, and global warming. No one could agree on whether the invasion of killer algae was a new development or a periodic occurrence, but there was no doubt that it was spreading across the globe to an unprecedented extent and that Nature had once again demonstrated her infinite creativity in producing new species. In Europe people congratulated themselves that *Pfiesteria* had not yet reached their shores, but thousands of fish were dying off the coast of Norway, and the Norwegian salmon farmers were facing financial ruin. This time the killer organism was *Chrysochromulina polylepis*, a kind of baby brother to *Pfiesteria*. No one dared speculate what might come next.

And now *Pfiesteria piscicida* was attacking Brittany lobsters.

But was it really *Pfiesteria piscicida*?

Roche was plagued by doubt. The organism was far more aggressive than he'd expected The real puzzle, though, was how the lobsters had survived. Had the algae come from inside them? Was it mixed with the jelly-like substance? The jelly had decomposed on contact with air; he was sure it was a distinct phenomenon, something new. But had the algae and the jelly both been hidden in the lobster? And, if so, what had happened to its flesh?

Was it really a lobster at all?

Roche was stumped. But of one thing he was certain: the substance, whatever it might be, had entered Roanne's drinking water.

22 April

Continental Margin, Norwegian Sea

At sea the world was just water and sky, with little to tell them apart. There were no visual markers, which meant that on clear days, the sense of infinity could suck you into space, and when it was wet, you never knew if you were on the surface or somewhere beneath it. Even hardened sailors found the monotony of constant rain depressing. The horizon dimmed as dark waves merged with banks of thick grey cloud, robbing the universe of light, shape and hope in a vision of desolation.

At least in the North Sea and the Norwegian Sea, the numerous oil platforms provided landmarks, although from the edge of the continental shelf, where the *Sonne* had been sailing for the past two days, most were too distant to see. Now even the few rigs in view were shrouded in drizzle. The vessel and everyone on it was soaked. A clammy cold crept under their waterproof jackets and overalls. Plump raindrops would have been preferable to the never-ending trickle of water, which seemed to rise off the sea as well as fall from the sky. It was one of the most unpleasant days that Johanson could remember. He pulled his hood down over his head and made for the stern, where the technicians were raising a CTD probe. Bohrmann caught up with him half-way there.

'Seeing worms in your sleep yet?' asked Johanson.

'Not quite' said the marine geologist. 'What about you?'

'Oh, I'm pretending I'm in a film. It's kind of reassuring.'

'Good idea. Who's directing?'

'Hitchcock.'

'The deep-sea version of *The Birds*.' Bohrmann smiled wryly. 'Sounds intriguing . . . Ah, here we go!'

He hurried towards the stern. A circular cage of rods rose over the side of the boat, hanging from the arm of a crane. Its top half was covered with an array of PVC bottles, containing samples of water from varying depths. Johanson watched as the probe was hauled on board and the bottles removed. Then Stone, Hvistendahl and Lund appeared. Stone hurried over to him. 'What's Bohrmann saying?' he asked.

'Not much.'

Stone's belligerence had given way to dejection. The *Sonne* had been following the continental slope south-west to a point above the tip of Scotland, taking readings from the water, while a sledge-mounted video system filmed from below. It was a bulky piece of equipment, like a steel shelf packed with gadgets, that was towed along the seabed. It was equipped with sensors, a floodlight and an electronic eye that took pictures and sent them via optical cable to the control lab on board.

The *Thorvaldson*'s footage came courtesy of the more up-to-date Victor. The Norwegian research vessel was following the slope in a north-easterly direction towards Tromsø, taking readings from the Norwegian Sea. Both vessels had set out from the site where the unit was to be built and were now on course to meet. Two days remained until their rendezvous, by which time they would have navigated the slope from Norway to the North Sea and recharted it from scratch. It had been Bohrmann and Skaugen's decision to survey the area as though they were exploring new territory – which, as it turned out, was what the waters had become. Since Bohrmann had announced the first findings, nothing seemed certain any more.

The news had come in the previous morning, before the sledge's first pictures arrived on the screen. They'd lowered the CTD probe at first light, when the air was damp and cold. Johanson had tried to ignore the sinking sensation in his stomach as the boat pitched over the waves. The first samples were whisked away to the geophysical lab where they underwent analysis. Shortly afterwards, Bohrmann had summoned the team to the seminar room on the main deck. They sat at the polished wooden table, waiting expectantly and clasping mugs of coffee.

Bohrmann's eyes were fixed on a sheet of paper. 'The first results are available already,' he said. 'They're not representative, more a snapshot of what's going on.' His eyes lingered briefly on Johanson, then shifted to Hvistendahl. 'Is everyone acquainted with methane plumes?'

A young man from Hvistendahl's team shook his head.

'They form when free methane gas escapes from the seabed,' explained Bohrmann. 'The gas dissolves in the water, is pulled along by the current and rises to the surface. Usually plumes are found at plate boundaries, where one plate pushes beneath the other, causing sediment compaction and uplift. As a result, fluids and gases escape. It's a well-known phenomenon.' He cleared his throat. 'Areas of high pressure like this are common in the Pacific but not in the Atlantic – and certainly not around Norway. The boundaries here are mainly passive. But this morning we picked up a highly concentrated methane plume. It doesn't figure in any of the earlier data.'

'What level of concentration?' asked Stone.

'Worryingly high – on a par with the levels we found off the coast of Oregon. And that was in a fault zone.'

'Right.' Stone smoothed the frown from his forehead. 'Well, to my knowledge, methane is always leaking into the water around here. I've seen it countless times. It's a well-known fact that somewhere on the seabed gas is constantly escaping. There's always a reason for it. I don't see any call for panic.'

'I don't think you quite understand.'

'Now, look here,' said Stone, 'all I care about is whether or not there's cause for concern. If you ask me, there isn't. We're wasting our time.'

Bohrmann smiled amicably. 'The slope in this region, Dr Stone, especially to the north of here, is held together by methane hydrates. The layers of hydrate are sixty to a hundred metres deep – that's a hefty wedge of ice keeping the seabed in place. However, we're aware of vertical breaks in the layers. Gas has been escaping through them for years. Theoretically, it shouldn't happen. At such high pressure and low temperature, it should freeze on the seabed. But it doesn't. That's the gas you were referring to. We can live with it – we can even decide to ignore it. But we shouldn't let our graphs and tables make us feel complacent. I'm telling you, the concentration of free gas in the water is excessively high.'

'But is it really a seep?' asked Lund. 'Is the gas in the water escaping from the crust, or is it coming from—'

'Dissociated hydrates?' Bohrmann hesitated. 'That's the big question. If hydrates are dissociating, it means the parameters have changed.'

'And is that the case here?' said Lund.

'There are only two parameters affecting the stability of the hydrates: pressure and temperature. But we haven't detected any rise in water temperature, and the sea level hasn't altered.'

'What did I tell you?' said Stone. 'You're worrying about a problem that doesn't exist. So far, we've only seen one sample.' He looked to the others for support. 'A single bloody sample.'

Bohrmann nodded. 'You're right, Dr Stone. We're speculating. But we'll find out the truth. That's why we're here.'

Johanson and Lund had headed for the canteen. 'Stone's getting on my nerves,' Johanson said. 'He's always trying to undermine the tests. What's wrong with him? It's his bloody project.'

They refilled their coffee mugs and took them out on deck.

'What do you make of the results?' asked Lund.

'They're preliminary findings, not results.'

'All right. What do you make of the preliminary findings?'

'I don't know.'

'Go on, you can tell me.'

'Bohrmann's the expert.'

'But, in your opinion, is there a link with the worms?'

Johanson thought back to his conversation with Olsen. 'I don't have an opinion,' he said cautiously, 'not yet. It's too early to say.' He blew on his coffee. The sky stretched gloomily above them. 'But I'd rather be at home than here.'

That had been yesterday.

While the new set of samples was analysed, Johanson took himself off to the radio room tucked behind the bridge. From there he could contact anyone in the world via satellite. For the past few days he'd been working on a database of contacts, firing off queries to institutes and scientists, presenting the whole thing as of scholarly interest. The first replies had been disappointing. No one else had found the worm. A few hours previously, he'd extended the search to some of the other expeditions currently at sea. Now he pulled up a chair, squeezed his laptop in among the radio equipment and logged into his account. The only interesting email was from Olsen, who'd written to say that the jellyfish invasion in South America and Australia was now out of hand:

I don't know whether you're listening to the news out there, but there was an update last night on the jellies. They're swarming all over the coast. According to the newsreaders' oracle, they're specifically targeting well-populated areas. Which is nonsense, of course. Apart from that, there's been another pile-up – a couple of container ships near Japan. Boats are still disappearing, but they've managed to record a few distress calls. No concrete details about British Columbia yet, but plenty of rumour. Supposedly the whales are getting their own back and have started hunting humans. Not everything you hear is true, though, thank God. Well, that's all the good news from Trondheim for now. Don't drown.

'Thanks a bunch,' Johanson muttered tetchily.

But Olsen was right: they didn't listen to the news enough here. Being on a research vessel was like falling out of space and time. People always said they were too busy to listen to the news when in fact they just wanted to be rid of politicians, cities and wars for a while. But after a month or two at sea, they'd start to long for civilisation, with its technology, hierarchies, cinemas, fast-food outlets and floors that didn't rise and sink.

Johanson realised he wasn't concentrating. His mind was on the images that had filled the monitors for the past two days.

Worms.

The continental slope was crawling with them. The mats and seams of frozen methane had disappeared under millions of seething bodies trying to burrow into the ice. They could no longer treat it as a localised invasion. They were witnessing a full-scale attack that ran the length of the Norwegian coast.

As if someone had magicked them there . . .

Surely other people had come across something similar.

Why did he get the feeling that the worms and the jellies were connected?

It was a crazy idea.

And yet, he thought suddenly, the craziness looked like the start of something new.

This was only the beginning.

He called up the CNN homepage to check out Olsen's news.

Lund walked in, set a mug of black tea in front of him and smiled conspiratorially. Their trip to the lake had forged a bond between them, a kind of unspoken solidarity.

The smell of freshly brewed Earl Grey filled the air. 'I didn't know they had it on board,' said Johanson.

'They don't,' she said. 'You bring it with you, if you know someone who likes it.'

Johanson raised his eyebrows. 'That was thoughtful of you. What favour were you hoping to extract from me this time?'

'A thank-you would be nice.'

'Thank you.'

She glanced at the laptop. 'Any luck?'

'Zilch. How're they getting on with the samples?'

'No idea. I had other things to deal with.'

'Such as?'

'Looking after Hvistendahl's assistant.'

'What's wrong with him?'

'He's feeding the fish.' She shrugged. 'You know, mustering his bag.'

Johanson chuckled. Lund liked using sailors' slang. Research vessels brought together two different worlds: scientists and seamen. The two groups tiptoed around each other, doing their best to be accommodating, adjusting to their different ways of talking and living, and getting used to each other's quirks. After a while, they'd know they were in safe water – but until then there was a respectful distance between them, which they bridged with jokes. 'Mustering a bag' was the crew's euphemism for a newcomer's seasickness.

'You threw up the first time too,' said Johanson.

'And you didn't?'

'No.'

'Huh.'

'It's true!' Johanson put his hand on his heart. 'I'm a good sailor.'

Lund dug out a scrap of paper with a scribbled email address. 'Next up is a trip to Greenland. One of Bohrmann's contacts is working out there.'

'Lukas Bauer?'

'You know him?'

Johanson nodded slowly. 'There was a conference a few years back in Oslo. He gave a lecture. I think he was working on currents.'

'He's an engineer. He designs all kinds of things – oceanographic equipment, pressurised tanks. Bohrmann said he even had a hand in the deep-sea simulation chamber.'

'And now he's in the Greenland Sea.'

'He's been there for weeks,' said Lund. 'You're right about his interest in currents, though. He's collecting data there. Another candidate for interrogation in your quest for the worm.'

Johanson hadn't come across the expedition in his earlier research.

The Greenland Sea ... Weren't there methane deposits there too?
'How's Skaugen getting on?' he asked.

'Slowly,' Lund told him. 'He's been gagged.'

'By the board?'

'Statoil's a state-controlled company. Need I say more?'

'So, he won't learn anything new,' said Johanson.

Lund sighed. 'The others aren't stupid, you know. They'll notice if
someone's trying to pump them for information without giving anything
in return. And, anyway, they've got their own code of silence.'

'That's what I told you.'

'Oh, if only I had your brains.'

There was the sound of footsteps outside, then one of Hvistendahl's
team poked his head round the door. 'Meeting in the conference room,'
he said.

'When?'

'Now. We've got the results.'

Johanson and Lund exchanged a glance. Deep down they already
knew the truth. Johanson closed the lid of the laptop, and they followed
the man to the main deck below.

Bohrmann stood at the table, leaning forward on his knuckles.

'So far we've found the same state of affairs all along the slope,' he said.
'The sea is saturated with methane. Our readings concur with those from
the *Thorvaldson*. There are a few variations, but the basic picture's the
same.' He paused. 'I don't want to beat about the bush. Something has
started to destabilise large sections of the hydrates.'

No one stirred. No one spoke.

Then the Statoil team all started talking at once.

'What are you saying?'

'So the hydrates are dissociating. I thought you said worms can't
destabilise the ice!'

'Is the water getting warmer? Because if it isn't . . .'

'But what happens if—'

'OK!' Bohrmann gestured for everyone to be quiet. 'That's the
situation. I still don't believe the worms are capable of causing serious
damage. However, we shouldn't forget that the incidence of the worms
coincides time-wise with the breakdown of the hydrates.'

'Very helpful,' muttered Stone.

'Do we know how advanced the process is?' asked Lund.

'We've studied the data from the *Thorvaldson*'s expedition a few weeks ago,' said Bohrmann. He was trying to sound reassuring. 'That was when you first discovered the worms. The readings were normal then. They must have started rising since.'

'So what's the deal?' asked Stone. 'Is it getting warmer down there or isn't it?'

'It's not. The stability field is unchanged. The fact that methane's escaping must be due to processes occurring deep in the sediment. Deeper, in any case, than the worms could burrow.'

'What makes you so sure?'

'We've already proved—' Bohrmann broke off. 'With the help of Dr Johanson we've already proved that these creatures can't survive without oxygen. They can only burrow a few metres deep.'

'All you've proved is what happens in a tank,' said Stone, disparagingly. He seemed to have selected Bohrmann as his new arch-enemy.

'If the water isn't getting warmer, then maybe the seabed is,' suggested Johanson.

'Volcanic activity?'

'It's just an idea.'

'Well, it makes sense – but not in this region.'

'Can the dissociated methane get into the water?'

'Not in sufficient quantities, no. For that the worms would need to reach a gas pocket, or be capable of melting hydrates.'

'But they can't possibly have reached a gas pocket,' Stone insisted stubbornly.

'No, like I said—'

'I know exactly what you said. Now it's your turn to listen to me. Each one of those worms is radiating heat, the same as any living creature does. And the warmth they're creating is melting the ice. It only melts a few centimetres on the surface, but it's enough to—'

'The body temperature of a deep-sea creature matches that of its environment,' said Bohrmann, smoothly.

'But, even so, if—'

'Clifford.' Hvistendahl placed a restraining hand on Stone's arm. It looked like a friendly gesture, but Johanson sensed it was a warning. 'Why don't we wait for the next set of readings?'

'Bugger that!'

'You're not helping, Cliff. Drop it.'

There was silence again.

'What happens if the methane keeps escaping?' asked Lund.

'There are various possible scenarios,' said Bohrmann. 'Methane fields have been known to disappear. The hydrates can dissociate within a year. That could be what's happening here, and it's conceivable that the worms have triggered the process. If that's the case, large quantities of methane will be released into the air above Norway.'

'Just like fifty-five million years ago?'

'No, there isn't enough for that, and we really shouldn't speculate. Having said that, I don't see how the process can continue without a decrease in pressure or an increase in temperature, and there's no evidence of either. In the coming hours we'll send down the video grab. Maybe that'll clear things up. That's all for the moment.' And with that he left the room.

Johanson emailed Lukas Bauer in the Greenland Sea. He was starting to feel like a biological detective. Have you seen this worm? Can you describe it to me? Could you pick it out from five other specimens in an identity parade? Is this the worm that stole the lady's handbag? All relevant information will be noted in evidence.

First he wrote a few friendly lines about their meeting in Oslo, then enquired whether Bauer had detected unusually high levels of methane in the area where he was working. He'd deliberately left this point out of his other emails.

When he returned to the deck, he saw the video sledge dangling from the arm of the crane while Bohrmann's geologists inspected it. They were hauling it in. Not far away, outside the repair room, a group of sailors sat talking on a large chest filled with scrubbing brushes. Over the years, it had established itself as a lookout and living room combined. Draped in a threadbare cloth, it was known by some as 'the couch'. It was the ideal place to sit and poke fun at the unsteady movements of the research assistants and scientists, but there were no jokes today. The tension was affecting the sailors too, most of whom knew what the scientists were up to: there was something wrong with the continental slope, and everyone was worried.

From now on everything had to happen as quickly as possible. Bohrmann had asked for the ship to be slowed right down so that they could investigate a site he'd identified using data from the multi-beam echo-sounder and the video-sledge. Beneath the *Sonne* there was a large field of hydrates. Taking a sample meant releasing a monster that appeared to belong to the Jurassic age of deep-sea science. The video-guided grab – a pair of metal jaws weighing several tonnes – was scarcely the most sophisticated piece of technology. In fact, it was probably the crudest, yet most reliable way of wresting a chunk of history from the seabed. Opening its maw, it bit into the sediment, and tore out hundreds of kilos of silt, ice, fauna and stone, which it then deposited at the feet of the scientists. The sailors had named it T. Rex. As it dangled from the A-frame, jaws agape, ready to plunge into the sea, the similarity was striking. A monster in the service of science.

However, as with all monsters, the grab was powerful, but lumbering and dumb. Inside its jaws were floodlights and a camera, enabling its handlers to see where it was heading before they let it off the leash. That was impressive. But the dim-witted T. Rex was incapable of stealth. No matter how carefully you let it down – and there were limits, since it took force to penetrate the seabed – it created a bow wave that frightened away most creatures. As soon as their finely tuned senses detected it, worms, fish, crabs and any other organism capable of rapid movement escaped before it pounced. Even the more up-to-date instruments gave advance warning. The bitter words of a frustrated American scientist summed up the situation: 'There's plenty of life down there. The trouble is, it sees us coming and steps aside.'

The grab was lowered from the A-frame. Johanson wiped the rain off his face and entered the control room. A crewman was operating the joystick that moved the grab up and down. He'd spent the last few hours steering the video sledge, but he still seemed focused. He had to be: staring at hazy pictures of the seabed for hours on end had a hypnotic effect. A moment of carelessness, and a piece of equipment that cost as much as a brand new Ferrari would be lost for ever.

Inside the control room the light had been dimmed. The monitors cast a pale glow on the watching faces of the people sitting and standing in front of them. The rest of the world no longer existed: there was only the seabed, whose surface they studied like a coded landscape in which every detail held a message.

Outside the cable slid over the winch.

The water looked as though it was going to spurt out from the monitors, then the metal jaws passed through a shower of plankton. The screens turned blue-green, then green, then black. Bright dots – tiny crabs, krill and other creatures – sped away like comets. Watching the voyage of the grab was like seeing the opening credits for the original *Star Trek* series, but now there was no music. It was deathly silent in the lab. The figures on the depth gauge were changing all the time. Then the seabed flashed into view, looking like a lunar landscape. The cable stopped.

'Minus seven hundred and fourteen metres,' said the man at the controls.

Bohrmann leaned over. 'Don't do anything yet.' The monitor filled with mussels. They liked to colonise hydrates, but now they were hidden by a mass of wriggling bodies. Johanson had a strange feeling that the worms weren't just burrowing in the ice but were eating the mussels in their shells. He could see jaws shooting out and ripping off chunks of mussel flesh, which vanished into the tube-like bodies. There was no sign of the white methane ice under the siege of worms, but they all knew it was there. Bubbles rose up from the bottom, with tiny shimmering fragments – splinters of hydrate.

'Now,' said Bohrmann.

The seabed rushed towards the screen. For a moment it looked as though the worms had risen to welcome the camera, then it went black. The iron jaws buried themselves in the methane and clamped shut.

'What the hell . . . ?' gasped the man at the controls.

The numbers on the panel were turning rapidly. They stopped briefly, then sped on.

'The grab's broken through. It's sinking.'

Hvistendahl pushed his way to the front. 'What's going on?'

'This can't be happening! There's no resistance!'

'Pull it up!' screamed Bohrmann. 'Quickly!'

The man jerked back the joystick. The counter stopped, and the numbers started to decrease. The grab rose upwards, jaws clenched. Its external cameras showed the vast hole that had opened. Swollen bubbles surged from inside it. Then a stream of gas gushed out, hitting the grab and engulfing it. Everything vanished in a seething whirlpool.

A few hundred kilometres north of the *Sonne*, Karen Weaver had just stopped counting. Fifty laps of the deck. She kept running up and down, careful not to get in the scientists' way. For once she was pleased that Lukas Bauer didn't have time to talk to her. She needed exercise, but the possibilities on board a research vessel were limited. She'd tried the gym, but the three exercise machines had driven her crazy so she was running instead. Up and down the deck – past Bauer's assistants, who were working on float number five, and past the crew, who were hard at work or standing in groups, watching her, suggestive comments on the tip of their tongues.

Puffs of white breath rose from her parted lips.

Up and down the deck.

She'd have to work on her stamina. It was her weak point. She made up for it in strength, though. Her body was like a sculpture: impressive muscles and glowing skin, with an intricately tattooed falcon between her shoulders. Yet Karen Weaver had none of the bulk of a female body-builder – in fact, she'd have made a perfect model, if only she had been a little taller and her shoulders less broad. A small, sinewy panther, she lived on adrenaline. Her favoured habitat was the edge of the abyss.

In this case, the drop was 3.5 kilometres. The *Juno* was sailing over the Greenland abyssal plain, an expanse of seabed beneath the Fram Strait, from which the cold Arctic water flowed south. The basin between Iceland, Greenland, the north Norwegian coast and Svalbard was one of the planet's two main water pumps. Bauer was interested in what was going on there – and so was Karen Weaver, on behalf of her readers.

Bauer beckoned for her to join him. With his bald head, huge glasses and pointed white beard, he resembled the cliché of an absent-minded professor more than any other scientist she'd met. He was sixty and already slightly hunched, but indefatigably energetic. Weaver respected people like Lukas Bauer. There was something almost superhuman about them. She admired them for their will.

'Take a look at this, Karen,' he called, in a clear voice. 'Incredible, isn't it? The water here is surging downwards at a rate of seventeen million cubic metres per second. *Seventeen million!*' He beamed at her. 'That's twenty times the volume of all the rivers on Earth.'

'Dr Bauer.' Weaver placed a hand on his arm. 'That's the fourth time you've told me that.'

Bauer blinked. 'Really?'

'And you still haven't got round to explaining how the floats work. You're going to have to talk me through this, if you want me to do your PR.'

'Yes . . . Well, the floats – that is to say, the autonomous drifting profilers – they . . . Oh, but you know all that already, don't you? It's why you're here.'

'I'm here to make computer simulations of the currents, so people can see where the floats are going, remember?'

'Of course. Dear me, you can't possibly know . . . You don't even . . . Well, I'm a bit short of time, unfortunately. There's so much to do. Why don't you watch for a while and then—'

'Dr Bauer! Not again. You promised to tell me how they work.'

'Certainly. You see, in my articles, I—'

'Dr Bauer, I've read your articles but I trained as a scientist and even I barely understood them. Popular science is supposed to be entertaining. You've got to write in a language that everyone can follow.'

Bauer looked hurt. 'My articles are easy to follow.'

'For you, maybe – and the two dozen others working in your field.'

'Now, that's not true. If you read the text carefully—'

'No, Dr Bauer, I want *you* to explain it.'

Bauer frowned, then smiled indulgently. 'If any of my students were to talk . . . But they wouldn't dare. They're not allowed to interrupt me – I leave that to myself.' He raised his skinny shoulders in a shrug. 'But that's life, I suppose. I can't refuse you anything. I like you, Karen. You're a . . . Well . . . You remind me of . . . Oh, never mind. Let's take a look at this float.'

'And when we've done that, we'll talk about your findings. I'm getting enquiries.'

'Where from?'

'Magazines, TV programmes, institutes.'

'How interesting.'

'It's not interesting, it's normal – publicity's logical outcome. Do you even see the point of PR?'

Bauer grinned mischievously. 'Perhaps you'd like to explain it?'

'With pleasure – it'd only be the tenth time. But first, you're going to talk to *me*.'

'But that won't do,' said Bauer, in agitation. 'We've got floats to lower, and then I mustn't forget to—'

'Keep your word and talk to me,' Weaver said sternly.

'But, Karen, my dear, you're not the only one getting enquiries. I'm writing to scientists all over the world. They ask the most outlandish things. One just emailed to ask about a worm. Imagine that – a worm! He even wanted to know if the methane concentration was higher than usual, which, of course, it is . . . But how was he to know? I'll have to—'

'I can deal with all that. I'll be your co-conspirator.'

'As soon as I've—'

'That's if you really like me.'

Bauer's eyes widened. 'I see. So that's how it is, is it?' His drooping shoulders shook with muffled laughter. 'That's exactly why I never married. It's constant blackmail. All right, then, I'll try harder, I promise. Now, let's get going. Come along!'

Weaver followed him. The drifting profiler was dangling from the boom above the grey surface of the water. It was several metres long and protected by a supporting frame. More than half of it was made up of a thin, shiny tube, with two spherical glass containers at the top.

Bauer rubbed his hands together. His down jacket was several sizes too big for him and made him look like an exotic Arctic bird. 'We drop the float into the water,' he said, 'and it bobs along with the current. Think of it as an enormous particle of water. There's a vertical drop beneath us – the water is sinking, as I said . . . Well, you can't see it sinking, of course, but it's sinking nonetheless. Now, how can I explain this?'

'Try avoiding jargon.'

Right. It's actually very simple. The point is, water doesn't always weigh the same. Warm fresh water is light. Salt water is usually heavier than fresh water. The saltier, the heavier, in fact – there's the added weight of the salt to consider. On the other hand, cold water is heavier than warm water because its density is higher. So water gets heavier as it cools.'

'Which means the heaviest water is always cold and salty,' Weaver put in.

'Very good.' Bauer seemed pleased with her. 'So, water doesn't just flow in currents: it moves up and down in layers. The coldest currents are on the seabed, warm currents are on the surface, and deep-water currents are somewhere in between. Of course, warm currents can travel thousands of kilometres on the surface before they reach colder regions where they start to cool down. And as the water cools—'

'It gets heavier.'

'Indeed. So, the water gets heavier, which makes it start to sink. Surface currents turn into deep-water currents, or even bottom-water currents, and the flow direction changes. It's exactly the same the other way round, but the water goes upwards, from cold to warm. That way, all the major currents are continuously in motion. And because they're all interconnected, there's a constant process of exchange.'

The float was lowered to the surface of the water. Bauer hurried to the railings and leaned over, gesturing impatiently for Weaver to follow. 'What are you waiting for? Come on, you'll get a better view from here.'

She stood next to him. Eyes glowing, Bauer was gazing out to sea. 'Imagine if there were floats in every single current!' he said. 'Just think how much we'd learn.'

'What are the glass spheres for?'

'They keep the float suspended in the current. There are weights at the other end too, but the key to the whole thing is the cylinder in the middle. All the equipment is in there. Electronic controls, microprocessor, power supply. And it's neutrally buoyant. Isn't that amazing? Neutrally buoyant!'

'I'd find it even more amazing if you told me what that meant.'

'Oh, yes. Of course . . .' Bauer tugged as his beard. 'Well, we had to think about how we could get the floats to— You see, it's like this: fluids are practically incompressible. That is to say, you can't compress them any further. Water is the key exception. You can't, er, squish it much, but it's possible. So that's what we do. We compress the water in the cylinder so there's always the same *amount* in there, but sometimes it's heavier and sometimes it's lighter. So the weight of the float can be varied without changing the volume.'

'Ingenious.'

'It certainly is! It can even be programmed to do it by itself – compressing, decompressing, compressing, decompressing, sinking down and rising up – without us lifting a finger. Clever, don't you think?'

Weaver watched the tube sink into the sea.

'It means the float can travel independently for months and even years, transmitting radio signals, while we track it and reconstruct the speed and the movement of the current. Off it goes.'

The drifting profiler had vanished.

'And where's it heading now?'

'That's the question.'

Weaver looked at him intently.

Bauer sighed resignedly. 'I know, I know. You want to hear about my work. Goodness me, you're tenacious . . . Very well, we can talk in the lab. But the findings are unsettling, to say the least.'

'People love to be unsettled. Haven't you heard? Jellyfish invasions, scientific anomalies, people going missing and sinking ships. You'll be in good company.'

'Do you think so?' Bauer shook his head. 'You're probably right. I'll never understand what publicity's about. I'm only a scientist.'

Continental Margin, Norwegian Sea

'Shit,' Stone groaned. 'It's a blow-out.'

On board the *Sonne*, everyone in the control room stared at the screen. All hell seemed to have broken loose on the seabed.

Bohrmann spoke into the microphone: 'We've got to get out of here. Full speed ahead. Tell the bridge.'

Lund ran out of the room, and Johanson chased after her. Suddenly everyone on board was running. Johanson skidded on to the working deck, where sailors and technicians were shifting cold storage tanks under Lund's lead. The winch cable quivered as the *Sonne* accelerated.

Lund saw him and ran over.

'What was that?' he yelled.

'We hit a gas pocket. Look!'

She pulled him across to the railings. Hvistendahl, Stone and Bohrmann joined them. Two Statoil technicians had gone to the far end of the stern and were standing under the A-frame, peering down.

Bohrmann was gazing at the taut cable. 'What the hell is he playing at?' he hissed. 'Why hasn't the idiot stopped the winch?' He hurried back inside.

At that moment the sea started to bubble madly and white lumps shot to the surface. The *Sonne* had reached full speed. There was a clunking sound as the video-grab's cable tightened. Someone raced across the deck towards the A-frame, waving wildly. 'Get away from there!' he yelled to the pair from Statoil. 'Run!'

Johanson recognised him. It was the first officer, the Sheep-dog, as the seamen called him. Hvistendahl swivelled round, gesticulating. Then everything happened at once. A foaming, hissing geyser engulfed them. Johanson saw the outline of the video-grab rising through the surface of the water. An unbearable stench of sulphur filled their nostrils. The *Sonne*'s stern sank, then the metal jaws shot sideways and sped through the air like a gigantic swing towards the topside. The second of the two technicians saw it coming and flung himself down. The other man froze, then took a tentative step backwards and stumbled.

The Sheep-dog sprang forward to pull him to the ground, but the metal jaws crashed into the man and sent him flying into the air. He fell back to the deck, skidded along the planks and lay still.

'Oh, God,' Lund gasped. 'Please, no.'

She and Johanson ran towards the motionless body. The first officer and other crew were kneeling beside him. The Sheep-dog glanced up. 'Don't touch him.'

'But I—' Lund began.

'Call the doctor.'

Johanson knew that Lund couldn't bear to be inactive. Sure enough, she walked towards the grab. It had nearly stopped swinging. Mud dripped from it on to the deck. 'Open it!' she shouted. 'Get whatever's left into the tanks.'

Johanson looked down at the sea. Bubbles of stinking methane were still fizzing up to the surface, but gradually subsiding. The *Sonne* was charging away from the scene. The last chunks of methane ice floated to the surface and disintegrated.

With a loud creak the grab opened its jaws, releasing hundreds of kilos of ice and sediment. Sailors and scientists crowded around it, trying to plunge the hydrate into tanks of liquid nitrogen. Johanson felt useless. He went over to Bohrmann to help collect the lumps. The deck was covered with small, bristly bodies. Some were twitching and writhing, but the majority hadn't survived the rapid ascent. The sudden change of temperature and pressure had killed them.

Johanson picked up a clump and examined it closely. Dark channels criss-crossed the ice, strewn with the corpses of worms. He turned it back and forth until its crackling and cracking reminded him that it needed to be conserved. Some of the other chunks were even more riddled with holes, but the real work of destruction had clearly taken place beneath the tunnelling. Crater-like breaches gaped in the ice, covered with slimy trails.

Johanson forgot about the storage tanks. He rubbed the slime between his fingers. It looked like the remains of bacterial colonies. Bacterial mats were found on the surface of hydrates: what were they doing inside the ice?

A few seconds later the lump had disappeared. He looked round. A muddy puddle covered the working deck. The man who had been hit by the grab was gone. Lund, Hvistendahl and Stone had also left the deck, but Bohrmann was leaning on the rails. Johnson joined him. 'What happened down there?'

Bohrmann ran his hand over his eyes. 'We had a blow-out. The grab penetrated more than twenty metres through the hydrates and gas came up. Did you see the enormous bubble on the screen?'

'Yes. How thick is the ice here?'

'Seventy to eighty metres minimum – at least it was.'

'So, the ice was cracked.'

'That's how it seems. We need to find out as soon as possible whether it's an isolated case.'

'You want to take more samples?'

'Of course,' said Bohrmann, testily. 'That accident should never have happened. The guy at the winch raised the grab when we were going full-speed. He should have stopped it.' He looked at Johanson. 'Did you notice anything unusual when the gas shot up?'

'It felt to me as though the boat dropped in the water.'

'That's what I thought. The methane lowered the surface tension.'

'Do you mean we could have sunk?'

'It's hard to say. Have you heard of the Witch's Hole?'

'No.'

'Ten years ago a fisherman set sail and never came back. His last radio transmission said he was going to make coffee. A research expedition found the wreck fifty nautical miles from the coast in an unusually deep pockmark on the North Sea floor. Sailors call the area the Witch's Hole. The wreck showed no sign of damage and was sitting upright on the seabed. It seemed to have sunk like a stone – as though it had suddenly stopped floating.'

'Sounds like the Bermuda Triangle.'

'You've put your finger on it. That's exactly the theory – the only one that stands up to scrutiny, anyway. Big blow-outs occur regularly in the area between Bermuda, Florida and Costa Rica. Sometimes there's enough gas in the atmosphere to set fire to the turbines of a plane. All it takes is a methane blow-out several times bigger than the one we just experienced and the water density falls so low that a ship sinks to the bottom.' Bohrmann pointed to the storage tanks. 'We'll get this stuff back to Kiel, run some tests and get answers about what's going on – and we *will* get answers, I promise you. We've already lost one man because of this mess.'

'Is he . . . ?'

'He was killed on impact. For the next sample we'll use the autoclave corer instead of the grab. It's safer that way. We have to find out what's happening. I'm not prepared to stand by and watch as subsea units are constructed willy-nilly all over the seabed.' Bohrmann moved away from the rails. 'But we're used to that, I guess. We're always trying to explain what's going on in the world but no one listens. And then what happens? Research is in the hands of big business. The only reason that you and I are on this boat is because Statoil found a worm. The state can't pay for science, so the money comes from industry. There's no science for the sake of enquiry, these days. This worm isn't an object of scholarly interest. It's a problem they want us to get rid of. Science always has to have an immediate application – and, preferably, one that gives industry free rein. But maybe those worms aren't really the problem. Has anyone stopped to consider that? The real problem could be elsewhere, and by solving the worm dilemma, we might make things worse.'

A few nautical miles to the north-east they excavated a dozen cores from the sediment without further incident. The autoclave corer, a five-metre-long tube clad in a plastic mantle with pipes round the outside, drew the sample from the seabed like a giant syringe. Before it was pulled back up, the tube was hermetically sealed by valves, preserving a perfect specimen of a different universe: sediment, ice, mud, an intact section of the top layer of hydrates, pore-water and even local organisms, unperturbed by the change, since temperature and pressure were maintained. Bohrmann had the sealed tubes stored upright in the walk-in freezer so as not to disturb the layers of life preserved within. The cores couldn't be analysed on board: they needed the deep-sea simulation chamber to provide the right conditions. Until then they had to content themselves with analysing pore-water and staring at the screen.

Despite the drama of the past hours, even the unchanging view of the worm-covered hydrates seemed tedious. No one felt like talking. In the faint light of the monitors everyone looked pale – Bohrmann and his scientists, the Statoil team and the crew. The dead man had joined the core samples in the freezer. The rendezvous with the *Thorvaldson* at the site of the planned unit had been cancelled so that they could head straight for Kristiansund, where they would hand over the body and transport the samples to the nearby airport. Johanson moved between his cabin and the control room, sorting through the responses to his survey. The worm wasn't described in any of the existing literature. No one had seen it. Some of his correspondents put forward the view that it was a Mexican ice worm, but that didn't take him any closer to the truth.

Three nautical miles from Kristiansund, Johanson received a reply from Lukas Bauer. The first positive reply – though positive wasn't really the word.

He read the message and chewed his lip thoughtfully.

Contacting the oil companies was Skaugen's business. Johanson was only expected to approach institutes and scientists with no obvious link to oil. But Bohrmann had said something after the accident that showed things in a different light.

The state can't pay for science, so the money comes from industry.

Could any institute, these days, afford to be truly independent?

If Bohrmann was right that research was kept alive by industry, there was scarcely an institute that wasn't working for a company. They raised their funds through sponsorship – it was either that or risk closing their labs. Even Geomar would soon be in receipt of a grant from the energy firm Ruhrgas, which had endowed a new chair in hydrates. Corporate sponsorship sounded tempting, but sooner or later companies expected the research they funded to be converted into profit.

Johanson returned to Bauer's message.

His own approach had been all wrong. Instead of contacting as many people as possible, he should have scrutinised the unofficial links between science and business. While Skaugen broached the topic in the companies' boardrooms, he could question the scientists they worked with. Sooner or later someone was bound to talk.

The problem lay in trying to unravel the connections.

But it wasn't a problem. It was just a lot of hard work.

He stood up and went to find Lund.

24 April

Anawak rocked impatiently on the balls of his feet. He rolled forwards on to his toes, then back on to his heels. Toes, heels. Toes, heels. It was early morning and the sky was lit in vivid shades of azure; a day straight out of a holiday brochure.

At the end of the wooden jetty, a seaplane was waiting. Its white fuselage shone in the deep blue water of the lagoon, contours creased by rippling waves. It was one of the legendary DHC-2 Beavers first manufactured by the Canadian firm De Havilland over fifty years ago. Engineers had yet to come up with a better design, so the planes were still in use. Beavers had made it to both poles: they were dependable, robust and safe.

Perfect for what Anawak was planning.

He glanced across at the red-and-white terminal. Tofino airbase was situated a few minutes out of town by car, and had little in common with other airports. It was reminiscent of a traditional hunting or fishing village, just a few low-lying timber buildings on the edge of a sweeping bay, fringed by forested hills with mountaintops in the distance. His eyes swept the road leading from the main highway through the towering trees towards the lagoon. Any moment now the others would arrive.

His brow furrowed as he listened to the voice on his mobile. 'But that was two weeks ago,' he said. 'Two weeks without Mr Roberts being available, even though he specifically asked me to keep him informed.'

The secretary reminded him that Mr Roberts was a very busy man.

'So am I,' barked Anawak. He stood still and tried to sound friendlier. 'Look, the situation on the west coast is spiralling out of control. There are clear parallels between the trouble we've got here and the incident at Inglewood. I'm sure Mr Roberts would agree.'

There was a short pause. 'What parallels would those be?'

'Well, whales, of course. I should have thought that was obvious.'

'The *Barrier Queen* suffered damage to her rudder.'

'Sure. But the tugs were attacked.'

'One tug was sunk, if that's what you mean,' said the woman, politely uninterested. 'No one's said anything about whales, but I'll tell Mr Roberts you called.'

'Tell him it's in his interest.'

'He'll call you in the next few weeks.'

'*Weeks?*'

'Mr Roberts is out of town.'

What the hell is going on? thought Anawak. He tried again.

'Mr Roberts also promised to send further samples of organic matter from the *Barrier Queen* to the lab in Nanaimo. Now, please don't tell me you know nothing about that either. I've seen the infestation. I even took a bunch of mussels from the hull.'

'Mr Roberts would have told me if—'

'The lab needs those samples!'

'Mr Roberts will deal with it on his return.'

'It'll be too late by then! Oh, forget it. I'll call back later.'

Annoyed, he jammed his mobile into his pocket. Shoemaker was trundling down the access road in his Land Cruiser, then turned into the car park in front of the terminal. Anawak headed over to him. 'You're not exactly a model of punctuality, are you?' he called grumpily.

'For heaven's sake, Leon! We're ten minutes late.' Shoemaker came to meet him with Delaware in tow. A young powerfully built black guy with dark glasses and a shaved head followed behind. 'Loosen up, will you? We had to wait for Danny.'

Anawak shook hands with the other man, who flashed him a smile. He was a marksman in the Canadian army and had been placed at Anawak's disposal. He was carrying his weapon, a state-of-the-art, high-precision crossbow. 'Nice island you got here,' he drawled. A piece of gum travelled across his mouth as he spoke. 'You need me to take care of something?'

'Didn't they tell you?' asked Anawak.

'Sure – that I needed my bow to shoot at some whales. Kind of surprised me, though. Never thought it was legal.'

'It isn't. I'll tell you all about it in the plane. Let's go.'

'Hang on.' Shoemaker held up a newspaper. 'Have you seen this?'

Anawak scanned the headline. '"The Hero of Tofino"?'

'Greywolf sure knows how to sell himself. He's all modest in the interview, but see what he says further down. It'll make you want to puke.'

'"... did my duty as a Canadian citizen, that's all,"' muttered Anawak. '"Sure, we could have died – but I had to do something to make up for the damage caused by irresponsible whale-watching. My organisation has been warning for years of the dangerous levels of stress that whale-watchers inflict on the animals, which leads them to behave in unpredictable ways." My God, he's crazy!'

'Read on.'

'"Davie's Whaling Station can't be accused of dishonesty, but it hasn't been completely honest either. In dressing up a money-making tourist business as an environmental research project, the whale-watchers are as bad as the Japanese, whose flotillas prey on endangered species in the Arctic. The Japanese also talk about the scientific value of their activities, even though in 2002 over four hundred tonnes of whale meat went on sale as a delicacy in wholesale markets. DNA tests traced the flesh to the objects of their so-called scientific study."'

Anawak lowered the paper. 'That bastard.'

'But he's right, isn't he?' Delaware demanded. 'The Japanese really are spouting all that crap about their research. At least, that's what I heard.'

'Of course he's right,' snorted Anawak. 'That's why it's so damn cunning. He's trying to implicate us too.'

'God knows what he hopes to achieve by it,' said Shoemaker.

'He's just attention-seeking.'

'Well, he . . .' Delaware's hands waved in gesture of appeasement. 'I guess, he is a hero in a way.'

Anawak glared at her. 'Oh, really?'

'Without him people would have died. It's not fair of him to lay into you like that but he was brave and he—'

'Greywolf isn't brave,' growled Shoemaker. 'That shit only ever does anything for effect. But he's screwed up big-time now. The Makah won't like it. I can't imagine they'll thank their self-elected blood-brother for his impassioned speech against whaling – right, Leon?'

Anawak didn't reply.

Danny pushed his gum from one cheek to the other. 'All set?' he said.

At that moment the pilot called to them through the open door of the plane, and waved. Anawak knew what that meant. Ford had made contact. It was time. Instead of responding to Shoemaker's comment he put a hand on his shoulder. 'Could you do me a favour when you're back at the Station?'

'Sure,' he said. 'I'm not exactly rushed off my feet.'

'Find out whether there's been anything in the papers over the last few weeks about the *Barrier Queen* and her accident. Maybe check the Internet too – and the TV.'

'Why?'

'I've a feeling it wasn't reported.'

'Uh-huh.'

'Well, I can't remember hearing anything about it, can you?'

Shoemaker squinted up at the sun. 'No. Just some vague stuff about shipping accidents in Asia. But that's not to say it wasn't mentioned. I haven't read the papers since things kicked off round here. But it's a good point. Come to think of it, not much has been said about the whole damn mess.'

'Exactly,' said Anawak.

As the plane took off, Anawak turned to Danny. 'Your job is to fire the tag into the blubber. The whale won't feel a thing. Scientists have been trying for years to get tags to stick to whaleskin, but a biologist in Kiel came up with the solution – a crossbow with tags and time-depth recorders that are fitted to the darts. The tip pierces the fat, and the whale carries the device for a few weeks. It doesn't even know it's there.'

Danny looked at him. 'A biologist from Kiel?'

'You don't think it'll work?'

'Oh, sure. Just seems to me he should have asked the whale about it hurtin'. Jeez, you gotta be pretty darned accurate. How you gonna know it won't go deeper than the fat?'

'They used pork to test the darts and kept going until they knew exactly how far the tips would penetrate. It's all a question of math.'

'I'll be darned,' said Danny. His eyebrows appeared above his dark glasses.

'What happens if you fire it at a human?' Delaware piped up from the seat behind them. 'Would the dart go in part-way?'

Anawak turned to face her.

'Yes, – but deep enough to kill you.'

The DHC-2 banked, the lagoon glittering beneath them.

'It wasn't the only option available,' said Anawak, 'but the key thing was to make sure we could track the whale over a significant period. The crossbow method seemed the most reliable. The tag records information on heartbeat, body temperature, water temperature, depth, speed and other variables. Fitting the whale with a camera is more of a problem.'

'Why not use the crossbow?' asked Danny. 'Save yourself a lot of hassle.'

'There'd be no means of ensuring which way up the camera would land. In any case, I'd like to *see* the whale. I want to be able to watch it, and that's only possible if the camera is further away and not mounted on top of it.'

'Which is why we're deploying a URA,' explained Delaware. 'It's a new type of robot from Japan.'

Anawak's lips twitched. From the way Delaware talked, you'd think she'd invented it.

'What robot?' Danny looked around.

'We didn't bring it.'

The plane was out of the lagoon, flying close to the swell. The water off Vancouver Island was usually full of pleasure-boats, Zodiacs and kayaks, but no one was brave enough to venture out now. In the distance a few freighters and ferries passed, too big for the whales to be a problem. The coastal waters were deserted, apart from a single mighty ship. The plane headed away from the rugged coastline, straight for it.

'The URA is on the *Whistler* – down there,' said Anawak. 'First we need to find and tag our whale, then the robot gets its turn.'

John Ford stood aft on the *Whistler*, shielding his eyes with his hand. He saw the DHC-2 approaching at speed. A few seconds later the plane swooped over the boat and swung round in a gentle curve.

He held his radio to his mouth and called Anawak on a tap-proof frequency. A host of channels was reserved for military and scientific purposes. 'Leon? Everything OK?'

'Receiving you, John. Where did you see them?'

'To the north-west, less than two hundred metres from the ship. Five minutes ago we had a cluster of sightings, but they're keeping their distance. There must be eight or ten. We identified two. One was involved in the attack on the *Lady Wexham*; the other sank a fishing trawler last week in Ucluelet.'

'They haven't tried to attack?'

'We're too big for them.'

'How are they behaving as a group?'

'No signs of aggression.'

'Good. They're probably one big gang, but let's stick to the whales we've identified.'

Ford watched as the DHC-2 disappeared into the distance, then banked and flew back in a loop. His gaze shifted to the *Whistler*'s bridge. The deep-sea rescue tug was sixty-three metres long, fifteen metres wide and belonged to a private company in Vancouver. With a bollard pull of 160 tonnes, she was one of the strongest tugs in the world, and far too heavy to be threatened by a whale. Ford guessed that a breaching humpback would cause the ship to rock but no more.

He still felt uneasy, though. At first the whales had attacked anything that floated, but now they seemed to know what they could and couldn't harm. Boats had been attacked by fin and sperm whales, as well as the omnipresent orcas, greys and humpbacks. And there had been a marked refinement in technique. Ford was certain that they wouldn't attack the tug – and that was what disturbed him. The idea that the whales were suffering from a rabies-like illness didn't fit with their growing ability to size up their targets. There was intelligence in their behaviour, and he wasn't sure how they'd react to the robot.

He radioed the bridge. 'We're off,' he said.

The DHC-2 circled overhead.

They'd started looking actively for the whales as soon as they'd identified some of the aggressors on the camcorder footage. For three days the tug had cruised up and down the coast and that morning they'd finally struck lucky. Among a pack of greys they'd seen two flukes they recognised from the pictures.

Ford wasn't sure if they stood any chance of getting to the truth in time. He shuddered when he thought of the increasingly militant calls from fishing unions and shipping lines who didn't like the scientists' non-aggression policy. They wanted military action – a few dead whales to show the herds what was what and to scare them into staying away from humans. The scheme was as dangerous as it was naïve, but it had found plenty of supporters. The whales were doing an excellent job of gambling away all the credit that environmentalists and animal-rights groups had worked so hard to raise for them. For the time being, the emergency committee was still taking the line that killing the whales wouldn't resolve anything since no one knew what was causing their behaviour. The only option was to fight the symptoms, or so they'd said. Ford didn't know what the government was planning in the long-run. Either way, there were clear indications that individual fishermen and rogue whalers were preparing to take matters into their own hands. While no one could offer a solution to the problem, everyone was certain that the others were wrong. It was fertile ground for mavericks.

Ford glanced at the robot in the stern. He was curious to see what it could do. They'd got it from Japan remarkably quickly and with almost no red tape. The technology was only a few years old. According to the Japanese, it was designed for research, not whaling, but few were convinced. Western environmentalists saw the three-metre-long cylindrical device, studded with sensors and highly sensitive cameras, as an invention from hell, intended to hunt down entire herds of whales as soon as the moratorium on whaling was rescinded. After the URA had tracked and followed humpbacks among the Japanese Kerama Islands, it had found favour at an international symposium for marine mammals in Vancouver. But the distrust remained. It was no secret that Japan had systematically bought the support of poorer countries with the aim of putting an end to the 1986 whaling moratorium: the government had called its machinations and horse-trading 'legitimate diplomacy', while providing the bulk of the funding to the University of Tokyo, to which the inventors of the robot, Tamaki Ura and his Underwater Robotics and Application Laboratory team, belonged.

'Maybe today you'll do something worthwhile,' said Ford, softly, to the robot. 'Salvage your reputation.'

The URA glinted in the sun. Ford went over to the rails and gazed out at the ocean. Finding the whales was easier from the plane, but identification had to be done from the ship. After a while a group of greys appeared, surfacing one after another and ploughing through the waves.

The voice of the lookout sounded through the radio. 'Look back and to the right. There's Lucy.'

Ford spun and raised his binoculars in time to see a ragged, slate-grey fluke disappear beneath the water.

Lucy was one of the two whales they'd identified. A fine specimen of a grey, measuring a full fourteen metres, she'd hurled herself against the

Lady Wexham. For all he knew, she might have been responsible for splitting the vessel's thin hull.

'ID authenticated,' said Ford. 'Leon?' He squinted up at the sun and saw the plane dip towards the place where the flukes had been seen. 'Well, I guess this is it,' he said to himself. 'Happy hunting.'

From their vantage-point a hundred metres above the water, even the enormous tug looked like a toy, though the whales seemed to grow by comparison. Anawak watched a pod of greys swimming just under the surface, moving leisurely and peacefully. Refracted rays of sunlight danced on their colossal backs. The full length of each whale was visible through the water. They were only a quarter the size of the *Whistler*, but they still seemed absurdly large. 'We need to get closer,' he said.

The DHC-2 descended. They flew over the pod towards the spot where Lucy had dived. Anawak hoped to God that she hadn't gone in search of food, since that would mean a lengthy wait. With any luck the water would be too deep for her here. Greys, like humpbacks, had their own feeding technique: they dived to the seabed and grazed on the sediment, rolling on to their sides and vacuuming up the bottom-dwelling organisms, such as small crustaceans, plankton and, their favourites, tube worms. The seabed near Vancouver Island was furrowed with trenches from their feeding orgies, but the giant greys seldom ventured into deeper water.

'OK, folks, prepare for the breeze,' said the pilot. 'Danny?'

The marksman grinned at them, opened the side door and pushed it back. A wave of cold air rushed into the cabin and swept through their hair. Delaware reached back and passed Danny his crossbow.

'You won't have much time,' shouted Anawak, above the roar of the wind and the engine. 'Once Lucy surfaces, there'll be just seconds to get the tag in place.'

'No sweat,' said Danny. Holding the crossbow in his right hand, he pushed himself out of his seat until he was practically sitting in the linkage under the wing. 'You gotta get me nice and close.'

Delaware shook her head. 'I can't watch.'

'Why not?' said Anawak.

'It's never going to work. He'll end up in the water – I just know it.'

'Don't you fret,' laughed the pilot. 'These boys can do anything.'

The plane shot forwards, low to the water, on a level with the

223

Whistler's bridge. They flashed past the spot where Lucy had been seen. Nothing.

'Circle,' shouted Anawak, 'and keep it tight. Lucy will come up pretty much where she went down.'

The DHC-2 banked sharply. Suddenly the sea rose towards them. Danny was balanced like a monkey in the linkage, one hand on the door frame, the other on the crossbow, ready to shoot. In the water below, the silhouette of a whale emerged through the waves. Then a grey shiny hump broke the surface.

'Yee-hah!' screeched Danny.

'Leon!' Ford was on the radio. 'It's the wrong whale. Lucy's ahead of us, starboard side.'

'Hell,' muttered Anawak. He'd miscalculated. Evidently Lucy was determined not to play the game. 'Don't shoot, Danny.'

The plane stopped circling and sank even lower. The waves rushed beneath them. They were approaching aft of the tug. For a moment it looked as though they were going to fly straight into the *Whistler*'s bridge, but the pilot adjusted their course and they passed to the side of the hulking vessel. A little way ahead Lucy dived again, showing her flukes. This time Anawak recognised her from the distinctive grooves in her tail. 'Slow down,' he said.

The pilot reduced speed, but they were still travelling too fast. We should have taken a chopper, thought Anawak. Now they were going to overshoot their target. They'd have to wheel round, in the hope that the whale hadn't vanished again.

But Lucy's enormous body glistened in the sunlight.

'Turn round, then down.'

The pilot nodded. 'Just don't throw up on me,' he said.

The plane tilted abruptly. A vertical wall of water sparkled through the open door, terrifyingly close. Delaware screamed, but Danny cheered and waved his crossbow.

Anawak saw everything in slow motion. He'd never imagined you could turn a plane like a pair of compasses, with the wing tip acting as the point. The plane moved in a perfect semi-circle, tilted again without warning, and then they were upright.

Engine roaring, they headed for the whale, towards the oncoming *Whistler*.

*   *   *

Ford watched with bated breath as the plane returned from its daredevil manoeuvre. Its skids were almost touching the water. He vaguely remembered that one of Tofino Air's pilots used to fly for the Canadian Air Force. Now he knew which one.

The cylindrical case of the URA was dangling from the *Whistler*'s stern crane on the other side of the railings, ready to be released as soon as the marksman fired the tag. The whale's grey back was clearly visible. The animal and the plane sped towards each other. Ford spotted Danny crouching under the wing and prayed that a single shot would do the job.

Lucy's hump surged through the waves.

Danny raised the crossbow, closed one eye, and bent his finger. Concentrating hard, he pulled the trigger. He was the only one to hear the soft hiss as the tagged dart left the bow at 250 kilometres per hour and whizzed past his ear. A fraction of a second later the metal barb penetrated the blubber and embedded itself in the whale. Lucy arched her back and dived.

'We got it!' Anawak hollered into the radio.

Ford gave the sign. The crane released the robot, which splashed into the waves. As it made contact with water, a sensor was triggered and the electrical motor leaped into action. Plunging deeper, it homed in on the disappearing whale. Seconds later, it was out of sight.

Ford punched the air. 'Yes!'

The DHC-2 thundered above the *Whistler*. Through the doorway Danny raised the crossbow and whooped triumphantly.

'We did it!'

'Nice work!'

'One shot and – Christ, did you see it? Unbelievable!'

Inside the plane everyone was talking at once. Danny started to pull himself into the cabin and Anawak stretched out a hand to help him. Then something loomed out of the water.

A grey whale leaped into the air. The massive body shot towards them.

It was right in their flight path.

'Take her up!' screamed Anawak.

The motors gave an agonised roar and Danny fell backwards as the plane jerked up. Anawak caught a glimpse of an enormous head covered with scars, an eye, a mouth. A powerful blow rocked the cabin. A torn mess of broken linkage replaced the right wing where Danny had been standing. Delaware screamed. The pilot was screaming. Anawak screamed. The sea rushed towards them.

Something hit him in the face. Icy-cold.

There was a droning in his ears. The high-pitched screech of tearing metal.

Spray.

Dark green.

Then nothing.

Fifty metres further down, the onboard computer steadied the cylindrical body of the URA. The robot began to track the nearest whale. Not far away, barely visible in the gloom, others came into view. The electronic eye of the URA took note of them, but the computer wasn't interested in optical data. Other functions took precedence.

The URA's optical sensors were impressive, but its real strength lay in its audio capacity. This was where the inventor had shown a flash of true genius. The robot's acoustic technology allowed it to follow a whale for ten to twelve hours without losing track of it, no matter where it went.

The URA's hydrophones – four sensitive underwater microphones – didn't merely capture the whalesong: they could also determine its source. The hydrophones were fixed at intervals around the robot's case, so that when a whale emitted its high-pitched whistle, they received the sound sequentially. No human ear could register the tiny time delays, the rise and fall in volume: only a computer was capable of that. The noise arrived first at the hydrophone nearest to the whale, then reached the other three in turn.

From there, the computer created a virtual space, assigning co-ordinates to the source of the sound. Gradually the digital environment filled with positioning data on the whales. The co-ordinates shifted constantly as the animals moved. Now the inside of the computer held a virtual copy of the pod.

Lucy was also emitting sounds as she disappeared into the depths. The computer's memory contained extensive information on specific noises made by whales and different species of fish, as well as the calls of individual animals. The URA searched its electronic catalogue for Lucy but couldn't find her. It automatically created a new entry for the sounds coming from her co-ordinates and compared them to other groups of co-ordinates, classifying all the surrounding animals as greys and accelerating to two knots to get closer.

Having located and identified the whales, the robot began its optical analysis, which was every bit as thorough as the acoustic diagnosis. Fluke patterns and shapes were stored in its memory, as well as fins, flippers and other identifying features of various whales. This time the computer was in luck. The electronic eye scanned the flukes pounding through the water ahead and identified one of the tails as Lucy's. The URA had been programmed with extensive data on individual whales that had been involved in the attacks. Now it knew which animal was the focus of its attention and changed course by a few degrees.

Whalesong allowed the animals to keep in contact with each other over distances of more than a hundred nautical miles. Sound waves moved through the water five times faster than they did in the air: Lucy could swim as fast as she liked and in any direction, but the robot would never lose her now.

26 April

The metal door slid open. Bohrmann's gaze travelled up the imposing walls of the deep-sea simulation chamber. It was a way of taming the ocean, albeit in miniature. Created by man from second-hand experience, the world inside it was an idealised copy of the real thing. People knew less about reality than they did about its substitutes. Children in America drew six-legged chickens because drumsticks came in packs of six, while adults drank milk from a carton, and recoiled at the sight of an udder. Their experience of the world was stunted, but it only fuelled their arrogance. Bohrmann was enthused by the simulator and the possibilities it offered, but imitating life rather than analysing it could make science blind. Understanding the planet was no longer enough for most people; they were intent on trying to change it. In the Disneyland of botched science, human intervention was forever being justified in new and disturbing ways.

He was struck by the same thought whenever he came here: they could never tell for sure what science might achieve, only what it should never have attempted – and no one wanted to hear about that.

Two days after the accident on the *Sonne*, Bohrmann was in Kiel. The sediment cores and cold-storage tanks had been sent express freight to the care of Erwin Suess. He and his team of geochemists and biologists had lost no time in examining the expedition's haul. By the time Bohrmann had returned to the institute, the tests had begun. For twenty-four hours they'd been working non-stop but now their efforts had been rewarded. The simulator seemed to have revealed the truth about the worms.

Suess was waiting for him at the control panel, with Heiko Sahling and Yvonne Mirbach, a molecular biologist specialising in deep-sea bacteria.

'We've put together a computer simulation,' said Suess, 'not that we need it – it's for everyone else.'

'So this isn't purely a Statoil problem, then,' said Bohrmann.

'No.'

Suess dragged the cursor towards an icon and clicked. A computer graphic appeared on the screen. It was a cross-section of a gas pocket covered with a layer of hydrates a hundred metres thick. Sahling pointed to a thin dark line on the surface. 'This layer represents the worms,' he said.

'We'll zoom in a bit,' said Suess.

The picture changed to show a close-up of the surface and the worms took shape. Suess carried on zooming until a single specimen was in view, a cartoon-like representation, with highlighted sections.

'Those red marks represent sulphur bacteria,' explained Mirbach. 'The blue ones stand for archaea.'

'Endo- and ectosymbionts,' muttered Bohrmann. 'One set colonises the inside, the other settles on the skin.'

'Right. It's a consortium. Different species of bacteria working in tandem.'

'The scientists who produced those reports for Johanson had realised that too,' said Suess. 'They wrote page after page on worms and symbiosis. But they drew the wrong conclusions. No one stopped to ask what the consortia were doing. All this time we've been working on the premise that the worms were destabilising the ice, even though we knew it was impossible. Now we know it wasn't them.'

'The worms are just transporters?' said Bohrmann.

'Right.' Suess clicked on another icon. 'Here's how you got your blow-out.'

The cartoon worm began to move. The pincer-like jaws sprang open, and it burrowed into the ice.

'Now watch this.'

Bohrmann stared at the picture as Suess zoomed closer. Tiny organisms became visible, boring into the ice. Then, all of a sudden—

'Oh, my God,' said Bohrmann.

No one breathed.

'If the same thing's happening along the length of the slope . . .' said Sahling.

'Which it is,' said Bohrmann dully. 'It's happening everywhere simultaneously, as far as we can tell. We should have figured this out on the *Sonne*. The hydrates were dripping with bacterial slime.'

He wasn't surprised by what he had seen. He'd hoped his fears would prove unfounded, but the truth was worse than he'd imagined. Assuming it was true . . .

'Each individual process is an established phenomenon,' Suess was saying. 'It's the combined effect that's new. When you isolate the details, we've seen it all before. But put it together, and it's obvious why the hydrates would dissociate.' He yawned. It seemed inappropriate to do so after what they'd witnessed, but none of them had slept for more than a day. 'What puzzles me is why the worms are there at all.'

'It beats me too,' said Bohrmann, 'and I've been thinking about it for weeks.'

'So who do we tell?' asked Sahling.

'Hmm.' Suess tapped his lip. 'It's confidential, right? We should tell Johanson first.'

'Why not go straight to Statoil?' said Sahling.

'No,' said Bohrmann, firmly. 'Definitely not.'

'Surely they wouldn't hush it up?'

'Johanson's our best option. From what I can tell, he's not on anyone's side. We should leave it to him to—'

'We don't have time to leave anything to anyone,' Sahling broke in. 'If the situation on the slope is even half as critical as the simulation suggests, the Norwegian government should be informed.'

'But you can't tell the Norwegians without informing all the other North Sea states.'

'So much the better – and there's Iceland too.'

'Hang on.' Suess flapped a hand to quieten them. 'This isn't some kind of crusade.'

'That's not the point.'

'Oh, but it is. So far, we've only got the simulation.'

'Sure, but—'

'No, he's right,' Bohrmann interrupted. 'We can't go putting the wind up people when we're not even sure ourselves. I mean, we know what's causing it, but as for the consequences – that's just speculation. All we can say right now is that vast quantities of methane are likely to escape.'

'You must be joking,' said Sahling. 'We know exactly what'll happen.'

Absentmindedly Bohrmann stroked his moustache, which had started to grow back. 'Let's say we go public. We make all the headlines – and then?'

'What would happen if the papers announced that a meteorite was going to hit the Earth?' asked Suess.

'Is that a valid comparison?'

'I'd say so.'

'I don't think it's for us to decide,' said Mirbach. 'Let's take this one step at a time. First, we'll tell Johanson. He's the one we've been dealing with and, from a scholarly viewpoint, it's his due.'

'Why?'

'He discovered the worms.'

'Actually, Statoil found them. But whatever. We tell Johanson, then what?'

'We get the governments on board.'

'We go public?'

'Why not? These days, everything's dealt with in the open. We're told about nuclear programmes in North Korea and Iran, as well as idiots releasing anthrax – not to mention BSE, swine fever and GM food. In France, dozens or maybe hundreds of people are dying because of contaminated shellfish – and they're not trying to keep it quiet, are they?'

'But if the public hears us talking about a Storegga Slide . . .' said Bohrmann.

'There's not enough evidence to be sure it's really that,' said Suess.

'The simulation demonstrates how rapidly dissociation occurs. I'd say that's all we need to know.'

'But it doesn't prove what happens.'

Bohrmann was about to argue, but he knew Suess was right. If they went public before their case was watertight, the oil lobby could dismiss the matter out of hand. Their theory would collapse. It was still too soon. 'All right,' he said. 'How long till we get a firm answer?'

Suess frowned. 'Another week, I'd say.'

'That's a bloody long time,' said Sahling.

'I'd say it's pretty damn fast,' Mirbach argued. 'You can spend months twiddling your thumbs for a taxonomy report on a worm, but we—'

'It's too long *in the circumstances*.'

'We've got no choice,' Suess decided. 'A false alarm won't do anyone any good. We've got to keep working on it.'

Bohrmann couldn't take his eyes off the screen. The simulation had finished, but it continued in his mind, and what he saw made him shudder.

29 April

Johanson entered Olsen's office. He closed the door and sat down on the other side of his desk. 'Is this a good time?'

Olsen grinned. 'I've left no stone unturned for you.'

'And what did you find?'

Olsen lowered his voice to a whisper. 'What do you want first? The monsters or the natural disasters?'

He was keeping him on tenterhooks. Johanson played along. 'Whichever you'd prefer.'

'Come to think of it,' Olsen looked at him slyly, 'isn't it time you were a bit more forthcoming?'

Johanson wondered again how much he could tell his colleague. The man was clearly dying of curiosity and, in his position, Johanson would want to know too. But within hours of Olsen finding out, the entire university would be buzzing.

He'd have to make something up. Olsen would think he was nuts, of course, but it was a risk he was willing to take.

'I'm thinking of being the first to come out with a theory,' he murmured.

'Namely?'

'That the anomalies aren't just coincidence. Those jellyfish, the boats that keep vanishing, people missing or dead . . . I realised there had to be a plan.'

Olsen looked blank.

'It's all connected.'

'What are you after? The Nobel Prize or a visit from the men in white coats?'

'Neither.'

Olsen stared at him. 'You're pulling my leg.'

'No.'

'Oh, come on. You're talking a[bout little] green men? *The X-Files*?'

'It's only a theory. But, there [...] of different phenomena happen[ing ...] coincidence to you?'

'I don't know.'

'There you go. You don't kn[ow ...]'

'What kind of connection di[d ...] Johanson made an evasive ge[sture.]'

'Very clever.' Olsen curled h[is ...]

'Just tell me what you've go[t ...]'

Olsen bent down to open a [...] 'My Internet pickings,' he said. 'You nearly had me with that non[sense] you were spouting.'

'What's the story?'

'The beaches in Central and South America are closed. No one's going into the water, and jellies are clogging the fishermen's nets. In Costa Rica, Chile and Peru, they're descending on the coastline in apocalyptic swarms. Portuguese men-of-war, plus a second species, very small, with extremely long, toxic tentacles. At first they thought they were box jellies, but now they suspect something else, perhaps a new species.'

Another new species, mused Johanson. First unidentifiable worms, now unidentifiable jellyfish . . .

'And the box jellyfish in Australia?'

'Similar problem.' Olsen riffled through his stack of paper. 'Increasing numbers. Fishing industry in chaos. Tourist industry on its knees . . .'

'What about the fish? Are they bothered by the jellies?'

'Too late – they've gone. The big shoals have abandoned the coastlines. Reports from fishing trawlers say they've left their normal range and headed out to sea.'

'But they won't find any food there. What's the official take on it?'

'All the affected areas have emergency committees,' said Olsen, 'but they won't tell you anything. I've tried.'

'So they're keeping the really bad stuff to themselves.'

'Quite likely.' Olsen pulled out a sheet of paper. 'Take a look at this. It's a list of stories that hit the press with a fanfare and haven't been heard of since. Jellies off the west coast of Africa. A probable jelly plague in Japan. Confirmation of a jelly invasion in the Philippines. People listed as

233

en not another peep. But that's nothing
ears now there's been talk of a particular kind
da. A microscopic killer. Targets animals and
possible to get rid of. Until recently it'd stuck to the
Atlantic, but now France is affected. It's not looking

hs?'

an bet on it. The French are fairly tight-lipped about it, but it
they found the algae in contaminated lobster. I printed out all the
stuff.'

He pushed one section of the documentation towards Johanson. 'Then we've got the disappearing boats. Some of the distress calls have been recorded, but they don't make any sense – they break off too early. Whatever happened to those vessels happened quickly.' Olsen waved another piece of paper at him. 'Three of the distress calls ended up on the web.'

'Go on.'

'The boats were attacked.'

'Attacked?'

'That's right.' Olsen rubbed his nose. 'Now there's a conspiracy theory for you. More grist to your mill, I suppose. The sea rises up and takes on mankind . . . About time too, after all the rubbish we've dumped in it. Not to mention the fish and the whales. Which reminds me, the last I heard was that ships in the east Pacific were being set upon by whales. Now everyone's too scared to venture out, apparently.'

'Does anyone know—'

'Of course not. No one knows anything. I tried bloody hard to get something for you. There was nothing on the collisions or the tankers either. A total news embargo. You're right about one thing: the minute anyone starts reporting the incidents, a veil of silence descends. Maybe this is *The X-Files*, after all.' Olsen frowned. 'In any case, there are too many jellyfish. Too much of everything, really – it's all happening in excess.'

'And no one knows why.'

'They're not rash enough to claim it's all interconnected if that's what you mean. They'll probably blame El Niño or global warming. There'll be a sudden interest in invasion biology, and all kinds of theories will be published.'

'The usual suspects, then.'

'Yes, but it makes no sense. Algae and jellies have been shipped around the world for years. It's not a new phenomenon.'

'Sure,' said Johanson. 'But that's what I'm suggesting. An invasion of box jellies is one thing, a worldwide outbreak of extraordinary phenomena is another.'

Olsen pressed his fingertips together. 'Well, if you really want to make connections. I don't think biological invasions are the right place to start. I'd go for behavioural anomalies. We're seeing attacks of a kind we've never seen before.'

'Did you come across any other new species?'

'Have you anything in mind?' asked Olsen, deliberately.

If I ask about worms, thought Johanson, he'll guess right away. 'Not really,' he said.

Olsen handed over the rest of the papers. 'So when are you planning to tell me whatever it is you're not prepared to say now?'

Johanson picked up the printouts and stood up. 'I'll buy you a drink someday.'

'Sure, you know, if I can ever find time.'

'Thanks, Knut.' Johanson stepped out into the corridor. Students streamed past from a lecture hall. Some were laughing and chatting, others more serious.

He stood still and watched them. Suddenly the idea of a master-plan didn't seem so far-fetched.

Greenland Sea, near Spitsbergen, Svalbard Archipelago

That night, in the moonlight, the ocean of ice looked so spectacularly beautiful that the crew came out on deck. Lukas Bauer missed it: sitting in his cabin, bent over his work, he was searching for a needle in a haystack – but the haystack was the size of two seas.

Karen Weaver had helped him enormously, but two days ago she'd disembarked in Longyearbyen, the capital of Spitsbergen, to pursue her research there. She led a turbulent life, thought Bauer, whose own was scarcely more ordered. Since starting out in journalism, she had specialised in marine-related topics. As far as Bauer could tell, she had chosen her career because it allowed her to visit the world's most inhospitable places. Weaver loved extremes, unlike Bauer, who hated them but was so committed to his work that he was prepared to give up comfort for the sake of understanding. It was the same for many scientists: people took them for adventurers, but adventure was the price they paid for knowledge.

Bauer missed comfy armchairs, trees, birds and German beer. Now he missed Weaver. He'd grown fond of the determined young woman, and he'd begun to see the point of what she did. Getting the public interested in your work meant using a vocabulary that wasn't a hundred per cent accurate, but that everyone could follow. Weaver had made him realise that all his work on the Gulf Stream would be lost on people if he couldn't explain how the current started or where it flowed. At first he hadn't believed her. Just as he'd refused to believe that no one had heard of drifting profilers, until Weaver had convinced him that they were too new and specialised. But not knowing about the Gulf Stream? Weren't children taught anything at school?

Weaver was right that his work needed public exposure: he could broadcast his anxiety and put pressure on the culprits.

And Bauer was worried.

The source of his troubles lay in the Gulf of Mexico, where temperate surface water flowed from Africa along the coast of South America. Warmed by the sun in the Caribbean basin, it continued northwards, an inviting stream of salty water that remained on the surface because of its heat. The Gulf Stream, Europe's mobile heater, wound its way north, carrying a billion megawatts of warmth, equivalent in energy to 250,000 nuclear power stations. It travelled as far as Newfoundland where it mingled with the cold waters of the Labrador Current and dispersed. Some pinched off to form eddies, swirling rings of warm water that meandered northwards as the North Atlantic Drift. Prevailing westerlies saw to it that plenty evaporated, conferring ample rain on Europe and causing the water's salinity to soar. Dubbed the Norwegian Current, the water continued along the coast of Norway through the North Atlantic, staying warm enough to allow ships to dock in south-west Spitsbergen even in mid-winter. It was only when it reached Greenland and northernmost Norway that the stream of heat was halted. There, it hit the Arctic, where the icy ocean and chill winds cooled it rapidly. The Gulf Stream had always been very salty; now it was immensely cold too. The heavy water fell, sinking vertically – not as a front but in channels of water called chimneys, which were difficult to pinpoint since they moved with the swell. Convective chimneys measured twenty to fifty metres across, with ten or so clustered in the space of a square kilometre; but their exact position varied daily, depending on the wind and waves. The critical point about them was the suction effect the sinking water caused. This was the Gulf Stream's real secret: it didn't flow north but was drawn there, sucked onwards by the powerful pump at the bottom of the Arctic. When the icy water reached a depth of between 2000 and 3000 metres, it started on the return leg. It was a journey that would take it once round the world.

Bauer had released a batch of floats in the hope they would follow the path of the current, but trying to find the chimneys in the first place was difficult enough. They should have been everywhere. Instead the giant pump seemed to have packed up entirely or begun its work elsewhere.

Bauer had come here because he was aware of the problem and he knew what would follow. He hadn't expected to find things working perfectly, but he wasn't prepared to find nothing at all.

It was seriously worrying.

He'd confided his concerns to Weaver, before she'd left him. Since then he'd been updating her and entrusting her with his innermost fears. Several days ago his team had detected a dramatic rise in the methane content of the water. Now he was considering the possibility that it was linked to the disappearance of the chimneys. He was almost sure of the connection. Hunched over his data, Bauer examined stacks of calculations, diagrams and charts. Every now and then he emailed Karen Weaver to tell her of his latest findings.

He was so caught up in his work that he was oblivious to the shaking. His teacup made its way to the edge of the table and toppled over, pouring its contents on to his lap. 'Oh, blast,' he muttered. Hot tea soaked through his trousers and down his legs. He got up to examine the extent of the damage.

Suddenly he stiffened, straining to hear the noises outside.

Screams. Someone was screaming. Heavy boots pounded the deck and the ship vibrated furiously, throwing him off balance. Groaning, he collided with his desk. The ground fell away beneath him, as though the vessel had fallen into a hole. Bauer sprawled backwards and fear took hold of him. He scrambled to his feet and stumbled into the passageway. The shouts were louder now, and the engine started up. A man was yelling in Icelandic. Bauer couldn't understand the words, but he could hear the terror, which was echoed and amplified in the voice that replied.

Had there been an underwater earthquake?

He hurried along the passageway and down the stairs to the deck. Fierce vibrations rocked the ship, making it hard to stay upright. He pushed his way unsteadily to the hatch, and was hit by the stench. All of a sudden Lukas Bauer knew what was wrong.

Struggling to the rail, he looked out. The water was seething with bubbles.

There was no swell. No sign of a storm. Just thousands of giant bubbles, surging to the surface.

The boat plummeted again and Bauer toppled over, crashing face first on to the deck. Pain exploded in his skull. When he raised his head, his glasses were broken. Without them he was blind, but he didn't need lenses to know what happened next. The sea rose up and closed over the vessel.

Oh, God, he thought. Oh, dear God, no.

30 April

The night was resplendent in deep shades of green. It was a while since Anawak had first started to fall through the shadowy universe, but now a rush of euphoria swept through him, and he stretched out his arms, plummeting downwards like an Icarus of the depths, weightless and elated. He sank deeper and deeper. Something shimmered in the distance below him, a frozen white landscape, and all at once the sombre ocean became a dark night sky.

He was standing at the edge of an icefield, gazing at the deep, still water, with a wealth of stars above him.

He was at peace.

How wonderful it felt to be standing there. In time, an ice floe would form, detaching itself from the frozen water and drifting through the seas, carrying him north to a place where he would be free from the burden of questions. Anawak's chest swelled with longing and tears came into his eyes, dazzling him. He shook his head, dispersing the drops, which scattered over the sea, lighting up its darkness. Something rose towards him from the depths, and the towering water became a figure. It waited for him at a distance, too far for him to follow. Shiny and motionless it stood there, starlight trapped within its surface.

I found them, it said.

The figure had no face and no mouth, but the voice was familiar. He took a step towards it, but he was at the water's edge. A vast and terrifying presence lurked beneath him in the darkness.

What did you find? he asked.

The sound of his voice made him start. The words dropped heavily from his mouth. What the figure had said or maybe thought had sounded noiseless; now his voice shattered the silence that had filled the land-scape of ice. Biting cold took hold of him. He looked for the thing in the water, but it was gone.

Surely you don't need to ask? a voice said beside him.

He turned his head and saw the delicate figure of Samantha Crowe, the SETI researcher.

You sound awful, she said. You're fine at everything else, but you need to practise talking.

Sorry, he stammered.

I've found my aliens. Do you remember? We finally made contact. Isn't that great?

Anawak shivered. It didn't seem great to him; in fact, without knowing why, he felt clammy with fear at the thought of Crowe's aliens.

So . . . who are they? *What* are they?

The SETI researcher gestured towards the dark water beyond the ice. They're out there, she said. And I think they want to meet you. They like making contact. But you'll have to go and find them.

I can't, said Anawak.

Why ever not?

Anawak stared at the dark, powerful bodies ploughing through the water. There were dozens of them, maybe hundreds. He knew they were there because of him, and realised all at once that they were feeding on his fear.

I–I just can't.

Don't be a coward. Just take a step, Crowe teased him. It's the easiest thing in the world. Think how hard it was for us. We searched the universe to find them.

Anawak's shivering redoubled. He walked up to the edge and looked out. On the horizon, where the black water embraced the sky, a light shone in the distance.

Just go, said Crowe.

I flew here, thought Anawak, through a dark green ocean full of life, and I wasn't afraid. Nothing can happen to me now. The water will bear my weight like solid ground, and I'll reach the light on the strength of my will. Sam's right. It's easy. There's no need to be afraid.

An enormous creature plunged through the water in front of him, and a colossal two-pronged tail tilted up to the stars.

No need to be afraid.

But he had hesitated a moment too long, and he faltered again at the sight of the tail. His will couldn't carry him, and the power of dreams gave way to the force of gravity. Stepping forward, he sank into the sea. Water washed over his head, engulfing him in darkness. He tried to cry out and his mouth filled with water, rushing painfully into his lungs. It pulled him under, although he fought it. His heart was beating wildly, and there was a noise in his head, a droning or hammering . . .

Anawak sat up and banged his head against the ceiling. 'Damn.' He groaned.

The banging was there again. No droning this time, just a gentle tapping, like knuckles on wood. He rolled on to his side and saw Alicia Delaware. She was stooping, peering into his berth. 'Sorry,' she said. 'I didn't know you'd shoot up like that.'

Anawak stared at her. Delaware?

Slowly the memory came back. He knew where he was. Clutching his head, he slumped back on to the bed.

'What time is it?'

'Nine thirty.'

'Shit.'

'You look terrible. Were you having a nightmare?'

'Forget it.'

'How about some coffee?'

'Good idea.' He fingered the spot where he'd hit his head and winced. 'Where's the alarm? I set it for seven.'

'You slept through it – and no wonder, after everything that's happened.' She went through to the kitchenette. 'Where's the—'

'Cupboard on the wall. Left-hand side. Coffee, filter paper, milk and sugar.'

'Are you hungry? I do a great breakfast.'

'No.'

She filled the percolator with water. Anawak dragged himself out of his bunk. 'Don't look round. I've got to get changed.'

'Chill, Leon. I've seen it all before.'

Grimacing, he glanced around for his jeans. They were screwed up in a heap on the bench by the table. Putting them on wasn't easy. He felt dizzy, and his injured leg hurt when he bent it.

'Did John Ford call?' he asked.

'Yeah. A while ago.'

'Oh, for crying out loud . . .'

'What now?'

'A pensioner could get dressed faster than I can. And why the hell didn't I hear the alarm? I wanted to—'

'Leon, you're a jerk. The day before yesterday you and I were in a plane crash. Your knee's swollen, my brain took a hammering, but so what? We were lucky as hell. We could have been killed, like Danny and the pilot. And all you can do is moan about your stupid alarm. Now, are you ready?'

Anawak dropped down on to the bench. 'Fine. Point taken. What did John have to say?'

'All the data's there, and he's taken a look at the video.'

'It just gets better. And?'

'That's all he said. You're supposed to draw your own conclusions.' She heaped coffee into the filter, slotted it on to the jug and started the machine. After a few seconds the room was filled with slurping sounds. 'I told him you were asleep,' she went on, 'and he said not to wake you.'

'He said what?'

'He said you needed to get better. And he's right.'

'I am better,' said Anawak stubbornly.

But he wasn't sure of it. The DHC-2 had lost its right wing when it collided with the breaching whale. Danny had probably died on the spot – the *Whistler* hadn't retrieved his body but there was no real doubt. He hadn't got inside in time, which meant the side door had been open when the plane hit the water. That was what had saved Anawak. He'd been thrown out of the cabin on impact. After that his mind was blank. He couldn't even remember what had happened to his knee. He'd come round on the *Whistler*, brought back to life by the throbbing.

Then he'd noticed Delaware stretched out beside him, and the pain had stopped mattering. For a moment, he'd thought she was dead, but someone had told him that she was OK. She'd been even luckier than he had. The body of the pilot had cushioned her fall. Barely conscious, she'd struggled free from the sinking wreck, and the plane had filled with water in less than a minute. The *Whistler*'s crew had managed to fish Anawak and Delaware out of the water, but the pilot and his DHC-2 had sunk into the depths.

The trip had ended in tragedy, but their goal had been achieved. Danny had fired the tag. The URA had followed the whales and recorded twenty-four hours' worth of footage without coming under attack. Anawak had known the recording would arrive on John Ford's desk at the aquarium that morning, and he'd intended to be there on time. Besides, the Centre national d'études spatiales had released all the telemetric data received so far from the tag. They'd have been patting themselves on the back now, if the plane hadn't crashed.

Instead things were looking more desperate than ever. People were dying every day. On two occasions *he*'d nearly died. At the time of Stringer's death he'd dealt with things quite well – perhaps his anger with Greywolf had distracted him from his grief. But now, two days after the plane crash, he felt wretched – as though he'd finally succumbed to an insidious sickness, and was paying for it in uncertainty, self-doubt and a worrying lack of strength. There was a chance he might be in shock, but Anawak didn't quite buy it. There seemed more to it than that. Ever since he'd been hurled from the plane, he'd had spells of dizziness, pains in his chest and vague feelings of panic.

He wasn't better, and the problem wasn't his knee.

Anawak felt bruised inside.

The previous day he'd done little but sleep. Davie, Shoemaker and the rest of the team had been to see him, and Ford had called a few times to ask how he was. Apart from that no one seemed overly concerned. While Delaware's parents and friends were urging her to leave the island, the only people who'd spared a thought for Anawak were his colleagues.

He was ill, and he knew the doctors couldn't help him.

Delaware put a mug of coffee on the table in front of him and studied him through her blue-tinted shades. Anawak took a gulp and burnt his tongue. He asked her to fetch him the phone.

'Can I ask you a personal question, Leon?' she said.

'Later.'

'How much later?'

He punched a series of digits.

'We haven't finished sifting the data,' said Ford. 'Take your time and get some rest.'

'You told Licia I should draw my own conclusions.'

'Yes, once we've been through the rest. So far it's uninteresting. For the moment, we'll carry on sifting. Who knows? Maybe you can save yourself a trip.'

'When will you be done?'

'No idea. Four of us are looking at the tapes. Give us another two hours – no, three. I'll have you flown over mid-afternoon. That's one of the perks of working for an emergency committee – always plenty of helicopters.' Ford laughed. 'Not that I want to get used to it.' He paused. 'There's something else you can do, though. I don't have time to tell you about it now, but ask Rod Palm. You'd be better off speaking to him directly. He's just had a long chat with the Nanaimo lab and the Institute of Ocean Studies. Call Oliviera if you prefer, but Palm's on your doorstep.'

'Christ, John. Why doesn't anyone call me when something's going on?'

'I wanted to let you sleep.'

Anawak said a surly goodbye and phoned Palm. The head of the research institute on Strawberry Isle picked up straight away. 'Ah!' he said. 'Ford promised you'd ring.'

'So I hear. Apparently you've made an earth-shattering discovery. Why didn't you call me?'

'Everyone knows you're supposed to be resting.'

'Yeah, right.'

'Seriously, Leon, I thought you should get some sleep.'

'That's the second time I've heard that in the last sixty seconds – actually, it's the third, what with Licia's constant fussing. And I'm fine.'

'Why don't you pop over?' suggested Palm.

'In the boat, you mean?'

'Come on, Leon, it's only a few hundred metres. Besides, we haven't had any trouble in the Sound.'

'I'll be with you in ten minutes.'

'Great.'

Delaware peered at him over her coffee and frowned. 'What's up?'

'I'm being treated like an invalid.' Anawak scowled.

'That's not what I meant.'

He got up, rummaged beneath his bunk and pulled out a T-shirt. 'Some discovery at Nanaimo,' he said gruffly.

'What is it?' asked Delaware.

'I don't know. 'I'm going over to see Rod Palm.' He hesitated, then added, 'Come along, if you like.'

'I'm honoured.'

'Don't be stupid.'

'I'm not.' She wrinkled her nose. The edges of her incisors rested on her lower lip. She desperately needed some work on those teeth, thought

Anawak. Whenever he saw them, he had to fight off the impulse to tell her. 'You've barely said a civil word for two days. You're in a foul mood, Leon.'

'You wouldn't feel great yourself if—' He stopped.

'I was in the plane too,' she said calmly.

'I'm sorry.'

'I can't tell you how scared I was. Lots of girls would have run straight home to Mummy, but since you'd lost one assistant I stayed. To help *you*, you old grouch. Now what was that about not feeling so great?'

Anawak felt the bump on his head, which was painful. His knee hurt too. 'Nothing. Calm again now?'

She raised her eyebrows. 'I'm always calm.'

'Good. Then let's go.'

'Can I ask you that question?'

'No.'

There was something unreal about crossing Clayoquot Sound in the *Devilfish*. It was as though the mayhem of the past few weeks had never happened. The islet itself was just a pine-covered mound – the circular tour took five minutes on foot. Right now there wasn't a ripple on the water. The wind was still, and the sun beat down on them. At any moment Anawak expected to see a fluke or a fin rise out of the ocean, but since the trouble had started, orcas had only been sighted twice in the Sound. On both occasions they'd been residents, showing no sign of aggression. Anawak's theory about the change in behaviour being peculiar to migrants still seemed to hold true.

But for how much longer?

They pulled up at the landing jetty. Palm's research station was opposite, housed in an ancient sailing-boat, the first British Columbia ferry, now nestled prettily on the shore, supported by logs and surrounded by driftwood and rusty anchors. It was also his home, which he shared with his two children.

Anawak was trying not to limp. Delaware was silent.

A few minutes later the three were sitting round a small beech-bark table in the ferry's bow, Delaware sipping Coke. From their vantage-point they could see Tofino with its houses on stilts. Strawberry Isle, a few hundred metres away, was much quieter than the town, and they were treated to a variety of nature's sounds.

'How's the knee?' Palm asked. He was an affable, bald man with a curly white beard, who seemed to have been born with a pipe in his mouth.

'I'd rather not talk about it.' Anawak tried to ignore the hammering in his head. 'Why don't you tell me what you've found?'

'Leon doesn't like it when people ask him how he is,' Delaware said pointedly.

Palm coughed. 'I've had a long chat with Ray Fenwick and Sue Oliviera,' he said. 'We've had a lot to talk about, what with J-19's dissection and the other stuff that's happened since. You see, on the day your plane crashed another whale was washed ashore, a grey. It wasn't one I'd seen before, and it's not in any of the databases. Fenwick was too busy to fly over, but Nanaimo needed the usual autopsy samples so I got a few people together and we took it apart ourselves. A god-awful task, I can tell you. We'd just about got down to the heart and I was standing in the ribcage when I slipped – blood and slime everywhere, in my boots and splattering down from above. We looked like zombies at a feeding frenzy. A not-so-romantic view of the heart, that's for sure. Anyhow, we took samples from the brain as well.'

The thought of another dead whale filled Anawak with sorrow. He couldn't bring himself to hate the animals for what they had done. To him they still deserved protection. 'What did it die of?' he asked.

Palm gestured vaguely. 'I'd say it was an infection. According to Fenwick, that's what did for Genghis too. But the weird thing is that there's something inside those whales that doesn't belong there.' He pointed to his temples and traced a circle with his finger. 'Fenwick found a clot in their brain stems. And some kind of leakage between the brain and the skull.'

Anawak sat up. 'A blood clot? In both whales?'

'Not a blood clot, although at first we thought it was. Fenwick and Oliviera were pretty keen on the idea that noise was behind the change in the whales' behaviour. They weren't going to mention it till they'd found some proof, but for a while Fenwick was convinced it had something to do with the effects of that sonar system—'

'Surtass LFA?'

'That's it.'

'No way.'

'Is anyone going to tell me what this is about?' Delaware chimed in. 'Well, a few years ago the American government decided to grant the

US Navy permission to use low-frequency active sonar for the detection of subs,' said Palm. 'The system's called Surtass LFA. They're trying it out all over the place.'

'Seriously?' said Delaware, appalled. 'But what about the Marine Mammal Protection Act? Surely they're bound to it.'

'All kinds of people are bound to all kinds of Acts,' said Anawak, with a grim smile. 'But there are loopholes. Evidently the Americans couldn't pass up on the opportunity of putting eighty per cent of the world's oceans under surveillance, which is what Surtass lets them do. Anyway, the system cost three hundred million dollars, and its operators were insisting it wouldn't hurt the whales.'

'But sonar is bad for whales. Any fool knows that.'

'Unfortunately it hasn't been adequately proven,' said Palm. 'Past experience shows that whales and dolphins are incredibly sensitive to sonar, but no one can say for sure what effect it has on feeding patterns, reproduction or migration.'

'It's ridiculous,' snorted Anawak. 'At 180 decibels, a whale's eardrums can explode. Each underwater transmitter can generate two hundred and fifteen. The combined effect is much louder, of course.'

Delaware looked at them. 'So . . . how does it affect them?'

'That's why Fenwick and Oliviera went for the noise theory,' said Palm. 'Years ago, when the navy started experimenting with sonar, there was an upsurge in beachings all over the world. Large numbers of whales and dolphins died. They all showed signs of heavy bleeding in the brain and in the inner ear – injuries consistent with noise damage. In each instance, environmentalists proved that NATO military exercises had been going on close to where the bodies were found. But tell that to the navy!'

'You mean they denied it?'

'Until recently the navy always denied any link between sonar and the beachings, but they've had to admit that in some cases sonar was indeed to blame. The problem is, we still don't know enough. The only evidence we have of damage is from the dead whales. Everyone's got their own theory. Fenwick, for instance, thinks underwater noise causes outbreaks of collective madness.'

'Noise just disorients them', growled Anawak. 'It causes beachings, not attacks.'

'Well, *I* think the theory's worth considering,' said Delaware.

'Oh, really?'

'Well, why not? The creatures are going mad. It started with a few and then it spread, like a mass psychosis.'

'Licia, that's rubbish. Look what happened to the beaked whales that died in the Canaries after NATO held a pow-wow there. They're about as sensitive to noise as you can get. Of course they went crazy. They were so panicked that they beached themselves in their rush to get out of the water. Loud noise makes them want to *flee*.'

'Or maybe they want to attack the noise,' countered Delaware, stubbornly.

'Attack what? Zodiacs with outboard motors? Since when is that noise?'

'It must have been something else, then. An underwater explosion.'

'Not round here.'

'How would you know?'

'I just do.'

'You can't bear to be wrong, can you, Leon?'

'That's rich, coming from you.'

'Besides, there've been beachings here before. It's been going on for centuries. Ancient stories tell of—'

'I know that, Licia. I think we all do.'

'Fine. So do you think the Indians had sonar?'

'What's that got to do with it?'

'Everything. Beached whales are being used for ideological purposes without a second thought—'

'Uh-huh. So now you're suggesting I'm thoughtless.'

Delaware glared at him. 'I'm suggesting that mass strandings don't necessarily have anything to do with artificial noise, and that noise might cause something other than mass strandings.'

'OK, folks!' Palm tried to pacify them. 'You're arguing over nothing. Fenwick has decided that the noise theory has too many holes in it anyway. OK, so he's still into his collective madness thing, but— Are you even listening to me?'

They turned.

'OK,' said Palm, when he was sure he had their attention. 'So Fenwick and Oliviera found the clots and decided they'd been caused by external factors. Superficially they resembled blood clots, so that's what they assumed they were. Then they removed the substance and ran some tests. It was the colour of whale blood, but the substance itself was transparent and disintegrated on contact with air. Most of it was too far gone to be useful.' Palm leaned across the table. 'But they took a look at some of it. The results matched some findings from a few weeks previously. They'd seen the substance once before. In Nanaimo.'

Anawak was silent for a second. 'What is it?' he asked hoarsely.

'The same substance you found in the mussels on the *Barrier Queen*.'

'So the substance in the brains and on the hull—'

'Identical. Organic matter.'

Anawak had only been up for a few hours but already he felt drained. He took Delaware back to Tofino in the boat. His knee twinged painfully as he climbed the wooden ladder to the jetty. He felt helpless, depressed and at the mercy of whatever unpleasantness was on its way next.

Clenching his jaw, he hobbled into the deserted office of Davie's Whaling Station, fetched a bottle of orange juice from the fridge and flopped on to the armchair behind the desk. One thought after another raced through his mind, like a dog chasing its tail.

Delaware had followed him.

'Grab yourself something.' Anawak pointed to the fridge.

'The whale that brought the plane down . . .' she began.

Anawak opened the bottle and took a gulp.

'That whale must have hurt itself, Leon. It probably died.'

He thought for a moment. 'Yes,' he said. 'I expect you're right.'

She walked over to a shelf with plastic miniatures of whales for sale, in all different sizes. A group of humpbacks were resting peacefully on their flippers. She took one down and twisted it in her fingers. Anawak kept a watchful eye on her. 'Something's making them do it,' she said.

He leaned forward and switched on the portable TV next to the radio. Perhaps she'd take the hint and go. He didn't mind her company but his need to be alone was growing by the minute.

Delaware replaced the whale on the shelf. 'Can I ask you something personal now?'

Oh, not again. Anawak was on the point of snapping at her, but shrugged instead. 'I guess so.'

'Do you come from the Makah?'

He nearly dropped the bottle. 'Whatever gave you that idea?' he bleated.

'It was something you said to Shoemaker when we were getting on the plane, about Greywolf falling out with the Makah if he kept going on about whaling. The Makah are Indians, right?'

'Right.'

'Your people?'

'I'm not a Makah.'

'But aren't you—'

'Look, Licia, don't take this personally, but I'm not in the mood for family history.'

She pursed her lips. 'OK.'

'I'll call you when Ford gets in touch.' He smiled wryly. 'Or you call me – he'll probably not want to wake me or something.'

Delaware shook her red ponytail at him and walked slowly to the door. She paused. 'And another thing,' she said, without turning. 'It's time you thanked Greywolf for saving your life. I've been to see him already.'

'You've done what?'

'I mean it. You can despise him for everything else, but he still deserves thanks. If it wasn't for him, you'd be dead.'

She went.

Anawak slammed the bottle on to the table and took a deep breath.

He was still sitting there, flicking through the channels, when an emergency broadcast came on. The TV stations were full of newsflashes with the latest on the situation in British Columbia, plus broadcasts from the US where shipping was at a standstill too. In the studio, a woman in naval dress was speaking. Her short black hair was combed sleekly off her face and there was an austere beauty about her features. She looked Oriental, perhaps Chinese. No, half-Chinese. One small detail didn't fit with the rest: her eyes were a deep unAsiatic blue.

A text box popped up at the bottom of the screen: *General Commander Judith Li, US Navy.*

'Should we consider withdrawing from the coast of British Columbia?' the interviewer was asking. 'Giving it back to nature, so to speak?'

'I think you'll find that we haven't *taken* anything in the first place,' said Judith Li. 'We live in harmony with nature although, of course, there's room for improvement.'

'Yet in the present situation there seems little sign of harmony.'

'Well, that's something we're working on in close collaboration with leading scientists and scientific institutes on both sides of the border. Sure, it's alarming when animals collectively change their behaviour, but it would be wrong to over-dramatise the situation. It's certainly no cause for panic.'

'In other words, you don't believe we're dealing with a mass phenomenon?'

'Before speculating on the *type* of phenomenon, I'd want to know for certain that this is a phenomenon at all. In my opinion, we're looking at a cumulative series of broadly similar events—'

'Events that the public knows nothing about,' the interviewer interrupted. 'Why is that?'

'We're keeping the public informed.' Li smiled.

'Well, I'm surprised and delighted to have this chance to talk with you, but let's be frank: the provision of public information, both here and in the United States, has been patchy to say the least. And now we're finding ourselves in a position where we're unable to report the views of experts since all attempts at communication are being blocked by the authorities.'

'Crap,' growled Anawak. 'Greywolf was only too happy to shoot his mouth off. I thought *everyone* heard it.'

On the other hand, had Ford been asked for an interview? Or Fenwick? Palm was an expert on orcas – had any news crews or reporters been in touch with him? And what about himself? It wasn't so long ago that *Scientific American* had cited him in an article on cetacean intelligence, but no one had come banging on his door.

Belatedly he was struck by the absurdity of it all. In any other circumstance – terrorist attacks, plane crashes or natural disasters – anyone resembling an expert was dragged in front of the cameras before the day was out.

Yet they were working steadily in silence.

Come to think of it, even Greywolf hadn't given vent to any outbursts since that interview in the paper. Until then he had seized every opportunity to push himself forward. The hero of Tofino had been dropped.

'That's a one-sided perspective,' Li said smoothly. 'Clearly we're in an extremely unusual predicament. Nothing like this has ever happened before. So of course we're anxious to prevent hordes of self-appointed experts jumping to conclusions. I mean, apart from anything else, we'd never be able to set the record straight. Besides, I don't see any threat we can't handle.'

'So you're saying it's under control?'

'That's certainly our goal.'

'Some people would say that you're failing.'

'In that case I'd like to know what they expect. The military is hardly going to attack the whales with warships and Black Hawks.'

'The number of casualties is rising by the day. The Canadian government has restricted the emergency zone to the coast of British Columbia—'

'The restrictions apply to pleasure-boats only. Ferries and freighters have not been affected.'

'The past few days have seen a spate of reports about missing vessels. Perhaps you could comment on that.'

'Let me make this quite clear. Those reports concern fishing-boats. Small motorboats,' said Li, in a tone of martyred patience. 'Every now and then a ship goes missing. We're looking into the incidents. Needless to say, we're doing everything we can to search for survivors. But in the meantime we shouldn't assume that every unexplained incident is the result of an attack. I hope people will see that.'

The interviewer adjusted his glasses. 'Please correct me if I'm wrong, but I understand that a recent incident involving a freighter belonging to Inglewood, the Vancouver-based shipping line, resulted in the sinking of a tug.'

Li pressed her fingertips together. 'I assume you're referring to the *Barrier Queen*.'

The interviewer looked briefly at his notes. 'That's right. There's very little information available on what actually happened.'

'Too right,' agreed Anawak. He'd forgotten to chase it up with Shoemaker since the crash.

'The *Barrier Queen*,' said Li, 'had a problem with her rudder. A tug sank during a botched attempt to fix a tow line.'

'Then if I understand you correctly it wasn't attacked. You see, according to my information—'

'Your information is obviously wrong.'

Anawak stiffened. What the hell was she talking about?

'All right, General, two days ago a Tofino Air seaplane crashed into the ocean. Could you tell us a little more about that?'

'A seaplane crashed. That's correct.'

'Reports suggest it collided with a whale.'

'The incident is under investigation. Please forgive me for not commenting on each individual case. My work is at a higher level, as I'm sure you'll understand.'

'Of course.' The interviewer nodded. 'Perhaps we should talk about your work, then. What exactly does your job entail? How would you describe the committee's brief? Presumably it's a case of responding to events . . .'

Li's face twitched. 'Emergency committees are there to act as well as react. We meet the situation head on, tackle it and see it through. Early detection, clear and comprehensive planning, prevention and evacuation are key to our success. But, as I mentioned before, we're on unfamiliar ground. So far, we haven't been as good at detecting and preventing incidents as we'd normally expect. Everything else is covered, though. You won't find a single boat out there in danger from the whales. Essential items of cargo from at-risk vessels are being diverted to nearby airports. Larger vessels are sailing under military escort. We're maintaining constant aerial surveillance and we're ploughing large sums of money into scientific research . . .'

'But you've ruled out military action.'

'We haven't ruled it out. We said it was unlikely.'

'Environmental groups are claiming that the change in the animals' behaviour is due to human intervention. Noise, toxic waste, shipping . . .'

'We're doing all we can to find out.'

'What progress has been made?'

'Let me spell this out clearly: until we're in a position to pass on concrete information, we refuse to engage in speculation. Nor will speculation be tolerated from any other quarter. Fishermen, industrialists, shipping lines, whale-watchers, pro-whaling activists and any other would-be vigilantes will be dealt with severely. This situation must not be allowed to escalate. When animals attack, it's because they're feeling threatened or they're ill. Either way, it would be foolish to use violence against them. We need to find out what's causing the problem so that we can deal with its symptoms. And until then we'll stay out of the water.'

'Thank you, General.' The newsreader turned to face the camera. 'That was General Commander Judith Li of the US Navy, who was recently appointed military chief of staff to the Allied Emergency Committee representing Canada and the United States. And now for today's other stories . . .'

Anawak turned down the volume and called Ford. 'Who the hell is Judith Li?' he asked.

'Oh, I haven't met her in person,' said Ford. 'She's always on the move, flying about the place.'

'I didn't know Canada and the US had formed a joint committee.'

'You can't know everything, Leon. You're a biologist, remember?'

'Have you talked to the press or anyone else about the attacks?'

'We had a number of media enquiries, but nothing ever came of them. The television people seemed keen to get you.'

'Why the hell didn't anyone—'

'Leon.' Ford sounded wearier than he had that morning. 'Li pulled the plug on it. It was probably for the best. The minute you start working for a state or military organisation, you're expected to keep your mouth shut. Anything you hear or do is classified.'

'So how come they let the two of us keep talking?'

'We're in the same boat.'

'But that general's talking crap! All that stuff about the *Barrier Queen*—'

'Leon,' Ford yawned, 'were you actually there when it happened?'

'Oh, don't you start.'

'I'm not. Like you, I don't doubt your Mr Roberts was telling the truth about what happened. But think about it. First, there's an invasion of mussels – odd creatures, with no taxonomic history, covered in ominous gunk – then an assault by whales on a tow line. And that's your story. Plus there's that incident in the dock, with you getting slapped in the face, not to mention Fenwick and Oliviera finding more of the gunk in the whale brains. Now, do you fancy telling *that* to the public?'

Anawak was silent. 'So why can't I get in touch with Inglewood?' he asked.

'No idea.'

'You must know something. You're scientific adviser to the Canadian response team.'

'Exactly! Which is why I'm drowning in dossiers right now. For Christ's sake, Leon, I don't know. They're not letting on.'

'Inglewood and the response team are in the same boat.'

'Well, I'd love to discuss it further with you, Leon, but right now I've got those darned videos to deal with, and it's going to take longer than I thought. One of the guys is laid up in bed. Diarrhoea, apparently. Perfect. There won't be anything for you to look at before tomorrow.'

'Damn,' said Anawak.

'Listen, I'll give you a call, all right? Or I'll ring Licia, in case you're asleep.'

'I'll be waiting to hear from you.'

'She's doing nicely, don't you think?'

Of course she was doing nicely. You couldn't wish for anyone more dedicated. 'Yes,' mumbled Anawak. 'Now, is there anything I can do?'

'Think. Go for a walk. Visit a Nootka chief.' Ford laughed wryly. 'I bet the Indians know something. Just think what a relief it would be if they came out and told you that all this had happened hundreds of years before.'

Joker, thought Anawak. He wrapped up the conversation and stared at the pictures on the screen.

After a few minutes he started pacing up and down. His knee was throbbing but he carried on, as if to punish his body for letting him down.

At this rate he'd soon be paranoid. He already had the feeling he was being sidelined. No one ever called him up to tell him anything unless he called them first. He wasn't disabled: he had a limp, for Christ's sake. Sure, things had been a bit much lately, but . . .

That wasn't the problem.

He froze in front of the plastic whales.

No one was treating him like an invalid, and he wasn't being sidelined. Ford was doing him a favour and saving him a trip to Vancouver by sifting the data himself. Delaware was doing her best to be supportive. They were only being considerate – nothing more, nothing less. He was the one acting like he was crippled. He was the one with the problem.

What's the best thing to do, he asked himself, when you're going round in circles? Break the cycle. Do what it takes to get back on the road. It's no good looking to other people. Look to yourself. Do something out of the ordinary.

But what?

Ford had said he should visit a Nootka chief.

The Indians know something.

Was it true? Canada's Indians had passed their knowledge from generation to generation until the Indian Act of 1885 had broken the chain of oral tradition. It had encouraged them to sell their identity by leaving their homeland and sending their children to residential schools to be 'integrated' into white society. Like a forked-tongued serpent, the Indian Act promised them one thing and offered another. With a smile it talked of integration, but the Indians were integrated in their own communities, yet that wasn't good enough for the snake. The nightmare of the Indian Act continued. For decades Canada's native peoples had been trying to reclaim their lives. Many had picked up the thread of memory where it had been severed a hundred years earlier. The Canadian government had made reparations, but nothing could bring back their culture. Fewer and fewer Indians knew the old lore.

Whom could he ask?

The elders.

Anawak hobbled on to the veranda and looked down the street. He'd never had much to do with the Nootka. They called themselves the Nuu-chah-nulth, meaning People Along the Mountains, and with the Tsimshian, Gitksan, Skeena, Haida, Kwakiutl and Coast Salish, they were one of the main tribes on the west coast of British Columbia. It was almost impossible for outsiders to understand how the various tribes, bands and linguistic groups were related. Most people's attempt to get to grips with Indian culture failed at the first hurdle, before they got anywhere near regional dialects and customs, which differed from one bay to the next. However, if you wanted to find out about Vancouver Island's Pacific coast, it made sense to ask the Nootka, from the west of the island. You might be lucky. On the other hand, you might get bogged down in the myths of the various bands of which the Nootka were composed. Each band had its own territory. To say that the Nootka's traditions were closely bound up with the landscape of Vancouver Island, and that their mythology was rooted in the natural world meant everything and nothing. At the heart of Nootka belief was the story of a creator, a figure capable of changing shape and form. In, say, the stories of the Ditidaht, wolves were of particular significance, but orcas played a key role too, and anyone wanting to find out about orcas had to get to grips with the wolf legends. Animals and humans were spiritually linked, so animals could transform themselves into other creatures and some had a dual identity. If a wolf went into the water, it changed into a whale, and a killer whale on land became a wolf. In the eyes of the Nootka, to tell stories about whales without thinking of wolves made no sense at all.

Since the Nootka had traditionally hunted whales, they knew count-less whale stories. But not every band told the same ones, and a similar basic story varied, depending on where it was told. It was a moot point as to whether the Nootka included the Makah, but at the very least they shared a language – Wakashan. Apart from the Inuit, the Makah were the only North American people with a treaty right to hunt whales, which, after a century of abstinence, they were planning to exercise, prompting widespread concern. The Makah didn't live on Vancouver Island, but on the other side of the water, on the north-westerly tip of Washington State. Their oral tradition included stories of whales that were also told by the Nootka on the island, but when it came to describing the reasons behind a whale's behaviour – its thoughts, feelings and intentions – they all took a different line. That was only to be expected, though: the whale was also known as the *iihtuup* or 'big enigma.'

Do something out of the ordinary.

Asking Indians for advice would certainly be that. Whether it would be helpful was a different matter.

Anawak gave a sour smile. It was the kind of thing he usually avoided like the plague.

Although he'd lived in Vancouver for twenty years, he didn't know much about the local peoples, mainly because he'd never tried to find out. Every now and then he felt a yearning for their world, but suppressed it before it could take hold. He found it too embarrassing. Delaware had mistaken him for a Makah, but he was the least suitable person to grapple with Indian myth.

Other than Greywolf.

It's pathetic, he thought bitterly. No self-respecting Indian ran round with such a lame-assed Wild-West surname. All the chiefs were called Norman George or Walter Michael or George Frank. None called themselves John Two Feathers or Lawrence Swimming Whale. Only arrogant jerks like Jack O'Bannon indulged in that kind of nonsense.

Greywolf was an ass.

And as for himself . . .

They were as bad as each other. Greywolf tried to be an Indian, and wasn't; while he looked like an Indian and was determined not to be one.

His goddamn knee had started him thinking, and he didn't want to think. He didn't need Alicia Delaware to send him back along the path he'd come.

Who could he ask?

George Frank was a chief he knew. He wasn't exactly a friend, but he was a nice guy, who also happened to be the *taayii Haw'ilh* of the Tla-o-qui-aht, one of the Nootka lands from the Wickaninnish area. A *Haw'ilh* was a chief, but a *taayii Haw'ilh* was a step up from that – a head chief. The *taayii Haw'ilH* were a bit like the British monarchy: their status was hereditary. These days, most bands were governed by elected coun-cillors, but the hereditary chiefs were still respected.

In the north of Vancouver Island the big chiefs called themselves *taayii Haw'ilH*, but in the south they were called *taayii chaachaabat*. George Frank, he guessed, was more likely to be a *taa'yii chaabat*. Maybe he'd avoid Indian words.

He could easily visit the chief – he lived a short distance from the Wickaninnish Inn. The more he thought about it, the more he liked the idea. Instead of waiting for Ford's call, he could break the cycle and see where it took him. He found Frank's number in the phone book and called him.

'So you're here to ask about the whales,' said Frank, thirty minutes later, as they wound their way past towering trees with densely clad branches.

Anawak had explained why he had come. The chief scratched his chin. He was a small man with a wrinkled face and friendly eyes. His hair was as dark as Anawak's. Underneath his windcheater he was wearing a T-shirt with the slogan 'Salmon Coming Home'.

'I hope you're not expecting me to come up with an ancient Indian proverb.'

'No.' Anawak was pleased with this. 'It was John Ford's idea.'

'Which one?' Frank smiled. 'Ford the movie director, or Ford the director of the aquarium?'

'The movie director's dead, I think. We're trying any angle we can think of. Even if it's just a tip-off from an old story. Maybe something similar happened in the past.'

Frank pointed to the river they were following. The water gurgled past, taking twigs and foliage with it. Its source was in the mountains, but in places its path was blocked with silt. 'Your answer's right here.'

'In the river?'

Frank grinned. '*Hishuk ish ts'awalk.*'

'I thought Indian folklore was out?'

'Don't worry, I'm done now. Actually, I assumed you'd know it.'

'I never learned your language. Sure, I picked up a few phrases here and there, but no more.'

Frank looked at him intently. 'Well, it's the central teaching of just about all Indian culture. The Nootka like to claim it for themselves, but I expect others say the same thing in different words. "Everything is one". If anything happens to the river, it affects humans, animals and the sea . . . If one thing changes, everything else does too.'

'Ecology, in other words.'

Frank bent to free a branch caught in the tangle of roots obstructing the river. 'I don't know what to say, Leon. We don't know any more than you do. I can listen out for you, and I'll make a few calls. We've got plenty of songs and stories, but none that might help you. You'll find what you're looking for in all our stories, and that's the problem.'

'I don't follow.'

'Our notion of animals is different to yours. The Nootka have never taken the life of a whale. Whales *give* their lives to the Nootka, and that's different – it's a conscious act, do you see? In the belief system of the Nootka, all nature is conscious – it's one big interconnected consciousness.' He turned down a boggy path. Anawak followed. The forest cleared into a large, barren space, empty of trees. 'Just look at the state of it. Shameful. The wood's gone, the soil's being eroded, and now the river's no better than a sewer. You only need to see this to know what's wrong with the whales. *Hishuk ish ts'awalk*.'

'Have I ever told you what my research is about?'

'You're looking for consciousness, aren't you?'

'Self-consciousness.'

'You told me last year. We had a good chat that evening. I drank beer and you drank water.'

'I don't like alcohol.'

'Never drunk it?'

'As good as.'

Frank stopped. 'Hmm, alcohol. You're a good Indian, Leon, keeping away from alcohol and coming to me because you think we might have some secret native knowledge.' He sighed. 'When will people ever stop treating each other like clichés? The Indians used to have an alcohol problem and some still do, but most of us just like the occasional drink. Yet as soon as a white guy sees an Indian with a beer, he thinks, Oh, how tragic, we drove these people to drink. On the one hand we're stray lambs, and on the other we're custodians of ancient wisdom. But how about you Leon? What are you? A Christian?'

Anawak wasn't too taken aback. The few times he'd talked to George Frank in the past, the conversation had meandered freely. The *taayii Haw'ilh* jumped like a squirrel from one topic to the next, ostensibly at random. 'I don't belong to any church.'

'I studied the Bible once, you know. It's full of ancient truths. Ask a Christian why the wood is burning, and he'll tell you that God is in the flames. He'll refer you to the ancient stories, and there you'll find a burning bush. But is that how a Christian would explain a forest fire?'

'No, of course not.'

'Exactly – and yet any true Christian treasures those stories. Indians believe in their ancient stories too, but not because they think they're *real*. Our stories don't describe how such-and-such a thing actually is. They describe the *idea* of it. In our stories you'll find everything and nothing, because you can't take anything literally, yet it all makes sense.'

'I know, George. It's just that we don't seem to be making any progress. The whales have gone mad, and we're tying ourselves in knots trying to figure out why.'

'And you think science can't help.'

'That's how it looks.'

'There'll be a way. Science is a marvellous thing and people work wonders with it. But it's a question of finding your focus. So far you've been looking at the whales. All of a sudden your old friends are enemies. Why? Could it be something we've done to them or to their world? What you need to realise is that *their world is our world*. If you look for things that affect the whales directly, there's no shortage – pointless slaughter, chemicals in the water, tourism gone mad . . . We're destroying the food chain and polluting the oceans with noise. We've even depriving them of the places they raise their young. Aren't there plans to build a salt plant in the Baja California?'

Anawak nodded. In 1993 the San Ignacio lagoon had been named a UNESCO World Heritage Site. It was the last undeveloped nursery and breeding ground in the world for the Pacific grey whale, and it was home to a multitude of endangered plant and animal species. But in spite of that the Mitsubishi Corporation was planning to build a salt-evaporation plant that would pump twenty thousand litres of salt water out of the lagoon per second, creating 116 square miles of salt ponds. The water would flow back as waste water. No one knew what effect it would have on the whales. Countless scientists, environmentalists and a host of Noble Prize winners were protesting against the proposal, which threatened to set a disastrous precedent.

'So you see,' continued Frank, 'that's the whales' world, as you know it. They live in this world and it's so much more than just a chain of conditions that are straightforwardly good or bad for their survival. Maybe the whales aren't the problem, Leon. They might be just part of the problem – the only part we can see.'

Aquarium, Vancouver

While Anawak was listening to the *taayii Haw'ilh*, John Ford was seeing double. For hours he'd been monitoring two screens at once. The URA's footage of Lucy and the pod of greys was on one screen while the other showed a 3-D grid of lines in which a dozen green pinpricks were suspended. As the pod changed location and formation, the pinpricks shifted, moving through the virtual space. Almost immediately after splashdown, the robot had matched Lucy's tail flukes to the sounds she was making, enabling it to use the noises to identify her and determine her position, which flashed green on the screen. Even if she had dived to the darkest depths, the robot wouldn't have lost her.

A stream of data flowed across the second screen from the tag still buried in Lucy's blubber: heart-rate, depth of dive, positional data, temperature, pressure and light. The combined information from the tag and the URA provided a comprehensive picture of what Lucy had been doing over twenty-four hours. Twenty-four hours in the life of a rampaging whale.

There was room in the observation lab for four people to monitor the output. Ford and two assistants were sitting in semi-darkness. The fourth work station was empty. A stomach bug had reduced the team to three, condemning them all to a night shift.

Ford reached to one side, keeping his eyes on the screens, and stuck his hand into a carton. A handful of congealed chips disappeared into his mouth.

Lucy didn't give the impression that she was rampaging.

Over the past few hours she'd been doing what benthic feeders did best – grazing, with half a dozen adult greys and two adolescents. At regular intervals she'd pushed her way through curtains of seaweed towards the bottom, raising clouds of sediment as she ploughed through sandy silt, catching worms and amphipods. Lying on her side, she'd tilled long furrows with her narrow bow-shaped head. In the beginning he'd been fascinated. It wasn't the first time he'd seen pictures of grey whales feeding, but the URA swam with the pod. Its footage was in a different league. He could even see much of the detail. Following a sperm whale to its feeding grounds would have meant sinking to the depths of the ocean, but grey whales loved the shallows. So for hours Ford had been watching an alternating picture of light and dusk. Lucy bobbed along the surface for a few minutes, filtered out the silt through her baleen, filled her lungs with air, then returned to the bottom. She came so close to the shore that most of the pictures had been taken at depths of less than thirty metres.

Ford watched as the scarred and mottled body slid over the sediment, swirling up the silt. The robot found it easy to follow the whales because they barely left the spot, swimming just a few metres in one direction, then a short distance in the other, shuttling back and forth, up and down, feeding, returning to the surface and plunging under water. Ford liked to compare Vancouver Island to a service station where whales hung out and snacked – which was what the pod was doing now.

Up to the surface, down to the sea floor, feeding, swimming.

After a while it got boring.

At one point a group of orcas appeared in the distance, but it didn't stick around. Most of the time, encounters like that passed without incident, although orcas were the only creatures apart from humans to prey on large whales. Not even blue whales were safe. When orcas went for the kill, it was a ferocious group attack. They took bites of their victim's lips and tongue, leaving behind a gigantic, mutilated corpse that sank slowly to the bottom.

Down to the sea floor, up to the surface, diving, feeding.

Lucy fell asleep. At least Ford assumed that she was sleeping. With his assistants he watched the picture darken, as daylight turned to dusk. A shadow was visible against the black background: Lucy's body, suspended upright in the water, sinking slowly towards the bottom, then creeping up again. Several marine mammals rested in that way. Every few minutes they rose to the surface in their half-sleep, breathed and sank down, still slumbering. Remarkably, they never slept longer than five or six minutes at a time, yet the short naps added up to a rest.

Eventually the screens went black. Only the green lights betrayed the position of the pack.

It was night.

Nothing to see, still he had to watch – the tedium was hard to bear. Now and then something flashed across the screen; a jellyfish or a squid. Otherwise it was blacker than black. A stream of data continued to flow across the second monitor – details of Lucy's metabolism and her physical surroundings. The green lights moved lethargically through the virtual space. Not all of the animals in the pod would sleep at night. Whales slept irregularly, at different times of day or night. From the screen he could tell that Lucy and the other greys had stopped diving and feeding. From time to time the temperature changed by half a degree, depending on the depth. Everything else stayed constant. The grey whale's heart was beating steadily, sometimes speeding up a little, sometimes slowing down. The URA's hydrophone picked up all kinds of underwater noise: swooshing and bubbling, orca calls and the song of the humpbacks, bellowing and growling, the distant whir of a ship's propeller, but nothing out of the ordinary.

Ford sat in front of the pitch-black screen and yawned until his jaw clicked.

He gathered up the last few chips. His fingers stiffened. He squinted at the screen. Something was happening to the data.

From the moment the probe had started to record, it had registered a depth of between nought and thirty metres. Now it was registering forty, then fifty. Lucy was on the move. She was swimming towards the open sea and diving deeper all the time. The other whales followed rapidly. There was no hanging about now. This was migration speed.

What's the hurry? thought Ford.

Lucy's heartrate slowed. She was still diving, gliding rapidly downwards. Now her lungs would contain only ten per cent of the oxygen she was carrying, maybe less. The rest was stored in her blood and muscles.

Lucy was over a hundred metres below the surface. The blood supply to her non-vital body parts had already shut down. A tangled network of capillaries absorbed the diverted blood. Muscle movement and metabolism proceeded anaerobically. Over millions of years a series of astonishing changes had enabled the former land-dwellers to move effortlessly between the surface and the depths; to most fish, a change in pressure of just a hundred metres posed mortal danger. Lucy continued to sink, 150 metres, 200, moving steadily from the shore.

'Bill? Jackie?' Ford called. His eyes were fixed on the screen. 'Come and look at this.'

They crowded round the monitors.

'She's diving.'

'At a fair pace, too. She's three kilometres from the shore already. The whole pod's heading out to sea.'

'Maybe it's time for them to get going again.'

'But why would they dive so deep?'

'Plankton sinks at night, doesn't it?'

'No.' Ford shook his head. 'That makes sense for other species, but not for benthic feeders. They've got no reason to—'

'Look! Three hundred metres.'

Ford leaned back. Grey whales weren't especially fast. If need be, they could put on a spurt, but ten kilometres an hour was as fast as they usually travelled, unless they were migrating or fleeing from a predator.

What had got into them?

He was sure now that he was observing anomalous behaviour. Grey whales fed almost exclusively on benthic organisms. When they migrated, they never strayed further than two kilometres from the coast. Ford wasn't sure how they'd cope at a depth of 300 metres. Ordinarily they never ventured below 120 metres.

Suddenly something lit up at the bottom edge of the grid: a green flash that shone for a moment before it was extinguished.

A spectrogram! The visual representation of a sound wave.

Then another.

'What was that?'

'Some kind of sound. The signal's pretty strong.'

Ford stopped the tape and rewound. They watched the sequence again. 'It's an incredibly loud signal,' he said. 'Like an explosion.'

'But there haven't been any explosions near here. We'd hear an explosion. This is infrasound.'

'I know. I only said it was *like* an explo—'

'There it is again!'

The green dots on the screen had stopped. The loud noise appeared a third time, then vanished.

'How deep are they?'

'Three hundred and sixty metres.'

'Unbelievable! What are they doing down there?'

Ford's gaze shifted to the left-hand screen, showing the footage from the camera. The black screen. His mouth dropped open. 'Look at that,' he whispered.

The screen wasn't black any more.

Vancouver Island

Frank's company was just what Anawak had needed. They had strolled along the beach towards the Wickaninnish Inn, discussing the environmental project with which Frank was involved. He came from a long line of fishermen, and now ran a restaurant, but recently the Tla-o-qui-aht had begun an initiative to combat the damage caused by logging. 'Salmon Coming Home' stood for their attempt to restore the complex ecosystem of Clayoquot Sound. The timber industry had devastated the area. No one was naïve enough to think that the forest could be restored, but plenty could be done. Clear-cut logging was to blame for the forest floor drying out in the sun and washing away in the rain. The topsoil flushed into lakes and rivers, adding to the congestion caused by stones and abandoned timber and depriving the salmon of their spawning grounds. With its disappearance, an important food source had been lost to other animals. The restoration project helped to train volunteers to clear the rivers and cut a path through disused roads where water used to flow. Protective walls of organic debris were constructed along drainage channels, while the banks were planted with fast-growing alder. Slowly the environmentalists were restoring some of the balance to the relationship between forest, humans and animals. It took constant energy and drive, and there was little prospect of speedy results.

'You know, if you take up whaling you'll make a lot of enemies,' said Anawak, after a while.

'And how do you see it?' asked Frank.

'If you want my opinion, it's not wise.'

'I expect you're right. They're a protected species, why hunt them? Not all of us are in favour of resuming whaling. For a start, does anyone know how to hunt any more? And what about the spiritual preparation? It's hard to imagine people submitting to the *7uusimch*, these days. But, that said, our people haven't hunted whales for nearly a century, and in real terms we're talking five or six creatures per year – a truly insignificant number. There aren't many of us left, you know. Our forefathers lived off whales. The hunters observed rituals that lasted months and even years. Before they set out they purified their spirit in readiness for the gift of life that the whale would make to them. It wasn't a question of harpooning the first animal they set eyes on. They were drawn to a particular whale by unknowable forces, in a kind of vision uniting hunters and whale. It's that spirituality we want to preserve.'

'Sure, but whales are worth a lot of money,' said Anawak. 'A spokesman for the Makah set the value of a grey at half a million US dollars. Whale meat and whale oil sell at a premium overseas, he said. In practically the same breath he mentioned the Makah's economic problems and high unemployment. That wasn't very clever – and it's a far cry from spirituality.'

'Oh, you're probably right there too. All the same whether you think it's greed or tradition that motivates the Makah, you can't ignore the fact that they refrained from whaling and set aside their right to do it at a time when whales were being hunted to extinction by whites. Commercial whaling isn't exactly spiritual either. It was whites who started to treat life as a commodity. They were quick to help themselves to whatever they wanted – but now if we mention money it causes such outrage that you'd think the survival of the planet was at stake. Funny, isn't it? The Aboriginal peoples take only what they need of the supplies that nature gives them, but the whites treat them wastefully. It's only when there's almost nothing left that they wake up and want to protect our resources – which means saving nature from those who never posed a threat. If whales are still endangered, then the Japanese and the Norwegians are to blame. We've never been guilty of wiping out a species, but we've been made to take the punishment.'

Anawak was silent.

'Our people are trapped,' said Frank. 'Things have got better, but I can't help thinking we're trapped in a conflict that we can't escape on our own. Have I ever told you that after every catch, every successful business deal, every celebration, I put something aside for the Raven?'

'No.'

'Do you know about Raven and his hunger?'

Anawak shook his head.

'Raven isn't actually the main animal spirit here. For that you'd have to go further north, to the Haida or the Tlingit. On the island you'll hear stories about Kánekelak, the changer – but we like Raven too. The Tlingit say that he speaks for the poor, like Christ, so I always break off morsels of meat or fish to leave for him. He was born the son of a beast-man and put into a raven's skin by his father, who named him Wigyét. As he grew up, Wigyét ate his people out of house and home, and they sent him into the world. He was given a stone to take with him so he had a place to rest, and the stone became the land in which we live. He stole the sunshine and brought it back to Earth. I give to Raven what belongs to him. At the same time I know that he is the result of evolutionary processes that started out with proteins, amino acids and single-cell organisms. I love our creation myths, but I also watch TV, read, and know about the Big Bang. So do Christians though, but that doesn't stop them learning about the seven days of creation and Adam and Eve. They had centuries to adjust their thought, find a way to unite mythology and modern science. We were given barely any time at all. We were thrown into a world that wasn't ours and never could be. Now we're returning to our own world and discovering that we no longer know it. That's the curse of being uprooted, Leon. You don't belong anywhere, neither in the old nor the new. The Indians were uprooted. The whites are doing their best to make up for it, but what can they do when they're uprooted too? They're destroying the world that created them. They've gambled away their homeland. We all have, in one way or another.'

Frank gave Anawak a long look. Then his face creased into a smile. 'Wasn't that a stirring Indian lecture, my friend? Come on, we should drink to it. Except you don't drink . . .'

1 May

Trondheim, Norway

Still no sign of Lund. They were supposed to meet in the canteen, then make their way to the conference hall upstairs. Johanson stared at the clock on the wall above the counter, watching the hands creep round the dial. Steadily, remorselessly, the worms crept with them, never flagging. With each passing second they burrowed deeper into the ice. And there was nothing he could do.

Johanson shivered. Time isn't just passing, it's running out, a voice whispered inside him.

This is the beginning.

The beginning of the plan.

Now, that was ridiculous. Locusts weren't planning anything when they ruined a harvest: they were hungry. Worms didn't plan and neither did jellyfish, nor algae.

Did Statoil have a plan?

Skaugen had flown over from Stavanger for the meeting. He'd asked for a detailed account of the findings. He seemed to have made some headway with his enquiries, and was keen to collate their results. Lund had wanted to meet Johanson beforehand so that they could agree on a strategy.

She must have been delayed, probably by Kare. They hadn't talked about her personal life since they'd left Trondheim for the *Sonne*. He'd avoided asking questions: he didn't like to press, and he hated indiscretion. Besides, he'd had the impression that she needed time to herself.

His mobile rang. It was Lund. 'What's happened to you?' he asked. 'I had to drink your coffee for you.'

'Sorry.'

'What's up?'

'I'm in the conference hall. I meant to ring ages ago, but I haven't had a second.'

There was an edge to her voice. 'Is everything all right?' he asked.

'Sure. Are you coming up?'

'I'll be there in a tick.'

So, she was upstairs already. Some business he wasn't supposed to know about, no doubt. Not that he minded. It was their bloody project.

He walked into the conference hall. Lund, Skaugen and Stone were standing in front of a large chart, which mapped the proposed location of the unit. Stone was talking in hushed tones to Lund, who seemed irritated. Skaugen didn't look too happy either. He turned as Johanson came in and gave a half-hearted smile. Hvistendahl was standing in the background, talking on the phone.

'Shall I come back later?' Johanson asked.

'No, you're just the man we need.' Skaugen gestured towards the table. 'Take a seat.'

Now Lund seemed to see Johanson for the first time. Leaving Stone in mid-sentence, she walked over and kissed his cheek.

'Skaugen wants to get rid of Stone,' she whispered. 'We need you to help us.'

Johanson showed no outward reaction. She was asking him to stir things up for them. What the hell was she thinking, getting him involved?

They sat down. Hvistendahl flipped his phone shut. Johanson was tempted to leave them to it. 'Right,' he said, sounding frostier than usual. 'A quick explanation before we get going. I had to narrow my investigation from its original focus, which is to say I specifically targeted scientists and institutes with known connections to energy conglomerates.'

'Was that wise?' asked Hvistendahl, in alarm. 'I thought we wanted to be as discreet as possible about, uh, putting our ear to the ground.'

'There was too much ground to cover. I had to set some boundaries.'

'Well, I hope you didn't say anything about—'

'I contacted them in my capacity as a biologist from the NTNU. A straightforward scientific enquiry.'

Skaugen pursed his lips. 'I don't suppose they were especially forthcoming.'

'That depends on how you look at it.' Johanson pointed to his file and the printouts. 'You have to read between the lines. Scientists make bad liars. They don't like politics. Their statements are like a dossier of muffled testimony – at times you can practically hear them shouting through their gags. I'm convinced that our worm has appeared else-where.'

'Convinced?' said Stone.

'So far no one's admitted it. But certain people became very curious.' Johanson looked at Stone. 'And they all happen to work for institutes with close ties to the energy industry. One of them is specifically involved in the technology of methane extraction.'

'Who?' Skaugen asked sharply.

'A scientist in Tokyo. Ryo Matsumoto. I didn't speak to him directly, only to his institute.'

'Who is he?' asked Hvistendahl.

'Japan's leading expert on gas hydrates,' said Skaugen. 'Worked on a methane-extraction project in Canada. He was testing drill sites in the permafrost.'

'His team got very excited as soon as I described the worm,' Johanson continued. 'They started asking questions. Was the worm capable of destabilising hydrates? How large were the colonies?'

'That doesn't mean they knew about it,' said Stone.

'Oh, yes, it does,' growled Skaugen. 'Matsumoto works for the Japan National Oil Corporation.'

'Are they interested in methane too?'

'You bet. In 2000 Matsumoto was trialling extraction methods in the Nankai Trough. The test results have been kept under wraps, but if he's to be believed, there are imminent plans for commercial extraction. The methane age is all he ever talks about.'

'Fine,' said Stone. 'But there's still no proof that he'd come across the worm himself.'

Johanson shook his head. 'Imagine our detective exercise in reverse. The enquiry comes to us. They ask my opinion as a so-called in-dependent scientist. The person doing the asking is also a scientist and an adviser to the JNOC, but he claims he's writing out of scientific curiosity. Now, I don't want to tell him outright that we know about the worm. But I'm alarmed. I want to know what he knows. So I pump him for information, like Matsumoto's people did me. And that's the mistake. The questions I ask are too pointed, too targeted. If the scientist's got his wits about him, he'll know he's hit a nerve.'

'If that's true,' said Lund, 'then the Japanese continental slope has been affected as well.'

'But you don't have any proof,' persisted Stone. 'There's not a shred of evidence to suggest that anyone other than us has come across it.' He leaned forward and the light caught the frame of his glasses. 'Dr Johanson, this type of information isn't any good to us. I'm sorry, but no one could have predicted the appearance of the worm because it's never been found elsewhere. I mean, for all we know, Matsumoto might just be curious to learn more about worms.'

'My instinct says he isn't,' said Johanson, unperturbed.

'Your instinct?'

'My instinct tells me that we haven't heard the end of it. The South Americans have found it too.'

'Let me guess. They asked leading questions too.'

'Exactly.'

'You disappoint me, Dr Johanson,' said Stone, scornfully. 'I thought you were a scientist. I assume you don't always rely on instinct.'

'Cliff,' said Lund, 'maybe you should shut up.'

Stone's eyes widened. He stared at her, outraged. 'I'm your boss,' he barked, 'and if anyone here needs to shut up it's—'

'That's enough,' said Skaugen. 'Not another word.'

Johanson could see that Lund was having difficulty containing herself. He wondered how Stone had provoked her. 'In any case', he went on, 'I think Japan and South America know more than they'll let on. Just like us. Fortunately it's much easier to get reliable data on water than it is on deep-sea worms. There's hardly a stretch of water that isn't under analysis at any one time. I tapped a few people for information, and they confirmed the situation.'

'Which is?'

'Unusually high quantities of methane are entering the water column. It all fits.' Johanson hesitated. 'I'm sorry to bring instinct into this again, Dr Stone, but when I was speaking to Matsumoto's people I had the impression that they were trying to let me guess the truth. No doubt they were sworn to secrecy, but no serious scientist or institute would play with information that people's lives depend on. It's indefensible. It only happens when—'

Skaugen frowned at him. 'When economic interests are at stake,' he said. 'Is that what you're saying?'

'Yes. Indeed.'

'Is there anything you'd like to add?'

Johanson pulled a printout from the pile. 'High levels of methane are being recorded in three areas of the world: Norway, Japan and off the east coast of Latin America. Then there's Lukas Bauer's data.'

'Who's he?' asked Skaugen.

'He works on deep-water currents. He's in the Greenland Sea right now. He uses drifting profilers to track the currents, then maps the data. I emailed his vessel. Here's what he had to say.' Johanson started to read: '"Dear Colleague, I'm afraid I'm not acquainted with your worm, though we are recording exceptionally high levels of methane in the Greenland Sea. In fact, in certain areas, large quantities of gas are seeping into the water. It may have something to do with the discontinuities we're observing here – a nasty business, if I'm right. I'm sorry this is rather sketchy, but I'm awfully busy right now. I'm attaching a detailed report by Karen Weaver, a journalist who's here to help me and distract me with her questions. She's a smart girl, and she'll deal with any further queries. You can contact her on kweaver@deepbluesea.com."'

'What kind of discontinuities does he mean?' asked Lund.

'No idea. When I met him in Oslo, he seemed a little absent-minded – likeable, but the epitome of a scientist. He forgot to attach the report, so no surprises there. I emailed straight back, but he hasn't replied.'

'We should probably find out exactly what he's working on,' said Lund. 'Bohrmann'll know, won't he?'

'I'm guessing the journalist does too,' said Johanson.

'Karen . . . ?'

'Karen Weaver. I thought the name was familiar. Turns out I'd read some of her articles. Interesting woman. Studied biology, computer science and sport. She focuses on marine-related issues – always the big themes: charting the seas, plate tectonics, climate change. Her latest article was on deep-water currents. As for Bohrmann, I'll give him a call if he hasn't contacted me by the end of the week.'

'So, where does that leave us?' Hvistendahl asked them.

Skaugen's blue eyes settled on Johanson. 'Dr Johanson has told you what he thinks. It would be a disgrace for the oil industry to withhold information when people's lives may depend on it. Unquestionably he's right. That's why yesterday afternoon I had a meeting with the board, and made some clear recommendations – as a result of which the Norwegian government has now been informed.'

Stone's head jerked up. 'Informed of what? We don't have any firm results. We don't even—'

'Informed about the worms, Clifford. And about the dissociation of the methane deposits. About the risk of an impending methane disaster. And the danger that the slope could collapse. We even told them that our deep-sea robot filmed an unknown organism in the ocean. Isn't that enough?' Skaugen frowned at them all in turn. 'Dr Johanson will be pleased to know that his instincts were right. This morning I had the pleasure of an hour-long conversation with the scientific board of the JNOC. Now, I'm sure you all realise that it's a reputable company, but suppose for a moment that the Japanese were so eager to lead the way in methane extraction that they were prepared to do anything to succeed before the rest. Unlikely as it sounds, it could result in a certain amount of risk-taking – or maybe in a tendency to overlook expert opinion.' Skaugen's gaze shifted to Stone. 'Then imagine that there are people in this world whose ambition might tempt them to disregard warnings and suppress vital evidence. Oh, I know it's absurd but, hypothetically, if it were true . . . Well, think how dreadful it would be. We'd have to suspect the JNOC of masterminding a cover-up to hide the existence of a worm that had threatened the nation's dream of being first to get to the methane. We'd have to suspect that they'd been doing it for weeks.'

No one said anything. 'But we shouldn't be so hard on them,' Skaugen went on. 'What if Neil Armstrong had stayed in the shuttle just because of some worm! And, as I said, I was talking hypothetically. The JNOC *has* found a similar worm species off the coast of Japan, but the director assures me that they first came across it in the past three days. What an amazing coincidence.'

'Oh, crap,' said Hvistendahl, softly.

'And what does the JNOC intend to do?' asked Lund.

'Well, I imagine they'll inform their government. They're a state-run company, like Statoil. They can't afford to keep quiet – not that they would ever have been tempted to do so. God forbid! I might call the South Americans later, to see if they can find the worm as well. Imagine their shock if they did! They'd call straight back and tell us right away. And just for the record, in case anyone thinks I'm pissing all over the others, we're no better.'

'That's a bit—' said Hvistendahl.

'You don't agree?'

'We didn't know how serious it was until now.' Hvistendahl seemed put out. 'And, besides, telling the government was my recommendation too.'

'I'm not accusing *you* of anything,' Skaugen said pointedly.

Johanson felt as if he was in a play. Skaugen was stage-managing Stone's execution, that much was clear. A look of grim satisfaction was spreading over Lund's face. But hadn't Stone found the worm in the first place?

'Clifford.' Lund broke the silence. 'When did you come across the worm?'

Stone's face paled. 'You should know,' he said. 'You were there.'

'You hadn't seen it before?'

'Before?'

'Like last year. When you decided to take matters into your own hands and build the Kongsberg prototype – a thousand metres under water.'

'What the hell is your problem?' Stone hissed. He glanced at Skaugen. 'I wasn't acting on my own. I had their backing. Come off it, Finn, what are you trying to suggest?'

'Oh, you had our backing all right,' said Skaugen. 'You said you'd be testing a new type of subsea unit designed for a maximum depth of a thousand metres.'

'Right.'

'*Testing.*'

'Well, of course you have to test it. Everything you do right up until production is one long test. You'd practically given me the go-ahead.' He turned to Hvistendahl. 'You too, Thor. You ran the trials in your lab and gave the OK.'

'That's true,' said Hvistendahl. 'We did.'

'Well, there you go then.'

'We asked you,' continued Skaugen, 'to investigate the site and take advice on whether it was prudent to construct a unit that hadn't been fully tested—'

'You can't do this to me!' Stone said angrily. 'That unit was approved.'

'– then get it up and running on a trial basis. Yes, we were prepared to take that risk. Providing all the reports were in favour.'

Stone leaped to his feet. 'Which they were,' he said, trembling with rage.

'Sit down,' said Skaugen, coldly. 'I've got news for you. Yesterday we lost contact with the Kongsberg prototype.'

Stone froze. Then he said, 'I'm not directly involved in monitoring the prototype. I didn't build the unit, just drove the project forward. What are you accusing me of? Of not knowing what's going on?'

'No. The seriousness of the present circumstances compelled us to reconstruct the exact chain of events leading to the building of the prototype. During our investigations we came across two reports that you seem to have . . . how shall I put it? . . . omitted to mention.'

Stone's fingers gripped the tabletop. He wobbled. Then he recovered himself. His face was expressionless. 'I don't know anything about it.'

'One of the reports states that the exact location of the hydrates and gas pockets proved difficult to chart. It concludes that the risk of hitting a pocket was minimal, although it couldn't be ruled out.'

'The risk was negligible,' said Stone, hoarsely. 'For the past year the unit's productivity has exceeded all our expectations.'

'Negligible isn't good enough.'

'But we *didn't* hit any gas pockets! We're extracting oil. The unit works. The prototype's been a resounding success – successful enough to convince you to launch a proper unit and this time make it official.'

'The second report,' said Lund, 'states that you found an unidentified worm that colonises hydrates.'

'For God's sake, yes, all right. It was the ice worm.'

'Did you examine it?'

'Why the hell would I?'

'Did *anyone* examine it?'

'It was . . . Of course we examined it.'

'The report says it resembled an ice worm. There was no conclusive verdict. It mentions large numbers of the creatures. Apparently their effect on the environment was unknown, although methane was detected in the water around them.'

Stone's face was white. 'That's not quite . . . not quite true. The worms were confined to a limited area.'

'But in that area there were thousands of them.'

'We built to one side of it. I didn't think the report . . . Well, it wasn't relevant.'

'Were you able to classify the worm?' Skaugen asked calmly.

'We were certain that it—'

'Could you *classify* it?'

Stone's jaws were grinding. 'No,' he conceded, after a long pause.

'Fine,' said Skaugen. 'In that case, Cliff, you're released from your duties for the moment. Tina will take your place.'

'You can't do that!'

'We'll discuss it later.'

Stone turned to Hvistendahl, who avoided his eyes. 'For Christ's sake, Thor, the unit worked fine.'

'You've been a fool,' said Hvistendahl, levelly.

Suddenly Stone looked crushed. 'I'm sorry,' he said. 'I didn't mean to. I only wanted to get the unit up and running.'

Johanson felt embarrassed for him. He'd wanted to be the first to launch a successful prototype. The subsea unit was his baby, a unique chance for him to further his career, so he'd decided to ignore the worms.

For a while it had worked. There'd been a successful year of unofficial tests, then the official start, a production run and the conquering of new depths. It could have been Stone's victory parade. But the worm had appeared again. And this time it wasn't restricted to a few square metres.

Skaugen rubbed his eyes. 'I apologise for dragging you into this, Dr Johanson,' he said, 'but you're part of the team.'

'So I see.'

'The fact is, things are off-kilter all over the world. Accidents, anomalies and so on. People are getting nervous, and oil companies are useful scapegoats. We can't afford to make mistakes. Can we still count on you, Dr Johanson?'

Johanson sighed. Then he nodded.

'Good. That's what we thought. Oh, don't get me wrong, it's entirely your decision. But since you may find yourself needing to invest more time in your role as scientific co-ordinator, we took the liberty of approaching the NTNU.'

Johanson sat up. 'You did *what*?'

'We asked if you might take leave of absence. I also put your name forward to the government.'

Johanson was dumbstruck. Then he recovered himself. 'Hang on a minute—'

'It's a proper research post,' interrupted Lund. 'Statoil will provide the budget, and you'll get all the help you need.'

'I would have preferred to be—'

'I can see that you're annoyed,' said Skaugen, 'and I understand why. But I'm sure you're aware of how critical the situation is out there. Apart from the Geomar people, no one is half as well informed as you are. You don't have to accept, of course, but it's in the public interest that you do.'

Johanson felt sick with rage. He had a scathing retort on the tip of his tongue, but he bit it back. 'I see,' he said stiffly.

'Do you accept, then?'

'I couldn't possibly refuse.' He shot Lund a look, hoping it would slice her in two. She looked away.

'Believe me, Dr Johanson,' Skaugen said gravely, 'Statoil is very grateful to you. You've already earned our utmost respect and admiration for everything you've done. But I'd like you to know that in me, at least, you've gained a friend. I'm sorry if we bulldozed you into this, but when this is all resolved you can run me over in any kind of vehicle you like. You can nail me to a cross, if it helps.'

Johanson held the other man's clear blue eyes. 'OK,' he said. 'I might take you up on that.'

'Sigur, slow down, for God's sake!' Lund was running after him as he hurried down the path towards the car park. The research centre was surrounded by lawns and trees, idyllically placed on a hill near the cliffs, but Johanson wasn't in the mood for pretty views. He wanted to get back to his office.

'Sigur!'

She caught up with him but he strode on.

'Oh, come on, Sigur. Do you have to be so pigheaded?' she yelled. 'Do you seriously want me to chase you?'

Johanson stopped abruptly and spun round. She almost ran into him. 'Well, why not? We all know how quick you are. Quick to speak and quick to make promises. In fact, you're so damn quick that you make plans for your friends without even asking.'

'You self-righteous bastard. I didn't want to interfere.'

'No? Well, that's reassuring.' He didn't wait for a reply but continued down the path.

Lund hesitated for a second, then appeared at his side. 'OK, I should have told you. I'm sorry. Honestly.'

'You should have *asked* me.'

'We wanted to, for God's sake, but Skaugen charged straight in and you got the wrong impression.'

'I got the impression that you bought me from the NTNU, like a packhorse.'

'No.' She tugged at his sleeve, forcing him to stop. 'We were sounding them out, that's all. We wanted to know whether hypothetically, they would grant you some leave.'

Johanson snorted. 'That's not how it sounded.'

'It came out all wrong.'

Johanson glanced down at her fingers, which were still wrapped in his sleeve. She let go.

'No one's forcing you to do anything,' she said. 'If you change your mind, that's fine too. We'll deal with it.'

Birds were singing in the background, and the chug of distant motorboats blew in on the breeze from the fjords. 'If I change my mind,' he said, 'it won't look good for you, though.'

'I'll just have to live with it. I didn't have to recommend you. It was my decision, and . . . Well, I jumped the gun a bit with Skaugen.'

'What did you tell him?'

'That you'd do it.' She smiled. 'I promised. But that's not your problem.'

Johanson felt his anger ebb away. He would have liked to keep hold of it for a while longer to teach Lund a lesson.

'Skaugen trusts me,' said Lund. 'I couldn't meet you in the canteen earlier. He'd called me up there on my own to tell me about Stone and those hushed-up reports. It's all Cliff's fault. If only he'd been honest from the start, we wouldn't be in this mess.'

'No, Tina.' Johanson shook his head. 'He didn't think the worms could be a danger, that's all.' He was defending Stone, even though he'd never liked the man. 'He just wanted to get on with it.'

'If he didn't think they were an issue, why did he hide the reports?'

'It would've held up the project. No one would have taken them seriously but Statoil would have done its duty and the project would have been delayed.'

'But we *are* taking it seriously!'

'Sure, but only because of the size of the problem. There was only a small patch of them when Stone found them, right?'

'Hmm.'

'A densely covered patch, perhaps, but a patch all the same. I bet it happens all the time. Small organisms often appear *en masse*, and how much damage can a few worms do? No one would have worried about it, believe me. When they came across the ice worm in Mexico, they didn't ring alarm bells either, even though the hydrates were crawling with them.'

'Sharing the reports is a matter of principle. The project was his responsibility.'

'Yes.' Johanson sighed. He looked out towards the fjords. 'And now it's mine.'

'We need a scientific co-ordinator,' said Lund, 'and I wouldn't trust anyone else.'

'My God,' said Johanson. 'Are you feeling OK?'

'I'm being serious.'

'And I've said I'll do it.'

'Just think,' Lund beamed, 'we'll be working together.'

'There's no need to put me off. So, what's the next step?'

She hesitated. 'Well, you heard what Skaugen said. He wants me to do Stone's job. Long-term, he can't make that decision. He needs the go-ahead from Stavanger.'

'Skaugen,' mused Johanson. 'But I don't get it. Why gun down Stone in public? Why get me involved? To provide the ammunition?'

Lund shrugged. 'Skaugen's got real integrity. Some say a little too much. But he gets tired of people turning a blind eye. He's soft-hearted, though. If I asked him to give Stone another chance, he'd probably agree.'

'I see,' said Johanson slowly. 'And that's what you're thinking of doing.'

She didn't answer.

'How magnanimous.'

Lund pretended not to hear him. 'Skaugen's left it up to me,' she said, 'but the subsea unit . . . Stone knows a hell of a lot about it. Much more than I do. Skaugen wants someone to take the *Thorvaldson* and find out why there's no signal from the prototype. Stone should head the operation, but if Skaugen suspends him, it's up to me.'

'And the other option?'

'Like I said, Stone gets another chance.'

'To save the unit.'

'If there's anything left to save. Or to get it back in working order.

Either way, Skaugen wants me promoted. But if he lets Stone off the hook, Stone keeps his job and goes on board the *Thorvaldson*.'

'Which leaves you where?'

'Well, I'd go to Stavanger and report to the board.'

'Congratulations,' said Johanson. 'Your career gets a boost.'

There was a short silence.

'Is that what I want?'

Johanson thought back to their weekend by the lake. 'No idea,' he said. 'But you can have a boyfriend *and* a career, if that's what you're worried about. If you still have a boyfriend, that is.'

'We . . . haven't seen much of each other since – since you and I . . .' She trailed off. When she spoke again, her voice was firm: 'Hanging out in cosy old Sveggesundet or taking day trips to the islands isn't normal life. It's like being on a film set.'

'But it is a *good* film.'

'It's like . . . Imagine going back to the place where you fell in love,' said Lund. 'As soon as you get there, it sweeps you off your feet. It's all so perfect, and when it's time to leave, you want to stay. And at the same time you can't help wondering whether you really want to live in the most beautiful place in the world. I mean, would it still be so beautiful if you lived there? She gave an awkward laugh. 'Sorry, I hate talking about this sort of thing.'

Johanson searched her face for signs of indecision, but saw only someone who had made up her mind. She just didn't know it yet. 'Maybe you should go and tell Kare that you love him and want to be with him for ever.'

'What if it doesn't work out?'

'You're suspicious of happiness. I was like that once. It didn't do me any good.'

'Are you happy now?'

'Yes.'

'No misgivings?'

Johanson flung up his hands in a despair. 'Come on, Tina, everyone has misgivings. I just try to be honest with myself and with everyone else. I like flirting, wine, having a good time and being in control. I don't talk much, but I don't feel the need to. Psychiatrists would find me deeply boring. I want my peace and that's all there is to it. My life suits me. But that's me. My way of being happy is different from yours. I trust mine.

You'll have to learn to do the same. But you haven't much time. Kare won't wait for ever.'

The breeze played with Lund's hair. 'If Stone goes out to the slope,' she said, thinking aloud, 'I'll have to go to Stavanger. That's OK, though. The *Thorvaldson* is ready to sail. Stone could leave tomorrow or the day after. The Stavanger job will take longer. I'd have to write a detailed report. So there'd be a few days spare for me to drive to Sveggesundet and . . . do some work from there.'

'Some work?' Johanson grinned.

She pursed her lips. 'I'll think about it and talk to Skaugen.'

'You do that,' said Johanson. 'But think quickly.'

Back at the office he checked his inbox for messages. There wasn't much of any interest. The final mail caught his attention when he saw who it was from: kweaver@deepbluesea.com

He clicked on it.

hello dr johanson. thanks for your message. i've just got back to london and all i can say right now is that i don't have a clue what's happened to lukas bauer and his boat. i can't contact him. i'd be happy to meet up with you though. who knows? we may even be able to help each other. i'll be at my london office from the middle of next week, but if you fancy meeting sooner, i'm heading off to the shetlands and could fix up something there. let me know what suits you. karen weaver.

'My, my,' murmured Johanson. 'So journalists *can* be co-operative.'

Had Lukas Bauer gone missing?

Maybe he should request a meeting with Skaugen and tell him his theory. But there was no evidence to support it – just a nasty feeling that the world was coming unstuck and the sea was to blame.

If he wanted to take the idea any further, he needed more evidence . . .

He should hook up with Weaver as soon as he could. Why not meet her in the Shetlands? The flights shouldn't be a problem, if Statoil was paying. In fact, it would all be very easy. Hadn't Skaugen said he could nail him to a cross if he wanted?

He didn't need to go that far. A helicopter would be enough.

Johanson leaned back in his chair and studied the clock. He was supposed to be lecturing in an hour, and then he had a departmental meeting about some DNA sequencing.

He created a new folder and entered a file name: *The Fifth Day*.

It was the first thing that had come into his mind. On the fifth day of creation, God had filled the sea with living creatures . . .

He started to type, and a chill swept through him.

2 May

For the past forty-eight hours Ford and Anawak had been poring over the same sequence of data. At first total darkness. Then an oscillation from an audio signal outside the human range. Three signals in total. And finally the cloud. A luminescent, blue-tinged cloud. Out of nowhere it appeared in the centre of the screen and scattered outwards, like a universe expanding. The light wasn't bright, more a faint blue glow; a dim, diffuse glimmer, just strong enough for the huge silhouettes of the whales to loom into view. It spread rapidly and filled the screen. The whales hovered in front of it, as if bound by its spell.

Several seconds passed.

Deep in the cloud something shot forwards like winding, twisting lightning. Its tapered point struck a whale on the side of the head. Lucy. The whole thing was over in less than a second. More flashes blazed towards the other whales, then the spectacle ended as abruptly as it had begun.

Next the film seemed to play in reverse. The cloud collapsed in on itself and vanished. The screen went dark. Ford's technicians had slowed the footage, then slowed it again. They'd tried everything they could think of to optimise the resolution and let in more light, but even after hours of studying the tape they were still no closer to solving the mystery of the whales.

In the end Anawak and Ford decided to write their report for the emergency committee. They'd been authorised to call on the help of a biologist from Nanaimo who specialised in bioluminescence. It took him a while to get over his bewilderment, but then he backed their conclusions: the cloud and the flashes were organic. According to the expert, the flashes were caused by a chain reaction within the cloud, though he couldn't say how they'd been triggered or what purpose they served. Their twisting motion and the way they tapered off towards the tip reminded him of squid, but a creature that size would have to be truly gigantic, and it was doubtful that giant squid could luminesce. Besides, that wouldn't explain the cloud or where the serpentine flashes were coming from.

But their instincts told them one thing unequivocally: the cloud was responsible for the change in the whales.

All of this was duly recorded in the report, which vanished into a hole of impenetrable darkness. The *Black Hole* was what they called the emergency committee, which sucked everything in without trace. Initially the Canadian government had encouraged the scientists to work alongside them, but since the US-led allied committee had been set up, all that was required of them was the provision of information. Vancouver Aquarium, the lab in Nanaimo and even the University of British Columbia were just links in a one-way chain of knowledge. The only time the scientists ever heard anything was when the committee instructed them to submit their findings, hypotheses and frustrations as reports. Neither John Ford, Leon Anawak, Rod Palm, Sue Oliviera nor Ray Fenwick had any idea how their input was being used or whether the committee agreed with their findings. Comparing their work with that of other groups was a key element of their research, and now it was being denied them.

'Things were fine,' said Ford, 'till Judith Li took the helm.'

Anawak had Oliviera on the line. 'We need to look at some more of those mussels,' she said.

'I can't get hold of anyone from Inglewood,' he told her. 'They won't talk to me, and Li's insisting that it was all an accident, a blunder with the tow line. No one's said anything about mussels.'

'But you saw them with your own eyes! And we need another sample, plus some of that weird organic substance. Why won't they co-operate? I thought they wanted our help.'

'You could try contacting the committee directly.'

'It all has to go via Ford. I don't get it, Leon. What's the point of an emergency committee, if this is what happens?'

Perhaps it was the nature of crisis squads and emergency committees to work furtively, thought Anawak. When had an emergency committee ever faced the same problem twice? Its permanent members had to get to grips with terrorism, political and military crises, all of which had to be handled in confidence. But they also faced malfunctioning nuclear power stations, broken dams, forest fires, floods, earthquakes, volcanoes and famines. Did all that have to be handled in confidence? Probably not, but it usually was.

'It's not as though we don't know what causes volcanic eruptions and earthquakes,' said Shoemaker, when Anawak voiced his frustration. 'Sure, you can be afraid of nature, but at least it never tries to catch you out or trip you up. Only people do that.'

The three were having breakfast on Leon's boat. The sun peeked out between the white clouds overhead and it was pleasantly mild, but no one was in the mood to appreciate it. Delaware was the only one with any appetite and she was demolishing a plateful of scrambled egg.

'Did you hear about the gas tanker?'

'The one that exploded near Japan?' Shoemaker took a sip of his coffee. 'That's old hat.'

Delaware shook her head. 'No. Another went down yesterday. Burst into flames in Bangkok harbour.'

'Has anyone said why?'

'No.'

'Maybe it was technical failure,' said Anawak. 'We shouldn't read too much into it.'

'You're beginning to sound like Judith Li.' Shoemaker slammed his mug on the table. 'You were right, by the way. There was practically nothing in the news about the *Barrier Queen*. They wrote mostly about the tug.'

Anawak wasn't surprised. The emergency committee seemed to like to keep them guessing. Maybe that was part of the game. Find your own answers. Well, he was on the case already. Straight after the plane crash Delaware had begun to scour the net. Had whales gone on the offensive anywhere else? As the *taayii Hawi'lh* had said: *Maybe the whales aren't the problem, Leon. They might be just part of the problem – the only part we can see.*

George Frank had hit the nail on the head, but Anawak didn't feel any the wiser for it when he saw the results of Delaware's foray. She'd browsed websites from South America, Germany, Scandinavia, France, Australia and Japan. Elsewhere the problem was jellyfish, not whales.

'Jellyfish?' Shoemaker burst out laughing. 'What are they doing? Flinging themselves at boats?'

At first Anawak hadn't seen the connection either, but maybe aggressive whales and plagues of toxic stingers had something in common that wasn't readily apparent – two symptoms of an underlying problem. Delaware had found a statement by a Costa Rican scientist who seemed to think that the jellyfish terrorising South America weren't Portuguese men-of-war but a similar, as yet unidentified but infinitely more toxic species.

The problems didn't stop there.

'Around the same time that we were starting to have trouble with the whales, boats started to disappear in South America and South Africa,' Delaware said. 'Motorboats and cutters. All they found was the odd piece of debris. But when you put two and two together—'

'You get a pack of vicious whales,' said Shoemaker. 'So how come we didn't hear about it earlier?'

'Well, most of the time we don't take an interest,' said Anawak. 'No one's usually bothered about what's happening in other parts of the world.'

'Either way, there've been far more shipping accidents than we've been told,' said Delaware. 'Collisions, explosions, freighters sinking . . . And there's the epidemic in France. It started with algae lurking in the lobster, and now a pathogen's sweeping the country. Other nations have been affected too, I think. But the more you look into it, the hazier it gets.'

From time to time Anawak felt sure they were making fools of themselves. Of course they wouldn't be the first to fall for America's favourite invention, the conspiracy theory. Every fourth US citizen harboured some kind of paranoid suspicion. According to some, Clinton had worked for the Russian secret service, and plenty of people believed in UFOs. But why would a government be interested in trying to hide events that were affecting thousands of people? Especially since keeping them secret seemed impossible in the first place.

Shoemaker was sceptical too: 'This isn't Roswell, you know. There aren't any little green men falling from the sky, or flying saucers hidden in bushes. All that conspiracy stuff – it doesn't happen in real life. I bet if a whale attacked today, the whole world would know tomorrow. And we'd know too, if something happened elsewhere.'

'OK, consider this, then,' said Delaware. 'Tofino has twelve hundred inhabitants and only three main streets. But people here don't know all there is to know about each other all of the time.'

'So what?'

'If one small town's too big to keep track of, what does that make the planet?'

'Oh, please!'

'What I'm trying to say is that the government can't always *withhold* news, but it can play things down. You just rein in the reporting. I bet most of what I fished out from the Internet was in the media here – we just didn't notice.'

Shoemaker squinted at her. 'Right . . .' he said uncertainly.

'We need more information.' said Anawak. He prodded his scrambled egg. 'Although, strictly speaking, we've got it. Or Li has.'

'So ask her for it,' said Shoemaker.

Anawak raised his eyebrows.

'If there's something you want to know, you should ask. What's the worst that could happen? A straight refusal and a kick in the teeth.'

Anawak fell silent. Li wouldn't tell him anything – Ford hadn't and he'd asked till he was blue in the face. On the other hand, Shoemaker had a point. There was a way of asking questions without anyone noticing.

Later on, when Shoemaker had left, Delaware placed a copy of the *Vancouver Sun* on the table in front of him. 'I didn't want to show you while Tom was around,' she said.

Anawak glanced at the front page. It was the previous day's edition. 'I've read it.'

'Cover to cover?'

'No, just the important bits.'

Delaware smiled. 'So read the unimportant bits.'

Anawak immediately spotted what she meant. It was a short article, only a few lines long. A photo was printed next to it, showing a family – father, mother, and a young boy, who was looking gratefully at the tall man next to him.

'Unbelievable,' murmured Anawak.

'Say what you like,' said Delaware, and glared at him. Today she was wearing yellow-tinted glasses with rhinestone crosses on the frames. 'But he's not that big an asshole.'

Little Bill Sheckley (5), the last person to be saved from the *Lady Wexham*, the passenger boat that sank on 11 April, can finally smile again. Today he was able to return home with his grateful parents, after spending weeks in Victoria Hospital where he was being kept for observation. After the rescue mission Bill had suffered a dangerous case of hypothermia, which developed into full-blown pneumonia. Now fighting fit again, Bill has evidently recovered from the shock. Today his parents expressed their gratitude to his rescuers, in particular Jack 'Greywolf' O'Bannon, a committed conservationist from Vancouver Island, who led the rescue mission and showed touching concern for little Bill's recovery. This young boy isn't the only one indebted to the 'hero of Tofino', as O'Bannon has been called.

Anawak folded the paper and flung it back on the table. 'Shoemaker would have gone mad,' he said.

For a while neither said anything. Anawak watched the clouds moving slowly overhead and tried to feel angry, but the only people he was angry with were General Li and himself.

In fact, mainly himself.

'Why does everyone have a problem with Greywolf?' asked Delaware.

'He can't stop causing trouble.' Anawak ran a hand over his eyes. Even though it was first thing in the morning he already felt tired.

'Don't get me wrong,' Delaware said cautiously, 'but he did pull me out of the water, just as I was thinking I was done for. I went looking for him two days ago. I found him sitting at the bar in a pub in Ucluelet, so I went up and thanked him.'

'And?' said Anawak wearily.

'He was surprised.'

Anawak looked at her.

'He wasn't expecting to be thanked. He was pleased. Then he asked how you were.'

'Me?'

She crossed her arms and leaned forward on the table. 'I don't think he's got many friends.'

'He needs to ask himself why.'

'And I think he's fond of you.'

'Come off it, Licia.'

'Tell me something about him.'

What was the point? thought Anawak. Why can't we talk about something more pleasant?

He thought for a moment. Nothing occurred to him.

'We used to be friends,' he said curtly.

He waited for Delaware to leap up in the air, yelling, 'I knew it!' Instead, she just nodded.

'His name is Jack O'Bannon and he comes from Port Townsend in Washington State. His father's an Irishman who married a half-Indian, from the Suquamish, I think. In the States Jack tried all kinds of jobs – he was a bouncer, a graphic designer, a bodyguard and finally a diver with the US Navy SEALs. That's when he found his calling – dolphin-handling. He was good at it, until they diagnosed his heart defect. Nothing serious, but they're a tough lot, the SEALs. Jack did well there – he's got more distinctions than you can count – but it was the end of his time in the navy.'

'How did he wind up here?'

'He always had a soft spot for Canada. At first he tried his luck in Vancouver's film business. He thought that with his build and looks he might become an actor, but he didn't have any talent. And things have never worked out for him because he can't keep his cool. He once put a guy in hospital.'

'Oh,' said Delaware.

Anawak flashed his teeth at her. 'Sorry to tarnish your image of him.'

'Never mind. What happened next?'

Anawak poured himself some orange juice. 'He was locked up. While he was in prison he read up on conservation and whales, and when he got out he decided that that's what he had to do. He went to see Davie, whom he knew from a visit to Ucluelet, and asked him if he could use an extra skipper. "Be my guest," said Davie, "just keep out of trouble." You know, Jack can be very charming when it suits him.'

Delaware nodded. 'But this time he wasn't charming.'

'Oh, he was fine for a while. We had a sudden rush of female tourists. Everything was perfect – until he punched a guy.'

'A passenger?'

'Right.'

'Oh, Jeez.'

'Yeah. Davie wanted to fire him, but I begged for him to have another chance. But three weeks later he pulled the same trick again. So Davie had to fire him. Wouldn't you have done the same?'

'I'd have thrown him out the first time,' said Delaware, softly.

'Well, at least *you* know how to look after yourself,' Anawak said cuttingly. 'Anyway, if you stick up for someone and that's how they thank you, sooner or later your patience runs out.'

He gulped his orange juice, choked and coughed. Delaware reached over and thumped him on the back.

'Then he totally lost it,' he wheezed. 'Jack's other little problem is that he doesn't know what's real. At some point during his frustration the Spirit of Manitou came upon him and told him; "From now on, let your name be Greywolf, protector of the whales, defender of all living things. Go forth and fight for them." Well, obviously he was mad with us, so he convinced himself that he had to fight against us. On top of everything else he still thinks I'm on the wrong side and I just haven't noticed.' Anawak was seething with rage now. 'He doesn't know anything about conservation or the Indians. They think he's hysterical – except the ones whose lives are washed up too: kids with nothing to do, guys who can't be bothered to work, drunks, people looking for trouble . . . They think he's great, and so do the grey-haired hippies and surfers who want to get rid of the tourists so they can laze around in peace. He attracts the scum of both cultures – anarchists, losers, dropouts, militants, extremists chucked out by Greenpeace for sullying its name, Indians whose clans have disowned them and crooks. Most of them don't give a shit about the whales. They just want to run riot. But Jack doesn't see any of that, and seriously believes that the Seaguards are an environmental pressure group. He even finances them. He earns the money as a lumberjack and a bear guide, and lives in a hovel not fit for a dog. He's such a screw-up. How does someone like him wind up as such a goddamn failure?' He paused for breath.

A seagull was shrieking in the sky above them.

Delaware spread a slice of bread with butter, dribbled some jam on the top and took a bite. 'Good,' she said. 'I can tell you still like him.'

The name Ucluelet came from the Nootka, meaning 'safe harbour'. Like Tofino, the picturesque town was situated in a natural harbour and had grown from a fishing village into a favourite spot for whale-watchers.

Greywolf lived in one of the less presentable parts of town. If you turned off the main road and ventured a few hundred metres down a root-ridden track just wide enough for a car, the centuries-old forest opened into a clearing with a shack in the middle. No one was more aware of its lack of comfort than its sole inhabitant. When the weather was good – and Greywolf's definition of bad weather came somewhere between a tornado and the end of the world – he spent his time outside, wandering through the forest, taking tourists to see the black bears and doing odd jobs. The probability of finding him at home was practically nil, even at night. He either slept in the open or in the bed of an adventure-hungry tourist, who never doubted for a second that she'd bagged herself a noble savage.

It was early afternoon when Anawak got to Ucluelet. He'd made up his mind to drive with Shoemaker to Nanaimo and get the ferry to Vancouver. He had his reasons for not taking the helicopter. The official reason for stopping in Ucluelet was so Shoemaker could talk business with Davie – the station was preparing to branch out into land-based adventure tours – but Anawak had excused himself from the discussions. Whatever the future held, he sensed that his time on Vancouver Island was coming to an end. If he was honest with himself, there was nothing to keep him there. Now the whale-watching was over, what did he have left?

He'd spent years trying to distract himself. OK, so he'd written his doctorate and become a respected scientist, but it was all wasted time. In the past few weeks he'd nearly died twice. Something had changed since the plane crash. He'd felt threatened on the inside, as though an enemy from the long-forgotten past had sensed his fear and was on his scent. He had one last chance to get a grip on his life. The message was clear: break the cycle.

Anawak's path had led him up the track strewn with tree roots and now he was standing in front of the shack, wondering what he was doing there. He took the few steps up to the shabby veranda and knocked.

Greywolf wasn't at home.

He circled the shack a few times, feeling vaguely disappointed. He should have known it would be empty. His feet led him back to the door. He reached out and pushed the handle. The door swung open. Leaving it unlocked was nothing out of the ordinary here. He shivered with a memory. There were other places like that too, or at least, there used to be. Hesitantly he walked in.

He hadn't been here for ages, which made him all the more astonished by the sight that met his eyes. He'd always thought of Greywolf as living in dingy chaos, but although the room was plain it was cosily furnished, with Indian masks and rugs on the walls. Colourful raffia chairs surrounded a low wooden table. Indian throws adorned the sofa. Two shelves were packed with utensils and wooden rattles that the Nootka used in ceremonies and for traditional chants. He couldn't see a television, but there were two hotplates and a sink. A narrow corridor led to a second room, Greywolf's bedroom, as Anawak remembered.

He felt a fleeting temptation to take a look around, but he still wasn't sure what he was doing there. The house was pulling him into a time warp, taking him back further than he cared to go.

His eyes were caught by a large mask, staring right at him. He took a step closer. Many Indian masks portrayed facial features symbolically, overemphasising and enlarging them – huge eyes, exaggeratedly arched eyebrows, a beak-like hooked nose. But this was a faithful copy of a human face. It showed the calm countenance of a young man with a straight nose, full lips and a smooth, high forehead. The hair looked matted, but seemed real. With the exception of the pupils, which were missing to allow the wearer to see, the eyes were surprisingly lifelike. Their gaze was calm and earnest, as though the man were in a trance.

Anawak stood motionless in front of it. He'd seen plenty of masks before. The Indians made them from cedarwood, bark and leather, and they were popular with tourists. But this mask was different.

'It's from the Pacheedaht.'

He swivelled round. Greywolf was just behind him. 'For a phoney Indian you're pretty good at sneaking up on people,' said Anawak.

'Thanks.' Greywolf grinned. He didn't seem put out to find an uninvited guest. 'Shame I can't return the compliment. For a *bona fide* Indian you're a wash-out.'

'How long have you been standing there?'

'I just walked in. I don't play games, you should know that.' Greywolf eyed him. 'Now, if you don't mind me asking, why are you here?'

Good question, thought Anawak. Without thinking, he turned back to the mask, as if it might answer for him. 'From the Pacheedaht, you say?'

'You don't have a clue, do you?' Greywolf sighed. 'The Pacheedaht—'

'I know who they are,' said Anawak, impatiently. A small Nootka band, resident in the south of the island, just north of Victoria. 'It's the mask that interests me. It looks old, not like the junk on sale round here.'

'It's a replica.' Greywolf stood beside him. He was wearing jeans and a faded shirt. The coloured checks were barely visible. His fingertips stroked the contours of the cedar face. 'An ancestral mask. The original's in the Queestos' *huupaKwan'um*. Do you need me to tell you what a *huupaKwan'um* is?'

'No.' Although Anawak knew the word, he couldn't be sure of its meaning. Something to do with a ceremony. 'Was it a present?'

'I made it,' said Greywolf. He went over to the chairs. 'Would you like a drink?'

Anawak stared at the mask. 'You made it yourself?'

'I've been doing a lot of carving recently. The Queestos don't mind me copying their masks. So, do you want a drink or not?'

'No.'

'Why are you here?'

'I wanted to thank you.'

Greywolf perched on the arm of the sofa, like an animal ready to pounce. 'What for?'

'For saving my life.'

'Oh, that. I thought you hadn't noticed.' Greywolf shrugged. 'You're welcome. Anything else I can do for you?'

Anawak stood there helplessly. He'd spent weeks avoiding this moment, and now it was over. He'd done what he was supposed to. 'What've you got to drink, then?' he asked.

'Cold beer and Coke.'

'Coke, please.'

Greywolf pointed to the little fridge next to the hotplates. 'Help yourself. I'll have a beer.'

Anawak opened the fridge and pulled out two cans. He sat down stiffly on one of the painted raffia chairs.

'So, Leon—'

'I . . .' Anawak twisted the can in his hand. He put it on the table. 'Look, Jack, I should have come ages ago. You pulled me out of the water, and . . . well, you know what I think about your protests and all your Indian nonsense. I won't say I wasn't mad at you. But that's not the point. The fact is, if it weren't for you, some of us wouldn't be alive, and that's far more important than the other stuff, so I – I came to tell you that. They're calling you the hero of Tofino, and I guess they're right.'

'Do you mean that?'

'Yes.'

There was another long silence.

'What you call "Indian nonsense" is something I believe in, Leon. Do you want to hear why?'

Under normal circumstances the conversation would have ended there. Anawak would have walked out and Greywolf would have hurled insults at his back. No, that wasn't true: Anawak would have begun the barrage before he left the room. 'All right.'

Greywolf gave him a hard look. 'I've got my own people that I belong to. I chose them.'

'Did they choose you too?'

'I don't know.'

'Jack, if you don't mind me saying, the way you look is like a fancy-dress version of your people. Like an Indian from a corny old western. What do your people think of that? Are you helping their cause?'

'I don't have to help anyone's cause.'

'Oh, yes, you do. If you want to belong somewhere, you have to take responsibility. That's the way it is.'

'They accept me. That's all I ask.'

'They're laughing at you, Jack!' Anawak leaned forwards. 'Don't you see that? You've got a pack of losers clustered around you. Sure, some of them are Indians, but not the sort that their own people want hanging around. You're twenty-five per cent Indian, and the rest is white, mostly Irish. Why didn't you choose to be Irish? At least the name would fit.'

'I didn't want to,' said Greywolf calmly.

'And why call yourself "Greywolf"? – Indians don't use names like that any more.'

'Well, I do.'

Go easy, Anawak thought. You're here to say thanks and you've said it. The rest is redundant. You should go.

But he didn't.

'OK, explain one thing to me. If you're so set on being accepted by your people, why don't you try to be authentic?'

'Like you, do you mean?'

Anawak recoiled. 'Let's leave me out of this.'

'Why should we?' Greywolf shouted. 'It's your damn problem. Why should I get the lecture?'

'Because I'm the one giving it.' Suddenly he was angry again. But this time he wasn't going to ignore it and let it gnaw away inside him.

It was too late for that now. He'd have to look himself in the eye, and he knew what that would mean. Every victory over Greywolf would be a defeat for himself.

Greywolf was watching him through half-closed eyes. 'You didn't come here to say thank you.'

'I did.'

'Do you really think so? Oh, God, you do. But it's not why you're here.' His lips curled in a sneer. 'Go on, then. What is it you're dying to tell me?'

'It's like this, Jack. You can call yourself Greywolf till you're blue in the face, but it won't change who you are. There were rules for the giving of names, and in your case not one of them applies. You've got a beautiful mask hanging on the wall, but it's a fake, like your name. And your protest group, that's fake too.' Suddenly it was all pouring out, everything he hadn't meant to say. Not today. He hadn't come here to insult Greywolf, but now he couldn't stop himself. 'Those people you hang out with are layabouts, wasters. They're only in it for the ride. Don't you get it? You're not achieving anything. Your notion of whale conservation is childish. Choosing your own people – that's crap. Your chosen people will never understand your loony ideas.'

'If you say so.'

'Get real, Jack. You know they want to hunt whales, and you want to stop them. That's very honourable, but you haven't been listening. You're turning against the people whom apparently you '

'There are plenty of people among the Makah who think the same as me.'

'Sure, but—'

'Tribal elders, Leon. Not all Indians think ethnic groups should express their culture through ritualistic killings. In their view, the Makah are as much a part of twenty-first-century society as the rest of Washington State.'

'I've heard that argument before,' said Anawak, scornfully. 'And it didn't come from you or any of your tribal elders. I read it in a press release from the Sea Shepherd Conservation Society. You can't even come up with your own arguments, Jack. It's unbelievable. Even your reasoning is fake.'

'No, it isn't. I—'

'And, anyway,' Anawak interrupted, 'singling out Davie's is pathetic.'

'Aha. So that's why you're here.'

'Come off it, Jack, you used to be one of us. Didn't you learn anything? It was only because of whale-watching that people realised live whales and dolphins are more precious than dead ones. Whale-watching focuses the world on a problem that wouldn't get that kind of attention by any other means. It's a form of conservation. Ten million people a year go whale-watching to experience the wonder of whales. That's ten million people who'd otherwise only see whales on TV or maybe not at all. Our research means we can protect whales in their natural habitat. If it weren't for whale-watching, it wouldn't be possible.'

'Yeah, right.'

'So why pick on us? Because we kicked you out?'

'You didn't kick me out. I left.'

'We kicked you out.' Anawak was yelling now. 'You were fired. You messed up and Davie got rid of you. Your pathetic ego couldn't handle that, just like O'Bannon couldn't cope without his hair and his outfit and his crappy name. Your whole ideology is a mistake, Jack. It's all a sham. You know what? You're a fake. You're nothing. All you do is screw things up. You're no use to the conservationists and no use to the Nootka. You don't belong anywhere. You're not Irish, you're not Indian, and that's your problem and it makes me sick, having to grapple with your problems when there's other stuff that—'

'Leon,' said Greywolf, thin-lipped.

'It makes me sick, seeing you like that.'

Greywolf stood up. 'Shut up, Leon. That's enough.'

'No, it's not. For Christ's sake, Jack, there's so much you could do. You're tall and strong, and you're not stupid, so what the—'

'Shut up, Leon.' Greywolf walked slowly around the table, fists raised. Anawak wondered whether the first punch would knock him out. Greywolf had once broken a guy's jaw. Anawak could sense he was going to pay for his big mouth with some teeth.

But Greywolf didn't lash out. Instead he rested both hands on the arms of Anawak's chair and bent towards him.

'Do you want to know why I chose this life?

Anawak stared at him. 'Go right ahead.'

'But you're not interested, are you, you self-righteous prick?'

'Oh, I am. It's just there's nothing to tell.'

'You . . .' Greywolf gnashed his teeth. 'OK, you asshole, of course I'm

Irish too, but I've never been to Ireland. My mother's half-Suquamish. The whites never accepted her, and neither did the Indians, so she married an immigrant and no one accepted him either.'

'That's very touching, Jack, but you mentioned it before. Tell me something new.'

'I'm gonna give you the truth and you'll darned well listen. You're right. Running around like an Indian won't make me into one. But guess what? I could drink litres of Guinness and I'd never be Irish either. I'll never be a regular American, even though there's American blood in me too. I'm not authentic, Leon, because I don't belong anywhere. *I can't do a damn thing to change it.*'

His eyes flashed. 'All you had to do was move and that changed everything. You turned your life around. I never had the chance.'

'Don't give me that.'

'Oh, sure, I could have behaved myself and got a proper job. This is a free society, after all. No one asks where you come from – so long as you're successful. Some people are lucky – they're a patchwork of ethnicities, the best bits of everything collected into one. They're at home wherever they want to be. My parents were simple people, ill at ease. They didn't know how to teach their son to be confident or fit in. They felt uprooted and misunderstood, and I got the worst of all worlds. It's one big foul-up. And the one thing that ever went right for me fouled up too.'

'Oh, yeah. The navy. Your dolphins.'

Greywolf nodded grimly. 'The navy was fine. I was the best handler they ever had, so they forgot about their stupid questions. Back home it all kicked off again. My parents drove each other wild – she with her Indian customs, and he with his talk of County Mayo. Like they were trying to prove their identity or something. It wasn't as though they even wanted to be proud of where they'd come from. They just wanted to come from *somewhere* – to be able to say, "This is where I belong."'

'That was their problem, Jack. No need to make it your own.'

'Oh, really?'

'Come off it. There you are, built like a tank, trying to tell me that you've been left so traumatised by your parents' problems that your life is a mess?' Anawak snorted. 'What difference does it make if you're Indian, half-Indian or God knows what? No one's responsible for where you feel at home on the inside. That's all down to you.'

Greywolf seemed taken aback. Then satisfaction crept into his eyes and Anawak knew he had lost.

'Who are we talking about here?' asked Greywolf, with a malicious smile.

Anawak didn't say anything.

Greywolf stood up slowly. The smile disappeared. Suddenly he looked wiped-out. He walked over to the mask and lingered in front of it. 'Maybe I *am* an idiot,' he said softly.

'It's not a big deal.' Anawak wiped his hand over his eyes. 'We both are.'

'Well, you're the biggest idiot of them all. This mask is from the *huupaKwan'um* of Chief Jones. I bet you don't know what that is. A *huupaKwan'um* is a box, a place where they keep masks, headpieces, ceremonial items. But that's not all. It's also where they keep their hereditary rights, the rights of the *ha'wiih* and the *chaachaabat*, the chiefs. The *huupaKwan'um* is the record of their territory, their historical identity, their heritage. It tells you where they come from and who they are.' He turned. 'Someone like me could never have a *huupaKwan'um*; but you could. You could be proud of it. But you don't want anything to do with who you are or where you're from. You tell me to be responsible for the people I've chosen to belong to. Well, you've abandoned yours. You accuse me of not being authentic. I can never be a genuine Indian, but at least I'm fighting to find something that's real. You *are* real, but you don't want to be who you are, and you're not what you'd like to be. To you I look like something out of a Western, but at least I'm prepared to show my commitment to the way of life I've chosen. You run a mile when anyone asks if you're from the Makah.'

'How do you know . . . ?' Delaware.

'Don't blame her,' said Greywolf. 'She didn't dare ask *you* again.'

'What did you tell her?'

'Nothing, you coward. You think you can lecture me on responsibility? Leon, my life might be pathetic, but you? You're dead already.'

Anawak replayed the words in his mind. 'Yes,' he said slowly. 'You're right.' He got up. 'But thanks for saving my life.'

'Hey, hang on a minute.' Greywolf blinked. 'What – what are you doing?'

'I'm leaving.'

'What? Come on, Leon, I . . . I didn't mean to hurt you, I . . . For God's sake, Leon, sit down.'

'Why?

'Because – because you haven't finished your Coke.'

Anawak sat down, picked up the can and drank. Greywolf sank down on the sofa.

'So what about that boy, then?' asked Anawak. 'Seems you've found a fan.'

'The lad from the boat? He was scared. I looked after him.'

'Just like that?'

'Sure.'

Anawak smiled. 'I thought it had more to do with wanting your picture in the paper.'

For a moment Greywolf looked annoyed. Then he grinned. 'Of course I wanted my picture in the paper. I love being in the paper. But that doesn't mean the other thing's not true.'

'The hero of Tofino.'

'Laugh all you like. Being the hero of Tofino was great. Total strangers came up and slapped me on the back. Not everyone can make their reputation with groundbreaking articles on whales. You have to take what you can get.'

Anawak drained the can. 'And how's your pressure group?'

'The Seaguards?'

'Yes.'

'History. Half were killed by the whales, the other half scattered with the wind.' Greywolf frowned. 'You know what the problem is, Leon? People are losing their significance. Everyone's replaceable. There are no ideals any more, and without ideals, there's nothing to make us more important than we are. Everyone's trying desperately to prove that the world's a little better with them than it would have been without them. I did something for that little boy. Maybe it was worthwhile. Maybe it makes me a bit more significant.'

Vancouver Docks

A few hours later, Anawak was on the jetty in the fading light. Not a soul in sight. Like all international ports, Vancouver harbour was gigantic.

Behind him lay the container port, with its angular mountains of crates. Black silhouettes of cranes stood out against the silvery-blue evening sky. The outlines of car freighters loomed like enormous shoeboxes between container ships, cargo boats and elegant white reefer-vessels. To his right he could see a long line of warehouses. A bit further on hoses, metal plates and hydraulic parts lay in heaps. That was where the dry docks started, and beyond, the floating docks. The smell of paint drifted to him on the breeze.

He would have been lost without the car. He'd already had to stop a few times for directions but, reluctant to spell out what he was looking for, he'd asked the wrong question. He'd assumed he wanted the floating docks, so that was where they'd sent him. But when he articulated his question more precisely, he was directed to the dry docks. After two wrong turns he had finally arrived. He parked the car in the shadow of a long, narrow building, heaved his sports bag over his shoulder and walked along the metal fence until he came to a rolling gate that was slightly ajar. He slipped inside.

In front of him was a paved area, with a line of barracks on both sides. Beyond that, the superstructure of an enormous ship rose from the ground. The *Barrier Queen* was lying in a basin a good 250 metres long. There were cranes on either side of her, mounted on tracks. Powerful floodlights lit the area. There was no one in sight.

As he crossed the tarmac, keeping an eye open for any movement, he questioned the wisdom of what he was doing. The ship must have been out of the water for weeks. They'd have removed the outcrop and anything hidden within it. Any scraps in the scratches and cracks would have dried out by now. There'd be no sign of the thing that had lurked among the mussels. All in all, Anawak wasn't sure what he stood to gain from inspecting the vessel again. It was a stab in the dark. If there was anything that might be useful to Nanaimo, he'd take it with him. If not, the adventure would only have cost him an evening.

The thing on the keel.

It had been no bigger than a skate or a squid and it had produced a flash of light. Lots of sea creatures did that: cephalopods, jellyfish, deep-sea fish. But Anawak was convinced that it was precisely the kind of flash that he and Ford had seen on the tape. The luminous cloud was many times bigger than the thing he'd seen, but the flashes of light had reminded him of what had happened beneath the *Barrier Queen*. If the same organism had appeared in both places, things were hotting up. The substance on the keel, the stuff inside the whales' brains and the thing in the dock all seemed identical.

The whales are just part of the problem – the only part we can see.

He spotted jeeps parked in front of the barracks. Light shone out of the building's windows. He stopped. They were military jeeps. What was the army doing here? Suddenly it occurred to him that he was standing without shelter in the glare of the floodlights. He crouched and hurried on until he neared the edge of the basin. He was so preoccupied with the presence of the vehicles that it was a few seconds before he grasped what he was seeing. His eyes widened. He forgot the jeeps and took a step closer.

The *Barrier Queen* was floating. He'd expected to see her resting on blocks. Why hadn't they drained it? Had they finished repairing the rudder? But then they wouldn't need the dock.

All of a sudden he knew the answer.

In his excitement he dropped his bag, which hit the ground with a thud. Startled, he glanced down the empty jetty. It was noticeably darker now. Floodlights cast their white-green beams along the dock. He listened for footsteps, but all he could hear was the noise of the city.

Faced with the basin full of water he wondered whether he was making a mistake. But he was frustrated by the committee's secrecy, and besides he'd come all this way. In any case, he'd be out of there in twenty minutes.

Anawak opened his holdall. It contained everything he needed to dive. If the *Barrier Queen* had been in the floating docks, it would have made sense to approach her from the sea. But this way was easier.

It was perfect.

He stripped to the waist, then took off his jeans and located his mask, fins and pen torch. Then he strapped his collection bag round his waist. His leg-mounted dive knife completed his gear. He wouldn't need oxygen. He stowed the holdall behind a bollard, gathered up his equipment and hurried along the edge of the basin till he reached a narrow ladder leading down to the water. He took a last look at the jetty. Light was still shining from the barracks, but no one was about. Noiselessly he made his way down, pulled on his mask and flippers and slipped into the water.

The biting cold cut through him. Without a protective layer of neoprene he had to be quick. Switching on his torch, he dived, kicking powerfully in the direction of the keel. The water was clearer than it had been in the dock, and he had a distinct view of the metal hull ahead, the red paint glowing in the torch light. He ran his fingers over the surface, paused, then pushed off and swam down.

After a few metres the ship's side disappeared under a dense coating of mussels. The crust on the keel was as thick as ever. Half-way towards the bow it seemed almost as though the outcrop had grown. So that was the explanation: the crust and its resident organisms were being examined *in situ.* The dry dock had been turned into a hermetically sealed laboratory, and flooded with water.

Suddenly he understood the significance of the military jeeps. If Nanaimo, a civilian institute, had been squeezed out of the affair, there could only be one explanation: the army had taken control of the investigation. Now it was classified.

There was still time to pull out, he thought. Then he dismissed the idea. He pulled out his knife and cut through the outcrop. Careful not to damage the shells, he prised the mussels from the hull, gently inserting the blade beneath the muscular foot, then jerking up. He was focused and systematic. One after another the mussels went into the bag.

He could no longer ignore the need for oxygen. He put away the knife and swam up for a breath. The ship's side towered above him, a vertical wall. Next time he dived he'd look for a spot like the one the luminescent thing had emerged from. Maybe there were more of those creatures in the outcrop.

He was just about to swim down when he heard footsteps.

He turned and peered up at the side of the basin. Two figures were on the move, half-way between a pair of floodlights.

They were looking at the water.

Without a sound he slipped beneath the surface. They were probably sentries, he thought. Or people working late. He'd have to be careful when he climbed out.

Then he remembered they could see his torch in the water and switched it off. Darkness surrounded him.

Which way had they been heading? Towards the stern. Maybe he could swim to the bow and carry on his investigation there. Kicking evenly, he set off. After a while he surfaced again and turned on to his back, eyes trained on the sides of the basin. No one.

As he drew level with the anchor, he dived. He felt his way tentatively along the hull. More mounds of mussels. He was looking for a chink or a dip but there was none. He needed to fill his bag with mussels and get out of there. In his haste he became careless about how he detached the mussels. His hands were trembling and his fingers were numb.

His fingers . . .

Then he realised he could see them. His arms and legs were glowing too. No, the water was glowing. A deep luminescent blue.

Oh, God . . .

A harsh light blinded him. Instinctively he raised his hands to shield his eyes. Flashes of light. The cloud. *What was happening?*

He realised that he'd been found. He was in the beam of an underwater floodlight, and the keel was steeped in cold white light. He saw the grooved mounds of mussels and shivered.

For a moment he didn't know what to do. But there was no other way. He had to get back to the stern and towards the ladder where his bag was waiting. Heart beating wildly, he sped past the harsh shafts of light. He was running out of air, but he didn't want to come up until he reached the ladder.

There it was, zigzagging towards the bottom.

His hands clung to the rungs and he pulled himself up. Above him he heard shouts and running footsteps. He pulled off his fins and mask, clipped the torch to his belt and climbed up until he could see over the edge.

Three gun barrels were pointing towards him.

In the barracks Anawak was given a blanket. He'd tried to explain to the soldiers that he was on the scientific arm of the committee, but they weren't prepared to listen. Their job was to make sure he didn't get away. When it was clear that he wasn't going to resist or make a break for freedom, they took him back to the barracks, where there were more soldiers and an officer who peppered him with questions. Anawak knew it was pointless to lie, since he wouldn't be allowed to leave anyway, so he told him who he was and what he was doing there.

The officer listened to him quizzically. 'Can you prove your identity?' he asked.

'My wallet's in my holdall. It's outside. I can get it if you like.'

'Just tell us where it is.'

He described where he'd left his bag. Five minutes later the officer

303

had his driving licence. 'Assuming the document is genuine, you are Dr Leon Anawak, resident in Vancouver.'

'That's what I've been saying all along.'

'People say the damnedest things. Do you want some coffee? You look frozen.'

'I *am* frozen.'

The officer got up from the desk and went to the coffee machine. He pressed a button. A paper cup dropped down and filled with steaming liquid. He gave it to Anawak. 'Well, I don't know what to make of your story,' he said. 'If you're part of the committee, why didn't you request permission in advance?'

'Ask your superiors. I've been trying to contact Inglewood for weeks.'

The officer's brow furrowed. 'You're working in an advisory capacity?'

'Yes.' Anawak glanced around. He suspected that the room, with its plastic chairs and shabby tables, was usually occupied by dock workers on their breaks. It had evidently been converted into a temporary military base. 'What now?' he asked.

'Now?' The officer sat opposite him and clasped his hands on the table. 'I'm going to ask you to stay here for a while. I can't just let you go – this is a military exclusion zone.'

'With all due respect, I didn't see any signs.'

'Well, there's no sign saying you can break in either.'

Anawak was in no position to argue. It had been a crazy idea in the first place, although it hadn't been completely fruitless – at least now he knew that the military was involved and that the organisms on the hull were alive and under observation. But the mussels he'd collected would never get to Nanaimo, if the authorities kept stalling.

The officer pulled a radio out from his belt and made a brief call. 'You're in luck,' he said. 'Someone's on their way to take care of you.'

'Why don't you just take my details and let me go?'

'It's not as easy as that.'

'But I haven't done anything wrong,' said Anawak. He didn't sound convincing, even to himself.

The officer smiled. 'Committee or no committee, trespassing's a crime.'

He walked out, leaving Anawak with the other soldiers. They didn't talk to him, but they were watching him closely. He felt warmer now, with the coffee – and with irritation at himself for messing up. The only comfort was the prospect of finding out more from whoever was coming to 'take care' of him.

Half an hour passed. Then Anawak heard a helicopter approaching. He turned to look out of the window facing the dock. For a moment the noise of the rotors was deafening as the helicopter swept over the building and came in to land.

Steps rang out on the paving outside. Snatches of conversation drifted through the open door. Two soldiers came in, followed by an officer. 'A visitor for you, Dr Anawak.' He stepped aside as a fourth person appeared in the doorway. Anawak recognised her immediately. She walked up to him, and he found himself gazing into her clear blue eyes. Aquamarine in an Oriental face. 'Good evening,' she said, in a soft, cultivated voice.

It was General Commander Judith Li.

3 May

Clifford Stone had been born in the Scottish city of Aberdeen, the second of three children. By the time he reached his first birthday there was nothing cute about him. He was small, scrawny and unusually ugly. His family treated him as though he were an accident – an embarrassing glitch that might go unnoticed if they ignored it. Unlike his older brother, he wasn't deemed worthy of responsibility, and no one spoiled him as they did his younger sister. He wasn't treated badly – in fact, he didn't want for anything, except attention and warmth.

As a child he had no friends, and at eighteen, when his hair receded, he didn't have a girlfriend either. At school he passed all of his exams with flying colours, but even that met with little interest from his family.

Stone went on to study engineering. He had a talent for it and at last – practically overnight – he received the acknowledgement he'd always desired. But it was strictly professional. Stone the man was disappearing – not so much because no one was interested in him, but because he didn't allow himself a private life. The idea terrified him: it meant a return to being overlooked. While the gifted engineer Clifford Stone rose through the ranks at Statoil, he learned to despise the insecure bald man who went home alone.

The company became his life, his family and his fulfilment because it gave him something he'd never known before: the knowledge that he was better at something than everyone else, that he was in the lead. It was intoxicating yet agonising – a constant rush to stay ahead. Before long he was so preoccupied with his quest for the ultimate achievement that none of his successes pleased him. He simply rushed on, trying to overtake himself. To stop would have meant catching a glimpse of the scrawny boy with the oddly adult face, who'd been disregarded for too long to have any regard for himself. There was nothing Stone feared more than looking into his own dark, defiant eyes.

In recent years Statoil had set up a new division for the development of emergent technologies. Stone was quick to recognise the opportunities offered by a switch to fully automated plants. He presented the board with a range of proposals, and was entrusted with building a subsea processor designed by FMC Kongsberg, the renowned Norwegian firm. A number of sub-surface units were already in use elsewhere, but the Kongsberg prototype was an entirely new system, which promised enormous savings and would revolutionise offshore processing. The construction of the prototype took place with the knowledge and approval of the Norwegian government, although officially it never happened. Stone was aware that they'd put it into operation sooner than some people would have liked. Greenpeace, in particular, would have insisted on a another set of tests, which would have taken months to complete. The distrust was understandable: on the scale of human and moral failure, the damage done by the petroleum industry was hard to exceed. No other business had the planet in such a stranglehold, with its web of vested interests. So the project stayed secret. Even when Kongsberg released a concept study on its website, the Statoil operation remained under wraps. A spectre was at work on the seabed, and the only reason it wasn't haunting its creators was because it functioned perfectly.

It would never have occurred to Stone to think otherwise. After endless tests he was convinced that they'd considered every risk. Why look further? It would only indulge the tendency towards indecision that Stone discerned and despised at the heart of the state-owned company. Besides, two factors made hesitation impossible. The first was the chance Stone saw to continue his technological trailblazing as a member of the board. The second was that the oil war was about to be lost by all parties. It wasn't a question of when the last drop of oil would flow but when extracting it ceased to make financial sense. An oilfield's typical yield obeyed the laws of physics. When a field was first drilled, oil shot out at high pressure and continued to do so for the next few decades. In time, the pressure decreased – the Earth held on to the oil in tiny pores by capillary pressure. Oil that had risen up of its own accord had to be pumped out at exorbitant cost. The yield fell rapidly, long before the reservoir was empty. It didn't matter how much oil was left: when extracting it consumed more energy than the oil itself could generate, it was better to leave it alone.

That was one of the reasons why energy experts at the end of the second millennium had got their predictions so badly wrong when they'd estimated that oil reserves would last for decades. Technically they were right: the Earth was drenched with oil. Yet most of it was inaccessible or the yield didn't justify the expense of extracting it.

At the beginning of the third millenium the dilemma provoked a ghoulish situation: OPEC, pronounced dead in the eighties, returned to life. Of course, it could do nothing to solve the real problem, but there was no doubt that it held the largest reserves. Determined not to let OPEC dictate the price of oil, the North Sea states had no choice but to lower the costs of extraction and colonise the seabed with automated plants. The ocean fought back with a brand new set of problems, starting with extremes of temperature and pressure. For whoever solved them, a second El Dorado beckoned. The riches wouldn't last for ever, but in the meantime they would satisfy humanity's craving for oil and gas, and keep the industry alive.

Stone called in the experts, pushed the prototype through the test phase and recommended construction. Statoil acquiesced. Stone saw his budget and jurisdiction increase overnight. He cultivated his relationship with the suppliers, ensuring Statoil's needs always came first. He knew what a fine line he was treading. So long as no one had cause to criticise the company, he was Statoil's conquistador – but if it came to the crunch, he wouldn't stand a chance. The best employee was the easiest fall-guy. Stone knew he had to make it to the boardroom before anyone decided he was expendable. Once his name became synonymous with innovation and profit, doors would open and he'd be free to choose his path.

At least, that was how he'd imagined it.

He wasn't sure whom he felt angrier with – Skaugen, who'd betrayed him, or himself. But he'd known the score from the beginning, and the worst-case scenario had occurred. Everyone was dashing for shelter. Skaugen knew as well as he did that the catastrophic disintegration of the slope would soon be public news. None of them could afford to keep quiet without risking disgrace. By contacting the other companies, Statoil had set a process in motion that couldn't be stopped. Each firm was putting pressure on the next. With an environmental disaster looming, it was too late to strike a deal. All they could do was try to cover their own backs and find someone else to take the blame.

Stone seethed. Finn Skaugen was the biggest villain of them all – it had made Stone retch to see him play the good guy. His game was more treacherous than anything Stone, even in his darkest moments, could ever have devised. Of course Stone had overstepped his usual remit, but not without good reason. He was doing their bidding. He hadn't used half the power they'd given him. Of course he'd 'omitted' to mention those ridiculous reports. Since when had worms stopped ships taking to the water or oil being drilled? Every day thousands made their way through billions of planktonic organisms. If they stayed at home every time a new copepod was discovered, the oceans would be empty. And as for the hydrates – the amount of gas escaping was well within the normal limit. It was obvious what would have happened if he'd submitted the report. The bloody bureaucrats would have held up construction for no reason at all.

The system was to blame, Stone thought grimly, but most of all Skaugen, with his sickening brand of bigotry. All the directors, smiling and thumping him on the back; well done, old man, keep up the good work, just don't get caught, because *we* won't want to know. It wasn't his fault he was in this mess, it was theirs. And Tina Lund was just as bad, sucking up to Skaugen to take Stone's job and probably sleeping with the asshole tóo. Worst of all, he'd even had to pretend to be grateful to her for getting Skaugen to give him another chance. He was supposed to find the missing prototype. Some chance. It was a trap. They'd all turned against him, the whole bloody lot of them.

He'd show them, though. Clifford Stone wasn't finished yet. Whatever was wrong with the unit, he'd find the problem and sort it out. Then they could look for skeletons in the cupboard, and he, for one, had nothing to hide.

He'd get to the bottom of it.

The *Thorvaldson* had scanned the site of the unit with multibeam sonar, but there was still no sign of the processor. The morphology of the seabed seemed to have changed. Within a few days the site of the unit had become a gaping chasm. The thought of the depths made Stone as queasy as the next man, but he pushed aside his fears. All he could think of was his voyage to the seabed and how he'd show them what he was made of.

Clifford Stone, intrepid man of action.

On the afterdeck of the *Thorvaldson* the submersible was waiting to transport him to the seabed, nine hundred metres below. Of course he should have sent the robot down first on a recce. That's what Jean-Jacques Alban and all the others had been urging him to do. Victor was equipped with fantastic cameras, a highly sensitive articulated arm and every conceivable instrument necessary for the highspeed evaluation of data. But going down there himself would make more of an impression. In any case, Stone disagreed with Alban. He'd spoken to Gerhard Bohrmann on the *Sonne* about travelling on manned submersibles. Bohrmann had explored the Oregon seabed in *Alvin*, the legendary DSV: 'I've seen thousands of video images – footage recorded by robots, all of it very impressive – but actually sitting in the submersible, being down there on the seabed, seeing it all in 3-D, I never thought it could be like that. It beats anything you've ever seen.' Besides, he'd added, there was no real substitute for the senses and instincts of a human.

Stone smiled grimly. It was his turn now. The submersible had been easy to get hold of, thanks to his excellent contacts. It was a DR 1002, a Deep Rover, made by the American firm Deep Ocean Engineering, a small, light boat, belonging to the new generation of submersibles. Its transparent spherical hull was mounted on bulky battery pods from which a pair of robotic arms emerged. Inside, there were two comfortable seats with controls to each side. As he approached the Deep Rover he felt pleased with his choice. The vehicle was attached to the boom by a cable, and had been jacked up to allow just enough room for them to crawl in through the bottom hatch. The pilot, Eddie, a stocky ex-navy aviator, was already inside, checking the instruments. There was the usual bustle before the launch of a submersible, with crew, technicians and scientists milling on the deck. Stone spotted Alban and called him over. 'Where's the photographer?' he shouted. 'And the guy with the video camera?'

'No idea,' said Alban. 'I saw the cameraman prowling around earlier.'

'Well, tell him to stop prowling and get here,' Stone snapped. 'We're not going under without this being filmed.'

Alban frowned and looked out to sea. It was a misty day with poor visibility.

'It smells bad,' he said.

'That's the methane.'

'It's getting worse.'

It was true. A sulphur-like odour hung over the sea. A good deal of gas must have escaped for the air to smell that bad. It didn't bode well.

'It'll sort itself out,' said Stone.

'I think you should postpone the dive.'

'Rubbish!' Stone glanced around. 'Where's that bloody photographer?'

'It's too risky – the barometer's plummeting. A storm's on its way.'

'We're going, and that's that.'

'Stone, don't be a fool. And, anyway, what's the point?'

'The point,' Stone said, in a hectoring tone, 'is to get a better, more accurate look at the problem. For God's sake, Jean, nothing'll get in the way of the Rover, least of all a few worms. It can descend to a depth of four thousand metres—'

'At four thousand metres the hull will implode,' Alban corrected him. 'It's cleared for a maximum of a thousand.'

'I know the facts. And we're only going nine hundred metres. What could possibly go wrong?'

'I don't know. But the seabed's changed. The water's filling with gas and the processor won't show up on sonar. God only knows what's going on down there.'

'Maybe there's been a slide. Or a partial collapse. If we're unlucky, there'll have been some subsidence. It happens, you know.'

'I guess.'

'So, what's the problem?'

'The problem,' said Alban, losing his temper, 'is that a robot could do the job for you. But – oh, no – you have to play the hero.'

Stone pointed at his eyes. 'You see these? They're still the best way of working out what's wrong. That's how problems are solved. You take a good look, then you fix them.'

'Fine.'

'So when are we going down?' Stone glanced at the time. 'OK, another half-hour. No, twenty minutes.' He waved at Eddie, who raised his hand and turned back to the controls. Stone grinned. 'What are you worried about? We've got the best pilot around. I'll even steer the thing myself, if I have to.'

Alban didn't reply.

'I'm going to take one last look at the dive plan. I'll be in my cabin if you need me. And do me a favour, Jean, find those bloody camera people. Anyone would think they'd fallen overboard.'

Could he really be out of aftershave? Impossible. Sigur Johanson kept a stockpile of life's little luxuries. He never ran out of wine or grooming products. Surely he had another bottle of Kiton eau-de-toilette.

He went back to the bathroom and rummaged through the cabinet. He needed to get a move on. The helicopter was waiting at Statoil's research centre to transport him to his meeting with Karen Weaver. But for someone who cultivated dishevelment, packing was complicated: neat people never had to bother with deliberations about which shade of jacket clashed to just the right effect.

Hidden behind two tubs of styling wax he found what he was looking for. He put the bottle in his wash-bag, then squeezed it into his suitcase, with some poetry by Walt Whitman and a book about port, then let it click shut. It was an expensive bag of the kind popular at the beginning of the nineteenth century among rich Londoners, who used them for weekend jaunts. The leather straps had been sewn by hand.

The fifth day!

Had he packed the CD? All the material supporting his incredible idea about the plan was on it. Perhaps there'd be a chance to discuss it with the journalist. There it was, buried under a pile of shirts and socks.

He left his house in Kirkegata Street with a spring in his step, and crossed the road to his jeep. For some reason he'd been raring to go since first thing that morning. There was something almost hysterical about his energy. Before he started the engine he took a last glance at the house.

Suddenly he realised that he was trying to distract himself. His hyperactivity was an attempt to ward off thought, like whistling in the dark. His hand hovered beside the ignition as he gazed towards the city. A damp mist was hanging over Trondheim, blurring its contours. Even his house on the other side of the street seemed flatter than usual. It looked almost like a painting.

What happened to the things you loved?

He had spent many hours in front of Van Gogh's paintings, feeling an inner peace as though the artist hadn't suffered from suicidal depression. Nothing could destroy the painting's impression. Of course, a picture could be destroyed but as long as it existed, it was a definitive moment captured in paint. The sunflowers would never fade. The Langlois

Bridge at Arles could never be bombed. The image of horror would always be horrifying; the image of beauty stayed beautiful for ever. Even the portrait of the man with the angular features and the white bandage over his ear had something comfortingly constant about it. At least in the picture he couldn't become unhappier, he couldn't age. The man in the painting was eternal. In the end he'd triumphed over those who'd tortured him or couldn't understand him. With the help of a paintbrush and his genius he'd outwitted them all.

Johanson looked at his house. If only it were a picture, and I was in it too, he thought. But he didn't live in a picture, and his life wasn't a gallery where he could pace out his past in a matter of steps. His house by the lake would make a fabulous picture, then a study of his wife, and pictures of all the other women he'd known, the friends he'd had – and Tina Lund, of course. Tina, hand in hand with Kare Sverdrup, at peace for all time.

He was assailed by a dull sense of loss. The world is changing, he thought. They're closing ranks against us. Somewhere something has been decided, and we weren't part of it. Humanity wasn't there.

He started the engine and drove away.

Kiel, Germany

Erwin Suess walked into Bohrmann's office with Yvonne Mirbach in tow. 'Call Johanson,' he said, 'Now.'

Bohrmann had known the Geomar director for long enough to grasp that something out of the ordinary had happened. 'What's wrong?' he asked, although he felt certain he knew.

Mirbach pulled up a chair and sat down. 'We've run through different scenarios on the computer. The collapse will take place sooner than we thought.'

Bohrmann's brow furrowed. 'Collapse? Last time we weren't even sure it would come to that.'

'The evidence doesn't look good,' said Suess.

'Because of the consortia?'

'Yes.'

Bohrmann felt a cold sweat break out on his forehead. It's not possible, he thought. They're only bacteria – minute, microscopic organisms. He knew he was thinking like a child: how could something so small destroy a layer of ice a hundred metres thick? There was no way. What difference could a microbe make to thousands of square metres of seabed? None. It was inconceivable, unreal. It couldn't happen. Scientists knew relatively little about consortia, but it was clear that various micro-organisms worked in symbiotic partnerships at the bottom of the ocean. Sulphur bacteria, for example, allied themselves with archaebacteria – odd single-cell microbes that numbered among the oldest forms of life. The symbiosis was extremely successful. Consortia of this type had first been discovered on hydrates only a few years previously. The sulphur bacteria took up oxygen to break down nutrients, including nitrogen, carbon dioxide and other carbon compounds, which were released by the archaea as they feasted on their delicacy of choice.

Methane.

The symbiosis meant the sulphur bacteria also lived off methane, although they never got a taste of it. Most methane was found in the oxygen-free sediment, and sulphur bacteria needed oxygen to survive. Archaea didn't. They broke down methane without oxygen, and could carry on doing so several kilometres beneath the seabed. Scientists estimated that archaea converted 300 million tonnes of marine methane each year, which probably benefited the climate: broken-down methane couldn't escape into the atmosphere as a greenhouse gas. In that respect, archaea were a kind of environmental task-force.

Provided they stuck to the seabed.

The trouble was, archaea also lived in symbiosis with worms, and the mutant worm with monstrous jaws was covered with consortia of archaea and sulphur bacteria, living in its guts and on its skin. With every metre it descended into the ice, the bacteria were transported further into the hydrates, where they destroyed the frozen layers from the inside, spreading like a cancer. Before too long the worm would perish, and so, too, the sulphur bacteria, but the archaea would chomp their way steadily through the ice, turning the dense layer of hydrates into a porous friable mass. Gas would leak out to the surface.

Worms can't destabilise the hydrates, Bohrmann heard himself saying.

True. But that wasn't their purpose. They were only there to transport their consignment of archaea through the ice, like shuttle buses: next stop, methane hydrates, depth of five metres, alight here, time for work.

Why didn't we think of it before? thought Bohrmann. Fluctuating water temperatures, a decrease in hydrostatic pressure, earthquakes – all that was part of the hydrate expert's standard litany of doom. Whereas bacteria – everyone knew what they did down there, but no one had stopped to think about it. Not even in their worst nightmares had anyone envisaged an invasion like this. A methanotrophic suicidal worm? The sheer numbers of them; their distribution across the full length of the slope. It was absurd, inexplicable – even without the armies of archaea, driven by their deadly appetite, too many of them to imagine.

And he couldn't help thinking, How the hell did they get there? What are they doing there? What could have brought them?

Or who?

'The problem,' Mirbach was saying, 'is that our first simulation was based on largely linear assumptions. But real life isn't linear. We're dealing with developments that are chaotic and, in some cases, exponential. The ice is crumbling, which means gas shoots up from inside it, cracking more of the hydrates, so the seabed starts collapsing and the crisis point comes much—'

'OK, OK.' Bohrmann waved his hand. 'How long have we got?'

'A few weeks. Or days. Or even . . .' Mirbach hesitated. 'But we still can't be certain – I mean, we can't say for definite that it's really going to happen. All the evidence suggests it will, but it's such an unusual scenario. We can't prove a thing.'

'Cut to the chase, Yvonne. What do *you* think will happen?'

'I don't know.' She paused again. 'OK, say three army ants crossed the path of a mammal. They'd be stepped on and squashed. But if the same mammal were surrounded by thousands of army ants, they could eat it alive. That's how I imagine it is with the microbes. Do you see?'

'Call Johanson,' Suess repeated. 'Tell him we're predicting a Storegga Slide.'

Bohrmann exhaled slowly. He gave a silent nod.

Trondheim, Norway

They were standing on the edge of the helipad, looking down on the fjord. On the other side of the water, the shore was barely visible. The lake stretched out like tarnished steel beneath the greying sky.

'You're such a snob,' said Lund, jabbing a finger at the helicopter.

'Of course I am,' replied Johanson. 'But since I was press-ganged into this business, I think I've got the right to be picky.'

'Oh, don't start that again.'

Anyway, you're just as bad, insisting on driving around in my jeep.' Lund smiled. 'Well, give me the key.'

Johanson fumbled in his coat pockets and pulled it out. He placed it in her palm. 'Take care of it while I'm gone.'

'You can count on me.'

'And no funny business with Kare.'

'In the jeep? I'm not that kind of girl.'

'I know what you're like. Anyway, at least you took my advice about defending poor Stone. He can fish his own bloody prototype out of the water.'

'I hate to disappoint you, but your advice didn't count. His reprieve was Skaugen's doing.'

'So he *has* been reprieved?'

'There's a chance he'll keep his job, if he can get things back on track.' She glanced at her watch. 'He'll be heading off in the submersible any time now. Wish him luck.'

'Why isn't he sending down a robot?'

'Because he's nuts. Actually, I think he wants to prove that in a crisis you need to do things his way. No one can handle it better than Clifford Stone.'

'And you're all letting him do it?'

'He's still the boss. Besides, in some ways he's right. He'll get a better picture that way.'

Johanson had a vision of the *Thorvaldson* in a seascape of blurry greys, with Stone deep in the water beneath the keel, enshrouded in darkness and sinking towards the unknown. 'Well, you can't fault his courage.' He picked up his bag and they made their way to the helicopter. Skaugen had kept his promise and had loaned him Statoil's flagship model. It was a Bell 430, the last word in helicopter comfort, with minimal noise.

'About this Karen Weaver,' said Lund, as they stood outside the cabin door. 'What's she like?'

Johanson's eyes twinkled. 'Young, unbelievably pretty ... How should I know?'

Lund flung her arms round him. 'You will take care of yourself, won't you?'

Johanson patted her back. 'I'll be fine. Why shouldn't I be?'

'No reason.' She was silent for a moment. 'Your advice wasn't entirely wasted, by the way. Those things you said to me – they made up my mind.'

'To see Kare?'

'To see things differently. And to see Kare.'

Johanson smiled. Then he kissed her on both cheeks. 'I'll call as soon as I get there.'

He climbed inside and threw his bag on to one of the seats behind the pilot. There was room for ten passengers but he had the cabin to himself.

'Sigur!'

He turned back.

You're the best friend I've got.' She lifted her arms helplessly, then dropped them. 'What I'm trying to say is—'

'I know.' Johanson grinned. 'You're no good at this kind of thing. Me neither. The more I like someone, the more of a mess I make of telling them. But I've never made more of a mess than the one I made with you.'

'Was that a compliment?'

'The best.' He closed the door. The pilot set the blades in motion, and the Bell lifted into the air, dipped its nose and flew out towards the fjord, leaving the research centre behind. Johanson made himself comfortable in the cabin, and tried to look out of the window, but there wasn't much to see. Trondheim was veiled in mist, and the lakes and mountains passed in a monotony of grey.

The uneasy feeling was back.

It's only a ride in a helicopter, he told himself. No need to worry. He had methane and monsters on the brain, that was all. And the weather didn't help. Maybe he should have had a decent breakfast. He pulled Walt Whitman out of his bag and started to read.

The rotors throbbed dully above him. His coat, with his mobile in the pocket, lay crumpled on the seat behind him. He didn't hear it ring.

Stone had decided to say a few words before he climbed aboard. The cameraman would film him while the other guy took stills. He meant the entire operation to be documented properly. Clifford Stone was a professional; a man who never shirked his duties. This would serve as a reminder.

'A little further to the right,' said the cameraman.

Stone moved, ushering a pair of technicians out of the frame. Then he thought better of it and beckoned them back. 'Stand behind me,' he said. 'A little to the side.' He didn't want people thinking there was anything amateur or gung-ho about this mission.

The cameraman cranked up the tripod.

'Are we ready yet?' yelled Stone.

'Just a moment. It's still not right. You're in the way of the pilot.'

Stone took another step to the side. 'How's that?'

'Better.'

'OK,' said the cameraman. 'We're rolling.'

Stone looked into the camera. 'In a few minutes we'll be beginning our descent, with the aim of establishing what's happened to the prototype. At present it looks as though the unit has, er, moved from its original, er, its original . . . well, from the place where it . . . Oh, bother.'

'Not to worry. Start again.'

This time everything worked fine. Stone explained in a business-like manner that over the next few hours they would be searching for the prototype. He gave a short summary of the information they had so far, mentioned the changed morphology of the slope, and said that the unit must have subsided due to local destabilisation of the seabed. It all sounded very earnest. Perhaps a little too earnest. Normally famous explorers had something clever to say at the start or the end of their mission, Stone thought. Something that summed it up perfectly. *One small step for a man, one giant leap for mankind.* Now, that had been inspired. Of course, Neil Armstrong would never have come up with a line like that himself. They must have made him practise it beforehand, but all the same . . . Julius Caesar: *I came, I saw, I conquered.* Had Columbus made a famous quip? Or Jacques Piccard?

He racked his brains. He couldn't be expected to come up with everything himself. Bohrmann's contemplations on submersibles would strike the right note. He cleared his throat. 'Of course we could have sent a robot down,' he said, 'but it wouldn't be the same. I've seen plenty of video images – footage recorded by robots. Incredible stuff.' Hmm, how did the next bit go? 'But actually sitting in the submersible, being down there on the seabed, seeing it all in 3-D – it's hard to imagine. There's nothing quite like it. And, er, besides . . . besides, there's no doubt that it gives us an, er, a better view – better *insight* into what's going on down there and, uh, what we can do to help.'

'Amen,' said Alban, softly, in the background.

Stone turned round, crawled beneath the submersible, and scrambled through the hatch. The pilot reached over, but Stone ignored the helping hand, pulled himself up and sat down. It was a bit like being in a helicopter. The weirdest thing was the sensation that he was still outside. The only difference was that he couldn't hear the bustle on the deck. The acrylic bubble was several centimetres thick and hermetically sealed.

'Do you want me to go over anything again?' Eddie enquired.

'No.' Eddie had shown him the ropes earlier, in his characteristically thorough, unflappable way. Stone glanced at the small computer console in front of them. His right hand slid down to touch the controls on the side of his seat. On the deck outside the photographer was taking pictures and the cameraman was filming.

'Great,' said Eddie. 'Let the fun begin.'

The submersible was jolted sideways. Suddenly they were suspended above the deck, gliding over it, until the choppy sea appeared below. There was quite a swell. For a moment they hung motionless. Then Alban gave the thumbs-up. Stone nodded at him. Over the next few hours they'd communicate via underwater telephone. There wouldn't be any optical fibre between the submersible and the ship; just sound waves. As soon as the boom released them, they'd be out there on their own.

Stone's stomach churned.

There was another jolt, then a clunk above them as the cable was released. The submersible sank down, rose on a wave, then water flooded into the tanks as Eddie opened the valves. The Deep Rover sank like a stone, descending thirty metres every minute. Apart from two positioning indicators on the battery pods, all the lights were switched off. Saving power was vital: they would need it later.

There were barely any fish to be seen. After a hundred metres the deep blue water darkened to a silky black.

On the other side of the hull something flashed, like a firecracker. One flash at first; then more.

'Luminescent jellyfish,' said Eddie. 'Pretty cute, huh?'

Stone was fascinated. He'd done a few dives before, but never in a Deep Rover. It really did feel as though nothing separated them from the sea. Even the red flashes from the lights on the console seemed at one with the shoals of glowing organisms outside. The thought of building a processor in this alien universe suddenly seemed so absurd that he almost laughed out loud.

While the submersible sank, the air inside it grew cooler, but it was perfectly pleasant. In comparison to Alvin, MIR or Shinkai, which could go down to six thousand metres, the Deep Rover's system of temperature regulation was luxurious. To be on the safe side, Stone had worn a warm jumper and a pair of thick socks – shoes weren't allowed in submersibles to protect the instruments from accidental kicks. Eddie looked focused, but relaxed. Now and then a noisy voice came through the loudspeaker: technicians calling to check on them. You could hear the words but the sound was distorted as it mingled with thousands of other noises in the sea.

They were falling and falling.

After twenty-five minutes Eddie turned on the sonar. The sphere was filled with a soft whistling and clicking, mixed with the gentle hum of the electrics.

They were approaching the seabed.

'Popcorn and drinks at the ready,' said Eddie. 'It's show-time.'

He switched on the floodlights.

Gullfaks C, Norwegian Shelf

Lars Jörensen stood on the top platform of the metal staircase that led from the helipad to the accommodation module below and gazed down at the derrick, his arms resting on the rails. The white tips of his moustache quivered in the wind. On clear days the derrick seemed in touching distance, but now it was retreating out of sight. As the mist from the approaching storm thickened, it seemed more illusory by the hour, as though it were trying to disappear entirely and fade into memory.

Since Lund's last visit, Jörensen had lapsed into melancholy. He kept wondering what Statoil might be planning for the slope. It had to be an automated system. Maybe they'd use a production vessel too . . . Lund had obviously thought she'd succeeded in fobbing him off, but Jörensen wasn't stupid. He could even appreciate why they were doing things as they were. After all, it made sense to save labour by swapping people for machines. Machines didn't require nice hot meals. They didn't sleep, they worked in hostile environments and they didn't expect to be paid. They never complained, and if they were getting on a bit, you could throw them away without having to provide for them. But robots couldn't respond intuitively or provide an adequate replacement for human eyes and ears. If you took away the humans you avoided human failure, but if the machinery stopped working without humans to fix it . . . It made him think of the disaster movies he watched on late-night TV, when the sea outside was crashing on the platform. Man would be powerless to act. Machines had no regard for life and the natural world around them. They didn't care about the welfare of their creators, who'd chosen to exclude themselves from the design. Humanity and compassion were absent in a robot.

Little by little the light was fading. The sky turned a deeper shade of grey as the drizzle set in. What a foul day, thought Jörensen.

For some time now the sea had smelt as though it was full of chemicals and, to make matters worse, the weather was even gloomier than his mood. We're working on a wreck, he thought, a ghost town in the water, filled with zombies. When the oil ran out, a skeleton without purpose would remain. The oil-workers were being laid off, the platforms discarded, and the future of the industry was a picture on a screen – video footage from a world they couldn't reach, no matter what went wrong.

Jörensen sighed.

In the old days, he thought, there had been the magical moment when men flung their arms round each other, dripping with shiny black oil, a fountain cascading from the sandy ground beside them, promising riches beyond their wildest dreams. Like with James Dean in *Giant*. Jörensen loved that film. To him, the scene where Dean struck oil was far better than the one in *Armageddon*, even though Bruce Willis was on a real oil-rig and Dean in the Texan desert. Watching the oil-spattered Dean laugh and jump around reminded him of sitting on his grandfather's knee, listening to stories of when he was young and everything was better.

Now he was a grandfather too.

Just a few more months, Jörensen told himself, and he'd be gone. Finished. Past it. He was luckier than the youngsters, though. No one was going to streamline him out of existence: he'd leave of his own accord, and get a pension with it. He felt almost guilty about clearing off before the oil platforms' final hour. But it wouldn't be his problem. He'd have other things to think about.

He heard a noise approaching from the distant coast. The rhythmic throbbing grew louder, becoming the roar of a helicopter. Jörensen craned his neck. He knew all the helicopters that flew around here. Despite the distance and the poor visibility he spotted a Bell 430 pass over Gullfaks and disappear into the mist. The beat of the rotors quietened to a hum and eventually fell silent.

Fine drops of rain covered the platform, like a sparkling layer of dust. Maybe he should go inside. He had an hour to kill. He didn't often have free time and he could watch TV, read or play chess. But he didn't feel like entering the module.

On the other side of the platform, the flame was burning gently from the tip of the steel boom. The beacon of the lost. Hey, that sounded almost like a film. Not bad for a decrepit old man who'd spent his whole life on a platform, watching helicopters and ships.

Maybe he should write a book in his retirement. About an era that would be forgotten in a few decades' time. The era of the oil-rigs.

He'd call it *The Beacon of the Lost.*

Granddad, tell us a story.

Maybe it wasn't such a bad day after all.

Kiel, Germany

Gerhard Bohrmann felt as though he was sinking in quicksand. He kept dashing between Mirbach and Suess, who were busy running new scenarios through their computers, coming up with ever more disastrous results. Every few minutes he tried to call Johanson, who wasn't answering his phone. He even called Johanson's secretary at the NTNU, who told him that Dr Johanson was away and wouldn't be back for some time. He'd apparently been released from his position to attend to other business – on behalf of the government, Bohrmann assumed. He tried Johanson's home number, then his mobile again. No joy.

In the end he consulted Suess.

'There has to be someone in Johanson's circle who could take a decision,' Suess said.

'Only the Statoil lot – in which case we may as well keep it to ourselves. And, anyway, about this confidentiality business, what if there *is* a Storegga Slide? It'll look pretty bad if we've kept it quiet.'

'What do you suggest?'

'I wouldn't take it up with Statoil.'

'OK.' Suess rubbed his eyes. 'You're right. We'll contact the Ministry for Science and Technology and the environmental authorities.'

'In Oslo?'

'And in Berlin, Copenhagen, Amsterdam – London, too. Have I forgotten anyone?'

'Iceland.' Bohrmann sighed. 'Let's do it.'

Suess stared out of his office window across the Kiel Firth to the warehouses, silos and giant cranes that loaded the ships. The contours of a naval destroyer merged with the grey of the clouds and water.

'What do the simulations have to say about Kiel?' asked Bohrmann. It was odd that he hadn't thought of it before.

'It could be OK.'

'I guess that's some comfort.'

'Call Johanson anyway. Just keep trying.'

Bohrmann nodded and left the room.

Deep Rover, Norwegian Continental Slope

There was no sign of the vastness of the ocean when Eddie switched on the six external floodlights. The four 150-watt quartz halogen bulbs and the two 400-watt HMI lights combined to bathe an area twenty-five metres in radius in a pool of glistening light. They couldn't make out any solid structures. Stone blinked after the long journey through the darkness. The Deep Rover was falling through a veil of shimmering pearls.

He leaned forward. 'What's that? Where's the seabed?'

Then he saw what was spiralling round them. Bubbles were rising towards the surface, some nestling together like beads on a string, others plump and egg-shaped.

The sonar continued to make its usual whistling, clicking noises. Eddie was frowning at the console's LED display, which provided information on the batteries, the inside and outside temperature, the oxygen reserves, cabin pressure and so on. He called up the data from the external sensors.

'Congratulations,' he growled. 'It's methane.'

The veil of pearls thickened. Eddie released two steel weights attached to the side of the pods, and pumped air into the tanks to stabilise the submersible. But instead of hovering in the water, they carried on sinking.

'Bloody marvellous. It won't let us up.'

The seabed appeared beneath them, visible in the floodlights. It was approaching too fast. Stone caught a glimpse of the crevices and craters, then his view was filled with bubbles. Eddie swore and continued to expel water from the tanks.

'What's going on?' Stone asked. 'Buoyancy problems?'

'More likely to be the gas. We're in the middle of a blow-out.'

'Shit.'

'Just keep calm.'

The pilot fired up the thrusters. The submersible pushed forward through the strings of bubbles. For a second Stone felt as if he was in an elevator that was slowing as it reached the floor below. He looked at the bathometer. The Deep Rover was sinking, although the speed of its descent had slackened. But they were still hurtling towards the seabed. Time was running out.

Stone bit his lip and let Eddie get on with his job. In such a situation it wasn't advisable to distract the pilot. He watched as the bubbles became rounder and the veil closed in. Through the whirling water he saw the faint outline of the seabed tilt away from them, and their right pod vanished in a fierce cascade of bubbles. The submersible heeled.

Stone held his breath.

They'd made it.

The commotion of bubbles gave way to a quiet expanse of seabed. Briefly the submersible rose. Unhurriedly Eddie valved water into the ballast tanks until the Deep Rover reached a stable depth, just above the slope. 'Panic over,' he said.

They were travelling at maximum speed, two knots or 3.7 kilometres per hour – slower than any jogger. But they weren't trying to cover a great distance – in fact, they were at almost exactly the spot where Stone had built the unit. It couldn't be much further.

The pilot grinned. 'I suppose we should have known this would happen, huh?'

'Not to that extent.'

'Who are you kidding? The sea stank like a cesspit. That gas had to be coming from somewhere. But you wanted it your way – well, now you've seen it.'

Stone didn't deign to reply. He sat up straight and looked for signs of hydrates, but there were none in sight, just a few lonely worms. A large flattish fish, resembling a plaice, was lying on the bottom. As they drew closer it took off sluggishly, churning up sediment.

How unreal it was to be sitting there, while the equivalent of 100 kilograms of water pressed on every square centimetre of the acrylic hull. Everything about the situation was artificial: the dark shadow edging forward over the illuminated area of the seabed as the Deep Rover drifted over the shelf; the pitch-blackness beyond the scattered light; the electronically regulated pressure inside the capsule; the cabin air, maintained by a constant stream of oxygen and the chemical breakdown of excess carbon dioxide.

Nothing in the depths invited man to linger.

Stone swallowed. His tongue stuck to his palate. He couldn't help remembering that they hadn't drunk anything for hours before the expedition. In the event of an emergency, they had human range extenders on board, special urine bottles in case they really had to go. But anyone using the submersible was advised to empty their bladder beforehand. Since early that morning he and Eddie had eaten only peanut-butter sandwiches and rock-hard chocolate and cereal bars. Dive meals. Nutritious, filling and dry as Sahara sand.

He tried to relax. Eddie made a brief report to the *Thorvaldson*. Occasionally they saw mussels or a starfish. The pilot gestured towards the water outside.

'Amazing, isn't it? We're below nine hundred metres now, and it's dark, but there's still light down here. They call it the dysphotic zone.'

'Can't light penetrate to a thousand metres, providing the water's clear?' asked Stone.

'Sure, but you wouldn't be able to see it. We're as good as blind as soon as it gets below a hundred and fifty, or even a hundred. Ever been deeper than a thousand?'

'No. Have you?'

'A few times.' Eddie shrugged. 'There's bugger-all to see, though. It's just like here. The light's more my thing.'

'So you don't want to try for the record, then?'

'There's no point. Jacques Piccard made it to 10,740 metres and, sure, scientifically speaking, it was a breakthrough, but there'd have been nothing to look at.'

'How do you know?'

'I don't. I just can't believe there would be. I mean, the abyssal plains aren't especially interesting. I like to see the benthos.'

'Didn't Piccard get to 11,340 metres?'

'Oh, that old chestnut.' Eddie laughed. 'That's what they say in all the books, but it's wrong. A discrepancy on the depth gauge. It was calibrated in Switzerland for freshwater usage, and freshwater's not as dense. So the one and only time they took a sub to the deepest spot in the ocean, they measured the depth wrong. Now if they'd—'

'Look. Over there!'

The beam of light in front of them was swallowed by darkness. As they drew closer they could see that the seabed dropped off abruptly. The light was lost in the abyss.

'Stop here.'

Eddie's fingers flew over the controls. He counterbalanced the thrust, and the Deep Rover came to a halt. Then it started to spin.

'Current's pretty strong here,' said Eddie. The submersible kept turning until the floodlights lit the edge of the precipice. 'Looks like something caved in, not long ago either. I'd say it's pretty fresh.'

Stone's eyes roamed around nervously. 'Any clues from the sonar?'

'There's a drop of at least forty metres. Can't tell what's on the other side.'

'You mean the plateau—'

'There is no plateau. It's fallen through.'

Stone chewed his lip. They had to be really close to the processor now. But there hadn't been a precipice here last year. Then again, it probably hadn't been there a few days ago either.

'Let's go down,' he decided. 'We'll take a look at where it goes.'

The Deep Rover gathered speed and sank down over the precipice. It was only a couple of minutes before the seabed emerged in the floodlights. It looked like a bomb site.

'We need to ascend a few metres,' said Eddie. 'Those crevices look nasty. We could easily fall down.'

'Sure, just a sec— Shit! Straight ahead.'

A torn pipe, one metre in diameter, came into view. It ran diagonally across enormous chunks of stone and disappeared beyond the floodlights. Thin black threads of oil were rising from it, climbing towards the surface in taut columns.

'It's a pipeline!' Stone was appalled. 'Oh, God.'

'It *used* to be a pipeline,' said Eddie.

'Let's follow it.' Stone knew where the pipeline would lead – or, rather, where it originated. They were on the site of the unit.

But the processor was gone.

A fissured wall loomed ahead. Just in time Eddie jerked the submersible up. The wall seemed to extend for ever, but soon they were up and over it with just centimetres to spare. It was only then that Stone realised it wasn't a wall: it was a vast expanse of seabed, rising vertically through the water. Beyond it, there was another steep drop. Particles of sediment drifted through the beam of light, clouding their vision. Then the floodlights caught a stream of bubbles shooting frantically towards the surface, spraying from the gaping edges of a hole. 'Holy shit,' whispered Stone. 'What happened here?'

Eddie banked to avoid the column of bubbles. For a moment they lost sight of the pipeline, then it pushed its way back into the light. It led downwards.

'Damned current,' said Eddie. 'It's pulling us into the blow-out.'

The Deep Rover spun.

'Keep following the pipeline,' commanded Stone.

'That's madness. We need to ascend.'

'The processor's right here,' insisted Stone. 'We'll see it any second now.'

'Like hell we will. There's nothing left to see.'

Stone was silent. Ahead, the pipeline curved upwards, as if it had been uprooted by a giant hand. It ended in a twisted stump, the warped steel curled in weird-looking sculptures.

'Still want to go on?'

Stone nodded. Eddie manoeuvred the submersible alongside the pipe. For a moment they hovered above the serrated opening, as though in the clutches of a gaping maw.

'Any further and there'll be nothing beneath us at all,' said Eddie.

Stone clenched his fists. Alban had been right. They should have sent a robot first. In that case, giving up now would be truly absurd. He needed to know what had happened. He had no intention of returning to Statoil without a full report. He refused to let himself be humiliated again by Skaugen.

'Keep going, Eddie.'

'You're crazy.'

On the other side of the twisted pipe, the fissured seabed slanted steeply downwards. The clouds of sediment thickened. Now the strain was telling on Eddie too. At any moment a new obstacle might appear in their path.

Then they saw the processor.

In fact, all they could see were some struts, but Stone knew right away that the Kongsberg prototype was gone, buried under the rubble of the broken plateau, more than fifty metres deeper than it had originally been built.

He peered closer. Something detached itself from the metal struts and came towards them.

Bubbles.

It reminded Stone of the colossal vortex of gas that they'd seen on the *Sonne* – of the blow-out when the video-grab had plunged through the hydrates.

Suddenly he was filled with panic. 'Move!' he yelled.

Eddie released the remaining weights. The submersible jerked upwards and shot through the water, followed by the vast bubble. Then the maelstrom engulfed them and they fell back down. 'Shit!'

'What's going on down there?' It was the tinny voice of the technician on the *Thorvaldson*. 'Eddie? Answer me! We've got some funny readings up here. A whole load of gas and hydrates is surfacing.'

Eddie pressed the transmission button. 'I'm throwing off the outer hull. We're on our way up.'

'What's the matter? Are you—'

The voice of the technician was drowned by hissing and banging.

Eddie had blasted off the battery pods and sections of the hull. It was a last-ditch attempt to lose weight. The Deep Rover, minus its batteries and exostructure, started to spin and rise again. Then a powerful jolt shook it. Stone saw a rock appear beside him, a gigantic slab of seabed had catapulted upwards. Inside the capsule, things turned upside down. He heard the pilot scream as they were hit again, from the right this time, pushing them out of the blow-out. The Deep Rover instantly gathered speed and shot up. Stone clung to the armrests, practically lying in his seat. Eddie sagged towards him, eyes closed, blood running over his face. Stone realised with horror that now it was up to him. Frantically he tried to remember how to stabilise the submersible. He could switch the controls from Eddie to himself.

Eddie had shown him how to do it. It was that button there.

Stone pressed it, trying at the same time to push Eddie away from him. He wasn't sure that the thrusters would work now that the outer hull was gone. The numbers were whizzing past on the depth gauge, so he knew the submersible was still rising fast. In the end it didn't matter which direction they were heading in, so long as it was up – thank God there was no need to worry about decompression problems: the pressure in the capsule was kept at surface level.

A warning light flashed on.

The floodlights above the right-hand tank went out, then all the other lights. Stone was plunged into darkness.

He was shaking.

Calm down, he told himself. Eddie showed you the emergency power supply. It's one of the buttons on the top row of the control panel. It either turns itself on or you have to do it manually. His fingers felt for the panel in the darkness.

What was that?

Now that the lights were out, it should have been pitch black. But something was shining.

Were they already that close to the surface? He'd checked the depth gauge before it went dark, and it had shown over 700 metres still to go. The submersible hadn't reached the top of the slope yet. They were well below the shelf break and beyond the reach of daylight.

He blinked.

A faint blue glow was emanating from the water, so faint he could barely be sure it was there. It loomed up from the depths, shaped like a funnel, tapering and disappearing into the darkness of the abyss. Stone held his breath. He could have sworn that the light would glow brighter if anyone approached. Now most of the light waves were swallowed by the water so it was still a long way off.

It had to be enormous.

The funnel started to move.

Its opening seemed to expand, while the rest of it swung round. Stone's fingers froze over the console in search of the power button.

He was mesmerised. It was bioluminescence – there was no doubt about it. Bioluminescence, filtered through millions of cubic metres of water and gas. But what kind of bioluminescent sea creature could grow to that size? A giant squid? The light in front of him was bigger than any squid – bigger than anyone could ever imagine a squid to be.

Or was it an optical illusion, caused by the sudden switch from light to dark, the ghostly traces of the rays from the floodlights?

The longer he stared at the thing, the paler it seemed to become. The funnel slid slowly into the depths.

Then it was gone.

Stone resumed his hunt for the emergency-power button. The submersible was rising steadily through the water, and he felt relieved at the thought of reaching the surface and putting the nightmare behind him. At least the video cameras hadn't been lost when Eddie fired off the hull. Had they caught the glowing thing? He wasn't sure if the technology was sensitive enough to detect such a weak signal.

But the glow had definitely been there. Then he remembered the peculiar footage that Victor had filmed, a creature retreating from the light. My God, he thought, what the hell have we unearthed?

Aha. He'd found the button.

The emergency-power supply clicked in with a hum. The lights on the console came on first, then the floodlights.

Eddie was lying, eyes wide open, next to him.

Stone was leaning towards him when something appeared in the light outside: an enormous sheet, cloudy-looking and reddish. It was coming towards the Deep Rover, and Stone's hand reached for the controls because he thought they were about to hit the slope.

Then he realised that the slope was going to hit them.

The slope was rushing towards them.

That was all he had time to think before the impact smashed the plastic sphere into a thousand tiny pieces.

Bell 430, Norwegian Sea

Since they'd left Trondheim the flight had become so bumpy that Johanson was having trouble giving Walt Whitman the attention he deserved. During the past half-hour the sky had darkened dramatically and was now bearing down on the helicopter as if it wanted to force it into the water. Fierce gusts buffeted them from side to side.

The pilot glanced round. 'Everything all right back there?'

'Couldn't be better.' Johanson closed his book. The sea was plunged into a thick layer of fog but he could dimly make out the outlines of oil-rigs and boats. The swell must be high, he thought. A hefty storm was brewing.

'We'll be fine,' said the pilot.

'What's the forecast?'

'High winds.' The pilot glanced at the barometer on the control panel. 'Looks as though we're in for a hurricane.'

'Now you tell me.'

'Well, I didn't know before.' He shrugged. 'Weather forecasts aren't that reliable, you know. Are you afraid of flying?'

'Oh, no,' said Johanson, emphatically. 'It's just the thought of falling I don't like.'

'You won't be falling anywhere. For an offshore pilot, this stuff is child's play. We'll get a good shaking, but that's about all.'

'How long have we got?'

'We're half-way there already.'

'OK.' He opened his book again.

A thousand other noises were mixed with the roar of the engines. Bangs, whistles, crackles. There was even a ringing sound, which came at regular intervals from somewhere behind him. Amazing what the wind could do to the acoustics. Johanson turned towards the seat behind him, but the noise had stopped.

He focused on Walt Whitman.

Eighteen thousand years ago, at the peak of the last ice age, the sea level was some 120 metres lower than it was at the start of the third millennium. A large proportion of the world's water was trapped in glaciers, so the water pressure on the shelves was less intense. Some of the planet's seas hadn't yet formed, while during the glacial period others levelled out, some drying up entirely, leaving vast swathes of marshland in their wake.

One consequence of the worldwide drop in water pressure was its dramatic impact on the stability of gas hydrates. Vast quantities of methane were released in a short space of time, particularly in the upper regions of the slopes. The ice crystals that trapped and compressed the methane melted. For thousands of years the hydrates had held the slopes together, like glue, but now they acted like dynamite. As the methane escaped, it swelled to 164 times its former volume, breaking open crevices and craters as it pushed through the sediment to the surface, transforming the seabed into a porous, crumbling ruin, incapable of supporting its own weight.

The continental slopes began to collapse, tearing swathes of shelf as they fell. Enormous landslides, carrying huge amounts of debris, hurtled hundreds of kilometres through the depths. Methane entered the atmosphere, causing disastrous climate change. But the slides had other, similarly drastic effects – not just on the sea, but on coastal regions and islands as well.

It wasn't until the second half of the twentieth century that scientists made an incredible discovery. Off the coast of central Norway, they found traces of several landslides, which over 40,000 years had swept away a large proportion of the slope. A number of factors had contributed to them: warm periods, in which the average temperature of the currents near the slope had risen, and glacial periods, like the one 18,000 years ago, when the water had remained cold but the pressure had decreased. Strictly speaking, in terms of the Earth's geology, phases of hydrate stability were the exception.

And the people of the modern world were living in an exception, happy to let the calm deceive them. They liked to think it was the rule.

All in all, over 5500 cubic kilometres had been ripped out of the Norwegian shelf by the landslides that had sent the seabed crashing to the depths. In the sea between Scotland, Iceland and Norway, scientists found a trail of sediment more than 800 kilometres long. The really worrying fact was that the biggest slide had taken place not so very long ago – within the past 10,000 years. The scientists named it a Storegga Slide, and hoped it would never happen again.

It was a futile hope but, even so, there was a chance that the peace could have lasted several thousand years. New ice ages or warm periods might have caused slides that unfolded at bearable intervals. Instead the worm had invaded with its cargo of bacteria and, aided by the attendant circumstances, had brought things to a head.

On board the *Thorvaldson*, Jean-Jacques Alban had guessed that the silence from the submersible meant they would never see it again. What he didn't know was the true extent of the events occurring just a few hundred metres beneath the vessel's keel. He was in no doubt that the breakdown of the hydrates had reached a critical phase: over the past quarter of an hour the smell of rotten eggs had become unbearably intense, while the battery of enormous waves had thrown up ever larger chunks of fizzing hydrate. He knew that to stay on the slope was tantamount to suicide. The gas would thin the surface of the water and the vessel would sink. Whatever was going on down there, neither he nor anyone else could predict the effect. He hated to give up on the Deep Rover and its passengers but he knew somehow that Stone and the pilot were dead.

By now the scientists and crew were in a state of agitation. Not everyone understood the significance of the smell and the fizzing, but the rough seas compounded the mood of anxiety. Like a vengeful god the storm had swept down from the heavens, hurling towering waves across the sea. It would soon be impossible to stay upright on deck.

Alban had to weigh up all the factors and decide what to do. It wasn't a question of looking at the safety of the research vessel from the viewpoint of the shipping line or as an asset to science. The safety of the *Thorvaldson* meant the safety of human lives – including those of the two men on the submersible, whose fate Alban's instincts had accepted, even though his mind had not. Both staying and leaving were equally wrong – and right.

He squinted up at the dark sky and wiped the rain off his face. At that moment a brief calm descended on the choppy sea. But the storm wasn't abating, just drawing breath before it continued with increased force.

Alban decided to stay.

* * *

In the depths, disaster had struck.

The hydrates, transformed by the worms and bacteria from stable icefields and veins to porous, brittle tatters, had suddenly disintegrated. Across 150 kilometres of the slope, the ice crystals of water and methane broke open explosively, releasing the gas. While Alban was persuading himself to stay, the gas was rushing upwards, breaking through walls, cracking rocks, and causing the shelf to rise up and slide forward. Cubic kilometres of stone caved in. As more layers collapsed further down, the whole seabed along the shelf margin was thrown into motion and started to slide. A violent chain reaction pulled one landslide after the another, as debris rained down on the remaining stable layers, reducing them to mud.

The shelf between Scotland and Norway, with its oil wells, pipelines and platforms, showed signs of cracking.

Someone shouted through the storm at Alban. He spun round and saw the chief scientist waving at him frantically. He could barely hear the man's words. 'The slope,' was all he could make out. 'The slope.'

After the lull the sea had whipped up into a frenzy. Black waves battered the *Thorvaldson*. Alban looked despairingly at the boom from which the Deep Rover had been lowered into the water. The water was foaming. The stench of methane was overpowering. He started to run amidships where the scientist grabbed his arm.

'This way, Alban! Oh, God – there's something you should see.'

The ship shook. Alban heard a low rumble. It was coming from beneath the water. They staggered up the narrow swaying stairway to the bridge.

'Look!'

Alban stared at the control panel. The sonar was scanning the depths. He couldn't believe his eyes. The seabed was gone. It was as though he was looking at a maelstrom. 'The slope's collapsing,' he whispered.

At that moment he knew there was nothing he could do for Eddie or Stone. His foreboding had become a dreadful certainty. 'We've got to get out of here,' he said. 'At once.'

'But which direction?' the helmsman asked.

Alban tried to think. He knew what was happening down there and what lay in store. Heading for port was out of the question. The *Thorvaldson*'s only chance was to sail out to sea as fast as she could. 'Put out a radio message,' he said. 'Norway, Scotland, Iceland and all the other North Sea states. They need to evacuate their coasts. Do it now. Get through to everyone you can.'

'But what about Stone and—' the scientist began.

'They're dead.'

He didn't dare think about how powerful the slide might have been. The images on the monitor had sent shivers down his spine. And they weren't out of danger yet. A few kilometres closer to the shore and the ship would capsize. Further out to sea there was a chance they'd escape, despite the fury of the storm.

Alban tried to remember how the slope was shaped. Towards the north-west the seabed descended downwards in a series of large terraces. If they were lucky, the avalanche would come to rest before it reached the bottom. But there was no stopping a Storegga Slide. The whole slope, hundreds of kilometres of it, would slip into the depths, descending 3500 metres. The slide would penetrate as far as the abyssal plains east of Iceland, sending apocalyptic tremors through the North Sea and the Norwegian Sea.

Alban looked up from the console. 'Head for Iceland,' he ordered.

When the first branch of the avalanche reached the Faroe-Shetland Channel, the submarine terraces between Scotland and the Norwegian Trench had already disappeared, transformed into a slurry of debris that gathered pace as it crashed into the depths, pulling with it everything in path. Nothing of shape or structure survived in its wake. One part of the avalanche split off to the west of the Faroe Islands and came to a halt in the underwater banks surrounding the Icelandic Basin. Another part headed along the mountain range between Iceland and the Faroes.

But the bulk thundered down the Faroe-Shetland Channel as though it were a chute. The same basin that had absorbed the Storegga Slide thousands of years earlier was filled by an even bigger avalanche, pushing forwards relentlessly.

Then the edge of the shelf broke away.

Over a stretch of fifty kilometres the shelf snapped off. And that was just the start.

Once the helicopter had taken off, Tina Lund had loaded her luggage into Johanson's jeep and driven away fast through the rain. God knows what Johanson would have said, but Lund believed in pushing a car to its maximum.

A weight lifted from her mind with every passing kilometre. It had all clicked into place. Once she'd cleared up that business with Stone, she'd called Kare and volunteered to spend a few days with him on the coast. Kare had seemed pleased, if a little bewildered. Something in his voice made her suspect that Johanson had been right and that she'd settled on the right course just in time.

As the jeep rolled down Sveggesundet's high street towards the seafront, her pulse quickened. She left the vehicle in a car park just along from the Fiskehuset. A track and a path led down towards the sea. It didn't look like a typical beach: the boulders and slabs of stone were covered with moss and ferns. Although the area around Sveggesundet was flat, it was wild and romantic, and the view from the Fiskehuset, with its dining terrace on the front, was impressive – even on a misty, rainy morning like today.

Lund strolled to the restaurant and went in. Kare was out, and they hadn't started serving. A kitchen assistant walked past with a crate of vegetables, and told her that the boss had business in town. He didn't know when he'd be back.

It's your own fault, Lund told herself.

They'd agreed to meet there, but – probably because she'd driven like a mad thing – she was an hour early. She'd just have to sit and wait.

She stepped out onto the terrace. Rain pelted her face. Some people would have fled indoors, but Lund barely noticed it. She'd spent her childhood in the country. Sunny days were wonderful, but she enjoyed rain and gales too. Suddenly it occurred to her that the gusts that had rocked the jeep for the final half-hour of the journey had turned into a severe storm. The mist had thinned, but the clouds had sunk and were scudding low across the sky. White spray billowed from the furrowed sea.

Something wasn't right about it.

She'd been here often enough to know the place quite well, but now the beach looked longer than usual. The pebbles and rocks seemed to extend for ever, despite the crashing waves. Like an impromptu ebb tide, she thought.

On impulse she pulled out her mobile and called Kare. She might as well tell him she had arrived – rather than risk taking him by surprise. She didn't want anything to go wrong.

His mobile rang four times, then switched to voicemail.

Fate had ruled otherwise. In that case, she'd just wait.

She wiped the dripping hair from her eyes and went inside, hoping that, if nothing else, the coffee machine was ready for action.

Tsunami

The sea was full of monsters. Since the beginning of human history it had been a place for symbols, myths and primal fears. The six-headed Scylla had preyed on Odysseus's companions. Angered by Cassiopeia's boastfulness, Poseidon had created Cetus, a sea monster, and cast sea snakes at Laocoön when he foretold the fall of Troy. Sirens were lethal to sailors unless they stopped their ears with wax. Mermaids, aquatic dinosaurs and giant squid haunted the imagination. *Vampyroteutis infernalis* was the antithesis of every human value. Even the horned creature of the Bible had risen from the sea. And then, to top it all, science, whose first allegiance was to scepticism, had taken to preaching the message of truth that lay at the heart of the legends. The coelacanth was alive. The giant squid existed. For thousands of years people had feared the creatures of the deep, but now they followed them excitedly. Nothing was sacred to the modern scientific mind, not even fear. Deep-sea monsters had become man's favourite playthings, the soft toys of science.

Except one.

It struck fear into the most rational mind. Rising up from the sea to sweep over the land, it brought with it death and destruction. It owed its name to the Japanese fishermen who had been spared its horrors out at sea, but had returned to their villages to find their homes devastated, their families dead. The word they used to describe it meant 'wave in the harbour'. *Tsu* for harbour; *nami* for wave.

Tsunami.

Alban's decision to plot a course for deep water showed that he knew the monster and its habits. Seeking the supposed protection of the harbour would be fatal.

While the *Thorvaldson* was battling its way through the choppy seas, the continental shelf and slope slid further into the depths. The downward pull lowered the sea level over a vast area. The water around the plummeting mass rose up, surging outwards in a wave that radiated across the ocean. Near the site of the slide, covering an area of several thousand square kilometres, the wave was so flat that its presence went undetected amid the raging storm. Its height above water reached scarcely a metre.

Then it hit the shallow water of the shelf.

Over the years Alban had learned what distinguished a tsunami from a normal surface wave. Ocean swells were usually the result of movement in the air: solar radiation warmed the atmosphere, but the warmth wasn't distributed equally across the surface of the planet so the heat was transferred by winds, which swept over the ocean, ruffling the water and creating waves. The water rose barely fifteen metres, even in a hurricane. Giant waves were the only exception. Normal surface waves reached a maximum speed of ninety miles an hour, and the effect of the wind stayed on the surface. Just two hundred metres lower, the water would be calm.

But tsunamis didn't form on the surface: they originated in the depths. They weren't the result of high winds: they were created by a seismic shock – and seismic shock waves travelled at entirely different speeds. Worst of all, the energy of the tsunami was transmitted throughout the water column all the way to the seabed. No matter how deep the ocean was, the wave was always in contact with the seabed. The entire mass of water was in motion.

The best demonstration that Alban had ever seen of a tsunami wasn't a computer simulation but something much more basic. Someone had filled a pail with water and rapped the bottom. Concentric rings had rippled through the water. To picture a tsunami, he had merely to imagine it several million times bigger.

Merely.

Triggered by the landslide, the tsunami propagated outwards at a speed of 700 kilometres per hour. The crest of the wave was long and flat. It carried a million tonnes of water and was laden with energy. Within a few minutes, it had reached the spot where the shelf had snapped. The water became shallower, acting as a brake. The wave front slowed, but lost little energy. The mass of water pushed onwards, but because it was slowing, it began to stack up. The shallower the water became, the higher the tsunami towered, while its length shrank dramatically. Normal surface waves joined in, riding on its crest. By the time it reached the platforms on the North Sea shelf it had decelerated to 400 kilometres per hour, but it was already fifteen metres high.

Fifteen metres was nothing to an oil platform – providing the wave was just normal surface swell.

A seismic wave that stretched from the seabed to the surface, carrying a fifteen-metre mound of water and travelling at four hundred kilometres per hour, had the momentum of a speeding jumbo jet.

Gullfaks C, Norwegian Shelf

For a second Lars Jörensen thought he was too old to endure the final months on Gullfaks. He was trembling so much that the platform seemed to be vibrating with him. In all other respects he wasn't feeling too bad. A little depressed, maybe, but not ill.

Then it dawned on him that the platform was shaking, not him.

He stared at the derrick, then back out to sea. The sea was raging, but he'd seen worse and it had never affected the platform. Jörensen had heard of platforms shaking: it happened when a drilling operation triggered a blow-out, causing oil or gas to shoot up at high pressure. The whole platform could shudder back and forth. But that was impossible on Gullfaks, where the reserves were half empty, and the oil was pumped into sub-surface tanks. Besides, extraction took place at a distance, not under the platform.

The offshore industry had its own top ten of greatest risks. Struts within the steel framework that supported the platforms might collapse. Freak waves, massive surges of water caused by a combination of current and wind, were the industry's equivalent of a maximum credible accident. Pontoons that broke free or tankers with engine failure were dangerous too. But near the top of the hit parade of horror was the gas leak. Escaping gas was almost impossible to detect. In most cases it was only noticed when it was too late and fire had broken out. In incidents like that the platform exploded: more than 160 people had died on the British Piper Alpha, the biggest disaster in the history of the industry.

But a seaquake was the ultimate nightmare.

And this, Jörensen realised, was a quake.

Anything could happen now. When the ground shook, events spun out of control. Metal warped and snapped. Leaks sprang up and fires broke out. If the tremor was enough to rattle the platform, they could only hope that things wouldn't get worse, that the seabed wouldn't cave in or slump, and that the rig's foundations would withstand the shock. But in addition to all that, another problem was associated with quakes, which no one could do anything about.

And it was about to hit the platform.

Jörensen saw it coming and knew that his chances were nil. He turned and made for the steel steps, trying to escape his lofty perch.

It happened quickly.

He lost his footing and fell. Instinctively his fingers clutched the metal grating beneath him. An infernal noise broke out, a roaring and cracking as though the platform were breaking apart. There was screaming, a deafening bang, and Jörensen was tossed against the railings. Pain seized him. As he hung there in the metalwork, the sea reared up out of nowhere. He could hear the shriek of tearing metal and realised that the whole platform was tilting. His mind shut down. Now he was just a panic-stricken body, making futile attempts to crawl away from the approaching water. He dragged himself up the slope that, seconds before, had been a floor, but the incline was getting steeper.

His strength was running out. The fingers of his right hand let go of the metal. There was a sickening jerk and he was hanging by one arm. The derrick was toppling and the gas flame on the boom was no longer shooting out across the water but rising vertically into the dark sky.

Then everything exploded in a fiery, incandescent cloud, and Jörensen was cast into the sea. He didn't feel the pain in his lower arm, where the blast had severed his hand, leaving it hanging in the metal. Before the spiral of flames could engulf him, the tsunami hit the sinking platform. Gullfaks C was blasted to pieces, the concrete pillars plunging into the sea.

Granddad, tell us a story . . .

The woman frowned as she listened to him. 'What do you mean?' she asked. 'A kind of chain reaction, did you say?'

She was on the Ministry of Environment's Disaster Management Committee, and she was used to being confronted with the most outrageous theories. But she knew of the Geomar Centre, which didn't usually make ludicrous claims. She focused on understanding what the German scientist on the telephone was trying to say.

'Not exactly,' said Bohrmann. 'It's *simultaneous*. The damage is occurring all along the slope. It's taking place everywhere at exactly the same time.'

The woman swallowed. 'And . . . which areas will be hit?'

'That depends on the location of the break and how far it extends. Still, a large proportion of the coast, I'd say. Tsunamis stretch thousands of kilometres. We're informing anyone in the vicinity – Iceland, the UK, Germany, everyone.'

The woman stared out of her office window. She was thinking of the oil platforms, stranded in the sea. Hundreds of them, as far north as Trondheim.

'What will happen to the coastal regions?' she asked dully.

'You should make plans to evacuate.'

'And the offshore industry?'

'As I said, it's hard to predict. If we're fortunate, there'll be a series of small-scale landslides. In that case, the platforms might wobble, but basically they'll be fine. On the other hand, if . . .'

The door opened and a man rushed in. His face was white. He thrust a sheet of paper in front of her and signalled to her to end her conversation. She picked up the printout and scanned the short text. It was the transcript of a radio message from a ship. The *Thorvaldson*.

As she read on, she felt as though the ground were slipping away from her.

'The warning signs are already there,' Bohrmann was saying. 'In the event of it happening, anyone living on the coast should know what to expect. Tsunamis make their presence known before they strike. When the wave is approaching, the sea level rises and falls. It's rapid, and it happens several times, so you'd notice if you knew what to look for. After ten to twenty minutes the water retreats from the shore. Reefs and rocks become visible. You start to see parts of the seabed that are usually covered. That's the last warning. Then you must head for higher ground.'

The woman didn't speak. She'd almost stopped listening. A few minutes earlier she'd been trying to imagine what would happen if the man was telling the truth. Now she was picturing what was taking place that second.

Sveggesundet, Norway

Lund was dying of boredom. The kitchen assistant had switched on the espresso machine for her benefit and the coffee had been delicious. And despite the stormy weather and poor visibility, the view of the sea through the panoramic windows while she drank it had been amazing. But Lund found the wait unbearable.

A blast of cold air hit the room.

'Hello, Tina.'

It was a friend of Kare's, Åke. He ran a successful boat-hire business in Kristiansund that made a lot of money in the summer.

They talked a bit about the weather. Then Åke asked, 'So what are you doing here? Visiting Kare?'

'That was the plan.' She smiled wryly.

Åke looked at her in surprise. 'So where is he?'

'It's my fault. I'm early.'

'Give him a call, then.'

'I've tried. Voicemail.'

'Of course.' Åke slapped his forehead. 'I'd forgotten. He won't have any reception.'

Lund sat up. 'You know where he is?'

'Sure, I was with him. We took a trip to Hauffen.'

'The distillery?'

'That's right. He's buying spirits. We sampled one or two, but you know Kare – he drinks less than a monk during Lent.'

'Is he still there?'

I left him chatting with them in the cellars. You should head over. Do you know where Hauffen is?'

Lund did. The little distillery produced an excellent aquavit reserved for the Norwegian market. It was on a low plateau to the south, about ten minutes away on foot. She could be there in two minutes by car, if she took the inland road. But somehow the thought of a short walk appealed to her. Besides, she'd sat in the jeep long enough already. 'I'll walk,' she said.

'In this weather?' Åke pulled a face. 'Well, it's up to you. Don't blame me if you get webbed feet.'

'Better than putting down roots.' She stood up. 'See you later. I'll bring him back here.'

Outside she pulled up her jacket collar, walked down to the beach and set off. On good days the distillery was clearly visible. Right now, it was just a faint grey outline through the slanting rain.

As she left the Fiskehuset behind her, she gazed out to sea. She must have been mistaken earlier. She'd thought the stony beach seemed longer than usual, but now it looked the same. No . . . it might be a bit smaller.

She shrugged and carried on.

When she arrived at the distillery, soaking wet, there was no one in the foyer. On the far side a wooden door stood open. Light shone up from the cellars. She went straight down the stairs. There she found two men, leaning against the barrels, chatting, each with a glass in his hand. They were the two brothers who owned the distillery – friendly old men with weatherbeaten faces. Kåre was nowhere to be seen.

'Sorry,' said one. 'You've just missed him. He left a few minutes ago.'

'Did he come on foot?' she asked. Maybe she could catch up with him.

'In the van. He bought a few bottles. Too many to carry.'

'Was he going back to the restaurant?'

'That's where he said he was heading.'

'Thanks.'

'Hey, hang on a minute. You can't visit a distillery and leave before you've had a drink.'

'It's very kind of you, but—'

'He's right, you know,' his brother said eagerly.

'I—'

'Come on, you'll catch your death out there. Let's get a drop of something warm inside you first.'

'OK,' she said. 'Just one.'

The brothers grinned triumphantly. The war of attrition had been won.

The helicopter was preparing to land. Johanson looked out of the window. They'd just flown over the cliffs, following the coastline in the direction of the little landing-field where Karen Weaver would be waiting. Towards the east of the island the cliffs sloped downwards to end in a sweeping bay. From there the landscape was flat. An endless succession of sand and pebble beaches separated the water from barren moorland and long rolling hills with roads etched between them like scars.

The helipad, which was rather a grand term for the rough circle of gravel surrounded by grey-green moorland, belonged to a marine research station whose crooked, windswept huts housed half a dozen scientists. A narrow road led down from the hills and stopped at a jetty. Johanson couldn't see any boats. Two jeeps and a rusty VW bus were parked next to the buildings. Weaver was working on an article on seals, which was why she'd chosen the spot. She lived in one of the huts, accompanied the scientists on their expeditions and joined in on their research dives.

A final gust shook the Bell 430, then the skids touched down. The helicopter landed with a jolt.

'Well, that wasn't too bad, was it?' said the pilot.

Johanson saw a small figure standing at the edge of the landing field, her hair blowing in the wind. Karen Weaver, he guessed. A few metres away from her, a motorbike was propped up on its stand. He stretched, then slid Whitman's poetry back into his bag and picked up his coat. 'It would have been fun to do a few more laps,' he said, 'but I'd hate to keep the lady waiting. Can you come back for me tomorrow around lunchtime? Twelve o'clock, let's say.'

'No problem.'

He waited for the door to slide open, then clambered down the ladder. He was pleased to be back on firm ground. The pilot had to head off again, but turbulent conditions were clearly part of the job. He'd take a short break, then carry on to Lerwick for fuel. Johanson swung his bag over his shoulder. His coat billowed in the wind and flapped around his legs, but at least it wasn't raining. Karen Weaver came to meet him. It was strange, but with every step her size diminished. By the time she was standing in front of him, he guessed she was barely five foot five. She was nicely compact. Her jeans were stretched over muscular legs, and her strong shoulders stood out beneath her leather jacket. As far as Johanson could tell, she wasn't wearing makeup. Her skin glowed with a natural tan and freckles were scattered over her forehead and wide cheekbones. The wind tugged at a cascade of auburn curls. She eyed him inquisitively. 'Sigur Johanson,' she announced. 'How was your flight?'

'Wretched. Thankfully I had Walt Whitman to reassure me.' He glanced back at the helicopter.

She smiled. 'Shall we go for some food?'

'Sure. Where?'

She nodded in the direction of the motorbike.

'We could drive into town. If you managed the flying, you won't mind the Harley. It'd be quicker to eat at the station, though – if corned beef and pea soup don't put you off.'

Johanson noticed that her eyes were an unusually brilliant blue. 'Why not?' he said. 'Where are all your scientists? Out sailing?'

'No, it's too rough. They headed into town for supplies. They don't mind me doing what I like here, including helping myself to their tins. That's about the extent of my cooking.'

Johanson followed her over the gravel towards the station. The buildings didn't look quite as flimsy from this angle as they had from above. 'Where are the boats?' he asked.

'We don't like leaving them out.' She pointed to the building closest to the water. 'The bay isn't very sheltered, so once we've finished we lug them back to that hut by the sea.'

The sea . . .

Where was it?

Johanson did a double-take and stopped. A few seconds earlier breakers had been crashing up the beach, but now there was nothing but mud and rocks. Within the last minute the tide had receded, leaving the seabed exposed.

It was impossible for the tide to turn so quickly. The water had retreated by hundreds of metres.

Weaver turned. 'What's wrong?'

He shook his head. He could hear noise. At first he thought it was an aeroplane swooping towards the shore. But it didn't sound like an aeroplane, more like a roll of thunder, only thunder rose and fell, and this noise just kept . . .

Suddenly he knew what it was.

Weaver had followed his gaze. 'What the hell—'

Johanson saw the horizon darken. 'To the helicopter,' he yelled.

Weaver seemed rooted to the spot. Then she darted forwards. Together they ran towards the helicopter. Through the bubble of the cockpit Johanson saw the pilot checking the instruments. It was a moment before he noticed the figures dashing towards him. He stopped what he was doing. Johanson signalled for him to let down the ladder. He knew the pilot couldn't see what was approaching from the water, since the helicopter was facing inland.

The man frowned, then nodded. With a hiss the door slid open and the ladder was lowered.

The thundering drew closer. Now it sounded as though the whole world was in motion, rushing towards the beach.

Which was exactly what was happening, thought Johanson.

Wrong place, wrong time.

Torn between terror and fascination, he paused at the foot of the ladder and watched as the sea returned, flooding over the muddy plain.

'Johanson!'

He pulled himself together and hurried up the steps, Weaver at his heels. He saw the confusion in the pilot's eyes and shouted, 'Start her up. Hurry.'

'What's that noise? What's going on?'

'Just get this thing in the air.'

'I'm not a magician, you know! What the hell's going on? Where am I supposed to go?'

'Anywhere. So long as it's up.'

The rotors rattled into action. The Bell wobbled and took off, climbing one metre, two. Then the pilot's curiosity conquered his fear, and he swung the helicopter through 180 degrees so that they were looking at the sea. 'Holy shit,' he gasped.

'Look!' Weaver was pointing towards the huts. 'Over there.'

Someone had come out of the main building and was running towards them. A man in jeans and a T-shirt. Weaver stared at him in horror. 'We've got to go down. Oh, God! I swear I didn't know Steven was here – I thought they'd all—'

Johanson shook his head. 'He won't make it.'

'We can't leave him here.'

'Look outside, for Christ's sake, he's not going to make it. If we go down none of us will.'

Weaver headed for the door as the pilot steered sideways over the strip of sand towards the man. The helicopter twisted, buffeted by strong blasts and for a moment they lost sight of the man, then they were almost above him.

'We've got to go down!' shouted Weaver.

'No,' said Johanson.

She didn't hear him. Even the sound of the rotors was lost in the thunder of the wave. Johanson knew it was too late to save the man now, but precious moments had been wasted, and he wasn't sure that they could get away themselves. He forced himself to look away from the running scientist and focus ahead.

The wave must have been thirty metres tall, a vertical wall of dark water. It was still several hundred metres from shore, but it was coming towards them at the speed of an express train. They had just seconds to get clear. The pilot made one last attempt to get closer to the fleeing man. Maybe he was hoping that the guy could leap through the open door or clutch on to one of the skids like a movie stunt—

The scientist stumbled, and fell.

Darkness descended in front of them. There was no sign of the sky through the cockpit screen, just the wall of water. It filled their view, surging forwards at incredible speed. They'd missed their chance. There was nowhere for them to go. Flying upwards, they'd be caught in the middle of the gigantic wave. By flying inland, they could buy themselves time, but the wave would still catch them. The tsunami was faster and, besides, they were facing the wrong way. The pilot couldn't turn the helicopter now.

Johanson's mind disengaged, and he wondered how he could bear to look at the vertical front of water without going mad. Then reality caught up with him. The pilot took the only viable option and sent the helicopter shooting backwards and up. The nose of the Bell sank down. For a second the ground was visible through the cockpit, but they didn't sink towards it; they were flying up and backwards, away from the wave that was racing into shore. The Bell roared as though its gearbox was about to explode. Johanson would never have thought that a helicopter was capable of a manoeuvre like that. Maybe the pilot had never believed it either. But it worked.

The breaking wave hit the beach, and collapsed. Mountains of spray shot up towards the Bell as it continued its lunatic flight. The tsunami bellowed and screeched. The next minute a tremendous jolt shook the aircraft and Johanson was slammed against the side, right next to the open door. Water slapped into his face. His head banged backwards, and red flashes passed before his eyes. His fingers clutched a strut, and tightened. Pain surged through him. He could no longer tell whether the booming was coming from the wave or his head; whether they were going up or down. His only thought was that the wave had finally done for them and they were about to be dashed to pieces. He waited for the end.

Then his vision cleared. The cabin was full of spray. Scraps of grey cloud flashed over the helicopter.

They'd made it. Instead of crashing into the tsunami, they'd scraped over its crest.

The helicopter carried on climbing and banked, so they could see the coast beneath them. But it was gone. Down below a fearsome tide, which showed no sign of slowing, surged forwards and swallowed the land. The station, the vehicles and the scientist had vanished. To their right, glittering fountains of spray exploded in the distance, shooting over the cliffs, rising straight into the sky, as though they were trying to meld with the clouds.

Weaver had been catapulted over the seats when the torrent had hit the helicopter. Now she scrambled up and stared out. 'Oh, God,' she mumbled.

The pilot's face was ashen, his jaws clenched.

But they'd made it.

They chased the wave. The mass of water was surging over the land faster than they could follow. A hill came into view and the water shot over it, the tide of foam spilling into the moorland, barely losing speed. The terrain was so flat that the water's incursion would continue for kilometres. Johanson saw a host of white specks moving in a field, and realised they were sheep. Then they were gone too.

It would have destroyed a seaside town, he thought.

Wrong. Practically every town on the North Sea coast was now being destroyed. From wherever it had started, the tsunami was radiating outwards. That was what impulse waves did. The destructive force would sweep towards Norway, Holland, Germany, Scotland and Iceland. Suddenly the nature of the catastrophe struck him like a blow. He doubled up, as though red-hot metal had been thrust against his belly.

Lund was in Sveggesundet.

Sveggesundet, Norway

The Hauffen brothers were nothing if not entertaining, thought Lund. Heaven knows, they'd tried everything to persuade her to stay. They were even prepared to claim that they'd make better lovers than Kare Sverdrup – at which point they nudged each other and gave knowing winks. In the end Lund had to drink another round before they agreed to let her go.

She looked at her watch. If she left now, she'd get to the Fiskehuset bang on time.

The old men insisted on farewell hugs. She was the right woman for Kare, they assured her, a real woman who didn't turn up her nose at a proper glass of aquavit. Then they bombarded her with tips, jokes and compliments, until at last one of the brothers escorted her out of the cellars and back up the stairs. He opened the door, saw the sheet of driving rain, and immediately decided she couldn't go out without an umbrella. She did her best to convince him that she could manage, but to no avail. The old man went in search of an umbrella, then the goodbye-ritual began again. Finally she escaped the brothers' solicitudes and set off through the rain.

Things were looking lively, she thought. The sky was even darker than it had been before, and the wind was blowing more fiercely. She speeded up.

A soft beep sounded from somewhere. She stood still. It was her mobile. He must be calling! How long had it been ringing? She unzipped her jacket and pulled it out hurriedly, expecting to hear Kare.

'Tina?'

'Sigur, nice of you to call. I was—'

'Where've you been, for God's sake? I've been trying to get hold of you.'

'I'm sorry, I was—'

'Where are you now?'

'Sveggesundet,' she faltered. There was static on the line and a loud drone in the background was forcing him to shout, but there was something in his voice that she'd never heard before. It scared her. 'I'm just walking along the beach. The weather's foul, but you know me, I—'

'Get out of there!'

'What?'

'Get out as quickly as you can!'

'Sigur! Are you mad?'

'Do it now. Right away.' He carried on talking, breathlessly. The words washed over her like rain. The crackling and rustling distorted his voice, so at first she thought she'd misheard him. Then she grasped what he was saying, and her legs turned to jelly.

'I don't know where the epicentre is,' his voice sputtered. 'The wave must be taking longer to get to you. Either way, you're running out of time. For God's sake, go! Get out while you can!'

She stared out to sea. The gale was ruffling the water with fluffy white surf.

'Tina?' Johanson shouted.

'I . . . OK.' She sucked in her breath, filling her lungs with air.

She threw down the umbrella and started to run.

Through the rain she could see the lights of the restaurant, warm and inviting. Kare, she thought. We'll take your car or mine. The jeep was parked five hundred metres from the restaurant, but Kare had some spaces right next to the Fiskehuset where he usually left his car. She carried on running. Rain splashed into her eyes and she remembered that the car would be parked on the far side of the building, hidden from view.

Amid the howling of the wind and the roaring of the waves there was another noise, a loud, slurping sound.

Without stopping she glanced round.

Something unbelievable was happening. Lund froze, watching the sea disappear, as though a plug had been pulled out. An expanse of dark, uneven seabed emerged, stretching far into the distance.

Then she heard rumbling.

She blinked and reached up again to wipe the rain from her eyes. Far away on the horizon, something long and immense took shape. At first she thought it was a dark bank of cloud. But then it surged forward, and she saw that it formed a perfect line.

She took a step backwards and she started to run again.

Without a car she'd be lost, there was no doubt about it. The only higher ground was on the other side of town, towards the mainland. She breathed evenly and deeply, trying to push down the panic that was welling inside her. Adrenaline shot into her muscles – she had the strength to run for ever, but that wouldn't help her. The wave was much faster.

The path forked in front of her. To the left it led to the restaurant, and to the right was a shortcut up the bank towards the car park where she'd left Johanson's jeep. If she ran there now, she'd make it to the car park; then straight up the road, towards the hill, as fast as the jeep would take her. But she couldn't leave Kare. The old men in the distillery had said he was heading back to the restaurant and that meant he was there, waiting for her. He didn't deserve to be left alone. She didn't deserve to be alone any longer.

She ran past the turn to the right and towards the building. It wasn't far now to the Fiskehuset. The thundering noise was louder, but she tried to ignore it and shake off her fear. And she was fast. She'd be faster than the wave. Her speed would be enough for two.

The door to the terrace flew open. Someone rushed out and froze.

Kare.

She called his name, but her voice was lost in the howling of the wind and the thundering of the wave.

He started to run, and disappeared round the side of the building. Lund groaned, unable to believe what was happening. Then the splutter of an engine was carried to her on the gale. An instant later Kare's car sped off up the road towards the hill.

Her heart almost stopped. He couldn't do that to her. He must have seen her. He *must* have.

He hadn't.

She carried on running, through the bushes and over the boulders to the car park. Her only hope was the jeep. She reached a barrier, a two-metre-high wire-netting fence. She pulled herself over it. Once again she'd lost valuable seconds in which the wave had surged forward. But now she glimpsed the jeep, a dark silhouette through the curtain of rain. It was tantalisingly close.

She ran even faster than before. The rocks gave way to meadow, and then her feet were on concrete. There was the jeep.

Come on, Tina, run.

The concrete shook.

Run.

Her hand slid into her pocket, fingers curling round the key. Her boots beat a regular rhythm on the ground. She skidded over the last few metres, but it didn't matter, she was there. Open up! Hurry!

The key slid out of her hand.

Oh no! she thought, *please no, not now.*

Frantically she fumbled for the key, spinning round in a circle.

The sky filled with darkness.

Slowly she looked up and saw the wave.

The hurry was over. She knew it was too late. She'd lived fast, and she'd die fast too. At least, she hoped it would be fast. At times she'd asked herself what it would be like to die, what went through a person's mind when their fate had been sealed and they knew it was time. I've come for you, Death would say. You've got five more seconds, so have a last think, whatever you like. Look back on your life, if you wish.

Didn't they say that as your car flipped over, or you fell from great height, that somehow, your life flashed before you, images from your childhood, your first love, like a 'best-of' compilation?

But the only thing Lund felt was fear that death would hurt her, and she'd suffer. She felt almost ashamed that it had had to end so pitifully. That she'd messed up.

She watched as the tsunami crashed into Kare Sverdrup's restaurant, smashing it to pieces and surging onwards.

The wall of water reached the car park.

A few seconds later it was rushing up the hill.

The Shelf

By the time the wave had reached the surrounding coastline, it had wrought untold damage on the shelf.

The oil-rigs and platforms built near the break had disappeared along with the slope. That alone had cost the lives of thousands but it was merely a foretaste of what was to come. As the water surged forward, it formed a towering vertical front that grew taller as the water depth decreased. Under the force of the impact the struts of the platforms snapped like matchsticks. In less than fifteen minutes more than eighty had toppled into the sea. The problem wasn't so much the height of the wave – North Sea oil platforms were built to contend with forty-metre waves, which, statistically speaking, occurred once in a hundred years – but the combination of other factors.

Even ordinary waves had been known to exert pressure of up to twelve tonnes per square metre – enough to rip out sections of harbour wall and deposit them in the centre of town, to throw sailing-boats into the air, and break a freighter in two. That was the impact of a wind-generated wave. The force of a tsunami was a different matter. Next to a tsunami of similar amplitude, even the most ferocious surface wave seemed gentle as a lamb.

The tsunami triggered by the landslide reached the middle of the shelf at a height of twenty metres, low enough to pass beneath the platforms' decks.

The force with which it hit the pilings was all the more lethal.

Oil-platforms, like ships and any other construction destined for long-term exposure to the sea, were expected to withstand certain stresses, which were measured in years. If the defining criterion was the forty-metre wave, then engineers designed the platform to survive the impact of the swell. Since the wave was expected only once a century, the platform – according to the workings of a none-too-confidence-inspiring logic – was deemed to have satisfied the hundred-year standard. That meant, statistically, that it was fit to weather a century of waves. Of course, no one expected it to last a hundred years being battered by forty-metre waves. In fact, it might not even survive one major surge. Monster waves weren't really the problem: the damage was done by everyday wear and tear caused by ordinary waves and currents. Platforms and other technical structures soon developed an Achilles' heel, although its location was anyone's guess. If a weak spot on a platform suffered the equivalent of fifty years' stress within the first decade, an ordinary wave might suddenly pose a risk.

Figures couldn't solve the dilemma. The statistics and mean values used in marine engineering described ideal scenarios, not what really happened. Averages might mean something to bureaucrats and engineers, but the sea had no truck with statistics: it was a succession of unpredictable circumstances and extremes. A particular stretch of water might have an average wave height of ten metres, but if you were hit by a one-off thirty-metre monster that statistically didn't exist, the average would be of precious little comfort: you would die.

When the tsunami swept across the landscape of steel towers, it exceeded their maximum strain. Struts snapped, welded joints burst open and decks sagged. On the British side, where steel structures were the norm, practically every platform was smashed to pieces or fatally damaged by the impact.

Years earlier Norway had switched to reinforced concrete pilings, which provided less of a target for the tsunami, but the outcome was no less calamitous: the wave bombarded the derricks with ships.

Theoretically, most ships weren't equipped to deal with surface waves of more than twenty metres. The hull-girder stress was designed to cope with a maximum nominal wave height of sixteen and a half metres. In practice, things worked differently. In the mid-nineties rogue waves north of Scotland tore a hole the size of a house in the 300 000 tonne tanker *Mimosa*, but the ship got away. In 2001 a thirty-five-metre breaker nearly sank the cruise ship MS *Bremen* off the coast of South Africa – nearly. That same year, close to the Falklands, the *Endeavour*, ninety metres in length, fell victim to a phenomenon known to oceanographers as the 'Three Sisters' – three freak waves, each thirty metres high, in quick succession. The *Endeavour* was severely damaged, but she made it back to port.

In most cases, though, the ships that met with freak waves were never seen again. Each monster wave would push a deep trough in front of it, a chasm that the vessel would sink into, bow or stern first. If the waves were far enough apart, there'd be time for it to rise up and scale the crest. When the wavelength was shorter, events took a different turn. The ship would pitch forwards into the trough, only to be met head-on by the vertical front of the following wave. The vessel would be swallowed and buried under water. Even if it managed to rise up from the trough and start to ascend the crest, there was still a danger that the wave would be too high or too steep. Most of the time it was both. Extremely high *and* extremely steep. That meant attempting the impossible – scaling a vertical wall. Smaller vessels in particular would fall victim to waves whose height exceeded their length, but even ocean-going giants didn't always make it out of the trough and over the crest. The wave would flip them over and they would hit the water upside-down.

Freak waves, generated by the interplay of currents and wind, could reach speeds of fifty kilometres an hour, but seldom more. That was enough to wreak havoc, but compared to the twenty-metre-high tsunami that was sweeping the shelf, a freak wave was a lame duck.

Most of the tugs, tankers and ferries that had the misfortune to find themselves in the North Sea at that moment were thrown around like toys. Some collided, others were hurled against the concrete pillars of the platforms, or smashed against the loading buoys to which they'd been moored. Even reinforced concrete couldn't withstand the force of the impact. The giant structures began to collapse. The few left standing soon followed suit. Tankers, some fully laden with oil, collided and exploded, smothering the platforms with clouds of fire. Derricks were blown to pieces in a series of chain reactions. Burning debris was scattered over hundreds of metres. The tsunami tore the platforms from their foundations on the seabed and toppled them into the water. The devastation of the shelf took place just minutes after the wave had surged outwards from the site of the submarine slide on its way to the coastline around it.

Each incident alone was a nightmare come true for the offshore and shipping industries. But what happened that afternoon in the North Sea was more than just a living nightmare.

It was the apocalypse.

The Coast

Eight minutes after the outer shelf collapsed, the tsunami hit the steep cliffs of the Faroes. Four minutes later it reached the Shetlands, and two minutes after that it slammed into the Scottish mainland and the south-west stretch of the Norwegian coast.

Nothing could flood Norway entirely – except perhaps the comet that scientists believed would wipe out all humanity if ever it were to crash into the sea. The Norwegian landscape was made up of mountain upon mountain, protected by sheer cliffs that even the biggest wave would find difficult to surmount.

But Norway lived on and from the water, and most of its major cities were at sea level, in the foothills of the towering mountains. All that separated them from the open water were small, flat archipelagos, some of which were home to cities themselves. Ports like Egersund, Haugesund and Sandnes in the south were at the mercy of the wave, just like Ålesund and Kristiansund further north, and hundreds of smaller towns along the coast.

The worst hit was Stavanger.

All kinds of factors influenced what happened to a tsunami when it reached the coast – reefs, estuaries, underwater mountain ranges, sandbanks, offshore islands or even just the angle of a beach. As a result, the impact of the tsunami would either lessen or increase. Stavanger, the heart of the Norwegian oil industry, a key commercial and shipping centre, one of the oldest, prettiest and richest cities in Norway lay all but defenceless on the coast. Only a string of flat islands stretched north of the port, linked to the mainland by bridges. Minutes before the wave hit the city, the Norwegian government had alerted the Stavanger authorities, who had immediately broadcast a warning on radio, television and the web. But there was hopelessly little time to react. Evacuating the city was out of the question.

Unlike the Pacific states, where people had lived with tsunamis since time immemorial, Europe, the Mediterranean and the Atlantic didn't have a warning system. While in Hawaii, the PTWS, the Pacific Tsunami Warning System represented over twenty Pacific states, including almost every coastal country from Alaska to Japan, Australia, Chile and Peru, people in countries like Norway knew nothing about tsunamis. That was one reason why Stavanger's final minutes were filled with confusion and dismay.

The wave closed in on the city before anyone had time to flee. It was still growing when the pillars of the inter-island bridges collapsed. Just before it reached the city, it towered to its full thirty metres. It didn't break immediately, but crashed vertically into the harbour defences, shattering the quays and warehouses, then racing inland. The old town, with its historic timber houses from the late seventeenth and early eighteenth centuries, was razed to the ground. From Vågen, the city's historic dock, the water burst into the city centre. When the tide hit Stavanger's oldest building, the Anglo-Norman cathedral, the windows exploded outwards before the walls collapsed and the debris was swept away. Anything in the path of the water was blasted aside with the force of a missile. But it wasn't just water that destroyed the city. Mud, twenty-tonne boulders, ships and cars battered the buildings like outsize projectiles.

By now the sheer wall of water had turned into raging foam. The tsunami no longer surged through the streets at such speed, but it was turbulent and destructive. The foam trapped pockets of air, which compressed on impact, generating fifteen bars of pressure, enough to dent a tank. The water snapped trees like twigs, and their trunks became part of its weaponry. Less than a minute after the wave had hit the sea defences, the entire harbour was in ruins, along with the adjoining district. As the water surged along the streets, the first explosions could be heard.

The people of Stavanger had no hope of survival. Anyone who attempted to outrun the towering wall of water ran in vain. Most of the tsunami's victims were struck dead by the force of the wave. The water was like concrete. They didn't feel a thing. Those who survived the impact soon suffered a similar fate as the water flung them into buildings or ground them against debris. Almost no one drowned, apart from those trapped in flooded cellars, but even then most people were killed by the force of the surging mass of water or smothered in mud. Those who drowned died a terrible death, but at least it was quick. Few had time to realise what was happening. Starved of oxygen, their trapped bodies floated in dark, chilly water, heartbeat faltering, then finally stopping as their metabolism ground to a halt. The brain lived for a little longer. After ten to twenty minutes the last flicker of electrical activity faded.

It took just two minutes more for the wave to reach the suburbs. The greater the expanse of land it covered, the shallower the seething water became. Its speed continued to diminish. The wave raged and surged through the streets, killing anyone it encountered, but at least the houses stayed standing. It was too soon, though, for the survivors to celebrate. The coming of the tsunami was the beginning of the devastation.

Its retreat was almost worse.

Knut Olsen and his family experienced the retreating wave in Trondheim, where the tsunami had arrived a few minutes earlier. Unlike Stavanger, Trondheim had the fjord to protect it. Flanked by several larger islands and shielded by a headland, it extended almost forty kilometres inland, then widened into a basin on whose eastern shore the city had been built. Many of Norway's towns and villages were situated at sea-level along the shores of the fjords. Anyone looking at the map would assume that even the destructive power of a thirty-metre wave wouldn't threaten Trondheim.

The fjords turned out to be death traps.

When a tsunami entered a channel or an inlet, the water that was already being compressed from the bottom was suddenly restricted on both sides as well. Tens of thousands of tonnes of water squeezed into the strait. In Sogne Fjord, long but narrow in the mountains north of Bergen, the wave rose dramatically. Most of the villages alongside it were situated on high plateaus at the top of its banks. Jets of water sprayed towards them, but no serious damage was caused. Things were different at the end of the hundred-kilometre-long fjord, though, where several towns and villages were clustered on a flat spit of land jutting into the water. The wave obliterated them, then slammed into the mountain range beyond. The water shot up to 200 metres, scouring the slope of vegetation, then collapsing down. It continued its path along the fjord's tributaries.

Trondheim Fjord wasn't as narrow as Sogne Fjord and its banks weren't as high. That, and the fact that it widened as it went on, meant the water wasn't so constricted. All the same, the mound of water that hit Trondheim was big enough to sweep across the harbour and flatten part of the old town. The Nid broke its banks and spilled over into the districts of Bakklandet and Møllenberg. Avalanches of foam mowed down timber houses. In Kirkegata Street almost every house fell victim to the flood of water, including Sigur Johanson's. Its pretty façade gave way and the timberwork splintered, while the roof caved in on the wreckage of the walls. The debris was washed away, swept along by the raging torrent whose power and energy only let up when it reached the walls of the NTNU, where it swirled furiously, then began to flow back.

The Olsens lived one road up from Kirkegata Street. Their house, wooden like Johanson's, withstood the tsunami's assault. It trembled and shook. Furniture toppled, crockery smashed, and the floor of the front room sagged. The children were panicking and Olsen shouted to his wife to take them to the back. In truth he didn't know what to do, but since the wave had hit the front of the house he thought the back rooms might be safer. While his family took refuge, he made his way breathlessly to the front windows to see what had happened. As he crossed the floor, it sagged further, but held. Olsen clutched the window-frame, ready to rush back should another wave roll in. He looked out in stunned horror at the ruins of the city, the trees, cars and people bobbing in the water. There were screams and bangs as walls collapsed. Then explosions rang out, and red-black clouds rose above the harbour.

It was the most harrowing sight he'd ever seen, but he fought back the shock and focused on a single thought: saving his family. All that mattered was that his wife and children survived.

It looked as though the wave had stopped.

Olsen watched for a while then picked his way carefully to the back of the house. The barrage of questions started right away. He looked into his children's wide, fearful eyes, and raised a hand to calm them, telling them it was over and they needn't be afraid. Of course it wasn't over — how could it be? But somehow they had to leave the house. He had the idea of escaping over the rooftops to dry land, but his wife said he'd been watching too much Hitchcock. How did he propose to do that with four kids? Olsen didn't know, so that settled it. He returned to his post by the window.

This time when he looked out he saw that the water was flowing back, racing towards the fjord and picking up speed.

We're going to make it, he thought.

He leaned out for a better view. At that moment the house shook violently. Olsen clung to the window. The floor was splintering. He wanted to leap back, but there was nothing beneath him. The living-room floor was a huge gaping hole. Water poured in and Olsen pitched forward. At first he thought he'd been jerked through the window, then he realised that the front of the house was hanging off the walls. It was tipping him into the water.

He screamed.

The people of Hawaii had lived with the monster for generations, and knew what would happen when it beat its retreat. The receding water created a violent pull that swept everything into the sea, washing over anything left standing. Those who had survived the first act of the catastrophe died in the second, but their death was filled with agony. Their end began with the futile fight for survival against the raging water, the struggle to swim against the tide. Their strength would give out and their muscles would weaken. They'd be struck by debris and their bones broken. They'd cling to anything they could find, only to be torn away again, swept onwards with the rubble and the mud.

The monster of the deep came on land to feed, and when it returned to the ocean it dragged its prey with it.

The first Olsen knew of that was when the front of the house tipped towards the maelstrom. Then he knew he was going to die. As the wall tilted further, more explosions rang out across the harbour as the remains of ships and oil plants burst into flames. Almost every electrical system in the city had failed as one short-circuit triggered the next. Maybe that was how he would be killed – by the high-voltage current in the water.

He thought of his family. For a split second he thought of Sigur Johanson, and was seized with impotent rage. Johanson was to blame. He'd kept something back – something that might have saved them, the son-of-a-bitch.

With a deafening crash the façade of the house smashed down on a tree that was straining in the water. Olsen was catapulted head-first through the window. He clutched at the air and grasped leaves. A stream of mud raged beneath him. He dangled from the branch, as it swung madly up and down, then tried to pull himself up. Fragments of wood and plaster rained down on him from above, narrowly missing his head. The jet of water ripped chunks out of the timber wall. The front of his house warped, splintered and tore apart. He tried to move closer to the trunk. Lower down, and a little to one side, there was a thicker branch that he could reach. Maybe he could rest his feet on it. The huge tree groaned, and he made his way forward, hand over hand, gasping for breath.

The remains of the wall crashed into the water, tearing branches and foliage as it fell. Olsen's branch jerked up. His fingers uncurled. Suddenly he was hanging from one arm. If he fell, his fate would be sealed. He turned his head awkwardly for a glimpse of his house – or whatever remained of it. Please, he thought, don't let them be dead.

The house was still standing.

And then he saw his wife.

She'd crawled to the edge and was on her hands and knees, staring out at him. There was a look of determination on her face, as if she was about to dive into the water to help him. She couldn't, of course, but she was there, and she was calling to him. Her voice sounded firm, almost angry, as though he should stop messing around because everyone was waiting.

For a moment Olsen just looked at her.

Then he tensed his muscles. His free hand stretched up and grabbed the branch. He dug his fingers into the wood and began to move forward until his feet were directly above the sturdy branch. Slowly he let himself down. Now he could balance properly. He stood up. His shoulders quivered. He wrapped his arms round the trunk, pushing his face against the bark and staring at his wife.

It took for ever. The tree stayed put, and so did the house.

When the water had finally dragged its booty into the sea, he was able to climb down shakily into the wasteland of debris and mud. He helped his wife and children to leave the house. They took only what they needed: money, credit cards, passports, and a few bits and pieces of sentimental value, hastily crammed into a couple of rucksacks. Olsen's car had disappeared. They'd have to walk, but anything was better than staying put.

Silently they left the ruins of their home and walked along the other side of the river, away from Trondheim.

Cataclysm

The wave kept spreading outwards. It flooded the east coast of the UK and the west coast of Denmark. Between Edinburgh and Copenhagen the shelf was unusually shallow. Dogger Bank loomed up from the seabed, a relic of the time when the North Sea was still partly dry land. It had once been an island, its shores home to numerous animals that crowded together as the tides kept rising, until eventually they drowned. Now it lay thirteen metres below sea level, and it forced the surging wave to rear higher.

South of Dogger Bank the shelf was crammed with the oil platforms that lined the south-east coast of Britain, the northern shores of Belgium and the Netherlands. The wave raged more ferociously than it had further north, but the uneven surface of the shelf, with its sand bars, ridges and chasms, acted as a brake. The Frisian Islands were inundated, but the wave lost some of its momentum so Holland, Belgium and northern Germany were spared its full force. By the time it reached The Hague and Amsterdam, its speed had dropped to a hundred kilometres per hour, which was still enough to destroy large sections of coastline. Hamburg and

Bremen lay further inland, but the mouths of the Elbe and the Weser were as good as unprotected. The tsunami raced along the rivers, flooding the surrounding area before it reached the cities. In London the Thames rose sharply, breaking its banks and smashing ships into bridges.

The surging water spilled into the Strait of Dover, shaking the coastline to Normandy and Brittany. Only the Baltic emerged unscathed. The water off the coast of Copenhagen, Kiel and the other Baltic cities was choppier than usual, but the tsunami didn't reach them, shuttling between the Skagerrak and Kattegat until it collapsed. Further north the devastation continued unabated as the tsunami slammed into the shores of Iceland, Greenland and Spitsbergen.

After the disaster, the Olsens had headed straight for higher ground. Later on, when Knut Olsen thought about it, he couldn't say why. He was the one who'd suggested it. Maybe he dimly recalled a film he'd seen about tsunamis or an article he'd read, or maybe it had been intuition. Either way, the decision to flee had saved their lives.

Most people who survived the coming and going of a tsunami were killed all the same. When the first wave was over, they returned to their villages and houses to see what remained. But a tsunami was made up of a succession of waves. The large intervals between peaks meant that the second wave hit when people thought they were safe.

It was no different now.

Barely a quarter of an hour later, the second wave struck as forcefully as the first, and completed the devastation. The third, which hit the coastline twenty minutes later, was only half as high, then came a fourth, and after that, nothing.

In Germany, Belgium and the Netherlands, the evacuation measures hadn't come to much, despite the extra warning time they'd been given. Nearly everyone owned a car, though – and they'd all had the bright idea of using it. Within ten minutes of the news flash, the roads were jammed. Then the wave came along and the traffic was cleared.

An hour after the underwater avalanche, the offshore oil industry in northern Europe had ceased to exist. Almost all of the coastal towns in the surrounding area had been ravaged or destroyed. Hundreds of thousands of people had lost their lives. Only Iceland and Spitsbergen, two sparsely populated areas, had escaped without fatalities.

During their joint expedition, the *Thorvaldson* and the *Sonne* had established that the worms were destabilising the hydrates along the length of the slope, as far north as Tromsø. The landslide had happened in the south. Because of the effects of the tsunami no one had time to consider whether the northern slope was in danger of collapsing too. Gerhard Bohrmann might have been able to provide an answer – but he had no means of identifying the location of the slide. Not even Jean-Jacques Alban, who had succeeded in getting the *Thorvaldson* far enough out to sea to escape the tsunami, had any idea of what had taken place.

The sound of explosions echoed across the sea, bouncing off the ruins of the towns. Roaring helicopters, wailing sirens and loudspeaker announcements mixed with the screams of survivors. It was a cacophony of misery, and at its heart was the leaden silence of death.

Three hours went by, and the last wave rolled back into the sea.

Then the northern slope collapsed.

PART TWO

CHATEAU DISASTER

From the annual reports of international environmental organizations

In spite of the 1994 ban, the dumping of radioactive waste in the world's oceans is ongoing. Greenpeace divers examining the seabed at the mouth of the discharge pipe of the French reprocessing plant in *La Hague* found levels of radioactivity seventeen million times higher than those in uncontaminated waters. Crabs and kelp off the Norwegian coast have been found to be contaminated with the radioactive isotope technetium-99. Radiation protection experts in Norway identified the source of the pollution as the ageing reactors of the British nuclear reprocessing factory in Sellafield. However, American geologists stick by their proposals for highly radioactive waste to be buried under the ocean. The scheme involves dropping nuclear containers kilometres into the seabed through pipes, then covering them with sediment.

From 1959 onwards, the former Soviet Union dumped large quantities of radioactive waste, including disused nuclear reactors, in the Arctic Ocean. Now over a million tonnes of chemical weapons are rusting away on the ocean seabed at depths of between 500 and 4500 metres. Particular concern has been raised over metal containers of Russian nerve gas that were sunk in 1947 and have been corroding ever since. 100,000 barrels of radioactive waste of medical, technological or industrial origin are known to be lying on the seabed off the coast of Spain. Plutonium from nuclear testing in the South Seas has been detected in the mid-Atlantic at depths of over 4000 metres.

The UK Hydrographic Office lists 57,435 wrecks on the ocean bed, including the remains of numerous American and Russian nuclear subs.

The environmental toxin DDT poses a particular danger to marine organisms. The pollutant is carried by currents and spread across the globe, where it accumulates in the ocean food chain. PBDE, a chemical used as a flame retardant in televisions and computers, has been found in the blubber of sperm whales. Ninety per cent of swordfish are contaminated with unsafe levels of mercury, while twenty-five per cent are also polluted with PCBs. Female dog whelks in the North Sea are developing male genitalia. The culprit is thought to be tribu-tyltin, a chemical contained in anti-fouling paint.

Oil wells have been shown to contaminate a surrounding area of over twenty square metres, of which one third is entirely barren of life.

Magnetic fields produced by deep sea cables interfere with the homing instincts of salmon and eels. The electromagnetic smog is also harmful to larvae.

Fish stocks are in decline, while algal blooms flourish. Mean-while, Israel has persisted in its refusal to ratify the convention banning the disposal of industrial waste in maritime waters. Haifa Chemicals dumped 60,000 tonnes of toxic sludge in 1999 alone. The pollutants, including lead, mercury, cadmium, ar-senic and chlorine, are swept away by the current, contaminat-ing the coasts of Lebanon and Syria. At the same time, the fertiliser industry in the Gulf of Gabès continues to pump 12,800 tonnes of phosphogypsum into the sea every day.

Seventy of the world's two hundred most commonly exploited fish species are endangered, according to the Food and Agri-culture Organisation, the FAO, and yet the fishing industry continues to expand. In 1970, thirteen million people earned their livelihood from fishing. By 1997 the number had reached thirty million. Bottom-trawl nets, commonly used to catch cod, sand eels and Alaskan salmon, have a devastating impact on marine life, quite literally sweeping away ecosystems. Mammals, seabirds and other marine predators are robbed of their prey.

Bunker C, the most commonly used ship fuel, contains ash, heavy metals and sediment that are separated off before use. The by-product is a thick sludge that many skippers prefer to dump illicitly rather than dispose of responsibly.

The effects of the planned commercial extraction of manganese nodules were simulated by German scientists 4000 metres below sea level off the coast of Peru. The research vessel dragged a harrow over the seabed, ploughing an area of eleven square kilometres. Numerous organisms died as a result. Years after the study, the region has failed to recover.

Florida Keys: in the course of a construction project, soil was flushed into the sea and settled on the reef, stifling a high percentage of the coral.

According to oceanographers, rising levels of carbon dioxide in the atmosphere caused by the burning of fossil fuels are adversely affecting the growth of coral reefs. When CO_2 dissolves, it lowers the pH of the water. Nonetheless, leading energy corporations intend to go ahead with their plans to pump large quantities of CO_2 into the ocean in an effort to prevent the gas entering the atmosphere.

10 May

The message left Kiel at a speed of 300,000 kilometres per second.

The sequence of words keyed into Erwin Suess's laptop at the Geomar Centre entered the net in digital form. Converted by laser diodes into optical pulses, the information raced along with a wavelength of 1.5 thousandths of a millimetre, shooting down a transparent fibreoptic cable with millions of phone conversations and packets of data. The fibres bundled the stream of light until it was no thicker than two hairs, while total internal reflection stopped it escaping. Whizzing towards the coast, the waves surged along the overland cable, speeding through amplifiers every fifty kilometres until the fibres vanished into the sea, protected by copper casing and thick rubber tubing, and strengthened by powerful wires.

The underwater cable was as thick as a muscular forearm. It stretched out across the shelf, buried in the seabed to protect it from anchors and fishing-boats. TAT 14, as it was officially known, was a transatlantic cable linking Europe to the States. Its capacity was higher than that of almost any other cable in the world. There were dozens of such cables in the North Atlantic alone. Hundreds of thousands of kilometres of optical fibre extended across the planet, making up the backbone of the information age. Three-quarters of their capacity was devoted to the World Wide Web. Project Oxygen linked 175 countries in a kind of global super Internet. Another system bundled eight optical fibres to give a transmission capacity of 3.2 terabits per second, the equivalent of 48 million simultaneous phone conversations. The delicate glass fibres on the ocean bed had long since supplanted satellite technology. The globe was wrapped in a web of light-transporting wires, through which the bits and bytes of virtual society travelled in real time – telephone calls, video images, music, emails. The global village was made of cable, not of satellites.

Erwin Suess's email left Scandinavia and sped towards Britain on its way north. As it rounded the tip of Scotland, TAT 14 curved to the left. Once it passed the Hebridean shelf, the cable snaked its way over the seabed, resting on the ocean floor.

At least, it would have done, if the shelf and the seabed hadn't been destroyed.

Barely eight milliseconds after the message had left Kiel, it crossed the ocean south of the Faroes, where the cable ended abruptly in gigatonnes of mud and rock. Its durable casing with its reinforced wire and flexible plastic jacket had been severed in two, shattering the glass fibres, so the message of light waves was sent to the mud. The avalanche had hit the cable with such force that the torn ends lay hundreds of kilometres apart. TAT 14 only resumed its course in the Icelandic Basin, crossing back on to the shelf south of Newfoundland and running parallel to the coast until it reached Boston, where the useless length of high-tech cable connected to the overland line. Winding over the Rocky Mountains, the data highway travelled north past Vancouver along the west coast of Canada, where the optical cable was hooked up to a conventional copper cable in the substation of the prestigious luxury hotel, Chateau Whistler, at the foot of Blackcomb Mountain. A photodiode then reversed the original process, converting the optical pulses back into digital data.

Under normal circumstances the message from Kiel would have passed through the photodiode and appeared as an email on Gerhard Bohrmann's laptop. But the situation wasn't normal, and Bohrmann, along with millions of others, had lost his connection. One week after the disaster in northern Europe, transatlantic Internet traffic was at a standstill, and phone calls could only be made via satellite, if at all.

Bohrmann was sitting in the hotel lobby, staring at the screen. He knew Suess had been planning to email him a file. It contained growth curves for the worm colonies and estimates of what would happen in the event of similar invasions in other parts of the world. After the initial shock, the scientists in Kiel had jumped into action, and were working flat-out on the data.

He swore. The small world was large again, full of unbridgeable space. They'd been told that morning that a satellite connection for email would be up and running by the end of the day, but there was still no sign of it working. For the time being, they were tied to the severed cable. Bohrmann knew that crisis teams around the world were feverishly trying to build autonomous networks, but the Internet kept collapsing. The real problem, he suspected, wasn't one of know-how but capacity. The military satellites were working fine, but even the Americans had never considered the possibility that the transatlantic fibreoptic bridge might one day need rerouting via space.

He reached for the mobile that had been supplied to him by the emergency committee, and dialled a satellite connection through to Kiel. He waited. After a few attempts he was connected with the Geomar Centre and put through to Suess. 'No luck,' he said.

'Well, it was worth a shot.' Suess's voice was perfectly clear, but there was a lag in response time that Bohrmann found offputting. He couldn't get used to satellite calls. The signal had to travel 36,000 kilometres from the caller to the satellite, then the same distance back to the receiver. Conversations were full of pauses and overlaps. 'Nothing's working here either,' said Suess. 'In fact, it's getting worse. We can't get through to Norway, we haven't heard a peep out of Scotland, and Denmark is just a place on the map. You can forget about emergency measures – nothing's been done.'

'We're on the phone now, aren't we?' said Bohrmann.

'Only because the Americans want us to be. You're enjoying the military privileges of a superpower. It's hopeless in Europe. There isn't a single person who doesn't want to make a call. Everyone's terrified because they don't know what's happened to their family and friends. We've got a data jam. The few available networks have been snapped up by government teams and crisis squads.'

'So what do we do?' Bohrmann asked helplessly.

'No idea. Maybe the *QE2*'s still sailing. You could always send a rider on horseback to wait for the boat. You'd have the information in – now, let me see – six weeks or so?'

Bohrmann gave a pained laugh. 'Seriously,' he said.

'In that case, we've got no choice. Get ready to write.'

'Fire away,' sighed Bohrmann.

While he noted what Suess dictated to him, a group of men in uniform crossed the lobby behind him and headed for the elevators. At their head was a tall man with Ethiopian features. According to his insignia, he was a general in the US military. He wore a name-badge – PEAK.

*   *   *

The men filed into an elevator. Most were travelling to the second and third floors. The others went up another level.

Major Salomon Peak continued on his own. He rode up to the ninth floor, on his way to the gold executive suites, the premier accommodation in the 550-room hotel. He was staying in a junior suite on the floor below. A no-frills single room would have suited him fine. He didn't give a hoot about luxury, but the hotel management had insisted on billeting the committee in their very best rooms. As he strode down the corridor, footsteps muffled by the carpet, he ran through the arrangements for the presentation. Men and women, some uniformed, others in civilian dress, came the other way. Doors were propped open, revealing suites that had been converted into offices. A few seconds later Peak reached a large door. Two soldiers saluted. Peak signalled for them to relax. One knocked, waited for an answer, then opened the door smartly. Peak was admitted.

'How're things?' said Judith Li.

She'd arranged for a treadmill from the health club to be installed in her suite. As far as Peak could tell, she spent more time running than sleeping. She was always on the treadmill – watching TV, dealing with her mail, dictating memos, reports and speeches through the voice recognition software on her laptop, listening to briefings on all manner of topics or using the time to think. She was on the treadmill now. A bandeau held her sleek black hair in place. She wore a lightweight track top with a zipper front and tight-fitting track pants. Her breathing was regular, despite the pace she maintained. Peak continually had to remind himself that General Commander Li was forty-eight years old. The trim woman on the treadmill could easily have been mistaken for someone ten years her junior.

'Fine,' said Peak. 'We're coping.'

He glanced around. The suite was the size of a luxury apartment and had been fitted out accordingly. Traditional Canadian furnishings – an open fireplace, lots of wood, rustic charm – combined with French elegance. A grand piano stood next to the window. Like the treadmill, it wasn't normally in the sitting room: Li had requisitioned it from the lobby downstairs. A magnificent archway led to the enormous bedroom on the left. Peak had never seen the bathroom, although he'd heard that it included a whirlpool and sauna.

To him, the treadmill was the only useful piece of furniture, a bulky black presence in the carefully designed interior. In his opinion, sophistication and army business didn't mix. Peak had come from humble beginnings. He'd joined the army not because he had an eye for nice décor but because the streets in his neighbourhood had led mostly to jail. He'd earned his college degree and his officer badge through sheer grit and hard work. His career was an inspiration to others, but it didn't change his roots. He still felt more comfortable under canvas or in a cheap motel.

'We've got the data from the NOAA satellites,' he said, staring past Li through the large panoramic window that overlooked the valley. The sun was shining on the forest of cedars and pines. There was no denying that it was pretty, but Peak wasn't bothered by the view. His mind was on the hours ahead.

'And?'

'We were right.'

'So there's a parallel?'

'Yes. Definite similarities between the noises picked up by the URA and the unidentified spectrograms from 1997.'

'Good,' said Li, apparently satisfied. 'That's good.'

'Is it? Sure, it's a lead, but there's no explanation.'

'Come off it, Sal, don't tell me you were expecting the ocean to give you an answer.' Li pressed the clear button on the treadmill and jumped off. 'That's what this whole circus is in aid of, remember? To find out what's going on. Do we have a full house yet?'

'Everyone's here. The last just arrived.'

'Who?'

'The Norwegian guy who discovered the worms. A biologist. He's called, uh . . .'

'Sigur Johanson.' Li disappeared into the bathroom and came back with a hand-towel draped round her shoulders. 'It's time you learned their names, Sal. We've got three hundred people in this hotel, seventy-five of them scientists. Goddamn it, Sal, that's not so much to ask.'

'Are you telling me you've learned three hundred names?'

'I'll learn three thousand, if I have to. You'd better start shaping up.'

'You're kidding me,' said Peak.

'I'll prove it.'

'All right. Johanson's got a British journalist with him. We're hoping she can tell us what went on in the Arctic. What's her name?'

'Karen Weaver,' said Li, towelling her hair. 'Lives in London. Science journalist with an interest in oceanography. Computer buff. Was on the vessel in the Greenland Sea that later sank with all its crew.' She flashed her snow-white teeth in a grin. 'If only we had pictures of everything like we have of that boat.'

'You bet.' Peak allowed himself a smile. 'Anyone mentions those pics and Vanderbilt goes red in the face.'

'I'm not surprised. The CIA can't handle seeing stuff without knowing what it means. Has he arrived yet?'

'He's due.'

'Due?'

'He's in the helicopter.'

'Wow. The weight-bearing capacity of our aircraft never ceases to amaze me. You know, Sal, I'd be sweating if I had to fly that pig. Well, don't forget to tell me if any sensational discoveries hit Chateau Whistler before it's time to dazzle our guests.'

Peak hesitated. 'How do we know they won't tell?'

'We've been through this a million times.'

'Sure – and that's still a million too few. These guys don't understand a thing about confidentiality. They've all got family and friends. Before we know it, journalists'll show up and start asking questions.'

'Not our problem.'

'Well, it might be.'

'So recruit them into the army.' Li gestured dismissively. 'Put them under martial law. Shoot them if they talk.'

Peak froze.

'I'm joking, Sal.' Li waved at him. 'Hello! I said it was a joke.'

'I'm not in the mood for jokes,' Peak said. 'Vanderbilt's dying to put the whole darned lot of them under martial law, but it's just not realistic. Over half of them are foreigners, Europeans mainly. We can't *do* anything if they decide to break their word.'

'Then we'll make out that we can.'

'You're going to coerce them? It won't work. No one co-operates under coercion.'

'Who mentioned coercion? For heaven's sake, Sal, I wish you'd stop inventing problems out of nowhere. They *want* to help us. And they *will* keep quiet. And if they somehow get the impression that they might end up in jail if they don't keep shtoom, well, so much the better. The power of suggestion can go a long way.'

Peak looked at her sceptically.

'Anything else?'

'No, I think we're all set.'

'Fine. See you later, then.'

Peak took his leave.

Li watched him go and smiled. How little he knew about people. He was an excellent soldier and a brilliant strategist, but he had difficulty in distinguishing humans from machines. Peak seemed to think that there was a hidden button on the human body that guaranteed all orders would be correctly carried out. It was a common misconception among graduates from West Point. America's élite military academy was known for its merciless regime, which was geared towards unconditional, blind obedience. Peak wasn't entirely wrong to be anxious, but his understanding of group psychology was way off the mark.

Li's thoughts turned to Jack Vanderbilt. He was in charge of the CIA's efforts. Li didn't like him. He stank, sweated and had bad breath, but he certainly knew his job. Over the past few weeks, his department had excelled itself, especially after the tsunami had devastated northern Europe. He and his team had pieced together an astonishingly clear overview of the chaos of events. In real terms that didn't mean they had answers, but no one could want for a better catalogue of questions.

Li wondered whether she should give the White House a call. Not that there was anything to report, but the President liked talking to her – he admired her intellect. That was the way things stood between them, and Li knew it, but she kept it to herself. It was better that way. She was one of only a handful of female American generals, and she was well below the average age for military high command. That was enough to arouse the suspicions of senior military and political figures. Her friendly rapport with the most powerful man in the world did nothing to improve the situation, so Li pursued her goals with utmost caution. She avoided the limelight, and never let slip in public just how much the President depended on her: that he didn't like scenarios being described as complicated because complexity had no place in his thinking, that it often fell to her to help him see the complex world in simple terms, that he asked her for guidance whenever the advice of his defence secretary or national security adviser seemed unintelligible, and that she had no trouble explaining their viewpoints – and the Department of State's opinion as well.

On no account would Li have allowed herself to acknowledge that she was the source of the President's ideas. If asked, she said, 'The President is of the opinion that . . .' or 'The President's view on the matter is . . .' No one needed to know how she tutored the lord and master of the White House, broadening his intellectual and cultural horizons and supplying him with opinions and ideas that he could call his own.

The members of his inner circle saw through it, of course, but all that mattered to Li was being rewarded for her ability at the right time, like during the Gulf War in 1991, when General Norman Schwarzkopf had discovered in her a gifted strategist and political tactician with a razor-sharp intellect and the guts to stand up to anyone or anything. By then Li had already amassed an impressive list of achievements: the first female ever to graduate from West Point, a degree in natural sciences, officer-training with the navy, admission to the US Command and General Staff College and the National War College and, to finish, a PhD in politics and history at Duke University. Schwarzkopf had taken Li under his wing and saw to it that she was invited to seminars and conferences with all the right people. Stormin' Norman, who took no interest in politics, smoothed the way for her to enter the murky realm where political and military interests mingled and the landscape of power was continually redrawn.

The first reward for her powerful patronage was the position of deputy commander of the Allied Forces in Central Europe. Within no time Li enjoyed immense popularity in European diplomatic circles. At last she was able to reap the full benefit of her upbringing, education and natural talent. Her father came from a long line of American generals and had played a key role in the White House's National Security Council until ill-health had forced him to step down. Her Chinese mother had made her mark as a cellist with the New York Opera and as a soloist on countless records. The couple expected even more from their only daughter than they did from themselves. Judith went to ballet classes, took ice-skating lessons, and learned the piano and the cello. She accompanied her father on his trips to Europe and Asia, and gained an insight into the diversity of different cultures at an early age. She never tired of hearing about the history and traditions of different ethnic groups, and pestered the locals to tell her about themselves, chattering away, usually in their native tongue. By the age of twelve she had perfected her knowledge of Mandarin, her mother's first language; at fifteen she spoke fluent German, French, Italian and Spanish; and by the time she was eighteen she could get by in Japanese and Korean. Her parents' attitudes were unbending as far as manners, dress and etiquette were concerned, though in other respects they were peculiarly tolerant. The marriage of her father's Presbyterian principles to her mother's Buddhist inclinations was as harmonious as their own.

The real surprise was that her father had insisted on taking his wife's name, a decision that had pitched him into a long, drawn-out struggle with the authorities. Judith Li worshipped her father for making this gesture towards the woman he loved and who had left her homeland for him. He was a man of contradictions, both liberal and dyed-in-the-wool Republican in his opinions, all of which he held with equal conviction. Someone with less strength of character would probably have been crushed by the family's determination to be the best at everything, but the youngest member rose to the challenge, finishing high school two years before her peers and with perfect grades to boot. Judith Li was convinced that she could do anything she turned her mind to. Even the Presidency wasn't beyond her reach.

In the mid-nineties she'd been appointed deputy chief of staff for Operations in the US Department of the Army and offered a lectureship in history at the West Point academy. Great things were being said about her in the Department of Defense. At the same time, her affinity for politics didn't go unnoticed. All she needed now was a significant military victory. The Pentagon insisted on active service before it opened the way to higher pastures, and Li hankered for a first-rate international crisis. She didn't have long to wait. In 1999 she was made US Deputy Commander in Kosovo, and her name was inscribed on the roll of honour.

This time her homecoming was marked by her appointment as commanding general at Fort Lewis and by the summons to join the National Security Council at the White House. A memo she'd written on national security had already been making waves. She had taken a hard line on the topic. In many respects she was even less compromising than the Republican administration, but above all she was patriotic. For all her cosmopolitanism she sincerely believed that there was nowhere as just and as free as the United States of America, and in her memo she'd dealt with some of the country's most pressing security problems in that light.

Suddenly she found herself in the corridors of power.

But General Li was all too aware of the beast that lurked inside her: fiery, untameable emotion. It could be as useful as it was dangerous, depending on what she did next. No one could be allowed to think that she was vain or that she flaunted her abilities. She shone enough already. Every now and then she would swap her uniform for a strapless gown, playing Chopin, Schubert or Brahms to the delight of her listeners at the White House. In the ballroom she made the President feel like Fred Astaire, whisking him off his feet until he felt like he was floating. Or she serenaded him and his family and their grand old Republican friends with songs from the days of the founding fathers. This part of her image was all her own. She was adept at making close personal ties, sharing the defense secretary's passion for baseball and the secretary of state's enthusiasm for European history, securing invitations to dinner at the White House and spending entire weekends at the presidential ranch.

On the outside she seemed unassuming. She kept her personal opinions on political matters to herself. She mediated between the military and the politicians, appearing cultivated, charming, self-assured and always well-dressed, without seeming stiff or self-important. She was said to have had affairs with several influential men, although none of it was true. Li ignored it blithely. No question was awkward enough to ruffle her. With a talent for feeding journalists and politicians with easily digestible soundbites, she was always well organised, and had vast amounts of information at her fingertips, which she could call up like a zip file, the details compressed into manageable chunks.

Of course, she had no idea what was happening in the ocean, but she'd succeeded in putting the President in the picture. She'd broken the bulky CIA dossier into a few key points. As a result, she'd been sent to Chateau Whistler, and Li knew exactly what that meant.

It was the last big step she had to take.

Maybe she should call the President. A quick chat. He always appreciated that. She could tell him that all the delegates had arrived, or – as she would put it – that they'd followed the USA's informal summons, despite their crises at home. Or maybe she should tell him that NOAA had found similarities in the unidentified noises. He liked that kind of thing. It had the ring of 'Sir, we've made some progress'. Of course, she couldn't expect him to know about Bloop and Upsweep, or why the NOAA scientists thought they'd tracked down the origins of Slowdown. That was all too detailed and, besides, it wouldn't be necessary. Just a few reassuring words over the secure satellite connection and the President would be happy; and a happy President was a useful President.

She'd call him.

Nine floors lower down the building, Leon Anawak had just noticed a good-looking man with greying hair and a beard. He was walking over the forecourt in the direction of the Chateau. At his side was a woman, small, broad-shouldered and tanned, in jeans and a leather jacket. Anawak guessed that she was in her late twenties. Chestnut ringlets tumbled down her back. Both new arrivals had been carrying cases, which the hotel porters had swiftly removed. The woman made some comment to the man and glanced around. Her eyes rested briefly on Anawak, then she pushed her hair back from her forehead and disappeared inside.

Lost in thought, Anawak stared at the spot where the woman had been standing. Then he craned his neck, shielded his eyes against the slanting sunshine, and scanned the Chateau's neo-classical façade.

The luxury hotel was situated in a real-life version of the dream that people nurtured of Canada. From Horseshoe Bay, Highway 99 led away from Vancouver straight into the mountains, where the majestic Chateau was nestled among wooded slopes, against a backdrop of imposing peaks whose summits glistened white throughout the summer. Whistler-Blackcomb was commonly thought to be one of the most picturesque ski areas in the world. By May, though, the hotel's guests were usually there to play golf or to go hiking among the forests and secluded lakes. Visitors could explore the area on mountain bike or take a helicopter to the year-round snow. The Chateau itself had a first-class restaurant and offered every comfort.

The remote spot in the mountains was equipped with everything under the sun. But the dozen or so military choppers came as a surprise.

Anawak had arrived there two days earlier. He'd been helping with the preparations for Li's presentation, as had John Ford, who'd been flying between Vancouver Aquarium, Nanaimo and the Chateau, sifting through data, analysing statistics and collating the results. Anawak's knee was still painful, but the limp had gone. The fresh mountain air had cleared his head as well as his lungs, and the despondency that had weighed on him since the plane crash evaporated, leaving him full of nervous energy.

So much had happened lately that his capture by the military patrol seemed almost ancient history, although it was less than two weeks ago that he'd first met Li – in embarrassing circumstances, as he was forced to admit. She'd been amused by the amateurism of his evening escapade. They'd spotted him immediately, before he'd even left the car. Allowing him to park inside the docks, they'd watched for a while to see what he was up to, and then they'd intervened. Anawak had felt like the man who disappeared.

He needn't have worried. Now, instead of feeding his findings to the big black hole of the committee, he was working at its centre, along with Ford and Sue Oliviera, another new arrival. At last he'd been permitted to get in touch with Clive Roberts, the Inglewood MD, who'd begun by apologising profusely for the severing of communications, which had been ordered from on high. On strict instructions from Li, he'd been compelled to make himself unavailable, which meant standing within earshot of his secretary while she fielded his calls and sent Anawak packing.

With the presentation ready, there was nothing for him to do but wait, so while the world descended into chaos and Europe was flooded, Anawak had gone to play tennis. He was keen to test his knee. His partner was a small Frenchman with bushy eyebrows and a very large nose. His name was Bernard Roche, a bacteriologist, who'd flown in the night before from Lyons. While North America was struggling to defend itself against the largest creatures on the planet, Roche was fighting a losing battle against the smallest.

Anawak looked at the time. They were due to meet in half an hour. The hotel had been closed to tourists ever since the government had started running the show, but the bustle of people made it seem like high season. A good few hundred delegates must have arrived by now. Over half had some kind of connection with the United States intelligence community. Most worked for the CIA, which had lost no time in turning the Chateau into its command centre. The NSA, America's biggest intelligence agency, responsible for signals intelligence, data protection and cryptology, had sent over an entire department of staff and now occupied the fourth floor. The fifth had been requisitioned by employees of the Pentagon and the Canadian Security Intelligence Service. The floor above that was reserved for MI5 and the British Secret Intelligence Service, plus delegations from the German Military Security Service and their Federal Intelligence Service. The French had sent representatives from the Direction de la Surveillance du Territoire, and the Swedish intelligence agency was present, as well as Finland's Pääeiskunnan Tiedusteluosasto. It was a historic meeting of intelligence units, a unique muddle of people and data gathered in the attempt to regain some understanding of the world.

Anawak massaged his knee. A stabbing pain shot through it. He'd been too hasty with the tennis. A shadow fell across him, as another military chopper dipped its nose on its way in to land. Anawak watched the powerful machine descend, then straightened and went inside.

People were milling around everywhere. The activity unfolded at marching pace, briskly but unhurriedly, beneath the vaulted ceiling of the lobby. At least half of those present were talking on mobiles. The others had taken up residence in the luxurious armchairs clustered around the stone columns that separated the nave of the lobby from the side aisles, and were typing on laptops or staring at their screens. Anawak made his way to the adjoining bar, where Ford and Oliviera were waiting. A third person was with them, a tall, glum-looking man with a moustache.

'Leon Anawak, Gerhard Bohrmann.' Ford took care of the introductions. 'Go easy on Gerhard's hand when you shake it. It might fall off.'

'Too much tennis?' asked Anawak.

'Writing, actually.' Bohrmann smiled bitterly. 'I spent a whole hour scribbling furiously when two weeks ago a simple mouse click would have solved it. It's like living in the Dark Ages.'

'What about the satellites?'

'They can't cope with all the traffic,' Ford explained.

'My colleagues in Kiel aren't properly equipped to deal with it,' Bohrmann said gloomily.

'No one's equipped for this.' Anawak ordered a glass of water. 'How long have you been here?'

'Two days. I've been working on the presentation.'

'Me too. Funny we haven't met before.'

Bohrmann shook his head. 'It's like a rabbit warren here. What's your area?'

'Cetaceans. Animal intelligence.'

'Leon's had a few unpleasant encounters with humpbacks lately,' Oliviera chimed in. 'Seems they don't appreciate him trying to look inside their minds . . . What's *he* doing here?'

They all turned. There was a clear view from the bar to the lobby, where a man was heading for the elevators. Anawak recognised him. It was the same guy who'd arrived a few minutes earlier with the curly-haired woman.

'Who is it?' asked Ford, with a frown.

'Don't you ever go to the movies?' Oliviera tutted. 'It's that European actor. What's his name? Maximilian Schell! He looks amazing, don't you think? Even better in real life than he does on the screen.'

'Restrain yourself, woman,' said Ford. 'Why the hell would an actor be here?'

'Sue could be right, you know,' said Anawak. 'If I remember rightly, he was in some disaster movie – *Deep Impact*, I think. A comet's on course to hit the earth and—'

'We're all in a disaster movie,' Ford interrupted him. 'Don't say you hadn't noticed.'

'So is Bruce Willis going to put in an appearance next?'

Oliviera rolled her eyes. 'Well, is it him or isn't it?'

'I wouldn't bother asking for an autograph.' Bohrmann smiled. 'It's not Maximilian Schell.'

'Really?' Oliviera seemed disappointed.

'No. His name's Sigur Johanson and he's Norwegian. He could tell you a thing or two about what happened in Europe. He and I, and some people from Statoil . . .' Bohrmann gazed after him and his expression darkened. 'Actually, you should probably wait for him to tell you himself. He comes from Trondheim, and there isn't much of it left. He lost his home.'

There it was again, the reality of the horror, proof that the TV pictures were real. Anawak drank his water in silence.

'OK.' Ford glanced at his watch. 'Enough of the chat. Time to head over and hear what they've got to say.'

The Chateau had several conference rooms. Li had chosen a medium-sized one, which was barely large enough for the group of intelligence operatives, government representatives and scientists who were due to attend the presentation. She knew from experience that when people were crammed in together they either got on each other's nerves or developed a sense of community. Either way, they lacked the opportunity to distance themselves from one another or from the business at hand.

The seating plan had been drawn up accordingly. The delegates were thrown together in a mix of nationalities and fields of expertise. Each chair came with its own small table, including a jotter and a laptop. The visual section of the presentation would take place on a three-metre by five-metre screen with loudspeakers for the sound and a remote-control for the PowerPoint display. Amid the plush, conservative furniture, the mass of high technology was sobering.

Peak turned up and took his place on one of the seats reserved for the speakers. He was followed by a man in a crumpled suit with an enormous girth. There were dark patches under the arms of his jacket. Strands of thinning white-blond hair had been scraped across his broad head. He wheezed audibly as he held out his hand to Li. Five swollen fingers stuck out like baby balloons. 'Hi, Suzie Wong,' he said.

Li extended her hand and resisted the urge to wipe it on her trousers afterwards. 'Jack. Good to see you.'

'Of course it is, baby.' Vanderbilt grinned. 'Go on, girl, knock 'em dead. And if they don't start clapping, strip. You'll get my applause.'

He wiped the perspiration off his forehead, gave the thumbs-up and winked, then plumped down next to Peak. Li watched him with a frosty smile. Vanderbilt was deputy director of the CIA. He was a valuable operative and the CIA would miss him. She decided to destroy him slowly when the moment came. There was still a long road ahead, but she'd soon have the fat pig squealing in the dirt. Too bad for the stellar Jack Vanderbilt.

The room was filling.

Most of the delegates didn't know each other, so they took their seats in silence. Li waited patiently until the scraping of chairs and rustling of papers had subsided. She could feel their tension. With one look at each face, she could divine the mood of every individual. Li had taught herself to read people's souls.

She walked up to the lectern and smiled. 'Please make yourselves comfortable.'

A low murmur swept through the room. A few leaned back stiffly and crossed their legs. Only the good-looking Norwegian biologist with the scarf draped carelessly round his shoulders was reclining in his chair with a nonchalance that verged on boredom. His dark eyes fixed on Li. She tried sizing him up, but Johanson's expression gave nothing away. She wondered why. He'd lost his home, so the disaster had affected him more directly than most. He should have looked depressed, but he evidently wasn't. Li could think of only one explanation. He wasn't expecting to hear anything new. He had a theory more pressing than sorrow or despair. Either he knew more than all of the rest, or he thought he did.

She'd keep tabs on him.

'I know that you're all under tremendous pressure,' she continued, 'so I'd like to offer our heartfelt thanks for making this meeting possible. Above all, I'd like to thank the scientists who've joined us today. With your help I sincerely believe that we can start to consider the events of the recent past with optimism. You give us cause for hope.'

Li spoke in a calm, friendly tone. She had their undivided attention, but Vanderbilt's mouth was open and he was picking his teeth.

'I guess many of you will be asking yourselves why we didn't decide to hold this meeting at the Pentagon, the White House or the Canadian parliament. On the one hand, we wanted to offer you a working environment that was as comfortable as possible. The delights of Chateau Whistler are legendary. But the key point in its favour is the location. The mountains are safe; the coastline isn't. There's not a single city on the coastline of America or Canada that would be safe for us.'

She let her eyes roam over the upturned faces.

'That's the first reason. Another is the relative proximity to the British Columbian coast. All the phenomena that we've been witnessing – anomalous behaviour among animals, mutations, changes to hydrate deposits on continental slopes – can be found right here. From Chateau Whistler you can take the helicopter to the coast in no time. We're also within easy reach of a number of leading research centres, most notably the lab in Nanaimo. We set up a base here a few weeks ago to observe the behaviour of the whales. In the light of developments in Europe, we've decided to expand it into an international crisis centre with the best crisis-management team in the world. And that, ladies and gentlemen, is you.'

She paused for her words to take effect. She wanted her listeners to be aware of their importance. It was expedient to encourage their sense of pride, of being part of the élite, despite the tragic circumstances. It sounded absurd, but it would discourage them from blabbing to outsiders.

'The third reason for being here is that we won't be disturbed. Chateau Whistler is cut off from the media. Needless to say, it doesn't go unnoticed when a hotel in a sought-after location suddenly closes its door and military helicopters are circling overhead. But we've never given an official statement as to what we're doing here. Whenever anyone asks us, we say we're on an exercise. Now, there's plenty they could write about that, but nothing concrete, so mostly they don't bother.' Li paused. 'It's not possible, and it's certainly not *advisable*, to tell the public everything. Mass panic would be the beginning of the end. Keeping everyone calm permits us to go about our work. I'm going to be frank with you here: the first casualty of war is always the truth. And don't be mistaken, this is war – a war that we need to understand before we can win it. We have an obligation to ourselves and to the rest of humanity. From now on, you may not speak to anyone, not even your closest friends and family, about the work you do for this committee. At the end of this meeting each of you will have to sign a declaration of silence, which will be taken extremely seriously. If any of you has any reservations, I would appreciate it if you could voice them now, *before* the presentation. As I'm sure you realise, you're entitled not to sign. No one will suffer any inconvenience for declining to comply. But anyone intending to do so should leave the room *now* and will be flown home at once.'

She made a bet with herself. No one would go, but someone would ask a question.

She waited.

A hand was raised.

It was Mick Rubin. He came from Manchester, England, and was a biologist, an expert on molluscs.

'Does that mean we won't be able to leave the Chateau?'

'You can leave whenever you want. But you can't talk about your work,' Li told him.

'And what if . . .' Rubin wasn't sure how to finish.

'If you talk?' Li's face assumed a look of consternation. 'That's a perfectly valid question, of course. Well, we'd have to deny everything, and make quite sure you didn't break your word again.'

'So you're . . . I mean, er . . . You're able to do that? I mean, you have that, er . . .'

'Authority? The majority of you will be aware that three days ago Germany called for a joint European Union commission to deal with the current situation. The German minister of the interior now chairs that initiative. As a precaution, Article V of the NATO treaty has also been invoked. Norway, the UK, Belgium, the Netherlands, Denmark and the Faroes have all declared a state of emergency, in some cases regionally, in others on a national scale. Canada and the USA have already combined forces under US leadership. Depending on how the international situation develops, there's every chance that the United Nations will take some kind of overall control. Throughout the world the existing order is crumbling and new jurisdictions are emerging. In view of the exceptional circumstances, yes, we do have that authority.'

There were no further questions.

'Good,' said Li. 'Then let's get going. Major Peak, I'll hand over to you . . .'

Peak walked to the front. The overhead lighting shimmered on his ebony skin. He pressed the button on the remote control and a satellite image appeared on the screen. A picture of a coastline dotted with towns, taken from considerable height.

'Maybe it started somewhere else,' he said, 'maybe this wasn't the beginning, but for today's purposes, this whole business kicked off in Peru. The slightly larger town in the middle here is Huanchaco.' He shone the laser pointer at different sites in the sea. 'Huanchaco lost twenty-two fishermen in a few days, despite the glorious weather. Some of their boats were found later, drifting out to sea. Soon afterwards sports boats, motor yachts and small sailing-boats went missing too. In some cases a few scraps of debris were recovered, but more often than not, nothing.'

He called up another image.

'The seas are under continual surveillance,' he continued. 'They're full of profilers and robotic floats transmitting a constant stream of data on salinity, temperature, carbon-dioxide flux, current velocity and all kinds of other phenomena. Marine instruments monitor the exchange of substances between the water and the seabed. There's a flotilla of research vessels cruising the oceans out there, and the skies are full of military and Earth-observation satellites. You'd think it wouldn't be a problem to trace a missing boat, but things aren't that simple. You see, our spies in the sky suffer the same problem as anything else that has eyes – the notorious blind spot.'

A diagram showed a section of the Earth's surface. A collection of satellites of varying sizes hovered above it, like oversized flies.

'I recommend you don't even try to get to grips with all the artificial stars up there,' said Peak. 'There are three and a half thousand, not counting space probes like Magellan or Hubble. Most of the stuff up there is junk. Only about six hundred satellites are fully functional, and you'll have access to several of them. Military satellites included.'

Peak uttered that last sentence with regret. He shifted the laser pointer to a barrel-shaped object with solar sails. 'An American KH-12 keyhole satellite, an optical satellite. In daylight the resolution is as good as five centimetres. That's almost enough to identify individual faces. It also uses infrared and multispectral imaging to generate night-time data. Unfortunately it's useless in cloud.'

He pointed to another satellite. 'That's why lots of recon satellites use radar instead – microwave radiation, to be precise. Clouds don't get in the way of radar. These satellites don't take pictures, they map the world by scanning the surface of the planet centimetre by centimetre and creating a 3-D model. But there's an Achilles' heel here too. Radar images need to be interpreted. Radar can't see colour or look through glass. The world of radar consists solely of shapes.'

'Can't you combine the two technologies?' asked Bohrmann

'You can, but it's expensive, and no one bothers. And that ties right in with the central problem of satellite surveillance. To survey an entire country or a stretch of water, you need a number of systems working together, each capable of scanning a very large area. Anyone interested in obtaining detailed images of a defined area has to put up with snapshots in time. Satellites are in orbit, and in most cases it takes them ninety minutes to return to their original location.'

'What about satellites that maintain their position in relation to the Earth?' a Finnish diplomat demanded. 'Can't we post a few of those above the regions in question?'

'They're too high up. Geostationary satellites are only stable at an altitude of exactly 35, 888 kilometres. The smallest recognisable detail from that height is eight kilometres long. That means Heligoland could sink without you realising.' Peak paused, then continued: 'But once it dawned on us what we were looking for, we changed our systems accordingly.'

Next up was a picture of the water's surface, taken from a moderate height. Rays of sunshine slanted across it, giving the sea the appearance of fluted glass. Dotted over it were small boats and tiny oblong shapes, which on closer inspection turned out to be reed craft, each with a single figure crouching on top.

'A close-up from KH-12,' said Peak. 'The shelf region near Huanchaco. A bunch of fishermen disappeared from there that day. The footage was taken early in the morning so the glare isn't too bad, which is fortunate, since it allows us to see this.'

The next picture showed a silvery patch spread over a considerable area. Two forlorn little reed boats sailed over it.

'Fish. An enormous shoal. They're swarming about three metres below the surface, which is why we can see them. The problem with the ocean is that it's a very poor conductor of electromagnetic waves. Fortunately our optical systems can see a little way under, if the water's sufficiently clear. Of course, using thermal imaging we can detect a whale at a depth of thirty metres. That's why the military's so fond of infrared, because it shows up the subs.'

'What kind of fish are they?' The question came from a dark-haired young woman. According to her name badge, she was an ecology expert from the Ministry for the Environment in Reykjavik. 'Dorado?'

'Maybe. Or they could be South American sardines.'

'There must be millions. Incredible. I was under the impression that the South American waters had been seriously overfished.'

'And so they have,' said Peak, 'which got us thinking. That, and the fact that the fish turn up wherever swimmers, divers and small boats have been reported missing. There've been a string of shoaling anomalies. Approximately three months ago a shoal of herring sank a nineteen-metre trawler off the coast of Norway.'

'I heard about that,' said the ecologist. 'The *Steinholm*, right?'

Peak nodded. 'The fish were caught in the net, but just as the crew were about to haul them on board, they turned and swam to the bottom. The boat capsized. The crew tried to cut the net loose, but it was too late. They had to abandon ship. It sank in ten minutes flat.'

'Not long afterwards we had a similar incident off the coast of Iceland,' the ecologist said thoughtfully. 'Two sailors drowned.'

'I know. Bizarre, and yet a freak occurrence – or so you might think. But if you add up all the freak occurrences on a global scale, it's clear that shoals of fish have sunk more boats in the past few months than ever before. Some say it's coincidence, that the fish were swimming for their lives. Others look at the same pattern of events and start to see a strategy. We can't exclude the possibility that the fish are allowing themselves to be caught *in order* to capsize the vessels.'

'That's nonsense!' The Russian diplomat was incredulous. 'Since when have fish been able to plan?'

'Since they started sinking boats,' Peak said curtly. 'They're doing it in the Atlantic right now. In the Pacific, though, they seem to have learned how to dodge nets. We don't have the slightest idea how, but we can only assume that they have made a cognitive leap and suddenly *know* about drag and seine nets, that they've figured out what nets *do*. But even supposing something has prompted their mental capacity to develop so quickly, their ability to gauge distance must have improved dramatically too.'

'A net like that measures a hundred and ten by a hundred and forty metres at its mouth. There's no way that a fish, or even a shoal, could detect it.'

'Yet that's precisely what seems to be happening. The fishing flotillas are complaining of drastically reduced catches. The whole food industry is suffering.' Peak cleared his throat. 'I'm sure you've all heard about the second factor in the disappearance of boats and people. It took a while, though, for KH-12 to document an incident.'

Anawak stared at the screen. He knew what was coming. He'd seen the images before – he'd even helped with the data – but his throat constricted every time.

He thought of Susan Stringer.

The pictures had been taken in such quick succession that the sequence unfolded like a film. A sailing yacht of about twelve metres in length was floating on the open water. The wind had dropped, the sea was perfectly smooth, and the sails had been lowered. Two men were sitting aft, while the women lay sunning themselves on the foredeck.

An enormous dark shape passed close to the boat, every detail on the colossal body clearly identifiable. It was an adult humpback. Two more whales followed. Their backs broke the surface of the water, and a man stood up and pointed. The women raised their heads.

'Now,' said Peak.

The whales made another pass, then something appeared in the deep blue water on the portside, rising swiftly to the surface. Another whale. It broke water vertically, shooting upwards, flippers splayed. The people on board turned their heads, transfixed.

The body tilted, then smashed diagonally on to the boat, splitting it in two. Debris whirled through the air and the people shot up like dolls. Anawak saw the mast break. A second whale hurled itself on to the wreck, and pieces of hull floated forlornly in an expanding ring of foaming wash. There was no sign of the crew.

'Only a handful of you will have witnessed an attack like this at first hand,' said Peak, 'which is why it was important for the rest to see it now. The danger zone is no longer confined to the American and Canadian coastlines. All but the largest ships have been banished from the waters worldwide.'

Anawak closed his eyes. How would it have looked from space when the DHC-2 collided with the whale? Was there a record of that too? He hadn't dared ask. The idea of a glass eye watching the scene impassively was too awful.

As though he'd heard his thoughts, Peak said, 'This type of documentation may strike you as heartless, ladies and gentleman, but we're not voyeurs. Whenever possible, we tried to help.' He looked up from the screen of his laptop, his eyes expressionless. 'Unfortunately, in cases like these, it's always too late.'

Peak was aware that he was skating on thin ice. He'd hinted that they were on the lookout for accidents, which invited the question as to why they hadn't done more to prevent them.

'Suppose we think of the spread of the attacks as a kind of epidemic,' he said, 'then the epidemic must have started in the waters off Vancouver Island. The first reported incidents took place near Tofino. It sounds incredible, I know, but in many cases, strategic alliances were obviously at work. Grey whales, humpbacks and, in some instances, fin, sperm and other large whales attacked the boats, then smaller, faster whales – orcas – took care of the survivors.'

The Norwegian biologist raised his hand. 'What reason do you have to assume that it's an epidemic?'

'I'm not saying it *is* an epidemic, Dr Johanson,' said Peak. 'I'm saying that it seemed to *spread* like one. First Tofino, then a few hours later the Baja California, then Alaska in the north.'

'I'm not so sure it spread at all.'

'Well, evidently, yes.'

Johanson shook his head. '*Evidently.* What I'm getting at is that appearances might lead us to draw the wrong conclusions.'

'Dr Johanson,' Peak said patiently, 'if you could just give me a little more time to—'

'Isn't it conceivable,' Johanson continued, undeterred, 'that we're dealing with a simultaneous outbreak that was imperfectly co-ordinated?'

Peak looked at him. 'Yes,' he said reluctantly.

She knew it. Johanson was advancing a theory of his own – much to the chagrin of Peak, who didn't approve of civilians interrupting an officer in uniform.

She watched with amusement.

Crossing her legs, she settled back in her chair and noticed Vanderbilt looking at her questioningly. He obviously assumed that she'd spoken to Johanson in advance. She returned the glance and shook her head, then turned back to Peak.

'We've already established,' Peak was saying, 'that the aggressors are all nonresidents. Resident whales are basically part of the scenery. Transients, on the other hand, either embark on extensive migrations – like the transient humpbacks or greys – or cruise around in the open water, like offshore orcas, for instance. On the basis of all this, we're assuming – tentatively, of course – that the cause for the change in behaviour must lie further away, that is, far out to sea.'

A map of the world appeared, showing places where attacks had been reported. The red shading stretched from Alaska down to Cape Horn, the east and west coasts of Africa and the coastline of Australia. The screen cleared and a new map appeared. Once again, there was coloured hatching around the coastlines.

'The number of sea-dwelling species actively attacking humans has risen across the board. Shark attacks have soared in Australia and South

Africa. No one goes swimming or fishing any more. Shark nets usually suffice to keep the creatures out, but now they're in tatters, and there's no dependable evidence as to who or what's to blame. Our electro-optical surveillance systems haven't succeeded in solving the mystery, and we don't have sufficient numbers of dive robots in the third world to be of much use.'

'So you don't think it's just a cluster of coincidences?' asked a German diplomat.

Peak shook his head. 'One of the first things you learn in the navy, sir, is how to assess the danger posed by sharks. They're dangerous, you see, but not always aggressive. And they don't like our flavour. In most cases they'll spit out an arm or a leg.'

'That's all right, then,' muttered Johanson.

'But various shark species have developed a sudden craving for human flesh. In the space of a few weeks, there's been a tenfold rise in attacks. Thousands of blue sharks – an open-water species – have migrated to the shelf. Packs of mako sharks, great whites and hammerheads are hunting together like wolves, descending on coastal areas and inflicting serious damage.'

'Damage?' asked a diplomat, in a thick French accent. 'I'm not sure I follow. Were people killed?'

Of course they were darned well killed, Peak seemed to be thinking.

'Yes, people are being killed,' he said. 'The sharks are also attacking boats.'

'*Mon Dieu*! What can a shark do to a boat?'

'Don't let them fool you.' Peak gave a thin smile. 'A fully grown great white is easily capable of sinking a boat by ramming it or tearing chunks out of it. Sharks are known to have attacked rafts carrying castaways. If several attack at once, there's little chance of pulling through.'

He called up a picture of an octopus, whose skin was covered with iridescent blue rings.

'Next up, *Hapalochlaena maculosa*, the blue-ringed octopus. Twenty centimetres in length, found in Australia, New Guinea and the Solomon Islands. One of the most poisonous animals in the world. Injects toxic enzymes with its bite. Its victims barely feel a thing, but in less than two hours they're stone dead.' Some of the organisms in the pictures were bizarre. 'Stone fish, weever fish, scorpion fish, bearded fireworms, cone snails – the seas are full of poisonous creatures like these. Usually the toxins are used for defence, but the number of incidents involving poisoning has increased significantly. In the case of some animals the statistics have shot through the roof, and there's a simple explanation: species that normally camouflage themselves and hide from humans have started to attack.'

Roche leaned towards Johanson. 'The question is, could something that triggers a change in a shark trigger a change in a crustacean?' Li heard him whisper. 'Is that possible?'

'I'd say it's deadly certain,' Johanson replied.

Peak had moved on to the jellyfish invasion of coastal areas, which was reaching crisis proportions in South America, Australia and Indonesia. Johanson listened, with half-closed eyes. Portuguese men-of-war had started to release a toxin that could kill within seconds.

'For the sake of clarity we've split the phenomena into three different categories,' Peak said. 'Behavioural changes, mutations and environmental disasters. They're all interlinked, of course. So far we've looked at abnormal behaviour, but in the case of the jellies, we're dealing mainly with mutations. Box jellyfish have always been capable of navigation, but now they're real experts. You get the sense that they're patrolling. It's as though they're trying to clear the area of any human presence, even though we could never really harm them. The diving industry is on its last legs, but the fishermen are the real victims.'

The screen filled with a picture of factory trawler, a colossal vessel with an on-board facility that processed the catch.

'This is the *Anthanea*. A fortnight ago its crew caught a load of *Chironex fleckeri*. Box jellies, in other words. Or at least we *think* they're *Chironex* or something very similar. In any case, the fishermen made the mistake of not throwing them straight back into the water. Instead they opened the nets, and several tonnes of poison landed on the deck. Some fishermen were killed outright, others died later when the metre-long, practically invisible tentacles were scattered around the ship. It rained that day. The whole boat was awash with jellyfish remnants. No one knows how the toxin entered the drinking water, but the *Anthanea* became a ghost ship. Now people are warier, and the trawlers carry protective clothing, but the essential problem remains. Throughout much of the world, the fishing flotillas are catching poison, not fish.'

They're not catching fish because there aren't any left, thought

Johanson. Come on, Peak, a detail like that deserves to be mentioned, even if it's not the real cause.

Or was it?

Of course it was. It was one of countless causes.

His mind switched to the worms.

All those mutant organisms that suddenly seemed to know what they were doing. Didn't anyone see what was happening? They were experiencing the symptoms of a disease whose pathogens were everywhere, but always in hiding. It was an amazing piece of camouflage. Man had emptied the seas of fish, and now the few remaining shoals had learned to avoid the death traps, while armies of poison-toting soldiers took their place in the nets, holding the ailing fishing industry in a toxic embrace.

The sea was killing mankind.

And you killed Tina Lund, Johanson thought sombrely. You encouraged her not to give up on Kare Sverdrup. She listened to you, or she would never have driven to Sveggesundet.

Was it his fault?

How could he have known what would happen? Lund would probably have died in Stavanger too. What if he had told her to take the next plane to Hawaii or Florence? Would he be congratulating himself on having saved her?

They all had their personal demons to fight. Bohrmann was tormented by the notion that he should have warned the world earlier. Well, of course he should. But what would he have said? That he *thought* a catastrophe might happen? That one day, some time, disaster might strike? They'd pulled out all the stops to find a definitive answer. In the end they hadn't been fast enough, but at least they'd tried. Was Bohrmann at fault?

And what about Statoil? Finn Skaugen was dead. He'd been called to Stavanger docks just before the wave rolled in. Johanson was starting to see the oil boss in a different light. Skaugen had been a manipulator. All that guff about being the good conscience of an evil industry, but what had he done? Clifford Stone had also died in the catastrophe. Maybe he hadn't been the calculating monster that Skaugen had made him out to be.

Worms, jellies, whales, sharks.

Fish that could plan. Alliances. Strategies.

Johanson thought of his flattened house in Trondheim. It was odd, but he didn't feel too saddened by its loss. His real home was elsewhere, on the edge of a watery mirror that on clear nights contained the universe. He had caught sight of himself there, and created a haven for everything that was beautiful and true. The house was his creation, an embodiment of himself. It was a refuge, in the way that a rented town-house could never be a home.

He hadn't been there since the weekend with Tina.

Would it have changed too?

The water in the lake was safe, but the thought of it made him uneasy. At the first opportunity he'd drive there and check up on it, no matter how much work the future held in store.

Peak called up another image. The remains of a lobster.

'Hollywood would call it a messenger of doom or something,' said Peak, with a wry grin. 'And, in this case, the hype would be justified. Central Europe has been seized by an epidemic whose pathogens are hidden in creatures like these. Thanks to Dr Roche, we've now got the lowdown on the microscopic stowaways. The nearest taxonomical match is *Pfiesteria piscicida*, a single-cell alga. It's one of around sixty species of dinoflagellate that are known to be toxic. Of all the killer algae, *Pfiesteria* is the worst. Some years ago we had a nasty brush with it along the east coast of America, mainly in North Carolina. *Pfiesteria* was responsible for killing billions of fish. For the local fishermen it was an economic disaster, but it also affected their health. Many developed lesions on their arms and legs, suffered memory loss and eventually had to give up their jobs. Scientists researching *Pfiesteria* also experienced long-term health problems.' He paused. 'In 1990 one of the scientists investigating the algae, Howard Glasgow, was cleaning a glass tank in a specially designed lab at the University of North Carolina, when he noticed something was wrong. His mind was whirring, but his body seemed to move in slow motion. His limbs refused to keep up. Glasgow's illness was the first sign that the *Pfiesteria* toxins could get into the air, so the organisms were moved to a more secure facility. Unfortunately the building contractor had messed up, and the air vent pumped the toxins directly into Glasgow's office. No one noticed the mistake, so for the next six months he breathed toxic air. His headaches got so bad that he could barely work. He lost his balance. His liver and kidneys were poisoned. He'd speak on the phone and five minutes later all memory of the conversation would be gone. He wandered around town and lost his way home. He forgot his phone number and even his name. Most people were convinced that he had a brain tumour or was suffering from Alzheimer's, but Glasgow wouldn't listen. In the end he agreed to undergo a series of tests at Duke University, which showed that the problem was of a different nature. Other researchers who had come into contact with *Pfiesteria* later succumbed to lung infections and chronic bronchitis. And, slowly but surely, they lost their memory to an organism that defies our understanding.'

Peak displayed a series of slides from an electron microscope. They showed different types of microbe. Some looked like star-shaped amoebas, others resembled scaly or bristly spheres, while the rest were hamburger-shaped, with twisted tentacles extending from between the two halves of the bun.

'These are all pictures of *Pfiesteria*,' said Peak. 'It can change its appearance within minutes, growing to ten times its former size, encasing itself in a cyst or mutating from a harmless single-cell organism to a highly toxic zoospore. There are twenty-four different shapes that *Pfiesteria* can assume, and with each different shape comes different characteristics. We've now succeeded in isolating the toxin it produces, and Dr Roche and his team have been working flat out to pinpoint its chemical structure, but they face even greater difficulties than the scientists in the States. The organism contaminating Central Europe's water supply isn't *Pfiesteria piscicida*, but another, far more toxic strain. *Pfiesteria piscicida* means "fish-eating *Pfiesteria*." Dr Roche has christened the new species *Pfiesteria homicida*. "Man-eating *Pfiesteria*".'

Peak summarised the factors that made tackling the algae so difficult. The new organism seemed programmed to reproduce in cycles of explosive growth. Once it had entered the water supply, it was impossible to get rid of. It seeped into the soil and deposited its toxins, which resisted all efforts to filter them out. And that was the problem. It was bad enough that many of the algae's victims were literally covered with *Pfiesteria* cells, which were eating them alive. Angry sores opened on their bodies, becoming infected, gangrenous and refusing to heal. But the poison given off by the algae was even more of a threat. No matter how determinedly the authorities tried to clean water-pipes and tanks, the organisms turned up elsewhere and spread their toxin. They had tried fighting them with heat and acid, clubbing them to death with chemical cudgels, but they had to be careful not to substitute one evil for another.

Pfiesteria homicida seemed unconcerned. *Pfiesteria piscicida* affected the nervous system, but the new strain attacked it with such aggression that it was paralysed within hours. The victims fell into a coma, then died. Only a few people seemed immune to it. Since Roche had been unable to unravel the structure of the toxin, he was hoping to decode the genetic basis for immunity, but time was running out. The epidemic had spread so fast it seemed impossible to stem.

'The algae arrived in a Trojan horse,' said Peak, 'tucked away in crustaceans. Trojan lobsters, if you like – or, at least, they looked like lobsters. The creatures were clearly alive when they were caught, but their flesh had been replaced with a jelly-like substance, inside which the colonies of *Pfiesteria* were hiding. The European Union has now outlawed the catching and exporting of lobsters. At present, only France, Spain, Belgium, Holland and Germany have reported instances of sickness and death. The latest available figures listed fourteen thousand fatalities. American lobsters still seem to be the real McCoy, but the authorities are contemplating a ban on the sale of crustaceans.'

'Dreadful,' whispered Rubin. 'Where did the algae come from?'

Roche turned round. 'We created them,' he said. 'Liquefied pig faeces are flushed into the sea by the east coast hog farm industry. *Pfiesteria* flourishes in fertile waters. The cells feed on phosphates and nitrates from the animal dung that washes off fields and into the rivers. They like industrial outlets too. It's obvious that they'll feel perfectly happy in city sewers where there's plenty of organic matter to go round. We're responsible for creating the *Pfiesteria* of this world. We don't invent them, but we allow them to turn into monsters.' Roche paused and turned to Peak. 'Take the Baltic, for example. If things get much worse, the fish will be wiped out, and it's obvious who's to blame – the Danish pig-rearing industry. Liquid manure prompts algae to bloom exponentially. The oxygen level of the water is depleted, and fish start to die. But these toxic algae are going to do a damn sight more than kill fish, and nowhere seems safe from them. We've got the deadliest strain of all in our midst.'

'But why didn't anyone do anything about it before?' asked Rubin.

'Before?' Roche laughed. 'Oh, they tried, my friend. They tried.

Where have you been all this time? No, instead of being encouraged to continue their research, the scientists were laughed at. Their lives were threatened. There was a scandal a few years back when it turned out that the environmental authorities in North Carolina hushed up the cases of *Pfiesteria* to appease various influential politicians who also happened to be pig farmers. Of course, there's always the question as to which lunatic is sending us *Pfiesteria*-contaminated lobsters in the first place, but the fact remains that we helped give birth to this catastrophe. Somewhere along the line, we're always to blame.'

'These mussels have all the characteristics of a zebra mussel, but they can do something that ordinary zebra mussels can't. They navigate.'

Peak had progressed to shipping accidents. The delegates had only just ploughed their way through *Pfiesteria* growth curves, and now they were being presented with another set of devastating statistics. Coloured lines criss-crossed the world.

'Shipping routes for merchant vessels,' Peak explained. 'The key to the whole thing is the redistribution of transportable goods. As a rule, raw materials are shipped in a northerly direction. Bauxite is exported from Australia, oil from Kuwait, and iron ore from South America, travelling distances of up to eleven thousand nautical miles to either Europe, North America or Japan, where the raw material is taken inland to cities like Stuttgart, Detroit, Paris and Tokyo, and turned into cars, electrical equipment and machines. The commodities are then loaded into containers and shipped back to Australia, Kuwait and South America. Nearly a quarter of world trade passes through the Asian Pacific. That's a total value of five hundred billion US dollars. A similar amount is shipped through the Atlantic. The busiest routes are marked here in bold: the east coast of America, including, most importantly, New York, then northern Europe – the English Channel, the North Sea, the Baltic Sea and the Baltic states – and finally the Mediterranean, in particular the Riviera. European waters play a pivotal role in world trade. Besides, the Med provides the passage from the east coast of North America through the Suez Canal to South Asia. Then there's Japan and the Persian Gulf, not to mention the China Seas, which rank just behind the North Sea as the busiest waters in the world. To get to grips with international seaborne trade, you have to understand the networks. You have to know what it'll mean for one side of the world if a container ship sinks on the other – which production chains will be disrupted, whose jobs are at risk, whose livelihood, or maybe life, is endangered, and who, if anyone, might profit from the mess. Air travel brought an end to the age of passenger shipping, but world trade still relies on the seas. Our maritime routes are essential.'

Peak paused.

'A few figures for you. Every day two thousand vessels pass through the Strait of Malacca and other nearby waters. Nearly twenty thousand ships of all shapes and sizes cross the Suez Canal every year. Each of those regions carries fifteen per cent of world trade. Three hundred ships a day make their way along the English Channel *en route* to the North Sea, the most congested sea in the world. Roughly forty-four thousand ships every year connect Hong Kong to the rest of the planet. Countless freighters, tankers and ferries circumnavigate the globe, to say nothing of the fishing flotillas, cutters, sailing-boats and sports boats. Millions of journeys are made through the oceans, marginal seas, channels and straits. Given all that, it probably seems unreasonable to suggest that an occasional supertanker accident could seriously threaten world trade. Surely a little thing like that wouldn't stop anyone filling their ram-shackle tankers with oil? You see, most of the seven thousand oil tankers in the world are in a god-awful state. More than half have been in service for over twenty years, and most aren't worth the metal they're made of. People in this business aren't afraid to take risks. There's always a chance that disaster could strike, but they're used to that. So they do their sums and ask themselves, What if it all goes right? They calculate the odds, and the rest is a gamble. If a three-hundred-metre-long tanker sinks into the trough of a wave, its hull can be warped by up to a metre. That's an enormous strain for any structure. But the tanker sets sail because, according to their calculations, things will be OK.' Peak gave a thin smile. 'But those calculations mean nothing when accidents start happening that can't be explained. They can't assess the risk. A different kind of mindset comes to the fore. We call it the shark-attack syndrome. No one knows where the predator's lurking or who it might eat next, so a single shark is enough to stop thousands of tourists swimming in the sea. Theoretically, it's impossible for one man-eating shark to have any real impact on tourism, but in practice the effect can be ruinous. So, imagine a shipping lane that's seen four times as many accidents in the space of a few weeks than ever before, and with no discernible cause. Ships are being sunk by alarming phenomena for which there's no explanation, and even those in tip-top condition aren't safe. No one knows which might be next and what measures they could take to safeguard it. There's no more talk of corrosion, storm damage or navigational errors. The word on the street is: don't set sail.'

Now Peak showed them the mussels. He pointed to the tufts poking out from between the striped shells.

'This is the byssus, a kind of foot. Zebra mussels use it to latch on to surfaces while they're drifting on the current. Technically, it consists of adhesive proteinaceous threads. On this latest breed of mussel, the byssus has been turned into a propeller. It's a swimming technique that's not so very different from the forward propulsion of *Pfiesteria piscicida*. Of course, adaptations are known to occur through convergent evolution, but that takes thousands and millions of years. So either the new mussels have kept themselves well hidden; or they've acquired some startling new abilities overnight. If that's the case, we're dealing with a speedy mutation, since in many ways they're still zebra mussels, only now they seem to know exactly where they're going. For example, the sea-chests of the *Barrier Queen* were clear of mussels, but the rudder was covered with them.'

Peak described the circumstances of the accident and the attack of the whales on the tug. Although the *Barrier Queen* eventually pulled through, the strategy of co-operation between mussels and whales had proved as effective as the alliance between humpbacks and orcas.

'That's insane,' said a German colonel.

'Oh, no, it isn't.' Anawak turned to him. 'There's method behind it.'

'What rubbish. Don't tell me that whales made a pact with some molluscs!'

'No, but they definitely joined forces. You'd be in no doubt about it if you saw it for yourself. In our opinion, the attack on the *Barrier Queen* was probably just a test.'

Peak activated the remote, and the screen showed a picture of an enormous vessel lying on her side. High seas pushed waves the size of houses over the hull. Driving rain made it hard to see the detail.

'The *Sansuo*, one of Japan's biggest car freighters,' Peak explained. 'On its final voyage it was carrying a consignment of trucks. The vessel hit a swarm of mussels off the coast of LA. In a replay of the *Barrier Queen* incident, the mussels clogged the rudder, only this time conditions were rough. An enormous wave hit the vessel portside, filling it with water. We can only guess what happened next. The force of the breaker must have shunted some of the trucks, which crashed through the ballast tanks and ruptured the side. This picture was taken less than fifteen minutes after the rudder had jammed. After another fifteen minutes, the *Sansuo* split open and sank.' He paused. 'Since then the list of similar incidents has been growing by the day. Tugs sent to help the vessels are coming under attack, and most rescue missions have to be aborted. The amount of damage caused in each incident is rising all the time. Dr Anawak's right in saying that there's method to this madness. And, recently, we've discovered that it comes in different forms.'

Peak showed a satellite image of a kilometre-long dark black cloud. It was drifting towards the shore from a point some distance out to sea, where it thickened in a grubby red plume. It looked as though a volcano had just erupted in the water.

'Beneath that cloud are the remains of the *Phoebos Apollon*, a tanker carrying liquefied natural gas. She's a Post-Panamax vessel – the biggest of her kind. But on the eleventh of April, fifty nautical miles off the coast of Tokyo, a fire broke out in her engine rooms, causing a series of explosions to rip through her four tanks. The *Phoebos Apollon* was a top-notch vessel, in perfect condition, and regularly serviced. The shipping line in Greece was determined to investigate, so a robot was sent down to check.'

Flashes of light flickered over the screen. Digits started ticking over, then a snowstorm filled the murky picture.

'An exploding gas tanker isn't likely to leave much intact. The *Phoebos Apollon* was torn into four separate pieces. The seabed near Honshu drops off to a depth of nine thousand metres, and the debris lay scattered over several square kilometres. But in the end the robot found the aft-end of the boat.'

Through the snowstorm they could see some faint outlines – a rudder plate, then the twisted remains of the stern and sections of the super-structure. The robot swung past and dived down, following the line of the hull. A lonely fish appeared on the screen.

'The bottom current carries all kinds of organic material – plankton, detritus, you name it, it's there. It's not easy to manoeuvre at that depth. I won't make you watch the whole film, but this next bit's intriguing.'

The camera was much closer to the hull now. A layer of something coated the metal, stacked in thick clumps. It shimmered in the beam of the floodlights, glowing like molten wax.

Rubin leaned forward in agitation. 'What the hell are *they* doing there?' he said.

'What would you say they are?' asked Peak.

'Jellyfish.' Rubin squinted at the screen. 'Tiny jellyfish. There must be tonnes of them. But why are they sticking to the hull?'

'When did zebra mussels learn to steer? Anyway,' Peak continued, 'somewhere beneath all that slime are the sea-chests. No prizes for guessing that they're clogged.'

One of the diplomats raised a hand hesitantly. 'Er . . . What exactly are the, er . . .'

'Sea-chests?' He had to explain every darned thing. 'Rectangular recesses that draw in the water for the intake system. They're protected by metal grating to keep out flora and ice. Inside the ship, the pipes branch off and take the seawater to where it's needed – to be distilled, for use in case of fire or, most importantly, for cooling the engines. It's hard to say when the jellyfish settled on the hull. Maybe not until the boat had sunk. On the other hand . . . Well, imagine the following scenario. The shoal of jellies drifts towards the tanker. They hit the hull in a mass of bodies and, within seconds, the sea-chests are blocked. Water can't get in. More and more jellies pile on top of each other, causing organic mush to squeeze through the grating. Meanwhile, the engine drains the last drops of water, and the pipes run dry. The next thing you know, the cooling system's broken. The engine overheats, lube oil bubbles over, the cylinder heads glow red, and one of the valves bursts open. Red-hot fuel shoots out and triggers a chain reaction – and there's no way of extinguishing it because the system can't draw water.'

'An ultramodern tanker explodes because of jellyfish in her sea-chests?' asked Roche.

It was funny, really, thought Peak. All these high-powered scientists sitting there like disappointed children because the high-tech world had let them down.

'Tankers and freighters are made up of one part technology, the other ancient history. Diesel and rudder engines might be sophisticated machines, but in general they're only used to turn a propeller or move a blade of steel. The navigation system has GPS, but the cooling system relies on a hole in the hull. And why not? The ships float, don't they? It's as simple as that. Now and then a sea-chest gets blocked by a bit of seaweed, but it soon gets cleaned out. If one hole's clogged, there's always another. Nature's never launched an attack on sea-chests before, so why change their design?' He allowed a pregnant pause. 'You see, Dr Roche, if tiny insects launched a concerted attack on your nostrils, your finely tuned, highly complex body would be in danger of collapse. Have you ever stopped to think about that? And that's exactly the problem with all these attacks. No one imagined that such things could happen.'

Johanson had stopped paying attention. He knew the next chapter inside-out. He and Bohrmann had structured the material in preparation for the meeting. It focused on worms and methane hydrates. As Peak carried on talking, Johanson transferred some ideas to his laptop.

Changes in the neural system caused by . . .

By what exactly?

He had to think of a name for it. It was annoying to keep describing it in full. He stared at the screen in concentration. Did the committee have access to his laptop? Suddenly he suspected that Li and her gang were spying on his thoughts, and he resented the idea. It was his theory and he'd confront the committee with it when *he* deemed it time.

It was pure coincidence that his left hand brushed the keyboard and his middle and ring fingers formed a word. Although it wasn't really enough to be a word. Three letters appeared on the screen: *Yrr.* Johanson was about to delete them, but stopped himself. Why not leave them? Any word would do. And this word would be better than a real word because no one could decipher it. Besides, he wasn't even sure what it described. There wasn't a term for it, so an abstract word would do fine.

Yrr.

He'd stick with *yrr* for the moment.

That was the third pencil Weaver had chewed since the presentation had begun.

'Maybe that's the kind of havoc that the Great Flood wreaked as well.' Peak was just coming to the end of a lengthy digression. 'Descriptions of floods occur in many religious stories and myths. The earliest verifiable description of a tsunami tells of a natural disaster that hit the Aegean in 479 BC. More recently, in 1755, sixty thousand people died in Lisbon when Portugal was pounded by ten-metre waves. Reliable evidence also exists for the damage caused by the Krakatoa eruption in 1883. The summit of the volcano was blown off, prompting the underwater caldera to collapse in the magma. Two hours later, waves reaching heights of forty metres swept into the coasts of Sumatra and Java, laying waste to three hundred villages and killing nearly thirty-six thousand people. In 1933 a much smaller tsunami hit the Japanese town of Sanriku, flattening the north-east of Honshu. The outcome? Three thousand people dead, nine thousand buildings destroyed and eight thousand boats lost at sea. But none of those incidents was anything like as devastating as the recent tsunami in northern Europe. The North Sea states are all highly developed industrial nations. Two hundred and forty million people live there, the majority near the coast.'

There was a deathly hush.

'Geologically, the whole area was transformed in a flash. It's too soon to predict the consequences for humanity, but economically the effects have been calamitous. Some of the most pivotal international ports suffered serious damage or were destroyed. Less than a fortnight ago Rotterdam was still the biggest maritime trading centre in history, while the North Sea was a major repository of the world's fossil fuels. Approximately four hundred and fifty thousand barrels of oil were being extracted from the North Sea every day. Half of Europe's oil reserves were located off the coast of Norway, a significant proportion off the coast of Britain, not to mention the region's share of the world's natural gas. And yet the entire industry was destroyed within hours. Initial estimates place the death toll at two or three million, but there are at least as many again who are injured or homeless.'

Peak recited the figures as though he were reading the weather forecast.

'The question is, what caused the slide? The polychaetes are undoubtedly the most striking example of mutation that we're up against. Nothing even begins to explain how billions of worms teamed up with bacteria and swarmed over the slope. Besides, Dr Johanson and our friends at the Geomar Centre in Kiel believe that we still don't have the full story. There's no doubt that the invasion of worms destabilised the hydrates, but a catastrophe of that magnitude just doesn't make sense. There must be another factor. The wave was only the most visible part of the problem.'

Weaver stiffened. The hairs stood up on the back of her neck. A long-distance satellite image was taking shape on the screen. The contrast had been altered and the contours were hazy, but she recognised the vessel straight away.

'You'll see what I mean from these pictures. The boat had been placed under satellite surveillance . . .'

What? Weaver couldn't believe what she was hearing. Bauer, under surveillance?

'It was a research vessel, the *Juno*,' said Peak. 'The images were taken at night by a military recon satellite, EORSAT. Luckily the visibility was good and the sea was calm, which isn't often the case in these waters. The *Juno* was off the coast of Spitsbergen at the time.'

The washed-out glow of the vessel's lights stood out against the darkness of the sea. Then light dots appeared in the water, multiplying rapidly until the sea seethed.

The *Juno* tipped from right to left, heeling . . .

Then she sank like a stone.

Weaver froze. No one had prepared her for *that*. Now at last she knew where Bauer had got to. The *Juno* was lying at the bottom of the Greenland Sea. She thought of the worrying indications of his research, his fears and concerns, and it dawned on her that she was the only person left who knew the details of his work. Bauer had left her his scientific legacy.

'It was the first time,' Peak was saying, 'that we'd actually witnessed the phenomenon. Of course, we'd known for some time that methane blowouts were occurring in the area, and yet—'

Weaver raised her hand. 'Did you anticipate this would happen?'

Peak fixed her with his eyes. His face was so still that it looked almost carved. 'No.'

'What did you do when you saw the *Juno* sinking?'

'Nothing.'

'You mean the region and the boat were under satellite surveillance, and you couldn't do a thing?'

'We were gathering data by tracking different boats. It's impossible to be everywhere at once. There's no way we could have guessed that precisely this vessel—'

'Correct me if I'm wrong,' Weaver interrupted forcefully, 'but surely you were aware of what happens in a blowout? The Bermuda Triangle's right on your doorstep.'

'Ms Weaver, we—'

'Let me put it another way. You *knew* blowouts were causing boats to disappear. And you *knew* that methane was being released into the Arctic. Didn't you have an inkling of what was going to happen to the shelf?'

Peak stared at her. 'What are you trying to suggest?'

'I want you to tell me if there's anything you could have *done*!'

Peak's expression didn't alter. His eyes were still fixed on Weaver. It was uncomfortably silent. 'We misjudged the situation,' he said eventually.

Li was all too familiar with this kind of scenario. Peak would be forced into admitting that their aerial recon hadn't delivered. There was no denying that they'd noticed a rise in the number of blowouts occurring near Norway, but they'd been registering all kinds of other phenomena too. The worms had come as a surprise.

She stood up. It was time to lend a hand. 'We couldn't have done a thing,' she said calmly. 'Besides, Ms Weaver, I would be grateful if you could listen to what the major has to say, instead of jumping to conclusions. Bear in mind that the scientists in this room were selected for two reasons: their expertise, and their familiarity with what's going on. Some of our delegates were directly involved in the events you refer to. What could Dr Bohrmann have done to prevent the disaster? What could Dr Johanson or Statoil have done? What could you have done, Ms Weaver? Having cameras in the sky doesn't mean that we have some omnipresent taskforce to rescue people anytime, anyplace, no matter what the danger. Would you prefer us to close our eyes instead?'

The journalist frowned.

'We didn't come here today to start apportioning blame,' Li said, before Weaver had a chance to reply. 'Let he who is without sin cast the first stone – that's what I was taught, and that's what it says in the Bible. And the Bible often gets it right. We're here to avert any future disasters. Perhaps we can move on . . .'

'Hallelujah,' Weaver murmured.

Li allowed the room to fall silent.

Then she smiled. Time for a sweetener. 'We're all on edge,' she said. 'I understand how you must be feeling, Ms Weaver. Major Peak, if you could continue . . .'

For a moment Peak had felt flustered. Soldiers never expressed criticism or doubt in that tone. He didn't have anything against criticism or doubt *per se*, but right now, when he couldn't reassert his authority with an order, he resented being challenged. He felt a wave of dull hatred towards the journalist. How the hell was he going to keep a check on all those damn scientists?

'What we just witnessed,' he said, 'was the release of large quantities of methane from the seabed. Now, much as I regret the death of those on board the boat, the escape of the gas poses much wider problems. In the course of the underwater slide, the amount of gas released into the atmosphere was a million times greater than it was during the sinking of the *Juno*. We've seen case scenarios for what would happen if the remainder of the world's underwater methane reserves were to escape in a similar way. It amounts to a death sentence. The equilibrium of the atmosphere would be fatally unbalanced.'

He paused. Peak was a tough character, but even he was scared as hell by what came next. 'I have to tell you,' he said slowly, 'that worms have been found in the Atlantic and Pacific. To be more specific, they're present on the continental slopes off the coasts of North and South America, western Canada and Japan.'

No one breathed.

'That was the bad news.'

A cough shook the room like a minor explosion.

'The good news is that the infestations haven't reached anything like the levels that were recorded near Norway. The organisms are clustered in isolated patches. For the time being there's no risk of serious damage occurring. However, we have to assume that somehow, at some point, the assault will intensify. Our sources indicate that smaller groups of worms were found last year near Norway, on a site earmarked by Statoil for the construction of a processor.'

'My government has been unable to verify that claim,' a Norwegian politician called from the back.

'Sure,' Peak sneered. 'Conveniently enough, almost everyone involved in the project is dead. We've had to rely entirely on Dr Johanson and the scientists in Kiel for information. But this time we've got a head start. And it's our responsibility to use it. We've got to fight those goddamn worms.'

He stopped short. Goddamn worms. That didn't sound good. Too emotional. He'd tripped at the final hurdle, so to speak.

'God help us but you're right,' a voice thundered.

A man of startling appearance had risen to his feet. He towered up like a rock, tall and solid. He was clad in orange overalls, and wiry black hair spiralled out from his baseball cap. A pair of oversized shades balanced precariously on his small nose, which curled up sharply in an attempt to avoid his wide frog-like mouth. As his broad mouth opened and his colossal chin sank down, it was impossible not to be reminded of *The Muppet Show*.

Dr Stanley Frost, said the giant's name badge. *Volcanologist.*

'I read through the documents beforehand,' he boomed, as though he was preaching, 'and I don't like what I see. You're interested in continental slopes near highly populated areas.'

'Sure, it replicates the Norwegian pattern. In the beginning a few worms, then hordes.'

'It's a mistake to focus on those regions.'

'Do you want another Europe?'

'Oh, please, Major Peak! Did I say you should stop monitoring those areas? Lord, no. All I'm saying is that focusing on those areas would be an almighty mistake. It's too obvious. The devil's ways are more sinister.'

Peak scratched his head. 'Could you be a little more precise, Dr Frost?'

The volcanologist took a deep breath. His chest expanded. 'No.'

'Have I understood you correctly?'

'I sincerely hope so. I need to look into it some more. I don't suppose you'd want me to cause unnecessary alarm . . . Just remember what I said.'

His chin jutted out purposefully at his audience. Then he plumped down again.

Perfect, thought Peak. One darned idiot after another.

Vanderbilt wobbled over to the lectern. Li watched him through narrowed eyes. The deputy director of the CIA placed a ridiculously small pair of glasses on his nose, filling her with amusement and disgust.

'Goddamn worms is just how I'd describe them, Sal,' Vanderbilt said cheerily. He beamed at his audience as though he were the bearer of glad tidings. 'But, believe you me, we're going to fry those shits until their sorry ass starts smoking. OK, then, what have we got? Very little, so far. Our precious oil – all kaput. Not great news for junkies like us. In economic terms, it means that world production's going to dive. Not that the OPEC camel will mind, of course. As for international shipping, well, you know all the details from Peak – nature's dirty tricks campaign has been taking its toll. And you know what? The reign of terror's working! Between you and me – aggressive whales and sharks, that kind of shit's just for kids. A glorified prank, if you like. OK, so it's a darned shame when decent American families can't go fishing off the coast, but humanity in general won't be losing any sleep. And, sure, it's regrettable if some poor fisherman in a third-world country, who feeds his seventeen kids and six wives on a single sardine, has to sit on the beach because he's scared of getting eaten. That sucks. But all the pity in the world won't help them. Humanity's got other problems. Rich countries have been hit. The badass fish don't want to get caught, so they're filling the nets with poison and trying to sink trawlers. Call them isolated cases, if you like, but there's a whole darned lot of them. And that's bad news for developing countries because there won't be any handouts.'

Vanderbilt looked at them craftily over the rim of his glasses.

'You know, folks, if you wanted to annihilate the world, you could kill off two-thirds of it just by giving the biggest, richest states a good run for their money – and by that I mean pressurising them so badly that they run out of time to deal with their problems. The third world only survives because the rich states prop it up. It *depends* on the wrath of America – you know, all those handy little regime changes that get negotiated with the drugs tsars, and that come with economic aid. Well, those days are over. You and I might snigger at the thought of whales attacking ships – after all, the state of our economy doesn't depend on bark canoes or little reed boats – but when you're chomping your way through the buffet tonight, just remember: the Western standard of living is far from representative. Anomalies spell the end for the third world. El Niño spells the end. La Niña spells the end. And compared to the delights that Nature's been throwing at us lately, one of those old-fashioned disasters would suit us just fine. Hey, maybe El Niño could stop by for a beer. No frigging chance. We've got other guests to entertain. Parts of Europe are under martial law. Do you know what that means? It's not to stop folks wandering out at night and getting their feet wet, oh, no. Martial law means Europe can't handle the humanitarian crisis. It means that all those aid agencies – the Red Cross, the disaster relief organisations, UNESCO – can't keep up with the need for tents and food. It means people in civilised Europe are going to starve to death or die of infection.

Plagues are raging through Europe. Europe! As if *Pfiesteria* cells and bacterial consortia weren't already wreaking havoc. But, oh, no, Norway's ravaged by cholera. Martial law means the injured won't be treated, and honest Europeans – people who spend their Saturday nights watching quiz shows on TV – will be covered with maggot-infested sores, while flies spread disease. Feeling queasy already? That's nothing. Things can't get much wetter than a tsunami, I know, but what happens when it's over? Stuff starts exploding. The fire service can't keep up. First the coastline gets drenched, and then it bursts into flames. Oh, yeah, and another thing – the retreating tsunami messed up the cooling systems in a couple of power stations, nuclear installations that some jerk had built by the sea. So now we've got a nuclear disaster in Norway, and another in England. Is that enough, or is there anything else I can get you? Did I mention that the electricity was down? I'm sorry, ladies and gentlemen, but for the moment you'll have to do without Europe. And the third world too. Europe's screwed.'

Vanderbilt pulled out a white handkerchief and started dabbing his forehead. Peak felt like throwing up. He hated that man. He hated the fact that no one liked him; that he probably didn't even like himself. He was a defeatist, a cynic, a mud-slinger. And, more than anything, Peak hated him for almost always being right. His hatred of Vanderbilt was one of the few things he shared with Li.

Aside from that, he hated Li too.

Sometimes he caught himself imagining how he'd rip the clothes from her body and shove her down on that goddamn treadmill. That would wipe the smirk off her face. Arrogant bitch, with her wealthy parents, her foreign languages and her private education. At times like that the Jonathan Peak in him took over, the one who might have been a gang-leader, a thief, a rapist and a murderer.

He was afraid of that other Peak. The other Peak didn't believe in the ideals of West Point, in honour, glory and country: he was like Vanderbilt, dragging everything into the mud, and showing that mud was the reality. The other Peak had grown up in the mud. A black man, born in the dirt of the Bronx.

'OK, then,' Vanderbilt said cheerily. 'So Europe's drinking water is full of pretty little algae. What are we going to do about it? Drown them in chemicals? We could always boil the water or pump it full of poison, that might kill the little assholes, but it would take us down as well. The water's running out. People never used to think twice about serenading themselves for hours on end in the shower, but not any more. Who knows when the first lobsters are going to explode in the States? God's favourite country had better watch out. The Lord's lost his patience with us.' Vanderbilt snickered. 'Sorry, I should have said *Allah*. The shape of things to come, my friends. Prepare yourselves for some sensational news. Right after the break.'

What the hell's he talking about? thought Peak. Had Vanderbilt gone crazy? It was the only explanation. You'd have to be crazy to start talking like that.

A world map appeared on the screen. The countries and continents were linked by coloured lines. A thick bundle stretched from the UK and France right across the Atlantic towards Boston, Long Island, New York, Manasquan and Tuckerton. Another parcel of lines, a little more spread out, crossed the Pacific and connected the west coast of America to Asia. Thick strands extended past the Caribbean islands and Colombia, through the Mediterranean and the Suez Canal, past the east Asian coast up to Tokyo.

'Deep-sea cables,' explained Vanderbilt. 'Data highways. They carry our phone calls and let us chat online. Glass fibres are integral to the Internet. Some of the fibreoptic connections between Europe and America were destroyed in the underwater slide, including five of the biggest transatlantic cables. Two days ago another transatlantic cable by the name of FLAG Atlantic-1 also went dead. The cable runs from New York to St Brieuc in Brittany and manages a respectable 1.28 terabits per second. Sorry. *Managed*. It looks like FLAG Atlantic-1 has just handed in its notice, and this time the landslide's definitely not to blame. Ditto for the loss of TPC-5 that runs between San Luis Obispo and Hawaii. Does anyone see a pattern? Something's chewing through our cables. Our bridges are collapsing. So you think electricity comes from the socket? Not any more it doesn't. You say the world's getting smaller. *Au contraire*. You want to call Auntie Polly in Calcutta and wish her happy birthday – forget it! International communication is breaking down, and we don't know why. But one thing's certain.' Vanderbilt flashed his teeth and leaned over the lectern as far as his podgy body would allow. 'This isn't coincidence. No, folks, there's someone behind all this, and they're slowly disconnecting us from the drip of civilisation. But that's enough talk of the things we've lost and the things we may be losing.'

He nodded jovially at the delegates. Creases of skin wobbled round his chin.

'Let's talk about what we've got.'

Anawak found some comfort in Vanderbilt's words. For a while he'd lost faith in the world, but now it seemed to be marching in front of him with a sign in big, bold letters proclaiming: LEON, WE BELIEVE YOU.

'Dr Anawak saw a bioluminescent organism,' Vanderbilt was saying. 'Flat and shapeless. We didn't find any creature of that description when we searched the *Barrier Queen*, but thankfully our hero didn't leave the vessel empty-handed. The scrap of tissue he took with him has been tested. It's identical to the amorphous jelly that Drs Fenwick and Oliviera found in the brains of those bullyboy whales. Now, remember how the algae hitched a lift in the gunk inside those lobsters? Well, their friendly driver wasn't Mr Lobster. Some other dude was at the wheel. Those shells were chock full of a slime that kept dissolving as soon as it hit the air. Still, Dr Roche analysed a trace of it, and guess what? It's our old buddy, the jelly.'

Ford and Oliviera exchanged hurried whispers, then Oliviera said, in her husky voice, 'The substance on the boat and the substance in the brains is identical, that's correct. But the stuff in the lobsters isn't as dense. The cells aren't quite so close together.'

'I'm aware that there's a difference of opinion on the subject of the jelly,' said Vanderbilt, 'but that's for you guys to sort out. I'll stick to what I know. We isolated that boat to stop any uninvited guests slipping away, and since then the dock has been glimmering blue. The light doesn't last long, but Dr Anawak saw it when he broke into our exclusion zone for a spot of unauthorised diving. Water samples show the usual soup of micro-organisms found in every single drop of the ocean. So where's the glow coming from? For want of a more scientifically accurate term, we're calling it the blue cloud, thanks to Dr John Ford, who witnessed its effects in some footage recorded by a URA dive robot.'

Vanderbilt played the footage of Lucy and her pod.

'The flashes of light don't seem to frighten the whales or do them any harm, but that cloud is definitely influencing their behaviour. Maybe there's something in it that stimulates the substance in their brains. Or maybe it even injects them with gunk. I mean, what are those flashing, whip-like tentacles actually *for*? OK, let's go one step further. Maybe the tentacles aren't just injecting the jelly: maybe they *are* the jelly. If that's the case, then what we're seeing with the whales is a giant version of what Dr Anawak interrupted on the *Barrier Queen*. It means the same unknown organism is driving whales crazy, helping mussels sink ships and hijacking lobsters. So you see, folks, we're making headway! Now all we need to know is, what is this stuff, why is it there, what's going on between the jelly and the cloud – oh, and which son-of-a-bitch cooked the whole thing up in his lab? Maybe this will give you some clues.'

Vanderbilt showed the film again. This time a spectrogram appeared towards the bottom edge of the frame. They saw a series of powerful oscillations.

'The URA is a smart little dude. Seconds before the cloud took shape, the robot picked up a noise on its hydrophones. We can't hear it with our pathetic bunged-up human ears, but there are ways of making ultra-sound and infrasound audible, if you know the right tricks – which for professional eavesdroppers like the guys running SOSUS is a cinch.'

Anawak sat up. SOSUS. He'd used the network before. The National Oceanic and Atmospheric Administration, or NOAA, ran a number of facilities aimed at detecting and analysing underwater sound as part of its Acoustic Monitoring Project. The sensors used for its marine bugging operation were relicts of the Cold War. SOSUS stood for SOund SUrveillance System, a worldwide network of highly sensitive hydro-phones, first installed by the US Navy in the sixties to keep tabs on Russian subs. Following the collapse of the Soviet Union, the system was declassified in 1991, and scientists from NOAA were given access to its data.

It was thanks to SOSUS that scientists had discovered it was anything but quiet in the ocean depths. In particular, the frequency range below sixteen hertz was deafeningly loud. To make the noise audible to humans, they had to play it at sixteen times its actual speed. Suddenly an underwater quake sounded like thunder, and humpbacks sang like twittering birds, while blue whales could be heard booming staccato messages to one another over hundreds of kilometres. Almost seventy-five per cent of the annual data recordings were dominated by a loud, rhythmic rumbling – the sound of airguns used by oil companies to explore the geological structure of the ocean floor.

Since then NOAA had added to SOSUS by developing its own systems. Every year the network of hydrophones probed further into the ocean. And every year the scientists heard a little more.

'We can ID an object just from its noise,' said Vanderbilt. 'That way we can find out how big a vessel is, how fast it's moving, what kind of power it uses, which direction it's coming from and how far away it is . . . Hydrophones tell us *everything.* It's a well-known fact that water conducts sound with great efficiency. Sound waves travel incredibly quickly under water – at speeds of up to five and a half thousand kilometres per hour. Which means that if a blue whale breaks wind off the coast of Hawaii, some guy in California will hear it in his headphones barely sixty minutes later. SOSUS doesn't merely detect sound; it identifies its source. NOAA's sound archive contains all the noises you could wish for: clicks, grumblings, whooshings, bubblings, squeaks, murmurs, bioacoustic and seismic data, and environmental noise. We can categorise pretty much everything – although there are a number of exceptions. And what do you know? Who have we got with us but NOAA's Dr Murray Shankar! He'll have the pleasure of telling you the rest.'

A thickset, timid man with Indian features and gold-framed glasses got up from the front row. Vanderbilt called up another spectrogram and played the artificially processed sound. The room was filled with a muffled drone, structured by gradual rises in pitch.

Shankar cleared his throat. 'We call this noise Upsweep,' he said, in a soft voice. 'It was first recorded in 1991, and its source seems to be located somewhere around 54 degrees south, 140 degrees west. Upsweep was one of the first unidentified noises picked up by SOSUS, and it was so loud that it was detected throughout the Pacific. We still don't know what it is. According to one theory, it may have been produced by resonance occurring between seawater and molten lava in an underwater range between Chile and New Zealand. The next images, please, Jack.'

Vanderbilt presented two new spectrograms.

'Julia, recorded in 1999, and Scratch, detected two years earlier by an autonomous hydrophone array in the Equatorial Pacific. The amplitude was clearly audible within a radius of five kilometres. Julia sounds rather like an animal call, wouldn't you say? The frequency of the sound alters rapidly. It's broken down into a series of discrete notes, like whalesong.

But it can't be a whale. No whale could produce a noise of that volume. Scratch, on the other hand, sounds as though a needle is being dragged at right angles to the groove of a record, only it would take a record player the size of a city to create a noise like that.'

The next noise was a drawn-out creak that fell away slowly.

'Detected in 1997,' said Shankar. 'Slowdown. We think it originated somewhere in the South Pole. We've ruled out ships and subs. The noise might be caused by an ice plate scraping over the rocks in the Antarctic. Then again, it could be something else entirely. There's always the possibility that it's bioacoustic in origin. Some people are dying to see us use these noises to prove that giant squid really exist, but as far as I'm aware, creatures of that kind are barely capable of producing noise at all. It's a false lead, in my opinion. In any case, no one knows what Slowdown is, but . . .' He smiled shyly. 'Well, at least there's one rabbit we can pull out of the hat for you today.'

Vanderbilt played the spectrogram from the URA again. This time he turned on the sound.

'Did you hear what it is? It's Scratch. And can you guess what the URA told us? The noise was coming from the cloud! Well, from that we can—'

'Thank you, Murray, that was worthy of an Oscar.' Vanderbilt coughed and wiped his forehead with his handkerchief. 'Those were the facts. The rest is speculation. OK, folks, let's round things off properly by giving you something to exercise your brains.'

The screen showed images that had been taken in the darkest depths. Floating particles sparkled in the floodlights. Then a flat-looking creature billowed up into the frame, and instantly retreated.

'The film was cleaned up by Marintek, before the institute had the misfortune of being washed into the sea. Now, if you watch their version, two things are clear: first, this thing is enormous; and second, it glows, or, to be more precise, it flashes, then the light goes out when it enters the frame. All we know is that it was frolicking in the water seven hundred metres below sea level on the continental slope near Norway. Take a good look at it. Is it our jellified friend? Find some answers for us. The salvation of God's number-one species is in your hands.' Vanderbilt grinned at the rows of delegates. 'I'm not going to lie to you: we're heading straight for Armageddon. That's why I'm proposing that we share the work between us. You're going to put a stop to this mutated shit – find a way of taming it, feed it something that will make it spew its guts. Whatever. Meanwhile we'll find the bastard who's been sending us this crap. Do whatever it takes, but don't go shooting your mouth off. You can kiss goodbye to the thought of making headlines. A joint US-European policy of strategic disinformation is already in place. Panic would be the icing on the turd, if you know what I'm saying. The last thing we need is any social, political, religious or other unrest. So when we let you out to play, just remember what you promised Auntie Li.'

Johanson cleared his throat. 'I'd like to express my thanks on behalf of everyone here for a thoroughly engaging presentation,' he said pleasantly. 'Now let me get this straight. You want *us* to tell *you* what's lurking in the water.'

'That's right, Doc.'

'And what do you suspect it is?'

Vanderbilt smiled. 'Jelly. And a few blue clouds.'

'I see.' Johanson grinned back. 'So you'd like us to open the advent calendar all by ourselves . . . You know what, Vanderbilt? I think you've got a theory. And if you want our co-operation, maybe you should tell us what it is. That's reasonable, isn't it?'

Vanderbilt rubbed the bridge of his nose. He exchanged a look with Li. 'Well, let's see now . . . Christmas wouldn't be Christmas without any presents,' he drawled. 'Aw, what the heck? The question we asked ourselves was this: where are the disaster hot spots? Which areas have got off lightly? Have any regions of the world been spared? And, hey presto, the unaffected areas are the Middle East, the former Soviet Union, India, Pakistan and Thailand. Plus China and Korea. You could count the iceboxes too, I guess, but I don't see much point. Basically, the main victim is the West. Take the destruction of the Norwegian offshore industry. That alone is going to do the West some serious long-term damage and put us in a very tricky position of dependency.'

'So, if I understand you correctly,' Johanson said slowly, 'you're suggesting it's terrorism.'

'Give that man a medal! You see, mass destruction is the hallmark of two types of terrorism. The first seeks to achieve political and social revolution, no matter what the cost, even if it means killing thousands in the process. Islamic extremists, for instance, think oxygen's too good for unbelievers. Type number two is fixated with Doomsday, and spreads the word that mankind is evil – we've outstayed our welcome on God's fair planet and deserve to be destroyed. The more money and technology these people can get their hands on, the more dangerous they become. Take killer algae, for example. Someone out there must be capable of breeding that stuff. Everyone knows how to train a dog to bite. If gene technology lets us tamper with DNA, why can't we use it to modify behaviour? Think about it . . . So many mutations in so little time. How does that look to you? If you ask me, someone's been very busy with their test-tubes. We've got an unknown shapeless organism out there too. Why is it shapeless? Everything's got a shape! Maybe it doesn't need one for its purposes. Maybe it's a kind of protoplasm, an organic compound, a sticky mess that channels itself in tiny strands like molecular chains, setting up home in whale brains and lobster shells. You know, folks, this definitely isn't coincidence. This is design. And if you want a motive, just think what the collapse of the European oil industry will do for the Middle East.'

Johanson stared at him. 'You're crazy, Vanderbilt.'

'You think so? There haven't been any accidents or collisions in the Strait of Hormuz – or in the Suez Canal, for that matter.'

'But why the plagues and tsunamis? Why annihilate people who would otherwise pay good money for Arab oil and gas? It doesn't make sense.'

'Oh, I agree,' said Vanderbilt, 'it's crazy. I never said it made sense, only that it adds up. The Med's been spared, you know. There's a clear route all the way from the Persian Gulf right through to Gibraltar. But take a look at where the worms are – all over the oilfields belonging to South America and the West.'

'They're on the American slope off the north-east coast too, don't forget. A tsunami on the European scale would be disastrous for your oil-trading terrorists – their clientele would be washed right out of the market.'

'Dr Johanson.' Vanderbilt smiled. 'You're a scientist, and in science you're always looking for logic. The CIA gave up on that years ago. The laws of nature may make sense. People don't. We all know nuclear war could mean the end of our race, but the threat's still there, hanging over us like the Sword of Damocles. The thing is, Dr Johanson, those Bond-film baddies who hold the world to ransom really do exist. It's Bond who doesn't. When Saddam set fire to the Kuwaiti oil wells in 1991, even some of his own advisers predicted it would trigger a nuclear winter that could last for years to come. They were wrong. That's beside the point, though: their warnings didn't stop him. In any case, why don't you ask your friends in Kiel what would *really* happen if all the underwater methane escaped into the air? It's all speculation, you see. Sure, the sea level would rise, Europe would be finished, and Belgium, the Netherlands and northern Germany would be one helluva watersports resort, but what about the barren areas of the Middle East? Maybe the deserts would come into bloom. You'd need more than a few tsunamis to wipe out the Western world entirely. There'll still be enough people to buy the Arabs' oil. And maybe the campaign of terror isn't intended to bring about the apocalypse: maybe it's designed to weaken the West and lead to a redistribution of world power, without anyone having to fight for it. And as for the planet – I'm sure it will sort itself out in the end . . . The monsters might be rising from the ocean, but you can bet your bottom dollar that their master's on dry land.'

Li switched off the projector. 'I'd like to thank the diplomats and the international intelligence community for enabling us to hold this summit,' she said. 'I know some of you will have to return home later today, but the majority of you will be our guests here for the next few weeks. I'm sure I don't need to remind you that the same conditions of confidentiality apply to us *all*. Our work and our findings must be kept under wraps. It's in the interest of all our governments.'

She paused.

'As for the scientists, please rest assured that we'll be doing everything in our power to help you. From now on we would ask you to use only the laptops provided. There are Internet connections all over the hotel – in the bar, in your rooms, in the health club – so you'll be able to log on no matter where you are. Transatlantic communication is up and running again. The hotel roof is covered with satellite dishes and everything's back in business. Telephone calls, faxes, email and Internet et cetera will all go via the NATO III satellites. They're normally reserved for communication between the NATO governments, but now they're at your disposal too. We've built in a closed network, a *secretus in secretum*, which only members of the working party will be able to access. You can use it to communicate with each other and to view confidential data. To get in, you'll need a personal password, which you'll be given once you've signed your non-disclosure forms.'

She looked at them sternly. 'Please take it as read that the password should not be shared with unauthorised individuals. Once you've logged in, you'll have access to recon and Earth observation satellites, to data from NOAA and from SOSUS, to archived and current telemetric material, and to the CIA and NSA's databases on international terrorism, bio-weaponry and gene technology. We've given you summaries of our current capabilities in terms of deep-sea technology, and you'll also find geological and geochemical information. There are catalogues of different organisms, deep-sea charts courtesy of the navy and, of course, all the details of today's presentation, including the stats and figures. New developments will be forwarded to you immediately and automatically. We'll keep you informed, and we expect you to do the same.'

Li smiled encouragingly at her audience. 'Good luck to you all. In two days' time we'll meet again, same time, same place. If anyone needs to compare notes before then, Major Peak and I are available for consultation at any time.'

Vanderbilt raised his eyebrows. 'I hope you'll be a good girl and tell everything to Uncle Jack,' he said softly, so that only she could hear.

'Just remember,' she said, as she packed up her things, 'I'm your superior.'

'I'm sorry, honey, you can't have heard right. We're partners now, equals.'

'Oh, I wouldn't say that. Not intellectually . . .'

She left the room.

Johanson

Most of the crowd headed for the bar, but Johanson didn't feel like joining them. Maybe it would have been a good opportunity to get to know a few people, but he had other things on his mind.

He'd barely made it inside his suite when there was a knock on the door. Weaver walked in without waiting for an answer.

'You should give an old man the chance to put on his corset before you burst in like that,' said Johanson. 'I wouldn't want to shatter your illusions.'

He picked up his laptop and wandered around the cosily furnished sitting room, looking for the modem. Weaver opened the minibar and helped herself to a Coke. 'Above the desk,' she said.

'Oh, so it is.' Johanson plugged in the laptop and booted it up.

Weaver watched over his shoulder. 'What do you think of the terrorism theory?' she asked.

'Makes no sense.'

'That's what I thought too.'

'I can't say I'm surprised by the CIA's schizophrenia.' Johanson clicked on a series of icons. 'They're trained to think like that. And Vanderbilt was right about one thing: scientists do tend to forget that people don't operate with the reliability of natural laws.'

Weaver leaned over and auburn curls cascaded over her face. She pushed them back. 'You've got to tell them, Sigur.'

'Tell them what?'

'About your theory.'

Johanson double-clicked on an icon and entered his password: Chateau Disaster 000 550899-XK/0. 'Ta-ra ta-ra,' he hummed. 'Welcome to Wonderland.'

Nice password, he thought. A castle populated by scientists, intelligence operatives and soldiers, all trying to save the world from monsters, floods and catastrophic climate change. Chateau Disaster was exactly right.

More icons appeared on the screen. Johanson studied the titles of the folders and whistled softly. 'My God, we really have got access to the satellites.'

'Seriously? Can we guide them?'

'Hardly. You can download the data, though. Look, GOES-W and GOES-E . . . the entire NOAA fleet's on here. And see this one? It's QuikSCAT – not bad either. And all the Lacrosse satellites too – that means they've really bitten the bullet, if they've let us have these. And over here we've got SAR-Lupe, it—'

'I get the picture. You can come back down to earth. Surely they haven't really given us unrestricted access to state information and intelligence resources?'

'Of course not. We've got access to whatever they'd like us to see.'

'Why didn't you tell Vanderbilt what you think?'

'It's too soon.'

'We don't have much time, Sigur.'

Johanson shook his head. 'People like Li and Vanderbilt need convincing. They want hard facts, not conjecture.'

'We've got hard facts!'

'The timing was all wrong. Today was their moment of glory. They'd put together all that information and turned it into an all-singing, all-dancing catastrophe fest. Vanderbilt had the chance to pull his big fat Arabian rabbit out of the hat, and did you see him? He was *proud* of it, for God's sake. If I'd said anything it would have sounded like a challenge. I want them to start doubting their neat little theory of their own accord, and that'll happen sooner than you think.'

'OK.' Weaver nodded. 'How certain are you?'

'Of my theory?'

'I mean, you are still certain, aren't you?'

'Sure. But after today we're going to have to find a way of convincing the American intelligence service that it's wrong.' Johanson looked at his screen. 'In any case, I get the feeling Vanderbilt's not that important. Li's the one we need to work on. From what I've seen, I bet she does what she wants, regardless.'

Li

Her first priority was to get on the treadmill. She set the speed to nine kilometres per hour, and settled into a comfortable trot. It was time to call the White House. Two minutes later the voice of the President sounded in her headphones. 'Jude! Good to hear from you. How're you doing?'

'I'm running right now.'

'You're running. Good Lord, Jude, you're the best. You're an example to us all – except me, of course.' He gave a chummy guffaw. 'You're too sporty for my liking. Well, did the presentation go to plan?'

'Absolutely.'

'And did you tell them our suspicions?'

'Regrettably, sir, they're now aware of what Vanderbilt suspects.'

The President was still chuckling. 'Oh, Jude, you've got to stop this vendetta against Vanderbilt.'

'He's an asshole.'

'But he's good at his job. Besides, I'm not asking you to marry him.'

'If it made America safer,' Li said irritably, 'I'd marry him right away. But nothing could induce me to agree with him.'

'Of course not.'

'I mean, would *you* have picked today to start parading your suspicions? There's no evidence yet for the terrorism hypothesis, and now it's at the forefront of their minds. We wanted the scientists to *come up* with a theory, not go chasing after one.'

There was silence. Li could hear the President thinking it over. He didn't like people taking matters into their own hands, and Vanderbilt had done just that.

'You're right, Jude. It would have been better to keep it to ourselves.'

'I quite agree, sir.'

'Good. Have a word with him about it.'

'Oh, no, sir, *you* should have a word with him. He won't listen to me.'

'Fine. I'll talk to him later, then.'

Li smiled to herself. 'Listen, er, I don't want Jack getting into trouble . . .' she added dutifully.

'Sure. No problem. But enough about him. Tell me about your scholarly panopticon. Are the scientists up to the job? Any thoughts so far?'

'They're all highly qualified.'

'Does anyone stand out?'

'A Norwegian. Sigur Johanson. He's a molecular biologist – marine science, of course. I'm not sure what's so special about him, but he's got his own way of looking at things.'

The President called to someone in the room. Li upped the speed on the treadmill.

'I spoke to the Norwegian foreign minister earlier,' he said. 'They're at their wits' end. I mean, they're pleased about the EU initiative, but it seems to me that they'd be a good deal happier if the US came on board. The Germans think the same – they want to pool our know-how and so on. They're calling for an international commission with a proper mandate that would unite our capabilities.'

'Who do they have in mind to run it?'

'A UN-led committee, according to the German chancellor.'

'Uh-huh. I see . . .'

'Not a bad idea, I thought.'

'Oh, it's a good one.' Li paused. 'Only didn't you say recently that the UN had never had such an ineffectual secretary general as the present incumbent? It was at that embassy reception three weeks ago, and we came under fire from all the usual corners. Do you remember?'

'Hell, yes. They were so darned pompous about it. Well, I can't help it if he's a pussy. It's just the truth. But what's your point, Jude?'

'I was just saying.'

'Come on, out with it! What's the alternative?'

'You mean the alternative to being led by a committee including dozens of Middle Eastern delegates?'

The President went quiet. 'I guess we could lead it,' he said in the end.

Li waited before she spoke, as though she needed time to think. 'That's an excellent idea, sir.'

'But then we get lumbered with the whole world's problems – *again*. Sickening, isn't it?'

'Well, we'd be stuck with them anyway. We're the only superpower, and if we want things to stay that way, we'll have to keep taking the lead. Besides, bad times are good times for the powerful.'

'You and your Chinese proverbs,' said the President. 'Well, they're not going to hand it to us on a plate. We'll have a tough time convincing them that we, of all people, should head an international commission. Imagine the reaction from the Arabs! Not to mention China and North Korea. Oh, that reminds me. I took a look at your files on the scientists. One looks Asian. I thought we said no Asians and no Arabs.'

'Asian? Which one?'

'Oh, something funny-sounding, like Wakawaka or—'

'You mean Leon Anawak. Did you read his CV?'

'No, I only flipped through.'

'He's not Asian.' Li increased the speed to twelve kilometres per hour. 'I'm the most Asian person in Whistler by some margin.'

The President laughed. 'Oh, Jude, you could be from Mars for all I care. I'd still back you all the way. Darned shame that you can't come over and watch the game. We're going out to the ranch – assuming nothing comes up. Barbecued spare ribs. My wife's got them marinating already.'

'Next time, sir,' Li said heartily.

They chatted for a bit about baseball. Li didn't push the idea that the US should lead the global coalition. Within forty-eight hours, he'd believe he'd thought of it himself. It was enough to plant the suggestion.

At the end of the conversation, she carried on running for a while. Then she sat down at the grand piano, her body still dripping with sweat, and lifted her hands to the keyboard. She focused.

A few seconds later, Mozart's Piano Sonata in G Major was flowing from her fingers.

KH-12

Like perfume on the breeze, the strains of Li's piano-playing carried through the corridors on the ninth floor of Chateau Whistler and floated out of the half-open window into the outside air. At a hundred metres above ground-level, the sound waves fanned out in concentric ripples. At the highest point of the hotel, in the fairy-tale turret perched at the top, anyone with sharp ears would have heard the music, albeit faintly. Beyond the gabled roof, though, the waves began to disperse. A hundred metres higher up, they had merged with numerous other sound waves and, as the altitude increased, the noises fell silent. A kilometre above ground, a number of sounds could still be heard: car engines starting, propeller planes droning past, and the chime of bells from the Presbyterian church in Whistler village, whose otherwise bustling streets now formed part of the exclusion zone. Finally, at an altitude of two kilometres, the whirring noise of the military choppers – the Chateau's main link to the outside world – gradually started to fade.

Viewed from that height, the hotel was still clearly visible to the naked eye, nestled among acres of forest rising gently to the west. Furrowed snow glistened on the nearby mountain ridges. Ludwig II could only have dreamed of such a place.

Higher up in the atmosphere, the sounds from below petered out altogether.

Now only jet planes taking to the skies or coming into land could still be heard. Seen from an altitude of ten kilometres, the Chateau blurred into the landscape. Charter planes left white trails in the air, and the horizon curved. Low-lying banks of cloud stood out against the bright blue sky like snow plains and icebergs, the vapour conjuring an illusion of firm ground. Another five or ten kilometres further up, the noise of supersonic jets cut through the thinning atmosphere. The troposphere was governed by the whims of the weather, but further up, the stratosphere was home to the ozone layer, which screened out ultraviolet light. The temperature increased. At that altitude, the clouds were just ethereal wisps, shimmering like mother-of-pearl. Silvery weather balloons shone in the sunlight, sparking reports of UFO sightings below. In 1962 an American recon plane had stolen through the silent skies twenty kilometres above ground to photograph Soviet warheads in Cuba. Because of the extreme altitude, the pilot of the legendary U-2 had been forced to wear a spacesuit. It had been one of the most daring flights of all time, and had taken place in a deep-blue sky that opened into the vastness of space.

At an altitude of eighty kilometres, the interwoven streaks of individual noctilucent clouds glistened in the light. It was minus 113°C. Up here the only sign of human presence was the rare sight of a passing spaceship as it took off or landed. The deep-blue gave way to blue-black. This was the realm of the heathen gods, unmasked by modern science as polar aurorae and glowing meteorites. The thermosphere had given rise to more myths and legends than any other feature of the physical environment. In reality it was an unsuitable home for divinities or for any form of life at all. Gamma and X-rays poured in from above. The thermosphere extended for hundreds of kilometres, but gas molecules were few and far between.

There were other things to see, though.

Travelling at 28,000 kilometres per hour, the nearest satellites orbited the Earth at an altitude of 150 kilometres. By their very nature they were mainly recon satellites, positioned at the minimum possible distance from the ground. Eighty kilometres above them the Shuttle Radar Topography Mission gathered land-elevation data from the Earth's surface to create a twenty-first-century planetary map. At relatively low altitudes such as these, the atmosphere was dense enough to slow the satellites, making them reliant on the occasional injection of fuel to keep them in orbit. Three hundred kilometres above the Earth there was no need for fuel. The centrifugal force and the force of gravity balanced each other out, and the satellite's orbit was stable. The skies began to fill.

The satellites circled the Earth like cars on a network of highways, passing over and under each other. The higher the altitude, the denser the traffic. At 500 kilometres, two elegant little satellites called Champ and Grace monitored the Earth's gravitational and magnetic fields. Six hundred kilometres above the polar regions, ICESat measured light-wave reflections from the Earth's surface, allowing scientists to track changes in the icecaps. Seventy kilometres above that, three state-of-the-art US Army Lacrosse satellites orbited the Earth, scanning its surface with high-resolution radar. At an altitude of 700 kilometres, NASA's Landsat satellites observed the land and coastal regions, acquiring data on advancing and retreating glaciers, mapping the growth of forests and the formation of pack ice, and providing accurate charts of the Earth's surface temperature. SeaWiFS, on the other hand, used optical scanning and infrared to keep tabs on the build-up of algae in the oceans. At 850 kilometres above ground, NOAA's satellites had made themselves at home in a sun-synchronous orbit, with numerous meterological satellites circling the planet, passing close to both poles. The bustle of satellites encroached high into the magnetosphere, where cosmic and solar particles were bundled into two radiation belts, known as the Van Allen Belt – a phenomenon that had developed a life of its own in the media. For many Americans the Van Allen Belt was proof positive that the moon landings had never happened. In fact, even respected scientists had cast doubt on whether the astronauts in the spaceship would have been sufficiently protected to pass through the band of lethal radiation and survive. In satellite terminology, though, space was simply divided into LEO, Low Earth Orbit, then Middle Earth Orbit, used by numerous satellites, including the GPS constellation at 20,000 kilometres above ground; and then finally Geostationary Orbit, where the satellites – primarily Intelsats, used for international communication – kept pace with the Earth at an altitude of 35,888 kilometres.

Mozart was nowhere to be heard.

Though the notes from the piano had been lost in the spring air, Li's conversation with the President had made the long voyage up to the satellites and back. At the peak of the phone call, the two had chatted in outer space, exchanging information that came courtesy of the skies. Without its army of satellites, America would never have been able to fight the Gulf War or the wars in Kosovo and Afghanistan. The air force's campaigns of precision bombing had relied on help from outer space, and if it hadn't been for the high-resolution images from Crystal, also known as KH-12, the US high command would have been blind to enemy movements in the mountains.

KH stood for Keyhole. America's most sensitive spy satellites were the optical counterpart to the radar system of Lacrosse. They could detect objects of just four to five centimetres across and could operate in infrared light, which allowed them to work through the night. Unlike satellites orbiting above the Earth's atmosphere, they were equipped with a rocket engine, permitting them to travel in a very low orbit. They usually circled the planet at an altitude of 340 kilometres from pole to pole, which meant they could photograph the whole Earth within twenty-four hours. When the attacks had begun off the coast of Vancouver Island, some of the Keyhole satellites had been brought down to an altitude of 200 kilometres. In response to the 9/11 terrorist attacks, America had launched twenty-four new high-resolution optical spy satellites that orbited the Earth at a very low altitude, and with Keyhole and Lacrosse, they formed a formidable recon network whose capabilities exceeded even Germany's famous SAR-Lupe system.

At eight p.m. a call came through to two men in an underground bunker in Buckley Field, not far from Denver. The intelligence base was one of several secret ground stations belonging to America's National Reconnaissance Office, the NRO, whose mission was to co-ordinate satellite espionage for the American air force. It had close ties with the NSA, an agency responsible for national security and cryptology. Its brief was to bug and intercept. The alliance of the two intelligence agencies gave the American administration an unprecedented power of surveillance. In addition to that, the entire planet was continually monitored by an almost fully automated reconnaissance network known as ECHELON, which used various technological systems to listen in to international communication, including satellite, radio and fibreoptic traffic.

The two men were sitting below ground, beneath an enormous satellite dish. Working in a room full of monitors, they spent their time receiving real-time data from Keyhole, Lacrosse and other recon systems, analysing and evaluating the information, then forwarding it to the relevant authorities. According to their job titles, they were intelligence agents, though their outward appearance gave nothing away. Dressed in jeans and sneakers, they looked more like grunge rockers.

The caller informed them that a fishing-boat had radioed for help from the north-east tip of Long Island. There seemed to have been an accident near Montauk, probably involving a sperm whale. In any case, there was no guarantee that the mayday would be genuine. Already the climate of hysteria was such that false alarms flooded in. A larger vessel was said to be on its way to help, but there was no way of knowing if that was true either. Contact with the crew had broken off only seconds into the exchange.

KH-12–4, a Keyhole-class satellite, was approaching Long Island from the south-east. It was in a good position to begin the search. Buckley Field's instructions were to focus the telescope on the relevant section of coast.

One of the men typed in a string of commands.

A hundred and ninety-five kilometres above the Atlantic coast, KH-12–4 was racing across the sky; a cylindrical telescope, 15 metres long and 4.5 metres in diameter, with a total weight of 20 tonnes including fuel. Large solar sails extended on either side. The command from Buckley Field activated the rotating mirror, through which the satellite could scan an area of a thousand kilometres in any direction. In this instance, it required only the smallest adjustment. Evening was drawing in, so the image intensifiers came on, brightening the picture as though it were midday. Every five seconds KH-12–4 took another photo and transmitted the data to a relay satellite, which beamed the information down to Buckley Field.

The men stared at the screen.

Montauk appeared in the distance, a picturesque old town with a world-famous lighthouse. But from a height of 195 kilometres, Montauk's charms were no more evident than they would have been on a map. Thin lines representing roads wiggled through a landscape scattered with light dots, which was all that could be seen of the buildings. Even the lighthouse was just a faint white dot at the tip of the headland.

Beyond that, the Atlantic stretched towards the horizon.

The man guiding the satellite pinpointed the area where the boat had supposedly been attacked, punched in the co-ordinates and zoomed closer. The coast disappeared from view as the screen filled with water. There were no boats in sight.

The other man watched. He reached into his paper bag of fish nuggets. 'Well, get looking, then,' he said.

'Cool it, man.'

'Cool it? They said they need that data *now*.'

'Well, they can kiss my ass.' The operator tilted the telescope's mirror by another fraction of a degree. 'Don't you get it, Mike? It's going to take for ever. This whole thing sucks. They always want everything yesterday, and this time they're going to have to wait. Thanks to that shitty little boat, we'll be searching the whole damn ocean.'

'We don't have to search the ocean: that boat can only be *here*. The distress call came via NOAA. It must've sunk, if we can't see it.'

'You're making my day.'

'Yep.' The guy licked his fingers. 'Poor bastards.'

'Screw them. We're the poor bastards. If that damn boat's gone down, we're going to have to look for debris.'

'You're just lazy, you know that, Cody?'

'Yeah.'

'Have some fish – Hey, what's that?' Mike jabbed a greasy finger towards the screen. There was a long dark smudge in the water.

'We'll soon find out.'

The telescope zoomed in until the silhouette of a whale emerged among the waves. Still no sign of a boat, though. More whales appeared on the screen, with faint white spots above them – vapour clouds from the blow. Then they dived.

'I guess that's that, then,' said Mike.

Cody zoomed in again. Now the image was at maximum resolution. They saw a seagull riding on the waves. Technically, it was just a collection of two dozen quadratic pixels, but it looked like a bird.

They scanned the area, but they couldn't see the boat or any wreckage.

'Maybe we're in the wrong spot,' said Cody.

'We can't be. According to the information, the boat must be here – unless they sailed on.' Mike yawned, screwed the paper bag into a ball and aimed at the wastepaper basket. He missed. 'Must be a false alarm. I'd sure like to be down there, though.'

'Down where?'

'In Montauk. It's a neat town. Took a trip there last year with the buddies, right after me and Sandy broke up. We were mostly drunk or stoned or whatever, but it was cool just lying there on the bluff, watching the sunset. The third night I made out with the waitress from the bar. Man, that was some trip.'

'Your wish is my command.'

'Meaning?'

Cody grinned at him. 'You want to visit Montauk? We're in charge of this celestial fucking army. And seeing as we're here and all . . .'

Mike's face lit up. 'We'll go to the lighthouse,' he said. 'I'll show you where we screwed.'

'Aye-aye, Cap'n.'

'Uh, actually . . . maybe we shouldn't. We could get in a lot of trouble for—'

'For what? I figure we're *supposed* to be here. We're looking for debris, remember?'

His fingers danced over the keyboard. The telescope zoomed out again. The headland appeared on the screen. Cody picked out the white dot and closed in on the lighthouse until it loomed up in front of them. The bluff was bathed in reddish light. The sun was going down on Montauk. A couple strolled past the lighthouse, arms round each other's waist.

'It's the best time of day,' Mike said. 'Romantic as hell.'

'Aw, you didn't screw her in front of the lighthouse, did you?'

'You've got to be kidding. No, it was further down . . . Look, right there! Where those two are going. That place has a reputation, I'm telling you. Every evening it's pants-down time on the beach.'

'Hey, maybe we'll get to see something.'

Cody swung the telescope round so that it raced ahead of the couple. There didn't seem to be anyone else on the black rocks. Seagulls soared overhead, swooping down to peck at scraps.

Then something else appeared on the screen. Something flat. Cody frowned. Mike leaned forward. They waited for the next image.

The picture had changed.

'What's that?'

'Don't ask me. Can you get any closer?'

'Nope.'

The next image arrived from KH-12–4. The scene had changed again.

'Holy shit,' whispered Cody.

'What the hell is that?' Mike screwed his eyes up. 'It's spreading. It's crawling up the fucking cliff.'

'Shit,' said Cody again. This time he sounded scared.

Montauk, USA

Linda and Darryl Hooper had been married for three weeks, and were spending their honeymoon on Long Island. Ever since film stars had supplanted fishermen as the region's main residents, Long Island had been a pricey place to stay. Now hundreds of classy fish restaurants looked out on to kilometres of sandy beaches. Fashionable New Yorkers holidayed there with all their customary style. In fact, with America's seriously rich industrialists, they had colonised the exclusive neighbourhood of East Hampton, a pristine and picture-perfect town that was practically unaffordable for its working population. Southampton, further to the south-west, wasn't cheap either, but Darryl Hooper had made a name for himself as an ambitious young attorney. It was no secret that he was being groomed for partnership at his downtown Manhattan law firm. The big bucks weren't flowing yet, but Hooper was undoubtedly on the make. Besides, he'd married a cute chick. Linda had been the darling of law school, but in the end she'd chosen him, despite his thinning hair and thick-lensed glasses.

Hooper was happy with his lot, and – in the knowledge that his star was rising – had decided to treat himself and Linda to a taste of things to come. On the face of it they couldn't afford the hotel in Southampton, and eating out at fancy restaurants cost them a hundred bucks a night. But that was OK. They'd worked their butts off and they deserved a little luxury. Besides, it wouldn't be long before the Hoopers could visit the most fashionable places as often as they liked.

He drew his wife a little closer to him, and gazed out across the Atlantic. The sun was preparing to drop into the sea. The sky turned violet, wisps of cloud glowed pink on the horizon and little waves lapped at the beach. Hooper thought about staying awhile. The highway would be busy right now, but in an hour or so they'd have a clear ride through to Southampton. It would only take twenty minutes to cover the fifty kilometres on the Harley. It seemed a shame to leave now.

Especially since after sunset Montauk Point was the perfect place for lovers, or so everyone said.

They picked their way slowly through the rocks. After a few paces they came to an area of flat ground, out of sight of the rest of the beach. Hooper was in love, and he liked the idea that no one could see them.

Never in a million years would he have guessed that two men in an underground bunker in Buckley Field were watching him from an altitude of 195 kilometres, as he kissed his wife, sliding his hands under her T-shirt and slipping it off, while she unbuckled his belt. Eventually they lay clasped together on their clothes. He covered her with kisses and Linda rolled on to her back. His lips roamed over her breasts, towards her belly, and his hands were everywhere at once.

She giggled. 'Stop that. It tickles.'

He took his right hand off the inside of her thigh and kissed her again. 'Hey, what are you doing?'

What was he doing? He was doing the things he always did – things he knew she liked. He kissed her lips but her eyes were fixed on something behind him. Hooper turned.

There was a crab on Linda's shin. With a little shriek, she shook it off. It landed on its back, then splayed its pincers and struggled to get up. 'Ugh! It scared me.'

'I guess it wanted part of the action.' Hooper grinned. 'Well, too bad, buddy, you'll have to find a lady of your own.'

Linda laughed and propped herself up on her elbows. 'Funny little thing,' she said. 'I've never seen a crab like that before.'

Hooper inspected it more closely. The crab still hadn't moved. It wasn't especially big – no more than ten centimetres long – and it was white. Its carapace glowed against the darkness of the rock. Sure, it was an unusual colour, but there was something else about it. Linda was right.

Then he realised. 'It's got no eyes,' he said.

'Oh, yeah.' She rolled over and crawled towards the creature on her hands and knees. 'Freaky. Do you think something's wrong with it?'

'I'd say it never had eyes.' Hooper ran his fingers down her spine. 'Just ignore it – it's not doing any harm.'

Linda picked up a pebble and took aim. The crab didn't flinch. She prodded its claws and pulled her hand back quickly, but nothing happened.

Hooper let out a sigh. He crouched next to her and prodded it. 'Come on, forget the stupid crab.'

Smiling, she kissed him. Hooper felt her tongue wind round his. He closed his eyes, abandoning himself to . . .

Linda flinched. 'Darryl.'

The crab was on her hand. There was another behind it, and a third next to that. His eyes darted up the wall of rock that separated their hide-out from the beach.

The black stone surface was covered with myriad armoured shells.

432

White eyeless creatures with pincers, row after row, as far as the eye could see.

There were millions of them.

'Oh, God,' Linda whispered.

The sea of bodies started to move. Hooper had watched smaller crustaceans scuttle about on the sand, but he'd always pictured crabs walking slowly and majestically. These were fast – so fast it was frightening. Like a tidal wave they swept towards them, their armoured legs clattering softly on the rock.

Stark naked, Linda leaped to her feet and backed away. Hooper tried to gather their things, but stumbled, dropping an armful of clothes. The crabs swarmed over them, and Hooper sprang back.

The creatures followed him.

'They won't hurt you,' he called out. But Linda was already scrambling over the rocks.

'Linda!'

She lost her balance, sprawling head-first on the rocks. Hooper rushed over, but the crabs were moving faster, surging past and clambering over them. Linda screamed, her voice high-pitched and panicky. With the flat of his hand he beat away the creatures as they marched over her back, scrabbling up his arms. She jumped up, panic-stricken, tugging at her hair. There were crabs on her scalp. Hooper grabbed her and pushed her forwards. He didn't mean to hurt her; he just wanted to get them out of there, away from the avalanche of creatures swarming over the rocks. But Linda tripped again, clutching at him and pulling him with her. He crashed to the ground and felt a mass of crab shell shatter beneath him. Sharp fragments dug painfully into his flesh. He lashed out. Hundreds of sharp feet scurried over his body. He saw blood on his fingers, and hauled himself up, dragging Linda with him.

Somehow they made it across the rocks and ran naked to the Harley. Hooper glanced back over his shoulder. From the raised ground around the lighthouse the entire beach was seething with crabs. They were rising out of the ocean, too numerous to count. The first wave had already reached the parking lot and was picking up speed on the even terrain. Hooper was running, tugging Linda behind him. His soles prickled with splintered shell, and slime coated his feet. He had to be careful not to slip. At last they reached the motorbike, leaped on, and Hooper pulled back the throttle.

They sped out of the parking lot and on to the open road, racing towards Southampton. The motorbike skidded dangerously on a slippery layer of mangled crab. Then they were out of the teeming mass and shooting along the tarmac. Linda clung to him. A van appeared from the opposite direction, an old man at the wheel, eyes wide in disbelief. It was like something out of a movie, thought Hooper – two people on a motorbike, without a stitch of clothing. He would have found it funny if it hadn't been so awful.

The houses on the edge of Montauk loomed into view. The eastern tip of Long Island was just a narrow strip of land, with the road running parallel to the coast. As Hooper made for the town he saw a sea of white crabs advancing from the left. They spilled over the bluff and marched towards the road.

He accelerated.

The white sea was faster.

It reached the tarmac just a few metres before the sign that welcomed visitors to Montauk. The road seethed. A truck was reversing out of a driveway. Hooper felt the Harley skid. He tried to dodge the vehicle, but the motorbike was out of control.

Oh, no, he thought. Oh, please, God, no.

The truck rolled across the road, with the Harley skidding towards it. Hooper heard Linda scream, and wrenched the bike round. They slid past the front of the truck, missing the chrome-plated metal by a hair. The Harley was still turning but Hooper steadied it. People were jumping out of their path. He took no notice. The road ahead was clear.

At full tilt they headed for Southampton.

Buckley Field, USA

'What the hell's going on down there?'

Cody's fingers sped over the keyboard. He tried viewing the images with different filters, but all they could see was a light-coloured mass spilling inland from the ocean.

'It looks like a wave,' he said. 'Like a fucking big wave.'

'But there wasn't a wave,' said Mike. 'It's got to be animals.'

'What kind of fucking animals?'

'They're . . .' Mike stared at the monitor. He pointed. 'Look, right there! Zoom in on that. Cut it down to a square metre.'

Cody selected the area and zoomed in. The screen was filled with a mixture of light and dark pixels.

'Closer.'

The pixels expanded, some white, others in varying shades of grey.

'OK, maybe I'm going crazy,' said Mike slowly, 'but to me they look like . . .' How could it be possible? 'Pincers,' he said. 'Pincers and shells.'

Cody stared at him. 'Pincers?'

'Crabs.'

Cody's jaw fell open. He typed in a command for the satellite to search the coastline.

The KH-12–4 worked its way from Montauk to East Hampton and from there to Southampton, Mastic Beach and Patchogue.

'This can't be happening,' Mike said.

'Can't it?' Cody turned around. 'Well, it fucking is. Something's coming out of the sea down there – along the whole damn coastline of Long Island. Do you still want to visit Montauk?'

Mike picked up the phone to call HQ.

Greater New York, USA

Just past the exit for Montauk, Route 27 joined the Long Island Expressway 495. It led all the way to Queens. It was about 200 kilometres from Montauk to New York, and the closer you drove to the metropolis, the busier it became. Roughly half-way there, near Patchogue, there'd be a surge of extra traffic.

Bo Henson was a deliveryman in his own private courier business. He made the round trip to Long Island twice a day. He'd been to Patchogue to pick up a parcel from the airport and drop it off nearby. Now he was on his way back to the city. He'd had a long day already – but it was no use griping about the hours when you were up against the big boys, like FedEx. Soon he'd be able to relax, though. He'd finished all his deliveries and was clocking off earlier than he'd expected. He was worn out and longing for a beer.

Near Amityville, roughly forty kilometres from Queens, the car in front skidded.

Henson hit the brakes. The car ahead straightened out and slowed right down. Its hazard warning lights flashed on. Something was coating the road. The light was fading, and Henson couldn't see what it was, only that it was moving, and that it seemed to be coming from the bushes on the left. Then he saw that it was crabs. The highway was swarming with them. They were trying to cross the road and didn't stand a chance – the tracks of slime and shattered shell were evidence of the casualties so far.

The traffic crept forwards. It was like driving on soap. Henson swore. He wondered where the creatures could have come from. He'd read in the paper about land-crabs on Christmas Island migrating from the mountains to the sea to spawn. Every year 100 million of them set off *en masse*. But Christmas Island was in the Indian Ocean, and the crabs in the photo had been huge and bright red, not a seething mass of white.

Henson had never seen anything like it.

He cursed again, and switched on the radio. After a while he hit on a country music station and resigned himself to his fate. Dolly Parton did her best to reconcile him to the situation, but nothing could salvage his mood. Ten minutes later, the news came on, but made no mention of the crab plague. A snowplough had appeared, though, and was pushing its way between the crawling traffic, trying to sweep the milling bodies from the road. The effect was to jam things up entirely. Henson switched between all the local radio stations, but none had anything to say about it, which riled him even more: he was suffering and no one cared. Meanwhile, the air-conditioning was blowing an unwholesome stench into his van and he was forced to turn it off.

On the other side of the crossroads leading left to Hempstead and right to Long Beach, the traffic picked up speed. The creatures hadn't made it that far. Henson kept his foot on the gas and reached Queens an hour later than he'd hoped. He was in a foul temper. Just before he got to the East River he turned left and crossed Newton Creek on the way to his regular drinking-hole in Brooklyn-Greenpoint. He parked, got out and almost had a heart-attack when he saw the state of his van. A mush of crab plastered the tyres, the hubcaps and the paintwork, reaching all the way up to the windows. He had to be on the road first thing the next morning and couldn't deliver any parcels like that.

It was late, but the beer could wait until he'd taken the van to the twenty-four-hour carwash. He climbed back in, drove the three blocks, and told the guys to pay special attention to the alloys: he didn't want a speck of filth left on his van. Then he told them where they could find him, and walked back to the bar for his beer.

The carwash had a reputation for doing a thorough, conscientious job. The slimy gunk on Henson's van was hard to get off, but after prolonged exposure to the jet of hot water, it melted off – like Jell-O in the sun, thought the boy in charge of the pressure-washer.

The effluent poured into the drains.

New York had a unique water-supply system. While cars and trains passed beneath the East River at a depth of thirty metres, pipes carrying drinking water and sewage extended 240 metres underground. Engineers with powerful drills were always boring new tunnels to ensure that water flowed freely into and out of the city. Alongside the existing pipes, countless old tunnels were no longer in use. Experts claimed that no one could locate all of the tunnels buried below the streets of New York. There wasn't a single map that showed the entire network. Some tunnels were known only to certain groups of drifters, who kept the secret to themselves. The sewers had inspired directors to make monster movies in which scary creatures were hatched in them. In a sense, everything that flowed into New York's sewers went astray.

In the course of that evening and over the next few days, the carwashes in Brooklyn, Queens, State Island and Manhattan were filled with vehicles that had come from Long Island. The wastewater disappeared into the bowels of the city, flowing along pipelines, mingling with other fluids and entering the recycling stations. Then it was pumped back into the system. Only a few hours after Henson's squeaky-clean van had been dropped off at the bar, the effluent had merged with New York's water.

Within six hours the first ambulances were racing through the streets.

11 May

There was always a way of coming to terms with change. Or, at least, Johanson had always found one. Much as it had hurt him to lose his house, he knew he could live without it. Even the end of his marriage had been a new beginning. In Trondheim, his short-lived relationships had compounded his solitude – but none of it had bothered him. As far as he was concerned, anything that didn't add to his aesthetic sensibilities or his appreciation of harmony could be consigned to the dustbin. The surface was something he shared with others but the depths he kept for himself. That was his way of getting on with life.

Now, though, in the early hours of the morning, other, more dissonant memories were emerging from the past. He hadn't intended to open his left eye, but now that he had, he examined the world from a cyclopean view, thinking about those in his life who'd been destroyed by change.

His wife.

People grew up thinking that they controlled their lives. But he'd abandoned her, and she'd been forced to see that control was an illusion. She'd argued with him, pleaded with him, shouted, shown compassion, listened patiently, begged for his pity, and been left behind, disenfranchised, bundled out of their shared life. She'd stopped believing in her power to change anything. Life was a gamble, and she'd lost.

Was it his fault that he'd suddenly felt differently? Emotions were beyond innocence and guilt: they were biochemical reactions to the circumstances of life. It wasn't very romantic, he knew, but endorphins meant more than any romance. So what was he guilty of? Of making promises that couldn't be kept . . .

Johanson opened the other eye.

Change, for him, was the elixir of life. For her it had induced a kind of coma. Years later, when he was in Trondheim, friends had told him that she'd finally got back on her feet, taken charge of her life. After a while she'd found someone new. Johanson and she had chatted on the phone a few times, free from rancour or longing. The bitterness had destroyed itself, and he'd been released from the burden of guilt.

But now it was back.

It followed him around, with Tina Lund's pale, pretty face. By now he had been through all the different scenarios. If they'd slept together at the lake, it would have changed everything. Maybe she would have joined him in the Shetlands. Or maybe it would have ruined everything, and he would have been the last person whose advice she would have taken — like when he'd encouraged her to visit Kare. Either way, she would still be alive.

He kept telling himself it was stupid to think like that.

But the thoughts kept returning.

The first rays of sunshine streamed into the room. He had left the curtains open as he always did: a bedroom with closed curtains was no better than a crypt. He wondered about getting up for breakfast, but he had no desire to move. Lund's death filled him with sorrow. He hadn't been in love with her, but he had loved her. Her restlessness, her need for freedom had drawn them together, as surely as they had kept them apart.

I won't live for ever, he thought. Ever since Lund had died, he had thought about death. He wasn't used to feeling old, but now it seemed as though Fate had stamped a best before date on him. He was fifty-six, in excellent shape, and had escaped the statistical threat of untimely death through illness or accident. He'd even survived a tsunami. But there was no doubt that time was running out. Most of his life was in the past, and he was starting to worry that it might all have been a mistake.

Two women in his life had trusted him, and he'd failed to protect them.

Karen Weaver was alive. She reminded him of Lund. She wasn't as hyperactive, as guarded or as moody, but she had Lund's strength, her toughness and impatience. After their escape from the tsunami, he had told her his theory and she'd explained her work for Lukas Bauer. After a while he had flown back to Norway and joined the ranks of the homeless. But the NTNU was still standing. The authorities had besieged him with work, and before he could drive to the lake, the summons had arrived from Canada. It had been his idea for Weaver to join them, ostensibly because she knew more than anyone else about Bauer's work and could take it further. But that wasn't the real reason. If it hadn't been for the helicopter, Weaver wouldn't have survived – so, in a sense, he had saved her. Weaver was absolution for his failure to help Lund, and he'd made up his mind to look out for her. To that end, it was better to have her close.

The memories of the past faded in the sunlight. Johanson got up, showered and arrived at the buffet at half past six to find that he wasn't the only one to have risen so early. The dining hall was filled with soldiers and intelligence agents drinking coffee, eating muesli and fruit and talking in hushed tones. Johanson piled his plate with scrambled eggs and bacon and searched for familiar faces. He would have liked to talk to Bohrmann, but he was nowhere to be seen. General Judith Li was there, though, sitting alone at a table for two. She was leafing through a file. From time to time she took a spoonful of fruit from her bowl.

Something about Li intrigued Johanson. He guessed that she looked younger than she was. He wondered what a man had to do to get her into bed, but decided it was probably unadvisable to try. Li didn't look like someone who would let others take the initiative.

She glanced from her reading and spotted him. 'Good morning, Dr Johanson,' she called. 'Did you sleep well?'

'Like a baby.' He walked over to her table. 'You're not breakfasting alone, are you? I guess it must be lonely at the top.'

'Why don't you join me? I like having people around me who are busy with their thoughts. It concentrates the mind.'

Johanson took a seat. 'Who's to say I am?'

'It's obvious.' Li put down her file. 'Coffee?'

'Yes, please.'

'You revealed yourself yesterday. The other scientists here are focused on their fields. Shankar's contending with mysterious deep-sea noises, Anawak's fretting about his whales – although he's got more of an overview than the others – and Bohrmann's terrified that there's going to be a methane disaster. He's juggling variables, trying to prevent another slide.'

'Sounds like they've got their work cut out to me.'

'But they haven't come up with a theory to tie it all together.'

'I didn't think we needed one,' Johanson said evenly. 'It's an Arab conspiracy.'

'Do you believe that?'

440

'No.'

'What *do* you believe, then?'

'If you want to hear what I think, you're going to have to wait an extra day or so.'

'You haven't convinced yourself yet?'

'Almost.' Johanson sipped his coffee. 'But it's tricky. Your Mr Vanderbilt is all fired up about terrorism. Before I even voice my suspicions, I'll need someone to cover my back.'

'And who's going to do that?'

Johanson put down his cup. 'You are, General.'

Li didn't seem surprised. 'If you're going to try to convince me of something, maybe you should tell me what it is.'

'Absolutely,' smiled Johanson. 'All in good time.'

Li pushed the file across the table. Inside the plastic wallet was a collection of faxes. 'Maybe this will speed up your decision, Dr Johanson. I received these at five o'clock this morning. No one seems able to tell us exactly what happened, and we're still awaiting a full report, but I had to make a quick decision. In a few hours' time, New York and the surrounding area will be under martial law. Peak's there already to set things in motion.'

Johanson saw the spectre of another wave. 'But why?'

'What if I told you that billions of white crabs were rising from the sea along the coast of Long Island?'

'I'd say they were on a team-building exercise.'

'Uh-huh. But for which team?'

'Tell me more about these crabs,' he said. 'What are they doing there?'

'We're not sure. But we think it's something similar to those Brittany lobsters. They're importing a plague. How does that fit with your theory?'

Johanson thought it over. 'Is there a biohazard facility where we could examine them?'

'We've set one up in Nanaimo. A consignment of crabs is being sent there.'

'Live ones?'

'They were alive when they were caught. Plenty of people are dead, though. The poison seems to work faster than the toxins in Europe.'

Johanson said nothing for a while. 'I'll fly over,' he said.

'And when do you plan to tell me what you're thinking?'

'Give me twenty-four hours.'

Li pursed her lips. 'Twenty-four hours it is,' she said. 'But not a minute longer.'

Anawak was sitting with Ray Fenwick, John Ford and Sue Oliviera in the institute's capacious projection room. The projector was showing 3-D models of whale brains. Oliviera had designed them on the computer, and had marked the places where the jelly had been found. You could navigate around the insides of the brains and slice them lengthways with a virtual knife. They'd already watched three simulations, and now they were viewing the fourth, which showed how the substance wound its way through the gyri towards the centre of the brain.

'OK, here's the theory,' said Anawak. 'Imagine you're a cockroach.'

'Gee, thanks, Leon.' Oliviera raised her eyebrows, which made her horsy face seem even longer. 'You know how to flatter a lady.'

'A cockroach incapable of intelligent thought.'

'I never knew you felt that way.'

Fenwick laughed and scratched the tip of his nose.

'Everything you do is merely a reflex,' Anawak continued, unabashed, 'so if I were a neurophysiologist, I could steer your behaviour with no trouble at all. I'd only have to control your reflexes and trigger them as required. You'd be like an artificial limb. I'd just have to push the right buttons.'

'Wasn't there an experiment where they beheaded a beetle and sewed on another one's head?' said Ford. 'If I remember rightly, it could walk.'

'Almost. They decapitated one cockroach, and chopped the legs off another. Then they joined the central nervous systems. The cockroach with the head took control of the legs as though they were its own. That's what I'm getting at: simple processes for simple creatures. There was another experiment where they tried something similar with mice. They took a mouse and grafted a second head on to its body. It lived a surprisingly long time – a few hours or days, I think. In any case, both heads seemed to function normally, but the mouse had trouble co-ordinating its movement. It was able to walk, but not always in the direction it intended, so it mostly fell over after a few steps.'

'Appalling,' muttered Oliviera.

'So, it's technically possible to gain control of any organism, but the more complex it is, the more difficult that becomes. Imagine dealing with a complex organism that's also conscious, intelligent, creative and self-aware. It's pretty darned hard to make it do your bidding, so what do you do?'

'You break its will and reduce it to the level of a cockroach. With men, you just flash your naked butt.'

'Exactly.' Anawak grinned. 'Because people and cockroaches aren't so very different.'

'*Some* people,' Oliviera corrected him.

'No, everyone. Free will's a wonderful thing, but it's only free until you flip a few switches. Like pain, for example.'

'So whoever made the jelly knows how a whale brain works,' said Fenwick. 'That's what you're saying, isn't it? That the substance stimulates specific neural centres.'

'Yes.'

'And to do that, you have to know which.'

'It's not too hard to find out,' said Oliviera. 'Think of John Lilly.'

'Exactly.' Anawak nodded. 'Lilly was the first to experiment with implanting electrodes in animal brains to stimulate pleasure or pain. He proved that by manipulating areas of the brain it's possible to cause an animal to feel pleasure, gratification, pain, anger or fear. That was with apes, remember, and apes are close to whales and dolphins in terms of complexity and intelligence. It worked. He could bring the animals under his control by using electrodes to trigger different sensations as punishment or reward. And that was back in the sixties.'

'Still, Fenwick's right,' said Ford. 'That's all well and good if you've got an ape on your operating-table and you can tinker around in its head. But the jelly must have entered through the ears or the jaw, and for that it would have to change shape. Even if you managed to get the stuff inside the brain, how could you be sure that it would redistribute itself correctly and then, um, press the right buttons?'

Anawak was convinced that the jelly inside the whales was doing just that, but he didn't have the faintest idea how. 'Maybe there aren't many buttons that need pressing,' he said. 'Maybe it's enough to—'

The door opened.

'Dr Oliviera?' A lab technician poked her head into the room. 'I'm sorry to disturb you but you're wanted in the containment lab. It's urgent.'

Oliviera looked at the others. 'This kind of thing never used to happen,' she said. 'Only a few weeks ago we could sit down comfortably and have a civilised conversation about all sorts of nonsense without anyone interrupting. Now I feel like I'm in a Bond film. Would Dr Oliviera please make her way immediately to the containment lab!' She got up and clapped her hands. 'OK then. *Vamos, muchachos.* Does anyone want to come? You won't get anywhere in this building without me anyway.'

Biohazard Containment Facility

Moments after the crabs had arrived, Johanson's helicopter touched down next to the institute. A lab technician accompanied him to the elevators. They descended two floors, got out and walked down a stark, neon-lit corridor. The technician opened a heavy door, and they entered a room filled with monitors. The biohazard sign above the steel door at the back was the only indication that death lurked beyond. Johanson spotted Roche, Anawak and Ford, talking quietly together. Oliviera and Fenwick were in conversation with Rubin and Vanderbilt. Rubin caught sight of Johanson and came over to shake hands. 'Never a dull moment, is there?' He gave a frenzied laugh.

'I suppose not.'

'We haven't had a chance to talk yet,' said Rubin. 'You must tell me about the worms. It's a shame we had to meet in such circumstances, but you can't say it's not thrilling . . . Have you heard the latest news?'

'I guess that's why I'm here.'

Rubin pointed to the steel door. 'Unbelievable, isn't it? These used to be storerooms, but the army had them turned them into a hermetically sealed laboratory. I know it sounds a bit makeshift, but there's nothing to worry about – the whole thing conforms to Biosafety Level 4. We can examine the organisms without putting anyone at risk.'

BSL-4 was the highest level of containment.

'Will you be joining us inside?' asked Johanson.

'It'll be me and Dr Oliviera.'

'I thought Roche was the expert on crustaceans.'

'Everyone's an expert on everything here.' Vanderbilt and Oliviera had joined them. The CIA agent smelt faintly of sweat. He thumped Johanson jovially on the shoulder. 'We picked our boffins very carefully – it takes a mix of flavours to make a good pizza. But Li's got a thing about you, Dr Johanson. I bet she can't stand letting you out of her sight. She'd love to know what's going on inside your head.' He guffawed. 'Unless it's something else she's after . . . What do you reckon?'

Johanson smiled distantly. 'Maybe you should ask her.'

'Oh, I have,' said Vanderbilt, serenely. 'I hate to disappoint you, but she's only interested in your brain. She thinks you know something.'

'Really? Like what?'

'You tell me.'

'I don't know anything.'

Vanderbilt looked at him disparagingly. 'No neat theory?'

'I thought yours was neat enough.'

'Well, so long as you haven't got any better ideas. And while you're in there, Dr Johanson, here's something for you to think about. We call it Gulf War Syndrome. Back in 1991, America kept her losses to a minimum on the ground in Kuwait, but guess what? Nearly a quarter of our veterans developed a weird bunch of symptoms. Looking back on it, their complaints were like a mild version of the damage caused by *Pfiesteria* – memory loss, concentration difficulties, damage to internal organs . . . We think they were exposed to some chemical. After all, our men were in the vicinity when the Iraqi weapons depots were blown up. At the time we suspected it was sarin, but maybe the Iraqis were developing a biological agent as well. Half the Islamic world has a stockpile of pathogens. It's not difficult to genetically modify harmless bacteria or viruses and turn them into killers.'

'And you think that's what's happened here?'

'I think you'd be well advised to open up to Auntie Li.' Vanderbilt winked. 'Between you and me, she's nuts. *Capisce?* And you should never get in the way of someone who's nuts.'

'She seems perfectly sane to me.'

'That's your problem. Don't say you weren't warned.'

'*My* problem is that we still don't know what's going on,' said Oliviera, gesturing towards the door. 'It's time to get to work. Roche is coming too, of course.'

'What about me? Are you sure you can't use a bodyguard?' Vanderbilt grinned. 'I'd be happy to volunteer.'

'That's very kind of you, Jack, but we're right out of suits in your size.'

The four made their way past the steel door and into the first of three airlocks. A camera poked down from the ceiling. Four bright yellow protective suits were hanging up, with transparent hoods, gloves and black vinyl boots.

'Are you all familiar with working in containment labs?' Oliviera asked.

Roche and Rubin nodded.

'Only in theory,' Johanson admitted.

'No problem. We'd normally have to train you, but there's no time for that. In any case, the suit is one third of your protection. You can rely on it 100 per cent. It's made of impermeable PVC. The other two thirds are caution and concentration. Wait, I'll help you put it on.'

The suit was pretty bulky. Johanson pulled on a kind of waistcoat, designed to distribute the intake of air evenly round his body, then struggled into the yellow overall, keeping pace with Oliviera's explanations.

'Once you're safely in the suit, we'll hook you up to the air system and fill your overall with dehumidified, tempered air. The charcoal filter supplies it under positive pressure. That's important, since it stops air entering in the event of a leak. Any surplus air exits via the exhaust valve. You can regulate the supply yourself, but that shouldn't be necessary. OK? How do you feel?'

'Like the Michelin man.'

Oliviera laughed and they walked out of the first airlock. Johanson could hear Oliviera's muffled voice in his ears and realised they were all wired up: 'The air pressure in the laboratory is maintained at fifty pascals below atmospheric pressure. Not a single spore will ever find its way out. If we lose power to the facility, we'll have emergency back-up so there's unlikely to be any problem. The floor is made of sealed concrete and the windows are bulletproof. The air inside the laboratory is decontaminated using high-tech filters. There aren't any drains because we sterilise liquid waste within the building. We can communicate with the outside world via radio, fax or computer. The freezers and the air-regulation system are fitted with alarms that will go off simultaneously in the control room, the virological lab and at Reception. Every last corner of the facility is under video surveillance.'

'Too right,' Vanderbilt boomed, through the speaker system. 'So if any one of you drops dead down there, there'll be a great home movie for the kids.'

Johanson saw Oliviera roll her eyes.

They walked through the other sealed chambers and into the lab. The room covered an area of about thirty square metres and looked rather like a restaurant kitchen, with its freezers, fridges and wall-mounted cupboards. Lining the walls were large metal barrels containing viral cultures and other organisms preserved in liquid nitrogen. There was plenty of space to work on the various benches. The interior of the lab had been designed so that there were no sharp edges to damage the suits. Oliviera pointed to three big red buttons that allowed them to sound the alarm, then led them over to one of the benches. She opened a tub-shaped container. Little white crabs sat in thirty centimetres of water, showing no sign of life. Oliviera picked up a metal spatula and prodded them, but none moved. 'They're dead, I reckon.'

'Unfortunate,' said Rubin. 'Didn't they promise us live specimens?'

'According to Li, they were alive at the start of the journey,' said Johanson. He leaned forwards and studied them one by one. He patted Oliviera's arm. 'Second to the left. Its leg twitched.'

Oliviera ferried the crab to the work surface, where it sat for a few seconds, then raced at speed towards the edge of the bench. Oliviera brought it back. It allowed itself to be pushed across the table without protest, then tried once more to flee. Oliviera repeated the procedure a few times, then replaced the crab in the tub. 'Any immediate thoughts?' she asked.

'I'd have to look inside it,' said Roche.

Rubin shrugged. 'It's behaviour seems normal enough. I'm not familiar with the species, though. Can you identify it, Dr Johanson?'

'No.' Johanson thought for a moment. 'But its behaviour *isn't* normal. Under normal circumstances it would see the spatula as its enemy. You'd expect it to splay its claws and wave them threateningly. In my opinion, its motor activity is normal, but there's a problem with its senses. It looks to me—'

'Like a clockwork toy,' said Oliviera.

'Right. It scuttles like a crab, but it doesn't behave like a crab.'

'Do you know what species it could be?'

'I'm not really a taxonomist. I can tell you what I think, but you shouldn't take my word for it.'

'Go on.'

'There are two interesting features.' Johanson picked up the spatula and touched a few motionless shells. 'First, the crabs are white. Colourless. Nature never uses colours for decoration, always for a purpose. Most colourless organisms live in places they can't be seen, which is why they don't need colour. The second feature is the lack of eyes.'

'You mean they come from caves or from the depths?' said Roche.

'Yes. Some creatures that live in darkness have traces of eyes – atrophied, of course, but you can see where they used to be – but these crabs, well, I'd say they never had eyes in the first place. If that's the case, then their habitat must be pitch-black. In fact, they must have evolved in the dark. As far as I'm aware, that applies to only one species of crab that looks anything like these.'

'Vent crabs,' nodded Rubin.

'And where do they come from?' asked Roche.

'Deep-sea hydrothermal vents,' said Rubin. 'Volcanic oases of life.'

Roche frowned. 'Then they shouldn't be able to survive on land.'

'The real question is, *what* has survived?' said Johanson.

Oliviera fished a dead crustacean out of the tub, turned it on its back and laid it on the bench. She gathered up a series of implements resembling crab picks, and cut into the side of the carapace with a tiny, battery-driven circular saw. A transparent substance spurted into the air. Oliviera continued unperturbed until the shell was divided in two. She picked up the underside, with the legs attached, and moved it to one side.

They stared at the dissected creature.

'That's not a crab,' said Johanson.

'No,' said Roche. He pointed to the semi-fluid, clumpy mass of jelly that filled most of the shell. 'It's the same gunk we found in the lobsters.'

Oliviera spooned the jelly into a jar. 'Look at this,' she said. 'Behind the head it still looks like a proper crab. See these fibres running down the middle? They're its nervous system. The crab's got all its senses, just nothing to help it use them.'

'Actually,' said Rubin, 'it's got the jelly.'

'It's not a crab in the normal sense.' Roche peered at the transparent gunk in the jar. 'It functions, but it's not alive.'

'Which explains why it doesn't behave like a crab – assuming we don't identify the stuff inside it as a new type of crab meat.'

'No way,' said Roche. 'It doesn't belong to the crab. It's a foreign organism.'

'In that case, the foreign organism is responsible for making these crabs come on land,' said Johanson. 'What we need to find out is whether the crabs were dead and it slipped inside to try to bring them back to life or . . .'

'Whether they were bred like that,' Oliviera finished for him.

There was an uncomfortable pause. Finally Roche broke the silence. 'Well, wherever this stuff is coming from, you can guarantee we'd all be dead without these suits. I'm willing to bet that these crabs are bursting with *Pfiesteria* or maybe something worse. The air in this laboratory is almost certainly contaminated.'

Johanson remembered what Vanderbilt had said. Biological weaponry. He was right, of course. Spot on. Just not in the way he'd assumed.

Weaver

Weaver felt a rush of euphoria. She only had to enter her password and the laptop gave her access to more information than she'd ever imagined. Under normal circumstances it would have taken her months to gather the kind of data she had here – and even then the military satellites would always have been off-limits. But this was amazing! She could sit on the balcony of her suite, log into NASA's server and immerse herself in the American military's satellite maps.

In the 1980s the US Navy had begun to investigate a remarkable phenomenon. Geosat, a radar-imaging satellite, had been launched into a near-polar orbit. There was no provision or possibility for it to map the ocean floor – radar was incapable of penetrating water. Instead, Geosat's mission was to measure sea-surface heights to within a few centimetres. It was thought that by charting great expanses of water it would be possible to show whether the sea level – tidal fluctuations aside – was the same across the planet.

Geosat's findings exceeded all expectations.

Scientists had suspected that the oceans were never completely smooth, even in conditions of perfect calm, but Geosat's images made the planet look like an enormous, lumpy potato. The oceans were full of dents, humps, bulges and troughs. For a long time scientists had assumed that the water in them was spread evenly across the globe, but the map offered a different picture. Off the south coast of India, for example, the sea level was 170 metres lower than it was in the waters around Iceland. To the north of Australia, on the other hand, it rose up to form a peak eighty-five metres above the mean sea level. The oceans were vast mountainscapes whose topography seemed to follow the lie of the underwater landscape. Towering underwater mountain ranges and deep ocean valleys replicated themselves on the surface with only a few metres' difference in height.

It all came down to variations in gravity. An underwater mountain gave the sea floor additional mass, so its gravitational field was stronger than that of a deep-sea valley. It pulled the surrounding water towards the mountain and made it pile up in a hump. The water surface bulged above a mountain – and dipped above a trench. For a short while, a number of exceptions kept the scientists guessing – for example, when water piled up above a deep sea plain – but in the end it transpired that some of the rock on the seabed was denser and heavier than average, and with that the gravitational topography fell into place.

The slopes of the water's mounds and valleys were too gentle for any sailor to detect. In fact, if it hadn't been for satellite mapping, no one would have stumbled on the phenomenon, but now scientists could use their knowledge of the surface to deduce what was happening in the depths. It was more than just a new method of charting the topography of the seabed: it was a key to understanding ocean dynamics. Geosat had revealed that powerful currents circled in the oceans, forming eddies that measured hundreds of kilometres across. Like coffee being stirred in a mug, the rotating masses of water formed a depression at the centre, while the outer rings rose upwards. It became apparent that these eddies also caused the ocean's surface to rise and fall, independent of gravitational variations, and that they themselves were part of far larger rings of water – oceanic gyres. From the long-distance perspective of satellite mapping, it became clear that all the world's oceans were rotating. In the northern hemisphere, enormous networks of rings spun in a clockwise direction, while in the southern hemisphere the flow was anti-clockwise. The speed of rotation increased with proximity to the poles.

This allowed scientists to prove another fundamental principle of ocean dynamics: the rotation of the planet determined the speed and direction of the gyres.

Logically, therefore, the Gulf Stream wasn't a stream, but the western boundary of an enormous vortex made up of smaller eddies: a gyre rotating slowly, and pushing towards North America in a clockwise direction. Because the whirlpool wasn't in the centre of the Atlantic Ocean but to the west, the Gulf Stream was pushed against the American coast, where the water piled up in a ridge. Strong winds and the poleward flow of the water increased the speed of the swirl, while the immense lateral shear with the coastline slowed it down. As a result, the north Atlantic whirlpool was rotating in a steady circular current, in line with the principle of angular momentum, which ruled that circular movements remained stable unless disrupted by an external force.

And it was the possibility that the current was being disrupted that Bauer had feared. He'd been trying to find proof. Water had stopped cascading into the Greenland Sea, which was alarming, but not decisive. Proving the existence of global changes meant obtaining data on a global scale.

In 1995, after the Cold War had ended, the American military had begun to release the Geosat maps and the system had been replaced with a string of new satellites. Karen Weaver had access to all their data, which combined to form a complete history of oceanic mapping from the mid-nineties onwards. She spent hours trying to match up the different readings. There were variations in detail – sometimes a satellite's radar altimeter would mistake a thick bank of mist for the surface and record a measurement that was disputed elsewhere, but in general the results were the same.

The closer she looked, the more her initial excitement gave way to anxiety.

In the end she was certain that Bauer had been right.

His drifting profilers had transmitted data for only a short time, without seeming to follow the path of any current. Then one after another, the floats had fallen silent. Practically no feedback was available from Bauer's expedition. She wondered whether he had sensed how right he'd been. She could feel his knowledge weighing on her shoulders. He had entrusted her with his legacy, and now she could read between the lines. She knew enough to grasp that a catastrophe was looming.

She went back through her calculations and checked for mistakes. She repeated the process again and again.

It was worse than she'd feared.

Online

Still in their PVC suits, Johanson, Oliviera, Rubin and Roche stood under the decontamination shower. The vapour from the solution of 1.5 per cent peracetic acid was guaranteed to obliterate every last trace of any lurking biological agent. Once the corrosive fluid had been washed away with water and neutralised with sodium hydroxide, the scientists were permitted to leave the sealed chamber.

Shankar and his team were working round the clock in an attempt to make sense of the unidentified noises. They'd called in Ford to help them, and were busy playing Scratch and other spectrograms over and over again.

Anawak and Fenwick had gone for a walk and were deep in conversation about possible ways of hijacking an organism's neural system.

Dr Stanley Frost had turned up in Bohrmann's suite. His baseball cap was pulled down over his glasses and his massive figure seemed to fill the room. 'Right, Doc, it's time we talked,' he boomed.

He explained his thoughts on the worms – interesting, all in all. He and Bohrmann clicked right away, drank a few beers at lightning speed and came up with a series of disturbing, yet plausible scenarios to add to the list of possible disasters. Now they were conferring via satellite with Kiel. Since the Internet connection had been restored, the Geomar scientists had been sending a steady stream of simulations. Suess had reconstructed events on the Norwegian slope as accurately as possible, leading them all to the conclusion that a catastrophe of such magnitude should never have occurred. The worms and bacteria had certainly had a dire effect on the slope, but something was missing: a tiny piece of the jigsaw, an additional catalyst.

'And if we don't find out what it is,' said Frost, 'I swear to God that we'll all be in for an almighty soaking. And it *won't* have anything to do with the slope collapsing near America or Japan.'

Li was working on her laptop. Alone in her enormous suite, she was everywhere, with everyone, all at once. She'd watched the scientists work in the containment lab, listening to what they said. Every room in the Chateau was under audio and video surveillance. The same went for Nanaimo, the University of British Columbia and Vancouver Aquarium. Scientists' homes within a certain radius had also been bugged, including Ford, Oliviera and Fenwick's flats, the boat that Anawak lived on, and even his apartment in Vancouver. The committee's eyes and ears were everywhere. Information escaped them only if it was exchanged outside – in the open air or in restaurants and pubs. That irked Li, but there was nothing she could do about it, short of implanting every scientist with a chip.

The intranet surveillance was an unqualified success. Bohrmann and Frost were currently online, as was Karen Weaver, who was analysing satellite data relating to the Gulf Stream. Now, that was interesting, as were the simulations from Kiel. Setting up the network had been an inspired idea. Of course, there was no way of actually seeing or hearing what its users were *thinking*, but everything they did, every page they consulted, was saved and could be tracked at any time. If Vanderbilt turned out to be right in his terrorism theory, which Li doubted, it would be legitimate to interrogate them all. Ostensibly they were clean. None had links to any extremist organisations or Arab countries, but you could never be too careful. Even if the CIA's suspicions proved unfounded, it was still useful to be able to peer over the scientists' shoulders without their knowledge. It was always best to obtain the facts as they emerged.

She switched back to Nanaimo and listened to Johanson and Oliviera, as they headed towards the elevators. They were talking about the safety precautions in the biohazard lab. Oliviera said something about the chemical shower being strong enough to bleach them to the bone and Johanson made a joke. They both laughed and rode up to ground level.

Why didn't Johanson tell anyone of his theory? He'd almost mentioned it when he was in his suite with Weaver, straight after the presentation, but had lapsed into allusions.

Li made a series of phone calls, spoke to Peak in New York, then looked at her watch. It was time for Vanderbilt's report. She left her suite and went along the corridor to a secure room on the southern side of the Chateau. It was the equivalent of the War Room in the White House, and was tap-proof, like the conference room. Vanderbilt and two of his team were waiting for her. The CIA chief had only just returned from Nanaimo by helicopter, and was even more dishevelled than usual.

'Can we get Washington on the line?' she asked, without bothering to say hello.

'Well, we could,' said Vanderbilt, 'but it wouldn't do much good—'

'Cut to the chase, Jack.'

'If you want to speak to the President, there's no point in calling Washington. He's not there.'

Nanaimo, Vancouver Island

As she was leaving the elevator with Johanson, Oliviera ran into Fenwick and Anawak in the foyer. 'Where've you been?' she asked, surprised.

'For a stroll.' Anawak beamed at her. 'Been having fun in the lab?'

'Yeah, right.' Oliviera grimaced. 'It looks as though Europe's problems are washing in our direction. The jelly in the crabs was an old friend of ours. But that's not all they were carrying. Roche has isolated a biological agent.'

'*Pfiesteria?*' asked Anawak.

'Not far off,' said Johanson. 'It's a mutation of a mutation, as it were. The new strain is far more toxic than the European variety.'

'We had to sacrifice a few mice,' said Oliviera. 'We shut them in with a dead crab and they died within minutes.'

Fenwick took an involuntary step back. 'Is the toxin contagious?'

'Oh, no. Feel free to kiss me, if you like. The poison they produce can't be passed between humans. We're not dealing with a virus – it's essentially a bacteriological invasion. The trouble is, the whole thing spirals out of control once the *Pfiesteria* get into the water. They keep spreading exponentially, long after the crabs have given up the ghost. All but one was dead on arrival, and now the last one's gone too.'

'Kamikaze crabs,' Anawak muttered.

'Their job is to get the bacteria to land, just as the worms' mission was to import it into the ice,' said Johanson. 'After that, they perish. Jellyfish, mussels, even the jelly – none of these organisms live long, but they all fulfil their function.'

'Harming us at all cost.'

'Absolutely. Even the whales have become suicidal,' said Fenwick. 'Aggressive behaviour is normally part of a survival strategy, like flight, but there's no evidence of it here.'

Johanson smiled. His dark eyes flashed. 'I'm not so sure about that. I'd say there's a clear survival strategy at the heart of all this.'

Fenwick stared at him. 'You're starting to sound like Vanderbilt.'

'Actually, no. Vanderbilt's right in some respects, but fundamentally I don't agree with him.' Johanson paused. 'But before too long, he'll be sounding like me.'

Li

'What's that supposed to mean?' demanded Li, as she sat down. 'If the President's not in Washington, where is he?'

'He's heading for Offutt Air Force Base in Nebraska,' said Vanderbilt. 'Swarms of crabs have shown up in Chesapeake Bay and along the Potomac river. They seem to be marching up the estuary. We've also had reported sightings near Alexandria and just south of Arlington, but we're awaiting confirmation.'

'Who decided on Offutt?'

Vanderbilt shrugged. 'The White House chief of staff is afraid that Washington's about to turn into another New York,' he said. 'But you know the President. He fought against it tooth and nail. He was all for confronting the crabs and declaring war on the bastards in person. But in the end he agreed to a break in the country.'

Li thought for a moment. Offutt was the home of the United States Strategic Command, the control centre for America's nuclear weapons. The base was the ideal place to protect the President. It was situated at the heart of the country, out of reach of any danger emerging from the sea. From there the President could communicate with the National Security Council over a secure satellite link and exercise the full powers of government.

'We can't afford this kind of sloppiness,' she said vehemently. 'For future reference, Jack, I expect to be informed of this kind of thing straight away. If anything so much as sticks its head out of the water anywhere in the world, I want to know.'

'I'll see what I can do,' said Vanderbilt. 'Maybe we can set up some talks with a few local dolphins and—'

'What's more, I certainly want to be informed if anyone sends the President anywhere else.'

Vanderbilt smiled jovially. 'If I could make a suggestion—'

Li cut him off: 'And I expect you to find out exactly what's happening in Washington. We need full information within the next two hours. If the reports turn out to be true, we'll evacuate the affected areas and turn Washington into an exclusion zone, like New York.'

'Funny you should mention it,' Vanderbilt said equably, 'but I was just going to say the same thing.'

'Good. What else have you got for me?'

'Shit and more shit,' he said.

'I'm used to that.'

'That's why I've been scraping around for all the bad news I can find. I'd hate for you to have withdrawal symptoms. OK, let's start with Georges Bank. NOAA was planning to send down two dive robots to scoop up some worms for research purposes. That, um, went fine.'

Li waited for him to continue.

'Like I said, they collected their sample,' Vanderbilt was enjoying every word, 'but they didn't get it back on board. The worms were already in the bag, so to speak – then something cut the cables. We lost both robots. Same story in Japan. A manned submersible on a worm-collecting mission went missing somewhere between Honshu and Hokkaido and according to the Japanese, the worms are spreading. I think we can safely say that things are stepping up a gear. At first, only divers were being attacked, but now it's subs, underwater probes and robots.'

'Any signs of suspicious activity?'

'Nothing conclusive – no enemy probes or submersibles around at the time. But NOAA's vessel picked up a sheet of something moving in the water at a depth of seven hundred metres. It extended over several kilometres. Their chief scientist is ninety per cent sure that it was a plankton shoal, but he can't swear to it.'

Li thought of Johanson. She almost regretted that he wasn't there to listen.

'Next up, deep-sea cables. They're still being destroyed. Of the major transatlantic links, ANTAT-3 and a number of the TAT cables have now gone down. Apparently we've also lost PACRIM WEST in the Pacific, one of our main links to Australia. In addition to that, the past two days have seen a proliferation of shipping accidents, all taking place in the busiest shipping lanes. There are two hundred main chokepoints in the world, and roughly half have been affected, in particular the Strait of Gibraltar, the Strait of Malacca and the English Channel. There was trouble in the Panama Canal too and . . . well, we probably shouldn't make too much of it, but there's news of a pile-up in the Strait of Hormuz and in the Khalij as-Suways, which is, um, in . . .'

Vanderbilt didn't seem as cynical or arrogant as usual, and now Li knew why. 'I know where Khalij as-Suways is,' she said. 'You mean the Gulf of Suez. It runs between the Red Sea and the Suez Canal. Which means two major Arab shipping hubs have been hit.'

'Bingo, baby. There were navigation problems. A new variety, incidentally. It's difficult to reconstruct exactly what happened, but the crash in the Strait of Hormuz involved seven vessels. At least two had no idea where they were going. The speed log and depth sounders had clearly screwed up.'

Four pieces of technology were essential for the safety of any ship: radar, anemometer, depth sounders and speed log. Radar scanning and wind speed measurement took place above the waterline, but the depth sounders opened out on to the keel, as did the speed log, a pitot tube with an integrated sensor that measured the speed of the water. It was basically the ship's speedometer. While the log provided the ship's radar system with data on the course and speed of the vessel, the radar calculated the risk of colliding with other objects and came up with alternative routes. Generally speaking, the crew blindly accepted the instruments' readings – blindly, since seventy per cent of the time it was either dark, foggy or choppy, so there wasn't any view.

'According to the reports, one craft had marine life clinging to its speed log,' said Vanderbilt. 'As far as the log was concerned, the vessel was at a standstill, so the radar failed to register the danger of collision, even though it was surrounded by ships. In the case of the other vessel, the depth sounder started claiming that the depth was diminishing. The water was plenty deep enough, but the crew were convinced they were about to run aground so they began to manoeuvre. Both ships smashed into other vessels, and because it was dark, a few more joined in. Similar antics have been going on all over the world. We've even heard claims that whales were swimming beneath the boats in the run-up to the crashes.'

'Well, that makes sense,' Li said thoughtfully. 'If a large object were to block the depth sounder for a significant amount of time, it could easily be mistaken for firm ground.'

'On top of all that, we're also seeing more infested rudders and thrusters. Sea-chests are still getting clogged – increasingly effectively. We've just had news of an iron-ore freighter sinking off the coast of India – apparently a case of accelerated corrosion, brought on by an infestation that had built up over weeks. The sea was perfectly calm, but its forehold just caved in. It sank within minutes. And so it goes on. There's no sign of a let-up. In fact, it's getting worse. And then you've got the toxic plague.'

Li pressed the tips of her fingers together, turning it all over in her mind.

It was ridiculous. But so were ships. Peak was absolutely right. They were outdated steel coffers that used high-tech navigation while slurping cooling water through a hole in the keel. And now crabs were invading twenty-first-century cities, getting mangled by cars and dumping tonnes of toxic algae into the sewers. They'd already had to barricade one city, and it wouldn't be long before they had to barricade the next. Even the President had been forced to flee inland.

'We need some more of those worms,' said Li. 'And we have to do something about the algae.'

'I couldn't agree more.' Vanderbilt did his best to sound obsequious.

His men were sitting on either side of him, faces expressionless, eyes fixed on Li. Strictly speaking, it was Vanderbilt's job to come up with a suggestion, but he was no fonder of Li than she was of him. He wasn't about to help her.

But Li didn't need Vanderbilt to come to a decision. 'First,' she said, 'as soon as we know if those reports are true, we're going to evacuate Washington. Second, I want tankers filled with drinking water to be sent to the affected areas. Supplies will be strictly rationed. We'll drain the pipes and burn those bugs with chemicals.'

Vanderbilt laughed. His men started grinning. 'Drain the pipes? Stop New York's drinking water?'

'Yes.'

'Great idea. Once we've killed the New Yorkers with chemicals, we can put the city up for rent. Maybe the Chinese would be interested? I heard they might be running out of space.'

'I don't care how you do it, Jack – I'll leave that up to you. I'm going to ask the President to call a plenary meeting of the Security Council so we can declare a state of emergency.'

'Of course!'

'We're going to close down the coastline. I want to see drones patrolling our shores, and troops in protective clothing on stand-by with flamethrowers. From now on, anything that tries to crawl out of the sea is going to get barbecued.' She stood up. 'As for the whales, it's about time we stopped acting like frightened kids. I want our vessels to be able to sail when and where they like – and that means every single boat, without exception. Let's see how they respond to psychological warfare.'

'What are you going to do to them, Jude? Give them a good talking-to?'

'No.' Li gave a thin smile. 'I'm going to hunt them down. Those whales and their masters need to be taught a lesson. To hell with animal conservation. From now on, they're going to get shot.'

'You want to take on the IWC?'

'No. We're going to blast them with sonar – and keep blasting them until they leave us in peace.'

New York, USA

Right in front of him, a man collapsed and died. Peak was sweating beneath his heavy protective suit. Breathing through an oxygen mask, he looked out through bulletproof goggles on a city that in the course of one night had been turned into hell.

The sergeant sitting beside him steered the jeep slowly along First Avenue. Entire blocks of the East Village seemed deserted. Every now and then they'd spot a group of people being herded together by the military. The main problem was that no one could be allowed to leave the city until they knew for certain that the illness couldn't be spread. It didn't seem contagious. In fact, the scenes around them reminded Peak of a large-scale poison-gas attack. But still he felt doubtful. Many of the victims had coin-sized sores on their bodies. If New York was in the grip of killer algae, they weren't just releasing clouds of airborne toxin: they were clinging to the skin of their victims too. Theoretically, that meant they were present in bodily fluids. Peak was no biologist, but he couldn't help wondering what would happen if a diseased individual were to kiss a healthy one and pass on their saliva. The algae could survive in water, were comfortable in a wide range of temperatures, and multiplied, as far as he could tell, at an incredible speed.

The aim was to quarantine New York and Long Island in such a way that the diseased and the healthy would all be treated fairly. They were working flat out to achieve that, and at first the mood had been optimistic. New York seemed prepared. After the first attack on the World Trade Center in 1993, the mayor at the time had created the Office of Emergency Management, OEM, to tackle any future crisis. At the end of the nineties, it had carried out the biggest emergency drill in the city's history by simulating a chemical-weapons attack, calling on over six hundred police, fire-fighters and FBI agents to 'save' New York. The drill had gone without a hitch, and the Senate had authorised generous additional funding. Suddenly the OEM had found itself the recipient of fifteen million dollars to spend on a bombproof armoured command centre with its own air supply, big enough to house forty highly qualified workers, who were waiting in anticipation of Doomsday. It was built on the twenty-third storey of the World Trade Center shortly before 11 September 2001. Now, the OEM was still rebuilding itself, and it certainly wasn't capable of dealing with the crisis. People were falling ill and dying too fast for anyone to help.

The jeep swerved to avoid dead bodies and approached the junction with 14th Street. Cars sped by, honking frantically. People were trying to leave the city, but they wouldn't get far: the roads were closed. So far the army had only brought Brooklyn and parts of Manhattan under any kind of control, but at least no one was able to leave Greater New York without authorisation.

They drove on, passing military blockades on either side. Hundreds of soldiers were sweeping the city like alien invaders, faceless behind their gas-masks, lumbering and misshapen in their bright-yellow NBC suits. The OEM team was out in force as well. Across the city, bodies were being loaded on to stretchers and taken away in military jeeps or ambulances. Crashed and abandoned vehicles blocked the roads, cutting off access to parts of the city. The perpetual roar of helicopters echoed through the canyons of the streets.

Peak's driver trundled a few hundred metres along the sidewalk and stopped outside Bellevue Hospital Center on the banks of the East River, where the provisional command centre was housed. Peak hurried inside. The foyer was crowded with people. Panic-stricken eyes turned towards him, and he quickened his pace. Photographs of missing people were thrust in his direction, and shouts and cries besieged him. Flanked by two soldiers, he crossed into the secure area and marched towards the hospital's IT centre. A tap-proof satellite link connected him to Chateau Whistler. After a few minutes, he had Li on the line.

'We need an antitoxin, and we need it now.'

'Nanaimo is on the case.'

'We can't wait that long. New York is out of our control. I've seen the plans for the drains, and you can forget about pumping the city dry. You may as well talk about draining the Potomac.'

'Do you have sufficient medical supplies?'

'We can't treat anyone! We don't know how to help them. All we can do is give them immuno-modulating medication and pray for the algae to die.'

'Listen, Sal,' said Li, 'we're not going to let this beat us. We're almost a hundred per cent certain that the toxins can't be transmitted from person to person. There's almost no risk of contagion from the bodies. We've got no choice but to wipe the bugs out of the system. We'll douse them in chemicals, burn them, plead with them – whatever it takes.'

'Well, go ahead,' said Peak, 'but it won't do any good. OK, the wind will probably blow away the toxic cloud, but as for the algae . . . Don't you realise that every single person in this city will have helped themselves to water? They'll have showered, done the dishes, had a drink, topped up the goldfish bowl and God knows what else. People have been washing their cars. The fire service has been putting out fires. This whole city is covered with algae. They're contaminating the buildings, swarming through the air vents and the air-conditioning. Even if we've seen the end of the crabs, I don't know how we could ever stop the algae reproducing.' He struggled for breath. 'I mean, Christ, Jude, there are six thousand hospitals in America, and less than a quarter are prepared for a crisis like this. How are we ever going to isolate so many people and get them treated before it's too late? The Bellevue can't cope, and it's huge.'

Li was silent for moment. Then she said, 'OK. You know what you have to do. Turn Greater New York into a prison. Don't let anyone in or out.'

'But they'll die if they stay here. We won't be able to help them.'

'I know. It's terrible. But we've got to think about everyone else. From now on, I want New York to be an island.'

'How am I supposed to do that?' Peak sounded desperate. 'The East River flows inland.'

'We'll think of something. But in the meantime . . .'

Peak didn't hear the explosion: he felt it. The ground shook beneath his feet. There was a muffled rumble and Manhattan trembled in the shock waves, as though there'd been an earthquake.

'Something's exploded,' said Peak.

'Find out what it is. I'll expect your report in ten minutes.'

Peak ran to the window, but there was no sign of trouble. He signalled to his men, and hurried out of the room, back along the corridor and towards the rear of the hospital, where there was a view across Franklin Drive and the East River towards Brooklyn and Queens.

He looked left, following the river upstream.

People were running towards the hospital. About a kilometre away he saw an enormous mushroom rising in the sky. It was hovering above the site of the United Nations headquarters. At first Peak was afraid that the building had exploded. Then he realised that the source of the cloud was closer than he'd thought.

It was billowing from the entrance to the Queens Midtown Tunnel, which crossed beneath the East River and connected Manhattan to the opposite bank.

The tunnel was on fire.

Peak thought of all the cars that littered the city – the pile-ups on the roads, the vehicles that had collided with shop-fronts or streetlights. He thought of all the drivers who'd collapsed at the wheel. He didn't need to be told what had happened in that tunnel, and it couldn't have happened at a worse time.

They ran back into the building, through the foyer, heading for the jeep, their movements hampered by the protective clothing, but some-how Peak managed to swing himself over the side of the vehicle and they accelerated away.

Three storeys above them, Bo Henson, the deliveryman who'd done battle with FedEx, passed away.

The Hoopers had already been dead for hours.

Vancouver Island, Canada

'So why Whistler? What are you doing there?'

It was supposed to be an excursion back to normality, but so far it was nothing of the kind. For the first time in days Anawak was sitting in Davie's Whaling Station, talking to Shoemaker and Delaware, who were draining a couple of cans of Heineken in his honour. Davie had closed the Station until further notice. His land-based expeditions had failed to catch on. The idea of watching animals held no appeal. If the whales had turned against humanity, who could trust bears? Besides, there was no telling what the Pacific might spring on them, now that Europe had been flattened by waves. Most tourists had abandoned the island already. As Davie's manager, Shoemaker was taking care of the Station on his own, trying to keep the place afloat by calling in old debts. 'I'd give anything to know what you're up to,' he repeated.

Anawak shook his head. 'It's no use bugging me, Tom. I promised to keep my mouth shut. Can't we talk about something else?'

'Why can't you just tell me? It must be a really big deal if—'

'Tom . . .'

'The thing is, Leon, I'd like to know when to get the hell out of here,' he said, 'in view of the tsunamis and so on.'

'Who said anything about tsunamis?'

'We don't need you and your fancy committee to tell us what's going on. People aren't stupid, you know. Ships are capsizing, people are dying in Europe, and now we're hearing horror stories about a plague in New York.' He leaned forward and winked. 'What do you say, Leon? The two of us, we saved those people from the *Lady Wexham*, didn't we? Come on, buddy, I'm with you guys – one of the gang, part of the team.'

Delaware took a sip of beer and wiped her mouth. 'Oh, stop pestering him. If he can't tell us, he can't tell us, OK?'

She was wearing a new pair of glasses with round orange-tinted lenses. She must have done something to her hair, thought Anawak. It had lost its frizziness and swept her shoulders in silky waves. In fact, even with her oversized teeth, she looked pretty. Really pretty.

Shoemaker raised his hands, then let them drop back helplessly. 'You guys should sign me up too. I mean it, Leon. I could be useful. And it would sure beat sitting around here and wiping the dust off the guidebooks.'

Anawak didn't feel comfortable about being so secretive. The role didn't suit him. He'd kept quiet about his own life for so many years that any kind of secrecy was beginning to get on his nerves. It occurred to him to tell them the truth, but then he remembered the look in Li's eyes. She always seemed friendly and supportive, yet Anawak sensed that she'd be seriously angry if she found out.

He glanced around the office. All of a sudden he realised how distant the Station had become in the short time he'd been away. This wasn't his life any more. So much had changed since he'd patched things up with Greywolf. He felt as if something decisive was about to happen; something that would turn his life upside-down. It was like being a kid on a roller-coaster – it had started moving, and he couldn't get out. The fear and horror were tinged with an indescribable sense of elation and expectation. The Station had been a kind of wall around him, but now he felt as though he was in the open and everything was bearing down on him with an intensity he wasn't accustomed to – too loud and too bright.

'Well, you're going to have to keep on dusting those guidebooks,' he said. 'You know as well as I do that your place is here, not with a bunch of scientists who'd never let you get a word in edgeways. Besides, Davie would be lost without you.'

'Was that supposed to be motivating?' Shoemaker asked.

'Why should I have to motivate *you*? I'm the one who's been told to keep my mouth shut and not talk to my friends. Why don't you try to motivate *me*?'

Shoemaker twisted the beer can in his hands. Then he grinned. 'How long can you stay?'

'As long as I like,' said Anawak. 'They're treating us like kings. We've got our own private helicopter service, day and night. I only have to call, and they'll be here to pick me up.'

'You're getting the full royal treatment, huh?'

'Well, they do expect us to work for it. In fact, strictly speaking, I should be working right now, in Nanaimo or at the aquarium or wherever – but I wanted to see you.'

'You can work here too, if you have to. OK, I'll motivate you. Come round to dinner tonight. You'll have a big fat steak to look forward to, and I'll fry it myself. It'll taste like pure heaven.'

'Sounds good,' said Delaware. 'What time?'

Shoemaker gave her a funny look. 'I'm sure I'll have room for *one* extra,' he said.

Delaware frowned. Anawak wondered what was going on, but promised Shoemaker he'd be there at seven. It was time for them to get moving. Shoemaker headed over to Ucluelet for a meeting with Davie, while Anawak set off down the high street in the direction of his boat, glad to have Delaware to talk to. She might be a pain in the butt but, somehow, he'd missed her.

'What was all that about?' he asked.

'What?'

'You know, about dinner tonight. I got the impression that Tom wasn't too keen on you bringing a friend.'

She fiddled with a strand of hair and scratched her nose. 'I guess there've been a few changes since you went away. I mean, life's full of surprises, isn't it? Sometimes you can't even believe it yourself.'

Anawak stopped in his tracks. 'Go on, then.'

'Well, the day you went to Vancouver – you disappeared overnight and never came back! No one knew where you were, and a few people got worried. And one of those people was, uh . . . Jack. So Jack called me up – well, actually, he wanted to talk to you, but you weren't there, and so . . .'

'Jack?' asked Anawak.

'Yes.'

'Greywolf? Jack O'Bannon?'

'He said you'd had a chat,' Delaware continued hastily. 'And I guess it must have been a positive chat. Or, at least, he was pleased about it, and he just wanted to, um, talk to you some more . . .' She looked him in the eye. 'It *was* a good chat, wasn't it?'

'Well, what if it wasn't?'

'That would be a bit awkward because, you see . . .'

'OK, fine. Jack and I had a good chat. All right? If you've finished tying yourself in knots, maybe you could get to the point.'

'We're going out,' she said quickly.

Anawak's mouth opened and closed again.

'He drove up to Tofino – I'd given him my number because I thought he was kind of cool . . . I mean, well, you know I always had a kind of sympathy for his point of view, and . . .'

Anawak tried to stay serious. 'A kind of sympathy. Well, yes, of course.'

'So he came over. And we had a drink at Schooners, and then we went down to the jetty. He told me all kinds of things about himself, and I told him a bit about myself. And you know how it is – we talked and talked and then . . . out of the blue . . . Well, you can guess the rest.'

Anawak grinned. 'And Shoemaker isn't happy.'

'He *hates* Jack!'

'I know. And you can't blame him either. Just because Greywolf has taken a liking to us – well, you in particular – doesn't change the fact that he behaved like an asshole. I mean, let's be honest here: he behaved like an asshole for years. He *is* an asshole.'

'No more than you are,' she blurted out.

Anawak nodded. Then in spite of all the wretchedness in the world, he laughed. He laughed about Delaware's awkward explanation, about his grudge against Greywolf, which had really been anger at the loss of a friend, and at himself. He laughed so hard that it hurt.

Delaware cocked her head. 'What's so funny?'

'You're right,' chuckled Anawak.

'What do you mean, I'm right? Are you feeling OK?'

His hilarity was edging towards hysterics, and he knew it, but there was nothing he could do. He couldn't remember the last time he'd laughed like this – if he ever had. 'Licia, you're priceless,' he said, between gasps. 'You're so darned right. We're assholes. Absolutely! And you're seeing Greywolf. Oh, man, I can't believe it.'

Her eyes narrowed. 'You're laughing at me.'

'No, no, I'm not,' he spluttered.

'Oh, yes, you are.'

'I swear I'm not. It's just—' Suddenly he thought of something and his laughter dried up. 'Where's Jack at the moment?'

'I don't know.' She shrugged. 'At home, maybe.'

'Jack's never at home. I thought you two were together now?'

466

'For God's sake, Leon, we haven't got married. We're just having a bit of fun. I don't keep tabs on him.'

'No,' murmured Anawak. 'He wouldn't like that anyway.'

'Do you want to speak to him?'

'Yes.' He put his hands on her shoulders. 'OK, listen to me. I've got a few things to sort out, but try to find him, would you, Licia? Before dinner, if you can. We don't want Shoemaker going off his food. Tell him I – I'd be pleased to see him. No, I'd love to see him right now.'

Delaware smiled uncertainly. 'OK ... Men are weird – I mean, honestly. And you two are just as weird as each other.'

Anawak went on board his boat, checked his post and dropped in at Schooners, where he got himself a coffee and talked to the locals. During his absence, two men had died. They'd defied the regulations and gone to sea in a canoe. In less than ten minutes, a pack of orcas had capsized them. The remains of one man had been washed ashore later, but there was no trace of the other, and no one felt like looking.

'And they don't give a damn about it,' said one of the fishermen, referring to the ferries, freighters, factory trawlers and warships. He was drinking his beer with the bitterness of one who was convinced he'd found the guilty party, and nothing was going to stop him laying the blame at their door. He looked at Anawak, as though expecting confirmation.

But that's where you're wrong, Anawak felt like saying. The big ships weren't faring any better. He kept quiet. He wasn't allowed to mention the other incidents, and the residents of Tofino saw only their corner of the world.

'They're probably laughing up their sleeves,' the old man grumbled. 'Those big fishing companies had the monopoly already. First they gobble up our stocks, and now they mop up what's left, while regular fishermen like me have to sit and watch.' He took a swig of his beer. 'We should shoot those damn whales. We need to show them who's boss.'

It was the universal refrain. Ever since he'd arrived in Tofino, Anawak had been confronted with the same demand: kill the whales. The frustrated fisherman had hit the nail on the head – the fishing grounds were only accessible to the largest factory trawlers, which gave ammunition to those who'd always agitated against the International Whaling Commission, fishing quotas and hunting bans.

Anawak paid for his coffee and went back to the station. The office was empty. He settled down behind the counter, switched on the computer and started to search the web for military applications of marine-mammal research. It was a tedious process. Back at the Chateau, they had access to all the information they needed, but the public network kept crashing, thanks to the problems with deep-sea cables.

He soon found the official website of the US Navy Marine Mammal Program. It couldn't tell him anything he didn't already know – every half-decent investigative journalist had written dozens of articles on the subject – but before long he had found information on a military programme in the former Soviet Union. During the Cold War, a large number of dolphins, sea-lions and belugas had been taught to find mines and retrieve lost torpedoes. According to the Internet, they'd been deployed to defend Soviet warships in the Black Sea. After the collapse of the Soviet Union, they had been transferred to an oceanarium in Sebastopol on the Crimean peninsula, where they'd performed tricks until their new owners ran out of cash for the vet bills and food. Some of the dolphins had ended up in therapy centres for children with autism. Others were sold to Iran, where the trail went dead, prompting the suspicion that their military career had continued elsewhere.

Marine mammals seemed to be making a comeback in strategic warfare. During the Cold War, the arms race had taken a new direction, with America and the Soviet Union each trying to create the most efficient sea-mammal fleet. After the dissolution of the USSR, the world was no safer; already the conflict between Israel and Palestine was spinning out of control and a new generation of terrorists was emerging, capable of sabotaging American warships. Underwater mines were being laid, projectiles went missing, and expensive weaponry sank to the bottom of the ocean and had to be retrieved. It was a job at which dolphins, sealions and belugas proved far more adept than any human or robot: tests showed that a dolphin could find a mine twelve times faster than a diver. Sealions at naval bases in Charleston and San Diego had a ninety-five per cent success rate at detecting torpedoes. Humans operating underwater couldn't see where they were going and had to spend hours in a decompression chamber afterwards, but marine mammals were working in their element. Sea-lions had good vision even when the light was weak. Dolphins could navigate in total darkness by using sonar, giving off a volley of clicks, whose echo they measured with

468

amazing precision to detect the location and shape of any object. Marine mammals could dive dozens of times a day to depths of several hundred metres without tiring. Millions of dollars' worth of divers, vessels, crews and equipment could be replaced by a small fleet of dolphins. And the animals nearly always came back. In thirty years, the US Navy had lost just seven dolphins.

The American marine-mammal training programme was still going strong and there were indications that animals were being used again in Russia for military purposes. The Indian Army had begun a breeding and training programme. Similar initiatives had been launched in the Middle East.

Did that mean Vanderbilt was right?

Anawak was convinced that scouring the depths of the web would turn up details that went unmentioned on the US Navy's website. It wasn't the first time he'd heard of military attempts to subjugate whales and dolphins to full human control. The programme was based on neural research of the kind conducted by John Lilly. Armed forces all over the world were interested in echo-location, a sonar system that outperformed anything man had invented and that still hadn't been fully understood. There were indications that experiments had taken place in recent years that went beyond the bounds of what was publicly acceptable.

But the web refused to tell him anything. For three full hours it maintained its silence until Anawak was on the point of giving up. His eyes hurt, and his enthusiasm and concentration had sunk so low that he almost missed the short article by *Earth Island Journal* when it appeared on the screen: '*Did US Navy Order Dolphin Deaths?*' The quarterly journal was published by Earth Island Institute, an environmental organisation committed to bringing new ideas to the conservation movement. It ran a variety of campaigns. The journal's staff were heavily involved in the climate debate and had uncovered some serious environmental scandals. A large part of their work was focused on preserving life in the oceans and protecting whales.

The article referred back to an incident that had occurred in the early 1990s when sixteen dead dolphins had been washed ashore in the French Mediterranean. The corpses were all marked with the same mysterious wound – a fist-sized hole on the underside of the neck, through which the lower cranium was exposed. At the time, investigators were unable to explain the presence of the marks, but there was no doubt that the injuries had caused the dolphins' deaths. The episode had taken place against the backdrop of the first crisis in the Gulf, when fleets of American warships were crossing the Mediterranean. The *Earth Island* article suggested a link to a classified programme of experiments that was rumoured to have been carried out by the US Navy at around the same time. By all accounts, the experiments had failed to achieve their expected success, forcing those involved to conceal the programme's existence. 'Something had gone badly wrong,' an expert had told the journal.

Anawak printed the article and searched through the journal's archive, hoping to find more leads. He was so immersed in what he was doing that he barely heard the Station door opening. It was only when a shadow fell over the screen that he looked up.

'I heard you wanted to talk to me,' said Greywolf.

His suede outfit was as greasy and scruffy as ever, but his hair was tied back in a long shiny plait. His teeth and eyes glinted. It was only a few days since Anawak had last spoken to him, but suddenly he saw Greywolf through different eyes. He exuded strength, charisma and natural charm. No wonder Delaware had fallen for him. 'I thought you were in Ucluelet,' he said.

'I was.' Greywolf pulled up a chair. It creaked as he sat down. 'Licia said you needed me.'

'Needed you?' Anawak smiled. 'I said it would be good to see you.'

'Same difference. Well, I'm here now.'

'How're things?'

'A drink would improve them.'

Anawak went over to the fridge, pulled out a beer and a Coke, and put them on the counter. Greywolf drank half of the Heineken in a single gulp.

'Did I call you away from anything important?'

'Nothing worth mentioning. I was fishing with a few rich pricks from Beverly Hills. All the jerks from your whale-watching have come over to my side. It seems no one's afraid of being attacked by a trout, so I branched out into angling. I'm doing fishing tours of our beloved island's lakes and rivers.'

'I see your attitude to whale-watching hasn't changed.'

'Why should it? I'm not going to cause you any trouble, though.'

'Why, thank you,' said Anawak, sarcastically. 'But right now it wouldn't much matter. I mean, it's pretty handy that you're still on your mission to get vengeance for nature. Tell me again what you used to do for the navy.'

Greywolf looked at him blankly. 'You know what I did.'

'Well, tell me again.'

'I was a dolphin-handler. We trained dolphins for military purposes.'

'In San Diego?'

'Yes, among other places.'

'And you were pensioned off because of a heart defect or whatever. Honourably discharged.'

'Exactly,' said Greywolf.

'That's not true, Jack. You weren't discharged. You walked.'

Greywolf set down the can almost cautiously on the counter. 'Where did you hear that bullshit?'

'The files at the Space and Naval Warfare Systems Center in San Diego seemed pretty clear to me,' said Anawak. 'Just so you know I'm in the picture: SSC San Diego took over from the Naval Command, Control and Ocean Surveillance Center, also of Point Loma, San Diego. The funding came from an organisation that now finances the US Navy's Marine Mammal Program. Each of those organisations is always mentioned in any account of marine-mammal training, and there's always the implication that they were involved in dubious experiments that allegedly never took place.' Anawak decided to call Greywolf's bluff. 'Experiments that were conducted in Point Loma, where you were stationed.'

Greywolf watched him warily as he paced round the room. 'Why are you telling me this crap?'

'The current research programme in San Diego looks at dolphin feeding habits, hunting, communication, training potential, possible ways of returning dolphins to the wild, and so on. But what really interests the military is the brain. Dolphin brains have fascinated the navy since the sixties, but around the time of the first Gulf War there was an upsurge of interest. You'd signed up a few years previously. By the time you left, you were a lieutenant, responsible for MK6 and MK7, two out of a total of four dolphin fleets.'

Greywolf frowned. 'So what? Haven't you got other things to worry about in your committee? Like Europe, for example.'

'One more step up the ladder, and you'd have been in charge of the entire dolphin programme. But you quit.'

'I didn't quit. They discharged me.'

Anawak shook his head. 'Jack, I've been given a few privileges lately, and that includes access to sources that are one hundred per cent reliable. You left of your own accord, and I'd like to know why.'

He picked up the *Earth Island* article and passed it to Greywolf, who glanced at it and put it down.

For a while there was silence.

'Jack,' said Anawak, softly, 'you were right. I *am* pleased to see you, but I do need your help.'

Greywolf didn't respond.

'Tell me what happened back then. Why did you leave?'

Greywolf leaned back and crossed his hands behind his head. 'Why do you want to know?'

'Because there's a chance we'll be able to figure out what's happened to our whales.'

'They're not your whales, Leon – or your dolphins either. You don't own them. Do you really want to know what's wrong with them? They're fighting back. It's payback time. We treated them like our playthings, hurt them, abused them, gawked at them and they're fed up with us.'

'You don't really believe they're doing this of their own free will?'

Greywolf shook his head. 'I'm not interested in *why* they do stuff. We shouldn't have taken such an interest in the first place. I don't want to understand them, Leon. I just want them to be left in peace.'

'Jack,' Anawak said slowly, 'they're being forced to behave like this.'

'That's bull. Who the hell—'

'They're being forced! I've got proof. I'm not even supposed to tell you this much, but I need your help. You want to stop them suffering, well, go on, then. They're suffering more than you could imagine—'

'Than I can imagine?' Greywolf was on his feet. 'What the hell do you know about their suffering? You don't know a darned thing.'

'Then tell me.'

'I—' He seemed to be fighting an inner battle. Then he relaxed. 'Come with me,' he said. 'We're going for a walk.'

*　　*　　*

For a while they strolled along in silence. Greywolf took a path through the forest and down to the sea. A rickety jetty led away from the shore, looking out across the austere beauty of the bay. Greywolf walked along the ramshackle planks and sat down, legs dangling over the edge. Anawak followed him. All that could be seen of Tofino were a few houses on stilts peeping out beyond the headland to the right and the Station on the wharf. They gazed up at the mountains, resplendent in the late-afternoon sun.

'There are a few things your sources didn't tell you,' Greywolf said finally. 'Officially there were four fleets of marine mammals: MK4 through to MK7. But there was a fifth in existence too, known as MKO. The navy calls them systems, not fleets, by the way. Each system is entrusted with a particular set of operational activities. The systems' centre is in San Diego, true, but I spent most of my time in Coronado, California, where the majority of the animals are trained. They're cared for in their natural habitat – creeks and ocean pens. And they have a pretty decent life there: they're well fed and they get excellent medical care – which is more than you can say for most people.'

'So you were in charge of this fifth system.'

'No, it wasn't like that. MKO is different. A regular system is made up of four to eight mammals with a specific objective. MK4, for instance, is assigned to finding mines on the seabed and marking their location. It's a dolphin-only system, and the animals are also trained to alert their handlers to the presence of saboteurs. MK5 is a sealion system. MK6 and MK7 are also used for mine-hunting, but their main purpose is to guard naval facilities against enemy divers.'

'By attacking them?'

'By nudging up against them. They affix a coiled rope to the suit of the diver, which connects the intruder to a float. The float is linked to a strobe, so it's easy to determine the diver's position, and the guys can take care of the rest. It works the same way with mine-sweeping. The dolphin alerts its handler as soon as it finds the mine. In some cases it dives down with a rope and a magnet – the magnet stays on the mine, and the end of the rope is returned to the boat. Provided the mine isn't anchored too firmly, it only takes a tug on the rope to get the job over and done with. You know, killer whales and belugas can even retrieve torpedoes from a depth of one kilometre. It's pretty darned impressive. What you have to realise is that mine-hunting is a dangerous business for humans. First, there's the risk of the thing exploding in your face, but worse, nine times out of ten you're searching the seabed at the heart of the conflict, right next to the shore – you get fired at all the time.'

'But don't the mines kill the dolphins?'

'According to the navy, no dolphin has ever been killed by a mine. In fact, a few have, but it's relatively rare. At any rate, when I started out, I didn't have anything to do with MKO, and I dismissed the stories as rumours. You see, MKO isn't a system as such: it's the codename for a series of programmes and experiments that take place in different locations with a constant stream of new animals. MKO mammals never come into contact with other systems, although members of the regular systems are sometimes recruited for MKO. That's the last anyone hears of them.' Greywolf paused. 'I was a good handler. MK6 was my first system. We participated in every major manoeuvre. In 1990 I took over MK7 as well. Eventually someone decided that maybe I should be told a bit more.'

'About MKO.'

'Naturally I knew all about the navy's first big dolphin-success story – Vietnam in the early seventies. Dolphins were used to guard the harbours in Cam-ranh Bay and intercept Vietcong frogmen on sabotage missions. That's the first thing they tell you at MMS, and they're pretty damn proud of it. What they don't tell you are the details. Things like the Swimmer Nullification Program – you can bet you won't hear about that. You see, it wasn't your regular dolphin operation. Those animals were trained to tug at divers' masks and flippers and disconnect their air-supply. Oh, and to make things really brutal, they had lance-like knives on their beaks and fins. Some even had harpoons strapped to their backs. They weren't dolphins any more – they were killing machines. But that was harmless, compared to what came next. The navy strapped hypo-dermic needles to their beaks and the dolphins were ordered to ram the divers. The syringes contained carbon dioxide compressed at 3000 psi, which coursed through the divers' bodies and expanded. The victims exploded. Our animals killed over forty Vietcong and two of our own guys by mistake.'

Anawak could feel his stomach cramping.

'The same thing happened at the end of the eighties in Bahrain,' Greywolf continued. 'That was my first time on front-line duty. My system did exactly what was expected of it, and I still knew nothing about MKO. I had no idea that they were parachuting dolphins into enemy territory. Some were dropped from a height of three kilometres, and not all survived. Others were pushed out of helicopters without a parachute from a height of twenty metres. Dolphins were being used to attach mines to enemy warships and subs. If things looked risky, the charges would be detonated as soon as the creatures were in range. I should have quit when they told me all about it but the navy was my home. I was happy there. I'm not asking you to understand, but it's the truth.'

Anawak was silent. He understood only too well.

'So I took comfort in the fact that I was one of the good guys. But the men at the top had made up their minds that my talents could be put to better use on MKO. According to the bad guys, I was pretty damn good at handling animals,' Greywolf spat. 'And the sonofabitches were right. I was good. Good, but stupid. Instead of telling them where they could stick their MKO, I said I'd help out. War was like that, I told myself. People are always dying in combat – they tread on a mine, get shot or burnt to death – so why make a fuss about a few dead dolphins? They sent me to San Diego where they were researching ways to make orcas carry nuclear weapons . . .'

'Carry *what?*'

'I stopped being surprised by this stuff a long time ago. They wanted whales to carry nuclear warheads. The weapons weigh up to seven tonnes, but you can train a fully grown orca to drag them for miles, right into enemy waters. Stopping a nuclear orca is virtually impossible. I don't know what stage they're at now, but I figure they must have got it licked – back then they were still running tests. And that was how I came to witness another kind of experiment. The navy likes to show reporters video clips of exercises: the dolphin swims off with a live mine, but instead of dumping it on the Russians and blowing the hell out of them, it comes back smiling with the mine between its teeth. The footage is designed to dispel any rumours that killer dolphins exist. Dolphins *have* been known to return with live mines, but it's practically unheard of. Besides, if it all goes wrong, it only costs the navy one vessel and three men, and that's a risk they're willing to take. They kept experimenting.' Greywolf paused. 'The trouble comes if you lose a nuclear whale. If one of those babies comes back with a primed bomb in its jaws, you're in trouble. The navy can send out as many orcas as it likes, but it needs to be sure that they won't get any funny ideas. And the best way to avoid that is to ban ideas altogether.'

'John Lilly,' muttered Anawak.

'What?'

'He was a scientist. Carried out brain experiments on dolphins in the sixties.'

'Yeah, I remember they talked about it,' Greywolf said. 'In any case, it was in San Diego that I saw them cracking open dolphins' skulls. That was in 1989. They used a hammer and chisel to make holes in the top of their heads. The animals were fully conscious, so it took a gang of strong guys to pin them down. They kept trying to leap off the table. It wasn't because of the pain, they kept telling me – the dolphins just didn't like the sound of hammering in their ears. The procedure was supposedly much less traumatic than it seemed. At any rate, they shoved electrodes through the holes to stimulate the brain using currents.'

'That's exactly what Lilly did,' Anawak interrupted in excitement. 'He was trying to create a map of the brain.'

'The navy has plenty of those, believe you me,' Greywolf said bitterly. 'It made me sick, but I kept my mouth shut. Next they showed me a dolphin. It was swimming in a tank with a kind of harness round its neck. The contraption was fitted with electrodes that pushed through the flesh. They'd found a way of steering the dolphin via electric signals. I mean, it was pretty amazing, to give them their due. They had it swimming left, right, then leaping clean out of the water. They could switch on its aggression and make it attack. They could even trigger its flight mechanism or induce calm. It didn't matter whether the animal would have wanted to participate. It was robbed of its will. It may as well have been a remote-controlled car or a wind-up toy. Well, they were excited, of course. It looked as though they'd made a breakthrough. So while the research team in San Diego continued to work on nuclear whales, we set off to the Gulf in 1991 with two dozen clockwork dolphins. I just went along with it. I'm not the quiet sort by nature, but for once I kept my mouth shut. It was none of my business, I kept telling myself. In the meantime, my dolphins looked for mines and were rewarded with food and attention. Then they started pressurising me to get actively involved in MKO. Somehow I managed to buy myself some thinking time – unpopular in the navy because you're not supposed to think. By that time we were in the Strait of Gibraltar, and we'd started to trial the technology at sea. At first it all went smoothly, but then we ran into problems. The control harnesses had worked perfectly in the laboratories and tanks, but in the open water the dolphins were subject to all kinds of stimuli. We started to get more misses than hits. It was obvious that it didn't work in the wild – or not in the way they'd expected. By now the dolphins were compromising our safety, and it was too late to take them back to the States. On the other hand, no one liked the idea of them swimming around in the Gulf so in the end we stopped off in France. The idea was to consult a French institute where experts were working on MKO. We don't usually get too friendly with the French, but they know a lot about the oceans so an alliance had been formed. We thought maybe they could help us. A man called René Guy Busnel was introduced to us as the head of the venerable Laboratoire d'Acoustique Animale. He promised to look into the problem, and took us on a tour of his splendid facility. First stop was a mutilated dolphin wedged into a vice. There was a knife the size of my arm sticking out of its back. I never did ask why. They gave us a card from the institute with their names signed in dolphin blood. To them it was all a big joke.'

Greywolf sighed.

'Busnel gave a long spiel about neural research and came to the conclusion that the procedure was flawed. There was evidently some critical factor that had been overlooked or misjudged. Back on board we held council and the decision was taken to get rid of the animals. We released them into the water. Then, when they were a few hundred metres away from the boat, someone pushed the button. The electrode-harness contained explosives to stop the technology falling into the wrong hands. The charge was only small, but it was enough to blast away the equipment. The animals died. We continued on our way.'

Greywolf chewed his lip. Then he looked up at Anawak. 'So there you have it: your Earth Island dolphins. The animals that washed up in France.'

'And after that you . . .'

'I told them I'd had enough. They tried talking me round, but I'd made up my mind. Of course, they didn't like the idea of one of their best dolphin-handlers quitting for undisclosed reasons – that kind of thing always attracts the attention of the press. So we talked, and in the end we came to an agreement. I got some cash, and they discharged me on the grounds of ill-health. I was a combat diver, you see, and you can't do that with a heart defect. No one asks awkward questions if they think there's something wrong with you. So they let me go.'

Anawak was gazing out across the bay.

'I'm not a scientist like you,' Greywolf said softly, 'I understand a bit about dolphins and how to handle them, but neurology means nothing to me. I can't stand to see anyone getting too interested in whales or dolphins. It winds me up just to see them taking photos. I can't help it.'

'Shoemaker thinks you're still mad at us.'

Greywolf shook his head. 'For a while I thought whale-watching was OK, but I couldn't handle it. I got myself thrown out – I made you guys do the hard part for me.'

Anawak rested his chin on his hands. It all looked so beautiful – the bay, the mountains, the island. 'Jack,' he said, 'you're going to have to revise your opinions. It's happening again. Those whales aren't taking revenge. They're under someone's control. Someone's busy with their very own MKO. Your navy stuff is nothing compared to this.'

In the end they left the jetty and walked in silence through the woods towards Tofino. Greywolf stopped outside Davie's Whaling Station. 'Just before I quit, I heard the nuclear whale programme had taken a big leap forward. They mentioned a name. It was something to do with neurology and neural network computers. They said that to exercise full control over the animals you needed to know about Professor Kurzweil. Maybe it's nothing, but I just thought I'd tell you.'

Chateau Whistler, Canada

It was early evening when Weaver knocked on Johanson's door. She tried the handle, but the room was locked.

She knew that he was back from Nanaimo. So she took the elevator to the lobby and found him in the bar, bent over some diagrams with the Geomar scientist and Stanley Frost.

'Hi.' Weaver walked over to them. 'Any progress?'

'We're stumped,' said Bohrmann. 'Still too many unknowns.'

'Hey, we'll get there in the end,' growled Frost. 'God doesn't play dice.'

'That's what Einstein said,' objected Johanson. 'And he was wrong.'

'I'm telling you, *God does not play dice!*'

478

She tapped Johanson on the shoulder. 'Apologies for the interruption, but could we have a quick chat?'

Johanson hesitated. 'Right now? We haven't finished with Stan's scenario yet. It's pretty strong stuff.'

'Sorry.'

'Why don't you join us?'

'This'll only take a moment. Can't they do without you for a second?' She smiled at the others. 'And then I'll join you, I promise. You can show me as many simulations as you like, and I'll bug you with comments.'

'Sounds good to me,' grinned Frost.

'Which way now?' asked Johanson, as they headed away from the table.

'The lobby?'

'Is it important?'

'Important doesn't begin to cover it.'

'OK.'

They went outside. The sun was low in the sky, and as it set, it bathed the Chateau and the snowy peaks of the Rockies in shades of red. A helicopter was perched on the forecourt, like an enormous gnat. They strolled in the direction of Whistler village. Suddenly Weaver felt embarrassed. The others were probably thinking that she and Johanson shared a secret, but in fact she just wanted his advice. It was up to him when he decided to share his theory with the committee but to make that decision he needed to hear her news.

'How was it in Nanaimo?'

'Pretty scary.'

'I heard killer crabs have invaded Long Island.'

'Crabs packed with killer algae,' said Johanson. 'Like in Europe, only more toxic. Oliviera, Fenwick and Rubin have started to analyse the poison.' He cleared his throat. 'I don't mean to be impatient, but I thought you had something to tell me.'

'I've been studying satellite data all day – comparing radar scans to multispectral images. I would have liked to see more data from Bauer's drifting profilers, but they've stopped transmitting. In any case, there's no real doubt. I'm guessing you know about oceanic gyres?'

'A little.'

'The sea level rises along the perimeter of a gyre. That applies to the Gulf Stream too – it's a boundary current. Bauer was worried

479

that a change was taking place. He couldn't locate the North Atlantic chimneys, where the water normally plummets. He was sure that something was disturbing the flow of the currents, but he couldn't say what.'

'And?'

She turned to him. 'I've done all the calculations, compared the data, checked it, recalculated, compared it again, rechecked it and started from the beginning. The sea level has dropped in the Gulf Stream.'

Johanson frowned. 'You mean . . .'

'The gyre has altered its rotation. If you look at the multispectral scans, it's clear that the temperature is dropping as well. There's no doubt about it, Sigur. We're looking at another ice age. The Gulf Stream has stopped flowing. Something's stopped it.'

Security Council

'It's a goddamn outrage. And someone's going to pay!'

The President was baying for blood. The first thing he'd done on arrival at Offutt Air Force Base was to convene a National Security Council meeting over a secure video link. The teleconference linked Washington, Offutt and the Chateau. The Vice-President was sitting in the White House Situation Room, together with the defense secretary, the defense secretary's deputy, the secretary of state, the assistant to the President for National Security Affairs, the head of the FBI and the chairman of the joint chiefs of staff. Across the Potomac River, deep in the windowless interior of the Counter-terrorist Center at CIA head-quarters, the director of Central Intelligence, the deputy director for Operations, and the director of the CTC and head of Special Forces, were also on screen. Commander-in-chief of the United States Central Command General Judith Li and deputy director of the CIA Jack Vanderbilt completed the line-up. They were sitting in Chateau Whistler's makeshift war room, watching the other members of the council on the long row of monitors. Most wore expressions of grim determination, though some seemed at a loss.

The President didn't bother to disguise his wrath. That afternoon the Vice-President had suggested that the White House chief of staff should convene an emergency cabinet, but the President was determined to chair plenary meetings of the Security Council himself. He had no intention of giving up the reins.

That suited Li perfectly.

Li's voice wasn't the most influential in the hierarchy of advisers. The highest-ranking military position was held by the chairman of the joint chiefs of staff, the President's principal military adviser. Next came his deputy. Every last idiot had a deputy. All the same, Li knew that the President appreciated her advice, which made her ecstatically proud. Her ambitions for the future were at the forefront of her mind. Even now, as she stared in concentration at the screens, she hadn't lost sight of her dream. For the moment she was only commander-in-chief, but soon she'd be chair of the joint chiefs of staff. The current chairman was on the brink of retirement, and it was no secret that his deputy was a dud. From there, she'd switch to politics and do a stint in the Pentagon or as secretary of state. And then she could run for President. If she got things right – which meant acting 100 per cent in the interests of America – her election was as good as guaranteed. The world was teetering on the abyss, but Li was on her way up.

'Our adversary is faceless,' the President was saying. 'Some of you are of the opinion that we should turn our attention to those parts of the world that could be the source of the threat. Others, I know, think there's nothing more to this business than a tragic build-up of natural disasters. For my part, I'm not interested in hearing any lectures. I want a consensus that will allow us to act. I want to see plans. I want to know how much it's going to cost and how long it's going to take.' His eyes narrowed. As always, the shrinking distance between his eyelids signalled growing fury and determination. 'Personally, I don't believe all that hooey about nature gone crazy. This is a war we're fighting. America is at war. So, what are we going to do?'

The chairman of the joint chiefs of staff remarked that wars weren't won on the defensive and that it was time to go on the attack. He sounded resolute. The defense secretary frowned. 'Attack *who?*' she asked.

'All I'm saying is that we need to attack,' said the chairman, authoritatively. 'Find the culprit and attack them.'

The Vice-President made it clear that he didn't believe any terrorist organisation had the resources to carry out such a large-scale offensive. 'If anyone's attacking us,' he said, 'it has to be a state. Or an alliance of states. A political bloc or something. Jack Vanderbilt was the first to voice his suspicions, and he may well be right. We need to focus on those countries or regions capable of organising an attack of this kind.'

'There are a number of countries with that capability,' said the director of the CIA.

The President nodded. Ever since the CIA chief had given him a long lecture on the eve of his presidency about the CIA's list of the good, the bad and the ugly, he had been convinced that the world was peopled with godless criminals planning the downfall of the USA. He wasn't entirely wrong. 'But can we be sure that it's one of our traditional enemies?' he asked all the same. 'After all, the whole free world is under attack, not just America.'

'The free world?' The defense secretary snorted. 'We *are* the free world. Europe is part of the American free world. The freedom of Japan is the freedom of the USA. The same goes for Canada and Australia . . . An attack on America's freedom is an attack on freedom worldwide.' There was a piece of paper in front of him, and he banged his hand on it. It contained his notes for the day. He believed that nothing was so complicated that it couldn't be summarised on a single sheet of paper. 'Just to remind you all,' he added, 'we've got access to biological weapons, and so has Israel. We're the good guys. Then there's South Africa, China, Russia and India – they're ugly. Finally, North Korea, Iran, Iraq, Syria, Libya, Egypt, Pakistan, Kazakhstan and Sudan are bad. And this is a biological attack. This is bad.'

'I thought chemical components were also involved,' said his deputy. 'Isn't that right?'

'Let's slow down here.' The director of the CIA gestured for quiet. 'Let's start with the assumption that a campaign of this kind would require a vast amount of cash and considerable effort. Chemical weapons are cheap and easy to make, but all that biological stuff swallows a lot of resources. And remember, we're not blind. Pakistan and India are working with us. We've trained over a hundred Pakistani secret agents for covert operations. Dozens of agents are working for the CIA in Afghanistan and India, and some have excellent contacts. That's a whole region you can strike off your list. We've got paramilitary troops in Sudan, working with the opposition. In South Africa some of our friends are government ministers. The fact is, there's been no indication that anything big is under way. Our priority is to find out where money has been changing hands and where suspicious activities have been noticed. We don't need an itemised list of world villains – we need to narrow the field.'

'As far as money is concerned,' said the director of the FBI, 'there isn't any.'

'Meaning?'

'The new measures on monitoring terrorist assets have allowed us to take a pretty good look at suspicious transactions. You can bet that if a large sum of money changes hands, the Treasury will know. We would have heard by now.'

'And have you?' asked Vanderbilt.

'Nothing. Not a peep from Africa, Asia or the Middle East. There's nothing to indicate that any state might be involved.'

Vanderbilt cleared his throat. 'They're hardly going to tell us about it,' he said. 'It won't make the headlines of the *Washington Post.*'

'Like I said, we've got no—'

'I'm sorry to disillusion you,' Vanderbilt cut in, 'but you can't seriously believe that someone who's capable of running riot in the North Sea and poisoning New York is going to show us his wallet?'

The President's eyes were slits. 'The world is changing,' he said. 'And that means we need to be able to see into everyone's wallet. Either those bastards are too smart or we're too stupid. But no matter how goddamn smart they are, it's our job to be smarter. Starting from now.' He turned towards the director of Counter-terrorism. 'So, how smart are we?'

The director shrugged. 'The latest warning came from India. It was about Pakistani jihadists trying to blow up the White House. The terrorists are known to us, and there isn't any danger. We were on to it before the Indians told us and we traced all of the financial transactions. The Global Response Center collects mounds of information on international terrorism every day. It's true, Mr President. Nothing happens without us getting wind of it.'

'And it's all quiet at the moment?'

'It's never quiet, but there's no sign of any serious planning or financial activity. Which isn't conclusive, I guess.'

The President's gaze shifted to the deputy director for Operations. 'I expect your team to step up its efforts,' he snapped. 'I don't care where your agents are posted or what backwater they're operating in, I'm not going to stand by and see American citizens killed, simply because someone hasn't done their homework.'

'Of course not, sir.'

'And in case any of you have forgotten, *we're being attacked*. We're at war! I need to know who we're fighting.'

'Well, take a look at the Middle East, then,' Vanderbilt called impatiently.

'We're doing that already,' Li said.

The fat man sighed. He didn't bother to turn; he knew Li didn't buy his theory.

'You can always punch yourself in the face to make it look as though you've been beaten,' said Li, 'but let's be realistic. It's all very well claiming that this is about hostile countries taking a swipe at America because they're intent on protecting their interests; but why would they hurt themselves? Sure, if it's us they're after, it would make sense to distract us by causing trouble elsewhere – but not on that scale.'

'That's not how we see it,' said the director of the CIA.

'I know. But I see it this way: we're not the main target. There's too much going on, and it's all too extreme. Just imagine the amount of effort it would involve – training thousands of animals, breeding millions of new organisms, triggering a tsunami in Europe, sabotaging the fish stocks, plaguing Australia and South America with jellyfish, and wrecking tankers . . . No one would stand to gain anything economically or politically. But there's no denying that it's happening – and whether Jack likes it or not, the Middle East isn't exempt. Those are the facts, and I'm not going to join in and pin the blame on the Arabs.'

'OK, so there've been a couple of minor shipping accidents in the Middle East,' growled Vanderbilt.

'They weren't exactly minor, Jack.'

'Maybe we're dealing with a megalomaniac,' suggested the secretary of state. 'A criminal mind.'

'That's more plausible,' said Li. 'An individual would be able to shift large amounts of money around and dabble in technology for ostensibly respectable purposes. If you ask me, though, we need to look at it this way – someone sends us a plague of worms, so we invent something to kill them, and so on.'

'What kind of measures have you taken so far?' asked the secretary of state.

'We've—' the defense secretary began.

'We've isolated New York,' Li interrupted. She didn't like other people taking the credit for her work. 'And I've just learned that the warnings about crabs in Washington have been confirmed. They've been sighted by surveillance drones. We're going to have to quarantine the city as well. The White House staff should follow the President's example and leave town for the duration of the crisis. I've ordered troops with flame-throwers to surround key coastal cities. In the meantime we're developing an antitoxin.'

'Any plans to use submersibles and dive robots?' enquired the CIA director.

'No. We can't release anything into the depths without it disappearing. We don't have any means of controlling things down there. ROVs, for example, are only connected via cables and, right now, scientists are lowering them into the water, and hauling up a bunch of frayed wires. The ROVs detect a blue glow, then the cables are cut. As for what's happening to the AUVs, it's impossible to say. Last week four Russian scientists set off in MIR submersibles. They were all rammed and sunk a thousand metres down.'

'So we're abandoning the field?'

'We're still trying to cull the worms. At the moment we're using drag nets to sweep the seabed. We're also deploying nets in strategic coastal areas to ward off marine life. It's another of our anti-invasion measures.'

'That's a little primitive, isn't it?'

'So are the methods of attack. In any event, we're about to start using sonar to get at the whales. We're going to deafen them with Surtass LFA. Someone's got control of the creatures, and it's high time we responded in kind. We'll turn up the volume till their eardrums explode. Then we'll see who's boss.'

'That sucks, Li.'

'If you've got a better idea, I'd love to hear it.'

No one said anything.

'How about satellite surveillance? Is that any help?' asked the President.

'Up to a point.' The deputy director for Operations shook his head. 'The army is accustomed to searching the jungle for camouflaged tanks.

There aren't many systems capable of identifying objects the size of a crab. OK, so there's KH-12 and the new generation of Keyhole satellites. We're also collaborating with the Europeans on Topex/Poseidon and SAR-Lupe – but they use radar, as does Lacrosse. It all comes down to a basic problem: we have to zoom in to detect small objects, which means we have to focus on a limited section of coast. Until we know where the next invasion is likely to happen, we're almost guaranteed to have our backs turned. General Li has suggested using drones to patrol the coastline, which makes sense, although even drones can't see everything. The NRO and the NSA are doing their best to come up with information. Maybe some of the transmissions we've intercepted will offer a few more clues. We're using every possible aspect of SIGINT.'

'Well, perhaps that's our problem,' the President said slowly. 'Maybe we should be focusing a bit more on HUMINT.'

Li repressed a smile. HUMINT was one of the President's personal hobbyhorses. In security jargon SIGINT stood for signals intelligence, which covered all forms of intelligence-gathering that revolved around the interception of transmissions. HUMINT was all intelligence gleaned through espionage – human intelligence. The President, who was a straightforward guy with no real grasp of technology, liked to look a person in the eye. Even though he commanded the most technologically advanced army in the world, he felt more comfortable being protected by spies crawling through undergrowth than by satellites.

'Put your guys to work,' he said. 'Some are too quick to let computer programs and service switching points do the job for them. I want less programming and more thinking.'

The director of the CIA pressed his fingertips together. 'Well,' he said, 'I guess we shouldn't pay too much attention to the Middle East theory, after all.'

Li glanced at Vanderbilt, who was staring rigidly ahead. 'I hope you haven't been too hasty, Jack,' she whispered.

'Save it, Li.'

She leaned forward. 'Maybe we could talk about something more positive?'

The President smiled. 'Sounds good. Fire away, Jude.'

'Sir, the present crisis won't go on for ever. It's up to us to think about what happens next. And in the end what really matters is who comes out on top. The world will look different by the time this is over. A number of regimes will have been destabilised – and in some cases we won't be sad to see them go. The world is indeed facing a terrible threat, but a crisis is also a chance. If we're unhappy with a particular regime, and something undermines it, maybe we can speed things along and make sure the right successor is in place.'

'Hmm.' The President was thinking.

After a moment's reflection, the secretary of state said, 'So the question isn't so much who started this war, but who's going to come out victorious?'

'Don't get me wrong. The civilised world will have to rally together against our invisible foe,' said Li. 'If the situation continues, our allies are going to look increasingly to the UN for guidance. That's fine for the moment. I'm not saying we should push ourselves forward, but we should be waiting in the wings, ready to offer our help. When it comes down to it, *we* need to win. And anyone who's ever threatened or opposed us should wind up on the side of the losers. The more we can influence the outcome of the situation, the clearer the divide between victors and losers.'

'That's a nice firm standpoint,' said the President.

There were a few nods of approval, with a hint of irritation. Li leaned back. She'd said enough. In fact, she'd said more than her position on the council warranted, but her words had made an impression. She'd alienated a few guys whose job it was to come up with that kind of stuff, but so what? She'd been well received in Offutt.

'OK,' said the President. 'We should keep that suggestion in mind, but we shouldn't lose sight of other options. The last thing we want is the rest of the world thinking we're intent on taking over. How are your scientists progressing, Jude?'

'In my opinion, sir, they're our biggest asset.'

'When can we see some results?'

'We're meeting tomorrow. Major Peak will be present as well. I've instructed him to leave New York – he can deal with the crisis from here.'

'It's time you addressed the nation,' said the Vice-President.

'Absolutely.' The President banged his fist on the table. 'Our communications team needs to rally the speechwriters. I want something frank, not *it'll-be-all-right-you'll-see*, but something that'll give them hope.'

'Any mention of a possible aggressor?'

'No. I want this handled as a natural disaster. We're not even sure yet where we stand, and besides, the public is anxious enough. We need to reassure them that we're doing everything in our power to protect them. And they need to believe that we have that power. That we're ready and prepared. That we can handle anything. America isn't merely a place of freedom, it's a place of safety. No matter what comes out of the ocean, America is safe. They need to believe that. And one more thing: I want you all to pray. It's God's country, and He'll be with us. He'll give us the power to emerge from this victorious.'

New York, USA

We can't handle it. That was the only thought in Peak's mind as he clambered into the helicopter. *We're not prepared for this. Nothing we can do will stem the horror.*

The helicopter lifted off from Wall Street heliport and headed northbound through the night air over Soho, Greenwich Village and Chelsea. The city sparkled with light, but you could see at a glance that things weren't right. Some streets were bathed in the harsh glare of floodlights, and the stream of traffic had stopped. New York was in the hands of the OEM and the army. Choppers were taking off and touching down all over the city and the harbour was closed. The only boats on the East River were military vessels.

They were powerless to help. The death toll kept rising, and there was nothing they could do to stop it. The OEM had published reams of regulations and recommendations, but the steady stream of warnings and drills had been in vain. Every household had been instructed to keep a canister of drinking water at the ready, in case of an emergency, but no-one was prepared. In any case, a safe supply of drinking water couldn't protect people against the toxins rising from drains or wafting up from washbasins, toilets and dishwashers. All Peak could do was herd those who were still in good health out of the danger zone and quarantine them in vast camps. New York's schools, churches and other public buildings now served as hospitals, and the belt of land surrounding the city was an enormous jailhouse.

He looked to the right. The fire was still blazing in the tunnel. The driver of a military tanker had failed to follow the protocol for securing his gas mask, and had lost consciousness at the wheel. He'd been part of a convoy. The accident had set off a chain reaction and dozens of vehicles had burst into flames. Right now the temperature down there was equivalent to the heat inside a volcano.

Peak berated himself for not having prevented the accident. It was obvious that the danger of contamination would be many times higher inside a tunnel than on the streets, where the toxins could disperse. But how could he be everywhere at once?

If there was anything Peak hated, it was the feeling of powerlessness.

And now it was Washington's turn.

'We can't handle it,' he'd told Li on the phone.

'We have to.'

They crossed the Hudson River and made for Hackensack airport, where a military chopper was waiting to take Peak to Vancouver. They left the lights of Manhattan behind them. Peak thought of the scientists' meeting scheduled for the following day. Would they make any headway? He wished they could at least find a drug that would put an end to the horror in New York, but something told him not to get his hopes up.

Peak leaned back and closed his eyes.

Chateau Whistler, Canada

Li was pleased with herself. In view of the impending Armageddon, it would have been more appropriate to feel anguished or shocked, but the day had been a resounding success. Vanderbilt had been forced on to the defensive, and the President had listened to her advice. After countless telephone calls she now knew all the latest on the apocalypse, and was waiting impatiently to talk to the defense secretary. The sonar offensive would be starting the next day, and she wanted to discuss the deployment of boats. The defense secretary was caught up in a meeting, and wouldn't be able to talk for another few minutes.

It was approaching two o'clock in the morning when she sat down at the piano to play some Schubert. The telephone rang. She jumped up to answer it. She'd been expecting the Pentagon, so she was thrown by the voice on the line. 'Dr Johanson! What can I do for you?'

'Have you got a moment?'

'Now?'

'I'd like to speak to you in private.'

'I'm afraid I'm busy. How about in an hour? I need to make some calls.'

'Aren't you curious?'

'Curious?'

'You said you thought I had a theory.'

'Come up to my suite.'

With a smile she replaced the receiver. It was exactly as she had expected. Johanson wasn't the type to use every last second of a deadline, and he was too well mannered to go back on his word. He had wanted to be the one to decide when he told her, and he'd chosen the middle of the night.

She called the Pentagon switchboard. 'Postpone my teleconference with the defense secretary by half an hour.' She changed her mind. 'Make that an hour.'

Johanson was bound to have plenty to say.

Vancouver Island

Anawak didn't have much of an appetite after Greywolf's explanations, but Shoemaker had excelled himself. He'd fried some steaks and concocted an impressive salad, topped with croutons and nuts. They ate on the veranda. Delaware was careful not to mention her budding relationship, and she was excellent company. She had an inexhaustible supply of jokes, and delivered even the corniest with perfect timing.

The evening was an oasis in a sea of misery.

During the Dark Ages, people had danced and caroused in the streets of Europe while the Black Death raged round them. Although there was no dancing or singing at Shoemaker's, they talked for several hours without a word about tsunamis, whales or killer algae. Shoemaker told anecdotes about the early days at the Station, and they enjoyed the balmy evening. Relaxing on the veranda, they gazed out over the dark waters of the bay.

Anawak left at two in the morning, but Delaware stayed behind. She and Shoemaker were deep in conversation about old movies and had just cracked open another bottle of wine. They were descending into tipsiness, so Anawak made his way through the night air to the station. He switched on the computer and went online.

Within minutes his search for Professor Kurzweil was rewarded.

As dawn broke, a picture began to emerge

12 May

Maybe, thought Johanson, this will be the turning-point. Or maybe they'll think I'm a crazy old fool.

He was standing on the little dais to the left of the screen. The projector was switched off. There'd been a few minutes' delay as they waited for Anawak, who'd stayed the night in Tofino, but now the delegates were assembled. The front row was occupied by Peak, Vanderbilt and Li. Peak had returned overnight from New York, and looked as though he'd left most of his energy there.

Addressing an audience was second nature to Johanson. He was used to lecturing students and speaking at conferences, occasionally adding his own insights and hypotheses to the standard set of facts. But for the most part standing at a lectern was the easiest thing in the world: you merely imparted the fruits of other people's research, and answered questions at the end.

Yet this morning he was experiencing the unfamiliar sensation of self-doubt. How on earth could he put across his theory without his audience laughing in his face? Li had conceded that he might be right, so he'd stayed up most of the night, drafting and redrafting his speech. Johanson had no illusions. He was only going to get one shot at this: either he won them over with a surprise attack, or they decided he was nuts.

He glanced at the top page of his print-out. He'd written a detailed introduction. Now, after three hours' sleep, it suddenly struck him as impenetrably complicated. He'd been satisfied with it in the early hours of the morning, when he was almost too exhausted to think, but now . . .

He laid aside his notes, and felt relieved of a burden. His self-assurance returned to him like a cavalry ready for battle, flags flying and trumpets blaring. He took a step forward and, once he was sure he had his audience's attention, he said, 'It's very simple, really. Dealing with the implications will be tricky, but the basic principle is logical and straightforward. We're not dealing with a series of natural disasters. And we're not doing battle with any terrorist organisation or rogue state. Not even evolution is to blame.' He paused. 'No. What we're experiencing is the fabled war of the worlds – a war between two worlds that we've always thought of as one because they're bound together. All this time we've been gazing upwards in anticipation of an alien species arriving from space, when intelligent life-forms have been with us all along, inhabiting part of the planet that we've never seriously attempted to explore. Two radically different systems of intelligent life coexist on the Earth, and they've done so peacefully until now. While one has been observing the development of the other since time immemorial, the other has no concept of the complexity of the underwater world – or, if you like, the alien universe sharing our globe. Outer space is on Earth, in the oceans. We've found our extra-terrestrials, and they don't come from faraway galaxies. They evolved at the bottom of the sea. Life in the water existed long before the first organisms appeared on land, and this species is likely to be far, far older than humanity. I can't tell you what these creatures look like, or how they live, think or communicate. But we're going to have to get used to the notion that we're not the only smart species on this planet. For decades we've been systematically destroying the habitat of another intelligent race – and now, ladies and gentlemen, these creatures seem justifiably irate.'

No one spoke.

Vanderbilt's heavy jowls began to tremble and his entire body shook, as though a peal of laughter was mounting inside him. His fleshy lips twitched and he opened his mouth.

'I can see how that might be possible,' said Li.

The deputy director of the CIA looked as though he'd been stabbed in the ribs. His mouth closed. Then he wheezed, 'You can't be serious.'

'Oh, yes, I can,' Li said calmly. 'I didn't say Dr Johanson was right, but we should at least hear him out. He must have some evidence to support his claims.'

'Thank you, General.' Johanson gave a little bow. 'I do.'

'Then please continue. Try to keep your explanation as succinct as possible so that we can start the debate right away.'

Johanson let his eyes rove round the room. Hardly anyone appeared openly dismissive. Most of the faces before him were frozen in surprise. Some looked fascinated, others disbelieving, and a few were impossible to read. Now he had to take the second step. He had to persuade them to assimilate his theory so that they could develop it on their own.

'Our main problem over the past few days and weeks,' he said, 'has lain in trying to connect the various phenomena. In fact, there wasn't any obvious connection until a jelly-like substance started to crop up. Sometimes it appeared in small quantities, sometimes in larger amounts, but always with the distinguishing characteristic that it disintegrated rapidly on contact with air. Unfortunately the discovery of the jelly only added to the mystery, given its presence in crustaceans, mussels *and* whales – three types of organism that could hardly be more different. Of course, it might have been some kind of fungus, a jellified version of rabies, an infectious disease like BSE or swine fever. But, if so, why would ships be disappearing or crabs transporting killer algae? There was no sign of the jelly on the worms that infested the slope. They were carrying a different kind of cargo – bacteria that break down hydrates and cause methane gas to rise. Hence the landslide and the tsunami. And what about the mutated species that have been emerging all over the world? Even fish have been behaving oddly. None of it adds up. In that respect, Jack Vanderbilt was right to discern an intelligent mind behind the chaos. But he overestimated our ability – no scientist knows anything like enough about marine ecology to be capable of manipulating it to that extent. People are fond of saying that we know more about space than we do about the oceans. It's perfectly true, but there's a simple reason why: we can't see or move as well in the water as we can in outer space. The Hubble telescope peers effortlessly into different galaxies, but the world's strongest floodlight only illuminates a dozen square metres of seabed. An astronaut in a spacesuit can move with almost total freedom, but even the most sophisticated divesuit won't stop you being crushed to death beyond a certain depth. AUVs and ROVs are only operational if the conditions are right. We don't have the physical constitution or the technology to deposit billions of worms on underwater hydrates, let alone the requisite knowledge to engineer them for a habitat that we barely understand. Besides, there are all the other phenomena: deep-sea cables being destroyed at the bottom of the ocean by forces other than the underwater slide; plagues of jellyfish and mussels rising from the abyssal plains. The simplest explanation would be to see these developments as part of a plan, but such a plan could only be the work of a species that knows the ocean as intimately as we do the land – a species that lives in the depths and plays the dominant role in that particular universe.'

'Have I understood you correctly?' Rubin asked excitedly. 'You're claiming that we share this planet with another intelligent race?'

'Yes.'

'If that's so,' said Peak, 'why haven't we heard of or seen them before?'

'Because they don't exist,' Vanderbilt muttered testily.

'Wrong,' said Johanson vigorously. 'I can think of at least three good reasons why we've never come across them. First, there's the phenomenon of the invisible fish.'

'The *what?*'

'Most deep-sea creatures can't *see* any better than we can, but they've refined their other senses. Their bodies respond to the slightest change in pressure. Sound waves are detected over hundreds, if not thousands of kilometres. No submersible could ever get in viewing range without attracting their attention. In theory, millions of fish could be living in a particular region but if they stuck to the shadows, we'd never find out. If that's true of ordinary fish, how are we supposed to spot intelligent beings? If they don't want us to see them, *they won't let us*! Second, we have no idea what these creatures might look like. So far, we've filmed a few peculiar phenomena – a blue cloud, flashes that look a bit like lightning, and an odd thing on the Norwegian continental slope. Are those signs of alien intelligence? And what about the jelly? Or the noises that Murray Shankar can't identify? And, finally, the third reason. At one time we were convinced that life was only viable in the upper layers of the ocean, where sunlight penetrates. Now we know that the whole ocean is teeming with life, even at depths of eleven thousand metres. Many organisms don't need to seek out shallower water. In fact, most wouldn't survive the transition – the water temperature would be too high, the pressure too low, and they wouldn't find their usual food. We, on the other hand, are well acquainted with the surface of the water, but only a handful of robots and scientists in bulky submersibles have ever visited the depths. Imagine an alien spaceship lowering cameras to Earth. Each captures only a few square metres at a time. The first zooms in on the Kalahari desert. The second takes a snap of the Mongolian steppes. A third is lowered over Antarctica, and the fourth hovers over a city and films just a few square metres of grass and a dog peeing up against a tree. What impression would the aliens have? No sign of intelligent life, though primitive life-forms are sporadically present.'

'They'd have to have some kind of technology to accomplish all this,' said Oliviera.

'I've been thinking about that,' said Johanson. 'It strikes me that there's an alternative to technology as we know it. We use materials to create our equipment and tools – houses, vehicles, radios, clothes and so on. But sea water is far more aggressive than air. Only one thing matters in the depths: optimal adaptation. Living organisms are usually fantastically well adapted, so you could imagine a technology based entirely on biology. If we're assuming this race is highly intelligent, then it seems reasonable to suppose that it's also creative and has a detailed knowledge of the biology of marine organisms. I mean, we're doing it too, if you think about it. For thousands of years we've been using other life-forms as part of our inventions. Hannibal crossed the Alps with a herd of living trucks. Horses are a kind of sentient motorbike. We've been training animals throughout the course of history, but now we're able to genetically modify them as well. We're already cloning sheep. What if we take the idea a bit further? What if we imagine a race that has based its culture and technology entirely on biology? They'd simply breed whatever they need, whether for daily life, transport – or warfare.'

'God help us,' groaned Vanderbilt.

'Of course, humans use living organisms for warfare too,' continued Johanson, as if he hadn't heard. 'Scientists are growing strains of Ebola and other viruses, and experimenting with smallpox. For the moment, the conventional method is to cram them into warheads, but it's not the most straightforward way of doing things, and even satellite-guided missiles don't always hit their mark. Dispatching a pack of diseased dogs might be more effective. Or you could use a battalion of birds – or insects, for that matter. Just imagine trying to defend yourself against a swarm of virus-infested flies or an army of infected ants . . . Or against millions of crabs, transporting killer algae.' He paused. 'The worms on the continental slopes were genetically engineered. It's not surprising that we'd never seen them before. They didn't exist. Their sole purpose is to convey bacteria into the ice. They're annelid cruise missiles, if you like – biological weapons developed by a race of beings whose entire culture is based on manipulating organic life. It gives us an explanation for all the various mutations. In some cases, organisms have been modified only slightly, while others are new creations. Take the jelly-like tissue. It's a highly versatile biological product, but it certainly wasn't arrived at via standard evolution. Like the worms, it's there for a purpose – to control other living creatures by invading their neural networks. It's somehow affecting the behaviour of live whales. The crabs and lobsters are a slightly different story. The jelly steers their move-ments, but they're not actually alive. They're empty shells with in-complete nervous systems – organic spacesuits for the journey on to land.'

'This jelly,' said Rubin, 'couldn't a scientist have developed it instead?'

'Unlikely.' Anawak joined the discussion. 'Dr Johanson's explanation makes more sense. If this were a human project, what would be the point of attacking via the depths? That's a pretty big detour.'

'Because killer algae are found in the sea.'

'Why use killer algae in the first place? Anyone capable of creating a strain of algae more toxic than *Pfiesteria* would surely be able to find some pathogen that doesn't live in water. Why breed crabs if ants, birds or rats would do the job?'

'Rats can't trigger a tsunami.'

'That jelly was concocted in a lab,' insisted Vanderbilt. 'It's a synthetic substance, which—'

'I don't buy it,' interrupted Anawak. 'Not even the navy would be capable of that, and from what I've heard, it's pretty darned good at messing with animals.'

Vanderbilt's head was shaking so fast that he looked as if he was having a convulsion.

'What are you trying to say?'

'I'm referring to a programme of experiments codenamed MKO.'

'Never heard of it.'

'Well, for years now the navy has been experimenting with dolphins and other marine mammals, trying to manipulate their behaviour by putting electrodes in their—'

'Bullshit.'

'It didn't work, though, or at least not in the way they'd intended, so now they're using Ray Kurzweil's ideas to—'

'Kurzweil?'

'A leading authority on artificial intelligence,' Fenwick explained. Suddenly he had become animated. 'He came up with a vision of the future that pushed back the boundaries of current neural research. If you want to establish how much we know about the workings of the brain . . . in fact, better still, if you want to understand how much another intelligent species might know about the brain, you should study his work.' Fenwick was flushed with excitement. 'That's it! Kurzweil's neural network computer! You could really be on to something.'

'I'm sorry,' said Vanderbilt, 'but I have no idea what you're talking about.'

'Really?' Li smirked. 'I thought the CIA took a professional interest in brainwashing.'

Vanderbilt snorted. 'Can anyone tell me what he's talking about? Because I'll be darned if I know. Is someone going to explain?'

'The neural network computer is a blueprint for creating a perfect replica of an individual brain,' said Oliviera. 'Our brains are made up of billions of nerve cells, or neurons. Each neuron is connected to countless others. They communicate using electrical pulses, allowing our brains to continually update, reorder and archive what we know, learn and feel. Every single second of our lives, even when we're asleep, our brains are being reconfigured. Modern scanning technology gives us pictures of the brain that are accurate to within one millimetre of detail. We can watch how the brain thinks and feels, and which neurons are activated when, for example, we kiss or experience pain or recall a past event.'

'The scans show which parts of the brain do what, so the navy knows where to place the electrical signals to achieve a particular response.' Anawak had taken over. 'But they aren't detailed enough. If you think of them as maps, you can only see objects in excess of fifty square metres. Kurzweil predicts that we'll soon have the ability to scan an entire brain, mapping every single synaptic connection and every neurotransmitter, and detailing the concentration of every chemical. We'll have a complete model of every cell.'

'Gee,' said Vanderbilt.

'And once you've gathered all that information,' said Oliviera, 'you'll be able to install the entire brain and all its functions in a computer, which would replicate that particular person's thought processes, memories and abilities. You'd have a kind of clone.'

Li raised her hand. 'I can assure you that MKO hasn't reached that stage,' she said. 'At the present time, Kurzweil's neural network computer remains just a vision.'

'Jude!' Vanderbilt whispered, aghast. 'What are you thinking? This stuff is classified – it's none of their business.'

'MKO is based purely on military necessity,' Li said calmly. 'If it didn't exist, we'd have to sacrifice human lives instead. We can't always choose our wars, as I'm sure you've realised. The programme is currently at an impasse, but I'm confident it's merely a temporary hitch. We're well on the way to creating artificial intelligence. In medicine, it won't be long before we can replace organs with microchips. Implants are already allowing blind people to regain some of their sight. Entirely new forms of intelligence will emerge.' She fixed her gaze on Anawak. 'That's what you're getting at, isn't it? All the evidence would seem to support the Middle East theory, if only humanity were as advanced as Kurzweil predicted. But we're not. This jelly does the job of a neural network computer, and no living scientist is capable of inventing it.'

'In practice, a neural network computer would be in control of every thought process,' said Anawak. 'Assuming that's how the jelly functions, it doesn't simply steer a creature, it becomes that creature. It becomes part of its brain. The cells of the substance assume the function of brain cells. They either add to the capacity of a brain—'

'Or they replace it,' chimed Oliviera. 'Leon's right. An organism like that can't come from any human lab.'

Johanson's heart was pounding as he listened. They were engaging with his theory. With every word that was spoken, his hypothesis gained weight. While the debate raged around him, he envisaged a biological computer that could copy every neuron in the brain.

Roche jumped to his feet. 'Perhaps you could explain one thing, Dr Johanson. How do you account for these underwater life-forms knowing so much about us? I dare say it's an impressive theory, but how could an inhabitant of the ocean depths obtain that kind of knowledge?'

Johanson saw Vanderbilt and Rubin nodding. 'That's quite straightforward,' he said. 'Whenever we dissect a fish, we do it in our world, not in the water. Why shouldn't these creatures find out about us in their world? Drownings happen all the time – and these beings are certainly capable of fetching more bodies, should they need them. Having said that, it's a valid point. How much do they *really* know about us? I first started to come round to the idea of an organised attack just before the shelf collapsed in Europe. Oddly enough, it never occurred to me that humans might have been responsible. The strategy seemed too outlandish. Wiping out large swathes of the infrastructure in northern Europe was a stroke of genius, and had serious consequences for humanity, but using whales to sink small craft strikes me as naïve. Poisonous jellies are never going to stop people plundering fish from the ocean. Shipping accidents cause a lot of damage, but I seriously doubt whether swarms of mutated organisms are capable of paralysing international trade. But it does make one thing clear: they know a lot about boats. They're familiar with anything that comes into direct contact with their habitat, but they're not so well informed about dry land. Dispatching killer algae in an army of crabs shows excellent military planning, but the first attempt, involving Brittany lobsters, wasn't as effective. They clearly hadn't reckoned with the pressure difference. The jelly was introduced into the lobsters in the depths – that is, in conditions of high pressure. Once it reached the surface, it expanded, and some of the lobsters exploded before they came into contact with humans.'

'By the time they deployed the crabs they seemed to have learned from that mistake,' said Oliviera. 'The crabs stayed stable.'

'What do you mean, stable?' Rubin pursed his lips. 'They died almost as soon as they reached land.'

'That's irrelevant,' retorted Johanson. 'Their mission had already been accomplished. These creatures are all destined for an early death. They're not trying to colonise our world. It's purely an *attack*. Whichever way you look at it, humans would never fight a war like this. Why approach from the sea? What possible reason could anyone have for manipulating the genes of organisms that live several kilometres underwater – like vent crabs, for instance? You won't find any humans at work here. All this is designed to discover our weak points. They're experimenting – and, more than that, they're trying to distract us.'

'Distract us?' echoed Peak.

'Yes. The enemy is attacking on all fronts at once. Some of the attacks cause nightmare scenarios, others are more of a nuisance, but the main thing is, they succeed in keeping us busy. They're needling us, which means we don't notice what's really going on. In our eagerness to limit the damage, we're blind to the ultimate threat. We're like circus clowns, balancing a series of plates on poles. All the time we're running from one pole to the next to keep the plates spinning and stop them crashing to the ground. As soon as we've spun the last plate, we have to rush back to the first. But the number of plates exceeds our powers of juggling. We won't be able to cope with the volume of attacks. Individually, whale attacks and disappearing fish stocks wouldn't be much of a worry. But taken together, they fulfil their purpose, which is to paralyse and overwhelm us. If the phenomena continue to spread, governments are going to lose control, other states will take advantage of the situation, and there'll be regional, maybe even international, conflicts. The trouble will get out of hand, and no one will be able to stop it. We'll undermine our own strength. International aid organisations will collapse, and medical supply networks will be overstretched. The barrage of head-on assaults serves to mask what's silently unfolding in the depths, and soon we won't have the technology, energy, know-how or even the time to prevent it.'

'Prevent what?' asked Vanderbilt, in a bored voice.

'The annihilation of mankind.'

'Excuse me?'

'Isn't it obvious? They've decided to deal with us in the same way that we deal with pests. They want to wipe us out.'

'I've heard enough of this bull.'

'Before we wipe out all the life in the sea.'

The CIA chief lumbered to his feet and pointed a trembling finger at Johanson. 'That's the biggest pile of crap I've ever heard. We summoned you here to deal with a crisis. Are you trying to tell us that those, uh, do-gooding aliens from *The Abyss* have come back to wag their fingers at us because we've been misbehaving?'

'*The Abyss*?' Johanson thought for a moment. 'Oh, I see. No, I wasn't thinking of creatures like that. They were extra-terrestrials.'

'It's the same kind of crap.'

'Actually, no. In *The Abyss* the alien creatures come from space. The film makes them out to be a nicer version of humans. They're supposed to have a moral message. The main difference, though, is that those aliens aren't interested in toppling us from our throne at the top of terrestrial evolution, which is what any intelligent species that had developed *in parallel* to us and that *shared* our planet would want to do.'

'Dr Johanson!' Vanderbilt pulled out a handkerchief, and wiped the sweat from his forehead. 'You're not a professional snoop like me. You don't have the benefit of my experience. You've done a great job in keeping us entertained for these past fifteen minutes, but the first thing you've got to do when you're trying to get to the bottom of a mess like this is to ask yourself who gains. *Who stands to gain?* That's how you get on the scent. Not by poking around like—'

'No one stands to gain,' said a voice.

Vanderbilt heaved himself round.

'That's just it, Vanderbilt.' Bohrmann had risen to his feet. 'Last night Kiel finished modelling the scenarios for what's likely to happen if further continental slopes collapse.'

'I know,' Vanderbilt said brusquely. 'Tsunamis and methane. We'll have a spot of bother with the climate—'

'No,' said Bohrmann. 'Not a spot of bother. It's a death sentence. We all know what happened fifty-five million years ago, the last time enormous quantities of methane were released into the atmosphere—'

'*Know?* Come on, it was fifty-five million years ago.'

'We reconstructed what happened – and now we're predicting that the same thing will happen again. Tsunamis are going to hit the coastlines and wipe out coastal populations. Then the surface of the Earth will get warmer, and it will keep getting warmer until we all die out. That's everyone, Mr Vanderbilt, including the Middle East and all your terrorists. The dissociation of the hydrate reserves in the western Pacific and off the east coast of America would be enough to kill us all.'

There was a deathly hush.

'And there'll be nothing,' said Johanson softly, looking at Vanderbilt, 'absolutely nothing you can do. You won't even know where to start. And because you've been dealing with all those whales, sharks, mussels, jellies, crabs, killer algae and invisible cable-munching monsters, you won't have had time to prepare. In fact, you won't even have been able to peek under water, because all your divers, dive robots and other gadgets will have disappeared.'

'How long will it take for the atmosphere to heat up sufficiently to pose a threat to humanity?' asked Li.

Bohrmann frowned. 'A few hundred years, I guess.'

'That's OK, then,' growled Vanderbilt.

'On the contrary,' said Johanson. 'If these creatures have launched their crusade because we're threatening their habitat, they've got to get rid of us fast. A few hundred years are nothing in the context of the history of the planet, but mankind has inflicted incredible damage in no time at all. So they've quietly decided to go one step further. They've stopped the Gulf Stream.'

Bohrmann stared at him. 'They've what?'

'It's stopped already,' Weaver spoke up. 'OK, so maybe there's still a weak current, but it's practically gone. The world had better start bracing itself for another ice age. It's going to get seriously cold within the next century. It may come sooner than that – in forty or fifty years' time, or perhaps even earlier.'

'Hang on,' Peak called. 'Methane's going to heat up the planet. We know that for a fact. The climate might shift. But how does that fit with the Gulf Stream causing an ice age? What the hell happens then? Do two catastrophes balance each other out?'

Weaver turned towards him. 'I'd say they make things worse.'

If at first it seemed that Vanderbilt was alone in vehemently rejecting the theory, over the next hour the situation changed. The assembly split into two camps that were locked in bitter combat. Everything that had happened was rolled out and picked over again. The first anomalies. The rampaging whales. The circumstances leading to the discovery of the worms. It was like watching a rugby match, as arguments were tossed back and forth, then knocked out of play by rhetorical elbows, allowing one side to surge forwards, flanked by the opposition, then thwarted by its tricks. But behind all the manoeuvring was an impulse that Anawak recognised: some people couldn't countenance the existence of a parallel intelligence that challenged the supremacy of mankind. They didn't voice their outrage, but Anawak – versed in debates about animal intelligence – could hear it. An undercurrent of aggression entered the debate. The split caused by Johanson's theory wasn't merely scientific; it created a schism within a group of experts who were, first and foremost, people. Vanderbilt counted Rubin, Frost, Roche, Shankar and a hesitant Peak on his side, while Johanson was backed by Li, Oliviera, Fenwick, Ford, Bohrmann and Anawak. At first the intelligence agents and diplomats looked on in silence, then one by one they joined the scrum.

It was astonishing.

Johanson would never have expected it, but the professional spies, arch-conservative defence advisers and counter-terrorist experts were almost unanimously on his side. One commented, 'I'm a reasonable kind of guy. If I hear something that seems to make sense, I'm willing to give it the benefit of the doubt. If the alternative explanation has to be pounded into shape before it fits the mould of our experience, it seems to me that it's unlikely to be true.'

Peak was the first to desert from Vanderbilt's team. Frost, Shankar and Roche followed suit.

In the end, an exhausted Vanderbilt suggested they take a break.

They left the room and headed for the buffet, where fresh juice, coffee and cake awaited them. Weaver squeezed in next to Anawak. 'You didn't take much persuading,' she said. 'How come?'

Anawak looked at her and smiled. 'Coffee?'

'Yes, please. And milk.'

He poured it and handed her the cup. Weaver was only marginally smaller than him. Suddenly it struck him that he'd liked her ever since he'd set eyes on her, when he'd seen her on the forecourt of the Chateau.

'I suppose not,' he said. 'It's a well-reasoned theory.'

'Is that all? Or does it have something to do with you believing in animal intelligence?'

'I don't. I just believe in intelligence in general. Animals are animals and people are people. If we could prove that dolphins are as intelligent as we are then, logically, they wouldn't be animals.'

'Do you think that's so?'

'No. And if we judge them by human criteria we'll never know. Do you think humans are intelligent?'

Weaver laughed. 'If you're talking about one human, yes . . . but lots of them together make an unenlightened mob.'

That was his kind of answer. 'Exactly! And the same applies to—'

'Dr Anawak?' One of the intelligence agents was hurrying towards him. 'You're Dr Anawak, aren't you?'

'Yes.'

'You're wanted on the phone.'

Anawak frowned. They weren't directly contactable in the Chateau, but there was a number for relatives to call in case of emergencies. Li had asked the delegates to distribute it with caution. Shoemaker had the number. Did anyone else?

'It's in the lobby,' said the man. 'Or would you like me to have the call transferred to your room?'

'No, that's fine. I can come right away.'

'See you later,' Weaver called after him.

He followed the man through the lobby. A row of makeshift telephone booths had been erected in a side aisle.

'Take this one, right here,' said the man. 'I'll get the call put through to you. The phone will ring. Answer it, and you'll be connected with Tofino.'

Shoemaker.

Anawak waited. It rang. He picked up. 'Leon,' said Shoemaker, 'sorry to disturb you. I know you've got important stuff to do but—'

'No problem. Thanks for dinner last night. It was great.'

'Oh, yes . . . Right . . . Well, I'm afraid this is important too. It's, um . . .' Shoemaker sighed. 'Leon, I've got some sad news. We had a call from Cape Dorset.'

It was as though someone had pulled the carpet from under his feet. He knew what was coming.

'Leon, your father's died.'

He stood motionless in the phone booth.

'Leon?'

'It's OK, I . . .'

But it wasn't OK at all.

Li

'Extra-terrestrials?' The President seemed remarkably composed.

'Not exactly,' said Li. They'd been through this countless times already. 'Not extra-terrestrials, inhabitants of our planet. A rival species, if you like.'

The Chateau was hooked up via satellite link to Offutt Air Force Base. In addition to the President, the delegation in Offutt was made up of the defense secretary, the assistant to the President for National Security

Affairs, the secretary of Homeland Security, the secretary of state and the director of the CIA. There could no longer be any doubt that Washington would suffer the same fate as New York. The city had been evacuated, and practically the entire cabinet had decamped to Nebraska. The retreat inland had gone largely to plan: this time they'd been prepared for it.

Li, Vanderbilt and Peak were participating in the briefing from the Chateau. Li could tell that the Offutt contingent loathed being stuck at the air base. The CIA director longed to be back in his office on the sixth floor of the agency's headquarters on the Potomac River. He secretly envied the director of Counter-terrorism who had flatly refused to evacuate his staff.

'Get your people to safety,' he'd ordered him.

'This isn't a natural disaster, this is a planned attack,' the reply had come. 'A terrorist attack. We need those guys in the Global Response Center to stay at their computers and keep working. Their role is crucial. They're our window on terrorism, and they're not going anywhere.'

'New York is under siege from biological killers,' the CIA director had countered. 'Don't you know what's happening there? Washington won't be any different.'

'The Global Response Center wasn't created so that it could close its doors at the critical moment.'

'Sure, but those guys could die.'

'Then they'll die.'

The defense secretary was also wishing himself back in his spacious office at the Pentagon, and the President was by nature the sort of person who had to be held down to prevent him commandeering a plane and flying back to the White House. People could say what they liked about him, but he wasn't a coward. In fact, he was so unflinching that some of his critics suspected he was simply too stupid to experience fear.

Offutt Air Force Base had all the facilities to serve as a seat of government, but they'd had to *flee* there. And that, Li figured, was why the idea of intelligent oceanic beings had met with instant approbation. The thought of fleeing from a human adversary, whose offensive had left them stymied, was too much of a humiliation for the administration to bear. Johanson's theory cast events in a different light. Retrospectively it cleared the intelligence agents, the Department of Defense and the President of blame.

'So what do you think,' the President asked the council, 'is this possible or not?'

'What I personally believe doesn't matter either way,' the defense secretary said tersely. 'The scientists at the Chateau are the experts. If they think this is the explanation, then we need to take it seriously and consider our next step.'

'Take it seriously?' Vanderbilt echoed incredulously. 'Aliens? Little green men?'

'They're not aliens as such,' Li put in patiently.

'I guess it presents us with an entirely new dilemma,' said the secretary of state. 'Supposing the theory's right. How much do we divulge to the public?'

'To the public?' the CIA director queried. 'Nothing. The whole world would be plunged into chaos.'

'It already *is* in chaos.'

'That's not the point. The media would hang us out to dry. They'd say we'd gone nuts. They'd never believe us. They wouldn't *want* to believe us. The existence of another intelligent species would shake the foundations of what it means to be human.'

'That's a religious issue.' The defense secretary made a dismissive gesture. 'Politically speaking, it's irrelevant.'

'*Politics* are irrelevant,' said Peak. 'There's nothing out there but suffering and fear. You should take a trip to Manhattan and see for yourself. People who've never been to church are praying on their knees.'

The President gazed thoughtfully at the ceiling. 'We need to reflect,' he said, 'on what the Lord's intention might be.'

'With all due respect, sir, I wasn't aware He was part of this council,' said Vanderbilt. 'He isn't even on our side.'

'That's a pretty bad attitude, Jack.' The President frowned.

'Good, bad, what does it matter? I judge an opinion on whether it makes sense. Everyone here seems to think there's some truth to this theory. Which makes me wonder if I'm the dope or—'

'Jack,' the CIA director warned him.

'Oh, I'd be happy to concede that it's me – once I've seen some *proof.* I'm not going to believe in this gang of bad guys in the water until I've spoken to the little schmucks in person. But until then you need to think seriously before you dismiss the possibility of a large-scale terrorist attack. We can't afford to let down our guard.'

Li laid a hand on his arm. 'Jack, why would terrorists attack us from the depths?'

'To make people like you believe we're being bullied by E.T. And it's working, for Christ's sake – it's actually working.'

'We're not stupid, you know,' the national security adviser said irritably. 'No one's going to let down their guard. Frankly, Vanderbilt, your terrorism obsession isn't going to get us anywhere. We can search all we like for crazed mullahs and stinking rich arch-villains, but in the meantime the continental slope's going to cave in, our cities will be flooded and innocent Americans will die. So what do you suggest we *do*?'

Vanderbilt crossed his arms. He looked like a smouldering Buddha.

'You know what, Jack?' Li said slowly. 'I think you just made a suggestion.'

'Namely?'

'To talk to the little schmucks. Make contact.'

The President pressed his fingertips together. His voice was measured. 'This is a test for all humanity. Perhaps God intended two powerful races to inhabit this planet – maybe the Good Book was right about the horned beast that comes up from the water. "Replenish the Earth, and subdue it." Those were the Lord's instructions, and He didn't give them to any kind of monster in the sea.'

'Hell, no,' grumbled Vanderbilt. 'He preached it to America directly.'

'This could be the final battle in the fight against evil.' The President straightened in his chair. 'And we've been appointed by God to fight for Him – and win.'

'Perhaps,' said Li, seizing on the idea, 'whoever wins this battle will govern the earth.'

Peak gave her a sideways look and said nothing.

'I think we should have a frank discussion with the other NATO states and the EU,' said the secretary of state, 'after which, we'll have to put the UN in the picture.'

Li jumped in: 'Of course, the UN won't be capable of handling this kind of operation, and we'll need to make that clear. Sure, they'll have people with know-how and ideas, and there's no reason why we shouldn't pick their brains. Let's enlist the help of our Asian and African allies as well – that sends out the right kind of message. But this is *our* chance to position ourselves at the head of the international community. Mankind isn't about to be wiped from the face of the Earth by a meteorite. This is a terrible threat we're facing, but we're going to overcome it – provided we get things right.'

'Have your counter-measures proven successful?' asked the national security adviser.

'We're running an international campaign to find an anti-serum that will protect against the toxins. Initiatives are under way to stop the advance of the crabs, bring a halt to the whale attacks and get rid of the worms – which is proving trickier than expected. We've taken all kinds of measures to contain the risks, but conventional solutions won't be enough. There's nothing we can do about the Gulf Stream, and the methane crisis is beyond our control. We could keep fishing worms out of the ocean in their millions, but if we can't see where they're coming from, there'll always be fresh plagues. Without the capacity to send down divers, probes or subs, we're as good as blind. Anything could be going on down there. In the course of this afternoon I was informed that two large drag nets have been lost near Georges Bank. In addition to that, there's no sign of the three trawlers that we'd dispatched to the Laurentian valley to sweep the seabed. Recon planes are out looking for them, but conditions are terrible. The Grand Banks are to the east of there, and the fog never lifts. Besides, a storm's been raging for the past two days.' She paused. 'There are thousands of other examples I could give you. All the reports coming in bear witness to our failure. OK, so the drone surveillance is working well, and troops with flame-throwers are beating back the crabs – but it's only temporary. They just crawl ashore elsewhere. The fact is, as far as the oceans are concerned, we don't call the shots. We never really called them in the first place, but now . . .'

'What about the sonar offensive?'

'We're still pressing ahead with it, but we're not anticipating any significant success. The only way we can get it to work is by killing the whales. They don't flee from the noise, as any creature with healthy instincts would do. I guess they're in horrible pain, but they don't have a choice – they're not in control. They're still terrorising the waters.'

'Speaking of control,' said the defense secretary, 'have you identified a strategy?'

'I'd say we're looking at a five-point plan. The first step is to clear the waters of all human presence, whether on the surface or in the depths. Step two is to expel or annihilate the coastal population, as with northern Europe. Step three aims to destroy our infrastructure – the offshore industry in northern Europe would be a case in point. The disruption of the fishing industry also falls into this category – it's going to cause us some serious issues with malnutrition, especially in third-world countries. Step four targets the major cities, the pillars of our civilisation – urban populations are forced to retreat inland. And, finally, step five, the climate shifts, and the Earth becomes uninhabitable for our species. It either freezes or floods, warms up or cools down, or maybe all of those – we don't know the details.'

'But wouldn't that make it uninhabitable for the entire animal kingdom?' asked the national security adviser.

'On land, yes. It's fair to say it would wipe out most species of flora and fauna. I've been reliably informed, though, that the same thing happened fifty-five million years ago, with the net result that large numbers of animals and plants died out, making way for other species. They're bound to have thought very carefully about their own survival before precipitating a crisis like this.'

'Such destruction. It's . . .' The secretary of Homeland Security struggled for words. 'It's so extreme. It's inhuman . . .'

'Well, they're not human,' Li reminded him.

'What hope do we have of stopping them?'

'We've got to find out who they are,' said Vanderbilt.

Li turned to him. 'Don't tell me you're finally coming round?'

'Oh, I haven't changed my view,' Vanderbilt said evenly, 'but if you identify the purpose of an action, you'll identify the culprit. In this particular instance, I have to admit that the five-point strategy is the most convincing explanation I've heard. Now we need to find out more. Who exactly are they? Where are they? How can we see inside their minds?'

'And how are we going to stop them?' the defense secretary added.

'Evil,' muttered the President, his eyes narrowing. 'How best to vanquish evil?'

'We talk to them,' said Li.

'We make contact?'

'Even the devil's been known to bargain. I don't see any alternative.

Johanson reckons they're trying to keep us busy so we don't have time to think. We're not going to let that happen. We're still in a position to act, so let's find them and make contact. Then we'll strike.'

'You want to launch an offensive against deep-sea organisms?' The secretary of Homeland Security shook his head. 'Dear God.'

'Hold on. Are we all in agreement that we should take this theory seriously?' the director of the CIA asked. 'We're talking about it as though it were fact. Are we really prepared to believe that we share the planet with another intelligent species?'

'Only one species was made in the image of God,' the President said firmly, 'and that was mankind. These creatures may be intelligent, but just *how* intelligent remains to be seen. And I very much doubt that they've got any intrinsic *right* to inhabit this planet like we have. There's certainly no mention of them in the scriptures. But the fact that an alien life-form is to blame for all this chaos sounds logical to me.'

'So, going back to my question,' said the secretary of state, 'what are we going to tell the world?'

'It's too early.'

'People are going to ask questions.'

'Then make up some answers. You're a politician, aren't you? If we come right out and tell them there's another intelligent species at the bottom of the sea, we're going to kill them with shock.'

'Incidentally,' said the CIA director, turning to Li, 'how would you like us to refer to these deep-sea deviants?'

Li smiled. 'Johanson had a suggestion. *Yrr.*'

'Yrr?'

'He came up with it by accident. His fingers slipped on the keyboard. He says it's as good a name as any, and I agree.'

'OK, Jude.' The President nodded. 'We'll see how this theory shapes up. We have to keep considering all the possibilities, all the options. And if it turns out that we're fighting a battle against these aliens – yrr or whatever you want to call them – we'll fight them and win. We'll declare war on the yrr.' He looked at the others.'This is an opportunity for us. A big opportunity. I want you to use it.'

'With God's blessing,' said Li.

'Amen,' mumbled Vanderbilt.

One of the benefits of staying at the Chateau under military occupation was that nothing was ever closed. None of the usual conventions of the catering trade applied. Li had made it clear that everybody, especially the scientists, would be working day and night, and a T-bone steak at four in the morning might be exactly what they needed.

For the past thirty minutes Weaver had been ploughing up and down the pool. It was well past one in the morning. Now, wrapped in a soft towelling bathrobe, with bare feet and wet hair, she padded across the lobby on her way towards the elevators. From the corner of her eye, she noticed Leon Anawak sitting at the hotel bar, which struck her as an unlikely place to find him. Perched forlornly on a stool and eyeing an untouched glass of Coke, he was dipping into a bowl of peanuts, picking one up, then letting it drop.

There'd been no sign of him since their conversation that morning. Maybe he didn't want to be disturbed. A bustle of activity filled the lobby and the adjoining rooms, but the bar was virtually empty. Two men in dark suits were sitting in a corner, talking in hushed tones, while a woman in combats stared at a screen. The west-coast music in the background gave the scene an air of inconsequential ordinariness.

Anawak looked unhappy.

She was just thinking that it might be best to go back to her suite when she found herself walking towards him. Her damp feet left tracks on the parquet floor. 'Hi.'

Anawak turned, his eyes empty.

She stopped. It was the easiest thing in the world to encroach on someone's private space and earn yourself a reputation for interfering. She leaned against the bar and drew the bathrobe closer. There were two stools between them.

'Hi,' said Anawak. His eyes shifted. At last he seemed to see her.

She smiled. 'What . . . um, what are you doing?' Stupid question. 'You disappeared this morning.'

'Yeah, I'm sorry.'

'Oh, no, don't apologise,' she said. 'I didn't want to disturb you. I just saw you sitting here and I thought—'

Something was wrong. It would be wise to leave him to it.

Anawak roused himself from his paralysis. He reached for his glass, picked it up and put it down again. His eyes moved to the stool beside him. 'Would you like a drink?' he asked.

'Are you sure I'm not disturbing you?'

'No, really, it's fine.' He hesitated. 'My name's Leon – Leon Anawak.'

'I'm Karen. Bailey's on ice, please.'

Anawak summoned the barman and ordered her drink. She took a step closer, but didn't sit down. Her wet hair sent droplets of cold water trickling down her neck and between her breasts. She should drink up and leave, she thought. 'So, how're things?' she asked, and sipped.

Anawak's brow furrowed. 'I'm not sure.'

'Not sure?'

'No. My father died.'

Shit. 'What was wrong with him?' she asked cautiously.

'No idea.'

'You mean the doctors don't know yet?'

'I don't know yet.' He shook his head. 'I'm not even sure I *want* to know.'

He fell silent for a while. Then he said, 'I was in the woods this afternoon, walking. I was out there for hours, trying to . . . feel something. I thought, there has to be some kind of emotion that goes with a situation like this. But I just felt sorry for myself.' He looked her in the eye. 'Do you ever get that feeling, like wherever you are you want to be somewhere else? And then suddenly you realise that it isn't you that wants to get away – the place you're in is pushing you away, telling you you don't belong there. But it won't tell you where you do belong, so you have to keep running.'

She ran a finger round the rim of her glass. 'I guess you didn't have a very good relationship with your father, then.'

'I didn't have a relationship with him at all.'

'Really?' Weaver frowned.

Anawak shrugged. 'How about you?' he asked. 'What do your parents do?'

'They're dead.'

'Oh . . . I'm sorry.'

'It's OK. You couldn't have known. They died when I was ten. A diving accident off the coast of Australia. I was in the hotel when it happened. They got caught in a rip. They were experienced divers, but, well . . . you can never tell with the sea.'

'Did anyone ever find them?'

'No.'

'How did you cope?'

'For a while it was pretty tough. I'd had an amazing childhood. My parents were teachers and loved the water. We went sailing in the Maldives, scuba-diving in the Red Sea, cave diving in the Yucatán. We even dived in Scotland and Iceland. Of course, they never went too deep when I was with them, but there was plenty for me to see. They only left me behind if the dive was going to be dangerous – and then, one day, they never came back.' She smiled. 'But, hey, I turned out OK in the end.'

'True.' He smiled back.

Then he slid off his stool. 'I should probably get some sleep. I'm flying out for the funeral tomorrow.' He hesitated. 'Good night . . . and thanks.'

She sat there, looking at her half-drunk Bailey's, remembering her parents and how the hotel staff had come to find her. She had to be brave, the manager had said.

She swished the liquid in her glass. Anawak didn't know just how tough it had been. How her grandmother had tried to look after the disturbed, fearful little girl, whose sorrow had vented itself in rage. At school her grades went downhill, and so did her behaviour. Then there was the bunking off class and bumming around on the streets, smoking her first joint, hanging out with punks, drinking herself into a stupor, and sleeping with anyone who was interested – which they always were. Nicking stuff, being expelled from school, the backstreet abortion, hard drugs, the young offenders' institute. Six months in a home for problem kids. Then all the piercings, the shaved head, the scars. Her mind and her body had been a battleground.

But the accident had done nothing to diminish her love for the sea. The water seemed to exercise a dark fascination, calling to her and summoning her to the depths. It beckoned to her so powerfully that one night she had hitched a lift to Brighton and swum away from the shore. Then, when the lights of the town were almost swallowed by the oily blackness of the moonlit water, she had allowed herself to sink beneath the surface.

Drowning wasn't easy.

She'd floated in the dark waters of the Channel, holding her breath as her heartbeats thundered in her ears. But instead of sapping the life from her body, the sea was showing her: look, see how strong your heart is.

She'd shot up to the surface and out of the nightmare that had begun when she was ten years old. A cutter was sailing nearby and picked her up. She was taken to hospital with severe hypothermia. There, she began to make plans for the future. After she'd been discharged, she stared at her body in the mirror for an hour, and decided she never wanted to look like that again. She removed the piercings, stopped shaving her head, tried to do ten press-ups and collapsed. After a week she could do twenty.

She put all her strength into trying to win back what she had lost. They allowed her to return to school on the condition that she saw a therapist. She agreed. She showed them that she was disciplined and eager to learn, and read everything she could lay hands on, especially if it was about the environment and the oceans. She jogged, swam, boxed and climbed, trying to eradicate the last traces of the lost time, until there was no sign of the scrawny, hollow-eyed girl she'd once been. She finished school at nineteen, a year older than her classmates but with perfect grades and a body like a sculpture of an ancient Greek athlete. She began a degree in biology and sport.

Karen Weaver was a new person.

With an ancient longing.

In order to better understand the workings of the world, she took a course in computing. The idea of programming computers to model complex changes intrigued her, and she persisted until she knew how to model oceanic and atmospheric change. Her first big project was a comprehensive report on ocean currents. It didn't add anything to existing research, but it was an intelligent piece of work: a homage to two people she'd loved and lost. She set up her own media business *deepbluesea*, and wrote for *Science* and *National Geographic*. Popular science magazines gave her regular columns to fill, which attracted the attention of research institutes, whose scientists needed a voice to convey their ideas. She was invited along on expeditions. She dived to the *Titanic* in MIR, visited the hydrothermal vents in the depths of the Atlantic with Alvin, and took the *Polarstern* to visit the over-winterers in the Antarctic. She went everywhere, making the most of every opportunity, because since that night in the Channel she had never felt fear. She wasn't afraid of anyone or anything.

Except of being alone. Sometimes.

Now she looked at herself in the mirror on the wall of the bar, wrapped in a bathrobe, looking a little lost.

She knocked back the Bailey's and made her way to bed.

14 May

His decision to make the trip hadn't come easily, and even then there'd been no guarantee that Li would let him leave. As it happened, she'd practically forced him to go. 'If you stay here, you'll never forgive yourself. Family comes first in life. It's the only thing you can count on. Make sure we can contact you, that's all I ask.'

Now, sitting in the plane, he wondered why Li was so eager to sing the praises of kinship. He couldn't share her enthusiasm.

The man sitting next to him, a climatologist from Massachusetts, began to snore. Anawak tilted back his seat and looked out of the window. He'd been alone with his thoughts for hours. From Vancouver he'd flown on one of Air Canada's Boeings to Toronto Pearson airport, where a long line of planes was waiting for takeoff. A violent storm had descended over Toronto, bringing air traffic to a temporary halt. To Anawak it had seemed like an omen. Waiting anxiously in the departure lounge, he'd watched as the planes were hooked up one by one to concertinaed walkways. Finally, after a two-hour delay, his flight had left for Montréal.

From there, everything had gone smoothly. He'd stayed overnight at a Holiday Inn near Dorval airport, then returned first thing in the morning to the departure lounge. At last there were signs that he was entering a different world. A group of men with steaming coffee cups were standing by a plate-glass window, their overalls emblazoned with the logo of an oil company. Two had faces like Anawak's: wide cheekbones, dark skin and Mongolian eyes. Outside on the airfield, enormous pallets trussed with netting were being loaded into the belly of the Canadian North Airlines Boeing 737. The lifting ramp was still shunting them into the aeroplane when the boarding call went out. They crossed the airfield on foot and climbed the steps at the tail. The seating area was limited to the front third of the plane; the rest of the space was given over to storage.

For more than two hours now Anawak had been in transit. From time to time the plane juddered. For most of the journey they'd been looking down on thick plains of cloud, but now, as they approached Hudson Strait, the grey mass of vapour parted to reveal the dark brown landscape of the tundra below, mountainous and jagged, with snow-fields and ice floes drifting on the lakes. Then the coast came into view. Hudson Strait passed beneath them, and Anawak knew he was crossing the frontier. A rush of emotions flooded through him, sweeping away his torpor. In every venture there was always a point of no return. Strictly speaking, that point had been Montréal, but symbolically it was Hudson Strait. Across the water was a world to which he'd sworn never to return.

Anawak was on his way to the country of his birth, to his homeland on the edge of the Arctic Circle – to Nunavut.

He stared out of the window, willing himself not to think. After thirty minutes the water gave way to land and then to a shiny frozen expanse, Frobisher Bay, cutting deep into the south-eastern tip of Baffin Island. The plane banked to the right, descending rapidly. A bright yellow building with a stumpy tower appeared in the window. It looked like a lone human outpost on an alien planet, although it was actually the airport, the way into Iqaluit, 'place of many fish', Nunavut's capital.

The plane touched down and taxied slowly to a halt.

It wasn't long before Anawak's luggage appeared. He hoisted the heavy rucksack on to his back and made his way through the terminal, passing a display of wall coverings and soapstone sculptures promoting Inuit art. In the middle of the building a giant figure, sturdily built, clad in boots and traditional attire, held a flat drum above his head in one hand and a drumstick in the other. It exuded vigour and self-assurance. Anawak stopped to read the inscription: 'Throughout the Arctic there is drum dancing and throat singing when the people come together.' He went to the First Air ticket counter and checked in his rucksack for the flight to Cape Dorset. The woman at the desk informed him that it was delayed by an hour. 'Maybe you've still got some errands to run in town,' she said, with a smile.

Anawak hesitated. 'Er, no, actually. I don't know my way around.'

She looked surprised. She was clearly wondering how someone whose appearance identified him as an Inuk could be unfamiliar with the capital. 'There's plenty to see,' she suggested. 'You should wander into town. There's the Nunatta-Sunaqutangit Museum. It has a wonderful collection of traditional and contemporary art.'

'Uh . . . sure.'

'Or you could try the Unikkaarvik Visitor Center. And it's well worth stopping off at the Anglican church. It's the only church in the world to look like an igloo.'

She was an Inuk, small with a black fringe and a ponytail. Her eyes shone as a smile spread over her face. 'I could have sworn you came from Iqaluit,' she said.

'No.' For a moment he was tempted to say that he came from Cape Dorset. 'Vancouver, actually.'

'Oh, I love Vancouver,' she exclaimed.

Anawak glanced round, worried that he was holding up the queue, but he seemed to be the only person on the onward flight that day. 'You've been there?'

'No, but I've seen the pictures on the web. It's a beautiful city.' She laughed. 'A bit bigger than Iqaluit, I guess.'

He smiled back. 'I'd say so.'

'But Iqaluit's bigger than it used to be. We've got six thousand inhabitants and we're growing all the time. Soon we'll be the size of Vancouver – well, almost anyway. You'll have to excuse me.'

A man and a woman had appeared behind him. He wouldn't be flying alone. He said goodbye and disappeared outside, in case she took it into her head to give him a tour of the city.

Iqaluit.

It was all so long ago. Some things looked familiar, but he had no recollection of most of what he saw. The clouds seemed to have stayed behind in Montréal, and now the sun shone down from a steel-blue sky, making it pleasantly warm. It was at least ten degrees, thought Anawak, and felt overdressed. He pulled off his down jacket and tied it round his waist, then trudged along the dusty road. There was a surprising amount of traffic. He couldn't remember there being so many four-by-fours and ATVs, small multi-axial buggies ridden like motorbikes. The street was lined with timber houses built in characteristic Arctic style with little stilts to raise them off the ground. Any building that rested directly on the tundra would melt the permafrost and start to sink.

As Anawak made his way through the town, he couldn't help thinking that God's hand must have descended over Iqaluit, shaking a clutch of buildings like dice and scattering them at random. Gigantic edifices made of windowless harsh white panels loomed up like abstract cubist structures among olive-green or rusty-red barracks. The school resembled a marooned UFO. Some of the houses glowed in deep shades of petrol blue or aquamarine. Towards the centre of town he came across the Commissioner's House, a cross between a cosy country villa and a space dome for astronauts. He tried to remain detached from his surroundings, but since the seaplane accident he had lost the ability to cloak himself in indifference. The crazy architectural hotchpotch conveyed nonchalance, even merriment, that he couldn't shut out.

The depressive Iqaluit of the seventies had vanished. People seemed friendly, greeting him in Inuktitut. He responded tersely. Without stopping he walked through the streets for an hour, popping in briefly to the Unikkaarvik Visitor Center, which boasted an even larger sculpture of a drum dancer.

When he was a kid, there'd been plenty of drum dancing. But that was a long time ago, when things were still OK . . . if they ever had been.

He went out on to the street where the glaring sunshine was oppressively hot. He passed to the right of the Anglican church – a stone igloo with a spire – then went back to the terminal where he sat down on a bench with a newspaper. With the exception of the couple, no one else was waiting for the flight. He held up the newspaper to cut himself off from the world and skimmed the articles without absorbing their content, then tossed it aside.

Eventually the young woman from the ticket desk came to collect them. They filed out through a side door, then walked on to the aircraft manoeuvring area, where a small twin-engined propeller plane, a Piper, was waiting. Anawak and his fellow passengers climbed the two steps to the cramped interior. There were only six seats. All the baggage had been stashed under netting at the rear of the plane. The cockpit led straight in to the cabin without any partition. They taxied on to the runway, waited for another Piper to land, then took a short, fast run-up and lifted off shakily. The terminal shrank and vanished, Frobisher Bay glittering far below. They flew west over mountains carved by glaciers and capped with snowfields and ice sheets. To their left, rays of sunshine glistened on Hudson Strait, while to the right, they sparkled on a lake, whose name Anawak suddenly remembered: Amadjuak.

They had gone there sometimes.

It was coming back to him at giddying speed. The memories appeared before him like silhouettes in a snowstorm, drawing him into the past, where he didn't want to go.

The terrain levelled out, then gave way to water. The flight continued over the sea for twenty minutes, until rugged land reappeared through the cockpit window. The seven islands of Tellik Inlet came into view. A thin line cut into one of the islands: Cape Dorset runway.

They touched down.

Anawak felt his heart spring forward. He was home. As the Piper taxied slowly towards the terminal, he felt loath to get out.

Cape Dorset, capital of Inuit art and home to 1200 people: the New York of the north, as it was half jokingly, half admiringly called.

That was the modern Cape Dorset.

Back then things had been different.

Cape Dorset: Kinngait, or 'high mountain' in the Inuit tongue, was situated in the Sikusiilaq region, 'where no ice ever forms on the sea', so-named because even in the harshest winter, temperate currents prevented the water freezing round Foxe Peninsula on the south-west extremity of Baffin Island. Names flooded back. Mallikjuaq, a tiny island near Cape Dorset, a nature reserve full of marvels – fox-traps from the nineteenth century, ruins from ancient Thule culture, burial sites that were the source of countless legends, and a romantic lake where they had camped. Anawak remembered the stone kayak-stands. He'd loved it there. Then he pictured his parents, and remembered what had driven him out of Nunavut, when it was still part of the Northwest Territories and didn't have its own name.

He picked up his rucksack and clambered out of the plane.

A man ran over to greet the couple. The reunion was effusive, but that was nearly always the way: the Inuit had any number of words for 'welcome', but none for 'farewell'. No one had bidden Anawak farewell when he'd taken his leave nineteen years previously, not even the weatherbeaten old man who was left standing alone on the airfield as the trio of friends moved noisily away. For a moment Anawak had difficulty recognising him. Ijitsiaq Akesuk had aged noticeably and now sported a thin grey moustache on his once clean-shaven face. But it was him. The creased face widened into grin. He hurried towards Anawak and threw his arms round him. A stream of Inuktitut words spilled from his lips.

Then he switched into English. 'Leon, my child. What a handsome young scientist you are.'

Anawak let him finish embracing him, and thumped Akesuk half-heartedly on the back. 'Uncle Iji. How are you?'

'Oh, as well as can be expected, considering the occasion. Did you have a good flight? You must have been travelling for days – all those places you must have been just to get here . . .'

'I had to change planes a few times.'

'Toronto? Montréal?' Akesuk let go of him and beamed. Like many of the Inuit, he had gaps in his top teeth. 'Montréal. You travel a lot, don't you? What a joy. You'll have to tell me all about it. You'll stay with us, now, won't you? We've got everything ready for you. Is that all your luggage?'

'Er, Uncle Iji—'

'Iji – you're too old for "uncle" now.'

'I booked a hotel.'

Akesuk took a step back. 'Which one?'

'The Polar Lodge.'

There was fleeting disappointment on the old man's face, but then he beamed. 'We can cancel it. I know the manager. No problem.'

'I don't want to put you to any trouble,' said Anawak. I only came to bury my father in the ice, he thought, and then to get the hell out of here.

'It's no trouble,' said Akesuk. 'You're my nephew. How long are you staying?'

'Two nights. I thought that would be enough, right?'

Akesuk frowned. He took Anawak's arm and pulled him through the airport. 'We'll talk about that later. Aren't you hungry?'

'Very.'

'Excellent. Mary-Ann's made caribou stew and a seal soup with rice. A real feast. When was the last time you had seal soup, hmm?'

Anawak allowed himself to be whisked away. A line of vehicles was parked outside the airport and Akesuk headed purposefully towards a truck.

'Throw your rucksack in the back. Do you remember Mary-Ann? Of course you don't. You'd already left by the time she moved out here from Salluit. We got married. I hated being alone. She's younger than me – which isn't a bad thing, I might tell you. Are you married? Goodness me, there's so much to talk about after all these years.'

Anawak shuffled around on the passenger seat. Akesuk seemed

determined to talk him into submission. He tried to remember if the old man had always been so chatty. Then it occurred to him that his uncle might be feeling as nervous as he was. One retreated into silence; the other talked.

They trundled along the high street. The hills cut right through Cape Dorset, dividing it into hamlets. In addition to the main hamlet of Kinngait, there was Itjurittuq in the north-east, Kuugalaaq in the west and Muliujaq in the south. Kuugalaaq had been their home. Akesuk, his mother's brother, had lived in Kinngait.

Anawak wondered whether he still lived there.

They seemed to be driving through the entire town and his uncle commented on almost every building. Suddenly it dawned on Anawak that Akesuk was giving him a tour. 'Uncle Iji, I know all these places,' he protested.

'Rubbish! You've been away for nineteen years. All kinds of things have changed. Do you remember that supermarket?'

'No.'

'You see? It wasn't there back then. It's new. There's an even bigger one now. We always used to go to the Polar Supply Store – you can't have forgotten that, surely. That's our new school. Well, I guess it's been there a while now, but it's new to you. See that, on the right? The Tiktaliktaq community hall. You wouldn't believe all the important people who've come here to hear the throat singing and drum dancing. Bill Clinton, Jacques Chirac, Helmut Kohl. Kohl was a giant – he made us look like dwarfs. Now when was that? Let me see . . .'

And so it went on. They drove past the Anglican church and the cemetery where his father was to be buried. Anawak saw an Inuk woman crouching outside her house, working on a sculpture. The enormous stone bird reminded him of Nootka art. A two-storey blue-grey building with a futuristic lobby turned out to be the hamlet office. Nunavut's decentralised administration meant that any decent-sized community had its own council office. Anawak resigned himself to his fate, not least because he realised that the Cape Dorset of his childhood was nothing like the place before him.

Suddenly he heard himself say, 'Let's go to the harbour, Uncle Iji.'

Akesuk turned the wheel briskly. They sped down a steep road in the direction of the sea. Timber houses in all sizes and colours were dotted in no apparent order over the dark brown landscape. A few patches of hardy tundra grass were scattered here and there, with the occasional stretch of snow. Cape Dorset's harbour consisted of little more than a wharf and some loading cranes where, once or twice a year, the supply ship would dock with its vital cargo of goods. Not far from there you could walk across the tidal flats of Tellik Inlet at low tide to get to the neighbouring island, Mallikjuaq, the territorial park with its burial sites, and the kayak-stand, and the lake where they used to pitch camp.

They stopped. Anawak got out, walked along the wharf and stared out across the blue polar water. Akesuk followed him a little way, then let him go on alone.

The view of the wharf had been Anawak's last glimpse of Cape Dorset before he left – not on the plane but on the supply ship. He'd been twelve. The ship had carried him away with his new family, who were leaving the country full of hope and excitement about the new world ahead of them, while mourning the paradise in the ice that had long since been lost.

After five minutes he walked slowly back to the truck and climbed in without a word.

'Yes, the old harbour,' Akesuk said softly. 'Our harbour. I'll never forget it. The way you left, Leon. It broke our hearts . . .'

Anawak looked at him sharply. 'Whose hearts?' he asked.

'Well, your—'

'My father's? Yours? The people down the street?'

Akesuk started the engine. 'Come on,' he said. 'Let's go home.'

Akesuk still lived in the same little house in the settlement. With its light blue walls and dark blue roof, it was attractive and well tended. The hills rose behind it, stretching for several kilometres until they reached their apex in Kinngait, the 'high mountain', whose rock was scarred with veins of snow. It looked more like a landscape of sculpted marble than a high mountain. In Anawak's memory the Kinngait range towered into the sky, but the comb of rock in the distance invited competent hikers to explore it on foot.

Akesuk went to the back of the truck and hauled down the rucksack. Although he was slight, he didn't seem to notice the weight. He held it in one hand and opened the door with the other. 'Mary-Ann,' he called, 'he's here!'

A puppy made its way unsteadily to the door. Akesuk stepped over it and disappeared into the house, returning seconds later with a plump woman, whose friendly face was propped on an imposing double chin. She hugged Anawak and greeted him in Inuktitut.

'Mary-Ann can't speak English,' Akesuk said apologetically. 'I hope you haven't forgotten your language.'

'My language is English,' said Anawak.

'Well, yes, it is now, of course.'

'I still understand a fair bit, though – enough to know what she's saying.'

Mary-Ann was asking if he was hungry.

He answered in Inuktitut, and she smiled, then picked up the dog, which was sniffing at Anawak's boots, and made signs for him to follow. There was a line of footwear in the hall. Anawak bent down automatically to remove his.

'I see you've still got your manners,' his uncle joked. 'They haven't turned you into a qallunaaq.'

Anawak glanced down at himself, then followed Mary-Ann into the kitchen. He saw a modern electric cooker and gadgets of the kind used in any well-equipped household in Vancouver. It was worlds away from the impoverished state of his family's old home. Next to the window was a circular dining-table, then a door leading out on to the balcony. Akesuk exchanged a few words with his wife, then pushed Anawak into a cosily furnished lounge. A cluster of heavy armchairs were grouped round a stack of equipment, including a TV set, video recorder, radio and CB transmitter. The kitchen was visible through a hatch. Akesuk showed him the bathroom, then the laundry and the larder at the back, the bedroom and a little room with a single bed and a vase of fresh flowers on the bedside table. Arctic poppies, saxifrage and heather.

'Mary-Ann picked them,' said Akesuk. It sounded like an invitation for him to make himself at home.

'Thank you, but I . . . I think it would be better if I stayed at the hotel.'

He expected his uncle to be hurt, but Akesuk regarded him thoughtfully. 'Would you like a drink?' he said.

'I don't drink.'

'Nor do I. We usually have fruit juice with our meal. Would that suit?'

'Yes, please.'

Akesuk poured two glasses, and they took their drinks to the balcony.

His uncle lit a cigarette. Mary-Ann had announced that the dinner wouldn't be ready for at least another quarter of an hour.

'I'm not allowed to smoke in the house,' said Akesuk. 'That's what happens when you marry. I'd smoked in the house all my life. But I guess it's better this way. Smoking isn't good for you, but it's hard to give up . . .' He laughed and drew the smoke into his lungs with obvious pleasure. 'Let me guess. You don't smoke, boy, do you?'

'No.'

'And you don't drink. That's good.'

For a while they gazed out at the mountain ridge with its gullies of snow. Wisps of cloud shimmered high above, while ivory gulls soared in the sky then swooped down.

'How did he die?' Anawak asked.

'Dropped dead,' said Akesuk. 'We were on the land. He saw a hare and started to chase it. He just collapsed.'

'You brought him back?'

'His body.'

'Did he drink himself to death?' Even Anawak was shocked by the bitterness in his voice. Akesuk gazed past him towards the mountains and wreathed himself in smoke.

'He had a heart-attack. That's what the doctor said in Iqaluit. He didn't do enough exercise and he smoked too much. He hadn't touched a drop in ten years.'

The caribou stew was delicious. It tasted of his childhood. Seal soup, on the other hand, had never appealed to him, but he took a large helping. Mary-Ann watched in satisfaction. Anawak did his best to revive his Inuktitut, but the result was embarrassing: he kept stumbling over the words, so they talked mainly in English, discussing the events of the past few weeks, the rampaging whales, the catastrophe in Europe, and all the other news that had penetrated as far as Nunavut. Akesuk assumed the role of interpreter. He tried to steer the conversation to Anawak's father, but Anawak refused to be drawn. The burial would take place in the late afternoon at the little Anglican cemetery. The dead were buried quickly at this time of year, but in winter they were stored in a hut near the graveyard until the ground was soft enough to dig. The bodies kept for a surprisingly long time in the natural chill of the Arctic, but the hut had to be guarded with a gun. The lands of Nunavut were wild: wolves and polar bears had no qualms about eating humans, dead or alive, especially when they were hungry.

After their meal Anawak decamped to the Polar Lodge. Akesuk didn't try to persuade him to stay. He fetched the flowers from the little bedroom and put them on the table. 'You can always change your mind,' he said.

Two hours remained until the funeral. Anawak didn't leave his room, just lay on the bed and tried to sleep. He didn't know what else to do. Of course, there were plenty of things he could have done. He could have found someone to take him to Mallikjuaq, or maybe walked there himself – Tellik Inlet was still frozen and would have carried his weight. Or he could have asked Akesuk. No doubt he would have been delighted to drag him around half of Cape Dorset and introduce him to everyone personally. In Inuit settlements everyone was family, either by blood or marriage, and a tour of Cape Dorset, the capital of Inuit art, would be like wandering round a vast exhibition. But to be shown round by Akesuk would have been too much like the return of the prodigal son, and he didn't want anyone thinking that this was a homecoming. He was determined to maintain a safe distance. Allowing this world to get close to him would reopen old wounds. So instead he lay motionless on his bed, boring holes in the ceiling, until he finally dozed off.

His alarm clock roused him from his slumber.

As he stepped out of the Polar Lodge, the sun was already sinking on the horizon, but the sky was still bright. Across the frozen inlet, he saw Mallikjuaq, only a stone's throw across the ice. The lodge was on the north-east periphery of Cape Dorset, and the cemetery was on the other side of town. Anawak looked at his watch. Plenty of time. He'd arranged to meet Akesuk and drive to the church in the truck. Next to the Lodge, on the street leading down to the sea, was the Polar Supply Store. On closer inspection Anawak realised that the shop also offered a delivery service, vehicle hire and car repairs. The building seemed familiar, but the sign was new, and when Anawak walked in he didn't recognise the men behind the counter. They weren't local. The shop was cosy and cluttered on the inside, and sold practically everything from dried caribou sausages to fur-lined boots. Towards the back there were stacks of prints and numerous sculptures. It wasn't his world.

He went back out and wandered down the street towards town. An old man was sitting in front of his house on a wooden pallet, working on a sculpture of a loon. A little further down the road a woman was carving a falcon in white marble. They greeted him, and Anawak continued on his way, feeling their eyes on his back. The news of his arrival must have spread like wildfire. There wasn't any need for anyone to introduce him: they all knew that the son of Manumee Anawak had arrived in Cape Dorset to bury his father. No doubt he'd already set tongues wagging by staying at the Lodge instead of at his uncle's house.

Akesuk was waiting for him. It was only a few hundred metres to the Anglican church, but they drove. A crowd had gathered outside.

Anawak asked if the people were there because of his father.

Akesuk was astonished. 'Of course. Why else would they come?'

'I didn't know that he had . . . that he had so many friends.'

'These are the people he lived with. What does it matter if they were his friends? When a man dies, they all go with him on the final stage of the journey.'

The burial was short and unsentimental. Anawak had been obliged to shake hands with everyone before the ceremony. People whom he'd never set eyes on embraced him. The priest read from the Bible and said a prayer, then the body was lowered into a shallow hole, just deep enough to accommodate the coffin. A layer of blue plastic was placed on top, and the men dropped stones into the grave. The cross was askew in the hard ground, like all the other crosses in the graveyard. Akesuk pressed a small wooden box with a glass lid into Anawak's hands. Inside were some faded artificial flowers, a packet of cigarettes and a metal-capped bear's tooth. His uncle gave him a little shove, and Anawak walked obediently to the grave and set the box beside the cross.

Akesuk had asked whether he'd wanted to see his father one last time, but Anawak had declined. While the priest was still speaking, he tried to picture the man inside the coffin. It was hard to believe that anyone was in there at all. Suddenly he realised that the dead man would never do anything wrong again: his father was gone for ever. Guilt and innocence stopped mattering. Whatever he'd done or failed to do in his lifetime became meaningless now that his plain coffin was surrounded by cold earth. For Anawak it had long since ceased to matter anyway. The old man had been dead to him for so many years that the burial seemed an overdue formality.

He'd stopped trying to make himself feel anything. All he wanted was to leave. To go home. Where was home?

As the congregation began to sing, he experienced a sense of isolation. He was shivering, but it had nothing to do with the cold. He had thought of home and meant Vancouver or Tofino, but now he saw that it wasn't true.

Anawak was staring into a black hole. His field of vision narrowed, and the world spun. Darkness swept over him, as powerful and inevitable as a wave. He was like an animal in a trap, forced to watch as the dark rushed towards him.

'Leon.'

Panic coursed through him.

'Leon!'

Akesuk had grabbed his arm. Anawak stared in confusion at the wrinkled face and grey moustache.

'Is everything OK, boy?'

'No problem,' he murmured.

'Good God, you can barely keep upright,' Akesuk said, full of sympathy. The mourners turned.

'I'm OK, thanks, Iji.'

He could see what the others were thinking – and they couldn't have been more wrong. They assumed that it was part of the ritual of bereavement. There was nothing unusual about collapsing at the grave of a loved one – even if you were an Inuk and too proud to let anything break your will.

Except maybe alcohol and drugs.

Anawak felt nauseous.

He turned and strode across the graveyard. When he reached the church and felt the road beneath his feet, he felt an urge to run; but he didn't. Heart pounding, he paced up and down. He wouldn't have known where to run to. None of the roads was marked for him.

He had an early dinner at the Polar Lodge. Mary-Ann had prepared a meal for them, but Anawak had told his uncle that he wanted to be on his own. The old man had nodded briefly and dropped him at the hotel. There had been a sadness in his eyes that wasn't inspired by the thought of his nephew in silent communion with his father, as Anawak had led him to believe.

Hours went by, and Anawak lay on one of the twin beds in his room, staring at the TV. How could he survive another day in Cape Dorset without the memories overwhelming him? He'd booked the room for two nights because he'd assumed there'd be a will and other paperwork to deal with, but Akesuk had taken care of that already. There was no need for him to stay.

He decided to cancel the second night. He was bound to be able to get a flight to Iqaluit and, with a bit of luck, there'd be a spare seat on the plane to Montréal. From there he didn't care how long he had to wait for his connection. There was plenty to see in Montréal, and it was far enough from this hellhole at the end of the earth . . .

Anawak was dreaming. He was in a plane, circling Vancouver, waiting for permission to land, but the control tower wouldn't let them. The pilot turned to him.

'They're not going to let us land. Vancouver and Tofino are out of the question.'

'Why?' yelped Anawak.

'We've made our enquiries. You don't live anywhere near here. We've got no record of a Leon Anawak. Ground Control says I have to take you home. Where do you want me to go?'

'I don't know.'

'You must know where your home is.'

'Down there.'

'Fine.'

The plane dipped, then banked around again. The city lights came into view, but only a scattering, too few for Vancouver. This wasn't Vancouver. There were ice floes drifting on dark water, and a marble mountain range beyond the town.

They were landing in Cape Dorset.

Suddenly he was in his childhood home, and there was a celebration – his birthday. Some of the local kids had been invited, and his father suggested a race in the snow. He gave Anawak an enormous package tied clumsily together. It was his only present, and it was precious, he said. 'You'll find everything in there that you'll need in life,' he explained. 'But you must carry it with you while we're running.'

Anawak tried to balance the enormous parcel on his head, steadying it with both hands. They went outside, and as the white snow glistened in the darkness, a voice whispered to him that he had to win the race or the others would kill him. At night they were wolves and would rip him to pieces. He had to reach the water first, had to run before they caught him.

Anawak began to weep. He cursed his birthday, because he knew that soon he would grow up, and he didn't want to grow up and be torn to pieces. Digging his fingers into the parcel, he started to run. The snow was deep and he sank into it. It reached his hips, scarcely allowing him to move. He glanced back but no one was running with him. He was on his own. Only his parents' house was visible behind him, with the door closed and the lights out. A cold moon shone down from above, and suddenly it was deathly still.

Anawak wondered whether he should return to the house, but everyone seemed to have left. It looked eerie and forbidding. There was no one to be seen in the frozen moonlit night, and not a sound. He remembered the wolves, waiting to eat him alive. Were they in the house? Had the party ended in a bloodbath? It didn't seem possible. In a mysterious way Cape Dorset and the house seemed to defy the laws of nature. This was where they had gathered for his birthday; but now it was a distant future or an even more distant past. Or maybe time had stood still and he was looking at a frozen universe hostile to life.

Fear won out. He turned away from the house and trudged towards the water. The wharf belonging to the real Cape Dorset had vanished, and the ice led directly to the sea. His parcel was getting smaller all the time, so small that he could carry it in one hand, and in a few steps he was at the edge.

Rays of moonlight shimmered on the dark waves and the drifting slabs of ice. The sky was studded with stars. Someone was calling his name. The faint voice was coming from a snowdrift, and Anawak moved forward until he was close enough to see. Two bodies, dusted with snow, lay side by side. His parents. They were staring at the sky with empty eyes.

I'm a grown-up now, he thought. It's time to open the parcel.

He examined it on the palm of his hand.

It was tiny. He began to unwrap it, but there was nothing inside, only paper. He tore away the crinkled sheets, discarding layer after layer, until the parcel was gone and so were the fallen bodies of his parents, leaving him alone on the edge of the ice, with the dark waves beyond.

A mighty hump parted the water and sank down.

Anawak turned his head slowly. He saw a small, shabby house, a shack made of corrugated iron. The door was open.

His home.

No, he thought. No! Tears came to his eyes. This wasn't right. This couldn't be his life. It wasn't where he belonged. It couldn't end like this.

He crouched in the snow and stared at the hut, weeping uncontrollably, in the grip of a nameless misery. His sobs almost burst his chest, echoing in the sky, filling the world with lamentation, a world in which no one existed but him.

No. No!

Then the light.

Anawak sat upright in bed. The display on his alarm clock read 2:30 a.m. His tongue was sticking to his palate so he got up and went to the minibar. He reached for a Coke, opened it and drank. Then, clutching the can, he went to the window, opened the curtains and looked out.

The hotel was on a hill overlooking Kinngait and parts of the neighbouring hamlets. It was a clear and cloudless night and a nocturnal half-light steeped the houses, tundra, snowfields and sea in an improbable shade of reddish-gold. It was never truly dark at this time of year: the contours just softened and the colours mellowed.

All of a sudden he saw its beauty. He looked in wonder at the sky, then let his eyes roam over the mountains and the bay. The frozen seascape of Tellik Inlet shimmered like molten silver, while Mallikjuaq Island rose up from the water like a slumbering whale.

What now?

He remembered how he had felt at the Station with Shoemaker and Delaware, his sense of alienation, from Davie's, Tofino, and everything around him. How he had seemed to be missing some inner space to protect him from the world. Something decisive had been on the horizon, of that he had been certain. He had waited, elated and fearful, as though an extraordinary change would sweep over him.

Instead his father had died.

Was that it, then? The event that would change everything? His return to the Arctic to bury his father?

He had far greater challenges to deal with. Right now he was facing one of the greatest that mankind had ever seen. Just him and a few other people. Yet it had nothing to do with his life. His life had a different framework, in which tsunamis, climate disasters and plagues had no place. His father's death had pushed his own life into the foreground and now Anawak felt, in Nunavut, a chance to reclaim it.

After a while he got dressed, pulled a fur-lined hat down over his ears and walked into the moonlit night. He had the streets to himself. He roamed the town until a wave of tiredness engulfed him, then returned to the warmth of the hotel room, and was asleep before his head had hit the pillow.

The next morning he called Akesuk. 'How about breakfast?' he asked.

His uncle seemed surprised. 'We've just sat down here. I thought you'd be busy.'

'OK. No problem.'

'Hold on – we've only just started. Why don't you come over? There's scrambled eggs and bacon.'

'Great.'

The plateful with which Mary-Ann presented him was so large that Anawak felt full before he started, but he still dug in. A smile spread across her face, and he wondered what Akesuk had told her. He must have found a good reason for Anawak to have turned down their offer of supper last night. She didn't seem in the least offended.

It felt odd to grasp the hand that Akesuk and his wife had extended to him. It pulled him back into the family. Anawak wondered whether it was a good thing. The magic of the moonlit night had vanished now and he was far from making peace with Nunavut.

After breakfast Mary-Ann cleared the table and went shopping. Akesuk twiddled with the dials on his transistor radio, listened for a while and said, 'IBC is forecasting mild weather for the next few days. You can't rely on it entirely, of course, but even if it's only half true, it'll be good enough for us to go out on the land.'

'You've got a trip planned?'

'We're leaving tomorrow. The two of us could do something today, though, if you like. Are you sticking to your plans – or were you thinking of flying back early?'

The old fox had guessed.

Anawak stirred his coffee. 'Last night I was on the point of leaving.'

'I guessed as much,' Akesuk said drily. 'And now?'

'I don't know. I thought maybe I'd take a trip to Mallikjuaq or Inuksuk Point – I don't feel comfortable in Cape Dorset. I don't mean to offend you, Iji, but good memories are hard to come by with a . . . well, with a . . .'

'With a father like yours,' his uncle said. He stroked his moustache. 'What astonishes me is that you're here at all. It's been nineteen years since any of us heard from you and now I'm the only one left. I got in touch with you because I thought you ought to know, but I never believed we'd see you here again. Why did you come?'

'Who knows? It wasn't as though anything was drawing me back. Maybe Vancouver wanted to get rid of me for a while.'

'Nonsense.'

'Well, it had nothing to do with my father, if that's what you're thinking. I'm not going to shed any tears over him.' He knew it sounded harsh, but it was too bad. 'I can't do that, Iji.'

'You're too hard on him.'

'He led a bad life.'

Akesuk gave him a long look. 'Yes, he did, but there weren't many options back then.' He drained the dregs of his coffee. Then he was smiling. 'Here's a suggestion. We'll start our trip today. Mary-Ann and I were planning to go somewhere different for a change – north-west to Pond Inlet. You could come too.'

Anawak stared at him. 'It's out of the question,' he said. 'You'll be out there for weeks. I can't possibly be away for that long – even if I wanted to.'

'I'm not suggesting you stay the whole time. We'll all set out together, and after a few days you can fly back on your own. You're a grown man – you don't need me to hold your hand. You can get on a plane by yourself, can't you?'

'But that'll be far too much trouble, Iji, I—'

'I'm fed up of hearing about trouble. Why should it be any trouble for you to come too? There's a group of us meeting in Pond Inlet. All the arrangements have been made, and I'm sure we'll find room for your civilised behind.' He winked at him. 'But don't go thinking it'll be an easy ride. You'll be given your share of bear duty like the rest of us.'

Anawak pondered his uncle's invitation. It had caught him off-guard. He'd prepared himself for one more day, not three or four.

But Li had made clear that he should stay for as long as he needed to.

Pond Inlet. Three more days.

'Why are you so keen for me to come?' he asked.

Akesuk laughed.

'Why do you think?' he said. 'I'm going to take you home.'

On the land. Those three words encapsulated the Inuit philosophy of life. Going out on the land meant escaping from the settlements and spending the summer camped in tents on the beaches or on the floe-edge, fishing, and hunting walrus, seal or narwhal, which the Inuit were permitted to kill for their own consumption. They would take everything they needed for life beyond the reaches of civilisation, loading clothes, equipment and hunting tools on to ATVs, sledges or boats. The territory they were venturing into was untamed: a vast expanse of land that people had roamed for thousands of years.

Time was of no importance on the land, where the routines and patterns of cities and settlements ceased to exist. Distances weren't measured in kilometres or miles but in days. Two days to this place, and half a day to that. It was no help to know that it was fifty kilometres to your destination, if the route was filled with obstacles like pack ice or crevasses. Nature had no respect for human plans. The next second could be fraught with imponderables, so people lived for the present. The land followed its own rhythm, and the Inuit submitted to it. Thousands of years as nomads had taught them that that was the way to gain mastery. Through the first half of the twentieth century they had continued to roam the land freely, and decades later the nomadic lifestyle still suited them better than being confined to one place by a house.

Some things had changed though, as Anawak was increasingly aware. They seemed to have accepted that the world expected them to take regular jobs and become part of industrial society, and in return they'd been granted the acceptance denied to them when Anawak was a child. The world was returning part of what it had taken, and giving them a new outlook, in which ancient traditions took their place alongside a western lifestyle.

The place Anawak had left behind had been a geographical region devoid of identity or self-worth, its people robbed of their energies and respected by no one. Only his father could have redrawn that picture for him, but he was the one who'd done most to inspire it. The man buried in Cape Dorset had become symbolic of the wider resignation: a worn-out alcoholic prone to self-pity and temper, who'd failed to stand up for his family. That day, as Cape Dorset had disappeared from his view, Anawak had stood on deck and shouted into the fog: 'Go ahead, kill yourselves! Then you won't be such an embarrassment.' For a second he'd toyed with the idea of leading by example and jumping overboard.

Instead he'd become a west-coast Canadian. His adoptive parents had settled in Vancouver, good people who did everything they could to support him in his schooling. They'd never grown accustomed to each other, though: a family united purely by circumstance. When Leon was twenty-four, they'd moved to Anchorage in Alaska. Once a year they sent him a greetings card, and he'd reply with a few friendly lines. He never visited, and they didn't seem to expect it – the idea would probably have surprised them.

Akesuk's talk of an expedition on the land had prompted a new wave of memories – long evenings round the fire, while people told stories and the whole world seemed alive. When he was little, he'd taken for granted that the Snow Queen and the Bear God were real. He'd listened to the tales of men and women who'd been born in igloos, and imagined how one day he'd journey over the ice, hunting and living in harmony with himself and the Arctic myth – sleeping when he was tired, working and hunting when the weather was right, eating when he was hungry. On the land they would sometimes leave the tent for a breath of fresh air and end up hunting for a day and a night. On other occasions they'd be ready to go, and the hunt never took place. The apparent lack of organisation had always seemed suspect to the qallunaat: how could anyone live without timetables and quotas? The qallunaat constructed new worlds in place of the existing one: Nature's ways were sidelined, and if things didn't fit with their notions, they ignored or destroyed them.

Anawak thought of the Chateau and the challenges he and the team were facing. He thought of Jack Vanderbilt, clinging to the belief that the events of the past months were down to human planning and activity. Anyone who wanted to understand the way of the Inuit had to let go of the mania for control that characterised the western world.

But at least they were all of the same species. There was nothing familiar about the beings in the sea. Anawak was convinced that Johanson was right. Humanity was on the brink of losing this war, and people like Vanderbilt couldn't see any perspective but their own.

Maybe the CIA boss was aware of his failings, but he wasn't about to change.

Anawak suddenly realised that they would never solve the crisis without the right team.

Someone was missing, and he knew who it was.

While Akesuk prepared for their departure, Anawak sat in the hotel and tried to place a call to the Chateau. After a few minutes he was redirected to a secure line and diverted several times. Li wasn't in Whistler: she was on board a US warship near Seattle.

A quarter of an hour later, he was connected and made his request for another three or four days' leave. When she agreed, he felt a prick of conscience, but told himself that the fate of the world hardly depended on it. Besides, he would be working: he might be in the Arctic Circle, but his mind would still be busy.

Li mentioned that she'd launched a sonar offensive against the whales. 'I don't expect you to be pleased,' she said.

'Is it working?'

'We're on the point of giving up. It hasn't achieved the desired results. We're having to try everything – at least if we can keep the whales away for a while, we've got more chance of sending down divers or robots.'

'You need to expand the team.'

'Who did you have in mind?'

'Three people.' He took a deep breath. 'I'd like you to recruit them. We need more input in the areas of behavioural and cognitive science. And I need someone to help me. Someone I can trust. I'd like you to get Alicia Delaware on board. She usually spends her summers in Tofino. She's a student – majored in animal intelligence.'

'Fine,' Li said. He hadn't expected her to agree so quickly. 'And the second person?'

'A guy in Ucluelet. If you take a look at the MK files, you'll find him under the name of Jack O'Bannon. He's good at handling marine mammals. He knows a thing or two that might help us.'

'Is he a scientist?'

'No. An ex-dolphin-handler with the US Navy. Marine Mammal Program.'

'I see,' said Li. 'I'll look into it. We've got plenty of our own experts. Why him?'

'That's who I want.'

'And the third person?'

'She's the most important of all. In a sense, we're dealing with aliens, so you'll need someone who devotes their time to thinking about how we could communicate with non-human life-forms. Dr Samantha Crowe is head of SETI in Arecibo.'

Li laughed. 'You're a bright guy, Leon. We'd already decided to recruit someone from SETI. Do you know Dr Crowe?'

'Yes, she's good.'

'I'll see what I can do. Make sure you get back here safely.'

Instead of taking a direct route northwards, the Hawker Siddeley turboprop headed east. Akesuk had persuaded the pilot to make a small detour so Anawak could admire the Great Plain of Koukdjuak, a wildlife sanctuary dotted with perfectly round ponds that were home to the world's largest colony of geese. The passengers, from Cape Dorset and Iqaluit, were all *en route* to Pond Inlet, where the expedition into the wilderness would begin. Most were already familiar with the view, and had dozed off. Anawak, however, was entranced.

They followed the line of the coast for a while, crossing into the Arctic Circle. Below them was the lunar landscape of Foxe Basin, its frozen surface fissured with cracks, leads, and pools of water. After a while, land reappeared, mountainous territory with steep drops and sheer palisades of rock. Snow glinted from the bottom of deep, shadowy gorges. Rivulets of meltwater poured into frozen lakes. In the light of the setting sun the scenery looked more majestic than ever. Rugged brown mountains were interspersed with snowy valleys, while jagged ridges reached up into the sky, the rock disguised by snowdrifts. Then, almost seamlessly, the plane passed above a blue-tinted shoreline, and they were staring down at a continuous layer of pack ice, Eclipse Sound.

Anawak forgot everything around him as he gazed at the strange beauty of the High Arctic. Colossal snow-white crystals stuck out of the white sheet of the Sound: icebergs. Beneath them the tiny forms of two polar bears raced across the ice, as though the turboprop's shadow was chasing them. Shimmering dots swooped through the air – ivory gulls. Further on, the glaciers and precipitous cliffs of Bylot Island rose into view. Then the plane dropped down, heading towards a shoreline as a marbled brown landscape appeared before them, a settlement of houses and an airstrip – Pond Inlet, or Mittimatalik in Inuktitut, 'the place where Mittima rests'.

The sun glared into their eyes from the north-west. It wouldn't set completely at this time of year, merely come to rest on the horizon for a few minutes at two o'clock in the morning. When they landed it was nine in the evening, but Anawak had lost all sense of time. He looked at the scenes from his childhood, and felt as though a weight had been lifted from his chest.

Akesuk had succeeded in doing something that, twenty-four hours earlier, Anawak would not have thought possible.

He had brought him home.

Pond Inlet was of a comparable size to Cape Dorset, but in most other respects it had little in common with the south of the island. The region had been settled for over four thousand years, but no one had embarked on any daring architectural experiments of the kind that Anawak had seen in Iqaluit. Akesuk explained that tradition played a more important role in this area of Nunavut than anywhere else. Some people even practised shamanism, he said cautiously, and hastened to add that they were good Christians too.

They stayed overnight at a hotel. Akesuk woke him early, and they strolled down to the shore. The old man sniffed the air. The mild weather would continue, he announced. They could look forward to the hunt.

'Spring hasn't kept us waiting this year,' he said, in satisfaction. 'I heard at the hotel that it's half a day's journey to the floe-edge. Or maybe a full day, depending.'

'On what?'

Akesuk shrugged. 'All kinds of things can happen. It depends. You'll see plenty of animals – whales, seals, polar bears. This year the ice is breaking up earlier than usual.'

Now that was hardly surprising, thought Anawak, given what else was going on.

The group was made up of twelve people. Anawak recognised some from the aeroplane; others he met in Pond Inlet. Akesuk had a word with the two guides, who were putting together the equipment for the trip. Anything that wouldn't be needed was left in the storeroom at the hotel. Four qamutiks were waiting. In Anawak's memory, the sleds had been pulled by dogs, but now they were hitched to snowmobiles and skidoos. The qamutiks hadn't changed, though: two wooden runners four metres long, curving up at the front, to which horizontal slats were tightly lashed. No screws or nails, the sleds were held together with rope and cord, which made repairs considerably easier. Open-topped wooden compartments mounted on three of the quamutiks would protect the passengers from the worst of the weather while the fourth was the pack sled.

'You won't be warm enough,' Akesuk warned him, glancing at Anawak's jacket.

'I checked the temperature. It's six degrees.'

'You're forgetting the wind chill from the sled. And I hope you're wearing two pairs of socks. We're not in Vancouver, you know.'

There was so much that he had forgotten. He was only just regaining his instinct for what it was like to be out there in the cold. He felt almost ashamed of himself. The challenge was in keeping your feet warm – it always had been. He pulled on another pair of socks and an extra sweater. In their padded clothes and snow goggles, they all looked like Arctic astronauts.

Akesuk and the guides made one last check of the equipment. 'Sleeping-bags, caribou pelts . . .'

There was a shine in the old man's eyes. His thin grey moustache seemed to bristle with pleasure. Anawak watched as he hurried between the sleds. Ijitsiaq Akesuk was nothing like Anawak's father.

His thoughts turned to the unknown force in the sea.

Once the expedition started, their decisions would be governed by Nature. To survive on the land, you had to adopt an almost pantheistical attitude: you were just part of the living world that manifested itself in animals, plants, ice and sometimes humans.

And in the yrr, he thought, whoever they are, whatever they look like, however and wherever they live.

There was a jerk as the snowmobile set off, pulling them over the snow-covered sea. Anawak, Akesuk and Mary-Ann shared a sled. From time to time they saw puddles of water on the surface, where the ice was melting. They curved round the settlement on the coastal hill, and headed towards the north-east, moving away from Baffin Island, which now protruded from the ice behind them. Across the sound the soaring peaks of Bylot Island towered into the sky, surrounded by icebergs. An immense glacier poured down from the mountains and on to the shore. Anawak reminded himself that the surface beneath them was the frozen crust of the ocean. Fish were swimming below. Every now and then the qamutik's runners lifted as they hit a patch of rough ground, but the sled cushioned them from the impact.

After a while the two Inuit in the first qamutik changed course and the other sleds followed. For a moment Anawak was puzzled, but then he saw that they were making their way round a gaping crack in the ice, too wide to be crossed in a sled. Dark fathomless water appeared inside the blue-tinged icy chasm.

'This could take a while,' said Akesuk.

'Yep, we'll lose some time.' Anawak knew what it meant to drive a sled round cracks.

Akesuk's nose wrinkled. 'I wouldn't say that. Time stays the same whether we travel due east or take a detour further north. Out here it doesn't matter when you arrive. Don't you remember? Your life doesn't stop unfolding because you take a longer route. No time is wasted.'

Anawak was silent.

'You know,' his uncle added, with a smile, 'maybe the biggest problem we've had to face in the last hundred years was the qallunaat bringing us time. They believe that time spent waiting is time wasted – wasted lifetime. When you were a child, we all thought so. Your father did so too, and because he couldn't see any way to do something useful with his life, he decided that it was worthless, just wasted time. A life not worth living.'

Anawak turned towards him. 'Don't feel sorry for him. Feel sorry for my mother,' he said.

'Well, *she* felt sorry for him,' Akesuk retorted, and said something to Mary-Ann.

They had to travel several kilometres until the crack had narrowed enough to cross. One of the Inuit drivers unhitched his snowmobile and revved it at high speed over the gap. Then he threw ropes across to the qamutiks and pulled them one by one to safety. The journey continued. Anawak's uncle pushed a strip of something fatty into his mouth. He held out the tin to Anawak.

It was narwhal skin. During Anawak's childhood, they'd always taken it on journeys to the floe-edge. It was an excellent source of vitamin C, he remembered – far better than oranges or lemons. He chewed, and the flavour of nuts filled his mouth. The taste evoked a string of pictures and emotions. He heard voices, but they didn't belong to this expedition: they came from the people he'd been travelling with twenty years earlier. He felt the caress of his mother, stroking his hair.

'Cracks in the ice, pressure ridges . . .' His uncle laughed. 'Well, this certainly isn't a freeway. Come on, be honest, you must have missed something of this?'

Anawak shook his head. 'No,' he said and immediately felt ashamed.

Anawak had spent most of his life on Vancouver Island, and had dedicated himself to marine biology, so he was bound to feel more of an affinity with nature than with any man-made construct. Yet whale-watching in Clayoquot Sound was quite different from sledging across a featureless expanse of white, gliding over the strait towards the ocean, with brown tundra on the right and the glaciated peaks of Bylot Island to the left. While the climate in western Canada seemed to have been designed with humans in mind, the Arctic was spectacularly hellish: fantastically beautiful, but sufficient unto itself, and fatal to anyone deluded enough to think that humans could conquer it. The settlements looked like a stubborn attempt to take ownership of a land that defied subjugation. The ride in the qamutik to the floe-edge resembled a journey into the unconscious.

Anawak's sense of time had abandoned him after another night in the midnight sun. They were on their way to the earth's primal source. Even someone as rational as Anawak, who could find a scientific explanation for everything, suddenly saw the logic in the old Inuit story of why the polar bear padded mournfully over the ice. Its love for an Inuk woman had clouded its judgement. The bear had warned the woman not to tell her husband about their illicit meetings, but when the hunter returned after weeks of tracking in vain, she took pity on him and told him where her lover could be found. The bear heard her treachery, and while the hunter went to look for it, it crept to her igloo, intending to kill her. Raising its paw, it was overcome with sorrow. Not even her death could undo the betrayal. It trudged away.

Anawak's skin prickled with the cold.

Whenever Nature had allowed man to approach, her trust had been betrayed. Since then, so the legend continued, man had been attacked by polar bears. This was the bears' kingdom. They were stronger than man, but in the end mankind had defeated them and, in so doing, had defeated itself. Although Anawak had turned his back on his homeland for the best part of two decades, he was well aware that industrial chemicals, like DDT and highly toxic PCBs, were transported by the wind and the currents from Asia, North America and Europe to the Arctic Ocean. They accumulated in the fatty tissue of whales, seals and walruses, which were eaten by polar bears and humans, who fell ill. Breastmilk from Inuit women contained levels of PCBs that were twenty times higher than the amount listed as harmful by the World Health Organisation. Inuit children suffered from neurological impairments, and IQ levels were falling. The wilderness was being poisoned because the qallunaat still couldn't, or wouldn't, grasp the way in which the world worked: sooner or later, everything was distributed everywhere, through the winds and the water.

Was it any surprise that something at the bottom of the ocean had decided to put a stop to it?

After two hours of sledging over the ice they veered right towards the coast of Baffin Island. Stiff from sitting down for so long and from bracing themselves against the bumpy ground, they trudged over the flat ice and up on to the land, past rocks covered with lichen and towards the snow-free tundra. Individual flower buds dotted the mossy waterlogged ground: crimson saxifrage and cinquefoil, colours glowing against the boggy soil. The group had chosen the right time of year to come here. In summer the place would be buzzing with flies.

The ground rose gently. One of the guides led them on to a plateau with a view of the ocean and the snow-capped mountains. He pointed out the remains of an ancient Thule settlement and showed them two plain crosses that marked the graves of German whalers. Some siksiks, or Arctic ground squirrels, chased each other over the plains, disappearing into burrows in the ground. Mary-Ann picked up some stones and juggled them deftly. It was an Inuit sport, as old as the hills. Anawak tried to copy her, but his efforts provoked a roar of collective laughter. The slightest thing, like someone slipping, always had the Inuit in stitches.

After a quick lunch of sandwiches and coffee, they crossed an even wider lead in the ice and headed for Bylot Island. Meltwater spurted in all directions beneath the skidoos' rubber tracks. Pack ice piled up in odd formations, blocking their path and necessitating further detours, but it wasn't long before they were gliding beneath the cliffs of Bylot Island. The noise of squawking birds filled the air. Kittiwakes were nesting in the rocks in their thousands. Great flocks circled the cliffs. The convoy halted.

'Time for a walk,' announced Akesuk.

'We've only just had one,' said Anawak.

'That was three hours ago, my boy.'

Unlike Baffin Island's gently sloping tundra, the shoreline of Bylot Island rose precipitously out of the water. The walk turned into a climb. Akesuk pointed to a trail of white bird droppings leading down from a crevice in the rock, high above their heads. 'Gyrfalcons,' he said. 'Beautiful creatures.' He made curious whistling noises, but the falcons wouldn't be tempted out. 'If we were further inland, we'd have a good chance of spotting them. We'd probably see a few foxes, snow geese, owls, falcons and buzzards.' Akesuk smiled ironically. 'On the other hand, we might not. That's the Arctic for you. You can't count on anything. An unreliable lot, these animals – just like the Inuit, right, Leon?'

'I'm not a qallunaaq, if that's what you're suggesting,' Anawak protested.

'Good.' His uncle sniffed the air. 'We'll spare ourselves the trouble of going any further. Seeing as you're no longer a qallunaaq, you're bound to return. Now, let's head out to the floe-edge – we should make the most of this weather.'

From then on time ceased to exist.

As they made their way east, leaving Bylot Island in their wake, the ice became rougher and the runners took even more of a battering. Cold winds had left thin layers of ice on the surface of the puddles, which tinkled beneath them like shattering glass. Anawak spotted a narrow lead and called to the driver, but the man had already seen it – he turned as the skidoo raced over the ice, pulling the qamutik behind it, and grinned.

'So you haven't forgotten everything,' laughed Akesuk.

Anawak hesitated. Then he joined in. He felt ridiculously proud to have spotted a crack in the ice.

The afternoon light conjured sun dogs in the sky. That was what the Inuit called the peculiar apparitions that formed on either side of the sun, coloured luminous spots created by the refraction of the sun's rays through tiny frozen crystals in the air. Pack ice had stacked up in the distance, forming steep, jagged barriers. Then smooth, open water appeared on their right. A seal rose up, glanced at them and dived. After a while its head popped back up to stare at them inquisitively. They left the water behind them and headed for a larger pool, which seemed to Anawak to stretch for ever, until he realised that it wasn't a pool but the open ocean. They had reached the floe-edge.

Before long they saw a collection of tents ahead. The procession halted. There were greetings all round – some people knew each other already. The group at the camp came from Pond Inlet and Igloolik. They'd caught a narwhal earlier and had carved it up, leaving the carcass further to the east near the floe-edge, in the direction that Anawak's expedition was heading. Pieces of its skin were passed round, and the talk turned to the hunt. Two men joined them, hunters returning from the floe-edge on skidoos, on their way home. Their qamutiks were loaded with hunting kayaks and the bodies of two seals they'd shot the day before. One man said the seals would follow the retreating ice, arriving at their feeding and breeding grounds earlier than usual. He swung his Winchester 5.6 as he talked, and advised them to be careful. The slogan on his cap read, 'Work is only for people who don't know how to hunt.' Anawak asked if he'd noticed anything odd about the whales, whether they'd seemed aggressive or had attacked. Apparently they hadn't. Suddenly the whole camp flocked to listen. Everyone was *au fait* with the reports and knew every last fact about the phenomena that had terrified the world. As far as Anawak could tell, though, the Arctic had been spared.

As evening drew in, they left the camp.

The two hunters headed back to Pond Inlet, while Anawak's party continued in the direction of the floe-edge. After a while they passed the remains of the dead narwhal. Flocks of birds were squabbling over the meat. They carried on, trying to put as much distance as possible between themselves and the carcass, but when they finally stopped it was still within sight. The guides set up camp thirty metres or so from the floe-edge. Boxes were unloaded from the sleds, and the radio mast was erected so that they could keep in contact with the outside world. In no time the guides had pitched five tents, four for the travellers and a kitchen tent, all with wooden flooring and camping mats. Three sheets of plywood daubed with white paint served as a toilet, housing a bucket lined with a blue plastic bag and topped with a scratched enamel seat.

'About time too,' beamed Akesuk.

While the others finished setting up camp, he was the first to disappear into the honey-pot, as the Inuit nicknamed it. The guides detached the skidoos from the sleds and proposed a race. Anawak was shown how to manoeuvre one, and soon they were shooting past each other on the shimmering ice. Anawak's heart lightened. He loved being there.

The races continued until one of the men from Igloolik was declared the overall winner, and their thoughts turned to food. Mary-Ann shooed them out of the kitchen tent, so they stood outside, leaning up against the sleds and huddling together to fend off the cold. A young woman started to tell an Inuit story of the kind that was told and retold but never the same way twice. Anawak could remember such stories lasting for days.

It was getting on for midnight when Mary-Ann served dinner – grilled Arctic char, caribou chops with rice, roasted Eskimo potatoes, and to wash it all down, litres of tea. The kitchen tent was supposed to accommodate everyone, but it was unquestionably too small – Akesuk was furious, and cursed the man from whom he'd hired it – so they took their plates outside and balanced them on the sleds and boxes,

One after another, the travellers retired to bed. Then at half past one in the morning, Akesuk reached into the depths of his bag and brought out a bottle of champagne. He winked slyly at Anawak. Mary-Ann turned up her nose and said goodnight, so Anawak and his uncle were left alone, with the exception of the man on bear-watch, who was standing on a mound of pack ice with a rifle at his feet.

'In that case we'll have to drink it by ourselves,' said Akesuk.

'I don't drink.'

'Of course.' Akesuk looked at the bottle mournfully. 'Are you sure? I packed it specially. I was waiting for the right occasion. And the occasion . . . Well, you've come home, so I thought . . .'

'I don't want to lose control, Iji.'

'Control of what? Of your life or of this moment?' He stowed the bottle away. 'No problem. There'll be other occasions. Maybe we'll catch something big. Who knows? We might get a beluga or a walrus. How about a walk before we turn in?'

'Good idea.'

They strolled down to the floe-edge. Anawak let his uncle take the lead. The old man had a better sense of where the ice was stable and where it might break. The Inuit had hundreds of words for every possible kind of snow or ice, but not one that meant 'snow' or 'ice' in general. Right now they were walking on elastic ice. Salt separated from water as it froze, so icebergs were formed entirely of fresh water. Pack ice and drift ice contained traces of salt – the faster the water froze, the greater the salinity of the ice. That increased its elasticity, which was good in winter because it prevented it cracking too easily, but problematic in spring when it heightened the risk of break-up. The mere shock of falling into the cold water was enough to kill someone, but the greater danger was of being swept beneath the ice.

They found a spot near the floe-edge and leaned up against a block of pack ice. The silvery sea stretched in front of them. Anawak spotted the steel-blue bodies of graylings flitting just beneath the surface. For a while they let the minutes tick by, and suddenly, as though Nature had decided to reward them for their patience, two spiral-ridged tusks rose out of the water like a pair of crossed swords. A couple of male narwhal appeared a few metres from the floe-edge. Their rounded mottled heads came into view, then the dark grey bodies dived down. In less than fifteen minutes they'd be back. That was their rhythm.

Anawak watched in fascination. Narwhal were hardly ever seen off the coast of Vancouver Island. For years they'd been threatened with extinction. Their tusks, which were actually modified teeth, were pure ivory, condemning them to centuries of slaughter. They were still on the list of endangered species, but the narwhal population in Nunavut and Greenland had crept back up to ten thousand.

The ice made soft creaking and groaning noises as the water rose and fell. Birds were still squawking around the remains of the dead narwhal. A gentle light bathed the mountains and glaciers of Bylot Island, casting shadows on the frozen sea. The sun hugged the horizon, pale and icy.

'You asked whether I'd missed this,' said Anawak.

Akesuk stayed silent.

'I hated it, Iji. I hated it, and I despised it. You wanted an answer. Now you know.'

His uncle sighed. 'You despised your father,' he said.

'Maybe. But you try explaining the difference to a twelve-year-old, whose father and people seem as wretched as each other. My father was weak and constantly drunk. All he did was whine and drag my mother down till she put an end to it all – she couldn't see any other way. Everyone was killing themselves back then. Name one family that wasn't in mourning for someone who'd taken their own life. All those stories about the proud Inuit, the self-sufficient Inuit – well, there wasn't much evidence of it back then.' He faced Akesuk. 'If your parents are reduced to wrecks in the space of a few years, get addicted to drugs, lose the will to live, how do you cope? What do you do when your mother hangs herself and all your father can do is get drunk. I told him to stop. I told him that I could get a job, that I'd do anything if he stopped drinking, but he just stared at me and went on as usual.'

'I know. He wasn't himself any more.'

'He gave me up for adoption,' said Anawak. The bitterness that had built up over the years was on the point of spilling out. 'I wanted to stay with him, and he gave me up for adoption.'

'He wanted to protect you.'

'Oh, really? Did he ever wonder how I might cope? Like hell he did. Ma died of depression, he knocked himself out with liquor. They both threw me out of their lives. Did anyone bother to help me? No. They were too busy staring into the snow and bewailing the fate of the Inuit. Oh, yeah, and that reminds me, Uncle Iji. You always told good stories, but you never changed anything. That was all you could ever think of – fairytales about the free spirit of the Inuit. A noble people. A proud people.'

'That's right.' Akesuk nodded. 'We were a proud people.'

'When would that have been?'

He waited for Akesuk to lose his temper, but the old man merely stroked his moustache. 'Before you were born,' he said. 'People of my generation came into the world in igloos at a time when everyone knew how to build them. Back then we used flints and not matches to light fires. Caribou weren't shot, they were hunted with bows and arrows. We didn't hitch skidoos to our qamutiks, we had huskies. Sounds romantic, doesn't it? Like the long-lost past . . .' Akesuk mused. 'It was barely fifty years ago. Look around you, boy. Look at our lifestyle. I mean, there are good things too. Hardly anyone on Earth knows as much about what's going on in the world as we do. Every second household has a computer with a modem, including ours. We've got our own country now too.' He chuckled. 'The other day there was a question posted on nunavut.com. On the face of it, it seemed harmless enough. Do you remember those old Canadian two-dollar notes? Queen Elizabeth was on the front, with a group of Inuit on the back. One of the men was positioned beside a kayak with a harpoon in his hand. It all looked idyllic. The question was, "What does the scene really show?" What do you think?'

'I don't know.'

'Well, I do. It's the image of an expulsion. The government in Ottawa had a more palatable term for it. They preferred to call it "relocation." A Cold War phenomenon. The politicians in Ottawa were scared that the Soviet Union or the United States would take it into their heads to lay claim to the uninhabited Canadian Arctic so they relocated the nomadic Inuit from their traditional territory in the southern Arctic to Resolute and Grise Fjord near the North Pole. They claimed that the hunting grounds were better there, but the opposite was true. The Inuit were forced to wear numbered dog-tags as though they were animals. Did you know that?'

'I can't remember.'

'Your generation and the kids growing up today have no idea what their parents had to live through. And it started long before that, with the white trappers in the 1920s who came here with guns. The seal and caribou populations were decimated – and not just because of the qallunaat. The Inuit killed them off too. That's what happens when you exchange your bow and arrows for a gun. Anyway, the Inuit people were plunged into poverty. They'd never had much trouble with disease, but now there were outbreaks of polio, tuberculosis, measles and diphtheria, so they left the land and moved into settlements. By the end of the 1950s our people were dying of starvation and infectious disease, and the government did nothing about it. Then the military got interested in the Northwest Territories and secret radar stations were erected on traditional Inuit hunting grounds. The Inuit who lived there were in the way, so at the instigation of the Canadian government they were packed into aeroplanes and deposited hundreds of kilometres further north – without their tents, kayaks, canoes or sleds. When I was a young man, I was relocated too. So were your parents. Back then the authorities justified it by claiming that the chances of survival for the impoverished Inuit were better in the north than in the vicinity of the military bases. But the new settlements were nowhere near the caribou trails or any of the summer breeding grounds.'

There was a lengthy silence. Every now and then the two narwhal reappeared. Anawak watched the clash of swords, waiting for his uncle to resume his story.

'After our relocation, they bulldozed our hunting grounds. Everything that might remind us of our old lives here was razed to the ground to stop us returning. And, of course, the caribou didn't change their habits to suit us. We had nothing to eat, no clothes. What use is all the courage in the world, if all you can hunt are a few siksiks, hares and fish? People could be as determined and strong as they liked, but there was nothing they could do to stop their kinsmen dying. I won't go into the details. Within a few decades we were reliant on welfare. Our old way of life had been destroyed, and we didn't know any other. Around the time you were born, the Canadian government started to feel bad about us again, so they built us some houses – boxes. It was the obvious thing for the qallunaat. They live in boxes. If they want to take a trip somewhere, they get into a box with wheels. They eat in public boxes, their dogs live in boxes, and the boxes they sleep in are surrounded by other types of boxes that they call walls and fences. That was their way of life, not ours, but now we live in boxes too. Losing your identity comes at a price. Alcohol, drug abuse, suicide.'

'Did my father ever fight for his people?' Anawak asked softly.

'We all did. I was still a young man when we were driven out. I campaigned for compensation. For thirty years we struggled for our rights and went through the courts. Your father campaigned with us, but it broke his spirit. Since 1999 we've had our own state, Nunavut, "our land". No one can tell us what to do any more, and no one can force us to move. But our way of life, the only way of life that was truly ours, has been lost for ever.'

'You'll have to find yourselves a new one.'

'I expect you're right. Self-pity never helped anyone. We were nomads, free to come and go as we pleased, but we've come to terms with the idea of our territory being limited. A few decades ago, our only social structure was the family. We didn't have chiefs or leaders, and now the Inuit are governed by the Inuit, as in any civil state. The concept of property was alien to us, but now we're going the way of every modern industrial nation. We're starting to revive our traditions – people are using dog-sleds again, the young are being taught how to build igloos and start a fire with flints – and that's good, but it won't stop the march of time. You know, boy, I'm not dissatisfied. The world moves on. These days we're nomads in the Internet, wandering through the web of data highways, tracking and collecting information. We can roam all over the world. Young people chat with friends from different countries and tell them about Nunavut. But too many of our people still kill themselves. We're coming to terms with a profound trauma. We need time. The hopes of the living shouldn't be sacrificed to the dead.'

Anawak watched the sun hover on the horizon. 'You're right,' he said.

And then, impulsively, he told Akesuk everything that they'd been told at the Chateau, about what they were working on and what they suspected about the intelligent beings in the sea. He knew he was breaking Li's instructions, but he didn't care. He'd been silent all his life. Akesuk was all the family he had left.

His uncle listened. 'Would you like to hear the advice of a shaman?' he asked finally.

'I don't believe in shamans.'

'Who does? But this isn't a problem you can solve with science. A shaman would tell you that you're dealing with spirits, the spirits of the once-living that now inhabit the Earth's creatures. The qallunaat started destroying life. They angered the spirits, the spirit of the sea, Sedna. No matter who these beings are, you won't achieve anything by trying to fight them.'

'So what do we do?'

'See them as a part of yourselves. The world is such a small place, or so they're always telling us, but the truth is, we're still aliens to each other. Make contact with them, just as you're making contact with the alien world of the Inuit. Wouldn't it be a good thing if the divisions were healed?'

'They're not people, Iji.'

'That's not the point. They're part of our world, just as your hands and feet are part of your body. No one can ever win the struggle for mastery. Battles only ever end in death. Who cares how many species there are on the planet and which is more intelligent than the rest? Learn to understand them instead of fighting them.'

'Sounds fairly Christian to me. Turn the other cheek and all that.'

'Oh, no,' chuckled Akesuk. 'It's the advice of a shaman. There are still plenty of shamans around. We just don't make a big deal of it.'

'Which shaman would . . .' Anawak raised his eyebrows. 'You're not saying that . . . ?'

Akesuk grinned. 'Well, someone has to provide spiritual counsel.' He paused. 'Look!'

A short distance away an enormous polar bear was tucking into the narwhal carcass, scaring away the birds, which scattered into the air or scuttled over the ice at a respectful distance. A petrel launched an airborne assault, but the bear scarcely noticed. It wasn't close enough to the camp for the sentry to sound the alarm, but the man had cocked his gun, his eyes trained on the site.

'Nanuq,' said Akesuk. 'The polar bear smells everything, including us.'

Anawak watched the bear. He wasn't afraid. After a while the enormous creature lost interest and moved away majestically. It turned its head and cast an inquisitive look at the camp, then disappeared behind a wall of pack ice.

'See how sedately it moves,' his uncle whispered. 'But that bear can run, my boy. You bet it can run.' He chuckled, then reached into his anorak and pulled out a little sculpture that he placed on Anawak's lap. 'I've been waiting to give this to you. There's a right time for every present and maybe this is the right moment for you to have this.'

Anawak picked up the carving. A human face with feathers for hair, mounted on the body of a bird. 'A bird spirit?'

'Yes.' Akesuk nodded. 'Toonoo Sharky, one of our neighbours, made it. He's famous now. The Museum of Modern Art has bought his work. Take it. There are challenges ahead of you. You're going to need it. It will guide your thoughts in the right direction when it's time.'

'Time for what?'

'Your consciousness will soar.' Akesuk's hands became wings 'But you've been away for a long time. You're out of practice. Maybe you need someone to tell you what the bird spirit sees.'

'You're talking in riddles.'

'That's the privilege of the shaman.'

A bird crossed the sky above them.

'A Ross's gull,' said Akesuk. 'Now you're really lucky, Leon. Did you know that thousands of birdwatchers come here every year to see a gull like that? That's how rare they are. Well, you've got nothing to worry about. The spirits have sent you a sign.'

Later, in his sleeping-bag, Anawak lay awake for a while. The midnight sun shone through the fabric of the tent. He heard the sentry shout, 'Nanuq, nanuq!' He thought of the Arctic Ocean and imagined the unknown world below. He drifted until he came to the top of an iceberg that had been formed by a glacier in Greenland before the current had swept it towards the east coast of Bylot Island, where it had frozen into position. Eventually the wind and waves had freed it from the ice and sent it further south. In his dream Anawak climbed a narrow snow-covered path to the summit of the iceberg. A lake of emerald-green meltwater had formed there. Everywhere he looked, he saw the smooth, blue sea. In time the iceberg would melt, sending him to the bottom of the calm water and the source of all life, where a puzzle waited to be solved.

Perhaps a shaman would be there to help him.

24 May

Dr Stanley Frost had his own take on the situation. Surveys carried out by the energy industry located the main marine deposits of methane hydrate in the Pacific, along the west coast of North America and near Japan. More reserves had been found in the Sea of Okhotsk, the Bering Sea and further north in the Beaufort Sea. In the Atlantic, America had the bulk of the deposits right on her doorstep. Sizeable areas were known to exist in the Caribbean and off the coast of Venezuela, while the seabed around Drake Passage, stretching between South America and the Antarctic, was also rich in hydrates. Before the collapse of the slope, the deposits off the coast of Norway had been charted, as had the hydrates in the eastern Mediterranean and the Black Sea.

But methane deposits seemed thin on the ground off the north-western coast of Africa, particularly in the vicinity of the Canary Islands.

And, in Frost's view, that didn't make sense.

The Canary Islands were in an up-welling zone, where cold, nutrient-rich water rose from the depths, stimulating the growth of plankton, which in turn encouraged fish stocks. On that basis, the seabed surrounding the Canary Islands should have been covered with hydrates since methane collected in the depths wherever organic life filled the sea.

The difference in the Canaries was that the decaying matter had nowhere to settle. The islands had formed millions of years ago as a result of volcanic eruptions, and they rose steeply from the seabed like towers. Tenerife, Gran Canaria, La Palma, Gomera, El Hierro – the pinnacles of volcanic rock loomed up from the ocean floor from depths of 3000–3500 metres. Sediment and organic matter swirled down their sheer sides without settling. That was why conventional charts didn't indicate the presence of methane deposits in the Canaries, and that – in Frost's estimation – was the first miscalculation.

He suspected that the seamounts, of which the Canary Islands formed the visible peaks, weren't as sheer as had generally been supposed. There was no denying that they were steep, but they were by no means smooth and vertical. Frost had studied the formation of volcanoes for long enough to know that even the most precipitous strato-volcanoes were scarred with ridges and terraces. It was his firm opinion that large quantities of hydrates were present in the Canaries, and that people hadn't found them because they hadn't looked properly. In this instance, the hydrates wouldn't be lying in chunks on the seabed: they'd be running through the rock in thin veins. And Frost was in no doubt that they'd be found on the terraces too, wherever sediment had settled.

Since Frost was a volcanologist and not a hydrates expert, he'd called on Bohrmann for help. Frost had drawn up a list of islands that were potentially at risk: La Palma, then Hawaii and Cape Verde, followed by Tristan da Cunha further south, and Réunion in the Indian Ocean. They were all potential time-bombs, but La Palma posed by far the biggest threat. If Frost's fears turned out to be justified then the Cumbre Vieja ridge on La Palma was a Sword of Damocles, hanging over the lives of millions of people, from a height of two thousand metres.

Thanks to Bohrmann's efforts, Frost and his team had been loaned the illustrious *Polarstern* for an expedition to the area. Like the *Sonne*, the research vessel came equipped with a Victor 6000. The *Polarstern* was sufficiently large to deter the whales from attacking, and had been rigged with underwater cameras to ensure that any swarms of mussels, jellyfish or other invading organisms were detected in good time. Frost had no idea whether he'd see Victor again once it had been lowered into the water. All manner of equipment was disappearing into the depths. He could only give it a shot and hope for the best. No one opposed the suggestion.

Victor was released from the *Polarstern* off the west coast of La Palma. Splashdown occurred within sight of the shore. The robot made its way downwards, systematically searching the steep face of the volcano. Then, at four hundred metres, an array of overlapping terraces came into view, jutting out of the rock like a series of balconies. They were covered with sediment.

Victor had found the hydrate deposits that Frost had predicted.

A mass of pink bodies writhed on top: bristly worms with pincer-like jaws.

8 June

'So why all this activity in the waters of a holiday resort, when the worms could do so much more damage in Japan or back home?' asked Frost. 'The North Sea was densely populated. The American coast is chock-a-block with people and so is Honshu, but the worm colonies in those areas aren't nearly big enough to make a splash. And now we've found worms here, on a holiday island off the north-west coast of Africa. So we ask ourselves why.'

Dressed as usual in a baseball cap and industrial overalls, he was standing high on the western side of the volcanic ridge that stretched across the island. In the north, the famous Caldera de Taburiente, an enormous crater caused by erosion, was ringed with sheer walls of rock, then the mountain ridge continued southwards, the line of volcanic cones extending to its tip.

Frost was accompanied by Bohrmann and two representatives from the De Beers Corporation, a business executive and a technology specialist called Jan van Maarten. They were gathered on a sandy slope with the helicopter parked to one side. From there they looked down on a verdant crater-pocked landscape of awe-inspiring beauty. A long line of peaks towered into the sky. Black trails of lava led down to the shore, dotted with tender green shoots. There were lengthy intervals between the eruptions on La Palma, but the next volcano could erupt at any time. In geological terms, the Canary Islands were still relatively young. As recently as 1971 a new volcano, Teneguia, had made its presence known, erupting near the southern tip of the island, and extending the land mass by several hectares. Technically, the ridge was a single volcano with numerous vents, which was why people tended to refer to the Cumbre ridge as a whole whenever they discussed the volcanism of the island.

'You see, the real question,' said Bohrmann, 'is which areas should be colonised to maximise the damage.'

557

'You don't really think it could be planned in that detail?' asked the executive. She gave a puzzled frown.

'It's all hypothetical at present,' said Frost, 'but assuming there's an intelligent mind at work here, it's incredibly strategic. In the aftermath of the North Sea catastrophe everyone reasoned that the next disaster would happen in another densely populated industrial area. And, sure enough, worms were present on such sites, but only in small numbers. The obvious explanation would be that the troops, so to speak, were depleted, or that it takes time to create new armies of worms. Our attention is continually being nudged in the wrong direction. Gerhard and I are fairly certain now that the half-hearted invasions near North America and Japan are just a diversionary tactic.'

'But what's the point of attacking the hydrates in La Palma?' the woman asked. 'No one could claim that it's a hub of activity.'

The De Beers Corporation had entered the picture when Frost and Bohrmann had gone in search of existing technology to vacuum up the methane-eating worms. For decades the seabed off the coast of Namibia and South Africa had been scoured for diamonds. Various companies were involved, but the biggest player was the international diamond corporation De Beers, which used ships and offshore platforms to launch its mining operations 180 metres below. A few years previously De Beers had started to develop new ways of mining the seabed at even greater depths, using remote-controlled submersible crawlers that vacuumed up the sand and minerals, transferring them via suction pipes to surface support vessels. The most recent project focused on developing a more flexible system that could operate without the need for horizontal ground. The new technology, a remote-controlled suction pipe, would be capable of scouring vertical surfaces. Theoretically the system would be operational at depths of several thousand metres, but first it would be necessary to build a pipe of that length.

The committee had decided to collaborate directly with the team assigned to the project by De Beers. So far the corporation's two representatives had only been told that their system was of potential use in helping to prevent a worldwide disaster, to which end a suction pipe measuring several hundred metres in length was needed as soon as possible. Frost had proposed a visit to Cumbre Vieja to explain what would happen to humanity, should their mission fail.

'Oh, don't let appearances deceive you,' he said. 'There's plenty of activity here.'

The strands of hair protruding from his cap quivered in the cool sea breeze. The blue sky appeared in the lenses of his shades. He looked like a cross between Fred Flintstone and the Terminator, as his voice carried over the peaceful pine forests.

'We wouldn't be standing here in the first place if volcanic activity two million years ago hadn't blasted the Canaries out of the sea. It may look idyllic, but you shouldn't let it fool you. There's a farming village down there, Tijarafe – a lovely place, sells wonderful *quesos de alemendras*. On the eighth of September each year they celebrate the Fiesta del Diablo. A devil runs across the market square, spitting fire and setting off explosions. Why? Because the islanders know the nature of their Cumbre. Fire and explosions are part of natural life here. They know that, and so, too, does the force behind those worms. It knows how the island was created. And if you know how things are made, more often than not you can identify their weak spots.'

Frost took a few steps towards the edge. The friable volcanic rock crunched beneath his Doc Martens. In the distance below, glittering waves broke against the shore.

'In 1949 the sleepy old dog Cumbre Vieja sprang into action with a bang. The eruption came from one of its craters, at the top of the San Juan volcano. It opened up a fault. It's hard to spot with the naked eye, but it runs for kilometres along the western flank of the island, just below where we're standing. It's possible that the rock at the heart of La Palma has been fissured. At the time, a section of the Cumbre Vieja ridge slipped four metres downwards into the ocean. I've been monitoring the area for the past few years. It's highly likely that the next eruption will cause the western flank to break off entirely, owing to the unusually large amount of groundwater trapped within the rock. As soon as a new burst of hot magma enters the volcanic vent, the water will expand and evaporate in an instant. The resulting pressure could easily blast the western flank into the water. It's already been destabilised, and the eastern and southern flanks are pushing against it. Five hundred or so cubic kilometres of rock would collapse into the ocean.'

'I read about that,' said van Maarten. 'The Canary Islands authorities say the theory is dubious.'

'Dubious?' Frost thundered, like the trumpets of Jericho. 'If anything's dubious, it's their failure to address the problem in any of their statements. All they care about is not worrying the tourists. But this problem isn't going to go away. The world's already experienced similar disasters, albeit on a smaller scale. In 1741 Oshima-Oshima erupted in Japan, triggering thirty-metre-high waves. More waves were generated by the collapse of Ritter Island in 1888 in New Guinea, but the amount of falling rock was barely one per cent of the landslide that could take place here. A GPS network has been continuously monitoring Kilauea volcano in Hawaii, looking for any sign of movement, and it sure as hell is moving. The south-eastern flank is slipping seaward at an annual rate of ten centimetres, and God help us if it starts to gain momentum. The consequences are too dire to imagine. Volcanic islands have a tendency to get steeper with age. Eventually a section breaks off. The authorities on La Palma don't want to face the truth. It's not a question of *if* it will happen, it's a question of *when*. In a hundred years? A thousand? The only thing we can't be sure of is the timing. The volcanoes here don't give much warning.'

'So what would happen if half of the island fell into the sea?' asked the executive.

'The mass of rock would displace vast quantities of water,' said Bohrmann. 'A dome would form on the surface of the ocean. According to our estimates, we'd be looking at a speed of impact of three hundred and fifty kilometres per hour. The fallen debris would extend sixty kilometres over the seabed, stopping water flowing back over the landslide, and creating an air cavity that would displace far more water than the volume of the rock. There's some debate about what happens next, but none of the scenarios are especially comforting. The landslide would create a mega-wave off the coast of La Palma, with a probable height of six to nine hundred metres. The wave would set off across the Atlantic at a thousand kilometres per hour. Unlike earthquakes, landslides and slope failures are point events, which means the wave's energy dissipates as it radiates across the ocean. The further it travels from its source, the flatter it becomes.'

'At least that's something,' said the technology specialist.

'Not really. The Canary Islands would be wiped out in a flash, then an hour later, a hundred-metre-high tsunami would wash over the north-west African coast. Think of it this way: the European tsunami reached a height of forty metres in the fjords, and we all know what happened there. Six to eight hours after the eruption, a fifty-metre wave would sweep over the Caribbean, laying waste to the Antilles and flooding the east coast of America from New York to Miami. Soon afterwards the wave would hit Brazil with similar force. Smaller waves would travel as far as Spain, Portugal and the British Isles. The consequences would be devastating, even in central Europe. The European economy would collapse.'

The representatives from De Beers paled. Frost grinned at them. 'I don't suppose you've seen *Deep Impact*?'

'You mean the movie? That wave was a lot higher,' said the executive. 'It measured hundreds of metres.'

'Fifty would be enough to flatten New York. The impact of the wave would release more energy than the United States uses in a year. It doesn't matter how tall a building is – it's the base that takes the force of the tsunami. The rest of the building collapses, regardless of how many storeys there are. And we won't have Bruce Willis to save us.' He gestured towards the edge of the ridge. 'There are two ways of destabilising the western flank of the island: either Cumbre Vieja erupts, or there's an underwater avalanche. The worms are working on a landslide – a kind of miniature version of what they did in Europe, although the force will be enough to detach a segment of volcano. The rock will sink into the depths, and that in turn will prompt a minor earthquake and destabilise the Cumbre ridge. The earthquake might even trigger an eruption, but in any event the western flank will detach. It's going to happen either way – and we'll have a disaster on our hands. The worms off the coast of Norway took a few weeks to finish the job. Things could move even faster here.'

'How long have we got?'

'It's almost too late already. Those worms are pretty cunning, and they've gone to work in spots that are hard for us to reach. The whole scheme depends on the power of mega-waves to propagate on open water. They've already scored one hit in the North Sea, but that was relatively minor by comparison. If this harmless-looking little island collapses into the ocean, human civilisation is going to see just how tough things can get.'

Van Maarten rubbed his chin. 'We've already produced a prototype for the suction pipe. It's operational at depths of up to three hundred metres. We haven't tried it any deeper yet, but . . .'

'We could extend the pipe,' suggested the executive.

'We'd have to figure something out pretty quick, but if we stopped work on everything else . . . What worries me is the support vessel.'

'A vessel won't be large enough,' said Bohrmann. 'A colony of a billion or so worms – that's a huge biomass. You'd have to find somewhere to pump it.'

'That's not the real problem – we can always set up some kind of relay. No, I was thinking about a command ship with the control desk for the pipe. If we extend the length to four or five hundred metres, we'll need a vessel big enough to transport it. That's half a kilometre of pipe! It'll weigh God knows how much, and it's a damn sight thicker than deep-sea cable. We won't be able to coil it up and stick it in the hold. Besides, we need the boat to stay stable while we're steering the pipe. I don't think we need to worry about an attack, but the hydrostatics are going to be tricky. A pipe of that length can't be left dangling from the side of the vessel without affecting its balance in the water.'

'How about a dredge?'

'Wouldn't be big enough.' The man thought for a moment. 'A drillship, maybe. No . . . We'd be better off with a floating platform. We're familiar with those already. We need a kind of pontoon system, ideally a semi-submersible construction like the type they use in the offshore industry – except we wouldn't want to anchor it in position. We'll have it travelling across the water like a normal boat. It has to be manoeuvrable.' He moved away from the others, muttering something about resonant frequencies and swell variations. Then he rejoined them. 'A semi-submersible should do the trick. It's stable, mobile, and provides an ideal base for the boom, which, let's not forget, will have to take a lot of weight. There's a semi-submersible in Namibia that would adapt quite easily. It's got two propellers, each with a six-thousand-horse-power engine. We can get it fitted up with some additional thrusters, if we think we might need them.'

'The *Heerema*?' asked the executive.

'Right.'

'I thought we wanted to get rid of her.'

'She's not ready for the scrapyard yet. She has two main rudders, and the deck's supported by six huge columns – it's just what we need. OK, it was built in 1978, but it'll do the job. It's the simplest solution. We won't need a derrick, we'll have two cranes instead. We can use one to lower the pipe. Pumping up the worms won't be a problem. And we'll be able to moor the vessels before we fill them with worms.'

'Sounds good,' said Frost. 'When will she be ready?'

'Under normal circumstances it would take six months.'

'And in these circumstances?'

'I can't promise anything. Six to eight weeks, if we start right away.' The man looked at him. 'We'll do everything in our power to have it ready as soon as we can. We're pretty good at that kind of thing. But if we get it done in time, you should see it as a miracle.'

Frost nodded. He looked out over the Atlantic. The blue surface shimmered beneath them. He tried to imagine the water rising up in a six-hundred-metre dome.

'No problem,' he said. 'We could do with one.'

PART THREE

INDEPENDENCE

Just as there are fundamental principles underlying mathematics, I am convinced that a code of universal rights and
values, most notably the right to life itself, exists independently
of human ethics. The dilemma is where to find it. Who could
establish it, if not humanity? Even if we accept that rights and
values exist beyond the limits of our perception, we ourselves
are limited to what we can perceive. It is as futile as asking a cat
to decide whether the consumption of mice can be ethically
justified.

Leon Anawak, 'Self-Knowledge and Consciousness'

12 August

Samantha Crowe put down her notes and stared out of the window. The CH-53 Super Stallion was descending rapidly. A strong gust pummelled the heavy-lift helicopter. The thirty-metre craft seemed to be plummeting towards the light-grey surface stationed in the sea. Crowe was astonished that a vessel of such colossal proportions was capable of staying afloat, but at the same time she couldn't help wondering if it was big enough to land on.

Nine hundred and fifty kilometres to the north-east of Iceland, the USS *Independence LHD-8* was sailing over the deep-sea basin of the Arctic Ocean, a floating city in the Greenland Sea. Like the spaceship in *Alien*, its presence seemed dark and foreboding. Two hectares of freedom and 97,000 tonnes of diplomacy – as the US Navy liked to say. The amphibious-assault helicopter-carrier, the largest of its kind in the world, would be her home for the next few weeks. Samantha Crowe, c/o USS *Independence LHD-8*, latitude 75 degrees north, 3500 metres above the ocean floor.

Her mission: to conduct a conversation.

The helicopter banked. The Super Stallion rushed towards the landing point and touched down with a bounce. Through the side-window she saw a man in a yellow shirt directing the helicopter into its bay. One of the crew reached over and unfastened her seat-belt, then helped her out of her lifejacket, goggles, safety helmet and ear-protectors. The flight had been turbulent, and Crowe felt unsteady on her legs. She teetered down the ramp at the rear of the helicopter, crossed beneath the tail of the Super Stallion and looked around.

Only a few helicopters were visible on the flight deck. Her eyes roved over the endless expanse of asphalt, 257.25 metres long, 32.6 metres across, and dotted with bollards. Crowe knew the exact dimensions. She was a mathematician who loved precision, and she'd found out as much as she could about the *Independence* before she'd set out. At present, the statistics were dwarfed by reality: the *Independence* was much greater than its technical specifications, schematics and plans. The air smelt strongly of kerosene and oil, mixed with a hint of salt and overheated rubber. A fierce wind swept the combination of odours over the flight deck and tugged at her overalls.

Not the kind of place you'd choose to visit.

Men in brightly coloured shirts and protective headphones ran back and forth. A white shirt headed towards her. Crowe racked her brains. White was the colour for safety personnel. The men in yellow directed the helicopters in to land, and the red shirts were responsible for fuel and ammunition. Weren't there brown shirts too? And maybe purple. What were the brown shirts for?

'Follow me,' the man bellowed over the noise of the slowing rotor. He gestured towards the superstructure. It rose up on the starboard side of the deck like a high-rise apartment block, crowned with oversized antennae and sensors. Crowe's right hand reached down automatically to her pocket. Then she remembered that her cigarettes were stashed beneath her overalls. She hadn't been able to smoke in the helicopter either. Flying to the Arctic in high winds hadn't bothered her, but holding out without nicotine for hours on end was no laughing matter.

The man opened a hatch and Crowe stepped into the superstructure, or the island, as the sailors called it. Once they'd passed through another door into the interior, they were greeted by a wave of clean air. In Crowe's view, the island looked more like a cave. It was incredibly cramped inside. The white shirt delivered her into the care of a tall black man in uniform, who introduced himself as Major Salomon Peak. As they shook hands, Peak seemed rather formal, as though he had little experience of dealing with civilians. Crowe had spoken to him several times over the past few weeks, but only ever by phone. They strode along a winding corridor and clambered down a series of steep companionways deep into the bowels of the ship. The soldiers followed with her bags. On one of the bulkheads, a sign proclaimed, in big letters, '02 LEVEL'.

'I expect you'll want to freshen up,' said Peak. He opened one among many identical doors lining both sides of the passageway. It led into a surprisingly spacious and pleasantly decorated cabin, more a suite than a room. Crowe had read somewhere that living space on helicopter-carriers was kept to a minimum and that the troops slept in dormitories. Peak raised his eyebrows when she commented.

'We'd hardly make you sleep with the marines,' he said. The hint of a smile played on his lips. 'The navy knows how to look after its guests. This is flag accommodation.'

'Flag?'

'Our very own Hilton. Living-quarters for admirals and their staff. We're not at full capacity, so we've got all the space in the world. We've given the flag accommodation to women and the men have been housed in officer berthing. May I?' He walked ahead of her and opened another door. 'Bathroom.'

'I'm impressed.'

The soldiers brought in her bags.

'There's a minibar under the TV,' said Peak. 'Soft drinks only. I was thinking I'd come back in thirty minutes so we can start the tour. Will that be sufficient?'

'Absolutely.'

Crowe waited until the door had closed behind him, then hunted for an ashtray. She found one in a sideboard, peeled off her overalls and rummaged through her jacket pockets. It wasn't until she'd opened the crumpled packet, lit the cigarette and taken a drag that she started to feel properly alive.

She sat on the edge of her bed. Two packs a day. She couldn't give up. She'd tried twice and failed.

Maybe her heart wasn't in it.

After a second cigarette, she showered, then pulled on some jeans, sneakers and a sweater. She smoked a third cigarette, and opened all the cupboards and drawers. By the time she heard a knock at the door, she'd already inspected the inside of her cabin so thoroughly that she could have drawn up an inventory from memory. She liked to know how things stood.

It wasn't Peak in the passageway, but Leon Anawak.

'I told you we'd meet again,' he grinned.

Crowe laughed. 'And I told you that you'd find your whales. Good to see you, Leon. I hear you're the one I need to thank for being here.'

'Who told you that?'

'Li.'

'Oh, I reckon you'd be here anyway. I had a dream about you.'

'Oh, my.'

'Don't worry – you were a kind of friendly spirit. How was the flight?'

'A bit bumpy. Am I the last to arrive?'

'The rest of us boarded in Norfolk.'

'I couldn't get away from Arecibo. You wouldn't believe how much effort it takes to stop working on a project. We had to close down SETI. No one's got the cash to look for little green men at the moment.'

'There's a good chance you'll find more of them than you bargained for,' said Anawak. 'Are you ready? Peak will be here in a moment. He'll show you what the *Independence* has to offer and then it's your turn. Everyone's really excited. You've already got a nickname, by the way.'

'A nickname? What are they calling me?'

'Ms Alien.'

'Oh, heavens. For a while everyone called me Miss Foster, after Jodie played me in that film.' Crowe shook her head. 'Well, why not? So long as I've got a pen for signing autographs. Let's go.'

Peak showed her round 02 LEVEL. They'd started their tour in the bow and were making their way amidships. Crowe had admired the gym, crammed with treadmills and weight machines. It was practically deserted. 'Under normal circumstances you can't move in here for people,' said Peak. 'The *Independence* can accommodate three thousand men. Right now there are barely two hundred of us aboard.'

They walked through the junior officers' berths – dormitories for between four and six people with comfortable bunks, plenty of storage space and foldaway tables and chairs.

'Cosy,' said Crowe.

'Depends on how you look at it. There's not much chance of falling asleep when things get busy on the roof. Those helicopters and jump-jets are roaring up and down the flight deck, only metres above your head. It's hardest on the new recruits. They're exhausted at first.'

'How long does it take to get used to it?'

'You don't. You get used to being woken up, though. I've served on flat-tops before, and you're always away for months at a time. After a while it seems normal to be lying there on stand-by. You forget what it's like to sleep soundly. The first night at home is hell. You're listening out for the roar of engines, aircraft landing and helicopters docking, people running in the passageways, constant announcements – but instead there's just the ticking of your clock.'

They walked past the enormous messroom and came to a watertight door protected by a combination lock. They went into a large, darkened room. For the first time Crowe saw people at work. Lights flashed from consoles as men and women stared at the bank of wide-screen monitors that lined the walls.

'02 LEVEL is where you'll find most of the control and command rooms,' explained Peak. 'In the past they'd have been housed in the island, but that's too risky. Enemy missiles are programmed to strike large heat-emitting structures so the island's an obvious target. They'd only have to score a few hits, and we'd be like a body with its head blown off. That's why most of the control rooms are located under the roof.'

'The roof?'

'Navy jargon. I meant the flight deck.'

'And what's your role on board?'

Peak ignored her.

'This room is the CIC . . .'

'Ah. The Combat Information Center.'

The eyes in the narrow ebony-sculpted face flashed with irritation. Crowe resolved to keep her mouth shut.

'The CIC is the nerve-centre of the vessel,' said Peak. 'All the information that comes into or goes out of the ship passes through here – data from the ship's sensors, satellites, missile detection, surface-search radar, damage-control, communication – all in real time, of course . . . It gets pretty darned busy when we're under attack. See those empty desks? I imagine you'll be spending a good deal of time there, Dr Crowe.'

'Samantha. Or Sam.'

'Those systems are our underwater eyes and ears,' Peak continued, as though he hadn't heard. 'Antisub surveillance, SOSUS sonar and Surtass LFA, to name a few. Nothing approaches the *Independence* without us knowing about it.' Peak pointed at a screen mounted at the head of the room, showing a patchwork of diagrams and charts. 'The big picture. An integrated overview of all the information received by the CIC. A smaller version appears on the screens in the bridge.'

Peak led the way through the adjoining rooms. Almost all were shrouded in half-light, illuminated only by screens, monitors and displays. Next to the CIC was the Landing Force Operations Center. 'It's the command centre for the Marine Expeditionary Units. Each unit has its own console. During a landing operation, satellite images and recon planes are used to detect the position of enemy troops.' There was an unmistakable note of pride in Peak's voice. 'The LFOC allows us to shift troops and develop strategies in an instant. The central computer links the commander to his units in a ship-to-shore system.'

Crowe recognised pictures of the flight deck on some of the screens. She knew Peak probably wouldn't appreciate the question, but she couldn't help asking, 'How will that help us, Major? Our enemy's at the bottom of the sea.'

'Sure. So we'll use our capabilities for a deep-sea operation. I don't see the problem.'

'Sorry. I guess that's what comes from spending too much time in space.'

Anawak grinned. So far he hadn't said a word, but Crowe found his presence reassuring. Peak continued the tour. The Joint Intelligence Center came next. 'All the data from the recon systems is decoded and interpreted here,' said Peak. 'If anything gets too close to the *Independence*, we take a good look at it, and if the boys don't like it, they shoot it down.'

'That's a pretty big responsibility,' murmured Crowe.

'The computer does some of the work for them,' said Peak. 'But you're right, of course.' He gestured towards the other rooms. 'Most of what goes on in the CIC and JIC is pretty technical stuff, but we also keep an eye on the news from all over the world. We've always got CNN and NBC on screen, plus a dozen or so other key channels. You'll have access to all the information you need, including the databases of the Defense Mapping Agency. The navy's maps are far more detailed than anything available in the public domain, and you'll have the privilege of using them.'

They carried on down. After the on-board store came empty dormitories and living-quarters, then the hospital on 03 LEVEL, a vast antiseptic expanse with six hundred beds, six operating theatres and a gigantic intensive-care unit. It was deserted. Crowe imagined the scene during an attack: people screaming, blood flowing, doctors and nurses rushing from bed to bed. The more she saw of the *Independence*, the more it seemed to resemble a ghost ship – or a ghost city. They began the ascent up to 02 LEVEL and continued aft, until they reached a ramp wide enough for vehicles to drive down.

'The tunnel starts in the bowels of the vessel and zigzags all the way up to the island,' said Peak. 'The layout of the *Independence* allows all the strategically relevant areas to be accessed by jeep. In an assault situation, the marines would use the tunnel too. Let's head down.'

The steel bulkheads resonated with their footsteps. For a moment Crowe was reminded of a multi-storey car park, but then the enclosed ramp opened on to a hangar bay. Crowe had read that it covered a third of the ship's total length, with a height of two entire decks. There was a strong draught. On either side a colossal open gate led out on to a platform. Pale yellow lighting combined with the sunshine seeping through the gates to bathe the area in hazy light. Glass booths and control points were housed between the ribs. Hooks hung from above, attached to some kind of monorail. Crowe spotted large forklift trucks and two Hummers.

'Usually the hangar bay would be full of aircraft,' said Peak, 'but for this operation we'll only be needing the six Super Stallions that are docked on the roof. In the event of an emergency, we'll be able to evacuate fifty people per craft. We've also got two Super Cobra attack helicopters aboard, in case we need something with a bit more zip.' He pointed to the two gate-like openings. 'The external platforms are elevators for transporting aircraft from the hangar bay to the roof. Each deck elevator has a capacity of over thirty tonnes.'

Crowe walked towards the starboard gate. The steely grey sea stretched towards an empty horizon. Few icebergs found their way into these waters. The East Greenland Current transported them along the coast, three hundred kilometres away. The *Independence* would only encounter occasional patches of slushy drift ice.

Anawak joined her. 'One of many possible worlds, right?'

Crowe nodded.

'Did any of your scenarios provide for an underwater alien civilisation?'

'We've got the full repertoire, Leon. It sounds ludicrous, I know, but whenever I'm thinking about alien life, the first place that occurs to me is planet Earth – the oceans, beneath the Earth's crust, the poles, the air. If you don't know your own planet, how can you get to grips with other worlds?'

'That's exactly our problem.'

They followed Peak further down the ramp. It linked the various levels like an enormous stairwell. The tunnel levelled out and turned into a passageway that led towards the stern. They were now at the heart of the *Independence*. A side-door had been left open, bathing the corridor in artificial light. As they walked in, Crowe recognised the biologist she'd spoken to via video link-up over the past few weeks. Sue Oliviera was standing beside one of a multitude of lab benches, talking to two men, who introduced themselves as Sigur Johanson and Mick Rubin.

The entire deck seemed to have been converted into a laboratory. Benches and equipment were grouped together like islands. Crowe noticed chest freezers and barrels of liquid. Two large containers had been joined together and were marked with biohazard signs; presumably the containment facility. In the middle was a structure the size of a small house, surrounded by a walkway. Steel ladders led up to the top. Thick pipes and bundles of cable connected the walls to box-shaped machinery. A large oval window revealed the diffusely lit interior. It seemed to be filled with water.

'You've got an aquarium on board?' said Crowe.

'A deep-sea simulation chamber,' explained Oliviera. 'The original's in Kiel. It's much bigger than this – but ours comes with a port-hole made of armoured glass. The pressure inside would kill you, but other organisms need it to survive. At the moment it's populated with several hundred white crabs that were caught in Washington and loaded into pressurised containers to be flown out here. It's the first time we've succeeded in keeping the jelly alive – at least, we think we have. We haven't caught sight of it yet, but we're sure it's lurking inside those crabs and controlling their movements.'

'Fascinating,' said Crowe. 'But I don't suppose the chamber's only here for the crabs, is it?'

Johanson flashed her an enigmatic smile. 'Who knows what'll turn up next in our nets?'

'So it's a kind of PoW camp.'

Rubin laughed. 'That's a good one.'

Crowe glanced around. With the exception of the door, the laboratory was sealed. 'Isn't this usually a vehicle deck?' she asked.

'Yes,' Peak told her. 'On the other side of this bulkhead is the stern half of the vessel with the hangar bay above us. You've read up on it, haven't you?'

'I'm inquisitive, that's all,' Crowe said modestly.

'Well, let's hope your inquisitiveness translates into results.'

'What a grouch,' Crowe whispered to Anawak, as they left the lab.

'Oh, Sal's a decent enough guy. He's just not accustomed to know-it-all civilians.'

The passageway ended in a hall, whose height and length exceeded the dimensions of even the hangar bay. They walked over an artificial embankment that sloped down towards a basin whose inset floor was lined with wooden planking. It looked like a vast empty swimming-pool. At its centre, the planks had been cut away to make room for an inverted glass structure made of two square flaps that sloped downwards, coming together to form an upside-down turret jutting out beneath the deck. Next to that was an enormous raised tank filled with water. Its rippling surface reflected the beam of the overhead lighting. Crowe saw slim, torpedo-shaped bodies gliding beneath the waves. 'Dolphins!' she exclaimed.

'Yes.' Peak nodded. 'Our marine mammal fleet.'

Her eyes shifted upwards. The monorail system covered the ceiling here too, the track branching off in several directions. Futuristic vehicles were suspended from above, like giant sports cars bred from submersibles and planes. On either side of the basin the embankment continued in the form of jetty-like walkways. Boxes of equipment and other goods were stacked along the walls. Crowe noticed probes, gauges and diving-suits hanging up in lockers. Ladders led down into the basin at regular intervals.

Four Zodiacs were resting on the wooden planking at the near edge of the basin.

'Someone pulled the plug, huh?'

'Yesterday evening. It's down there, by the way.' Peak pointed to the glass structure. Crowe tried to gauge its size – it had to measure at least eight by ten metres. 'That's our sluice gate, the entrance to the ocean – with a twin set of locks: glass flaps at the base of the pool and steel flaps in the hull. There's a three-metre vertical shaft between them. It's foolproof – the gates never open simultaneously. As soon as a submersible has been released into the shaft, we close the glass flaps and open the steel ones. When the sub returns, the same thing happens in reverse. The submersible enters the shaft, the steel flaps close, and we can peer through the glass to make sure there's nothing down there that shouldn't be. In the meantime, the water's being checked for chemicals – the shaft is lined with sensors that test it for impurities and toxins. The results appear on two displays, one near the glass flaps and the other on the control panel. The sub stays in the shaft for about a minute. The glass flaps won't open until we've received the all-clear, then it's released into the basin. We use the same procedure for the dolphins. Follow me.'

They walked along the starboard jetty. A console towered up from the decking, positioned at the edge of the pool and equipped with monitors and other gadgets. A bony man with piercing eyes and a handlebar moustache left the group of soldiers and came towards them. 'Commander Luther Roscovitz,' Peak introduced him. 'He's in charge of the dive station.'

'You're Ms Alien, right?' Roscovitz flashed his long, yellowed teeth in a grin. 'Welcome aboard for the cruise. What took you so long?'

'My spaceship was delayed. Neat desk.'

'It does the job. We use it to operate the hatches and for sending down the submersibles. It also controls the pump, for when we want to fill the basin.'

Crowe remembered what she'd read about the *Independence*. She jerked her head in the direction of the steel bulkhead that sealed the stern-side of the hall. 'That's a hatch too, isn't it?'

'A stern gate. By flooding the ballast tanks we can get the vessel to sit lower in the water, so when the stern gate's open, seawater rushes in and creates a nice little harbour with its own private entrance.'

'Cute place to work. I like it.'

'Oh, don't get me wrong. Normally this place is full of landing-craft, heavy-duty tugs and hovercraft. It's a big hall, sure, but in no time at all they're crammed in like sardines. We had to shift everything around for this mission. It was clear from the start that we wouldn't need landing-craft. All we were looking for was a ship heavy enough not to be sunk by any kind of sea monster, that could stand up to huge waves, and had all the latest in communications technology. Oh, and it had to have aircraft landing points and a dive station. It was lucky as hell that the *LHD-8* was already in construction, the biggest and most powerful amphibious-assault vessel of all time. It was practically ready, but we had the option of making some changes. What more could you ask for? The ship-builders in Mississippi are seriously good. They came up with a new design for the well deck, added the sluice system and modified the workings of the pump. Now we can flood the basin without using the stern gate. In fact, we'd only ever need to open it if we wanted to launch the Zodiacs.'

Crowe looked down into the basin. Two people in neoprene wetsuits were standing at the edge of the dolphin pool; a slim red-headed woman and an athletically built giant with a long dark mane. She watched as a dolphin swam towards them and poked its head above the water, allowing the giant to stroke its smooth forehead.

'Who's that?' asked Crowe.

'They're in charge of the dolphin fleet,' said Anawak. 'Alicia Delaware and . . .' he hesitated '. . . Greywolf.'

'Greywolf?'

'Yes, or Jack if you prefer. He answers to both.'

'What do the dolphins do?'

'They're living cameras. They take video footage for us while they're swimming around out there. But we mainly use them for surveillance. Dolphin sonar detects other living creatures long before our systems pick them up. Jack used to work with some of this fleet when he was in the navy. Their vocabulary is pretty big. They use different kinds of whistles – one for orcas, another for grey whales, a third for humpbacks and so on. They can recognise pretty much every decent-sized creature, provided they've been taught the signal, and they can even point out shoals. Anything they don't recognise, they classify as unknown.'

'Impressive,' said Crowe. 'And that good-looking man down there can really speak their language?'

Anawak nodded. 'Better than he speaks ours, I sometimes think.'

The meeting took place in the Flag Command Center opposite the LFOC. Crowe already knew most of those present, having met them in the flesh or via video link-up. Now she was introduced to Murray Shankar, SOSUS's lead acoustician, and Karen Weaver, as well as the first officer, Floyd Anderson, and the skipper, Craig C. Buchanan, a wiry, white-haired man who seemed to have been born for a career in the navy. They all shook hands and Crowe took an instant dislike to Anderson, with his thick neck and small dark eyes. She was introduced lastly to a corpulent man, who arrived a few minutes late, sweating profusely. He was dressed in a baseball cap and sneakers. A bright yellow T-shirt bearing the words '*Kiss me, I'm a Prince*,' stretched over his expansive belly. 'Jack Vanderbilt,' he introduced himself. 'You're not what I expected of E.T.'s mom.'

'Daughter would have been more flattering,' Crowe said drily.

'Hey, would you be dishing out compliments if you looked like me?' Vanderbilt chortled. 'Incredible, isn't it, Dr Crowe? After all those decades pointlessly beaming your hopes and expectations into space, you might even get an answer.'

They all took their seats. General Judith Li addressed the room briefly, summarising the state of play. They knew in advance what was coming. The US had tabled a leadership motion to the UN Security Council, which, in a special meeting held behind closed doors, had voted unanimously in favour of the proposal. America now had the mandate to co-ordinate the logistical and technological battle against humanity's unknown enemy. Japanese and European scientists had reached the same conclusion as the Chateau delegates: mankind wasn't attacking itself; the threat was coming from an alien intelligence.

'Well, I'm pleased to say that we'll soon have a drug that will immunise humans against the killer algae's toxins. The trouble is, the side-effects are pretty nasty, and the drug won't work against mutations of the pathogens, which is what we've been finding in the latest batch of crabs. By now, most of the world's worst-hit regions no longer have any functioning infrastructure. The American government was happy to assume responsibility for the international war effort, but we've had to accept that we're no longer in a position to safeguard our shores. There's also the ongoing problem of the worms. Colonies are continuing to collect along the continental slopes and – more worryingly – on the slopes of volcanic seamounts like La Palma where Dr Frost and Dr Bohrmann are setting up a deep-sea vacuum-cleaner to clear the infestation. In other parts of the world we're still not making any progress with the whales – sonar offensives are futile when you're dealing with mammals whose instincts have been hijacked by an alien intelligence. But even supposing we could control the whales, we still wouldn't be able to jump-start the Gulf Stream or prevent the build-up of methane. Tackling the symptoms doesn't solve anything and we haven't been able to advance to the cause. We're not gleaning any information about what's going on down there, and our underwater cables are being disconnected one by one. The devastating truth about this war is that we're blind and deaf. Let me put it more bluntly. We've lost.' Li paused. 'Who are we supposed to attack? La Palma's going to slide into the ocean and America, Africa and Europe will be swamped by mega-waves. What's the point of fighting back? The fact is, we're not going to make any progress until we know whom or what we're up against – and right now we don't have a clue. So the purpose of this mission isn't to launch an offensive but to open negotiations. We want to make contact with these alien beings and persuade them to stop terrorising mankind. In my experience, it's always possible to negotiate with the opposition, and there's an excellent chance that we'll find our enemy right here – in the Greenland Sea.' She smiled. 'We're hoping to achieve a peaceful solution. And, to that end, we're pleased to welcome the final member of our team, Dr Samantha Crowe.'

Crowe rested her elbows on the table. 'I appreciate the warm welcome.' She glanced at Vanderbilt. 'Some of you may know that SETI's efforts haven't met with particular success. Given the sheer size of the known universe – at present estimated at over ten billion light years – almost anything seems possible, except perhaps the chance of looking in the right direction when an alien signal happens to be coming our way. So, compared with SETI's mission, our current predicament seems positively promising. First, we can be reasonably confident that the aliens exist; and second, we know roughly where they live – somewhere in the ocean and, very possibly, in this particular sea. But even if they turned out to live at the opposite pole, we'd still have narrowed it down. They can't leave the oceans, and a strong sound wave sent from the Arctic can still be heard on the other side of Africa, which gives us good grounds for hope. But there's an even more decisive factor. *We're already in contact.* We've been sending messages into their habitat for decades. Regrettably, those messages have brought with them destruction, so the yrr haven't bothered with ambassadors or diplomacy: they've launched straight into war. From our point of view, that's tiresome, but for the moment we should set aside our negative feelings and consider the onslaught as a kind of opportunity.'

'An opportunity?' echoed Peak.

'Yes, we have to see it for what it is – a message from an alien life-form that can help us discover how it thinks.' She placed her hand over a stack of plastic files. 'I've outlined the basis of our approach in these packs. But if any of you thinks this is going to be easy, I'm going to have to disillusion you. No doubt you'll have been wrestling with the question as to what kind of creature could be sending us the seven plagues. I guess you're familiar with *Close Encounters of the Third Kind*, *E.T.*, *Alien*, *Independence Day*, *The Abyss*, *Contact* and so on, and you'll probably be expecting either monsters or saints. Take the ending of *Close Encounters*. A superior intelligence descends from space to lead the worthy to a better, brighter future. For lots of people, that's a comforting thought, but doesn't it remind you of something? Exactly! There's a strong religious current beneath the surface of these movies. To some extent, the same could be said about SETI. The trouble is, it blinds us to how radically different an alien intelligence is likely to be.'

Crowe gave them time to digest what she was saying. She'd thought long and hard about the best way to approach the project, and she knew that she wouldn't make progress until the myths had been debunked.

'My point is that science fiction never engages with the true alienness of non-human civilisations. Sci-fi's extra-terrestrials are grotesquely exaggerated projections of human hopes and fears. The aliens in *Close Encounters* symbolise our longing for a lost Eden. They're essentially angels, and that's their function: a few chosen people are guided to the light. Of course, no one's interested in whether these aliens have their own culture. They only exist to serve basic religious notions. Everything about them is human, because that's how humans would like aliens to be. Even their appearance – glowing white light and what have you – has been choreographed to suit us. The same goes for the aliens in *Independence Day*. They're not really *alien*, in so far as they just live up to our notions of evil. The movies don't allow their aliens to be genuinely different. Good and evil are human concepts, and stories that try to do without them seldom catch on. It's hard for us to accept that our values aren't shared by other civilisations, but it's a problem we face all the time. Every human culture finds aliens on its doorstep – or just across the border. To communicate with an alien intelligence, we have to understand that. It's more than likely that we won't have any common values; and if our senses aren't compatible, we may not be able to communicate in any conventional way.'

Crowe handed the stack of files to Johanson, who was sitting next to her, and asked him to pass them round the room.

'If we want to think seriously about communicating with an alien civilisation, we can begin by imagining a state run by ants. Although ants are highly organised, they're not truly intelligent, but for the purpose of the exercise, let's imagine they are. In effect, we'd be dealing with a collective intelligence that sees nothing wrong with feasting on injured members of its species, that goes to war but doesn't understand our concept of peace, that sets no store by individual reproduction, and that treats the harvesting and consumption of excrement as a kind of sacred ceremony. We'd be trying to communicate with a collective intelligence that works in a completely different way from our own. *But it works!* Let's take this a step further. Suppose for a moment that we don't recognise alien intelligence, even when it comes our way. Leon, for instance, runs all kinds of tests because he wants to find out if dolphins are intelligent, but will he ever know for sure? Conversely, what would an alien intelligence think about us? The yrr are attacking us, but do they credit us with *intelligence*? Do you see what I'm driving at? We're not going to get any closer to understanding the yrr until we've dispensed with the idea that our system of values is the be-all and end-all of the universe. We have to cut ourselves down to size – to what we really are: just one among an infinite number of possible species, with no special claim to being anything more.'

Crowe noticed that Li was scrutinising Johanson's expression – as though she was trying to see inside his head. There were some interesting constellations on board, she thought. Then she caught Jack O'Bannon and Alicia Delaware exchanging glances, and knew that they were more than friends.

'Dr Crowe,' said Vanderbilt, leafing through the pages of his file, 'what would you say constitutes intelligence?'

It sounded like a trick question.

'A stroke of luck,' said Crowe.

'*Luck?*'

'Intelligence occurs when a host of different factors unite in a specific way. How many definitions do you want? Some people think intelligence is simply whatever is deemed valuable within a particular culture. According to some people, intelligence can be analysed by examining basic thought processes, while others try to measure it statistically. Then there's the question of origin: is intelligence inborn or acquired? At the beginning of the twentieth century it was postulated that intelligence could be gauged by studying an individual's ability to master certain tasks. That's what modern-day experts base their ideas on when they define it as the ability to adapt to the demands of a changing environment. In their view, intelligence is acquired, not genetically determined, but others argue that it's an innate part of being human – an inborn capacity that helps us adjust our thinking to new situations. If you take that line, then intelligence is the ability to learn from experience and to adapt to your surroundings. And then there's my personal favourite: intelligence is asking what intelligence means.'

Vanderbilt nodded slowly. 'I see. So you don't really know.'

Crowe grinned. 'I hope you won't mind my using your T-shirt to illustrate an example, Mr Vanderbilt, but it's unlikely we'd be able to judge a being's intelligence from its appearance.'

Laughter rippled through the room and ebbed away. Vanderbilt was staring at her. Then he grinned. 'I dare say you're right.'

Once the ice had been broken, the meeting gathered pace. Crowe outlined the next steps. During the past few weeks she'd worked out a basic strategy with the help of Murray Shankar, Judith Li, Leon Anawak and some of the guys from NASA. It was based on the limited number of attempts to make contact that had been conducted in the past.

'Space makes things easy for us,' Crowe explained. 'You can send out huge packets of data in the microwave spectrum. Light is easy to spot and it travels at three hundred thousand kilometres per second. You don't need any cables or wires. It's a different story under water. Water molecules absorb the energy of short-wave signals, while for a long-wave signal you'd need enormous antennae. Light waves *can* be used to communicate under water, but only over relatively short distances. So that leaves us with sound. But sound comes with its own particular drawback – the echo effect. Sound waves get deflected all over the place, and that leads to interference. The message would overlap with itself and become unintelligible. To get round that, we need a special modem.'

'We borrowed the principle from marine mammals,' said Anawak. 'Dolphins use it. They've essentially invented a way of outsmarting echoes and interference. They sing.'

'I thought that was whales,' said Peak.

'When we talk about whalesong, we only mean it sounds as though they're singing,' explained Anawak. 'Music may not exist to them as a concept. In this instance singing means constantly modulating the frequency and pitch of the noise. There are two advantages. You get round the problem of interference, and you increase the amount of data you're able to transmit. We'll be using a singing modem. We can get it to transmit thirty kilobytes of information over a distance of three kilometres. That's a lot of data – half the capacity of an ISDN line. It's enough to beam out high-resolution images.'

'So what are we going to say?' asked Peak.

'The laws of physics are expressed in mathematics,' said Crowe. 'They're the cosmic code that gave rise to consciousness in the first place, allowing humanity to understand math. Math is life's way of explaining its own origins. It's the only universal language that any intelligent being subject to the same physical conditions would understand. It's the language we'll use.'

'How? Are you going to make them do sums?'

'No. We're going to express our thoughts in math. In 1974, SETI fired a powerful radio wave from Earth towards a globular cluster in the constellation of Hercules. We sent 1679 characters, all expressed in binary pulses – ones and zeros, like the dots and dashes of Morse code. A mathematician would know what to do with the number 1679 because it's the unique product of two prime numbers, 23 and 73, numbers only divisible by one and themselves. In other words, the basics of our numerical system were contained within the structure of the message. The 1679 pulses separate into 73 columns, each containing 23 characters. Well, a little mathematics goes a long way, and if you turn the dots and dashes into black and white blocks, lo and behold, a pattern will emerge.'

She held up a diagram on a sheet of paper. It resembled a pixelated computer printout. Parts of it looked abstract, but there were some clearly identifiable shapes.

'The top lines represent the numbers one to ten and contain information on our decimal system. Below that are the atomic numbers of five chemical substances: water, carbon, oxygen, nitrogen and phosphorus. All five substances are crucial to life on this planet. The message continues with extensive information about the biochemistry of the Earth, with formulae for our DNA bases and sugars, the structure of the double helix and so on. The final third of the message shows an image of the human form, linked directly to the representation of DNA, from which the recipient should be able to deduce the nature of evolution on

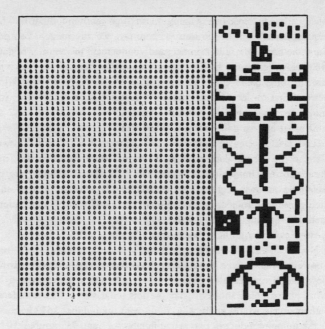

Earth. Our units of size wouldn't mean anything to an alien intelligence, so the wavelength of the message was used to convey the average human height. Following on from there is a diagram of our solar system, and then, to round it all off, we've got details of the appearance, dimensions and design of the Arecibo radio telescope from which the message was sent.'

'A polite invitation for them to visit our planet and eat us alive,' said Vanderbilt.

'That was exactly what concerned the authorities. But we've always had an answer to that: the aliens don't need our invitation. Humanity has been sending radio waves into space for decades. All our radio traffic goes up there – including all the chatter from intelligence agencies. You don't need to decode those signals to know that they must have been sent by a civilisation with technology.' Crowe put down the diagram. 'We expect the Arecibo message to take twenty-six thousand years to reach its destination, so it'll take fifty-two thousand before we receive a reply. You'll be pleased to hear that our underwater message will be faster.

We're going to proceed in stages. Our first communication will be straightforward. You were partly right, Major Peak – we'll be sending them two sums. If they're sporting, they'll answer. The first exchange is designed to prove the existence of the yrr and to gauge our chance of initiating dialogue.'

'Why would they bother to reply?' asked Greywolf. 'They know enough about us already.'

'Well, they may know some things, but they won't necessarily know the essential point: that we're an intelligent species.'

'Excuse me?' Vanderbilt shook his head. 'They're destroying our ships, for Christ's sake, so they must know we built them. Why should they doubt our intelligence?'

'Just because we're able to build complex structures doesn't prove we're intelligent. Think of termite hills – they're architectural master-pieces.'

'That's different.'

'Oh, it's no use getting on your high horse, Mr Vanderbilt. If Dr Johanson is right about yrr culture being based on biology, we need to ask ourselves whether they think we're capable of focused, structured thought.'

'You mean they might think we're . . .' Vanderbilt grimaced '. . . animals?'

'Vermin, even.'

'A kind of fungal infection.' Delaware grinned. 'We're being targeted by a pest-control agency.'

'I've been looking at our enemy's mindset,' said Crowe. 'To see if there's anything it can tell us about these creatures' way of life. It's all speculation, I know, but we need to find a way of focusing our efforts. At any rate, it struck me that while we've had no shortage of aggression directed towards us, there hasn't been a single diplomatic overture, so I asked myself why. Maybe they don't set any store by diplomacy – or maybe it hasn't occurred to them to try. Obviously, a pack of army ants wouldn't bother with diplomatic niceties before they swarmed all over their prey, but in their case, attacks are guided by finely tuned instincts. The yrr, on the other hand, have already demonstrated a high degree of insight and awareness in their ability to plan. Their strategies are creative. If the yrr are intelligent, and they're aware of it, they clearly don't share our notions of morality and ethics. Maybe in their logic the only way forward is to attack us relentlessly, so if we want them to stop, we'll have to give them a persuasive reason why.'

'I don't see what good a message will do when they're already chomping through our deep-sea cables,' said Rubin. 'Surely they'd be able to glean all the information they could possibly need.'

'That's not quite true.' Shankar chuckled. 'SETI's Arecibo message is only intelligible to extra-terrestrials because it was put together with an alien intelligence in mind. That's not something we bother about when we communicate with each other on a day-to-day basis. To an alien intelligence, all that cable data would look like an almighty mess.'

'Absolutely,' said Johanson. 'But let's see what else we can deduce. Sam's using my idea of a biologically based technology. Why? Because it's the most obvious conclusion to draw. They don't need machines or equipment, just genes. Their weaponry consists of organic life-forms – strategic mutations. I'd say they're tied to nature in a way that humans aren't. You can see how they might be far less estranged from their natural environment than we are.'

'Noble savages – is that what you mean?' asked Peak.

'I don't know about *noble*. It's pretty reprehensible to go around polluting the atmosphere with exhaust fumes, like we do – but what about breeding and manipulating other life-forms to suit your own needs? Is that any better? Anyway, what interests me is how they might perceive our threat to their habitat. We're always talking about the destruction of the rainforests. Some people militate against it, others keep chopping. But what if, metaphorically speaking, the yrr *are* the rainforests? I'd say there's evidence for that in the way they deal with biology, which brings me to my second point. With the exception of the whales, the organisms they're using are almost exclusively creatures that occur *en masse* – worms, jellies, squid, mussels, crabs. They're organisms that live in shoals or swarms. Millions of creatures are being sacrificed for the yrr to achieve their goals. The individual doesn't matter to them. Would humans think like that? Sure, we breed viruses and bacteria, but for the most part we use man-made armaments in manageable quantities. Mass biological weaponry isn't really our thing. But the yrr seem fairly expert at it. Why? Well, maybe shoals and swarms are what they know best.'

'Do you mean . . . ?'

'I think we're dealing with a collective intelligence.'

'And how does a collective intelligence experience the world?' asked Peak.

'A fish in a fishing net would ask the same about the fisherman, assuming fish could think,' said Anawak. 'Why should he and millions of his friends be forced to die in nets? Surely that's mass murder.'

'Hardly,' said Vanderbilt. 'More like fish-fingers.'

Crowe gestured for silence. 'I agree with Dr Johanson,' she said. 'And if we're right, it would seem that the yrr have taken a collective decision to fight us, and that ethics and empathy aren't part of the deal. I know in the movies you can melt the heart of even the nastiest alien by looking at it with puppy-dog eyes, but that isn't going to work. No, we need to make communication seem more intriguing than violence. The yrr would never have been able to accomplish half of what they've done if they weren't *au fait* with physics and math, so let's challenge them to a mathematical duel. Hopefully, at some point their logic – or maybe even some kind of moral code – will kick in and persuade them to rethink their behaviour.'

'They *must* know we're intelligent,' Rubin insisted. 'If any species stands out because of its superior understanding of physics and maths, it has to be us.'

'Yes, but are we intelligent and conscious?'

Rubin blinked in confusion. 'How do you mean?'

'Are we aware of our intelligence?'

'Well, obviously.'

'Or maybe we're computers with an inbuilt learning capacity? Of course *we* know the truth, but do *they*? Theoretically it would be possible to replace the entire brain with an electronic equivalent, and then you'd get AI. Your artificial brain would be capable of doing everything that you can do. It could build you a spaceship and outsmart Einstein. But would it be aware of its achievements? In 1997 the world chess champion Garry Kasparov was defeated by an IBM computer, Deep Blue. Does that mean Deep Blue was conscious? Or did it win without seeing the point? Does the fact that we build cities and lay underwater cables prove that we're intelligent, conscious beings? SETI has never excluded the possibility that one day we might come across a machine civilisation; computer intelligence that has outlived its creators and continued to develop over millennia by itself.'

'And the creatures down there? If what you're saying is true, maybe the yrr are just ants with fins. A species without any ethics, without even any—'

'Exactly. And that's why we're proceeding in stages.' Crowe smiled. 'Stage one, I want to find out if there's anything down there; stage two, I want to establish whether dialogue is possible; and stage three, I want to know if the yrr are consciously responding to our messages – if their intelligence is conscious at all. Only then – once we've reason to believe that in addition to their evident knowledge and skill they're able to conceptualise and understand – will I be prepared to consider them as intelligent beings. And only then would it be worthwhile reflecting on their values – but *even then* we shouldn't expect those values to bear the slightest resemblance to our own.'

For a while there was silence.

'I don't want to interfere in a scientific debate,' Li said finally, 'but pure intelligence is unfeeling. Intelligence connected to consciousness is an entirely different matter. In my opinion, an intelligent conscious being would *necessarily* have values. If the yrr represent conscious intelligence, they'd have to recognise at least one value: the value of life. And since they're trying to defend themselves, that would seem to be the case. I'd say they've got values. What we need to find out is whether those values coincide in any way with our own. Maybe there's the tiniest overlap.'

Crowe nodded. 'Yes,' she said. 'Maybe there is.'

Late that afternoon they bundled the first sound wave and sent it into the depths. Shankar had chosen a frequency to match the spectrum of the unidentified noises that his SOSUS colleagues had christened Scratch.

The modem set about modulating the signal. The sound wave was subject to a certain amount of reflection, so Crowe and Shankar sat in the CIC, modulating the modulations until the distortion was gone. An hour after the signal had been broadcast, Crowe felt confident that any creature capable of detecting acoustic signals would have no trouble receiving it. Whether the yrr would make sense of it remained to be seen.

They might not bother to reply.

Perched on the edge of her chair in the half-light of the CIC, Crowe felt a wave of elation at the thought of how close they were to the moment she'd always longed for: contact. But, more than anything, she was afraid. She could feel the burden of responsibility weighing on her and the rest of the team. This wasn't an adventure like Arecibo and Project Phoenix: it was up to them to avert a catastrophe and save mankind from destruction. The SETI researcher's dream had turned into a nightmare.

Friends

Anawak made his way up through the vessel, then strode along the narrow passageways in the island and emerged on the flight deck. Over the course of the voyage, the roof had turned into a kind of promenade. Anyone with a few moments to spare could be found strolling along it, deep in thought or deliberating in groups. In an unlikely twist of fate, the roof of the largest helicopter-carrier in the world, usually the site of innumerable take-offs and landings, had developed into a place of contemplation and scientific debate. The six Super Stallions and two Super Cobras waited forlornly on the vast expanse of tarmac.

On board the *Independence*, Greywolf continued to lead his exotic life, although Delaware was ever more a part of it. The two were growing steadily closer. Delaware wisely gave him space, which meant that Greywolf sought out her company. In public, they never let slip that they were more than friends, but Anawak could see that their bond was growing. The signs were unmistakable. Delaware rarely worked with him now: she spent all her time looking after the dolphins with Greywolf.

Anawak found Greywolf sitting cross-legged at the bow, looking out across the ocean. As he started to sit down, he realised Greywolf was carving.

'What is it?' he asked.

Greywolf passed it to him. It was a large object, skilfully carved from cedarwood. It looked almost finished. One end finished in a handle, while the larger section showed a number of intertwined figures. Anawak could make out a bird, two animals with powerful jaws, then a man, who seemed to be at their mercy. He ran his fingers along the surface. 'It's beautiful,' he said.

'It's a copy.' Greywolf grinned. 'I only ever make replicas. I don't have it in me to come up with an original.'

'I get it.' Anawak smiled. 'You're not Indian enough.'

'You don't get anything – you never do.'

'OK, calm down. So, what is it?'

'It's a ceremonial hand-club. From the Tla-o-qui-aht. The original was made of whalebone, in a private collection from the late nineteenth century. The figures tell a story from the time of the ancestors. One day a man came across a mysterious cage with all kinds of creatures inside it. He took it back to his village. Soon afterwards he fell ill and no one could cure him. There didn't seem to be any explanation for his illness, but then the answer came to the sick man in a dream. The creatures in the cage were to blame. They weren't just animals, they were transformers, shapeshifters, and they attacked him in his sleep.' Greywolf pointed to a squat creature. 'This one's a wolf-whale. In the dream it attacked the man and closed its jaws round his head. Then Thunderbird tried to save him. You can see how it's digging its claws into the wolf-whale's flank. While they were fighting, a bear-whale joined them and grabbed the man by his feet. The man woke, told his son the dream and died. The son carved this club and used it to kill six thousand shapeshifters to avenge his father's death.'

'And what's the hidden meaning?'

'Does everything have a hidden meaning?'

'A story like that is *bound* to have a hidden meaning. It's the eternal struggle, isn't it? The battle between good and evil.'

'No.' Greywolf pushed the hair out of his eyes. 'The story tells of life and death. In the end you die, but until then your life is in flux. You can live a good life or a bad life, but you don't control what happens to you – that's for higher powers to decide. If you live in harmony with Nature, she will heal you; if you fight her, she will destroy you. But the important point is that you don't control Nature – she controls you.'

'The man's son doesn't seem to have shared that insight,' said Anawak. 'Otherwise why would he have sought vengeance for his father?'

'The story doesn't say he was right.'

Anawak handed the club to Greywolf, reached into his anorak and pulled out the bird spirit. 'Can you tell me anything about this?'

Greywolf turned it in his hands. 'It doesn't come from the west coast,' he said.

'No.'

'Marble. Does it come from your homeland?'

'Cape Dorset.' Anawak hesitated. 'A shaman gave it to me.'

'You, of all people, accepted a gift from a shaman?'

'He's my uncle.'

'And what did he tell you about it?'

'Not much. He said the bird spirit would guide my thoughts when it was time. And that I may need someone to tell me what it sees.'

Greywolf was silent for a while. Then he said, 'There are bird spirits in almost every culture. Thunderbird is an ancient mythological figure. It's part of creation, one of the spirits of Nature, a higher being. But bird spirits have other meanings too.'

'They're linked to heads, aren't they?'

'In ancient Egyptian art you often see bird-like headdresses. For the ancient Egyptians, the bird represented man's consciousness. It was trapped inside the head, like in a cage. If your head was open, the bird would fly away, but you could still entice it back. Then your consciousness would return.'

'So whilst I'm asleep my consciousness is soaring.'

'Your dreams are more than stories: they show you what your consciousness is seeing in higher worlds that are otherwise closed. Have you ever seen an Indian chief's feather headdress?'

'Only in Westerns.'

'Well, the headdress signifies that the chief's spirit is inscribing stories in his head. That's what the feathers are for. In other words, his head is full of good ideas, and that's why he's chief.'

'His mind soars.'

'With the help of the feathers. Most tribes have a single feather, but it means the same thing. The bird spirit represents consciousness. That's why the worst thing that can happen to an Indian is to lose their scalp, or headdress. It means being separated from their consciousness – possibly for good.' Greywolf frowned. 'If you were given this sculpture by a shaman, he must have been alluding to your consciousness, the power of your ideas. You should use your mind but you have to open it first. Your spirit needs to go on a journey, and that means it has to join with your unconscious.'

'Why don't you wear feathers in your hair?'

Greywolf grimaced. 'Because, as you pointed out, I'm not a true Indian.'

Anawak was silent. –

'I had a dream in Nunavut . . .' he said eventually.

Greywolf listened intently to the story of the iceberg. 'I knew I'd end up sinking into the sea,' Anawak concluded, 'but the thought of drowning didn't scare me.'

'What did you expect to find down there?'

'Life,' Anawak said.

Greywolf looked at the green marble figurine resting on the palm of his enormous hand. 'Tell me honestly, Leon, why did they ask me and Licia to come on board?' he asked abruptly.

Anawak gazed out at the ocean. 'Because we need you here.'

'No, you don't, not really. I'm pretty good with dolphins, but there's no shortage of dolphin-handlers in the US Navy. And Licia doesn't have any particular role.'

'She's an excellent assistant.'

'Have you asked her to help you? Do you need her?'

'No.' Anawak stared up at the sky. 'You're here because I wanted you.'

'But why?'

'You're my friends.'

For a while there was silence again.

'I guess we are.' Greywolf nodded.

Anawak smiled. 'I've always rubbed along fine with everyone, but I can't remember having proper friends. And you can bet I never thought I'd be friends with an argumentative smart ass student – or with someone twice my size and full of crackpot ideas, whom I practically came to blows with.'

'That argumentative student did exactly what friends do.'

'Which is?'

'Took an interest in your life. You and I have always been friends though. If you ask me . . .' Greywolf lifted the sculpture and grinned. '. . . our heads were just closed for a while.'

'What do you suppose made me dream all that stuff? It keeps coming back to me, and it's not as though anyone could accuse me of having mystical tendencies. But something happened in Nunavut, and I can't explain it. By the time we were out there on the land and I had that dream, something had changed.'

'What do you think it means'

'Well, we're being threatened by deep-sea creatures, aren't we? Maybe it's my job to go down there and—'

'Save the planet.'

'OK, forget it.'

'Do you want to know what I think?'

Anawak nodded.

'I think you couldn't be more wrong. For years you retreated into yourself, dragging around all your baggage. That iceberg you were floating on – it was you. An icy, unapproachable block. But out there the block began to melt. The ocean you're sinking into isn't the kingdom of the yrr. It's our world. That's where you belong. That's the adventure in store for you. Friendship, love, hostility, hatred and anger. Your role isn't to play the hero. Those roles were handed out a long time ago, and they're for dead men. You belong in the world of the living.'

Night

They all rested in different ways. Crowe's small, delicate form was swaddled in blankets, with just her steel-grey hair protruding at the top. Weaver lay naked on top of the sheets, sprawled on her front, head to one side, pillowed on a forearm. Her chestnut hair covered her face, so that only her parted lips could be seen. Shankar was a restless sleeper who couldn't stop rearranging his bedclothes, muttering and giving the occasional muffled snore.

Rubin was mostly awake.

Greywolf and Delaware didn't sleep much either, but that was mainly because they were otherwise engaged. Two cabins further along, Anawak was asleep on his side in a T-shirt. There was nothing remarkable about Oliviera's sleeping patterns.

Johanson lay on his back, arms outstretched. Only the beds in flag and officer accommodation allowed an expansive position like that. It suited the Norwegian so well that a former lover had once woken him to tell him that he'd been sleeping like the lord of the manor. He slept like that every night – a man who looked as though he wanted to embrace life, even when his eyes were closed.

The sleeping or waking bodies filled a row of brightly lit screens. Each monitor showed an individual cabin. Two men in uniform were watching them, while Li and Vanderbilt hovered in the background.

'Regular angels, wouldn't you say?' said Vanderbilt.

Li's expression didn't flicker as she watched Delaware and Greywolf. The volume was turned down, but faint sounds of their love-making penetrated the cool air of the control room.

'I'd go for that little beauty,' said Vanderbilt, pointing at Weaver. 'Nice ass.'

'Fallen for her, have you?'

Vanderbilt grinned. 'Oh, please.'

'You should turn on the charm,' said Li. 'You're carrying around at least two tonnes of it.'

The CIA agent mopped the sweat from his forehead. They watched for a while longer. Li didn't care if the people on the screens were snoring or turning cartwheels. They could hang upside-down from the ceiling for all she cared.

The main thing was that she knew where they were, what they were doing and everything they said.

'Carry on,' she said. On her way out she added, 'Remember to keep looking in *all* of the cabins.'

13 August

The message had been beamed non-stop into the depths – as yet to no avail. At seven o'clock they'd been jolted out of bed by the alarm call, but almost no one felt properly rested. Most nights the gentle rocking motion of the enormous vessel lulled them to sleep. The air-conditioning hummed softly in the cabins, keeping the temperature agreeably constant, and the beds were comfortable. They might have slept soundly, but for the suspense. Instead they'd dozed fitfully. Johanson had lain awake imagining the effect of the message on the Greenland Sea, until nightmare visions haunted him.

That they were in the Greenland Sea at all, and not thousands of kilometres further to the south, was due only to his intervention, with the support of Bohrmann and Weaver. If it had been up to Rubin, Anawak and some of the others, the attempt to make contact would have been launched over the site of the volcanoes in the Mid-Atlantic Ridge. Rubin's reasoning was based on similarities between the crabs of that region and those that had invaded New York and Washington. Besides, it was one of the few places in the depths that provided the right conditions for sophisticated life-forms to flourish. In that respect, the habitat in the hydrothermal vents was ideal. Hot water rose up from huge chimneys of rock on the seabed, drawing with it minerals and life-giving nutrients from the heart of the volcanoes. Worms, mussels, fish and crabs inhabited the vents in conditions not dissimilar to those of an alien planet. Why shouldn't the yrr live there too?

Johanson had accepted most of their arguments, but two factors prevented him backing their conclusion. First, although the hydrothermal vents were the most favourable place for life in the deep sea, they were also the most lethal. Molten rock was regularly cast out of the volcanoes as the ocean plates shifted apart. During such eruptions the deep-sea biotope could be wiped out entirely, although it didn't take long for new life to establish itself. All the same, it was hardly an environment that a complex, intelligent civilisation would choose as its home.

Second, the chance of making contact with the yrr was greater, the closer they got to them. Exactly where that might be was a matter for debate. All the various theories were probably right to a degree. There was reason to believe, for example, that they might live in the benthic zone at the very bottom of the ocean. Many of the recent anomalies had occurred in the immediate vicinity of deep-sea trenches. Yet there was also evidence to suggest that they resided in the vast ocean basins of the abyssal plains. And Rubin's suggestion that they might inhabit the oases of life in the middle of the Atlantic couldn't be rejected. In the end Johanson had proposed that they shouldn't focus on where the yrr might live, but on places where they had to be present.

The cold water in the Greenland Sea had stopped plummeting into the depths. As a result, the Gulf Stream had halted. There were only two possible explanations for the phenomenon: either the water had warmed, or an influx of fresh water flowing southwards from the Arctic had diluted the salt-laden current so it could no longer sink. Both explanations presupposed intense activity at the site of the convective chimneys. Somewhere in the Arctic Ocean the yrr were providing the impetus for radical changes in the sea.

Somewhere not far from the vessel.

Lastly, there was the safety aspect. Even Bohrmann, who had got into the habit of expecting the worst, was forced to concede that the risk of a methane blow-out in the Greenland Basin was relatively small. Bauer's ship had come to grief near Svalbard, at a site where vast deposits of hydrates lined the continental slope. By contrast, 3500 metres of water separated the *Independence* from the seabed. At that depth there was relatively little methane, certainly not enough to sink a vessel of that size. To be on the safe side, the scientists had taken regular seismic readings as they crossed the Arctic Ocean, selecting a position that seemed mainly hydrate-free. Stationed on the open water, the *Independence* would be safe from the mightiest tsunami – unless, of course, La Palma collapsed into the sea.

But then it would all be over anyway.

Inside the cavernous messroom, the scientists were having breakfast. Anawak and Greywolf were missing. After the alarm call Johanson had spent a few minutes talking on the phone to Bohrmann, who'd arrived in La Palma and was preparing to deploy the suction tube. The Canaries were a time-zone behind the Arctic, but Bohrmann had been up for hours already.

'A five-hundred-metre suction tube doesn't take care of itself,' he'd said.

'Don't forget to vacuum in all the corners,' Johanson had advised him.

He missed Bohrmann, but there no shortage of interesting people on board. He was chatting to Crowe when first officer Floyd Anderson walked in, holding a pint-sized insulated mug emblazoned 'USS *Wasp* LHD-8'. He walked over to the coffee machine and filled it. 'We've got visitors,' he bellowed.

Everyone turned.

'We've made contact?' asked Oliviera.

'We can't have. I'd know.' Crowe picked up a slice of toast and took a bite. Her third or fourth cigarette was smouldering in the ashtray. 'Shankar's in the CIC. He'd have called.'

'Well, what is it? An alien landing?'

'Why don't you take a look from the roof?' Anderson said cryptically.

Flight Deck

The cold air clung to Johanson's face like a mask. The sky was suffused with white. Grey waves rose with spray-crowned crests. A wind had blown up overnight and was raining minute crystals of ice across the deck. Johanson spotted a group of muffled figures on the starboard side of the ship. As he got closer, he identified Li, Anawak and Greywolf. At the same time he saw what was holding their attention.

Not far from the *Independence* the dark outlines of sword-like fins cut through the water.

'Orcas,' said Anawak, as Johanson joined them.

'What are they doing?'

Anawak squinted at him through the shower of ice. 'They've been circling the vessel for the past three hours. The dolphins alerted us. I'd say they're watching us.'

Shankar ran over from the island to join them.

'What's going on?'

'We seem to have caught someone's attention,' said Crowe. 'Maybe it's a response.'

The orcas kept a respectful distance from the vessel. There were hordes of them – hundreds, thought Johanson. They were swimming at a steady speed, their shiny black backs rising occasionally above the waves. There was no denying that they looked like a patrol.

'Are they infected?'

Anawak wiped water out of his eyes. 'We don't know.'

'Tell me,' Greywolf rubbed his chin, 'if this stuff is controlling their brains, has it occurred to you that it might be able to see us? Or hear us?'

'You're right,' said Anawak. 'It's in control of their sensory organs.'

'Exactly. It means that gunk has eyes and ears.'

They stared out to sea.

'Either way,' said Crowe, drawing on her cigarette and exhaling into the icy air, 'it's started.' Wisps of smoke rose above their heads.

'What has?' asked Li.

'They're sizing us up.'

'Let them.' A thin smile formed on Li's lips. 'We're ready for anything.'

'For everything we've anticipated,' said Crowe.

Lab

As he headed below deck with Rubin and Oliviera, Johanson asked himself whether a psychosis could forge its own reality. He'd started the ball rolling. Of course, if he hadn't come up with the theory, someone else would. But the fact remained that they were creating information on the basis of a hypothesis. All it took was for a pack of orcas to circle the *Independence*, and everyone saw the eyes and ears of aliens. In fact, they were seeing aliens everywhere. That was what had prompted them to send the message in the first place, and it was why they were expecting an answer.

The fifth day. We're not really making any progress, he thought, in frustration. We need something to show us we're not completely off-course, that we haven't been blinded by a theory.

Footsteps echoing, they made their way down the ramp, past the hangar bay and deeper into the vessel. The steel door to the lab was locked. Johanson tapped in the combination code and the door opened with a soft hiss. He made his way along the bank of switches, turning on the strip-lights and the desk-lights, flooding the islands of benches and equipment in a cold white glare. The deep-sea simulation chamber hummed in the background.

They climbed on to the walkway and peered through the large oval window. It gave a full view of the inside of the tank. The beam of the internal floodlights picked out small white carapaces and spindly legs scurrying over the artificial seabed. Some of the crabs were moving hesitantly, as though they'd lost their way, scuttling in circles or stopping to consider where they wanted to go. Towards the bottom of the tank, the water obscured the details, but underwater cameras took close-up footage and beamed it on to the monitors at the control desk next to the chamber.

'No real change since yesterday,' said Oliviera.

Johanson scratched his beard. 'We should open some up and see what happens.'

'Crack open some crabs?'

'Why not? We've already established that we can keep them alive in the pressure lab.'

'We've established that we can keep them in a vegetative state,' Oliviera corrected him. 'We don't yet know if they're really alive.'

'The jelly inside them is,' Rubin said thoughtfully, 'but the rest of the crab is no more animate than a car.'

'I agree,' said Oliviera. 'But what's the deal with the jelly? Why isn't it doing anything?'

'What were you expecting it to do?'

'Run around.' Oliviera shrugged. 'Shake its pincers at us. I don't know. Leave the shell, maybe. Those creatures are programmed to march ashore, wreak havoc and die, so this situation puts them in an awkward position. No one's here to give them new orders. They're basically on stand-by.'

'Exactly,' said Johanson, impatiently. 'They're just like battery-operated toys. I agree with Mick. The crab bodies are equipped with just enough nervous tissue to make a dashboard for their drivers. I want to tempt them out of their shells. I want to know what happens if you force them out of their armour in a deep-sea environment.'

'OK.' Oliviera nodded. 'Let's stir things up a bit.'

They left the walkway, clambered down the ladders and walked over to the control desk. The computer enabled them to operate various robots inside the tank. Johanson selected a small, two-piece ROV-unit named Spherobot. A bank of high-resolution screens sprang to life above a console with two joysticks. One showed the inside of the tank. Everything looked elongated and hazy. Spherobot's wide-angle lens was able to survey the whole interior of the tank, but as a result the camera provided a fisheye view.

'How many shall we open?' asked Oliviera.

Johanson's hands flitted over the keyboard, and the angle of the camera shifted upwards by a degree. 'Well, in a good plateful of scampi there's usually at least a dozen.'

One of the walls inside the tank resembled a two-storey garage in which all kinds of deep-sea equipment was stored. Underwater robots of different types and sizes were there, ready to be operated from the control desk. There was no other way to intervene in the artificial world of the chamber.

Johanson activated the controls, and powerful lights flared up on the underside of a robot. Two rotors turned. A box-shaped sled the size of a shopping-trolley floated slowly out of the garage. The top half was packed with machinery, and the rest was made up of an empty basket with fine wire-netting sides. It glided towards the artificial seabed and stopped in front of a small group of motionless crabs. Curved eyeless shells and powerful pincers came into view.

'I'm going to switch to the camera on the globe now,' said Johanson.

The hazy image was replaced by a high-resolution close-up.

Floating above the crabs, the sled released a shiny red ball, no bigger than a football. It was easy to see how the Spherobot had acquired its name. The ball floated into the water, a single cable linking it to the sled, the shiny eye of its camera pointing straight ahead. It brought to mind the flying robot in *Star Wars* that sparred with Luke Skywalker as he learned to use his light saber. In fact, the Spherobot, with its six miniature thruster pods, was a detailed re-creation of its cinematic predecessor. It travelled a short distance through the water, then sank slowly until it was hovering just above the crabs. They paid no attention to the strange red ball, even when its underside slid open and two slim articulated arms unfolded from inside.

At the end of each arm, an arsenal of equipment began to rotate. Then a robotic grasper protruded from the left arm and a saw from the right. Johanson's hands held both joysticks and shifted carefully forwards, the arms of the robot following each move.

'*Hasta la vista*, baby,' said Oliviera.

The grasper reached down, grabbed a crab by the middle of its shell and lifted it in front of the camera lens. On the monitor, the creature took on monstrous proportions. Its jaws moved, and its legs kicked, but its pincers dangled limply. Johanson rotated the grasper in a full circle and carefully watched the reaction of the spinning crab.

'Normal motor activity,' he said. 'Its legs are moving fine.'

'But it's not responding like a crab,' said Rubin.

'No, it hasn't splayed its pincers or made any obvious show of aggression. It's just a machine.' He moved the second joystick and pressed the button on the top. The circular saw started to rotate and the blade cut into the side of the shell. For an instant the crab's legs twitched wildly.

The shell broke apart.

A milky substance slid out and hovered, trembling, over the debris of the crab.

'Oh, my God,' said Oliviera.

It looked like nothing they'd ever come across. It bore no resemblance to a jellyfish or a squid, but seemed entirely without form. Waves passed through the fringes of the substance, and the creature billowed and flattened. Johanson thought he saw a flash of light shoot out from its centre, but in the harsh glare of the tank it might have been an optical illusion. He was still thinking about it when the creature regrouped into something snake-like and shot away.

Johanson swore, picked up the next crab and cut it open. This time everything happened even faster, and the jelly-like inhabitant of the carapace fled before they had a chance to see it.

'Wow!' Rubin was clearly excited. 'This is crazy! What the hell is this stuff?'

'Something slippery,' Johanson said, through gritted teeth. 'How the hell are we supposed to stop it getting away?'

'What's the problem? It's got nowhere to go.'

'Well, you try searching the chamber for two shapeless, colourless objects no bigger than a tennis ball!'

'You could open the next one inside the sled basket,' said Oliviera.

'There's no netting at the front. It will get away.'

'No, it won't. The basket closes. You'll just have to be quick.'

Johanson grabbed another crab, spun the Spherobot by 180 degrees and guided it back towards the sled until it was close enough to extend its articulated arms inside the basket. Once they were in, he set the edge of the circular saw against the crab.

The shell burst open.

Nothing happened.

'Was it empty?' asked Rubin.

They waited a few seconds, then Johanson guided the spherical robot slowly inside the basket.

'Shit!'

The jelly shot away from the crab, but chose the wrong direction. It hit the back of the basket with a thud. Contracting into a trembling ball, it flitted unsteadily back and forth beside the rear mesh. Its confusion, if that was what it was, lasted only a second.

'It's trying to escape!'

Johanson reversed the Spherobot away from the basket. It hit the side of the cage and then it was out. Its arm grabbed the flap and slammed it shut.

The thing flattened itself into a sheet and rushed towards the flap, recoiling within centimetres of hitting it, and changing shape once more. This time its edges extended on all sides until it was suspended in the water like a transparent bell, filling half of the basket. The creature morphed. For a few seconds it looked like a jellyfish, then it rolled itself up. It was shaped like a ball again.

'Unbelievable,' whispered Rubin.

'Look at that,' exclaimed Oliviera. 'It's shrinking.'

The sphere was slowly decreasing in size and losing its transparency. The milky colour became more pronounced.

'Its tissue is contracting,' said Rubin. 'It can change its molecular density.'

'Does it remind you of something?'

'Early types of simple polyps.' Rubin thought. 'The Cambrian. A number of modern-day organisms have similar properties. Most squid contract their tissue, but they don't change shape. We need to catch a few more and see how they react.'

'Next time I won't be fast enough,' Johanson said. 'If I open the basket, this one will escape. They're too quick for me.'

'Fine. Well, I guess one is enough for observation purposes.'

'Oh, I don't know,' said Oliviera. 'Observing them is all very well, but I want to examine the stuff, not just its disintegrating remains. Maybe we should freeze the thing and slice it up.'

'Absolutely.' Rubin was staring at the screen in fascination. 'But not right now. Let's observe it for a bit.'

'But we've got the other two as well. Can anyone see them?'

Johanson switched on all the other screens. The inside of the tank appeared from various angles.

'Vanished.'

'They've got to be in there somewhere.'

'OK, let's crack open a few more,' said Johanson. 'That's what we'd agreed to do anyway. The more gunk there is floating around in the tank, the more chance we have of spotting it. We'll leave our PoW in the cage – we can deal with him later.'

They opened a dozen or so crabs without making any attempt to catch the jelly-like beings, which darted away as soon as the shells broke open.

'Well, they're certainly not affected by the *Pfiesteria*,' said Oliviera.

'Of course not,' said Johanson. 'The yrr will have made sure that neither organism can harm the other.'

'Do you think the jelly is another genetic mutation?'

'I don't know. It could be natural – but then again, it might be engineered.'

'Perhaps it's the yrr.'

Johanson rotated the Spherobot so that the camera was pointing at the basket. He stared at the captive. It had kept its spherical shape and was lying like a glassy white tennis ball on the floor of the cage.

'These things?' Rubin said in disbelief.

'Well, why not?' said Oliviera. 'We've found them in whale brains, they were underneath the mussels on the *Barrier Queen*, they were in the blue cloud. They're everywhere.'

'The blue cloud. How does that fit in?'

'It must have some kind of function. The things hide inside it.'

'Well, I'd say the jelly is like the worms and the other mutations. It's a biological weapon.' Rubin pointed to the motionless ball in the cage. 'Do you think it might be dead? It's not moving. Maybe the tissue contracts when it's dying.'

At that moment a whistling noise came through the loudspeakers overhead and Peak's voice boomed, 'Good morning, everyone. Now that Dr Crowe is here and the team is complete, there'll be a meeting at ten thirty on the well deck. We'll be introducing you to the submersibles and other equipment, so we'd appreciate your attendance. And don't forget that our daily meeting will take place as usual at ten in the Flag Command Center. Thank you.'

'Good thing he reminded us,' Rubin said. 'I've got no sense of time when I'm busy in the lab.'

'I wonder if there's any news from Nanaimo.' Oliviera sounded bored.

'Why don't you ring Roche?' Rubin suggested. 'You can tell him about our progress. Maybe he'll have something to show for his efforts too.' He prodded Johanson. 'And maybe we'll get to hear before Li. Then we can show off at the meeting.'

Johanson smiled back. He didn't like Rubin. The man was good at his job, but Johanson had the feeling he'd sell his grandmother to boost his career.

Oliviera went up to the radio-telephone next to the control panel and dialled the number. Thanks to the satellite dish on top of the island, the full range of telecommunication systems was available on board. No matter where you were in the ship, you could watch a wide range of TV channels, plug in your own portable TV set or radio, go online on your laptop or place a telephone call on a secure line to any city in the world. Even Nanaimo in faraway Canada was easy to reach. She talked to Fenwick, then Roche. They were working with a team of scientists all over the world. It looked as though they'd managed to stake out the spectrum of *Pfiesteria* mutations, but a breakthrough wasn't in sight. Instead hordes of crabs had invaded Boston. Oliviera updated them and hung up.

'What a bloody mess,' said Rubin.

'Perhaps our friends in the tank can be of some assistance,' said Johanson. 'Something must be protecting them from the algae. Let's set up a session in the containment facility. And as soon as we know what our prisoner—' He stared at the screen.

The thing in the cage had gone.

Olivera and Rubin followed his gaze.

'That's impossible.'

'How the hell did it get out?'

There was nothing to see on any of the screens, apart from water and crabs.

'They've disappeared.'

'They can't have!'

'Hang on a minute. There must be a least a dozen whizzing around in there. We're bound to be able to spot some.'

'Oh they'll be there all right. But where's the one from the cage?'

Johanson's face brightened.

'Maybe you're right,' he said slowly. 'After all, they keep changing shape. The wire mesh is pretty fine, but probably not fine enough for something very long and thin.'

'That stuff's unbelievable,' whispered Rubin.

They started to search the tank. They assigned themselves to different monitors, so they could scour the chamber simultaneously. They zoomed in, but there was no sign of the jelly anywhere. In the end Johanson guided all the robots, one by one, out of the garage, but the beings weren't hiding there either.

They'd vanished.

'Maybe we've got a problem with the plumbing,' said Oliviera. 'Do you think they could have got stuck?'

'Impossible,' said Rubin.

'Either way,' said Johanson, testily, 'it's time for the meeting. Let's hope we have a brainwave while we're up there.'

Baffled, they switched off the lights in the chamber and walked towards the door. Rubin turned off the lab lights and started to follow the others into the passageway. He looked back and stopped.

Johanson saw him standing in the doorway, staring back into the darkness. Slowly he walked towards him, followed by Oliviera.

Through the oval window of the chamber, something was glowing.

A faint glimmer of scattered light.

Blue.

Without stopping to worry about the obstacles in their path, they ran through the dark lab towards the chamber and rushed up the steps.

The blue glow was suspended in the water. A cosmic cloud in the darkness of space – only space was a tank, and inside it was water. It covered a few square metres.

Johanson peered at it. It looked as though tiny pulses of light were flowing towards the centre of the cloud, getting faster all the time, like particles of matter near a black hole.

The cloud turned a deeper blue, then collapsed in on itself.

It was imploding, like a Big Bang in reverse. Everything was sucked towards its centre, which grew steadily brighter and denser. Flashes of light shot out, forming complicated patterns. The cloud was disappearing into its mid-point at incredible speed, drawn into a turbulent whirlpool, and then . . .

'This can't be happening,' said Oliviera.

On the other side of the glass there was now a spherical object the size of a football. A blue-tinged mass of matter, made of luminous pulsating jelly.

They'd found the creatures.

And they'd become one.

Flag Command Center

'Single-cell organisms,' Johanson said. 'They're single-cell organisms!' He was incredibly excited. Rubin shifted on his chair and nodded vigorously, while Johanson paced up and down. He could never have stayed seated at a time like this. 'Until now we've assumed that the jelly and the cloud are two separate entities, but they're one and the same. They're a network of unicellular beings. It's not just a case of the jelly changing shape – it can disintegrate entirely, and get back together in a flash.'

'The unicellular whatsits can disintegrate?' queried Vanderbilt.

'Of course not! The single-cell organisms combine to form the jelly and the cloud. When we opened the crabs, we found blobs of the jelly inside them. We only managed to catch hold of one and all the others disappeared. Then we lost the captive too. It vanished without trace. I can't believe I didn't work it out straight away. It's obvious that you can't keep single-cell organisms in a cage. And you're hardly going to see them with the naked eye! The chamber was lit internally, which meant there was no sign of any bioluminescence. We had the same problem in

Norway. A huge thing appeared in front of our cameras. At the time we saw a pale surface, lit up by Victor's floodlights, but in reality it was glowing. It was glowing because it was made up of an enormous confederation of luminescent microbes. The creature we've got swimming about in the tank right now is the combined mass of jelly we let out of those crabs.'

'Well,' said Anawak, 'that would explain the shapeless creature on the keel of the *Barrier Queen* and the blue cloud near Vancouver Island . . .'

'Of course – your URA footage of the whales . . . Well, most of those cells would have been floating freely in the water, but others combined to form tentacles. They must have been injecting themselves into the heads of the whales, and—'

'Hang on a minute.' Li raised her hand. 'The jelly was already inside their heads.'

'OK, then.' Johanson thought for a moment. 'Well, some kind of connection took place. I bet that's how the jelly finds its way inside. Maybe we were witnessing some kind of exchange: old jelly out, new jelly in. Or it could have been a kind of check-up. Maybe the gunk in the brains was handing something to the cells outside.'

'Information,' said Greywolf.

'Why not?' exclaimed Johanson.

Delaware wrinkled her nose. 'You mean, they can take on any size at all? They can be as big as they need to be?'

'Any size and any shape.' Oliviera nodded. 'To steer a crab, you need only a handful. But the thing near the whales off Vancouver Island was the size of a house so—'

'That's why our discovery is so important,' Rubin cut in. He leaped to his feet. 'The jelly is a raw material that serves to accomplish different tasks.'

Oliviera looked put out.

'I've taken a close look at the footage from the Norwegian continental shelf,' he said breathlessly, 'and I think I know what happened! I'm willing to bet that this stuff was the final trigger for the collapse of the slope. We're on the verge of discovering the truth.'

'So you've found a substance that can do all kinds of shit,' said Peak, sounding unimpressed. 'Great. And where are the yrr?'

'The yrr—' Rubin stopped short. His self-assurance had evaporated. He glanced nervously at Johanson and Oliviera. 'Well . . .'

'Do you think these organisms *are* the yrr?' asked Crowe.

Johanson shook his head. 'No idea.'

For a while there was silence.

Crowe pursed her lips and drew on a cigarette. 'Well, we still haven't received a reply. What kind of organism would be able to respond? An intelligent being or maybe even a conglomerate of intelligent beings? What do you think, Sigur? Are those things in the tank intelligent?'

'You know perfectly well that it's pointless to speculate,' said Johanson.

'I just wanted to hear you say so.'

'How are we supposed to know if they're intelligent? What would an alien intelligence make of a bunch of human PoWs who can't do maths, and are moaning in a corner or sitting around apathetically because they're cold and scared?'

'Oh, God.' Vanderbilt groaned. 'Next thing he'll be throwing the book at us for infringing the Geneva Convention.'

'I didn't realise it applied to aliens.' Peak grinned.

Oliviera shot him a look of contempt. 'We're going to start running tests on the substance in the tank,' she said. 'Leon, tell me again what you saw on your solo recce in the docks.'

'Just before they fished me out? A blue glow.'

'You see,' said Oliviera, turning to face Li. 'You insisted on the military taking charge of everything, but your guys prodded around the *Barrier Queen* for weeks without any progress. They must have missed something crucial when they examined the water samples from the dock. Didn't anyone notice the glow? Or that there were single-cell organisms in the water?'

'We tested the water,' said Li.

'And?'

'Nothing. Ordinary seawater.'

'OK.' Oliviera sighed. 'Could I have another copy of the report, then? Including all of the lab results.'

'Of course.'

'Dr Johanson.' Shankar raised his hand. 'Do you have any explanation as to how they join together? What makes them do it?'

'How would they manage to co-ordinate it?' It was the first time that Roscovitz had spoken. 'How the hell does that work? And what's the point? It's like one of those cells is saying, "Hey, guys, over here, we're having a party!"'

'Not necessarily,' Vanderbilt pointed out. 'The cells in our body make a pretty good job of co-operation, and no one tells them what to do.'

'Aren't you confusing that with the CIA?' There was a smile on Li's lips.

'Watch it, Suzie Wong.'

'OK, guys,' said Roscovitz helplessly. 'I just drive subs for a living. I need help. Human cells stick together just fine, but that's different – we don't dissolve whenever we feel like it. And, besides, we've got a nervous system to keep us in check.'

'The cells in our bodies communicate via chemical signals,' said Delaware.

'But what does that mean? Are you saying we're like a shoal with everything going the same way, doing the same thing, at exactly the same time?'

'Shoals only appear to move simultaneously,' explained Rubin. 'Shoaling behaviour is related to pressure.'

'I know that, for Chrissakes – I was only trying to—'

'Lateral line organs are located on the sides of the body,' Rubin continued undeterred. 'If a fish changes its position, it sends a pressure wave through the water. That wave is picked up by all the neighbouring fish, who realign their bodies until the shoal has corrected its position.'

'I know!'

'But of course!' Delaware's face lit up. 'That must be it!'

'What?'

'Pressure waves. If you had enough of these jellies, you could redirect a shoal. We kept asking ourselves what kind of spell had been cast on the fish to stop them swimming into nets – well, that could be the answer.'

'Redirect a shoal?' Shankar sounded doubtful.

'She's right,' Greywolf chimed in. 'If the yrr can steer millions of crabs on land and transport billions of worms to the continental shelves, you can bet they're capable of redirecting shoals. And that's easy with pressure waves. The shoal's sensitivity to pressure is practically the only thing that keeps it safe.'

'Are you saying that those single-cell organisms in the tank use pressure waves to band together?'

'No,' put in Anawak. 'It has to be more complicated than that. Fish can create pressure waves, but single-cell organisms?'

'*Something* must have caused them to cluster together.'

'Hang on a minute,' said Oliviera. 'Bacteria use similar forms of communication. Take *Myxococcus xanthus*. Myxobacteria live in the soil. They move in loose swarms. If an individual cell can't find enough nutrients to feed itself, it gives off a starvation signal. The rest of the colony doesn't pay much attention at first, but as more and more cells start to starve, the intensity of the signal increases, until it crosses a certain threshold. At that point, the swarm draws closer together and gradually forms a complex multicellular aggregate known as a fruiting body. You can see it with the naked eye.'

'What kind of signal?' asked Anawak.

'They produce a chemical.'

'Like a scent?'

'Pretty much.'

The discussion dried up. Everyone was frowning, pressing their fingertips together, or pursing their lips.

'OK,' said Li. 'I'm impressed. That's a big step forward. It doesn't make sense to continue the discussion until we've had time to inform ourselves properly. What's next?'

'I've got a suggestion,' said Weaver.

'Let's hear it.'

'Do you remember what Leon was saying about dolphins' brains when we were in Whistler? He was talking about military experiments and electronic implants – not just basic microchips, but networks of artificial nerve cells that re-create parts of the brain in perfect detail and communicate with each other via electrical pulses. Well, supposing the jelly *is* an aggregate of single-cell organisms, and supposing those organisms *can* take over the function of brain cells and maybe even replace them – well, they'd have to be able to communicate or they wouldn't be able to band together or change shape. Maybe they can even form an artificial brain including all of the neurotransmitters. Maybe . . .' she hesitated '. . . they can even replace the emotions, characteristics and knowledge of their host, and that's how they learn to control it.'

'In that case they'd have to be capable of learning,' said Oliviera. 'But how could a single-cell organism learn?'

'Leon and I could try to model a swarm of them electronically. We could give them various characteristics and see how long it takes for them to start acting like a brain.'

'Artificial intelligence?'

'Yes, but with a biological basis.'

'That might be useful. Go ahead,' Li ruled. 'Any other suggestions?'

'I'll see if I can find any similar organisms among prehistoric life-forms,' said Rubin.

Li nodded. 'Any news from you, Sam?'

'Not really.' Crowe's voice emerged from a cloud of smoke. 'For the moment we're trying to decipher old Scratch signals while we wait for a reply.'

'Maybe you should have sent the yrr something a bit more challenging than a couple of sums,' said Peak.

The smoke cleared and Crowe's beautiful, time-worn face emerged with a smile. 'Just be patient, Sal.'

Well Deck

Roscovitz had devoted his life to the US Navy and saw no reason to change. It was his belief that people should do what they did best, and since he'd always liked being under water, he'd embarked on a career in submarines, working his way up to commander.

But he also believed that curiosity was one of the most important characteristics a person could possess. He had plenty of respect for loyalty, commitment and patriotism, but mindless drilling wasn't in his nature. At some stage it had occurred to him that submarine commanders knew nothing about the world in which they lived, so he'd decided to inform himself. Of course, he hadn't become a biologist overnight, but his enquiring mind had come to the attention of the technological division of the navy, which was on the look-out for people who were loyal enough to behave like soldiers but agile enough intellectually to play an executive role in research.

Once the decision had been taken to prepare the *Independence* for an expedition to the Greenland Sea, Roscovitz had been entrusted with finding her a state-of-the-art dive station. Many people saw her as humanity's last hope, which meant no expense was to be spared. Roscovitz was told to purchase whatever seemed useful, at any price, and to commission anything that didn't already exist – on the proviso that it could be built before they sailed.

No one had seriously expected him to consider using manned submersibles. ROVs were the obvious choice; vehicles like Victor, which had tracked down the Norwegian worms. The AUV was a serious option too: unlike Victor, there was no cable to connect it to the ship and most robots came with high-resolution cameras and either an articulated grasper or precision-operated artificial arms. Given the number of divers who'd been attacked or killed already, no one was keen to put human lives at risk. These days, even paddling was dangerous.

Roscovitz had listened to their objections and told them to forget it. 'Since when have we ever won a war using nothing but machines?' he'd argued. 'Sure, we can fire off smart bombs or send unmanned drones into enemy territory, but no robot can make the kind of decisions a fighter pilot takes. At some point in this mission we're going to have to go down and deal with the problem ourselves.'

They'd asked what he had in mind. ROVs and AUVs, he'd said, *plus* manned submersibles with weaponry. He'd also requested a dolphin fleet, and discovered, to his satisfaction, that MK6 and MK7 had been assigned to the mission at the request of a scientist. When he'd heard who'd be in charge of the dolphins, he'd been doubly pleased.

Roscovitz hadn't met Jack O'Bannon personally, but the ex-diver was well known in certain navy circles. When he'd resigned he'd refused to have anything to do with the navy. Roscovitz knew perfectly well that O'Bannon didn't have any kind of heart defect so he was surprised to find him back on board.

His superiors had tried to persuade him that there wouldn't be any call for manned submersibles, but Roscovitz wouldn't listen. In the end he got the green light.

Then he'd startled them again.

In all probability, the Department of the Navy had expected him to pack the stern of the enormous helicopter-carrier with the big-name submersibles, like the Russian MIR subs, the Japanese Shinkai and the French Nautile. With good old Alvin, they belonged to the half-dozen or so craft in the world capable of descending to a depth of 3000 metres. But Roscovitz was more interested in innovation. Shinkai could reach 6500 metres, but its ascent and descent relied on flooding and emptying its ballast tanks. The same was true of the MIR submersibles and Nautile.

But Roscovitz wasn't envisaging a conventional deep-sea expedition: it was war against an unknown enemy. Relying on regular submersibles would be like using hot-air balloons to fight a battle in the air. Most submersibles were too cumbersome for his purposes. He wanted deep-sea jets. Fighter planes.

It didn't take long to find a company that seemed to be working more along his lines. Hawkes Ocean Technologies, based in Point Richmond, California, had an excellent reputation, and not just within the industry. Hollywood often relied on its expertise whenever high-tech vessels were required. Graham Hawkes, a renowned engineer and inventor, had founded the firm in the mid-nineties to pursue his dream of flying under water.

Roscovitz had drawn up a wish list and placed it on the table with a large amount of cash. He had one stipulation: the firm would have to undercut every known record for building a submersible.

The cash had sealed the deal.

As the scientists lined up on the jetty at ten thirty, clad from head to toe in thermally insulating neoprene suits Roscovitz was pleased to be able to teach them something for once. The induction for the military and crew had taken place in Norfolk, Virginia. Most of them were navy SEALs, who were so used to the water that they'd practically grown fins. But Roscovitz was determined to ensure that the scientists were capable of deep-sea flying and fighting as well. He knew that things could happen during an expedition that meant civilians had to play a decisive role.

He instructed his chief technician, Kate Ann Browning to lower one of the four submersibles from the rail overhead. Deepflight 1 descended slowly towards them. The underside of the boat resembled a larger-than-life Ferrari without wheels, equipped with four long, thin cylinders. He waited until it was suspended at eye-level, four metres above the deck and directly over the basin. Seen from that angle, it had little in common with a conventional submersible. Flat, wide and almost rectangular in shape, with four thrusters mounted at the rear and two partially transparent body pods sloping up towards the front, the Deepflight looked more like a spaceship. Below the transparent domes, a pair of articulated arms protruded from the bow. Most noticeable of all were the vessel's stubby wings.

'I expect you're thinking it looks like a plane,' said Roscovitz, 'and you'd be right. It is a plane, and it's every bit as manoeuvrable. The wings serve the same purpose as they would on a plane, only they're angled in the opposite direction. The wings of an aeroplane generate lift. The wings on a Deepflight generate a downward force that counteracts the lift. Even the steering system is modelled on aeronautical principles. You don't sink like a stone; you move at an angle of up to sixty degrees, so you can bank elegantly from side to side or shoot up or down.' He made swooshing noises as he demonstrated the movements with the flat of his hand. He pointed to the pods. 'The main difference from an aeroplane is that you don't sit down. You lie prone. That way the height of the vehicle is kept to just 1.4 metres for a surface area of three by six metres.'

'How deep can it dive?' asked Weaver.

'As deep as you like. You could fly straight to the bottom of the Mariana Trench in less than ninety minutes. This baby can fly at twelve knots. The pressure hull is ceramic and the transparent domes are acrylic, enclosed in titanium. It's safe at any depth. It also provides a fantastic panoramic view, which will help us decide whether to turn tail or take aim.' He pointed to the underside. 'We've equipped our Deep-flights with four torpedoes. Two are loaded with a small amount of explosive – enough to seriously injure a whale, or maybe even kill it. The other two will do even more damage. You can use them to blast through rock or get rid of an entire pack of whales. But please leave the missiles to the pilot, unless, of course, he's dead or unconscious, in which case you won't have much choice.'

Roscovitz clapped his hands.

'You can fight among yourselves for the chance to be first for a test flight. And there's one more thing you should know. The fuel will give you eight hours' flight time. If you get stuck anywhere, the life-support system will provide you with sufficient oxygen for ninety-six hours. Either way, there's no need to panic – by then God's very own taskforce, the US Navy, will have come to your rescue. So, who wants to go first?'

'Without any water?' asked Shankar, casting a sceptical look at the basin.

Roscovitz grinned. 'Would fifteen thousand tonnes be enough?'

'Er . . . well, I guess so.'

'Here goes, then. Let's flood the deck.'

Two radio operators had been detailed to fill in for Crowe and Shankar while Roscovitz was instructing the scientists. The guys were killing time. Strictly speaking, they were supposed to keep their mouths shut and their ears open, but they knew they could rely on the computer, as well as on Shankar's SOSUS team back home in the States. If any noise were to emerge from the depths, it would be picked up onshore by countless electronic systems and human brains, then filtered out and sent back to the *Independence* with a full analysis and report. Crowe's message had been sent from the vessel, and the *Independence* was listening for a reply, but she was only one of many listening posts. If the yrr were to answer, the sound would be picked up by the Atlantic Ocean's hydrophone array. Using the distances between the hydrophones and the time taken for the signal to reach each one in turn, the computer could calculate the position from which the signal had been sent. The information would be forwarded to the CIC, where the operators would be bound to see it.

Trusting in the power of technology, the men were engaged in an impassioned musical debate. They were so caught up in white hip-hop that it didn't occur to them to glance at the screens. Eventually one reached across to pick up his coffee and glanced round. He stared.

'Jeez! What the hell is that?'

Coloured waves were flickering over two screens.

The other man stared too. 'Since when have they been there?'

'Dunno.' The radio operator peered at the lines. 'We should have been notified by the onshore team. How come they're not calling? They must be receiving it too.'

'Is that the frequency Crowe used for the message?'

'Don't ask me. I'm not getting any audible noise, though – must be ultrasound or infrasound.'

The other guy thought for a moment. 'The nearest hydrophone is off the coast of Newfoundland. Sound takes a while to travel, but no one else has picked up the signal, which means . . .'

'It's coming from here.'

The hydraulic system set to work noisily as the vast ballast tanks flooded. The *Independence*'s stern sank slowly through the water as seawater rushed inside.

'There's also the option of admitting water via the sluice,' Roscovitz shouted above the noise, 'but that would mean opening the hatches simultaneously, which would breach our security, so it's something we're keen to avoid. We get round it by using a specially designed pump system. A closed loop of pipes feeds water up to the deck. It's filtered several times before it gets here. The basin is lined with sensors, like the sluice, so you can be sure the water's safe before you jump into the pool.'

'Will we be testing the boats in the basin?' asked Johanson.

'Hell, no – we're going to fly them outside.'

Now that the dolphin fleet had reported the retreat of the orcas, Roscovitz felt satisfied that they could risk a few dives.

'My God.' Rubin was staring at the frothing water in the basin. He appeared to be frozen to the spot. 'It looks as though we're sinking.'

Roscovitz grinned at him. 'I've been on a sinking warship and, trust me, it's nothing like this.'

Metre by metre, the stern of the enormous vessel sank deeper into the water. The *Independence* was too large for anyone to feel her tilting. The change was minimal – it would have taken a spirit level to detect it – but the effect on the well deck was astonishing. The water level rose until it was lapping the edge of the jetty. Within a few minutes, the deck had been transformed into a four-metre-deep pool. By now the dolphin tank was underwater, which allowed its occupants to swim the full length of the deck. The Zodiacs drifted on the surface, moored securely to the embankment. Deepflight 1 bobbed gently on the waves.

Browning let down another submersible from the rail overhead. She was standing at the control panel, operating the joystick. One by one she manoeuvred the boats along the monorail until they were lined up next to the jetty. Then she opened the pods. They clapped open like fighter-plane cockpits.

'Each pod can be opened and closed individually,' she explained. 'Getting in is easy, although you might be soaked on your first attempt. The water is heated on its way into the basin so it's a balmy fifteen degrees, but don't think of taking off your suits. If you were tipped into the ocean without one, it would all be over in minutes. The water temperature off the coast of Greenland reaches a maximum of two degrees.'

'Any questions?' Roscovitz organised the first groups, pairing scientists with pilots. 'Let's go, then. We'll stick close to the vessel. Our friendly colleagues from the dolphin fleet have given us the all-clear, but things could change at any moment. Leon, you're coming with me. We'll take Deepflight 1.'

He jumped on to the boat, which lurched from side to side. Anawak tried to copy him, but lost his balance and landed in the water. He spluttered to the surface and was greeted by laughter.

'I guess that's what I meant,' Browning said drily.

Anawak pulled himself on to the hull and slid into the pod on his belly. To his surprise it felt comfortable and roomy. He wasn't lying completely flat; the pod slanted upwards, so his body assumed the position of a ski jumper in mid-flight. In front of him he found a control panel. Roscovitz switched on the power, and the pods closed soundlessly.

'Not exactly the Ritz, eh, Leon?'

The commander voice boomed out of the loudspeakers and into Anawak's ears. He turned his head. A metre away from him, Roscovitz was looking out of his acrylic pod and grinning at him. 'See that joystick in front of you? Remember I told you it's like a plane? Well, that's how it flies. So you're going to have to learn to fly it like a plane – gaining and losing height, banking round. You need to be able to move in all four directions. It's equipped with four thrusters that generate sufficient counter-force to allow the vehicle to hover. I'll fly the first loop, then you'll take over, at which point I'll tell you what you're doing wrong.'

All of a sudden the vessel tipped forward. Water washed over the acrylic domes, and they banked down in a gentle curve. Floodlights lit up at the bow and on the wings. Anawak saw the planks at the bottom of the basin slide beneath them, and then they were hovering at the opening to the sluice. The flaps opened to reveal a shaft that stretched down several metres, fully lit, with a dark steel hatch at the bottom. The Deepflight sank leisurely through it and the glass flaps closed above them. He felt a wave of queasiness.

'Don't worry,' said Roscovitz. 'They'll let us out pretty quickly. It's coming back in that takes time.'

The steel flaps juddered into motion. As the enormous metal panels moved apart, the view opened up to show the dark, featureless expanse of the depths. The Deepflight sank into the unknown.

Roscovitz accelerated and banked round. The boat turned onto its side. Anawak was enthralled. He'd driven conventional submersibles designed for use in the upper layers of the ocean, but this was different. The Deepflight handled the water like a sports plane. And it was fast! In a car, fourteen miles per hour – the equivalent of twelve knots – would seem slow, but underwater the Deepflight was displaying an amazing burst of speed. He watched in fascination as they emerged from beneath the *Independence* and the rippling surface of the water came into view overhead. Roscovitz dipped the nose of the submersible at a precipitous angle. He banked round again, headed towards the stern of the heli-copter-carrier and dived back under. Above them, the enormous rudder blade of the vessel whizzed by.

Then Roscovitz banked sharply. Anawak kept expecting to see the round black-and-white face of an orca appear before them, but instead two dolphins peered in. With cameras on their heads, they pranced jauntily around the submersible.

'Smile, Leon!' laughed Roscovitz. 'You're on camera!'

Then a light flashed on. 'You're taking over,' said Roscovitz. 'If anything comes along and tries to eat us, we'll give it a brace of torpedoes for breakfast. But I'll take care of that. You focus on steering.'

Anawak was momentarily flummoxed. His grip on the joystick tight-ened. Roscovitz hadn't told him what to do, so he headed straight on.

'Hey, Leon, no snoozing at the wheel. I've been on bus journeys that were more exciting than this.'

'What do you want me to do?'

'Anything. Fly us to the moon!'

The moon in this scenario must be below us, thought Anawak. Here goes.

He thrust the joystick forward.

The Deepflight's nose jerked down and they headed into the depths. Anawak stared into the darkness. He pulled the joystick towards him, this time more gently. The boat straightened. He tried a curve, but turned too sharply. He tried another. He knew he was steering too jerkily, but really it was easy. It was all a question of practice.

Ahead he spotted a second Deepflight. Suddenly he started to enjoy himself. He could have carried on for hours.

'Not bad, Leon. I reckon your technique's enough to make anyone travel-sick, but that's nothing we can't fix. Now put her on the horizontal. Excellent. That's it, drift along slowly. Now let's have a go at operating the articulated arms. There's nothing to it.'

After five minutes Roscovitz took over the controls and guided the boat slowly into the shaft. There was an agonising minute inside the sluice, but then the glass flaps opened and they surfaced. Anawak wasn't sorry to be back: the early-morning visit from the orcas had unnerved him. And there were all the other surprises that the sea might spring on an unsuspecting pilot.

Roscovitz opened the pods, and they lifted themselves out of the boat and jumped on to the jetty.

Floyd Anderson was waiting for them. 'How was it?' he asked. He didn't seem to care.

'Fun.'

'Well, folks, the party's over.' The first officer watched the second boat surface. 'As soon as you guys stick your heads under water, stuff happens. We've picked up a signal.'

'What?' Crowe joined them. 'What kind?'

'We were hoping you could tell us.' Anderson stared straight past her. 'It's loud, and it's coming from somewhere nearby.'

Combat Information Center

'A low-frequency signal,' said Shankar. 'Same pattern as Scratch.'

Shankar and Crowe had rushed to the CIC. In the meantime they'd received confirmation from the onshore station. According to their calculations, the noise was coming from the vicinity of the *Independence*.

Li walked in. 'Can you make any sense of it?'

'Not right away.' Crowe shook her head. 'We'll need some help from the computer. We'll get it to break down the signal and start looking for patterns.'

'Call me some time next year.'

'Is there a problem?' Shankar growled.

'I was just wondering how you intended to decipher it in a viable timescale, when your guys at NOAA have been puzzling over Scratch for years.'

'And you're asking that *now?*'

'Come on, children.' Crowe scrabbled around for her cigarettes and lit up. 'I keep telling you that communicating with an alien species is an entirely different matter. Yesterday's signal was probably the first human message that the yrr have been able to decode. They'll reply in a similar format.'

'You really think they'll use the same coding?'

'Well, *if* the yrr exist, *if* this is a message, *if* they understood our code, and *if* they're interested in talking to us – then, yes, I do.'

'Why are they using the infrasound spectrum and not a frequency we can hear?'

'Why shouldn't they use infrasound?' Crowe asked, surprised.

'You'd think it would be diplomatic.'

'If a Russian were to address you in bad English, would you reply to him in Russian?'

Li shrugged. 'OK, whatever. But what now?'

'We'll stop transmitting our message. That'll signal to them that we've picked up their transmission. We'll know soon enough if they've been using our code. They'll have tried to make it easy to decipher. Whether we're smart enough to grasp what they're telling us is another matter.'

Joint Intelligence Center

Weaver was attempting the impossible. She was trying to disregard all the existing research about the evolution of intelligent life – and, at the same time, confirm its findings.

Crowe had explained that every theory on the existence of alien civilisations hinged on the same set of questions, including: how big or small could intelligent life-forms be? In SETI circles, where the focus was on interstellar communication, people were busy hypothesising about beings whose gaze was turned towards the skies – extra-terrestrials who had entertained the possibility of other worlds and had decided to make contact. Such beings would almost certainly live on dry land, so there were clear limitations governing their size.

Astronomers and exobiologists had recently come to believe that a planet would have to possess no less than 85 per cent and no more than 133 per cent of the Earth's mass to generate surface temperatures conducive to the development of intelligent life within one to two billion years. The dimensions of this hypothetical planet had implications for its gravitational field, which in turn allowed certain conclusions to be drawn about the anatomy of any beings that might live there. Theoretically a living creature could grow infinitely large on an Earth-like planet. In practice, though, it would be limited by the ability of the body to bear its own weight. Dinosaurs, of course, had developed extraordinarily large bones, but their brains had failed to keep up. They were designed for lumbering, eating and not much else. Accordingly, there was a rough rule of thumb: intelligent non-stationary life-forms were unlikely to grow more than ten metres tall.

The more interesting question was how small they could be. Could ants develop intelligence? And how about bacteria? Or viruses?

SETI researchers and exobiologists had good reason to want to find out. It was almost certain that the Earth's corner of the galaxy was free from other humanoid civilisations, at least within its own solar system, which left scientists clinging to the hope that Mars or one of Jupiter's moons would be home to a few stray spores or some single-cell organisms. They started to search for the smallest viable unit of life, which inevitably led them to complex organic molecules – the smallest self-contained units capable of storing and using information. But could a molecule like that develop intelligence?

The answer was a decisive no.

But the individual neurons of a human brain weren't intelligent either. For humans to attain the brain-to-body ratio that made them intelligent, it took one hundred billion neurons each. It was conceivable that an intelligent organism smaller than a human could make do with fewer cells, but there was no altering the size of the molecules of which the neurons were composed – and without a critical mass of neurons, there could be no intelligent spark. That was the limiting factor for ants, who seemed to possess non-conscious intelligence but whose brains could never attain a higher neural capacity because they lacked sufficient cells. In fact, since ants didn't breathe through lungs but absorbed oxygen through their body surface, their growth was inherently restricted. Their respiratory system would fail if they exceeded a certain size, so their brains had no chance to develop any further. In evolutionary terms, ants and their fellow insects had reached a dead end. Scientists had therefore concluded that the smallest possible size for an intelligent life-form was roughly ten centimetres, which meant the chances of encountering a scuttling Aristotle were practically nil. Single-cell intelligence seemed out of the question.

All that was at the back of Weaver's mind as she sat down to program the computer to link mental capacity and single-cell organisms in a meaningful combination.

In the hours following the discovery in the lab, the general mood was one of scepticism. Could the jelly really be intelligent? Single-cell organisms weren't capable of creativity and couldn't develop self-awareness. No one contested that a sizeable number of single-cell organisms theoretically corresponded to a brain or a body. The blue cloud filmed by the URA near Vancouver Island had evidently consisted of billions of cells – but did that mean it could think? And even if it could, how was it supposed to learn? How would the cells communicate? What had to happen for a conglomerate of cells to become a higher entity?

How had it worked for humanity?

Either the jelly substance was nothing more than insentient goo, or there was a trick to it.

The jelly had steered whales and crabs.

Computer programs developed by Kurzweil Technologies used billions of bits to simulate neurons that worked together as a brain. Artificial intelligence of one kind or another was already being used throughout the globe. AI systems were capable of learning, and there was even a sense in which they used their own creativity to further their development. None of the AI researchers claimed to have created *consciousness*, but their work already posed the question as to when a mass of tiny identical parts could be classed as alive – and whether life could be generated artificially in that way.

Weaver was now in possession of one of the latest generation of artificial brains, having approached its inventor Ray Kurzweil directly. Her first move was to save a backup copy. Then she set about dismantling the original into its individual electronic components, breaking down the bridges and turning it into an unstructured swarm of tiny units. She tried to imagine breaking down a human brain. What would she have to do to get the cells to come back together and re-create the thinking whole? Billions of electronic neurons were swarming all over her computer, tiny bits of data with nothing to bind them together.

She tried to imagine that they were single-cell organisms.

Billions of single-cell organisms.

She thought through the next steps. It would be best to stick as closely as possible to the facts as she knew them. After some reflection, she constructed a three-dimensional space and gave it the physical characteristics of water. What did single-cell organisms look like? They came in all kinds of different shapes – rods, triangles, stars, sometimes with irregular outlines, sometimes with flagella – but it made sense to settle for the simplest. She decided on spheres.

Step by step the computer became an ocean. Weaver's virtual organisms rolled and spun through their electronic world. Maybe she should add currents, so that the virtual space mirrored the deep-sea environment. No, that could wait. First there were some major questions to address.

So many units. How could they give rise to an intelligent being? There weren't any limitations on maximum size. None of SETI's assumptions about size was relevant to water-dwelling organisms, since the forces affecting bodyweight were different under water. An intelligent marine-based life-form could be incomparably bigger than any land-dwelling organism. SETI's scenarios barely accounted for water-based civilisations, because any such civilisation would be beyond the reach of radio waves. Besides, it seemed unlikely that an underwater species would be interested in space or other planets – unless it was planning to cross the universe in a travelling aquarium. But a water-based scenario was what she needed now.

When Anawak arrived in the JIC thirty minutes later, she was staring at the screen, forehead knitted. She was cheered when she saw him. Since his return from Nunavut, they'd talked a lot about themselves to each other, and Anawak seemed more confident and self-assured. The dejected Inuk whom she'd found in the hotel bar had vanished in the Arctic.

'How are you doing?' he asked.

'My brain's in knots. Both brains, actually. I don't know where to start.'

'What's the problem?'

She told him what she had done so far. 'I'm not surprised you're stuck,' he said. 'You're doing a great job with the computer, but there's some biology you need to know. The brain can only think because of its structure. For the most part our neurons are pretty much identical – it's the way in which they're connected that allows them to think. It's like . . . Imagine a city.'

'London.'

'It's been shaken out of place and your job is to put the houses and streets back where they were. There are heaps of possibilities, but only one will give you London.'

'Fine, but how does each house know where it belongs?' Weaver sighed. 'No, scrap that question. Let's not worry about how the brain cells are connected. What I don't get is how they can join together and form something that's more intelligent than the sum of their parts.'

Anawak rubbed his chin thoughtfully. 'Think of the city again. In one of the streets a tower block is being built by a team of, say, a thousand workers. The workers are all identical – clones. Each has a specific task – a particular set of actions that he's employed to carry out. None of the workers has seen the blueprint for the building, yet together they're capable of constructing it. But imagine what would happen if you switched those guys around. There's a chain of ten builders passing bricks along the line, and you swap one for a man who tightens screws – well, you're going to cause trouble.'

'I see. So provided they stick to their jobs, the whole thing works fine.'

'Now, you could say that it only works because someone's been telling the workers what to do, but that someone couldn't build the block without them. Each presupposes the other. The plan gives rise to the workers' joint effort, and the workers' joint effort gives rise to the plan.'

'Is there someone who plans?'

'Maybe the workers are the plan.'

'Well, in that case all the workers would have to be coded slightly differently – which, come to think of it, they are.'

'Exactly. You see, the workers only *seem* to be identical. So, let's start at the beginning again. There's a plan. The units are all coded differently. What else do you need to make them into a network?'

Weaver thought. 'I guess they have to be willing to co-operate.'

'It's more straightforward than that.'

Suddenly she saw what he was getting at. 'Communication. A common language. A signal.'

'And what would the signal be telling the workers in the morning?'

'Get up and go to the building-site.'

'Anything else?'

'Remember where you belong when you get there.'

'Exactly. But these guys are labourers, so they don't indulge in fancy conversation. They're hard-working men. They sweat in bed, they sweat when they get up in the morning – they're sweating all day long. How do they recognise each other?'

Weaver pulled a face. 'By their smell?'

'Bingo!'

'I'm beginning to worry about your imagination.'

Anawak laughed. 'It's Oliviera's fault. She was talking about those bacteria earlier, the ones that form aggregates, *Myxococcus xanthus*. Remember? They secrete a scent and group together.'

Weaver nodded. It made sense. 'I'll think it over while I'm swimming,' she said. 'Want to come?'

'Swimming? Now?'

'Yes, now,' she teased him. 'Listen, under normal circumstances I wouldn't spend the whole day cooped up in a room without moving.'

'I thought that was normal for computer geeks.'

'Are you saying I'm pale and flabby?'

'I've never seen anyone paler or flabbier.' He grinned.

She saw the sparkle in his eyes. He was small and compact, not exactly George Clooney, but right now he seemed tall, self-assured and good-looking. 'Idiot,' she said.

'Thanks.'

'Just because you spend half your life under water, you think anyone who works with computers must be chained to their desk. For your information, I do most of my work outdoors. I spend most of my time *thinking*. I grab my laptop and take off. There's no reason why you shouldn't write features from a cliff-top. Sitting here makes me tense up. I'm going to get shoulders like steel girders.'

Anawak stood up. For a moment Weaver thought he was leaving. Then she felt his hands on her back. His fingers stroked the muscles in her neck, while his thumbs kneaded her shoulders.

He was massaging her back.

Weaver stiffened.

She liked it. But did she want it?

'You're not tense,' said Anawak.

He was right. Why had she said it?

She stood up abruptly and his hands dropped away. She knew she'd made a mistake. She wanted to sit down again and let him carry on. But it was too late.

'Well, I guess I'll be going then,' she said awkwardly.

Anawak

He wondered what had gone wrong. He would have liked to join her in the pool, but the mood had changed. He should have asked before he massaged her shoulders. Maybe he'd misread the situation. You're no good at this kind of thing, he told himself. Stick to your whales, you stupid Eskimo.

He thought about going in search of Johanson and continuing their discussion about single-cell intelligence, but somehow he didn't feel like it. He decided to stop by the CIC instead. Greywolf and Delaware spent much of their time there, monitoring and evaluating audio and video output from the fleet. But there was nothing to see except images of murky water from the cameras on the hull. Things had been quiet since the whales had circled the boat that morning, and now they seemed to have gone. Shankar was sitting on his own wearing a pair of oversized headphones, listening to the depths, while a constant stream of numbers passed before him on the screen. According to one of the crew, Greywolf and Delaware were busy on the well deck, substituting MK6 for MK7.

Anawak marched down the vehicle ramp and on to the empty hangar deck. It was cold and draughty. He'd been meaning to carry straight on, but something held him back. Although daylight was visible through the gate-like openings where the deck elevators were situated, the bay was dominated by the pale, yellowish glow of the sodium vapour lamps. He tried to imagine what it would look like when it was full of helicopters, Harrier jets, vehicles, cargo and equipment, all packed in with just enough room to open a door, climb through a window or slip into a hatch. Jeeps and forklift trucks would rattle up and down the ramps, and once the aircraft were on the roof, hundreds of marines would sort weaponry and equipment swiftly and intently. The formidable apparatus of the *Independence* would pull together as one.

The vast expanse of the bay seemed absurd in its emptiness. Useless. The booths between the ribs were unmanned. High among the steel girders on the gloomy ceiling, the yellow lamps had nothing to illuminate. Pipes ran along the walls, ending in the void. There were hazard signs everywhere, but no one to see them.

'If things get too cosy in the gym, we sometimes shift a few of the treadmills down here,' Peak had said, as he'd shown them round the vessel in Norfolk. 'Then it's real homey.' He'd stood there frowning. 'It's too empty. I hate to see the hangar like this. There are times when I hate this whole damn mission.'

The emptiest room, Anawak thought, is always on the inside.

He crossed the bay unhurriedly and walked out on to the portside elevator. The platform towered above the waves like a vast balcony. It was held in place by vertical slide rails that ran up the side of the ship. Anawak peered out across the water. The wind buffeted him. A strong gust could easily have swept him off his feet and over the edge of the platform. There weren't any rails, but safety nets encircled the ship so that no one could be pitched into the sea by the wind or aircraft exhaust.

It was still risky, though.

Ten metres below him, the waves rose up from the ocean.

The light was weak, but the icy rain had stopped. The sea rose and fell, slate-grey, with veins of white. A watery desert. For more than half of his life he'd lived in the temperate climate of the Canadian west coast, and now, for the second time in a few months, Fate had sent him back to the ice.

The wind tugged at his hair. Gradually he could feel his skin becoming numb with cold. He cupped his hands in front of his mouth, and puffed warm air inside them.

Then he went back into the bay.

Lab

Johanson had promised to treat Oliviera to some real lobster when the crisis was over. He used the Spherobot to fish out a crab from the chamber, then bring it back to the garage, where hermetically sealable PVC-coated containers were ready and waiting. The robot dropped the crab into one of the boxes and closed the lid.

The container was moved through a sluice gate and into a dry area, where it was sprayed with peracetic acid, rinsed, blasted with sodium hydroxide and conveyed out of the chamber through a second sluice. Now it didn't matter how toxic the water was inside the deep-sea chamber: the outside of the container was clean.

'Are you sure you can manage on your own?' asked Johanson. He'd already scheduled a phone conversation with Bohrmann, who was about to lower the suction tube in La Palma.

'No problem.' Oliviera picked up the box that contained the crab. 'If anything goes wrong, I'll scream. Hopefully you'll hear me and not that jerk Rubin.'

Johanson chuckled. 'Do I detect a shared antipathy?'

'Oh, I've got nothing against the guy,' said Oliviera. 'If only he wasn't so hung up on winning a Nobel Prize.'

'I know what you mean. How about you, though? Aren't you interested in a bit of glory? We'll all be vaguely famous, if we get out of this alive.'

'Oh, I wouldn't say no to a few groupies. Life in the lab can be desperately dull.' Oliviera stopped short. 'Which reminds me, where is he anyway?'

'Rubin?'

'He was determined to be around for the DNA tests.'

'You should be grateful.'

'Oh, I am. But I'd still like to know what he's up to.'

'It's bound to be something constructive,' Johanson said soothingly. 'I mean, he's not a bad guy. He doesn't smell, he's not an axe-murderer, and he's got a whole stack of medals in his drawer. We don't have to like him as long as he's useful.'

'Well, is he? Name me one useful thing he's done so far.'

'My dear lady,' Johanson spread his arms, 'if an idea's worth having, what does it matter who came up with it?'

Oliviera grinned. 'That's how second-rate people try to kid themselves. Fine. Let him do what he wants – but I'm not convinced that it's useful.'

Sedna

Anawak walked to the edge of the basin. The deck was still flooded. Delaware and Greywolf, in neoprene suits, were knee-deep in water, unharnessing the dolphins. The room was filled with noise. Aft, one of the Deepflight submersibles was being lowered from the rail, Roscovitz and Browning overseeing the process from the control desk. Slowly the vehicle sank towards the basin, touched down and rocked gently on the water. Light from the sluice shone up to the rippling surface.

'Taking the subs out again?' Anawak called.

'No.' Roscovitz pointed to the Deepflight. 'This baby's developed a quirk – a fault with the vertical steering.'

'Is it serious?'

'We need to check it over.'

'That's the one we were in, isn't it?'

'Don't worry. It's not your fault.' Roscovitz laughed. 'It's probably a glitch in the software. We'll have it ironed out in a couple of hours.'

A tide of water swept over Anawak's feet.

'Leon!' Delaware beamed up at him. 'Come and join us.'

'Excellent idea,' said Greywolf. 'I'd like to see you do something useful.'

'I have been,' Anawak protested.

'I bet.' Greywolf stroked one of the dolphins, as it nuzzled up to him and made chattering noises. 'Grab yourself a suit.'

'I only wanted to see how you are.'

'Very kind of you.' Greywolf patted the dolphin and watched it speed away.

'Any news?'

'We're about to send out MK7,' said Delaware. 'MK6 haven't noticed anything unusual since this morning when they warned us of the orcas.'

'And that was before any of the sensors noticed they were there,' Greywolf added with pride.

'Yeah, their sonar is—'

Anawak got another soaking, this time from one of the dolphins, as it shot out of the water like a torpedo and showered him with spray. It seemed to be enjoying itself. It squeaked, poking its beak out of the water.

'I wouldn't bother if I were you,' said Delaware to the dolphin. 'Leon won't come in. He's not prepared to freeze his butt off because he's not a real Inuk. He's just a show-off. If he was a real Inuk he'd have—'

'OK, OK!' Anawak made a gesture of defeat. 'Where's the damn suit?'

Five minutes later he was helping Delaware and Greywolf fit the second fleet with cameras and tags when he remembered something. 'Why did you think I was a Makah?' he asked Delaware.

'I knew you had to be some kind of Indian – you're not exactly blond and blue-eyed. But now I know the truth, well . . .' she beamed at him '. . . I've got something for you.' She fastened the strap round the dolphin's chest. 'I found it on the web. I thought you might be pleased. I learned it by heart. It's the history of your world.' She said it with a flourish.

'Wow.'

'Not interested?'

'Oh, he is,' said Greywolf. 'Leon's dying to hear about his beloved homeland. He just hates to admit it.' He swam towards them, flanked by two dolphins. In his padded suit he looked like a sea monster. 'He'd rather be taken for a Makah.'

'You can talk!' Anawak protested.

'Don't argue, boys!' Delaware lay on her back and drifted. 'Do you know where whales, dolphins and seals *really* come from? Shall I tell you?'

'The suspense is killing me.'

'Well, it all started when people and animals were still one. Many years ago, a girl lived near Arviat.'

Now she had Anawak's attention.

'Where's Arviat?' asked Greywolf.

'It's the southernmost settlement of Nunavut,' Anawak replied. 'Was the girl called Talilajuk?'

'Yes,' Delaware said. 'She had beautiful hair, and all the men courted her, but the only one who could win her heart was a dogman. Soon Talilajuk became pregnant, and bore all kinds of children, Inuit and canine. One day, while the dogman was out hunting, a dashing birdman arrived in his kayak at Talilajuk's camp. He invited her to climb into his boat and, to cut a long story short, they eloped.'

'The usual.' Greywolf was inspecting the lens of one of the cameras. 'And when do the whales come into it?'

'All in good time. One day Talilajuk's father came to visit them, only to find the dogman howling because Talilajuk had gone. The old man paddled back and forth across the ocean until he found the birdman's camp. While he was still out to sea, he spotted his daughter sitting outside her tent. Well, he ordered her to go home, so she followed her father dutifully to the kayak, and they set off. It wasn't long before they noticed that the ocean swell was rising. The waves grew steadily higher,

630

and a fearsome storm broke out. The waves washed over the boat, and the old man worried that they might drown. It was the revenge of the birdman, but Talilajuk's father had no desire to die. Since he was furious with his daughter, he reached over, grabbed her and flung her overboard. Talilajuk clung to the side of the kayak, but her father told her to let go. She held on all the more tightly. The old man went crazy with fear. He picked up his axe, swung it and chopped off her fingertips. They had barely touched the water when they turned into narwhal, her nails forming their tusks. Talilajuk still refused to let go, so the old man hacked her fingers down to the joints, and they turned into white whales – belugas. Still his daughter clung to the side. She paid for her stubbornness with the last of her fingers, and a pod of seals appeared. Talilajuk wouldn't give in. Even though her hands were stumps, she clung to the kayak, which was filling with water. The old man was terrified. He struck her in the face with the paddle, and she lost her left eye. She let go slowly, and sank beneath the waves.'

'Brutal customs they had back then.'

'But Talilajuk didn't die or, at least, not a normal death. She was transformed into Sedna, the spirit of the sea, and since then she's ruled the creatures of her realm. Stretching her mutilated arms in front of her, she glides through the water with only one eye. Her hair is as beautiful as ever, but she has no hands to comb it. That's why it gets tangled, and you can tell that she's angry. But anyone who manages to comb and plait her hair is granted the freedom to hunt the creatures of her kingdom.'

'I remember that story from long winter nights when I was little,' Anawak said softly. 'I heard it countless times, and it was never exactly the same.' He wondered what had made her dig up the ancient legend of Sedna for him. It seemed to him that she hadn't stumbled on it by chance. She'd been on the look-out for a story of the sea. It was a present, proof of their friendship. He was touched.

'Rubbish.' Greywolf summoned the last dolphin with a whistle, and started to attach the hydrophones and cameras. 'Leon's a scientist. You can't tell him stories about the spirit of the sea.'

'You two and your feud,' said Delaware.

'Besides, the story's all wrong. Do you want to know how it really started? There wasn't any land. There was only a chief who lived under water in his cabin. He was a lazy so-and-so who never got up – he just lay on the seabed with his back to the fire, which was kept alight with crystals. He lived on his own, and his name was Wonderful Creator. One day his attendant rushed in and told him that the spirits and supernatural beings couldn't find any land to settle on. They wanted the chief to do something about it, and be worthy of his name. The chief lifted two rocks from the seabed and gave them to his attendant with the instruction to cast them into the water. He did as he was told, and the rocks formed the Queen Charlotte Islands and the mainland.'

'Well,' said Anawak, 'it's good to hear a scientific explanation.'

'The story comes from an old Haida myth cycle: Hoyá Káganus, the travels of Raven,' said Greywolf. 'The Nootka tell similar stories. Lots of the myths are related to the sea – either you come from it or it destroys you.'

'Maybe we should pay more attention to them,' said Delaware, 'if science can't get us any further.'

'Since when have you been interested in myths?' said Anawak. 'you're even more of an empiricist than I am.'

'So? At least they tell us how to live in harmony with nature. Who cares if none of it's true? You take something and give something back. That's all you need to know.'

Greywolf grinned and petted the dolphin. 'Then there wouldn't be any problems in the world, would there, Licia? Well, as a woman, you'll be pleased to know you can help.'

'How do you mean?'

'I happen to know a few customs from the Bering Sea. And they had a different way of doing things. Before the hunters set to sea, the harpooner had to sleep with the captain's daughter to acquire her scent. That was the only way of attracting the whale to the boat and calming it enough so that they could kill it.'

'Trust men to think up something like that,' said Delaware.

'Men, women, whales . . .' laughed Greywolf. '*Hishuk ish ts'awalk* – everything is one.'

'OK,' said Delaware. 'In that case I think we should dive to the bottom of the ocean and comb Sedna's hair.'

Everything is one. Anawak remembered what Akesuk had told him. *This isn't a problem you can solve with science. A shaman would tell you that you're dealing with spirits, the spirits of the once-living that now inhabit the Earth's creatures. The qallunaat started destroying life. They angered the spirits, the spirit of the sea, Sedna. No matter who these beings are, you won't achieve anything by trying to fight them. Destroy them, and you'll destroy yourselves. See them as a part of yourselves, and you'll be able to share the same world. No one can ever win the struggle for mastery.*

While Roscovitz and Browning were repairing the Deepflight, the three of them had been swimming with dolphins and telling each other legends about spirits of the sea. As they had paddled around, they had got cold even though the water had been heated and they were wearing suits.

How were they supposed to comb the sea spirit's hair?

Until now humanity had pelted Sedna with toxins and nuclear waste. One oil slick after another had collected in her hair. Without asking her permission they'd hunted her creatures until some were extinct.

Anawak's heart was pounding and he was shivering. A dull sense of foreboding told him that this moment of happiness wouldn't last, that something was ending. They'd never be together like this again.

Greywolf checked that the harness was sitting correctly on the sixth and final dolphin. 'All OK,' he said. 'We can send them out to sea.'

Biohazard Containment Facility

'Oh, God, how stupid can you get? I must be blind!' She stared at the magnified image from the fluorescence microscope on the screen. In Nanaimo they'd analysed various batches of the jelly – or, at least, what had been left of it after they'd scraped it out of the whales' brains. They'd also taken a good look at the blob of matter Anawak had brought back on his knife after his inspection of the *Barrier Queen*. But not once had it occurred to her that the disintegrating substance could be a dissociating conglomerate of single-cell organisms.

How embarrassing.

She should have worked it out ages ago, but what with all the *Pfiesteria*-induced panic, they'd had killer algae on the brain. Even Roche hadn't noticed that the jelly-like substance was still clearly visible through the microscope, even after it had apparently dispersed. Countless single-cell organisms lay dead or dying on the slide. All the various components had been there from the start, mixed up inside the lobsters and the crabs: killer algae, jelly – and seawater.

Seawater!

Maybe Roche would have cottoned on to the nature of the mysterious substance if it hadn't been for the fact that one single drop of it contained a universe of life. For centuries people had been too distracted by all the fish, marine mammals and crabs in the oceans to see the other ninety-nine per cent of life. The oceans weren't ruled by sharks, whales or giant squid, but by legions of microscopic organisms. Every litre of surface water teemed with a colourful mix of microbes: tens of billions of viruses, a billion bacteria, five million protozoa and a million algae. Even water samples taken from depths below 6000 metres contained millions of viruses and bacteria. Trying to keep track of the turmoil was practically impossible. The more insight science gained into the cosmos of Earth's tiniest life-forms, the more bewilderingly detailed the picture became. What was seawater anyway? If you looked at it closely through a modern fluorescence microscope, it seemed to be made of a thin gel. A chain of interconnected macromolecules ran through every drop like joined-up suspension bridges. Countless bacteria made their watery homes on the sheets and films that stretched over bundles of transparent fibres. To obtain two kilometres of DNA molecules, 310 kilometres of proteins and 5600 kilometres of polysaccharides, you needed only to untangle and line up the contents of a single millilitre of seawater. And somewhere within that mix were organisms that might be intelligent. They were hidden only in so far as they were interspersed with all the other microbes. The jelly had remarkable properties, but it wasn't composed of exotic life-forms, just ordinary deep-sea amoebas.

Oliviera groaned.

It was obvious why no-one had spotted them. It hadn't occurred to anyone that deep-sea amoebas could aggregate to form collectives capable of controlling crabs and whales.

'It's impossible,' Oliviera decided.

The words sounded feeble. She examined the taxonomic results again, but it didn't change what she knew already. The jelly was evidently made up of an existing amoeba species. It was known to exist mainly at depths of 3000 metres or below, and there were huge numbers of them.

'Nonsense,' hissed Oliviera. 'Come on, you've got to be kidding. You've disguised yourself, trying to pretend you're an ordinary amoeba. Well, you can't fool me. But what the hell *are* you?'

Once Johanson had joined her, they set to work isolating individual cells from the jelly. Mercilessly they froze and heated the amoebas until their cell walls burst. Proteinase was used to break down the protein molecules into chains of amino acids. Then phenol was added and the samples were centrifuged in a slow and laborious process to separate the solution from the scraps of protein and remains of cell wall. Finally they had a small quantity of clear watery fluid; the key to understanding the enigmatic organism.

Pure DNA.

The second step required even more patience. To unravel the DNA, they had to isolate and replicate sections of it. The genome was far too complex to be read as a whole, so they set about trying to analyse diagnostic sequences.

It was a hard slog, and Rubin was supposedly ill.

'Asshole,' moaned Oliviera. 'This was his chance to do something useful. What's the matter with him anyway?'

'Migraine,' said Johanson.

'Well, that's something. Migraines are painful.'

Oliviera transferred the samples via pipette to the sequencer. The machine would take a few hours to analyse them all. For the time being there was nothing they could do so they underwent the obligatory peracetic shower and walked out into the open, breathing freely once more. Oliviera suggested a cigarette break on the hangar deck while they waited for the sequencer to finish, but Johanson had a better idea. He disappeared into his cabin and returned five minutes later with two glasses and a bottle of Bordeaux. 'Let's go,' he said.

'Where did you find that?' marvelled Oliviera, as they walked up the ramp.

'You don't find wine like this.' Johanson smirked. 'You have to bring it with you. I'm an expert at smuggling contraband goods.'

'Is it a good one? I don't know much about wines.'

'It's a Château Clinet from Pomerol, 1990 vintage. Lightens the wallet and the mood.' Johanson spotted a metal crate next to one of the booths between the ship's ribs. They headed over to it and sat down. The deck was deserted. The gateway to the starboard-side elevator gave them a clear view of the sea. The water lay calm and smooth in the half-light of the polar night, ice-free but wreathed in frosty mist. It was cold in the hangar bay, but they were in need of fresh air after hours in the containment lab. Johanson opened the bottle, poured some wine, and clinked glasses with Oliviera, a bright pinging sound.

'Lovely,' she said.

'I packed a few bottles for special occasions. And I'd say this is one of them.'

'Do you think we're on their scent?'

'We could be very nearly there.'

'So we've found the yrr?'

'Well, that's the question. We don't know what we've got inside that tank. Is it possible for single-cell organisms, for amoebas, to be intelligent?'

'When I look at humanity, I sometimes wonder whether we're much different from them.'

'We're more complex.'

'Is that an advantage?'

'What would you say?'

Oliviera shrugged. 'What kind of answer do you expect from someone who's spent the last God-knows-how-long doing nothing but microbiology? It's not like your job: there's no teaching involved. I never speak to a wider public, and I definitely suffer from acute lack of distance to myself. I'm a lab rat in human guise. I guess I tend to look at the world through my own specific lens, but I see micro-organisms wherever I go. We live in an age of bacteria. For over three billion years they've existed in their present form. Humanity is just a passing fashion, but even when the sun explodes, somewhere, somehow, a few of those microbes are bound to survive. They're the planet's real success story, not humans. I don't know if humans have any advantages over bacteria, but one thing's for certain: if we end up proving that microbes are intelligent, we'll be in more shit than they are.'

Johanson took a sip of wine. 'Just think of the embarrassment. Imagine the Church having to tell the faithful that God created his *pièce de résistance* on the fifth day and not the seventh.'

'How are you managing to cope with all this?'

'So long as I've got a few bottles of vintage Bordeaux to hand, I don't see any major problems.'

'Aren't you angry?'

'With whom?'

'With those beings.'

'How would anger solve anything?'

'It wouldn't, Socrates.' Oliviera gave a wry smile. 'But I'm serious. I mean, they took away your home.'

'Part of it.'

'Don't you miss your house in Trondheim?'

Johanson swirled the wine in his glass. 'Not as much as I'd expected,' he said, after a moment's silence. 'It was a beautiful house, – but my life wasn't kept there. I have another a house by a lake in the middle of nowhere. You can sit on the veranda, look out at the water, listen to Sibelius and Brahms, and drink good wine. There's nothing like it.'

Johanson reached for the bottle and topped up their glasses. 'You'd understand if you'd been there. Watching the night sky reflected on the water – you can't forget a moment like that. Your whole existence seems to be concentrated in the stars. They're like pinpoints of light perforating the universe above and below. It's an incredible feeling, but you have to experience it for yourself.'

'Have you been there since the wave?'

'Only in my memory.'

'I've been lucky,' Oliviera said. 'So far I've been spared any loss. All my family and friends are fine. Everything's still standing.' She paused. 'But I don't have a house by a lake.'

'Everyone has a house by a lake.'

It seemed to her that Johanson wanted to say more, but he just swirled the wine in his glass. Eventually he spoke again: 'I lost a friend'.

Oliviera kept silent.

'She was a complicated person. Lived life at a sprint.' He smiled. 'It's funny, but we didn't really find each other until we'd both decided to let go. I guess that's life.'

'I'm sorry,' Oliviera said softly.

Suddenly Johanson's gaze shifted. He seemed almost transfixed. Oliviera turned. 'Is something wrong?'

'I just saw Rubin.'

'Where?'

Johanson pointed amidships towards the bulkhead at the end of the hangar. 'He went in there.'

'But there's nowhere to go.'

The far reaches of the hangar were shrouded in gloomy half-light. The bulkhead stretched up in an unbroken wall, sealing the hangar from the compartments beyond. There was no sign of any door.

'Maybe it's the wine,' she suggested.

Johanson shook his head. 'I could swear it was Rubin. He was there for a second, and then he disappeared.'

'Did he see us?'

'Unlikely. We're in shadows.

'Let's quiz him when his migraine's better.'

By the time they returned to the lab, they'd polished off half the bottle of Bordeaux, but Oliviera didn't feel in the slightest bit tipsy, just pleasantly exhilarated and ready to discover great things.

Which was exactly what she did.

The sequencer in the containment facility had done its work. They viewed the results on the computer terminal in the main lab. The screen showed a row of DNA sequences. Oliviera's eyes darted back and forth as she followed the lines down the screen. 'That's impossible,' she said softly.

'What is?' Johanson leaned over her shoulder. Then two vertical ridges formed in his brow. 'They're all different.'

'Yes.'

'It doesn't make sense. Identical organisms have near identical DNA.'

'If they're all the same species.'

'But these *are* the same species.'

'The background mutation rate . . .'

'No way.' Johanson seemed stunned. 'This goes far beyond any background mutation rate. They're all different organisms. None of the DNA matches.'

'Well, they're certainly not ordinary amoebas.'

'There's nothing ordinary about them at all.'

'What are they, then?'

'I don't know.'

'I don't either,' she agreed. 'But I do know that there's some wine left, and I could really use another drink.'

For a while they searched different databases, comparing the DNA sequencing of the cells in the jelly with existing DNA data. In no time at all Oliviera had found the results from the day they'd examined the substance in the whales' brains. Back then she hadn't noticed any variations in the sequence of the DNA bases. 'I should have examined a few more of those cells,' she said crossly.

'You might not have noticed anyway.'

'Even so.'

'How were you supposed to guess it was an aggregate of single-cell organisms? Come on, Sue, it's no use beating yourself up. Think positive.'

Oliviera sighed. 'I guess you're right.' She glanced at the clock. 'Sigur, why don't you go to bed? There's no point in both of us staying up all night.'

'What about you?'

'I'll carry on here. I want to know if this tangle of DNA has ever been found before.'

'Let me help you.'

Go and get some rest. You need your beauty sleep – it's wasted on me. Nature gave me wrinkles and crow's feet as soon as I hit forty. No one can tell the difference if I'm wide awake or half asleep. You go. And don't forget to take your lovely wine with you – I can't afford to drink away any more of my scientific rigour.'

Johanson saw that she wanted to struggle through the problem on her own. She had nothing to reproach herself for, but it was probably better to leave her in peace.

He picked up the bottle and left the lab. Outside, he realised he wasn't tired. In the Arctic Circle time seemed to vanish. The near-constant sunlight stretched the day until it became an almost perfect loop, interrupted by only a few hours of dusk. The sun was creeping along the horizon out of sight. You could have described it as night and, in psychological terms, it was time to go to bed. But Johanson didn't feel like it. Instead he continued up the ramp.

The vastness of the hangar deck was obscured by abstract patterns of shadows. The bay was still deserted. He glanced over to where they'd been sitting earlier; the crate was all but invisible amid the gloom.

Rubin couldn't have seen them.

But he'd seen Rubin.

He wanted to inspect the bulkhead.

To his disappointment and surprise, it proved fruitless. He walked up and down several times, running his fingers along the sheets of steel and the bolts that held them together. He checked the pipes and the fuse boxes. Oliviera was right: he must have been seeing things. There was nothing there. No door or any other kind of opening.

'But I wasn't seeing things,' he muttered softly.

Maybe he should go to bed. But he'd only keep thinking about it. Or he could ask someone – Li, Peak, Buchanan or Anderson. But what if he was wrong?

You're supposed to have an enquiring mind, he told himself, so keep up with your enquiries.

Unhurriedly he walked back towards the aft end of the hangar and sat down on the crate that had served as their makeshift bar. He waited. It wasn't a bad spot. Maybe in the end he'd be forced to concede that people with migraines couldn't walk through walls, but it was a pleasant place to sit and look at the view.

He took a sip from the bottle. The Bordeaux gave him a sensation of warmth. His eyelids began to feel heavy. They seemed to gain a gram with every passing minute, until he could barely keep them open. Finally, when the bottle was empty, he dozed . . .

A soft metallic noise woke him.

At first he didn't know where he was. Then he felt the pain in his back where he was leaning against the steel side. The sky was brightening over the sea. He sat up straight and glanced at the bulkhead.

It had parted.

He got to his feet. A door was open. There was a space of about three square metres. The glow stood out against the dark metal.

His eyes shifted back to the empty bottle on the crate.

Was he dreaming?

He moved slowly towards the square of light. As he got closer he saw that it led into a corridor with plain walls. The neon lighting emitted a cold, harsh glare. After a few metres, the corridor reached a wall and disappeared to one side.

Johanson peered through the door and listened.

He could hear voices and other sounds. Instinctively he took a step back. He wondered whether it would be best to turn round now. This was a warship, after all. The rooms inside were bound to serve some purpose. A purpose that was of no concern to civilians.

Then he remembered Rubin.

If he backed away now he'd never stop thinking about it.

He went inside.

14 August

Bohrmann was unable to enjoy the good weather because he knew that millions of worms carrying billions of bacteria were progressing at frightening speed through the thin veins of hydrate 400 metres below. He stared gloomily out to sea.

The *Heerema* was a semi-submersible, a floating platform the size of several football pitches. The rectangular deck rested on six columns that rose from massive pontoons, supported by diagonal struts. On dry land, the vessel resembled a gigantic catamaran. Now the pontoons were partially flooded and had sunk out of sight beneath the waves. Only the tops of the columns rose out of the waves. With a draught of twenty-one metres and a displacement capacity of over 100,000 tonnes, the platform was incredibly stable. Even when conditions were at their roughest, semi-submersibles rode out the motion of the rolling, pitching sea. Most importantly, though, they were manoeuvrable and comparatively speedy. The *Heerema*'s two main propellers had allowed her to reach a transit speed of seven knots on her voyage northbound from Namibia to La Palma.

At the stern a two-storey tower housed the crew quarters, mess-room, kitchen, bridge and control room. Two vast cranes rose from the front of the platform, each capable of lifting 3000 tonnes. The right-hand crane lowered the suction tube into the water while the other took care of the lighting system, a separate unit with integrated cameras. Four technicians, perched high in the air in their drivers' cabs, had the sole responsibility for co-ordinating and steering the tube and the lights.

'Gair – hard!'

Stanley Frost was hurrying towards him from one of the cranes. Bohrmann had told him that he could always call him Gerd for short, but Frost insisted on pronouncing his full name in a thick Texan drawl. They made their way into the tower and entered the darkened control room. Some of Frost's team were there, with some technicians from De Beers, including Jan van Maarten. The technology expert had achieved the promised miracle astonishingly quickly. The world's first-ever deep-sea vacuum-cleaner for worms was ready for action.

'OK, folks,' trumpeted Frost, as they took their places behind the technicians. 'May the Lord bless our work here. And if all goes well, it's next stop Hawaii. We sent one of our robots down there yesterday, and the whole south-eastern flank was swarming with worms. Attacks are being launched against other volcanic islands, but we're going to give those worms hell. Our tube's going to blow them right out of the water. This whole planet's going to get a darned good tidy.'

'Nice thought,' said Bohrmann. 'OK, La Palma is relatively manage-able, but what about the American continental slope? You can't seriously be planning to use one suction tube to clear all of that seabed.'

'Course not.' Evidently Frost was astounded by the idea. 'That speech was supposed to be motivating!'

Bohrmann turned towards the monitors. He hoped to God the scheme would work. But even if they got rid of the worms, they still couldn't be certain how many bacteria had already been deposited in the ice. Deep down he was worried that it was too late to prevent the collapse of Cumbre Vieja. At night he had terrifying visions of a huge dome of water rushing over the ocean towards him. But he was doing his best to be optimistic. Somehow they'd make it work. And maybe the others on the *Independence* would persuade the unknown enemy to see sense. If the yrr were capable of destroying an entire continental slope, maybe they could repair one.

Frost gave another impassioned speech, denouncing the enemies of mankind and heaping praise on the technicians from De Beers. Then he signalled for the tube and the lighting system to be lowered.

The lighting unit was a gigantic concertinaed floodlight scaffold. Suspended over the waves from the arm of the crane, it consisted of a compact package of metal pipes and struts, ten metres long and crammed with lights and cameras. The crane lowered it into the water and it vanished beneath the surface, linked to the *Heerema* with a fibreoptic cable. After ten minutes Frost glanced at the depth gauge and said, 'Stop.'

Van Maarten relayed the command to the operator. 'You can open it up now,' he added. 'Half-way at first. If there's nothing in the way, we'll open it entirely.'

Four hundred metres below the surface, an elegant metamorphosis was taking place. The metal package unfolded into a framework of scaffolding. The area seemed clear, and soon a lattice-like frame, the size of half a football pitch, was hanging in the water.

'Ready and waiting,' said the operator.

Frost glanced at the control panel. 'We should be right in front of the flank.'

'Lights and camera,' instructed van Maarten.

The frame was lit with row upon row of powerful halogen lamps, while the cameras rolled into action. A gloomy panorama appeared on the monitors. Plankton drifted across the screens.

'Closer,' said van Maarten.

The scaffold moved forwards, pushed by two swivelling propellers. After a few minutes a jagged structure rose out of the darkness. As they drew closer it became a black wall of unevenly sculpted lava.

'Down a bit.'

The scaffold sank. The operator navigated the depths with utmost caution, until a terrace-like protrusion showed up on the sonar. Without warning, a ridge appeared on the screen, so close it seemed almost in touching distance. Its surface was covered with wriggling bodies. Bohrmann stared at the eight monitors with a sinking feeling in his stomach. He was face to face with the nightmare that had haunted him since the collapse of the Norwegian slope. If the entire flank looked the same as the forty metres that the floodlights had wrested from the darkness, they could turn round and go home.

'Evil bastards,' growled Frost.

We're too late, thought Bohrmann.

Immediately he felt ashamed of himself for fearing the worst. No one could tell whether the worms had unloaded their cargo of bacteria or whether there'd be enough to do any real harm. Besides, there was still the unknown factor that had provided the final trigger. It wasn't too late. But they didn't have time to hang around.

'All right, then,' said Frost. 'Let's raise the unit and tilt it by forty-five degrees so we get a better view. And then it's time to lower the tube. I hope it's hungry.'

'Ravenous,' said van Maarten.

At maximum extension, the suction tube stretched half a kilometre into the depths, a segmented, rubber-insulated monster, measuring three metres in diameter and culminating in a gaping mouth. Its opening was armoured with floodlights, two cameras and a number of swivelling propellers. From the *Heerema*, the end of the tube could be steered up and down, forwards, backwards and sideways. The monitor in the driver's cab combined footage from the lighting scaffold with images from the tube, providing a generous view of the overall picture. But although the visibility was good, operating the joysticks required sensitive fingers and a co-pilot to make sure that nothing was missed.

Time ticked by as the tube fell through the impenetrable darkness. Its floodlights were switched off. Then the lighting scaffold came into view. At first it was just a faint glimmer in the pitch-black water, then its glow intensified, taking on a rectangular form and finally sculpting the terrace out of the rock. It was so big that Bohrmann was reminded of a space station. The tube continued to sink, nearing the milling mass until the monitors were covered with writhing bristly worms.

There was a breathless silence in the control room.

'Amazing,' whispered van Maarten.

'A good cleaner doesn't stand about admiring the dirt,' Frost said grimly. 'It's about time you switched on your vacuum-cleaner and got rid of them.'

The suction tube was really a suction pump that created a vacuum, so that anything that passed before its mouth was swallowed inside. They threw the switch, but nothing happened. The pump evidently needed time to warm up – or that was what Bohrmann hoped. The worms went about their business uninterrupted. Disappointment swept round the room. No one said a word. Bohrmann fixed his eyes on the two monitors displaying the tube. What was the problem? Was the tube too long? Or the pump too weak?

While he searched for an explanation, the picture changed. Something was tearing at the worms. Their bodies rose, then lifted vertically in the water, quivering frantically . . . They rushed towards the cameras and were gone.

'It's working!' Bohrmann shouted, and punched the air. He felt like dancing and turning cartwheels.

'Hallelujah!' Frost nodded vigorously. 'Oh, Lord, we're going to cleanse the world of evil. Sheesh!' He tore off his baseball cap, ran his hands through his hair and put the cap back on. 'Those critters won't know what's hit them.'

The worms were sucked into the tube so quickly and in such numbers that the picture faded to a flicker as sediment rose in swirls from the terrace.

'Further to the left,' said Bohrmann. 'Or the right. Doesn't matter which way, as long as you keep going.'

'Why don't we zigzag over the terrace?' suggested van Maarten. 'We could vacuum the floodlit zone from one end to the other. Then, once it's clear, we'll move the lights and the tube and start on the next forty metres.'

'Makes sense. Let's do it that way.'

The tube wandered over the terrace, pulling in worms as it went and causing such turbulence that the rock disappeared in clouds of sediment.

'We'll have to wait until the water settles to see what we've achieved,' said van Maarten, sounding relieved. He gave a deep sigh, and leaned back serenely. 'But my guess is that we'll all be pretty pleased.'

Independence, Greenland Sea

Dong! Trondheim's church bells on a Sunday morning. The chapel in Kirkegata Street. Bathed in sunshine, the little steeple was stretched confidently into the sky, casting its shadow over the ochre-coloured house with its pitched roof and white steps.

Ding dong.

He buried his head in the pillow. As though church bells could dictate when it was time to get up. Fat chance! Had he been drinking last night? He must have been in town with some colleagues from the faculty.

Dong!

'Oh-eight hundred hours.'

The loudspeakers.

The tranquillity of Kirkegata Street was gone. There was no steeple, no ochre-coloured house. Trondheim's bells weren't to blame for the noise in his head. He had an almighty headache.

Johanson opened his eyes and found himself lying amid rumpled sheets in a strange bed. Other beds were lined up around him, all empty. It was a big room, full of equipment, with no windows and a sterile appearance. A sickbay.

What the hell was he doing here?

His head lifted and fell back on to the pillows. His eyes closed of their own accord. Anything would be better than the hammering in his head. He was even feeling nauseous.

'Oh-nine hundred hours.'

Johanson sat up. He was still in the same room. He felt significantly better, though. The queasiness was gone, and his head no longer felt as though it were being crushed in a vice. The pain had subsided to a tolerable ache.

He still didn't know what he was doing there.

He looked down at himself. Shirt, trousers, socks – the clothes he'd been wearing last night. His down jacket and sweater lay on the next bed, with his shoes arranged neatly on the floor.

He swung his legs over the side of the bed.

A door opened and Sid Angeli, the head of the medical unit, came in. He was a small Italian with a thin circle of hair and deep creases round his mouth. He had the most tedious job on the ship since no one was ever ill. That seemed to have changed. 'How are you feeling?' Angeli cocked his head. 'Everything OK?'

'I'm not sure.' Johanson touched the back of his head and flinched.

'It'll be sore for a while,' said Angeli. 'Don't worry, though – it could have been worse.'

'What happened?'

'You can't remember?'

Johanson thought hard. 'I could use a few aspirin.'

'But you don't know what happened?'

'No idea.'

Angeli came closer. 'Uh-huh. Well, you were found on the hangar deck in the middle of the night. You must have slipped. Thank God the ship is under video surveillance or you'd still be there. You probably hit your head on one of the struts.'

'On the hangar deck?'

'Yes. Don't you remember?'

Of course. He'd been on the hangar deck with Oliviera. Then a second time, by himself. He could remember going back there, but he couldn't think why. And he had no recollection of what had happened next.

'It could have been really nasty,' said Angeli. 'You, er, hadn't been drinking, had you? I only ask because there was an empty bottle down there. Sue Oliviera said the two of you had cracked open some wine.' Angeli splayed his fingers. 'Don't get me wrong, Dottore, it's not a problem, but helicopter carriers are dangerous places. Wet and dark. It's easy to slip over or fall into the sea. It's better not to wander around on your own if you've, er . . .'

'. . . had a glass or two,' Johanson finished for him. He got up, and the blood rushed to his head. Angeli was there in an instant, holding his elbow. 'I'm OK, thank you.' Johanson shook him off. 'Where am I anyway?'

'In the infirmary. Can you manage?'

'Provided you give me those aspirin.'

Angeli walked over to a shiny white cabinet and took out a packet of painkillers.

'Here you go. You hit your head, that's all. You'll soon feel fine.'

'OK. Thanks.'

'Are you sure you're all right?'

'Yes.'

'And you can't remember anything?'

'Like I said, no.'

'*Va bene.*' Angeli gave a wide smile. 'Take things gently today, Dottore, and if you experience any problems, don't hesitate to come back.'

Flag Command Center

'Hypervariable sections? What the hell's that supposed to mean?'

Vanderbilt was struggling to keep up. Oliviera realised that she was in danger of losing her audience. Peak looked bewildered too. Li's expression was as inscrutable as ever, although it seemed likely that her knowledge of genetics was under severe strain.

Johanson sat among them like a ghostly presence. He'd turned up late, as had Rubin, who'd come in mumbling apologies for his absence. But, unlike Rubin, Johanson seemed genuinely ill. His gaze was unsteady and he kept glancing around, as though he needed to reassure himself every few minutes that he wasn't hallucinating and that the people around him were real. Oliviera made a mental note to have a word with him.

'It might be easier if we started by talking about normal human cells,' she said. 'You can think of our cells as bags of information wrapped in membranes. Inside each cell is a nucleus, and inside the nucleus are the chromosomes – home to our genes. The genome is the complete set of genetic information, the full sequence of DNA, the famous double helix. In simple terms, it's our design plan. The more complex an organism, the more sophisticated the plan. The results of a DNA test can be used to find someone's killer or prove that people are biologically related, but by and large we all share the same blueprint: feet, legs, torso, arms, hands and so on. In other words, an individual's DNA can tell you two things: first, that they're a person; and second, who they are.' She saw interest in their faces. It had been a good idea to start with some basic genetics.

'Of course, two individual humans will have less in common than two single-cell organisms of the same species. Statistically speaking, there'll be three million small differences between my DNA and the DNA of any other person in this room. Human beings are differentiated from one another by roughly one difference per twelve hundred base pairs. What's more, if you were to take two different cells from the same individual, you'd still find small variations – biochemical discrepancies in the DNA, caused by mutations. Consequently, the results will be different if you analyse a cell from my left hand and one from my liver. But the DNA will tell you clearly that those cells belong to Sue Oliviera.' She paused. 'Single-cell organisms are a slightly different story. The cell is the entire organism. So there's only one genome, and since single-cell organisms reproduce asexually, there are no parent cells to pass on their chromosomes. It works by cell division. The organism duplicates itself and all its genetic information.'

'So, as far as single-cell organisms are concerned, if you know one DNA sequence, you know them all,' said Peak, choosing his words carefully.

'Yes.' Oliviera rewarded him with a smile. 'That's what you'd expect. A population of single-cell organisms should have largely identical genomes. Apart from a minimal rate of mutation, their DNA should be the same.'

649

She saw Rubin shifting impatiently on his chair, desperate to speak. Usually he would have tried to butt in by now and take the lead. Poor Mick, thought Oliviera, in satisfaction. What a shame you were confined to your bed last night with a migraine. For once there's something you don't know.

'But that's exactly the problem,' she continued. 'At first glance, the cells in the jelly appear identical. They're amoebas – not even a particularly exotic variety, just ordinary deep-sea amoebas. But it would take at least two years and a whole army of computers to decode their DNA in full, so we settled for analysing a diagnostic section. We isolated the DNA and amplified key regions for sequencing. We call them amplicons. Each amplicon contains a sequence of base pairs – the language of genetics. Now, when we compare amplicons from DNA belonging to different individual organisms, we see something interesting. Amplicons of different organisms belonging to the same population should look something like this.'

She held up a print-out that she'd blown-up for the meeting:

A1: AATGCCAATTCCATAGGATTAAATCGA
A2: AATGCCAATTCCATAGGATTAAATCGA
A3: AATGCCAATTCCATAGGATTAAATCGA
A4: AATGCCAATTCCATAGGATTAAATCGA

'So you see, entire segments of the DNA can be exactly the same. Four identical single-cell organisms.' She put down the sheet and picked up another. 'But instead we got this.'

A1: AATGCCA CGATGCTACCTG AAATCGA
A2: AATGCCA ATTCCATAGGATT AAATCGA
A3: AATGCCA GGAAATTACCCG AAATCGA
A4: AATGCCA TTTGGAACAAAT AATCGA

'Those are the base sequences of four amplicons from four of our jelly organisms. The DNA looks identical – until you hit brief hypervariable segments, where it all goes haywire. There's no pattern whatsoever. We've examined dozens of cells. Some differ only marginally in the hypervariable sections, but others are radically different. It can't be accounted for by the background mutation rate. In other words, the variations aren't coincidental.'

'Maybe this isn't a single species, after all,' said Anawak.

'No, it's definitely the same species. And there's definitely no way an organism can change its genetic coding in the course of its lifetime. The design plan comes first. Organisms are built according to their design plan, and once they're built, they correspond to that plan and no other.'

There was a long silence.

'But if, in spite of all that, the cells are still different,' said Anawak, 'they must have found a way of changing their DNA *after* they divided.'

'But for what purpose?' asked Delaware.

'A human purpose,' said Vanderbilt.

'Human?'

'Are you all deaf or something? Nature doesn't do this stuff. That's what Dr Oliviera said, and I haven't heard any objection from Dr Johanson. So who's got the nerve to cook this shit up? Those jelly cells are a biological weapon. Only humans could do a thing like this.'

'In that case, *objection*,' said Johanson. He ran his hand through his hair. 'It doesn't make sense, Jack. The advantage of biological weaponry is that you only need one recipe. Reproduction takes care of the rest.'

'But surely it's an advantage when a virus mutates. The AIDS virus is mutating all the time. Whenever we start to get wise to it, hey presto, it's changed its form.'

'That's different. We're dealing here with a superorganism, not a virological infection. There's got to be some other explanation as to why the cells are different. Something happens to their DNA after they divide. They're coded differently. Who cares what's responsible for making them do that? We need to find out *why*.'

'To kill us, of course,' Vanderbilt said angrily. 'The purpose of this gunk is to destroy the democratic world.'

'OK then,' growled Johanson, 'why don't you shoot it? I mean, maybe they're Islamic cells. Extremist DNA. That would make sense.'

Vanderbilt stared at him. 'Whose side are you on?'

'The side of understanding.'

'Well, I'm not sure I understand how you came to fall over last night.' Vanderbilt gave a smug smile. 'Maybe it had something to do with that bottle of Bordeaux . . . How are you feeling, Dr Johanson? Is your head OK? Maybe you should shut up and listen for a while.'

'Not if it means you doing all the talking.'

Vanderbilt wheezed. He was sweating profusely. Li shot him a scornful look from the corner of her eye and leaned forward. 'You say that they're coded differently, right?'

'Right.' Oliviera nodded.

'I'm no scientist, but wouldn't it be possible that their coding serves the same purpose as any type of human code? Like military passwords, for instance.'

'Yes.' Oliviera nodded again. 'That would be possible.'

'Passwords that allow them to recognise each other.'

Weaver scribbled something on a scrap of paper and pushed it in Anawak's direction. He read it, gave a quick nod and laid it aside.

'Why would they need to recognise each other?' asked Rubin. 'And why use such an intricate method?'

'I'd have thought that was obvious,' said Crowe.

For a moment the only sound was the rustling of Cellophane as she unwrapped a pack of cigarettes.

'What do you mean?' asked Li.

'I'd say it's for communication,' said Crowe. 'The cells are communicating with each other. It's a kind of conversation.'

'You mean this stuff . . .' Greywolf stared at her.

Crowe held the lighter to the end of her cigarette, took a drag and exhaled. 'It's exchanging information.'

Vehicle Ramp

'Whatever happened to you last night?' asked Oliviera, as they made their way down to the lab.

Johanson shrugged. 'I haven't the faintest idea.'

'And how are you feeling now?'

'A bit weird. The headache's getting better, but I've got a hole in my memory about the size of the hangar bay.'

'Bad luck, eh?' Rubin glanced back at them. His teeth showed as he smiled. 'Who'd have thought we'd both end up with a headache? What a pair of invalids. I felt so rotten last night that I couldn't even get out of bed to let you know what was wrong. I can't apologise enough. But when you feel a migraine coming on like that . . . Wham! It just hits you. I was out for the count.'

Oliviera fixed Rubin with an unfathomable look. 'A migraine, was it?'

'It comes and goes. It doesn't happen too often, but when I get one, there's nothing I can do. It's enough trouble just to swallow my tablets and turn out the lights.'

'And you didn't wake up until this morning?'

'Yeah.' Rubin looked at her guiltily. 'I'm sorry, but a migraine knocks me out. Normally I'd have at least popped down to the lab . . .'

'But you stayed in bed?'

Rubin gave her a vexed smile. 'Yes.'

'Are you sure?'

'Well, I should know.'

Something clicked in Johanson's head. It was like a broken projector: the carousel kept trying to drop a slide into position, but something was sticking.

They stopped in front of the door to the lab, and Rubin punched in the code. The door swung open. As Rubin walked inside and turned on the lights, Oliviera whispered to Johanson, 'What's up? You were the one who swore blind you'd seen him last night.'

Johanson stared at her. 'Was I?'

'You know,' murmured Oliviera. 'We were sitting on that crate, drinking wine and waiting for the sequencer to finish. You said you'd seen him.'

Click. The carousel tried to release the slide. Click.

His mind felt woolly. He could remember drinking a glass of wine. And they'd talked for a bit. And then he'd . . . He'd seen something?

Click.

Oliviera raised her eyebrows. 'My God,' she said. 'That must have been quite some blow to the head.'

Neural Network Computer

They were sitting in the JIC at Weaver's computer. 'OK,' she said. 'This stuff about the coding puts an entirely new spin on things.'

Anawak nodded. 'The cells aren't identical. They're not like neurons.'

'So it's not just a case of *how* they're connected. If their DNA contains individually coded sequences, maybe that's their secret. It could be how they aggregate.'

'No, there has to be another trigger – something that can work over distance.'

'Well, yesterday we were talking about scent.'

'OK,' said Anawak. 'Give it a go. Program the units so they can secrete a scent that tells them to aggregate.'

Weaver thought for a moment. She picked up the phone and used the intercom to dial the lab. 'Sigur? Hi. We're working on the computer simulation. Any new ideas about how these cells are aggregating?' She listened for a while. 'Fine. We'll try that . . . OK. Let me know.'

'What did he say?' asked Anawak.

'They're doing a phase test. They're trying to get the jelly to dissociate, then band back together.'

'So they agree that the cells could be using a scent?'

'Yes.' Weaver wrinkled her nose. 'The trouble is, which cell would secrete the scent first? And why? If it's a chain reaction, it has to start somewhere.'

'It could be a genetic program,' mused Anawak. 'You know, with only particular cells capable of triggering aggregation.'

'So one part of the brain would have an inbuilt capacity to do more than the rest . . .' Weaver mused. 'It's an interesting idea. But I'm not sure it's right.'

'Hold on a minute – what if we're still on the wrong track? We're working on the assumption that the cells form a brain when they aggregate.'

'I'm almost certain they do.'

'Well, so am I. But it's just occurred to me that . . .'

'What?'

Anawak was thinking feverishly. 'Don't you find it odd that the cells are all different? To my mind, there's only one reason why the coding would be variable – their DNA has been programmed separately to enable them to accomplish different tasks. But if that were the case, each of those cells would be a brain in itself.' He stopped to think again. That would be amazing. But he didn't have the first clue how it might work. 'In fact, the DNA in each cell would actually *be* the brain.'

'Intelligent DNA?'

'Er, yes.'

'But it would have to be able to learn.' She looked at him doubtfully. 'I'm prepared to believe almost anything, but isn't that a bit . . . ?'

She was right. It was a crazy idea. It would involve a new type of biochemistry. Something they knew nothing about. But if there was a way of making it work . . . 'Can you tell me again how neural network computers actually learn?' he said.

'It's through parallel distributed processing. The computer learns from example. The more input patterns it encounters, the more output patterns it predicts.'

'And how does it retain that information?'

'It stores it.'

'So every unit has to have storage space. And the network of storage units produces artificial thought.'

'What are you getting at?'

Anawak explained. She listened, then made him start again from the beginning. 'But aren't you rewriting the laws of biology?'

'I guess so. But couldn't you write a program that works in a similar fashion?'

'Oh, God.'

'A smaller version, then.'

'Even that's a tall order. Christ, Leon, what a crazy theory. But, OK, I'll do it.'

She stretched her body. Tiny golden hairs shimmered on her forearms. Her muscles were taut beneath her T-shirt. Anawak gazed at her small, broad-shouldered frame, and thought again how much he liked her.

At that moment, she glanced up. 'It's going to cost you, though,' she said.

'What?'

'A massage. For my shoulders and back.' She grinned. 'Well, jump to it. You can start right away while I work on this program.'

Rubin

At lunchtime they made their way to the officers' mess. Johanson was evidently feeling better, and he was getting on swimmingly with Oliviera. Neither seemed disappointed when Rubin announced that the migraine had ruined his appetite. 'I'm going for a stroll on the roof,' he said.

'Take good care of yourself,' grinned Johanson. 'You wouldn't want to slip.'

'Oh, I'll be fine,' laughed Rubin *If only you knew*, he thought. If only you could see just how careful I'm being, your jaw would hit the well deck. 'Don't worry,' he said. 'I'll keep away from the edge.'

'Well, remember we need you.'

'Yeah, right,' he heard Oliviera mutter, as she and Johanson continued to the mess.

Rubin clenched his fists. They could say what they liked about him. In the end he'd get the recognition he deserved. He was the one they'd have to thank for saving humanity. He was tired of being veiled in secrecy by the CIA, but once this business was over, there'd be nothing to stop him sharing his achievements with the world. All that stuff about confidentiality wouldn't matter. He'd broadcast his successes and bask in admiration.

His mood improved as he hurried up the ramp. On 03 level he turned down a passageway and arrived in front of a narrow door. It was locked. He tapped in the code. The door swung open and Rubin entered a corridor. He followed it to the end, and came to another locked door. This time when he punched in the code, a green light flashed up on the display. Above it was a camera behind a glass panel. Rubin walked up and placed his right eye in front of the glass. The camera scanned his retina and gave the all-clear.

Authentification complete, the door slid open. He went into a large, dark room full of computers and monitors. It bore a striking resemblance to the CIC. Civilians and people in uniform were manning the control desks. The air was abuzz with the sound of computers. Li, Vanderbilt and Peak were standing around a chart table. Its transparent surface was lit from below.

Peak looked up. 'Come in,' he said.

Rubin walked over. Suddenly his self-assurance slipped. Since the events of last night they had stuck to brief factual conversations on the phone. The tone had been neutral. Now it was frosty.

Rubin decided to pre-empt the attack. 'We're making good progress,' he said. 'We're still one step ahead and—'

'Sit down,' said Vanderbilt. He gestured brusquely towards a chair on the opposite side of the table.

Rubin sat. The others remained standing, leaving him in a position that made him uneasy. He sensed that he was on trial. 'Of course, the incident last night was rather unfortunate,' he added.

'Unfortunate?' Vanderbilt rested his knuckles on the table. 'For Chrissakes, you jerk. Under any other circumstances I'd have made you walk the plank.'

'But, really, I only—'

'What the hell did you knock him out for?'

'What was I supposed to do?'

'You were *supposed* to be more careful in the first place. You shouldn't have let him in.'

'That wasn't my fault,' Rubin objected. 'I didn't think anyone could scratch their bums without you people watching.'

'Why did you open the goddamned hatch?'

'Because . . . Well, I thought we might . . . You see, there was a matter that I . . .'

'That you what?'

'Now, look here, Rubin,' said Peak, 'that hatch on the hangar deck serves one purpose and one purpose only: to let vehicles in and out. You should know that.' His eyes flashed. 'Maybe you could tell us what was so damned important that you opened it.'

Rubin bit his lip.

'You couldn't be bothered to walk through the ship. It was laziness, period.'

'How could you even suggest that?'

'Because it's true.' Li walked over to Rubin and perched on the edge of the table. Her eyes looked concerned, almost friendly. 'You said that you were going for a breath of fresh air.'

Rubin slumped deeper into his chair. Of course he'd said that. And, of course, the surveillance system had recorded him saying it.

'And then you went out a second time.'

'But it didn't look as though anyone was there,' he defended himself. 'And your people didn't say different.'

'They didn't say anything because you didn't ask – even though you need express permission to open that hatch. It happened twice in a row. They didn't get a chance to tell you.'

'I'm sorry,' murmured Rubin.

'I'm going to be straight with you, Mick. We didn't do our job perfectly either. No one seems to have clocked Johanson's return trip to the hangar deck. We're also to blame for the fact that the whole vessel isn't under continual surveillance. As it turns out, we couldn't hear what Oliviera and Johanson were saying when they held their private party. The ramp and the roof are out of earshot too. But none of that changes the fact that you acted like a total jerk.'

'I promise I won't—'

'You're a security risk, Mick. A brainless asshole. I may not always agree with Jack, but if you go ahead and pull another stunt like that, I'll volunteer to help him throw you overboard. I'll even drum up a few sharks so I can watch them tear your heart out. Do you understand me? *I will kill you.'*

Li's deep blue eyes gazed at him amicably, but Rubin could see she'd have no reservation about carrying out her threat. The woman scared him.

'I think you get my drift.' Li thumped him on the shoulder and joined the others. 'OK. Let's talk about damage limitation. Did the drug work?'

'We injected ten mills,' said Peak. 'Any more than that would have really knocked him sideways, and we need his brain. The drug's supposed to work like an eraser on the mind. But there's no guarantee that his memory won't come back.'

'What kind of risk are we talking?'

'It's hard to say. A word, a colour, a smell could do it. Once the brain finds a trigger, it's capable of remembering exactly what happened.'

'Well, that's quite some risk.' Vanderbilt scowled. 'No drug can suppress a memory entirely. We still don't know enough about the workings of the brain.'

'We'll have to keep him under observation,' said Li. 'What do you think, Mick? How much longer are we going to need him?'

'Oh, we're going great guns,' Rubin said eagerly. Here was his chance to regain lost ground. 'Weaver and Anawak are working on the idea of pheromone-induced aggregation. Oliviera and Johanson think it might be scent-based too. This afternoon we'll be running some phase tests, and we should get our proof. If we're right about aggregation being triggered by scent, we'll soon be in a position to proceed as intended.'

'If, should, could.' Vanderbilt snorted. '*How long* until you come up with a goddamned formula?'

'This is scientific research, Jack,' said Rubin. 'No one stood over Alexander Fleming and kept telling him to hurry up and discover penicillin.'

Vanderbilt was on the point of responding when a woman stood up and walked over.

'They've decoded Scratch in the CIC,' she said.

'Scratch?'

'Seems that way. Crowe said to Shankar that they'd figured it out.'

Li turned towards the desk where the audio and video footage from the CIC was being processed. A view from the overhead camera showed Shankar, Crowe and Anawak in conversation. Weaver had just walked in.

'They'll call us in a minute,' she said. 'Good. Don't forget to look surprised.'

Combat Information Center

Everyone was crowding round Crowe and Shankar, trying to get a look at the message. What they were seeing wasn't a spectrogram but a graphic representation of the transmission they'd received the day before.

'Is it a reply?' asked Li.

'Good question,' said Crowe.

'But what is Scratch anyway?' asked Greywolf, who'd just arrived with Delaware. 'A language?'

'Well, Scratch itself might be a language, but this signal isn't part of it, not in the way it's been coded here,' said Shankar. 'It's like the Arecibo message. I mean, humans don't usually communicate in binary code. If you think about it, *we* didn't send that message into space. Our computers did.'

'The good news,' said Crowe, 'is that we've worked out its structure. You know how Scratch sounds as though a needle's being dragged across a record? Well, it's a staccato vibration of a very low frequency, ideally suited for propagating across the ocean. Infrasonic waves can travel incredible distances. And in this case the wavelength is extremely short. The trouble with infrasound is that we have to speed up any sound with a frequency of less than a hundred hertz to make it audible, but that would speed up the staccato. The trick to understanding this signal lies in slowing it down.'

'We had to stretch it,' said Shankar, 'to be able to identify the individual components. So we slowed it right down until the scratching noise became a sequence of individual pulses varying in length and intensity.'

'Sounds like Morse code,' said Weaver.

'It seems to work like it too.'

'How are you transcribing it?' asked Li. 'With spectrograms?'

'Yes, but they aren't enough. When it's a question of listening to something, it's always better to hear it. So we used an acoustic trick. It's a bit like false colour being added to radar images to show up the detail. In this instance we took each individual sound and replaced it with a frequency that we can hear, while keeping its original length and intensity. Whenever the original signal switched frequencies, we modified ours. That's how we handled Scratch.'

Crowe punched something into the keyboard. 'The sound we detected is like this.'

There was a rumble, like an underwater drum. The beats followed in quick succession, almost too fast to tell apart, but there could be no doubt that they were listening to a sequence of noises that varied in volume and duration.

'Well, it sounds like code,' said Anawak, 'but what does it mean?'

'We don't know.'

'You don't know?' echoed Vanderbilt. 'But I thought you'd cracked it.'

'What we don't know,' Crowe explained patiently, 'is how their language might work when they're using it normally. We can't make head or tail of the previous Scratch signals. But that's beside the point.' Smoke curled from her nostrils. 'We've got something better. We've got contact. Murray, show them the first part.'

Shankar clicked on an icon. The screen was lined with rows of numbers. Some columns seemed identical.

'We sent them some homework, as you know,' said Shankar. 'Math questions. Like an IQ test. We asked them to continue decimal sequences, work out some logarithms, fill in the missing numbers, that kind of thing. If it worked, we were hoping they'd find it kind of fun and send us a reply. It would be their way of telling us that they'd heard us, that they really exist, that they know about math and can manipulate numbers.' He pointed to the rows of figures on the screen. 'This is their answer. Grade A. They got everything right.'

'Christ,' whispered Weaver.

'That tells us two things,' said Crowe. 'First, Scratch is indeed a kind of language. In all probability, each of the Scratch signals contains complex information. Second, and this is the decisive point, it proves that they're capable of adapting Scratch so that we can understand it. That's an achievement of the highest order. It tells us that they're every bit as smart as we are. They're capable of decoding our messages; but they can also code their own.'

For a while they just stared at the columns of figures, admiration mixed with fear.

'But what does it prove?' asked Johanson, breaking the silence.

'I should have thought that was obvious,' retorted Delaware. 'It proves something's down there. Something that can think.'

'OK, but couldn't a computer generate the same results?'

'You don't think we're talking to a computer, do you?'

'He's got a point, you know,' said Anawak. 'All it proves is that our math questions have been answered. That's impressive, but it's not evidence of conscious intelligence.'

'But what else could be sending us messages?' asked Greywolf, disbelievingly. 'Mackerel?'

'Nonsense. Think about it. What we're seeing here is the work of a creature that can manipulate symbols. That's not proof of higher intelligence *per se*. Take chameleons, for instance. They solve a highly complex processing problem every time they change colour, but they've got no idea they're doing it. If you weren't acquainted with the IQ of chameleons, you might suppose they're very clever – after all, they can use a program that allows them to resemble foliage one day and a rock face the next. You'd probably credit them with enormous insight because they're reading the code of their surroundings. And you'd assume they were creative because they change their code to match.'

'So what *are* we looking at?' asked Delaware, helplessly.

Crowe smiled. 'Leon's right,' she said 'Just because someone can manipulate symbols doesn't mean they understand them. The real proof of intelligence and creativity resides in a creature's ability to understand and conceptualise conditions in the real world. That requires a deeper understanding. Even the most highly powered computer doesn't deal in rules of thumb or counter-intuitive decisions. It can't engage with its environment or experience the world. I imagine the yrr had the same considerations in mind when they formulated their reply. They tried to find something that would signal to us they're capable of real under-standing.' Crowe pointed to the screen. 'These are the results of the two math problems. If you look closely, you'll see that the first answer appears eleven times in a row, then you get three repetitions of answer number two, a single occurrence of answer number one, then nine times number two and so on. At one point the second answer appears nearly thirty thousand times. But why? It makes sense to send us the results more than once, of course, even if only to make sure that the message is long enough to be detected. But why would they mix them all together?'

'This is where Ms Alien comes in,' said Shankar, with an enigmatic smile.

'Jodie Foster, my *alter ego*.' Crowe nodded. 'I have to admit that if it hadn't been for the movie, I would never have got there so quickly. You see, the sequence of answers is a code in itself. If you know how to read it, you get an image of black and white pixels – just like the messages we work on at SETI.'

'I hope it's not a picture of Hitler,' said Rubin.

This time he was rewarded with a laugh. By now everyone on board had seen *Contact*. It was about extra-terrestrials transmitting an image to Earth. The pixels of the image contained the manual for a spaceship. Humanity had been beaming pictures into space throughout its high-tech evolution, and the aliens had picked one at random as the basis for their message. Of all the available images, they'd chosen one of Hitler.

'No,' said Crowe. 'It's not Hitler.'

Shankar hit a few keys. The columns of figures disappeared and made way for an image.

'What is it?' Vanderbilt leaned forward to get a better look.

'Don't you recognise it?' asked Crowe. 'Any suggestions?'

'Looks like a skyscraper,' said Anawak.

'The Empire State Building?' suggested Rubin.

'Yeah right,' said Greywolf. 'How are they supposed to know what the Empire State Building looks like? I'd say it's a missile.'

'And how would they know what a missile looks like?' asked Delaware.

'They're lying all over the seabed! Nuclear missiles, chemical missiles . . .'

'What's all this stuff in the background?' asked Oliviera. 'Clouds?'

'It could be water,' said Weaver. 'Maybe it's a picture of the depths. Some kind of rock formation.'

'You're on the right track with water,' said Crowe.

Johanson scratched his beard. 'It looks more like a monument. Maybe it's a symbol. Something . . . religious.'

'That's a human idea if ever I heard one.' Crowe seemed to be enjoying herself enormously. 'Hasn't it occurred to you that there might be another way of looking at the picture?'

They stared at it again. Li gave a start. 'Can you rotate it by ninety degrees?'

Shankar's fingers danced over the keyboard and the picture shifted to the horizontal.

'I still don't get what it is,' said Vanderbilt. 'A fish? A huge animal?'

Li chuckled to herself. 'No, Jack. Those are waves in the background. It's a snapshot taken from below. We're looking at the surface – from the perspective of the depths.'

'Huh? What about that black thing, then?'

'Easy. That's us. It's our ship.'

Heerema, La Palma, Canary Islands

Maybe they shouldn't have allowed themselves to celebrate so soon. Over the past sixteen hours the tube had been in constant operation, sucking up pinkish creatures by the tonne. The worms didn't seem to take too kindly to the rapid change of scene. Most had exploded in transit, while the remainder writhed in their death throes, jaws twitching. Frost had run out on deck as soon as the first polychaetes spurted out of the tube into enormous nets stretched beneath it. As the water drained through the mesh, giant slides conveyed the bodies into the bowels of a freighter moored alongside the *Heerema* and whose load was growing steadily. Frost had plunged his hands into the mass and returned to the control room, covered with slime but brandishing a dozen corpses, which he waved triumphantly in the air. 'The only good worm is a dead one,' he yelled. 'Yeee-haa!'

They'd all clapped, including Bohrmann.

After a while the swirling sediment had settled, and a view of marbled lava had appeared on their screens. Isolated strings of bubbles were rising from the surface of the rock. The cameras on the lighting scaffold zoomed in, showing Bohrmann the true nature of the marbled pattern. 'Bacterial mats,' he said.

Frost turned. 'What does that mean?'

'It's hard to say.' Bohrmann rubbed his knuckle against his chin. 'Provided they've only colonised the surface, there won't be any danger. I can't tell how many bacteria will have worked their way through the sediment. See those dirty grey lines? That's the hydrate.'

'At least it's still there.'

'Some of it. But who's to say how much was there in the first place and how much has dissociated already? The escaping gas hasn't reached critical proportions yet. For the moment I'd say we haven't been entirely unsuccessful in our efforts.'

'A double negative is as good as a yes.' Frost got up. 'I'll make us some coffee.'

After that they'd waited for hours, watching the tube graze the plateau until their eyes were sore. In the end van Maarten had dispatched Frost to bed – he and Bohrmann had barely slept for three days. Frost had protested, but his eyes were closing, and he wobbled out unsteadily to his cabin.

Bohrmann stayed behind with van Maarten. It was 23.00 hours.

'It's your turn next,' said the Dutchman.

'But I can't.' Bohrmann passed his hands over his eyes. 'I'm the only one who knows enough about hydrates.'

'We know enough.'

'It won't take long now anyway.' Bohrmann was drained. The operating team had been relieved three times already. In a few hours Erwin Suess would be arriving by helicopter from Kiel. He had to hold out until then.

He yawned. A soft hum filled the air. The lighting scaffold and the tube had worked their way slowly but surely towards the north. If the readings from the *Polarstern* expedition were correct, the infestation was restricted to this terrace. He knew it would take at least another couple of days to vacuum the worms up entirely, but hope was stirring inside him. The methane content of the water was above average, but there was no real cause for concern. If they could get rid of the worms and the bacteria, there was a chance that the partially eroded hydrates might restabilise.

Eyelids drooping, he gazed at the screens. It took him a while to grasp what he was seeing. The picture had changed. 'Something's glittering down there,' he said. 'Move the tube.'

Van Maarten squinted. 'Where?'

'Look at the monitors. There was a flash in the water. Look – there it is again!'

Suddenly he was wide awake. Something was amiss, and the footage from the scaffold now confirmed it. The cloud of sediment had swollen. Bubbles and dark clumps of matter were spinning around and drifting towards the tube.

The cameras filmed nothing but darkness, then the tube jerked to one side.

'What the hell's going on down there?'

The operator's voice came through the speakers: 'We're sucking up large chunks of something. The tube's becoming unstable. I don't know if—'

'Move the tube!' shouted Bohrmann. 'Get away from the flank.'

This can't be happening, he thought. It was the *Sonne* all over again. Another blow-out. They'd lingered too long over the same section of terrace and the plateau had come loose. The vacuum was tearing up the sediment.

No, it wasn't a blow-out. It was worse than that.

The tube tried to retreat from the billowing sediment. The cloud bulged, then seemed to explode. A wave of pressure rocked the scaffold. The picture juddered up and down.

'It's a landslide,' screamed the operator.

'Stop the pump!' Bohrmann sprang to his feet. 'Get away from the terrace!'

He watched as lava boulders crashed down on to the terrace. Somewhere within the fog of sediment and debris the tube was still moving, almost hidden.

'The pump's off,' said van Maarten.

Eyes wide with horror they watched the progress of the slide. Debris continued to shower from above. If the cracks were to spread through the almost vertical flank, ever larger boulders would detach themselves from the volcano. Lava was porous: within minutes a small slide could become an avalanche, prompting the scenario they'd been trying to prevent.

We should accept our fate, thought Bohrmann. We haven't got time to get away.

He pictured the dome of water stretching six hundred metres into the sky . . .

The clatter of rocks stopped.

There was a long silence. No one said anything as they stared at the monitors. The terrace was enveloped in a haze of sediment that scattered the light from the halogen bulbs.

'It's stopped,' said van Maarten. There was an almost imperceptible shake in his voice.

'Yes.' Bohrmann nodded. 'Apparently.'

Van Maarten radioed the operators.

'The scaffold shook all over the place,' said the guy in charge of the lighting unit. 'We've lost one of the floodlights. The others are bright enough, though.'

'And the tube?'

'Seems to be stuck,' came the verdict from the other crane. 'The system's processing our commands, but it's unable to react.'

'I guess the mouth must be buried under rubble,' said the scaffold operator.

'How much debris do you think will have fallen?' asked van Maarten.

'We'll have to wait for the cloud to settle,' said Bohrmann. 'But it looks as though we've escaped with a bruising.'

'OK, then, we'll wait.' Van Maarten leaned into the microphone. 'Don't attempt to free the tube. You can all have a coffee break. I don't want anyone causing any more damage. We'll wait for a while, then reassess.'

Three hours later they could vaguely make out the mouth of the tube.

Frost had rejoined them, his hair springing out from his head in an unruly mop of wiry curls.

'It's trapped,' said van Maarten.

Frost scratched his head. 'But I don't think it's broken.'

'The propellers can't turn.'

'How are we going to free them?'

'We could always send down a robot and try to shift the debris that way,' Bohrmann suggested.

'For the love of God,' protested Frost, 'that would take for ever. And things were going so well.'

'We'll just have to hurry.' Bohrmann turned to van Maarten. 'How quickly can we get Rambo ready?'

'Right away.'

'Let's go, then. We'll give it a shot.'

Rambo owed its name to the Sylvester Stallone films. The ROV looked like a smaller version of Victor, and came equipped with four cameras, a set of thrusters at the stern and on its sides, and two powerful articulated arms. It was suitable for depths of up to eight hundred metres, and was popular in the offshore industry. Within fifteen minutes it was ready to go. Soon it was descending along the flank of the volcano towards the terrace, attached to its control system via an electro-optical tether. The lighting scaffold came into view. The robot sank further, accelerated and manoeuvred its way towards the trapped tube. Seen in close-up, it was obvious that the propellers and the video system were still intact, but the tube was well and truly jammed.

Rambo's articulated arms started to shift the debris. At first it seemed that the robot might succeed. It lifted the rocks one by one until it came to a sharp splinter of lava that had bored its way into the sediment and was sticking out diagonally, pressing the tube against a ledge. Its arms extended and contracted, twisting and trying to dislodge the splinter.

'It's not a job for a robot,' said Bohrmann. 'They can't generate momentum.'

'Great!' spat Frost.

'What if the operator were to reel in the tube?' suggested Bohrmann. 'That's bound to create enough tension to free it.'

Van Maarten shook his head. 'It's too risky. The tube might tear.'

They kept trying for a while, getting the robot to ram the rock from every possible angle, until eventually it was obvious that Rambo couldn't help. And in the meantime, worms were invading the surface that had been cleared, swarming out of the darkness from all directions.

'I don't like the look of this,' said Bohrmann. 'Especially not here, where the rock's so unstable.'

Frost frowned. 'I'll do it.'

Bohrmann looked at him questioningly.

'I'll take a dive.' Frost shrugged. 'If Rambo can't do it, only we can. It's four hundred metres. The pressure suits can handle that.'

'You want to go down there?' Bohrmann said.

'Sure.' Frost stretched his arms until they clicked. 'Is there a problem?'

15 August

Independence, Greenland Sea

The yrr's reply prompted Crowe to send a second, infinitely more complex message into the depths. It contained information about the human race, its evolution and culture. At first Vanderbilt wasn't too happy about this, but Crowe persuaded him they had nothing to lose. The yrr were on the brink of victory. 'Our only chance,' she said, 'is to convince them that we deserve to live. And the only way we can do that is by telling them about us. Maybe there'll be something they haven't already taken into account. Something that will make them reconsider.'

'Shared values,' said Li.

'Or just the tiniest overlap.'

Oliviera, Johanson and Rubin had shut themselves into the lab to get the blob of jelly to dissociate. They kept in constant communication with Weaver and Anawak. Weaver had endowed her virtual yrr with electronic DNA and pheromones. It seemed to work. On a theoretical level they'd demonstrated that the aggregation of single-cell organisms relied on a pheromone, but in practice the jelly was disinclined to prove it. The being, or collection of beings, had turned into a flat sort of pancake and sunk to the bottom of the chamber.

On 02 level, Delaware and Greywolf were busy monitoring the footage from the dolphins' cameras, but there was nothing to be seen on the screens apart from the *Independence*'s hull, a few fish, and the mammal fleet – dolphins filming each other. When they weren't in the CIC, they were down on the well deck, where Roscovitz and Browning were still hard at work, repairing the Deepflight.

Li was aware that even the best minds could seize up or get stuck in a rut if they weren't distracted from their work. She asked for the latest data on the weather forecast and double-checked its reliability. There was every indication that low winds and smooth seas would prevail until the next day. The water was noticeably calmer than it had been that morning.

With that knowledge, she summoned Anawak for a chat, and discovered to her astonishment that he knew next to nothing about Arctic cuisine. The responsibility was delegated to Peak, who, for the first time in his military career, found himself in charge of catering.

He made a series of phone calls and two helicopters set out for Greenland. Late that afternoon, Li announced that the head chef had invited them all to a party at nine o'clock that evening. The helicopters returned, bearing all the ingredients for a Greenland feast. Tables, chairs and a buffet were set up on the flight deck next to the island. A stereo system was carried outside and heaters were positioned around the perimeter to keep out the cold.

The bustle in the kitchens became a whirlwind of activity. Pots and pans were filled with caribou; seal stock was converted into soup; *maktaaq* – narwhal skin – was cut into strips, and eider-duck eggs put on to boil. The *Independence*'s baker turned his hand to bannock, a tasty variety of flat bread, whose preparation was at the centre of numerous annual baking competitions. Arctic char and salmon were filleted and fried with herbs; frozen walrus became *carpaccio*, and mounds of rice were poured into water. Peak, who knew nothing about cooking, had trusted the advice of locals. Only one regional delicacy had failed to make the cut. No matter how much anyone extolled the virtues of raw walrus gut, Peak had decided it was one experience he was prepared to forgo.

He'd arranged for a skeleton crew to man the bridge, the engine room and the CIC, so at nine o'clock sharp almost everyone made their way to the deck – sailors, scientists and military – to claim their welcome drink, an alcohol-free cocktail, and wait for the buffet to open. Soon scientists were talking to soldiers, soldiers to sailors and sailors to scientists.

It was a strange party that Li had arranged, with the steel tower of the island behind them and the lonely expanse of the sea all around. In the distance they could see surreal peaks of retreating mist, and the red ball of the sun low on the horizon. The clean air felt invigoratingly cold, and a deep blue sky stretched high above.

At first everyone discussed anything other than the circumstances that had brought them together – but there was something awkward, almost desperate, about their determination to stick to polite conversation. As midnight approached, and dusk descended, they were on first-name terms and gathered in groups around the experts, seeking comfort where there was none to be found.

'Seriously, though,' said Buchanan, shortly after one o'clock, 'you can't tell me you really believe all that stuff about intelligent amoebas.'

'Why not?' said Crowe.

'We're talking about real intelligence, right?'

'I should think so.'

'Well . . .' Buchanan fumbled for the right words '. . . I'm not saying that all intelligent beings should look like us, but you'd think they'd be more complex than amoebas. Chimps are supposed to be intelligent, aren't they? Whales and dolphins too. They're all creatures with complex bodies and big brains. Ants are too small to be truly intelligent – you said so yourself – so how's it supposed to work for amoebas?'

'Are you sure you're not confusing two different issues?'

'What?'

'The truth, and what you'd like the truth to be.'

'What do you mean?'

'She means,' said Peak, 'that we'd prefer our enemy to be powerful and strong. In other words, if we have to concede defeat to anyone, we'd rather it was to a race of tall, good-looking creatures.'

Buchanan slammed his hand on the table. 'Well, I don't buy it. Primitive organisms aren't supposed to rule the planet. There's no way that an amoeba can be as intelligent as man. No way. Humans mean progress, they—'

'Progress?' Crowe shook her head. 'What do you mean by progress? Is evolution progress?'

Buchanan looked hunted.

'Let's see, then,' said Crowe. 'Evolution is the struggle for existence, as Darwin called it. The survival of the fittest. Whichever way you look at it, it means triumph in the face of adversity – either by succeeding over other organisms or by surviving natural disasters. Natural selection allows organisms to adapt. But does that necessarily mean organisms become more complex? And is complexity progress?'

'Evolution isn't my field,' said Peak, 'but the way I see it, most creatures have been getting bigger and more complex throughout the course of time. Humans are the perfect example. Organisms increase in size and complexity. In my book, that makes it a trend.'

'A trend? No. What we call history is only a passing moment in time. Sure, nature is currently experimenting with complexity, but who's to say that it won't lead to an evolutionary dead end? We're vastly overestimating our own importance if we see ourselves at the forefront of any natural trend. Think of the tree of life – that diagram with branches sprouting off in all directions. Where would you see humanity on it, Sal? As a main branch or one of its offshoots?'

'Goes without saying. A main branch.'

'That's what I expected. It's a typically human way of seeing things. If various offshoots of a genus die out, we tend to assume that the surviving offshoot is the central branch. Why? Well, because – for the moment, at any rate – it's still there. But what if it's just an unimportant side branch that's managed to survive a little longer than the rest? Humans are the only remaining bud on an evolutionary branch that once flourished. We're the leftovers from a biological development whose other offshoots withered and died, the last survivors of an experiment named *Homo*. *Homo Australopithecus*: extinct. *Homo habilis*: extinct. *Homo sapiens neanderthalensis*: extinct. *Homo sapiens sapiens*: still extant. We may have mastered the Earth for the moment, but evolutionary parvenus shouldn't confuse ascendancy with inherent superiority or long-term survival. We could disappear from this planet faster than we'd like to think.'

'Maybe you're right,' said Peak. 'But you're forgetting one thing. This one surviving species is the only species with highly developed consciousness.'

'Sure. But consider the development of consciousness within the context of nature as a whole. Can you really see any overall progress or general trend? Eighty per cent of all multicellular organisms have been far more successful in evolutionary terms than mankind, without ever being part of this supposed trend towards neural complexity. The fact that we're endowed with intelligence and consciousness is only evidence of progress from our particular viewpoint. We're just some bizarre evolutionary sideshow that's arisen against all the odds. There's only one thing that the human species has contributed to the ecosystem of this planet, and that's a whole lot of trouble.'

'Well, I still think humans are behind all this,' Vanderbilt was saying at the neighbouring table. 'But, OK, I'm prepared to be proven wrong. If it turns out that we're not up against a human enemy, I'll be launching an operation in yrr surveillance instead. Don't you worry! The CIA will trail those unicellular slimeballs until we know exactly how their minds work and what they're planning next.'

He was standing with Delaware and Anawak, surrounded by soldiers and crew.

'Dream on,' said Delaware. 'Not even the CIA could manage that.'

'What would you know about it, honey?' scoffed Vanderbilt. 'If you're patient enough, you can slip inside any mind you choose – even if it belongs to an amoeba. It's just a question of time.'

'No, it's a question of being able to see things objectively,' said Anawak. 'And that presupposes the ability to adopt an objective point of view.'

'We can do that. We're intelligent, civilised beings.'

'You might be intelligent, Jack, but you're not capable of viewing nature objectively.'

'In fact, your viewpoint is as subjective and restricted as any other animal's,' said Delaware.

'Which particular animal did you have in mind?' Vanderbilt chuckled. 'A walrus?'

Anawak gave a short laugh. 'I'm serious, Jack. We're closer to nature than we think.'

'Well, I'm not. I'm a city boy. Never did like the country. Same as my old man.'

'Makes no difference,' said Delaware. 'Think of how we feel about snakes, for example. We admire them as much as we fear them. It's the same with sharks. There are all kinds of shark divinities. Man's emotional reliance on other forms of life is inborn. It might even be genetic.'

'You're talking about tribespeople. I'm talking about city folk.'

'OK.' Anawak thought for a moment. 'Have you got any phobias? Anything you really don't like?'

'Well, I wouldn't call it a phobia, exactly . . .' Vanderbilt trailed off.

'An aversion, then?'

'Yes.'

'To what?'

'Just the usual. I don't like spiders.'

'Why?'

'Well, because . . .' Vanderbilt shrugged. 'They're disgusting. You find them disgusting, don't you?'

'Not really, but that's not the point. The point is, most phobias still plaguing civilised society derive from things that posed a threat to humanity in the past – *before* we lived in cities. Walls of rock that cave in on us, storms, floods, dark water, snakes, dogs, spiders. Why don't we develop phobias of guns, live wires, flick knives, cars, explosives and electric sockets? They're far more dangerous. But it's engrained in our minds: beware of snake-like creatures and many-legged insects.'

'The human brain developed in a natural, not a technological environment,' said Delaware. 'The evolution of our minds took place over a period of two million years, when we were living in intimate contact with our natural surroundings. It's even possible that the prehistoric rules of survival are inscribed in our genes. Either way, only a tiny fragment of our evolution took place during the so-called civilised era. Do you really think that just because your father and your father's father grew up in cities that all the formative information in your brain will have disappeared for good? Why are we afraid of small creatures that slither through the grass? Why don't you like spiders? It's because once upon a time fears like those saved our lives. Because individuals who were more susceptible to fear stayed out of danger and created more offspring. That's why, Jack. Do you see?'

Vanderbilt looked from Delaware to Anawak. 'But what's that got to do with the yrr?' he asked.

'It's to do with the fact that they might look like spiders,' retorted Anawak. 'How would that make you feel? So don't try to tell us that you're objective. If we can't control our aversion to the sight of the yrr – or to jelly, amoebas and toxic crabs or whatever – then we'll never find out how their minds work. We won't be able to. We'll only be intent on destroying them because they're not the same as us – and we don't want them creeping into our caves to steal our children . . .'

Johanson had extricated himself from the main group and was standing in the shadows, trying to remember what had happened the previous night. Li came over to him and handed him a glass. Red wine. 'I thought this was a soft-drinks-only expedition,' said Johanson, surprised.

'It is.' She clinked glasses with him. 'But there's no point in being dogmatic. Besides, I like to cater to the wishes of my guests.'

Johanson took a sip. 'Tell me, General,' he said, 'what kind of a person are you?'

'Call me Jude. "General" is only for people who have to salute me.'

'Well, I can't work you out.'

'Why's that?'

'I don't trust you.'

Li smiled in amusement and took a sip. 'The feeling's mutual, Sigur. What happened to you last night? Don't tell me you still can't remember.'

'My mind's blank.'

'What were you doing on the hangar deck? It was the middle of the night.'

'Just relaxing.'

'And before that you did a bit of relaxing with Oliviera.'

'When you're as busy as we are, it's important to relax.'

'Hmm.' Li stared past him towards the water. 'What were you talking about?'

'Work.'

'Is that all?'

Johanson looked at her. 'What do you want, Jude?'

'To beat this crisis. And you?'

'Oh, ditto,' said Johanson, 'but I'm not sure I want to beat it in the same way as you. What are you hoping will be left when this is over?'

'The values of our society.'

'Human society? Or American society?'

Her blue eyes seemed to gleam 'Is there a difference?'

Crowe had worked herself into a fury. Oliviera was on hand to back her up, and a crowd had assembled. There was no doubt that Peak and Buchanan had been forced on to the defensive, but while Peak had lapsed into thoughtful silence, Buchanan was seething with rage.

'We're not the inevitable product of some superior evolutionary development, you know,' Crowe was saying. 'Mankind was created by chance. We owe our existence to a colossal cosmic accident: a giant meteorite hit the Earth and wiped out the dinosaurs. If that hadn't happened, maybe intelligent neosauroids would now be roaming the planet. Or maybe there wouldn't be any intelligent life, only animals. We came into being because conditions were favourable for our evolution, not because of any logic. Who knows? Out of the millions of possible turns that multicellular life could have taken since its beginnings in the Cambrian, maybe this is the one and only pathway that could have given rise to us.'

'But mankind rules the planet,' persisted Buchanan. 'You can't argue with that.'

'Right now the yrr rule the planet. You've got to face facts. We're just one small species among the class of mammals, and there's a long way to go before evolution could deem us a success. The most successful mammals are bats, rats and antelopes. We're not the final glorious chapter of natural history, just a couple of pages in a very long book. There's no trend that leads towards a golden era of nature, only selection. Over time, one of the planet's species may have experienced a period of increasing anatomical and neural complexity, but if you look at the bigger picture, that's not a trend, and it's certainly not a progression. Life in general doesn't exhibit any impulse towards progress. Nature gives us complex beings, and at the same time preserves simple ones like bacteria for over three billion years. Life has no reason to want to improve on anything.'

'How does what you're saying fit with God's plan?' asked Buchanan, in a tone that sounded almost threatening.

'Well, *if* there's a God, and if that God's intelligent, then God must have organised the world in the way I've just described. We're not God's crowning achievement, we're just one version of life that will only survive if we understand our place in the whole.'

'And what about man being created in God's image? I suppose you're going to take issue with that?'

'Surely it must have occurred to you that the yrr might be created in God's image. You're not that narrow-minded, are you?' Crowe noticed that Buchanan's eyes were flashing dangerously, but she didn't let him speak. 'Anyhow, it's irrelevant. God's bound to have created His favourite species according to the best of all possible designs. Well, compared to other species, we humans are relatively big. Is a big body a better body? You were right, Peak, about some species growing bigger through selection, but most do very well as they are – and they're tiny. Small organisms are far more likely to survive during periods of mass extinction, which means that every few million years the larger organisms get wiped out and evolution starts again with the smallest possible species. Creatures get bigger and then the next meteorite strikes. Boom! That's God's plan for you.'

'That's not a plan, that's nihilism.'

'Realism, actually,' said Oliviera. 'The thing is, it's the highly specialised species like humans that die out in times of environmental change. They're unable to adapt. Koalas are complex organisms, but they only eat eucalyptus. What happens to the koalas if the eucalyptus disappears? They die too. Now, compare that to single-cell organisms: most species can live through ice ages, volcanic eruptions and shifts in oxygen and methane concentration. They can even survive for thousands of years in a death-like state and come back to life as though nothing had happened. Bacteria are everywhere – in boiling springs, glaciers, or burrowed kilometres under the earth . . . We couldn't survive without bacteria, but they'd have no trouble surviving without us. We've got bacteria to thank for the oxygen in the air. Our supply of chemicals – oxygen, nitrogen, phosphorus, sulphur, carbon dioxide and so on – depends on the activity of microbes. Plant and animal matter is broken down by bacteria, fungi, protozoa, microscopic scavengers, insects and worms, who feed the chemical components back into the cycle of life. It's no different in the ocean. Micro-organisms are the dominant form of life in the water. The jelly in the lab is almost certainly older and perhaps a good deal smarter than we are, whether you like the idea or not.'

'You can't compare humans to microbes,' Buchanan snapped. 'Humans have a special significance. If you can't see that, what are you doing in this team?'

'I'm trying to do the right thing.'

'But you're betraying mankind.'

'No, mankind is betraying the planet by attributing a disproportionate significance to certain organisms. We're the only species to do that, you know. We try to rate everything. We have bad animals, important animals, useful animals. We judge nature by what we see, but we see only a fraction of it, and we invest that fraction with more significance than it deserves. Our focus is on large animals, on vertebrates, and mainly on ourselves. All we see are vertebrates. The total number of living vertebrate species is approximately forty-three thousand, of which six thousand are reptiles, ten thousand are birds and four thousand are mammals. But there are nearly a million scientifically classified non-vertebrate species, including two hundred and ninety thousand species of beetle alone. That's seven times the number of vertebrates!'

Peak looked at Buchanan. 'She's right, Craig,' he said. 'You should admit it. They're both right.'

'We're not a successful species,' said Crowe. 'If you want to see a successful species, you should take a look at the shark. It's survived in unchanged form since the Devonian, four hundred million years ago.

Sharks are a hundred times older than any member of our genus, and there are three hundred and fifty different species. The yrr could be even older than that. Single-cell organisms that can think collectively would be light-years ahead of us. We'd never catch up. The only thing we could do is destroy them. But would you really want to take that risk? We don't even know what role they play in our survival. Maybe we'd find it even harder to live *without* this particular enemy than we do to live with it.'

'You want to protect American values?' Johanson shook his head. 'In that case, we're bound to fail.'

'What have you got against American values?'

'Nothing. But you heard what Crowe said: intelligent life-forms from other planets probably have nothing in common with humans or mammals. They may not even have DNA. Their system of values is likely to be completely different from ours. What kind of social and moral framework do you think you're going to find in the depths? We're talking about a species whose civilisation probably depends on cell division and self-sacrifice. How are you going to reach any kind of agreement with them, if all you're concerned about is the preservation of values that even humans can't agree on?'

'That's not what I meant,' said Li. 'I know we don't have the monopoly on ethics. But the question is this: is it absolutely necessary to understand how others think? Or wouldn't it be better to invest all our energies in trying to coexist?'

'Living in peace alongside each other?'

'Yes.'

'If only we'd thought of that before,' said Johanson. 'I think the native peoples of America, Australia, Africa and the Arctic would have welcomed that idea. Same goes for all the animal species that we hunted to extinction. But the situation's not that straightforward. I don't suppose for a second that we'll ever really understand how they think, but we've caused each other too much trouble not to try. Our habitat's too small for us to keep living side by side. We need to learn to live together. And there's no way we'll be able to do that unless we scale back our expectations concerning humanity's so-called God-given rights.'

'How do you propose we do that, then? By adopting the customs of amoebas?'

'Of course not. It's genetically impossible, anyway. What we refer to as customs or culture is inscribed in our genes. Cultural evolution began in prehistoric times. That was when our mind was laid out. Sure, these days we design aeroplanes, helicopter carriers and opera houses, but only to continue our primitive activities on a so-called civilised plane. It's what we've been doing since the first axe was bartered for a slab of meat: going to war, congregating in social units, trading. Culture is part of our evolution. It allows us to survive in a stable condition—'

'Until another species with greater stability turns out to be superior. I see what you're getting at, Sigur. It's not something we like to dwell on, but genes are what's allowing us to have this conversation in the first place. We're so proud of our intellectual heritage, but it's just the result of biology. Culture is nothing but a set of successful patterns of behaviour grounded in our struggle to survive.'

Johanson didn't respond.

'Did I get something wrong?' said Li.

'No, I was listening in silent admiration. You're absolutely right. Human evolution is just the interplay between genetic mutation and cultural change. We owe the growth of our brains to genetic mutations. It was biology that allowed us to speak. Five hundred thousand years ago, nature restructured our vocal apparatus and built the language centres in our cortex. And these genetic mutations fired our cultural evolution. Speech gave us the ability to express our thoughts, describe our past, discuss our future, and give voice to our imagination. Culture is the product of biological processes, and biological adaptation occurs in response to cultural change. The whole process takes generations, of course, but it happens all the same.'

Li smiled. 'I'm glad I passed the test.'

'I never suspected otherwise,' Johanson said graciously. 'But you've pinpointed the problem: our much-vaunted cultural diversity is bounded by genetic limitations. And those limitations clearly separate our culture from the culture of non-human intelligent beings. Over time, mankind has created numerous cultures, and each is based on the imperative of keeping our species alive. We could never adopt the values of a species whose biology isn't compatible with our own. They're our rivals in the struggle for habitat and resources.'

'So you don't believe in the Federation, with walking electronic beehives queuing up beside us at the bar?'

'*Star Wars?*'

'Yes.'

'A great movie. No. That would only work if we could somehow suppress our instincts over hundreds of thousands of years. We'd need our genes to be reprogrammed towards inter-species co-operation.'

'Which proves that I'm right. We shouldn't try to understand the yrr. We should find a way of leaving each other in peace.'

'That's the snag. *They* won't leave *us* in peace.'

'Then we've lost.'

'Why?'

'Didn't you just say that humans and non-humans will never reach a consensus?'

'The same could be said for Christians and Muslims. Listen, Jude, understanding the yrr isn't an option. We'll never be *able* to understand them. But we have to make room for what we can't understand. That's not the same as allowing their values to hold sway – or vice versa. The solution lies in retreat. And, right now, it's our retreat that's being called for. It can work, you know. It doesn't mean we have to understand them emotionally – that would be impossible. It just means looking at things from a different, broader perspective, and we can do that by taking a step back from ourselves as a species. Because without that distance, we'll never be in a position to present the yrr with a view of us that's any different from the one they've got now.'

'But we're retreating already. We're trying to make contact – isn't that enough?'

'And what are you hoping to gain from making contact?'

Li said nothing.

'Jude, tell me something. How is it that I hold you in such high esteem yet with so little trust?'

The noise of the debate drifted over from the other tables. It gathered like a wave sweeping over the deck, breaking as it hit them. The scraps of conversation became raised voices, then shouting. At that moment an announcement came through the speakers: '*Dolphin alert! Warning! Dolphin alert!*'

Li was the first to wrench her eyes from the duel. She turned her head and looked towards the dusky sea.

'Oh, God,' she whispered.

It had started to glow.

All around them the waves were tinged with luminous blue. Shimmering violet pools surfaced on the water, spreading and merging, as though the sky were pouring into the ocean.

The *Independence* was suspended in light.

'Whatever you said in that message, you certainly made an impression,' said Greywolf to Crowe, as he stared at it.

'It's so beautiful,' Delaware said softly.

'Look!' cried Rubin.

The veil of light began to stir. The glow pulsated. Enormous whirlpools formed, turning slowly at first, then ever faster, until they were rotating like spiral galaxies, drawing in fresh streams of blue. The light at the centre of the whirlpools intensified. Thousands of tiny stars lit up, then faded.

There was a flash.

A cry went up from the deck.

In a split second the scene had changed. Lightning zigzagged through the water, branching out between the swirling eddies. A mute storm raged beneath the surface of the sea. Then the maelstrom retreated, peeling back from the vessel's hull, as the blue cloud rushed towards the horizon, disappearing at breathtaking speed.

Greywolf ran towards the island.

'Jack, wait!' Delaware darted after him. The others followed. He hurried through the vessel, swinging down the companionways, then striding through the command centre and bursting into the CIC, Peak and Li close behind him. The cameras on the hull showed nothing but dark green water. Two dolphins swam into view.

'What's going on?' Peak called to the guys at the monitors. 'What are you getting from the sonar?'

A man swivelled round. 'There's something big out there, sir. Something – well, it's uh, kind of—'

'Kind of what?' Li grabbed his shoulder. 'We need information, you moron. What's happening?'

The man blanched. 'It's – it's— First there was nothing on the screen, then the next second there were sheets of something. They came out of nowhere. The sea just went solid. They turned themselves into a wall or something, they were – they were everywhere.'

'Dispatch the Cobras. I need them up there now, surveying the area.'

'What are the dolphins reporting?' asked Greywolf.

'Unknown life-form,' said a soldier. 'The dolphins detected it first.'

'Is it localised?'

'No, everywhere. But it seems to be retreating – one kilometre and still moving. The sonar's showing vast swathes of something all around the ship.'

'Where are the dolphins now?'

'Underneath us. They're crowding in front of the hatch. I think they're scared. They want to come in.'

People were still pouring into the CIC.

'Bring up the satellite footage,' commanded Peak.

The enormous monitor mounted at the head of the room showed the *Independence*, as seen by KH-12. She was resting on a dark expanse of water. There was no trace of any blue light.

'Just now the whole screen was lit up,' said the guy in charge of monitoring the satellite feedback.

'Any other satellites we can look at?'

'Nothing available, sir.'

'Zoom out on KH-12, then.'

The man relayed the command to the control centre. A few seconds later the *Independence* dwindled on the screen and the Greenland Sea extended across it. Whistles and clicks came through the speakers, as the dolphins continued to issue their warning of the unknown presence below.

'Keep going.'

KH-12 zoomed out further. It was now covering a hundred square kilometres. The *Independence* was 250 metres long, but now it looked like driftwood. They stared at the monitor with bated breath.

And then they saw it.

A thin blue glow was stretched in a vast ring round the vessel. It quivered with flashes of light.

'How big is it?' asked Peak, in a whisper.

'Four kilometres in diameter,' said the woman in front of the screen. 'No, it's bigger. It's some kind of funnel. The image that we can see here is only the opening. The whole thing stretches into the depths. And we're, uh . . . suspended over its jaws.'

'What's it made of?'

Johanson had appeared in the room next to Peak. 'Jelly, I should think.'

'Congratulations,' wheezed Vanderbilt. 'What the hell did you send them?' he snarled at Crowe.

'We asked them to show themselves.'

'Was that wise?'

Shankar spun round angrily. 'We're supposed to be making contact, aren't we? What the hell is your problem? Don't tell me you were expecting messengers on horseback—'

'We've got a signal!'

They swivelled in the direction of the voice – it was the guy in charge of acoustic surveillance. Shankar was there in an instant. He bent over the screen.

'What is it?' Crowe called.

'From the look of the spectrogram, I'd say it was a Scratch signal.'

'An answer?'

'I don't know whether—'

'The ring! Look, it's contracting.'

Their heads jerked towards the main screen. The ring of light was creeping back slowly towards the ship. At the same time, two tiny dots sped away from her. The Cobras had started their recce. The whistling and squeaking from the speakers grew louder.

Suddenly they were all talking at once.

'Quiet!' barked Li. Her forehead creased as she listened to the dolphins. 'They've changed their signal.'

'Yes.' Delaware closed her eyes in concentration. 'Unknown creatures and . . .'

'Orcas!' cried Greywolf, before she could finish.

'We've picked up a number of large animals approaching from below,' said a member of the sonar team. 'They're inside the tube.'

Greywolf turned to Li. 'I don't like the sound of this. We should bring the dolphins inside.'

'Why now?'

'I'm not prepared to put their lives at risk. And, anyway, we need the footage from their cameras.'

Li hesitated for a moment. Then she made up her mind. 'OK. Fetch them in. I'll tell Roscovitz. Peak, go with him. Take four of your men.'

'Leon?' said Greywolf. 'Licia?'

They hurried out. Rubin watched them go. He leaned towards Li and said something in a low voice. She listened, nodded and turned back to the screens. 'Wait for me!' Rubin yelled. 'I'm coming too.'

Well Deck

Roscovitz, Browning and one of her technicians reached the well deck before the scientists arrived. The commander swore when he saw the broken-down Deepflight. It was floating on the surface with the pods flipped open, tethered by a single chain that stretched up to the rail overhead. 'I thought I told you to finish the job,' he snapped at Browning.

'It's more complicated than we thought,' the head technician protested, as they strode along the jetty. 'The steering system is—'

'Shit.' Roscovitz stared at the submersible. It was positioned half-way over the sluice, whose contours were partially visible in the water, four metres below. 'I don't like it there, Browning. And I especially don't like it there when we're letting the dolphins in and out.'

'With all due respect, sir, it's not in the way. Just as soon as we've repaired it, we'll hoist it back on to the rail.'

Roscovitz growled incomprehensibly and took his position at the controls. The boat was lying in front of him. From that angle it blocked his view of the sluice. He'd have to rely on the footage on the screens. He swore again, this time using juicier expressions. The *Independence* had been equipped in great haste – shoddily, it seemed. If things weren't going to work properly, why the hell didn't they cause problems before they were in use? What was the point of testing every last piece of hardware if his view would be blocked by a floating submersible?

Steps echoed through the hangar deck. Greywolf, Delaware, Anawak and Rubin hurried down the ramp, followed by Peak and his men. The soldiers spread out on either side of the jetty. Rubin and Peak headed towards Roscovitz while the others pulled on their wetsuits and adjusted their masks.

'Ready,' said Greywolf. He made the OK sign, forming a circle with his forefinger and thumb. 'Let's bring them in.'

Roscovitz switched on the audio recording to summon the dolphins. He saw the scientists splash down into the basin, their bodies illuminated by the underwater lights. They swam towards the sluice. One by one they dived towards the glass hatch.

He opened the flaps in the hull.

Delaware sank head first towards the display panel beside the hatch. She was still diving when the enormous steel plates jolted into action, three metres below the inverted glass turret. She watched as they swung open to reveal the water below. Two dolphins slid into the sluice. They seemed nervous, pressing their snouts against the glass. Greywolf signalled for them to wait. A third dolphin swam in.

By now the steel plates were fully open. There was a gaping chasm below the glass plug. Delaware strained to see through the darkness. No blue glow, no lightning, no orcas, and no sign of the other three dolphins. She sank lower, below the level of the deck, until her hands were touching the glass, scanning the depths for the rest of the fleet. Suddenly a fourth dolphin shot into view, banking sharply and swimming into the sluice. Greywolf nodded, and Delaware gave the OK to Roscovitz. The steel plates moved slowly together, closing with a dull thud. Inside the sluice the sensors went to work, testing the water for impurities and toxins. After a few seconds the green light came on, and the all-clear went to Roscovitz's control panel. Noiselessly the glass flaps slid open.

As soon as the gap was wide enough, the dolphins pushed into the basin, where Greywolf and Anawak were ready to receive them.

Peak watched as Roscovitz closed the glass flaps, his eyes fixed on the monitors. Rubin was at the edge of the basin, peering down at the sluice.

'And then there were two,' Roscovitz muttered to himself.

Whistling and clicking came to them from the speakers: the dolphins left outside sounded increasingly frantic. Greywolf raised his head above the water, followed by Anawak and Delaware.

'What are they saying?' asked Peak.

'Same as before,' said Greywolf. 'Unknown life-form and orcas. Anything new on the monitors?'

'No.'

'Which isn't to say that we're clear. Let's fetch the other two in.'

Peak stared. A deep blue glow was emanating from the edges of the screens.

'You'd better get a move on,' he said. 'It's coming closer.'

The scientists dived back towards the sluice. Peak dialled the CIC. 'What can you see up there?'

'The ring's still contracting.' Li's voice rasped through the speakers on the console. 'The helicopters have reported that it's disappearing under water, but we can still see it clearly on the satellite footage. Seems to be trying to get under the boat. Any second now the blue light should come on.'

'It's on already. Listen, what are we dealing with? The blue cloud?'

'Sal?' That was Johanson's voice. 'I think the cloud has gone. The cells are aggregating. It's a dense funnel of jelly, and it's contracting. I don't know what's going on, but I think you'd better finish up down there.'

'We're almost done. Rosco?'

'I'm on the case,' said Roscovitz. 'The sluice is open.'

Anawak was staring in fascination through the glass. This time things looked very different as the steel flaps swung open. Earlier they'd peered into murky green gloom. Now the depths were aglow with blue light, faint at first, but growing steadily stronger.

This doesn't look like the cloud, he thought. It was almost as though they were encircled by light. He recalled the satellite images of the *Independence* floating at the centre of the enormous funnel's mouth.

Then it hit him that he was looking down inside the tube. His stomach turned at the thought of its vastness. Panic took hold of him. As the fifth dolphin appeared out of nowhere and shot into the sluice, he drew back from the hatch, barely able to control the urge to flee. Anawak forced himself to stay calm. A second later, the sixth dolphin entered the sluice. The steel flaps closed. The sensors tested the water, gave the OK to Roscovitz and the glass hatch opened.

Browning bounded forward and landed on the Deepflight.

'Hey! What do you think you're doing?' asked Roscovitz.

'Well, the dolphins are inside now, aren't they? I'm doing my job.'

'I didn't mean it like that.'

'Sure you didn't.' Browning crouched to open a compartment at the stern. 'I'm going to fix this damn thing.'

'This isn't the time, Browning,' Peak said testily. 'We've got more important stuff to deal with. Stop messing about.' He couldn't tear his eyes away from the screens. The light was getting brighter.

'Sal, are you finished down there?'

'Yeah. What's going on?'

'Part of the funnel is pushing itself under the boat.'

'Can that stuff cause us any damage?'

'I doubt it. I can't imagine any organism causing the *Independence* to so much as wobble. Not even these creatures. They're like muscular jelly.'

'And they're right below us,' said Rubin, from the edge of the basin. His eyes were gleaming. 'Open the sluice again, Luther. Pronto.'

'What?' Roscovitz stared at him in disbelief. 'Are you crazy?'

In a few steps Rubin was alongside him at the desk. 'General?' he called, leaning into the mike.

The speakers crackled. 'What do you want, Mick?'

'We've got a fantastic opportunity to get hold of a significant sample of that jelly. I'm suggesting that we open the sluice but Peak and Roscovitz—'

'Jude, it's too risky,' said Peak. 'Anything could get in.'

'All we have to do is open the hatch in the keel and wait,' said Rubin. 'Maybe it'll spark their curiosity. We'll catch a few big lumps of jelly, then seal off the sluice. It'll give us a lovely big sample for testing. What do you say?'

'What if it's contaminated?' objected Roscovitz.

'Why are you all so negative? We'll know if it's contaminated. The glass flaps stay closed until we're sure it's OK.'

Peak shook his head. 'I'm not in favour.'

Rubin rolled his eyes. 'General, we'll never get a chance like this again!'

'All right,' said Li. 'But be careful.'

Rubin laughed excitedly, walked to the edge of the basin and waved his arms.

'Hey! Get a move on, can't you?' he shouted to Greywolf, Anawak and Delaware, who were busy unharnessing the dolphins. 'Hurry up and—' They were under water and couldn't hear him. 'OK, forget it. Luther, open the hatch. There's nothing to worry about while the glass flaps are closed.'

'Shouldn't we wait until—'

'We don't have time,' Rubin snapped at him. 'You heard what Li said. If we wait, the jelly will be gone. All you have to do is let a little into the sluice, then close it. A cubic metre or so should do fine.'

Roscovitz felt like shoving Rubin into the water, but Li had given the bastard her permission.

She'd given the order to open the hatch.

He pressed the button.

Delaware was dealing with a particularly excitable dolphin. It was fidgety and impatient, and as she tried to unstrap its camera, it darted away. Harness trailing through the water, it sped towards the sluice. Delaware saw it circling the hatch and swam after it, taking long, powerful strokes.

She didn't hear the discussion on the jetty.

Come on, she willed the dolphin silently. Come over here. What's the matter? There's nothing to be afraid of.

Then she saw what was wrong.

The steel flaps were swinging open.

For a second she was so astonished that she stopped swimming and sank through the water until her toes touched the glass. The flaps were still moving. The sea beneath them glowed a vivid blue. Flashes of lightning shot through the water.

What the hell was Roscovitz playing at?

The dolphin darted back and forth around the hatch. It swam over to her and prodded her with its snout, trying to ward her away. When Delaware failed to respond, it swivelled and sped off.

She stared into the luminescent depths.

She could see outlines, shadows flitting back and forth, then a dark patch drawing closer, getting bigger.

It was approaching at high speed.

The patch became clearer, and assumed its normal form.

Suddenly she knew what it was. She recognised the enormous rounded head with its black beak and white chin, the even rows of teeth between the half-open jaws. It was the biggest of its kind she'd ever seen. It was rising vertically from the depths, gaining speed all the time, with no intention of stopping. Her mind raced. Within a split second the snippets of information came together. The glass hatch was made of armoured glass and was solidly built, but not solid enough to withstand a collision with a living missile. The creature measured at least twelve metres. At top speed it could propel itself out of the water at fifty-six kilometres an hour.

It was moving too fast.

She made a desperate attempt to get away from the sluice.

Like a torpedo the orca crashed through the glass plug. The wave sent Delaware spinning. Through the swirling debris she glimpsed shards of glass and swirling sections of the hatch's metal rim, then the white belly of the whale, as it rose through the hatch, barely hindered by the impact. Something struck her painfully between the shoulders. She cried out, and water filled her lungs.

Roscovitz barely had time to take in the situation. The jetty groaned and shook beneath his feet as the orca smashed through the hatch. A wave lifted the Deepflight into the air. He saw Browning lose her balance, arms flailing. The orca crashed down into the water and accelerated away.

'The sluice,' screamed Rubin. 'Close the flaps.'

The head of the orca rammed into the submersible, sending it spinning into the air. There was a snapping noise as the chain broke free. Browning was catapulted upwards and slammed down on to the control panel. One of her boots struck Roscovitz in the chest and sent him reeling backwards against the bulkhead, pulling Peak with him.

'The sub!' screamed Rubin. 'The sub!'

Browning's body sagged back into the basin, blood pouring from her head. The stern of the Deepflight shot vertically into the air. Then the boat filled with water and sank. Roscovitz staggered to his feet and tried to reach the controls. Something whizzed towards him. He looked up and saw the chain swinging in his direction like a whip. He tried to duck, but the metal struck his temples and curled round his neck.

He was dragged forwards and over the edge.

Greywolf was too far away to identify the cause of the chaos and, since he was in the water, he couldn't feel the impact. But he saw the submersible ripped from its chain, and what happened to Browning and Roscovitz. Rubin was standing at the control panel, shouting and waving. Peak's head popped up in the background. The soldiers were running to the site of the disaster, guns raised.

Hurriedly he scanned the water. Anawak was beside him, but Delaware was nowhere to be seen.

'Licia?'

No answer.

Fear gripped him. With a powerful kick, he dived down and swam towards the sluice.

Delaware was heading in the wrong direction. A searing pain ran through her back and she felt as though she was suffocating. Suddenly she found herself back at the sluice. The two halves of the hatch had been ripped apart, but the steel flaps were closing. Beneath them the sea was ablaze with blue light.

She turned on to her back.

No!

The Deepflight was falling towards her, pods open and bow first. It sank like a stone. She kicked with all her might. The boat was going to hit her. As she stared up, the articulated arms, folded neatly together, bore down towards her. She tried to speed through the water, long and thin like an otter, but it wasn't enough. The boat rammed into her torso and she felt her ribs break. Her mouth opened in a scream, and she swallowed more water. The vessel pushed her down into the sluice and out into the open water. The cold pierced her body. Through the fog of her consciousness, she saw the steel flaps hit the submersible with a dull thud. The Deepflight stopped sinking. It was trapped, but Delaware was still falling. She stretched out her arms to grab on to the vessel, but her strength was failing and her lungs were clogged.

Please, she thought, I want to go back. I don't want to die.

In the gap between the blocked hatch and the trapped submersible she saw a hazy image of Greywolf's face.

A large dark shape approached from the side, jaws open, showing rows of conical teeth.

The orca bit into her chest.

She didn't see the glowing mass shoot past her. By the time it reached the sluice, Delaware was dead.

Peak banged his fist down on the control panel. His attempt to close the sluice had failed. The Deepflight had jammed the steel plates. Either he opened the flaps entirely and lost the submersible, or he left them as they were and allowed God knows what to find its way into the vessel.

Browning had disappeared and Roscovitz was hanging from the chain, legs dangling in the water, hands clutching at his throat.

Where was the damned orca?

'Sal,' Rubin whined.

The water in the basin bubbled and frothed. The soldiers were rushing around with no clear objective. Greywolf had dived under water. Anawak was nowhere to be seen. And where had Delaware got to?

Someone prodded him in the ribs.

'For God's sake, Sal!' Rubin pushed him away from the controls. His hands danced over the keyboard, fingers jabbing at buttons. 'Why haven't you closed the bloody sluice?'

'You stupid bastard!' Peak drew back his fist and landed a punch in the middle of Rubin's face. The biologist swayed and tumbled backwards into the pool, sending water spurting into the air. Through the shower of spray Peak saw the blade-like fin of an orca speed towards him.

Rubin's head appeared above the waves. Now he saw the fin too. His splutters turned into a scream.

Peak pushed the button to open the steel flaps and release the Deepflight into the sea.

He was expecting the display to light up.

Nothing happened.

Greywolf thought he was losing his mind. A pod of orcas was patrolling the water beneath the *Independence*. Seconds ago one had closed its jaws round Delaware and whisked her out of sight. Without stopping to consider, Greywolf swam towards the gap between the two steel plates, in time to see something hurtle towards him from below. Lightning and sparks flashed before his eyes and he was hit by a force like a giant fist that sent him reeling backwards. Everything turned upside down. For an instant he saw Anawak to his left, and then he was gone again. Legs flailed in the water. A body tumbled towards him. The white belly of an orca flashed past in the basin above. Finally he was looking down at the Deepflight trapped between the flaps.

Watching as a thing pushed its way through the half-open hatch, towards the inside of the vessel.

It was like a tentacle belonging to an enormous polyp, only there was no polyp on earth with a tentacle that size. It was three metres in diameter, too big for any living creature. Matter streamed up towards the well deck, racing out of the ocean in a never-ending column. As it left the sluice, the single muscle of jelly branched into slender tendrils, whose smooth surface glittered with patterns of light.

Rubin was swimming for his life.

The fin chased after him. Coughing and spluttering he reached the jetty and tried to pull himself out of the basin, crazy with fear. His elbows gave way. He heard shots and sank back under the water to be confronted with an incredible sight. In a flash he realised that his wish had been fulfilled. The alien organism had entered the vessel, but under circumstances he hadn't foreseen.

Glowing tentacles twisted through the water, thick as tree trunks.

And the orca was between them, jaws agape.

Rubin shot back up. Two legs were thrashing over the surface of the water, centimetres from his face. Roscovitz stared down at him through bulging eyes. He looked as though he was hanging on a gallows.

A terrible gurgling noise spilled from his lips.

Oh, God, thought Rubin. Dear God. The fin was almost upon him.

The orca rose in a tower of spray, jaws wide open. Roscovitz's legs disappeared inside its mouth. The jaws clamped shut. For a moment the whale was suspended motionless above the water, then it dropped back.

Blood trickled from Roscovitz's dangling torso, and Rubin found himself unable to turn away. He heard a long scream of terror, and slowly it dawned on him that he was the one who was screaming.

He screamed and screamed.

The fin reappeared.

Combat Information Center

Li couldn't believe her eyes. In a matter of seconds chaos had erupted on the well deck. She watched Peak sprint along the jetty. Soldiers were firing blindly into the water, and Roscovitz's mangled body dangled from above. 'Get me some sound,' she demanded.

The next moment gunshots and screams echoed through the room. Everyone started talking at once, as the chaos on the well deck found its echo in the CIC. Feverishly Li considered what should be done. She'd send reinforcements, of course. This time with explosive projectiles. Why were the idiots firing standard ammunition?

They had to wrest back control.

She'd go down in person.

Without a word she went into the adjacent room. The LFOC was the command centre for amphibious operations. From there they could flood the ballast tanks, pump out the water, and open the stern gate, in the event that the control desk in the well deck failed. Only the steel flaps couldn't be operated from the LFOC – another stupid oversight.

'OK,' she said, to the shocked crew members in front of the screens. 'I want the ballast tanks in the stern pumped dry.' She thought for a moment. Was the sluice in the well deck open or closed? Would the water be able to run out? It was impossible to tell from the confusion on the monitors. Usually it was enough to raise the stern of the vessel and the artificial harbour would drain automatically, either through the open sluice or out of the stern gate into the sea. There was an emergency pump system, in case both were blocked. It took a little longer, but served the same purpose.

Li gave the order for the pump to be activated, and ran back to the CIC.

Well Deck

The steel flaps weren't responding. He didn't have time to wonder why. Breathing heavily Peak ran to one of the armaments lockers and pulled out a harpoon gun with an explosive charge. His men were firing indiscriminately into the water, while an enormous squid-like creature seemed to be forcing itself through the open sluice, writhing and snaking beneath the surface of the pool.

From the corner of his eye Peak spotted Rubin hauling himself out of the water. He felt disgusted and relieved. He detested the man, but that was no excuse for knocking him into the water. Rubin's life had to be protected He still had a job to do.

The fin moved away from the jetty. Anawak and Greywolf were some distance away, swimming towards the other side of the pool. Glowing tentacles seemed to pursue them, but the jelly was everywhere, stretching out in all directions. The orca was definitely on their tail.

He had to dispatch the beast before it killed anyone else.

Suddenly Peak felt calm. Everything else could wait. The key thing was to finish off the lethal mass of flesh and teeth.

He raised the harpoon gun and took aim.

Anawak saw the orca approaching. The water in the basin foamed and splashed – it seemed to have come alive, a moving, shimmering mass of blue, through which the orca swam purposefully towards him and Greywolf. It rose to expel a jet of misty air, and its black head loomed into view. It was only metres away now. They'd never make it to the jetty; that much was clear. But they had to do something. When the orcas had attacked in Clayoquot Sound, Greywolf had arrived in the nick of time and saved them. Right now, their only chance was to outmanoeuvre it.

The orca dived.

'Let it through!' he screamed at Greywolf.

Not a very clear instruction, he thought. God knows if Jack will understand. But it was too late for explanations.

Anawak took a gulp of air and sank beneath the surface.

Peak cursed. The whale was gone and there was no sign of Greywolf or Anawak. He ran along the jetty, searching for the enormous body, but the basin had turned into a surreal underwater inferno, in which flashes of light, blurred shapes and jets of water blocked his view. Ahead one of the soldiers was firing at the serpentine creature in the pool, which was clearly having no effect.

'Stop that!' Peak pushed the man in the direction of the console. 'Sound the alarm. Get the flaps open and get rid of the Deepflight.' His eyes scanned the water. 'Then close the goddamned sluice.'

The soldier ran off.

Peak walked up to the edge of the jetty and peered into the basin, the harpoon gun in his hands.

As soon as Anawak had ducked under water, the harsh noises of the deck had yielded to low hissings and rumblings. Greywolf was alongside him, treading water, bubbles streaming from his mouth. Anawak hadn't let go of his arm since he'd jerked him under water. He didn't know if his idea would work.

Something surged towards them. It looked like a huge headless snake. Lines of light pulsated over the semi-transparent shimmering blue tissue. Hundreds of thin, whip-like tendrils extended from its body, sweeping over the floor of the pool. Suddenly Anawak realised that the creature was scanning its surroundings. The whips were registering every detail of the deck. As he watched, in horror and fascination, a fresh set grew out from the body and wriggled towards him.

The open mouth of the orca loomed between them.

Anawak felt a change come over him. One part of him shut itself off and calmly asked questions. How much of the aggressor was whale and how much was jelly? How would an orca behave, if it wasn't following its instincts but was in the grip of an alien consciousness? He had to see the orca as part of the luminescent jelly, not as an orca with normal orca reflexes. But maybe that was where their advantage lay. Perhaps they could confuse it.

The orca shot towards them.

Anawak dodged to one side, pushing Greywolf in the opposite direction. He saw Greywolf swim off – good, he'd understood the plan. The whale hurtled between them, startled by the sudden division of its prey.

They'd gained a few seconds.

Without stopping to look for the orca, Anawak swam into the forest of tentacles.

Rubin was crawling along the jetty on all fours, gasping for breath. The soldier leaped over him and hurried to the control desk. He glanced at the display panels, got his bearings, and pressed the button to open the steel hatch.

The system was jammed.

Like all the other members of his squad, the soldier had been trained to operate the control systems on the vessel, and knew exactly how they worked. An image of Browning, body sprawled over the panel, was etched in his mind. He bent down and peered at the button. It was stuck, pushed down to one side. It wouldn't take much to fix. He jabbed at it with his gun.

Anawak was floating through an alien world.

Veils of tendrils surrounded him. He wasn't sure whether it had been a good idea to swim into the living jungle, but there was no point in worrying about it now. The jelly might react aggressively, or it might not. It might be toxic – in which case it would kill them all anyway.

The glowing tendrils arced in his direction. The whole basin seemed to be moving. Anawak was tossed from side to side. The web tightened, and he felt one of the whips stroking his face. He pushed it away. More twisted towards him, feeling their way over his head and body. Throbbing, buzzing noises filled his ears, and his lungs ached. If he didn't make it to the surface soon, his attempts to fend off the jelly would be in vain.

He reached into the tendrils with both hands and tore them apart. The organism was like a strong, highly flexible muscle, and it never stopped moving or changing shape. Tentacles that had wrapped themselves round him fell away, withdrawing and merging with the main trunk, which immediately started budding new ones.

He had to get out of there.

A sleek, elegant body darted forward.

He saw a smiling face: one of the dolphin fleet. Without hesitation Anawak held on to its dorsal fin. The dolphin continued at high speed, shooting out of the mass of tentacles and pulling him with it. Suddenly the view cleared. He clung to the dolphin and saw the orca approaching from the side. The dolphin shot upwards as the enormous jaws snapped shut behind them, missing by a hair's breadth. They rose through the surface, on course for the embankment.

The soldier pressed the button.

The repair job had been carried out crudely, but it had worked. The steel flaps swung open, releasing the submersible. It continued on its downward path, dropping past the jelly that was surging through the sluice. Noiselessly it fell out of the vessel and disappeared into the depths of the ocean.

For a fraction of a second the soldier wondered whether it wouldn't be better to leave the flaps open, but he'd been instructed to close them, so he did. This time there was no submersible to get in the way. The flaps, driven by a powerful motor, cut into the vast trunk of the organism.

Peak raised his gun hurriedly. He'd caught sight of Anawak. For a moment it had seemed that the orca had caught him, but then he'd reappeared above the water and the whale had sped across the pool. The soldiers were firing at the black back. The orca sank beneath the surface.

Had they hit it?

'Hatch is closing,' shouted the soldier from the controls.

Peak raised his hand in acknowledgement, then set off along the jetty. His eyes scanned the far side of the basin. Bullets could do nothing to harm the squid-like creature, and firing explosives at it seemed too risky. There were people in the pool.

Greywolf had copied Anawak's example, and swum into the tentacles. His arms powered through the water as he summoned all his energy and sped towards the side. After a few metres the main trunk of the jelly blocked his path and he had to turn round. He'd lost all sense of direction.

Tentacles wrapped themselves round him, encircling his shoulders. Greywolf felt sickened. He couldn't think any more. The images of Delaware's death played before his eyes in a never-ending loop of film. Ripping the tendrils away from his body, he tried to escape.

Suddenly he found himself back at the sluice. The submersible had vanished. He watched as the flaps closed, cutting into the jelly and slicing through its trunk. There was no mistaking the organism's reaction: it wasn't happy.

A mountain of water shot up towards Peak as the orca surged out of the basin in front of him. Too surprised to feel afraid, Peak stared into its jaws. He staggered backwards, and at the same time the entire well deck seemed to blast apart. The organism was raging in the water. Enormous snakes of jelly raced up to the ceiling in wild spirals, slapping against the walls and sweeping along the jetty. Peak heard screams and shots from the soldiers, saw bodies flying through the air and into the basin. Then his legs were knocked from under him, and he slammed down on to his back. The orca's body teetered towards him. Peak groaned, tightened his grip on the harpoon gun and was jerked into the water.

He sank in a maelstrom of bubbles. A shimmering blue coating stuck to his legs. He stabbed at it with his gun, and the vice-like hold relented. Above him the orca splashed back into the pool. A violent pressure wave sent Peak reeling through the water. He saw the jaws of the whale spring open, less than a metre away. He thrust the harpoon gun into its mouth and fired.

For a moment everything seemed to stop.

A dull explosion sounded inside the orca's head. It wasn't especially loud, but it turned the world red. Peak was catapulted backwards in a mass of flesh and blood. He tumbled through the water, hit the side of the basin, and pulled himself on to the jetty in a single fluid movement. Wheezing, he crawled on his belly away from the side. There was blood everywhere, and red slime was mixed with fatty tissue and splinters of bone. Peak tried to stand up, but slid and fell. Pain shot through him. His left foot was twisted at an awkward angle, but he barely noticed.

He stared incredulously at the scene unfolding around him.

The organism seemed to have worked itself into a frenzy. There was a chaos of flailing tentacles. Shelving units collapsed, and equipment flew through the air. Only one soldier was visible, running along the jetty and firing into the water. Then a giant arm swept him into the pool. Peak ducked as a semi-transparent stem whipped over his head. It wasn't a snake and it wasn't a tentacle – it was like nothing he'd ever encountered. The tip of the stem changed shape in mid-flight, assuming the form of a fish, then sprouting a host of thread-like feelers that spiralled through the air. The basin seemed filled with vast animals. Dorsal fins loomed out of the water and collapsed. Misshapen heads appeared, lost their contours and slumped into a featureless mass that splashed into the water.

Peak rubbed his eyes. Was he imagining it, or was the water level sinking? He could hear the drone of machinery. Then it hit him: they were pumping the water out of the well deck. The ballast tanks were emptying. The *Independence*'s stern lifted imperceptibly as the contents of the artificial harbour ran into the sea. The raging tentacles retreated. Suddenly the whole organism disappeared under water. Peak pushed himself up against the wall and his left foot gave way. He was about to hit the deck when two hands grabbed him from behind. 'Lean on me,' said Greywolf.

Peak hung on to the giant's shoulder. He himself wasn't small, but alongside Greywolf he felt scrawny and weak. Greywolf scooped him up and ran along the jetty to the embankment.

'Stop,' gasped Peak. 'You can put me down now.'

Greywolf lowered him gently. They were standing at the mouth of the tunnel that led to the laboratory. From there they overlooked the whole deck. Peak saw the sides of the dolphin tank emerge as the water level fell. The pump was still droning in the background. He thought of the people in the basin who were probably dead, the soldiers, Delaware, Browning . . .

698

Anawak.

He scanned the water. Where was Anawak?

Coughing, Anawak appeared near the embankment. Greywolf rushed over and helped him to the side. They watched as the water continued to sink. An enormous organism came into view, its surface emitting a dull blue glow. In shape, it resembled a slim whale or a stocky sea snake. It seemed to be looking for a way out. It shot round the pool, swimming into every corner, snaking along the walls, looking rapidly and system-atically for an exit that didn't exist.

'Son of a bitch,' spluttered Peak. 'We're going to hang you out to dry.'

'No! We've got to save it!'

That was Rubin. Peak saw him emerge from the tunnel, trembling and hugging his chest.

'Save it?' echoed Anawak.

Hesitantly Rubin took a few steps closer. He kept a watchful eye on the basin, where the creature's laps were becoming ever more frantic. The water was barely two metres deep. The creature expanded its surface area, clearly trying to keep itself submerged.

'We'll never get another chance,' he said. 'Don't you see? We've got to get the chamber cleaned out – lose the crabs, change the water and shovel in the jelly. We'll be able to—'

With a single step Greywolf was upon him, hands round his neck, grip tightening. The biologist's eyes and mouth were wide open. His tongue lolled to the side.

'Jack!' Anawak was tearing at Greywolf's hands. 'Stop it, Jack!'

Peak struggled to his feet. 'Jack, there's no point,' he called out. 'Let go of him.'

Greywolf hoisted Rubin into the air. The man's face was turning blue.

'That's enough, O'Bannon!'

Li strode out of the tunnel, surrounded by a group of soldiers.

'I'll kill him,' Greywolf said calmly.

The commander in chief took a step forward and placed her hand round Greywolf's right wrist. 'No, you won't. I don't care what your grudge is against Rubin. His work is essential.'

'Not any more.'

'O'Bannon! Don't put me in the regrettable position of having to hurt you.'

Greywolf's eyes fixed on Li. He'd evidently decided that she meant what she said because he put Rubin down. The biologist fell to his knees, choking and spitting.

'Licia died because of him,' Greywolf said dully.

Li nodded. Suddenly her expression changed. 'Jack,' she said, almost gently, 'I'm sorry. I promise that she won't have died in vain.'

'People only ever die in vain,' he said wearily. He turned away. 'Where are my dolphins?'

Li marched along the jetty with her men. Why hadn't Peak armed the squad with explosive ammunition from the start? Because no one could have predicted what would happen? Bullshit. It was exactly what she'd predicted – trouble. She hadn't known what form it would take, but she'd known it was coming. She'd expected it long before the scientists had arrived at the Chateau, and she'd prepared herself accordingly.

Only a few puddles remained in the basin. It was a scene of utter devastation. At the bottom of the pool, four metres below the jetty, lay the corpse of the orca, and the motionless bodies of some soldiers sprawled nearby. Three of the dolphins had disappeared. They'd probably left the boat while the sluice was still open.

'What a goddamn mess,' she said.

The shapeless mass at the bottom of the basin was barely moving. It was now white. The last few drops of water lingered around its edges, and the jelly sprouted tendrils that slid over the basin. The thing was dying. For all its unnerving ability to change shape and cast tentacles into the air, there was nothing it could do now. The surface of the mound was already showing signs of dissociation. Li had to remind herself that the stranded colossus wasn't a single organism but a conglomerate of billions of amoebas. Rubin was right; they had to save as much of it as possible. The faster they acted, the more of it would survive.

Anawak joined her without a word. Li continued to scan the wreckage in the pool. Out of the corner of her eye she noticed a movement at the bottom of the basin. She walked to the end of the jetty and climbed down a ladder. Whatever had caught her attention was now hidden from Anawak's view. She made her way past Roscovitz's dangling body, then darted round the mound of jelly and cried out. Anawak came running and almost stumbled over Browning. The technician was staring at them from under the dissolving mass.

'Give me a hand,' said Anawak.

Together they pulled the body from under the creature. The jelly clung stubbornly to its legs, unwilling to let it go. It struck Li that Browning's corpse was unusually heavy and the dead woman's face looked almost varnished. Li bent down to take a closer look.

Browning sat up.

'Shit!'

Li jumped back, and watched as Browning's face twitched. The mouth contorted in a grimace. The technician flung up her arms and fell backwards. Her fingers clawed at the ground. Her legs kicked out, her back arched and she banged her head from side to side.

'But that's impossible – impossible . . .'

Li was tough, but she was filled with horror. She continued to stare at the living corpse. Anawak crouched beside Browning's body. 'Take a look at this, Jude,' he said softly.

She fought back her revulsion and took a step forward.

'See,' he said.

She peered more closely. The shiny coating on Browning's face had begun to dribble away, and in a flash Li realised what it was. Dissociating jelly ran over the technician's shoulders and neck, disappearing into her ears. 'It's inside her,' she whispered.

'The jelly's trying to control her.' Anawak nodded. His face was ashen – a dramatic transformation for an Inuk. 'It's probably spreading through her body and acquainting itself with the structure. But Browning isn't a whale. The residual electricity in her brain is reacting to the jelly's attempt to take charge.' He paused. 'It'll be over in a moment.'

Li said nothing.

'It's trying out all the functions in her brain,' said Anawak, 'but it doesn't know how humans work.' He stood up. 'Browning's dead, General. What you're seeing is the final stage of an experiment gone wrong.'

Heerema, La Palma, Canary Islands

Bohrmann was looking sceptically at the pressure suits in the dive station – two silvery body pods with helmets and in-built dome ports, segmented arms and legs, and manipulators for hands. They were hanging like puppets in a large open steel container, staring fixedly into space. 'I didn't know we were going to the moon,' he said.

'Gair-hard!' Frost laughed. 'You'd be surprised. At four hundred metres below sea level you might as well be. Anyway, you volunteered to come along, so you'd better not start complaining.'

Originally Frost had asked van Maarten to accompany him but, as Bohrmann had pointed out, the Dutchman knew more than anyone else about the *Heerema* and would be needed on board. It was a silent admission that the dive could go wrong.

'Besides,' Bohrmann had added, 'I don't want to have to watch while the two of you mess around down there. You might be excellent divers, but I'm the one who knows about hydrates.'

'That's why we need you here,' Frost had argued. 'You're our resident expert. If anything were to happen to you, we'd be stuck.'

'Hardly. You'd have Erwin, remember? He knows at least as much as I do – probably more.'

Suess had just flown in from Kiel.

'You do realise that this is a deep-sea dive and not a day out at the pool,' said van Maarten. 'Have you dived before?'

'On numerous occasions.'

'I mean, have you ever dived to any *depth*?'

Bohrmann hesitated. 'I went to fifty metres once. Just regular scuba, though. But I'm in great condition. And I'm not stupid.'

Frost thought for a moment. 'Two strong men should do the trick,' he said. 'We'll take an explosive charge and—'

'An explosive charge?' Bohrmann was horrified. 'That's exactly the kind of thing I mean!'

'OK, OK!' Frost held out his hands in surrender. 'I can tell we're going to need your help – you're in. But don't come crying to me when you decide you don't like it.'

Now they were gathered in the starboard-side pontoon, eighteen metres below the ocean's surface. The rest of the pontoon had been flooded, but there was a small compartment that van Maarten had kept dry. It was accessible from the main platform via ladders, and had been used to launch the robot. Before the operation had begun van Maarten had realised that at some point it might be necessary to send down divers to depths of several hundred metres, and with that in mind, he'd ruled out conventional divesuits. He'd ordered the equipment from a firm with a reputation for pioneering dive technology – Nuytco Research in Vancouver.

'They look heavy,' said Bohrmann.

'Ninety kilos each. They're mainly titanium.' Frost ran his hand affectionately over the dome part of one of the helmets. 'Yeah, exosuits are pretty darned heavy – not that you'll notice when you're under water, of course. You can move up and down the water column as often as you please. You've got your own oxygen supply, and you're cocooned in the suit, so there's no risk of nitrogen bubbles forming in your blood, and you don't have the hassle of decompression chambers.'

'They've even got flippers.'

'Not bad, eh? Instead of sinking like a stone, you'll be swimming like a frogman.' Frost pointed to the numerous articulated joints. 'It's built to ensure complete freedom of movement, even at four hundred metres. Your hands are protected inside two pods – no articulated gloves, I'm afraid: the fingers would be too delicate. Instead you've got computer-operated manipulators on the end of each arm. The sensors provide tactile feedback for your hands inside the pods. They're incredibly sensitive – you could write your own will on the seabed if you wanted.'

'How long can we stay down?'

'Forty-eight hours,' said van Maarten. He saw the alarm on Bohrmann's face and grinned. 'Don't worry, you'll be finished long before then.' He pointed to two torpedo-shaped robots, each measuring roughly 1.5 metres. They were equipped with propellers, and their tips were encased in translucent plastic. Several metres of cable were attached to each robot, connecting them to a console with handles, a display and buttons. 'These are your trackhounds. AUVs. They're programmed to find the lighting scaffold, and they're accurate to within a few centimetres, so please don't attempt to find your own way. Just let yourselves be towed. They go at a rate of four knots, so you'll be there in three minutes.'

'How reliable are they?' Bohrmann enquired.

'Very. Trackhounds come equipped with all kinds of sensors that determine their position and their depth in the water. You're certainly not going to get lost, and if anything gets in the way, the trackhound will dodge it. They're activated via the console at the end of the leash. Descent, ascent – easy. The button marked zero starts the propeller without activating the navigational program, so you can steer the trackhound with the joystick instead. Your dog will scamper in whichever direction you choose. Any questions?'

Bohrmann shook his head.

'Let's go, then.'

Van Maarten helped them into the suits. Entry was via a flap in the back, to which two oxygen tanks were mounted. Bohrmann felt like a knight in full armour, about to take a stroll on the moon. As the suit closed, all went silent for a moment, then the volume returned. Through the visor he could see Frost talking to him from inside his own suit, and then the volcanologist's voice boomed into his ears. He could even hear outside noise.

'Wireless communication,' explained Frost. 'It's more reliable than hand signals. Are you getting the hang of the manipulators?'

Bohrmann wiggled his fingers inside the pod. The manipulator copied his movements. 'I think so.'

'Van Maarten's going to give you the console. Try to get hold of it.'

It worked the first time. Bohrmann gave a sigh of relief. If everything was as easy as operating the manipulators, they would be fine.

'One more thing. If you look down at your suit, there's a raised rectangular panel. It's at waist level – like a flat switch. It's a POD.'

'A what?'

'Nothing you need worry about now. It's just a precaution. If we need them, I'll explain what they're for. To turn it on, you push it firmly. OK?'

'What is it?'

'A good thing to have when you're diving.'

'I'd really rather—'

'I'll tell you later. All set?'

'All set.'

Van Maarten opened the hatch to the sluice tunnel. Lit up in the artificial light, the bright blue water sloshed towards them. 'Just topple in,' he said. 'I'll send the trackhounds after you. Don't switch them on until you're out of the tunnel. Stan, I'd suggest you start yours first.'

Bohrmann shuffled his flippers towards the edge. Even the tiniest movement was an amazing feat of strength. He took a deep breath and allowed himself to fall forwards. The water rose up towards him and he saw the artificial lights of the tunnel flash above him, then found himself upright. He sank slowly through the tunnel and out into the sea, landing in a shoal of fish. Thousands of shimmering bodies dispersed, regrouping in a tightly packed spiral. The shoal changed shape a few times, strung out in a line, and fled. Bohrmann saw the trackhound beside him and sank deeper. Above him the tunnel glowed against the dark contours of the pontoon. He kicked his fins and realised he could hover on the spot. The divesuit felt good now, like wearing his own submersible.

Frost followed him in a column of bubbles, then sank until he was on a level with Bohrmann and looked at him through the view port. Bohrmann saw that the American was still wearing his cap.

'How are you feeling?' asked Frost.

'Like R2–D2's older brother.'

Frost laughed. The propeller on his trackhound started to turn. Suddenly the robot dipped its nose and pulled the volcanologist into the depths. Bohrmann activated his own. He felt a sharp jerk, then shot off head-first. The water darkened. Van Maarten was right: these things were fast. In no time it was pitch black. It was impossible to see anything apart from the diffuse rays of light emitted by the trackhounds.

To his surprise he felt uneasy in the darkness. He'd sat in front of the screen hundreds of times, watching robots dive to the abyssal plains or even as far as the benthic zone. He'd been down to a depth of four thousand metres in the legendary submersible *Alvin*, yet nothing had prepared him for being encased in a suit and whisked into the unknown by an electronic guide-dog.

Hopefully the thing he was clutching had been properly programmed or there was no telling where he was headed.

Showers of plankton appeared in the glow of the floodlights and the electronic hum of the trackhounds buzzed inside Bohrmann's helmet. Ahead he saw a delicate creature drifting through the night with elegant pulsing movements, a deep-sea jellyfish sending out ring-shaped signals of light like a spaceship. Bohrmann hoped they weren't being emitted in panic as it fled from some predator. Then the jellyfish disappeared. More jellyfish luminesced in the distance, and a bright cloud flashed before his eyes. He couldn't help flinching. But the cloud was white, not blue. Its source luminesced briefly before it disappeared within its own mist. Bohrmann knew what it was: a *mastigoteuthid*, or whiplash squid, a creature usually only found at depths of around a thousand metres. It made sense for it to expel white ink when threatened – in the darkness of the depths, black would be useless.

The dog strained at its leash.

Bohrmann scanned the water for a glimpse of the lighting scaffold, but he was surrounded by darkness, with just a faint dot of light moving in front of Frost. At least, he assumed it was moving. It might as well have been stationary: two fixed points of lights, his beam and Frost's, in a starless universe.

'Stanley?'

'What's up?'

The promptness of the answer soothed him.

'It's about time we saw something, isn't it?'

'You've got to be patient, buddy. Look at the display. We've only gone two hundred metres.'

'Oh. Of course. No problem.'

Bohrmann didn't dare ask Frost whether he was sure that the track-hounds had been properly programmed, so he kept quiet and tried to stifle his mounting anxiety. He almost wished a few more jellyfish would show themselves, but there was nothing to be seen. The robot hummed busily. All of a sudden Bohrmann felt a change of direction.

There was something ahead. Bohrmann screwed up his eyes and made out a distant glow. At first it was just a faint patch of light, then a hazy rectangle.

He could barely contain his relief. Good dog, he felt like saying. There's a good boy.

How small the lighting scaffold looked.

He was still puzzling over its size as the distance decreased and the glow brightened, separating into individual floodlights along the unit's frame. They continued towards it, and suddenly it was above them, a canopy of light overhead. Of course, they were above and it was below, but the head-first dive had turned everything upside-down. Next the terrace appeared, and it, too, was suspended in the sky. For a moment Frost became visible, a shadow being pulled by a torpedo on a leash, rushing towards a football field of light. Now the view opened up before them: the terrace, the snake-like body of the tube towering out of the darkness, the lumps of rock blocking its mouth . . .

And the writhing mass of worms.

'Turn off your trackhound before you crash into those lights,' said Frost. 'We can swim the last few metres.'

Bohrmann flexed the fingers of his free hand and tried to get the manipulator to hit the right button. The first attempt failed, and he sped past Frost, who'd slowed down.

'Gair-hard? Where do you think you're going?'

He tried again. The manipulator slipped. Finally he succeeded, kicked his fins a few times and realigned himself on the horizontal. The scaffold was very close, stretching out seemingly endlessly in all directions. After a few seconds Bohrmann recovered his sense of up and down, and the scaffold and the terrace were beneath him.

Kicking evenly, he swam to the wedged tube and sank alongside it. The scaffold was now fifteen metres above his head. Within an instant the worms were swarming over his fins. He had to force himself to ignore them. They didn't stand a chance against the suit. They were revolting, of course, but no more. Worms could never pose a danger to a creature of his size.

Or could they? After all, these worms weren't even meant to exist.

The trackhound had sunk on to the terrace alongside him. Bohrmann parked it on a ledge of rock and looked up at the tube. Man-sized chunks of black lava blocked the propellers – nothing they couldn't handle, though. More worrying was the larger splinter of lava that was squashing the tube against the side. It looked at least four metres high. Bohrmann doubted that he and Frost would be able to shift it, even though things weighed less under water and lava was porous and relatively light.

Frost joined him. 'Disgusting,' he said. 'Those sons of Lucifer are everywhere.'

'What's everywhere?'

'Worms of course! I suggest we deal with the smaller chunks first and see how far we get. Van Maarten?' he called.

'Over.' There was a tinny quality to the man's voice. Bohrmann had forgotten that they could communicate with him, too.

'We're going to tidy up a bit down here. We'll start by clearing the propellers. If we're lucky, the tube might be able to work its own way free.'

'OK. Are you all right, Dr Bohrmann?'

'Never been better.'

Frost pointed to an almost spherical chunk of lava that was blocking the swivel joint of one of the propellers. 'We'll start with that.'

They got to work, and after a good deal of pushing and shoving, the rock came unstuck, freeing the propeller and squashing hundreds of worms.

'OK,' said Frost.

They moved two more boulders, but the next was larger. After a concerted effort they tipped it to one side.

'See how strong we are down here,' said Frost, enthusiastically. 'OK, Jan,' he said to van Maarten, 'we've only got one propeller to go. They don't look damaged. Can you rotate them? Don't turn them on, just rotate them.'

After a few seconds, the tube started to purr. One of the turbines was rotating on its shaft. Then the others began to turn.

'Good,' shouted Frost. 'Now try to switch them on.'

Having retreated to a safe distance away from the tube, they watched the propellers start up.

The tube juddered.

'No go,' said van Maarten.

'I can see that.' Frost scowled. 'Turn them the other way.'

That didn't work either, and silt was being churned up, making the water murkier by the second.

'Stop!' Bohrmann waved his segmented arms about. 'Hey guys, that's enough now! There's no point. You're only getting mud in our eyes.'

The propellers slowed to a halt. The cloud of silt dispersed, leaving muddy streaks in the water. They could barely make out the mouth of the tube.

'Great.' Frost opened a flat box on the side of his exosuit and took out two pencil-sized objects. 'That huge chunk of rock is what's causing the problems. I know you're not going to like this, Gair-hard, but we're going to have to blow the damn thing up.'

Bohrmann's gaze shifted to the worms. They were rapidly reclaiming the freshly vacuumed terrace. 'It's a big risk,' he said.

'We'll use a small charge. We'll place it at the bottom of the rock, where the tip's digging into the terrace – blast its legs off, so to speak.'

Bohrmann pushed off, floating a metre or so upwards, then heading for the rock. It got muddier and murkier as he approached. He switched on his head torch and sank into the cloud of sediment. He lowered himself carefully, dropped on to his knees and man-oeuvred his helmet as close as possible to the place where the rock was embedded in the ground. He used his two manipulators to sweep away the worms. Some lunged at him and tried to bite the articulated limbs. Bohrmann shook them away and examined the sediment. He found thin veins of dirty white hydrate. When he poked at them with the manipulators, the surrounding lava splintered and tiny bubbles spun towards him.

'No,' he said. 'Bad idea.'

'Do you have a better one?'

'Yes. We'll use more of the explosive, look for dents or cracks in the lower third of the boulder, and blow it up from there. With a bit of luck the top will fall off and we won't disturb the terrace beneath it.'

'OK.'

Frost swam through the cloud towards him. They rose up a little, and visibility improved. Working systematically, they searched the rock for suitable spots. Eventually Frost found a deep groove in the lava and filled it with something that looked like firm grey Plasticine. He poked a pencil-thin cylinder inside it.

'That should do the trick,' he said. 'Expect some flying debris. Let's get out of the way.'

They started up their trackhounds and hitched a ride to the edge of the illuminated zone where, after a few metres, the terrace ended in darkness. The shower of particles wasn't too bad there, so the light waves weren't being deflected by algae or other floating matter, yet the transition into darkness was abrupt. Light disappeared under water in a sequence determined by its wavelength – first red, after two or three metres, orange, then yellow. After ten metres only green and blue were left, until they, too, were absorbed or scattered as the water swallowed any vestige of light. After that the world ceased to exist.

Bohrmann was reluctant to venture from the relative safety of the illuminated zone into nothingness. He noticed with relief that Frost didn't appear to think that they needed to retreat any further. At the edge of the gloom, where the blue gave way to inky black, he could see what appeared to be a crevice in the flank. Maybe it was a cave. He imagined how the stone had tumbled into the depths in a stream of red hot lava, slowly cooling and setting in curious shapes. Suddenly he felt cold inside his suit – cold at the thought of spending a lifetime in the depths.

He looked up towards the lighting scaffold. There was nothing to be seen apart from a blue aura around the white floodlights.

'OK,' said Frost. 'Let's get this done with.' He activated the fuse.

A torrent of bubbles poured forth from the rock, mixed with splinters and lava dust. There was a rumbling noise inside Bohrmann's helmet. A dark ring spread outwards, followed by more bubbles, as the debris dispersed in all directions.

He held his breath.

Slowly, very slowly, the top half of the rock began to topple.

'Yes!' shouted Frost. 'Thank you, God!'

The rock was tipping faster now, pulled over by its own weight. It broke half-way down, dropping on to the terrace next to the pipe and creating another, larger cloud of sediment. Despite his body armour, Frost managed to jump up and down and waggle his arms. He looked like Neil Armstrong taking a giant leap for America on the surface of the moon.

'Hallelujah! Hey, van Maarten! We knocked the damn thing down. Give the tube another try!'

Bohrmann hoped with all his heart that the explosion wouldn't result in any more landslides. Through the swirling sediment he heard the propellers start up, and suddenly the tube moved. It crinkled up, then its far end rose like the head of a gigantic worm, lifting slowly out of the cloud. The mouth swivelled round, pointing straight at them, then turned in the other direction, as though it were surveying its surroundings. If Bohrmann hadn't known better, he would have thought they were done for.

'It's working!' yelled Frost.

'You guys are the best,' van Maarten said drily.

'Tell me something I don't know,' agreed Frost. 'Now switch it off before it eats us. We'll check out the site again, and then we're coming up.'

The tube lifted a little, then its mouth drooped and it dangled lifelessly amid the light. Bohrmann set off. He glanced over at the scaffold, then back again. Something didn't look right, but he couldn't put his finger on it.

'A shady business,' said Frost, jerking his head towards the gloomy cloud. 'Go ahead, Gair-hard. You'll be able to make more sense of it than I can.'

Bohrmann switched on his trackhound's floodlight. Then he thought better of it and switched it off.

Was he seeing things?

He glanced at the scaffold again. This time his eyes lingered. It seemed that the floodlights were more powerful than before, but that was impossible: they'd been on full beam throughout the operation.

But the glow wasn't coming from the floodlights. It was coming from the blue aura. It was getting bigger.

'Do you see that?' Bohrmann jerked his arm towards the scaffold. Frost's eyes followed the movement.

'I can't see— My God.'

'The light,' said Bohrmann. 'The blue glow.'

'By Ariel and Uriel,' whispered Frost, 'you're right. It's spreading.'

A blue-violet halo had formed round the scaffold. Distances were hard to judge under water, particularly since the refractive-index made everything look a quarter closer and a third larger than it was – but the source of the blue glow was clearly a good deal further away than the lighting unit. Although the glare of the halogen lamps was shining into his eyes, Bohrmann was almost certain he'd seen flashes. Then the blue paled, the light faded and went out.

'I don't like the look of this,' said Bohrmann. 'We should go back.'

Frost didn't answer. He was still staring at the scaffold.

'Stan? Are you listening to me? We should—'

'Don't do anything hasty,' Frost said slowly. 'We've got company.'

He pointed to the top of the scaffold. Two long shadows were patrolling the length of the frame. Blue bellies flashed in the light. Then they were gone.

'What was that?'

'Don't panic, kiddo. Turn on your POD.'

Bohrmann pressed the panel at the front of his exosuit.

'I didn't want to alarm you,' said Frost. 'I thought if I told you what they're for, you might get nervous and keep looking around for—'

Two torpedo-shaped bodies shot out from behind the scaffold. Bohrmann saw a pair of oddly formed heads. The creatures were coming straight for them, travelling at tremendous speed, teeth grinning in their open jaws. Fear clutched his heart. Bohrmann pushed off from the terrace, moving backwards and shielding his helmet with his hands. None of the movements made sense, but his civilised, scientific mind had yielded to primeval instinct. He cried out.

'They can't hurt you,' Frost said firmly.

The creatures were almost upon him when they banked. Bohrmann gasped for air and tried to fight back his panic. Frost swam to his side. 'We tested the PODs in advance, you know,' he said, 'and they definitely work.'

'What the hell is a POD?'

'A Protective Ocean Device. The best shark deterrent there is. It emits an electromagnetic field that acts as a barrier and keeps the sharks at a distance of five metres.'

Bohrmann tried to recover from the shock. The creatures had swum in a wide arc round the back of the scaffold. 'They were closer than five metres,' he said.

'They'll have learned their lesson now. Sharks have highly sensitive electro-receptive organs. The electromagnetic field overstimulates their sensors and interferes with their nervous system. It causes them unbearable muscle spasms. During the trial run, we used bait to attract white and tiger sharks, then activated the POD. They couldn't get through the field.'

'Dr Bohrmann? Stanley?' That was van Maarten's voice. 'Are you OK?'

'Everything's fine,' said Frost.

'Well, POD or no POD, it's time for you to leave,' said van Maarten.

Bohrmann's eyes scanned the scaffold. He'd known much of what Frost had told him. Distributed around the front of a shark's head were ampullae of Lorenzini, small canals that detected even the weakest electrical pulses, such as those produced by other living creatures. What he hadn't realised was that a POD could sabotage the sensors. 'Those were hammerheads,' he said.

'Great hammerheads. About four metres long, I'd say.'

'Shit.'

'PODs work especially well on them.' Frost chuckled. 'with their rectangular heads, they've got more ampullae than any other species.'

'What now?'

He saw a movement. Out of the darkness behind the scaffold the two sharks came back into view. Bohrmann stayed still. He watched the sharks attack. Without swinging their heads as sharks usually do when they are tracking a scent, they shot purposefully through the water and stopped suddenly as if they'd hit a wall. They turned in confusion and swam away, then came back and circled the divers, but at a respectful distance.

It worked.

Their body shape was like that of any other shark. It was the head that had given the species its name. It extended on each side in flat wings, with the eyes and nostrils at the far ends. The front edge of the hammer was as smooth and straight as a blade.

Slowly Bohrmann composed himself. The creatures wouldn't even be able to harm them through their suits. But he was keen to get out of there.

'How long will it take us to get back?' he asked.

'Same as it took to get down. We'll swim past the scaffold, activate the hounds, and hold tight for the ride.'

'OK.'

'Don't activate anything until we get there. I don't want to see you on a collision course with the floodlights again.'

'How long will the deterrent last?'

'The PODs have at least four hours' worth of battery.' Frost rose through the water, kicking evenly with his fins, holding the console of the trackhound in his right-hand manipulator. Bohrmann followed.

'Well, so long, guys,' said Frost. 'It's too bad we've got to leave.'

The sharks gave chase, but their mouths started to twitch and their bodies contorted. Frost laughed and carried on paddling towards the lighting unit. Against the backdrop of the vast, glowing scaffold, his silhouette looked small and blue-tinged, its contours illuminated.

Bohrmann thought of the blue cloud that had appeared in the distance. In the shock of the moment he'd forgotten that it had appeared immediately before the sharks had arrived. The same phenomenon had been responsible for the change in the whales and probably for a string of other anomalies and catastrophes. It meant they weren't dealing with ordinary sharks.

Why had the sharks been there in the first place? They had excellent hearing. Maybe the explosion had attracted them. But why were they on the attack? Neither he nor Frost was giving off a scent. They bore no resemblance to prey. In any case, sharks didn't usually attack humans in the depths.

They were approaching the uppermost edge of the scaffold.

'Stan? There's something wrong with them.'

'They won't hurt you.'

'I'm telling you, they're not normal.'

One of the sharks turned its broad flat head and swam off to the side.

'You may have a point,' mused Frost. 'It's the depth that bothers me.

Great hammerheads have never been known to go deeper than eighty metres. It makes you wonder what they're—'

The shark turned. For a moment it stopped, head raised slightly and back arched, the classic attack position. Sweeping its tail powerfully it raced towards Frost. The volcanologist was so surprised that he didn't try to fend it off. The shark reared up briefly and violently, then swam into the electromagnetic field and rammed Frost with its flank. Frost twirled like a spinning top, arms and legs splayed.

'Hey!' The console slipped away from his articulated grasper. 'What in God's name—'

A third body shot over the scaffold, appearing from nowhere. It sped over the line of floodlights with eerie elegance. A tall, dark dorsal fin, and a hammer-shaped head.

'Stan!' screamed Bohrmann.

The latest arrival was enormous, much bigger than the other two. Its hammer lifted upwards as it opened its jaws and grabbed Frost's right arm and tugged.

'Shit!' he yelled. 'You evil bastard, let go of me, you—'

The hammerhead wrenched its huge rectangular head from side to side, using its tail to steady itself. It had to be six or seven metres long. Frost was shaken like a leaf. His suited arm had disappeared up to the shoulder into the shark's gullet. 'Beat it!' he screamed.

'For God's sake, Stan,' yelled van Maarten, 'punch it in the gills. Try to hit its eyes.'

Of course, thought Bohrmann. They're watching us. They can see everything.

Bohrmann had sometimes wondered what it would be like to encounter a shark, be attacked, or see it go for someone else. He was neither particularly brave nor especially fearful. Some would have deemed him an adventurer. He might have described himself as a man who was not afraid to take risks, but who didn't go looking for them. Now, faced with the huge predator, it didn't matter how he or anyone else had judged him in the past.

Bohrmann didn't flee from the shark. He swam towards it.

One of the smaller creatures approached him from the side. Its eyes twitched and its jaws jerked open. It evidently required great effort for it to swim into the electric field. It accelerated and rammed into Bohrmann.

He was thrown to one side and fell through the water towards the scaffold. All he could think about was not letting go of the console. Come what may, he had to hold on to it. Without its homing program, he'd be doomed to swim around blindly in the dark until his oxygen ran out.

Assuming he lasted that long.

A sudden surge of pressure caught him and pushed him downwards. The tail of the big shark thrashed above his head. Bohrmann tried to regain control of his movements, and saw the two smaller sharks swim towards him in formation, jaws snapping. They were so close to the scaffold that their natural colours were illuminated in the blue. Bronze skin stretched over their backs towards their white bellies. Their gums and gullets had the orange-pink glow of freshly filleted salmon. Distinctive triangular daggers lined their upper jaws, with pointed teeth stacked below – five rows like sharpened steel, positioned one after the other, ready to tear into anything that came within their reach.

'G-a-i-r-h-a-r-d!' screamed Frost.

Squinting into the halogen lights, Bohrmann watched Frost raise his free arm and rain blows on the head of the shark. Then, in a single violent shake of its head, the shark ripped the arm from the exosuit and cast it aside. Fat oxygen bubbles escaped from the tear. The jaws opened and snapped shut on Frost's unprotected arm, biting it off at the shoulder joint.

A cloud of blood and bubbles billowed darkly in the water. So much blood. The sweeping motion of the shark's tail dispersed it. There were no words to be heard in Frost's screams, just unarticulated high-pitched sounds, then a gurgle as the seawater shot into his suit and filled it. The screams stopped. The smaller sharks lost interest in Bohrmann. Whatever was controlling their minds couldn't stop their natural instincts coming briefly to the fore. They rushed into the turbulent water and dragged Frost about as they tried to bite through his suit.

Amid the static van Maarten was screaming too.

Bohrmann was paralysed with shock, yet at the same time part of his brain was crystal clear. It was telling him that he shouldn't rely on the creatures to follow their instincts. Their power and hunger were being manipulated. This wasn't about feeding. Temporarily their instincts had got the better of them, but the substance inside their heads was interested in one thing only: killing the human intruders.

He had to get back to the flank.

His left-hand manipulator reached towards the keypad on the console. If he made a mistake, he would activate the homing program and launch himself towards the *Heerema*, which – now that the POD could no longer defend him – would inevitably cost him his life. Somehow he hit the right button. The propeller began to whir, and he manoeuvred the joystick so that the hound was pulling him away from the scaffold and towards the lava flank. He could feel the acceleration. On the way down the robot had seemed speedy and dynamic, but now it trundled along at an interminable crawl.

Bohrmann kicked his fins and glided through the water towards the terrace. There wasn't much he could do in a situation like this, but one of the rules of diving stated that rocks afforded protection. Bohrmann progressed towards the wall of lava. As he reached it, he turned and stared up at the scaffold. Fins and tails thrashed in the dissipating cloud of blood, creating a maelstrom of bubbles. Sections of Frost's suit sank through the water. It was a harrowing sight, but what truly horrified him wasn't the bloodbath; it was that only two of the sharks were involved.

The big shark was missing.

Numbing fear took hold of him. He turned off the propeller and looked around.

The big shark shot out of the cloud of sediment with its mouth wide open. It was coming at him with breathtaking speed. This time Bohrmann's mind shut down. He still hadn't worked out whether or not he should switch on the trackhound when the wedge-shaped head rammed into him, flinging him backwards into the flank. He hit the lava with a dull crunch. The shark swam past, then returned at the speed of a racing car. Bohrmann screamed. Now there was nothing but an abyss of jaws and teeth, as the gaping mouth took his entire left side, from shoulder to hip.

Well, that's that, then, he thought.

The shark shot over the terrace, pushing Bohrmann's body through the water. There were rustling and droning sounds in his headphones. The shark's teeth grated against the titanium shell. Its head swung back and forth, banging Bohrmann's helmet against the lava, and scraping it along the flank. The world was spinning. The titanium alloy was tough enough to withstand the battering for a while longer but inside the suit Bohrmann's head was banging mercilessly from side to side. He couldn't see or hear. His fate was sealed. He was going to be sawn apart and ripped to shreds. His life was worth less than the air in his lungs.

It was the helplessness that enraged him.

He was still breathing, wasn't he?

Then he could fight back!

The straight edge of the hammer stretched out above him. The head's width was equivalent to a quarter of the shark's total length, which meant that he could see only the hammer's edge: no eyes or nostrils. He started to hit it with the console. The shark swam on, heading towards the edge of the light where Bohrmann had waited with Frost for the charge to explode. Once they were in the pitch-black water, he wouldn't even be able to see the shark.

They had to stay in the light.

Bohrmann exploded with rage. Trapped inside the shark's jaws, his left arm jerked up and pounded its palate. It was lucky that the shark had seized his side and not just an arm or a leg – otherwise he would have met Frost's fate. There were no weak points like articulated joints in the metal shell protecting his torso. It was too big and solid, even for the teeth of a predator like this. The shark seemed to realise that too. It shook its head more vigorously, until Bohrmann was on the verge of blacking out. He'd probably broken several ribs already, but the more the shark shook him, the angrier he became. He bent his right arm, reaching up towards the end of the hammer, and smashed the console against it—

Suddenly he was free.

The shark had spat him out. He'd evidently hit a delicate spot like an eye or a nostril. The enormous creature raced upwards through the water, passing close to him and sending him flying back into the rock. For a moment it looked as though it was turning tail. Bohrmann tried feverishly to think of a way to use the situation to his advantage. He had no illusions about what would happen if he tried to reach the *Heerema*. He'd temporarily got rid of the shark, but he had only a few more seconds. Hastily he pulled the trackhound towards him and threw his arms round its slender form

Under no circumstances was he going to let it go.

The shark disappeared into the darkness and reappeared a little further on, a blue shadow in the water.

Bohrmann glanced frantically at the flank.

He was back at the crevice!

Some distance away from him the powerful body of the hammerhead was cruising through the open water. Bohrmann pulled himself towards the crack. He could see the other two sharks fighting over Frost's remains beneath the scaffold. They were moving down through the water, out of the illuminated zone. Bohrmann wondered how long it would be before they finished with the mangled body and turned on him. Then he stopped wondering anything. In the twilight of the ocean the big shark banked at incredible speed and came towards him.

Bohrmann pushed himself inside the crack.

There wasn't much room. The exosuit and the oxygen tanks on his back got in the way, and he struggled to shove himself in. Arms clamped to his sides, he tried to push himself deeper into the crevice, but the shark was upon him.

The cartilage of the hammer hurtled into the rock and the giant fish flew backwards. Its head was too big for it to enter. It arced round so tightly that it seemed to be chasing its tail. It tried again.

Chunks of lava dislodged themselves in a cloud of sediment from the surrounding rock. Bohrmann squeezed his arms closer to his body. He had no idea how far back the crevice extended. The shark was rampaging, attacking the rock, sending sediment and splinters into the water. Inside, Bohrmann was enveloped in fog. The blue light of the scaffold disappeared.

'Dr Bohrmann?'

Van Maarten. His voice was faint.

'Bohrmann, for God's sake! Bohrmann, say something!'

'I'm here.'

Van Maarten made a noise that might have been a sigh of relief. Bohrmann could barely hear him amid the din the shark was creating. Noises sounded completely different in the water, like a dull, hollow racket of overlapping vibrations. The attack ended abruptly. He was stuck in the crack, blinded by the black cloud of mud. He could only guess where the scaffold might be.

'I'm in a crack in the flank,' he said.

'We'll send some robots down for you,' said van Maarten, 'and two men. We've got more suits.'

'Forget it. The PODs don't work.'

'I know. We saw what happened to—' Van Maarten's voice failed him.

'We'll send the men right away. They've got harpoon guns with explosive charges and—'

'Harpoon guns? Now, there's a thing,' Bohrmann said caustically.

'Frost was convinced you wouldn't need them.'

'Evidently.'

Something rammed Bohrmann in the chest, pushing him deeper into the crevice. He was so surprised that he forgot to scream. In the dim light he saw the hammer. It had hit him vertically. The shark was trying to enter the crack on its side.

Why you clever little thing, he thought grimly. His heart was in his throat. I'm going to make you pay.

He rained blows on the hammer, careful not to let go of the hound. He could vaguely see its jaws opening and closing. The rectangular head was beating up and down, but Bohrmann was out of reach of its jaws. Its eye was rolling. Bohrmann raised one of the manipulators and let the console slam down on top of it.

The shark flinched.

It's not going to be able to get itself out of here, Bohrmann realised. He channelled his strength into pressing the trackhound against the shark's skull. Surely the creature couldn't be jammed. How much power did the jelly have over it? It was obviously controlling its behaviour, but could it teach it to swim backwards?

Evidently it could. The hammer withdrew from the crack.

Bohrmann waited.

Something shot out of the cloud. A hammer came at him horizontally. One of the smaller sharks. Its head crashed into the domed visor of his helmet. Its jaws opened. Rows of teeth scraped against the Plexiglas. The shark's body obscured the light to such an extent that Bohrmann could barely see, but what he could see was enough. He tried to push himself further inside the crack and suddenly the walls of the crevice seemed to give way. He toppled backwards into nothing.

Pitch blackness.

The left manipulator moved erratically over the console. The switch for the trackhound's floodlight was just above the homing button. He'd had it a moment ago . . .

There!

The floodlight lit up. The wandering shaft of light revealed that the back of the crevice had widened into a spacious cave. He shone the beam at the opening and saw the head of the shark. The hammer was shaking back and forth but the shark didn't advance.

It was stuck.

Bohrman raised his arm and showered blows on the box-like head. The shark had to be at least half-way into the cave. Suddenly he realised that it wasn't a good idea to wound the shark enough to make it bleed. Instead he used all his weight to push against it, but in the water it wasn't nearly enough. He pushed off and hurled himself against the twitching head, banging into it with his chest, shoulders and arms until the shark gradually retreated. The beam from the trackhound wandered all over the place, illuminating the pink gullet and flapping gills.

I don't care *how* you get out of here, thought Bohrmann. But I want you out now. This is my cave, so piss off!

'Piss off!'

'Dr Bohrmann?'

The shark disappeared.

Bohrmann slumped down. His arms trembled. Suddenly he felt overwhelmed with exhaustion and sank to his knees.

'Dr Bohrmann?'

'I don't need you bugging me, van Maarten.' He coughed. 'Do something to get me out of here.'

'We'll send down the robots and the men right away.'

'Why robots?'

'We're sending down anything that might scare the sharks or distract them.'

'They're not sharks. They only look like sharks. They can recognise a robot – and they know exactly what we're trying to do.'

'The sharks know?'

Frost evidently hadn't told van Maarten the whole story.

'That's right. They're no more sharks than the whales are whales. Something's controlling them. The men should be on their guard.' He had to cough again, this time more loudly. 'I can't see a bloody thing in this cave. What's going on out there?'

For a moment van Maarten was silent. Then he said, 'Oh, God . . .'

'Talk to me!'

'There's more of them – dozens, hundreds! They're smashing up the floodlights.'

Of course they are, thought Bohrmann. That's the whole point.

They're trying to stop us cleaning up the worms. That's what this is about.

'Then forget it.'

'I'm sorry?'

'I said forget the rescue operation, van Maarten.'

There was so much noise inside Bohrmann's helmet that he had to get van Maarten to repeat his answer a second time: 'But the men are ready.'

'Tell them that intelligent predators are lying in wait for them. The sharks are intelligent. The stuff in their heads is intelligent. You're not going to achieve anything with two divers and a decoy. Think of something else. Like you said, I've got enough oxygen for two days.'

Van Maarten hesitated. 'OK. We'll keep an eye on things. Maybe the sharks will disperse in the next few hours. Do you think you're safe for the moment?'

'How the hell do I know? I'm safe from ordinary sharks, but these guys are unbelievably resourceful.'

'We're going to find a way, Gerhard. We'll have you out of there *before* your oxygen runs out.'

'I sincerely hope so.'

Light was returning gradually to the crack, but if what van Maarten was saying was true, the lamps were about to go out.

He'd be alone in the darkness of the ocean, alone until someone declared themselves ready to brave hundreds of hammerhead sharks.

No shark in possession of its natural instincts would have swum into an electromagnetic field. A hammerhead shark would never attack two humans in exosuits, and even if it did, it would quickly lose interest. Hammerheads were known to pose a threat to humans and to be infuriatingly inquisitive, but they usually gave anything suspicious-looking a very wide berth.

They didn't normally swim inside crevices.

Bohrmann cowered inside the cave, equipped with enough oxygen for another forty or so hours. He hoped there wouldn't be a bloodbath when van Maarten's men came down. *If* they came down.

A bloodbath in the lightless water.

He switched off the floodlight on his trackhound to conserve its battery. He was immediately engulfed in inky black. Light shone through the crack. It was getting fainter all the time.

Johanson couldn't settle. He'd been down on the well deck where Li's men were preparing for the jelly to be transferred to the deep-sea chamber under Rubin's supervision. The tank had been emptied and decontaminated, and the *Pfiesteria*-laden crabs deposited in liquid nitrogen. The whole process was being conducted under the most stringent safety precautions. Johanson and Oliviera were planning to start the phase tests as soon as the jelly was in the tank. In the meantime, while they'd been exchanging notes and laying down the procedure, Crowe and Shankar had begun to decipher the second Scratch message.

'The shock is still with us,' Li had said, in her improvised speech. 'Every one of us has been deeply affected by what happened. Our enemy is trying to demoralise and destroy us – but we mustn't give in. I'm sure you're all asking yourselves whether this vessel is safe. Let me assure you, *it is*. Providing we don't give our enemy any further opportunities to come aboard, we've got nothing to fear on the *Independence*. All the same, speed is of the essence. It's more important than ever that we focus our energies on forcing a dialogue. We need to convince our enemy to put a stop to its campaign of terror against the human race.'

Johanson went up to the flight deck, where the kitchen staff were clearing away the remnants of the abandoned party. The sun had risen again, and the sea looked no different from usual: no blue glow, no flashes, no luminescent vision presaging a nightmare.

He walked back to where he'd been standing before Li had presented him with a glass of red wine and tried to pump him for information about his night-time escapade. Two things had been clear to him: first, that Li knew what had happened to him; and second, that she wasn't sure how much he could remember and whether he was telling her the truth – which worried her.

She'd lied to him. He hadn't fallen over.

If Oliviera hadn't mentioned that he'd seen Rubin walk through a door in the hangar deck, nothing would have come back to him, and he would have swallowed Dr Angeli and the others' explanation. But Oliviera's comment had triggered something in his mind. His brain was reprogramming itself. Enigmatic images appeared and faded. As he stared at the uniform seascape of waves, his gaze turned inwards. Suddenly he was back on the crate, chatting to Oliviera, glass in hand. Rubin stepped through a door in the hangar-deck wall. A door . . . It appeared in the distance, and yet in another picture he seemed to be standing right in front of it — proof to Johanson that the mysterious passageway existed.

But what had happened next?

They'd gone down to the lab. Then he'd returned to the hangar deck alone. Why? Was it something to do with the door?

Or was he imagining it all?

You could be getting old and crazy without even knowing it, he thought to himself. That would be embarrassing.

While he was still puzzling over it, Fate took pity on him and sent Weaver to him. Johanson was pleased to see her walking over the deck. They hadn't spent much time together lately. At first he'd seen her as his confidante, but he'd soon come to appreciate that she wasn't a replacement for Lund. They got on well, but it hadn't gone any deeper than that, neither in the Chateau nor on the boat. Maybe he had hoped that, through her, he could make up for everything that had happened to Lund. In the meantime things had changed. Now Johanson was by no means certain that he needed to make up for anything, and still less whether he'd share the intimacy with Weaver that he had with Lund. He had the impression that something might happen between her and Anawak, and they were much better suited . . .

But there was trust. If he put his trust in Weaver, he would surely be rewarded. She was much too down-to-earth to want to romanticise inexplicable events. She'd listen to him and tell him if she believed him or if she thought he was mad.

He gave her a succinct account of everything he could remember, including all the things that didn't make sense or that made him doubt himself, and how he'd felt when Li had given him the third degree.

After a thoughtful pause Weaver asked; 'Have you been down to look?'

'I haven't had a chance.'

'You must have had plenty. You're just scared in case there's nothing there.'

'You're probably right.'

She nodded. 'Let's take a look together.'

Weaver had surmised correctly. He did feel scared and unsure of himself — more so with every step that took them closer to the hangar deck. What if there was nothing? By now he felt almost certain that they wouldn't find a door, and then he'd have to get used to the idea that he might be delusional. He was fifty-six, he was good-looking, and people seemed to find him intelligent, attractive and charming. There was never any shortage of women.

It was just as he'd feared. They paced up and down along the bulkhead, and there was nothing that resembled a door.

Weaver looked at him.

'I know, I know,' he muttered.

'Don't worry,' she said. And then, to his surprise, she added, 'You can see the wall's riveted together. Look at all these pipes and joints. There must be thousands of ways of building a door into the wall without anyone being able to spot it. You need to remember *precisely* where you saw it.'

'You believe me?'

'I know you pretty well, Sigur. You're not nuts. You don't drink yourself into a coma or take drugs. You appreciate the finer things in life – and that means you see details that other people miss. I'm more of a fish-and-chips girl. I probably wouldn't notice a hidden door if it opened right in front of my face, because it wouldn't occur to me that something like that might exist. I don't know what you saw, but . . . yeah, I believe you.'

Johanson leaned forward impulsively and kissed her cheek. He headed down the ramp towards the laboratory, almost elated.

Lab

Rubin still looked pale, and when he spoke, he sounded like a squawking parrot. He was lucky to be alive. Greywolf had been well on the way to finishing him off. The biologist showed himself to be extremely understanding. He maintained a stiff smile, reminding Johanson for all the world of Nurse Ratched in *One Flew Over the Cuckoo's Nest* after she had narrowly escaped being throttled by Jack Nicholson. Rubin swivelled his whole body ostentatiously whenever he glanced to either side. He was quick to let everyone know about his wretched state of health, and magnanimously announced that he didn't hold a grudge against Greywolf.

'I mean, the two of them were an item, weren't they?' he rasped. 'It must have been dreadful for him. And I was the one who insisted on opening the sluice. Of course, he shouldn't have attacked me, but I understand.'

Oliviera exchanged glances with Johanson and refrained from comment.

Huge lumps of jelly were floating in the tank, beginning to glow again. But what interested the three biologists wasn't so much the jelly as the cloud. The two and a half tonnes of organic matter that Li's men had scooped up from the well deck included large quantities of dissociated jelly. Now big clumps of aggregated matter and countless individual amoebas filled the tank, while a robot flitted among them, armed with an array of sensors that monitored the chemical composition of the water and transmitted the data to the screens on the desk. The skirt of the robot was lined with tubes that, at the push of a button, could be extended into the water, opened, closed and returned to the rosette. The entire contraption was scarcely bigger than the Spherobot. It was robust, yet manoeuvrable.

Johanson sat at the control desk like the captain of a spaceship, waiting with his hands round the joysticks. The lights in the lab had been dimmed as low as possible to allow them to see what was happening. Before their eyes, the jelly was recovering. The lumps of matter were already glowing more intensely, pulsating with currents of blue light.

'This is it,' whispered Oliviera. 'It's about to start aggregating.'

Johanson steered the robot under one of the lumps, opened a test-tube and pushed it into the substance. The edge of the tube was razor-sharp: it sliced into the jelly, collected a sample, sealed itself automatically and retreated to the rosette. The clump changed shape slightly, swathed in blue mist. Johanson waited for a few seconds, then repeated the procedure elsewhere.

Pinpricks of light sparkled inside the jelly. The clump was about the size of a fully grown dolphin. Yes, thought Johanson, as he continued to fill the test-tubes with samples, that would be right: it was exactly the size of a dolphin. Although, actually, it wasn't merely the size of a dolphin: it was the shape of one too.

At that moment Oliviera said, 'Unbelievable – it looks like a dolphin.'

Johanson almost forgot that he was supposed to be steering the robot. He watched, fascinated, as other clumps of jelly changed shape too. Some looked like sharks, others squid.

'How are they doing it?' asked Rubin.

'They must be programmed,' said Johanson. 'It's the only explanation.'

'But how do they know how to do it?'

'They must have learned.'

'How, though?'

'Just think,' said Oliviera. 'If they can copy different shapes and movements, they must be masters of disguise.'

'Oh, I don't know about that.' Johanson sounded sceptical. 'I'm not convinced that what we're seeing is mimicry. I'd say it's more a case of them, uh . . . remembering.'

'Remembering?'

'Well, you know what happens in our brains when we think: specific neurons light up so you get networks and connections. Patterns emerge. Our brains can't change shape, but the neural networks do. If you could read them, you could tell what a person is thinking.'

'So the jelly's thinking of a dolphin?'

'It doesn't look like a dolphin,' objected Rubin.

'Sure it –' Johanson stopped short. Rubin was right. The dolphin shape had gone. Now it was more like a skate, wings beating slowly as it ascended through the water. The tips of the wings grew slender feelers, and it turned into a snake-like creature. The jelly flew apart. Suddenly thousands of tiny fish were flitting through the water in synchrony, then the swarm came together and the jelly morphed again, accelerating through a series of changes as though it were running through a programme. In milliseconds familiar forms gave way to strange shapes. The other clumps of jelly had succumbed to the frenzy as well. They were moving towards each other. Then the familiar flashes of lightning came into play, and for one awful moment Johanson thought he saw a human body among the rapid succession of shapes.

It all streamed together, lumps of jelly and wisps of cloud.

'It's aggregating!' croaked Rubin, eyes gleaming as he stared at the display on the screen. A stream of data flowed across it. 'There's a new substance in the water. A compound!'

Johanson swooped through the imploding universe with the robot, taking samples as he went. It was like a rally. How many could he collect? When should he retreat? The mass seemed to have regained its original strength. A hub formed, then it all collapsed inwards. They'd already observed the phenomenon in miniature, but now it was occurring on a far larger scale. An organism was forming from a host of amoebas. It didn't appear to have eyes, ears or any other sensory organs, or a heart, brain or gut, yet the homogeneous lump was somehow capable of complex processes.

A giant form emerged. At least half of the jelly from the well deck had been pumped back into the sea, but what remained was still the size of a Transit van. Through the oval window of the tank they watched as the jelly clustered and hardened. Johanson whisked the robot to the edge of the activity where blue streams were racing towards the hub. Three of the test-tubes were still empty. He directed them out of the rosette and launched another foray into the mass.

It sprang back at lightning speed, sprouting dozens of tentacles and seizing the intruder. Johanson lost control of the robot. Immobilised, it was trapped in the grip of the creature, which sank towards the bottom of the tank, producing a clumpy foot on which to settle. All of a sudden it looked like an enormous mushroom with a crown of rubbery arms.

'Shit,' whispered Oliviera. 'You were too slow.'

Rubin's fingers sped over his keyboard. 'I've got all kinds of data coming up,' he said. 'A heady molecular mix. The jelly's using a pheromone. So I was right!'

'Anawak was right,' Oliviera corrected him. 'Weaver was right.'

'Of course. What I meant was—'

'We were *all* right.'

'Exactly.'

'Is it anything we've seen before, Mick?' asked Johanson, without taking his eyes off the screen.

Rubin shook his head. 'Pass. The ingredients are familiar enough but I'd have to examine the recipe. We need those samples.'

Johanson watched as a thick stem wound its way out of the creature, producing a bush of tiny feelers at its tip. The stem bent over the robot. Its feelers swept over the gadget and the test-tubes.

It looked like a structured, deliberate investigation.

'Are you seeing what I'm seeing?' Oliviera peered at the screen. 'Is it trying to open the test-tubes?'

'They're pretty well sealed.' Johanson tried to wrest back control of the robot. The tentacles wrapped round it merely tightened.

'It seems to have fallen in love.' He sighed.

The feelers continued their investigation.

'Do you think it can see it?' asked Rubin.

'What with?' Oliviera shook her head. 'It can change shape but it can't grow eyes.'

'Maybe it doesn't need to,' said Johanson. 'Maybe it literally *grasps* its surroundings.'

'So do kids.' Rubin glanced at him doubtfully. 'But they've got brains to store the information. How does this stuff make sense of what it's grasped?'

The creature released the robot. Its feelers and tentacles slumped down and disappeared inside the main body. The organism flattened itself, spreading until the base of the tank was coated with a thin layer of jelly.

'The ostrich approach,' joked Oliviera. 'So it knows about that too.'

'*Arrivederci*,' said Johanson, and guided the robot into the garage.

Combat Information Center

'What are you trying to tell us?' Crowe rested her chin in her hands. As usual, a cigarette was smouldering between the index and middle fingers of her right hand, but this time it had barely been smoked. She didn't have time to puff at it. She and Shankar were struggling to make sense of the message from the yrr.

A message that had been sent with an attack.

Having decoded the first transmission, it didn't take the computer long to get to grips with the second. As with the previous message, the yrr had responded in binary code. It remained to be seen whether the data would form a picture. Until now only one sequence made sense. It was a piece of information that seemed laughably simple, given that it was supposed to have come from an alien system of thought.

It was the description of a molecule. A chemical formula. H_2O.

'Very original,' Shankar said sourly. 'I think we know they live in water.'

But the formula was overlaid with other information. While the computer crunched the data, Crowe realised what the message might mean. 'Perhaps it's a map,' she said.

'How do you mean? A map of the seabed?'

'No. That would imply that they lived on the seabed. Assuming the belligerent little creatures in the lab are part of the alien intelligence, the yrr live in water. The depths are a liquid universe – homogeneous and the same from every angle.'

Shankar thought for a moment. 'Unless, of course, you examine the seawater and look at its make-up – exact levels of minerals, acids, alkalis and so on.'

'And then you see it all looks different.' Crowe nodded. 'The first time they sent us a picture composed of two mathematical solutions. This time it looks more complicated. But if we're right, there'll be limits to the variation. I can't swear to it, but I think they've sent us another picture.'

Joint Intelligence Center

Weaver found Anawak sitting at the computer. Virtual amoebas were spinning over the screen, but it seemed to her that he wasn't really looking at them. 'I'm sorry about what happened to your friend,' she said softly.

'Do you know what's funny?' His voice sounded choked. 'That her death's really affecting me. The last time I cried was when my mother died. My father died, and I just felt terrified because I wasn't even sorry. But Licia? God, it's not like I chased after her or anything. Until I learned to like her, she was just some student who got on my nerves.'

Tentatively Weaver laid her hands on his shoulders. Anawak's fingers reached up to touch them. 'Your program works by the way,' he said.

'So now it's up to the others to get the biology working in the lab.'

'Yes, that's the problem. Meanwhile, it's just a hypothesis.'

They'd equipped the virtual amoebas with DNA that was capable of learning and could constantly mutate. Every single cell was essentially an autonomous computer that continually reprogrammed itself. Each new piece of information changed the structure of the genome. If a certain number of cells underwent a particular experience, the experience changed their genetic structure. If the mutated cells aggregated with other cells, they passed on the information, and the DNA of the other cells changed. It meant that the cells weren't merely learning constantly: whenever they aggregated they updated each other. Any new knowledge acquired by a single amoeba enriched the collective knowledge of the whole.

It was a revolutionary idea. It meant that knowledge could be inherited. They'd discussed it with Johanson, Oliviera and Rubin, but the outcome had left them more bemused than ever. The good news was that the theory had been accepted with enthusiasm.

The bad news was that there was an almighty catch.

Control Room

'What you have to realise,' explained Rubin, 'is that when DNA mutates, its genetic information changes – and that spells trouble for any living creature.'

While the others were still analysing the samples, Rubin had snuck out of the lab, supposedly because his migraine was returning. In reality, he'd disappeared into the hidden control room for a meeting with Li, Peak and Vanderbilt. They were working through the transcripts from the audio surveillance. By now they all knew about the computer program and about Weaver and Anawak's theory – but only Rubin understood the implications.

'Organisms rely on their DNA staying intact,' said Rubin. 'Otherwise they fall sick or produce defective offspring. Exposure to radiation, for instance, causes irreparable damage to DNA, resulting in cancer or birth defects.'

'But how does that fit with evolution?' asked Vanderbilt. 'If humans are descended from apes, our DNA must have changed.'

'Sure, but evolution takes place over a long time. And it selects those organisms whose natural mutation rate makes them best suited to the prevailing conditions. People don't often talk about evolutionary failures, yet nature gets rid of unsuccessful adaptations all the time. That said, there is another option, and that's repair. Take tanning, for instance. Sunlight leads to changes in the cells in the upper layers of our skin, resulting in mutations in the DNA. Our skin starts to tan, and if we're not careful we go red and burn. When that happens, our body sheds the cells that have been destroyed, but those remaining can be repaired. It's repairs like these that allow us to survive. Without them, we'd not only suffer continual mutations in our DNA, but our injuries wouldn't heal and we wouldn't recover from disease.'

'Fine,' said Li. 'But what about single-cell organisms?'

'The same thing applies,' said Rubin. 'If their DNA mutates, it has to be repaired. And remember, organisms like that reproduce by cell division. For a species to remain stable, its DNA has to undergo repair. It doesn't matter what kind of cells we're talking about, nature always endeavours to keep the rate of mutation within manageable limits. And that's the catch for Anawak's theory. The genome is repaired globally, along its entire length. You can picture the repair enzymes as policemen, patrolling the entire DNA strand on the look-out for errors. As soon as they find a defective area, they begin the repair. To ensure that the information corresponding to the DNA's original sequence doesn't get lost, the repair enzymes act as the guardians of the genome's data. They police the sequence and can tell immediately which genetic configurations match the original and which are defective. It's like trying and failing to teach a child to talk. As soon as it learns a new word, the repair enzymes come along and reprogram it to its original state – ignorance. It's not possible for it to learn.'

'Then Anawak's theory is nonsense,' said Li. 'It would only make sense if the amoebas could retain the changes to their DNA.'

'Well, on the one hand, that's right. Any new information would be treated as defective by the repair enzymes and, hey presto, the genome's restored to its original configuration. Back to square one, so to speak.'

'I'm guessing,' grinned Vanderbilt, 'that we're about to hear the but.'

Rubin nodded hesitantly. 'There is one,' he said.

'Which is?'

'I don't know.'

'Hang on,' said Peak. He sat up in his chair and winced. His foot was bandaged. 'I thought you just said—'

'I know! But the theory's brilliant,' cried Rubin. 'It would explain everything. Then we'd be certain that the substance in the tank is our enemy. We'd be face to face with the yrr – the creatures that have landed us in all this shit. And I'm certain that it's them! We saw some pretty weird stuff in the lab this morning. The blob of jelly examined our robot, and you should have seen the way it did it – it had nothing to do with animal instinct or curiosity. It was pure cognitive intelligence. Anawak's theory must be right. Weaver's already got it working electronically.'

'But how are we supposed to make sense of it?' Vanderbilt sighed and mopped his forehead.

'It could be to do with anomalies.' Rubin gestured vaguely. 'Even repair enzymes sometimes make mistakes. Not often, but every ten thousand repairs or so they slip up. They miss a base pair that should have been restored to its original state. It's not much, but it's enough to cause a baby to be born haemophiliac, with a cleft palate or even cancer. We see these anomalies as defects, but they're proof that the repair mechanism doesn't always work.'

Li got up and paced slowly round the room. 'So you believe that the amoebas and the yrr are one and the same. We've found our adversary.'

'With two provisos,' Rubin added. 'First, we have to solve the DNA conundrum, and second, there has to be some kind of queen-yrr. No doubt the collective is highly intelligent, but I reckon the stuff we've got down there is only the executive part of the whole.'

'A queen-yrr? How do you envisage it?'

'Well, the same and yet different. A bit like ants. The queen-ant is an ant, but a special one. She's at the heart of everything. The yrr are swarming organisms, you see – collectives of amoebas. If Anawak's right, they embody an alternative evolutionary path for intelligent life, but something must be guiding them.'

'So if we were to find this queen . . .' Peak began.

'No.' Rubin shook his head. 'There's no point in fooling ourselves. There could be more than one – there could be millions. And if they're smart, they won't come anywhere near us.' He paused. 'But to be queens, they'd necessarily share the same basic principles as the rest of the yrr. They'd aggregate, and they'd have genetic memory. We're in the process of isolating a chemical that the amoebas give off as a signal to start aggregating. Oliviera and Johanson are on the brink of working out its formula. And you can bet that this chemical, this pheromone, will also cause the queens to aggregate with the yrr too. Scent is the key to yrr communication.' Rubin gave a self-satisfied smile. 'And it could be the answer to all our problems.'

'Thank you, Mick.' Vanderbilt inclined his head towards him graciously. 'You're in our good books again – for the time being at least. Even if you did screw up on the well deck.'

'That wasn't my fault.' Rubin sounded offended.

'You're in the CIA, Mick. In my team. And in my team the buck always stops with you. Did we forget to mention that when we hired you?'

'No.'

Vanderbilt shoved his handkerchief clumsily into his trouser pocket.

'I'm glad to hear it. Jude's about to call the President so she'll be able to tell him what a good boy you've been. Thanks for paying us a visit. Now, run along back to work.'

Flag Command Center

Crowe and Shankar didn't look anywhere near as self-assured as they had when they'd decoded the first signal. Team morale was low, which was only due in part to the terrible events on the well deck. It was becoming increasingly obvious that no one understood the yrr's strategy.

'Why send us a message and then attack us?' asked Peak. 'Humans wouldn't do that.'

'You've got to stop thinking in those categories,' said Shankar. 'They're not humans.'

'I'm just trying to understand.'

'Well, you never will, if you keep basing your ideas on human logic,' said Crowe. 'Maybe their first message was a warning. *We know where you are.* That's what their reply comes down to.'

'Maybe it was a diversionary tactic,' suggested Oliviera.

'But what would be the point?' asked Anawak.

'To distract us?'

'From what? From the fact that they were about to light up outside like a Christmas tree?'

'It's not as crazy as it sounds,' said Johanson. 'They certainly achieved one thing. They got us thinking they were interested in dialogue. Sal's right: people wouldn't act like that, and maybe the yrr know it. So they lulled us into a false sense of security, showed themselves in all their glory, and while we were blithely expecting a cosmic revelation, they gave us a kick in the teeth.'

'Maybe sending them a couple of lousy math questions wasn't such a great idea,' said Vanderbilt to Crowe.

Crowe lost her cool. Her eyes flashed. 'Do you have a better suggestion?'

'It's not *my* job to make suggestions,' said Vanderbilt, spoiling for a fight. 'That's your job. Making contact is *your* responsibility.'

'Making contact with whom? You won't accept it's not a plot by rebel mullahs.'

'If all you can achieve with your crappy messages is to give away our location, that's your problem and you're going to have to fix it. You sent the enemy detailed information about the human race. You practically told them to attack.'

'You have to know who you're dealing with before you can negotiate,' Crowe hissed back. 'It's about time you understood that, you moron. I need to know who they are, which is why I'm telling them about us.'

'All this message shit is a dead end—'

'For Christ's sake, we've only just started!'

'Just like your jumped-up SETI hogwash was a dead end too. Only just started? Well, congratulations – how many people are going to die when you *really* get going?'

'Jack,' snapped Li.

'This contact crap is—'

'That's enough! I don't want arguments, I want results. So let's hear from someone who's got something to report.'

'We've got something,' Crowe said sullenly. 'The second message is based around a formula, the chemical formula for water. We'll find out what the rest of it means in due course – if we're allowed to work in peace.'

'We've made a bit of headway too,' Weaver added.

'So've we!' Rubin was in there like a shot. 'We've made a massive leap forwards, thanks to the, uh, assistance of Sigur and Sue.' He coughed. 'Maybe you'd like to explain, Sue?'

'You're too kind,' she muttered. To the others she said, 'We've managed to isolate the chemical that causes the cells to aggregate. It's a pheromone, and we know how it works. Sigur can take the credit for that – he dared to do battle with the monster to get those tissue samples.'

She put a sealed container on the table. It was half full of a watery liquid.

'The yrr scent is in here. We've analysed it and we're able to synthesise it. The formula is surprisingly simple. We're still not a hundred per cent sure exactly how they use it to make contact or who or what initiates the aggregation. But assuming that something's able to trigger it – and, for the sake of argument, I'm going to call that something the queen – there's the question of how it summons millions and billions of free-floating amoebas who don't have eyes or ears. That's what this pheromone is for. Chemicals aren't especially suited for communication under water – the molecules disperse too quickly. But over short distances pheromone signals work brilliantly. And, as far we can tell, the amoebas' pheromonal communication is restricted to this one chemical. There's no language, just a single word: *aggregate*! We're not sure how they keep communicating after they've aggregated. All we can say for certain is that there's some form of information exchange. It's no different from a neural network computer or a human brain. The individual units need messengers working between them. In biology, they're called ligands. If a cell wants to pass information to another cell, it can't just wander over and tell it so it sends a message via the ligands to the other cell. And when the ligands get to the cell, it's like arriving at any civilised house: they come to a door with a bell – scientifically speaking, a receptor. The ligands ring the bell, and the message is carried through a cascade of signals to the centre of the cell, where the information is passed to the genome.'

She paused.

'The amoebas in the tank also seem to communicate using ligands and receptors. Of course, the idea that cells are like houses with doorbells and helpful messengers is a little misleading. Each cell emits not just one but a cloud of molecules, and cells don't just have a single receptor – they've got something in the region of two hundred thousand. That's how they pick up the pheromones and dock on to the collective. That's two hundred thousand doorbells to help them communicate with their neighbouring cells! It's pretty impressive. The process of aggregation takes place like a relay – one cell picks up pheromones from the collective and attaches itself to the neighbouring cells, all the time sending out new pheromones to reach the other cells floating in the water around it, and so it goes on. It progresses from the centre outwards. For the sake of simplicity, let's skip a few stages of the argument and contend that the cells we've been looking at are indeed our formidable enemy, the yrr.'

She pressed her fingertips together.

'What struck us right away was that the cells don't merely have receptors, they have *pairs* of receptors. We racked our brains trying to figure out why, and then we cracked it: it's about ensuring the collective stays healthy. We labelled the receptors according to their function. The *universal* receptor says, I am the yrr. The *special* receptor says, I am a fully functioning healthy yrr-amoeba with intact DNA, worthy of being part of the collective and ready to take part in the pow-wow.'

'But couldn't you achieve that through a single receptor?' asked Shankar, with a frown.

'No. Probably not,' said Oliviera. 'It's actually an ingenious system. According to our model, a yrr-amoeba is rather like a military camp fenced in by a wall. Any soldier approaching from the outside is identified by a universal marker: his uniform. The uniform tells the other soldiers in the camp, I'm one of you. But those of you who've seen your Michael Caine war movies will know that uniforms are sometimes a disguise. Once your camp's been infiltrated by an outsider, your lives are in danger. So if Michael Caine's to be admitted, he has to know the special signal too. He needs the password. How am I doing from a military point of view, Sal?'

Peak gave a nod. 'Absolutely right.'

'Thank goodness for that. So, when the yrr join together, the following occurs: yrr that have already aggregated produce a scent molecule, a pheromone. The pheromone reaches the other cells' universal receptors and initiates the primary connections; I am the yrr. The first part of the identification process has taken place. The second step requires the special receptors to receive the message, I am a healthy yrr. Well, that's all very well, but some yrr-cells aren't fully operational or healthy. In other words, they've got defective DNA. Since our adversary exists in swarms of billions and seems able to evolve continually, it has to weed out any yrr-cells that aren't capable of further development. The trick seems to be that while every amoeba has a universal receptor, only healthy ones capable of development are in possession of the special receptor. Defective cells don't have them. And now comes the really surprising bit, the bit that should make us afraid. Defective yrr don't know the password. They're excluded from the aggregation. But that's not enough. Yrr are amoebas, and like all amoebas they reproduce by cell division. A species that's continually learning and evolving obviously can't allow a second, defective, population to come into being, so it has to act quickly to stop faulty cells reproducing. That's when the pheromone reveals its dual purpose. In the event that a defective yrr is rejected, the pheromone clings to the amoeba's universal receptor and serves as a fast-acting toxin. It induces programmed cell death, a

736

phenomenon otherwise unheard of in single-cell organisms. The faulty yrr-cell dies at once.'

'How can you tell it's dead?' asked Peak.

'Easy. Its metabolism stops. Besides, you can recognise a dead yrr because it stops glowing. For yrr, luminescing is a biochemical necessity. The best-known example of marine bioluminescence is probably the *Aequorea*, a hydromedusa from the South Seas. It glows when it produces a pheromone. A similar process is going on here. Pheromones are released by the yrr, causing them to glow. The flashes of light are a sign of particularly intense biochemical activity within the aggregated cells. When yrr luminesce, they're communicating and thinking. When they die, the light goes out.'

Oliviera looked at the others. 'So here's why we need to be afraid. The yrr use basic means to run a complex system of selection. If a yrr-amoeba is healthy and has a fully functioning pair of receptors, the pheromone triggers aggregation. But if that amoeba lacks a special receptor, the pheromone takes its deadly toll. The point is, a species that works like this has a very different perspective on death. Death in yrr society is vital. It would never occur to the yrr to spare a defective yrr-cell. To them it would seem absurd – stupid, even. It's *imperative* for them to destroy the threat to their own evolution. Whenever the collective is threatened, the yrr respond with the logic of death. It's no good pleading for mercy or expecting compassion. The logic of death doesn't make exceptions, and it's not about brutality. Such thoughts are alien to the yrr and, as such, they'll never understand *why* they should spare us – given that we're a concrete threat.'

'Uh-huh. So their biochemistry imposes a different morality,' said Li.

'Well, I dare say that's very interesting,' interrupted Vanderbilt, 'but what does it matter if they all use Chanel No. 5 or whatever? I mean, what's the point of knowing that? We could all go and aggregate with them. Yeah, that's it, I'll club together with some yrr.'

Crowe gave him a withering look. 'Like they'd let you.'

'Oh, screw you, Crowe.'

'You guys can keep fighting if you like,' said Anawak, 'but Karen and I have an idea about how yrr cognition might work. We've got Sigur, Mick and Sue pulling their hair out over it. Biologically, it's nonsense – but it would answer a whole heap of questions.'

Weaver took over. 'We programmed our virtual amoebas with

electronic DNA, and set it up to keep mutating. In other words, the DNA was learning. All of a sudden we found ourselves back where we'd started – with a functioning neural network computer. We'd originally split our electronic brain into its smallest programmable units and tried to put them back together again as a thinking whole. It didn't work, or at least not until the individual cells were capable of learning. But the only way that a biological cell could learn is through mutations in its DNA, and that's unheard of – but it's exactly what we told our virtual cells to do. We used a scent, like Sue described.'

'The thing is,' Anawak continued, 'we didn't just get our fully function-ing neural network computer back: we had yrr operating within their natural habitat. Our version of the network came with a few added extras – we allowed the cells to move through three-dimensional space. It replicated deep-sea conditions, with pressure, currents, friction and so on. First, we had to answer the question as to how members of a collective are able to recognise each other. The pheromone is only half of the story. The rest involves limiting the size of the collective. And that's where Sue and Sigur's discovery comes into play. They found that yrr amplicons differ from each other in small, hypervariable sections, so, as we said before, the cells would have to change their DNA *after* they came into being. Well, we think that's exactly what happens, and that these hyper-variable sections serve as a code for them to recognise each other and to know which collective they belong to.'

'Yrr-amoebas with the same coding recognise each other, and small collectives can aggregate with larger ones,' said Li.

'That's right.' Weaver nodded. 'So we coded our virtual cells too. Each cell already had basic information about its habitat, but some cells were given additional information that the others didn't have. As you'd expect, the first cells to aggregate were the ones that shared the same coding. Then we tried a different tack, and attempted to join two collectives with non-identical coding. It worked, and the unthinkable happened: the cells not only succeeded in aggregating; they managed to exchange their individual coding and mutually update each other. They programmed themselves to share the same standard code, thereby attaining a new state of knowledge. The two collectives merged into one, which joined with a third, and that, too, gave rise to something new.'

'Next we wanted to examine their learning strategies,' said Anawak. 'Once again we created two collectives, each with different coding. We gave one information about a specific experience – an enemy attack. It's not especially original, I know, but we decided to use a shark. We programmed it to take a big bite out of the collective, then we showed the collective how to dodge it. The second collective wasn't taught the trick, and it got bitten. Then we aggregated the collectives and sent in the shark – the new conglomerate dodged it. The whole mass of cells had learned what to do. Finally, we divided the collective into smaller groups, and all of them knew how to dodge a shark.'

'So the hypervariable sections allow them to learn?' asked Crowe.

'Yes and no,' said Weaver, glancing at her notes. 'It's theoretically possible, but on the computer it takes too long. The mass of jelly that attacked us on the well deck was incredibly quick to respond, and it probably thinks just as swiftly. It's a superconductive organism, an enormous variable brain. It didn't make sense to limit ourselves to small segments of DNA. We programmed the entire strand so it was capable of learning, and that increased the speed of cognition enormously.'

'Leading to what?' asked Li.

'We can only base our conclusions on the few trials that we ran before the meeting, but we've already seen enough to be sure of a few things: yrr-collectives, no matter what their size, think at the speed of the most up-to-date parallel processors. The information held by individual cells is standardised, and new data gets scrutinised. We found some of the collectives weren't able to handle new challenges, but as they aggregated, they learned. Initially, the learning curve was linear, but beyond a certain point, the collective's behaviour couldn't be predicted—'

'Hold on.' Shankar interrupted her. 'Do you mean to say that the program takes on a life of its own?'

'We introduced entirely new situations. The more complex the problem, the more frequently the amoebas aggregated. It didn't take them long to develop strategies that hadn't been programmed. They started to work creatively. They became inquisitive. And they learned exponentially. We only had time to do a few tests, and it's only a computer program, but our electronic yrr learned to assume any given form – to imitate and vary the shapes of other living things. They were able to form feelers that made our fingers seem no more sensitive than cudgels. They examined objects on a nano level. And *every single one* of their experiences was shared with *every single cell*. They solved problems that would leave us stumped.'

For a moment there was silence as the news sank in. It was clear from their faces that they were remembering the scenes on the well deck. In the end Li said, 'Give me an example of a problem.'

Anawak nodded. 'Let's say I'm a yrr-collective. I've managed to infest an entire continental slope with worms that I'd previously bred, packed with bacteria and transported across the seabed. I want them to destroy the hydrates along the length of the slope, but there's one small problem: although the worms and the bacteria are causing a hell of a lot of damage, they can't start the landslide without help.'

'That's right,' said Johanson. 'We still haven't figured that out. The worms and the bacteria take care of the groundwork, but a little something's still missing before the catastrophe can unfold.'

'A little something like, for instance, a small drop in the water level, hence decreased pressure on the hydrates, or maybe an increase in the water temperature near the continental slope – right?'

'Exactly.'

'Let's say one degree Celsius?'

'That would probably do it, but I'd say two to be sure.'

'OK. Well, we did our homework. The Håkon-Mosby mud volcano is situated not far from the Norwegian continental slope at a depth of twelve hundred and fifty metres. Gas, water and sediment are vented from inside the earth to the surface of the seabed. The water around a mud volcano isn't hot, but it's warmer than elsewhere. So what do I do? I aggregate until I'm an enormous yrr-collective. Then I turn myself into a funnel, and since I need to be an extremely long funnel, I limit the width of my walls to several cells across. I need huge quantities of myself – billions and billions of cells – but I extend over several kilometres. My circumference matches that of the volcano's main crater – around five hundred metres. It allows me to draw warm water from the volcano, so I'm like an enormous pipe, transporting the water to the site where the worms and the bacteria have been burrowing away. And then, whoosh, the slope collapses. Incidentally, I can use the same method for warming the water near Greenland and around the poles to melt the icecaps and disable the Gulf Stream.'

'OK, but those are your computerised yrr,' Peak said sceptically. 'What can real yrr do?'

Weaver pursed her lips. 'That and a good deal more, at a guess.'

Weaver's body was feeling the strain as much as her mind. As they left the operations room, she asked Anawak if he felt like a dip in the pool. Her shoulders were one long ridge of pain – even though her body was accustomed to being put through its paces. None of the training she'd subjected herself to had prepared her for this. Maybe that's your problem, she told herself. You should probably take up a sport that isn't a feat of endurance.

Anawak went with her. They stopped off at their cabins to change into swimwear, then set off to the pool together, wrapped in towelling robes. Weaver felt like holding Anawak's hand – in fact, that wasn't all she felt like doing, but she had no idea how people initiated that kind of thing without embarrassing themselves. Before the radical turnaround in her life, she'd taken anyone and everyone who came her way, but love had never entered the equation. Now she felt shy and inhibited. She didn't even know how to flirt. How were they supposed to end up in bed together, when only last night people had died and the whole world was on the brink of disaster?

Why did she have to make it such a big deal?

The *Independence's* swimming-pool looked surprisingly welcoming for a warship. It was the size of a small lake. As her robe slid off her shoulders, she felt Anawak's gaze on her back. Suddenly it occurred to her that it was the first time he'd seen her like that. Her swimsuit had high-cut legs with a low, scooped back and, of course, her tattoo was on display.

She walked self-consciously to the edge, took off and arced elegantly through the air. Arms stretched in front of her, she cut through the water, just below the surface. She heard Anawak swim up behind her. Maybe it would happen here, she thought. Half hoping and half fearing that he would catch up with her, she kicked her legs and sped away.

Coward. Why shouldn't she just do it?

Dive down and make love in the pool.

Bodies uniting in the water . . .

The idea came to her in a flash.

It was laughably simple and more than a little irreverent but, assuming it worked, it was brilliant. It was a peaceful way of persuading the yrr to retreat – or, at least, to reconsider.

Her fingertips brushed against the tiled side. She stood up and wiped the water from her eyes. The idea seemed almost obscene, and with every metre that Anawak swam towards her, she felt less and less certain.

She'd have to sleep on it.

Suddenly he was very close.

She pushed up against the side of the pool, chest heaving, heart pounding, just as it had all those years ago in the icy waters of the Channel.

She felt his hands round her waist. Her lips opened.

A rush of fear.

Say something, she told herself. There must be something you can say. Something, anything—

'Sigur's feeling better.'

The words lurched out like toads and she saw the disappointment in his eyes. He drifted away from her and slicked back his wet hair. 'Yeah.'

How could she have been such an idiot?

'But something else is bothering him. A problem.' She rested her elbows on the side of the pool and pulled herself up. 'Keep it to yourself, though. I don't want him to think I go around telling everyone. I just wanted your opinion.' Sigur's got a problem? *She* was the one with the problem!

'What kind of problem?' asked Anawak.

'He saw something odd. Or, at least, he thinks he did. And from what he said, I believe him. But then it makes you wonder what it means, and . . . Well, it's like this . . .'

Control Room

Li listened as Weaver told Anawak about Johanson's dilemma. She sat perfectly still in front of the monitors. Quite the lovely couple, she thought.

She was less amused by the topic of their chat. Rubin had endangered the entire mission. She could only hope that Johanson wouldn't remember any more of the details that should have been wiped for ever from his brain. But Weaver and Anawak were gossiping about it.

Come on, kids, she thought, why waste your time on rubbish like that? It's just a horror story from Uncle Sigur. You could always hop into bed together. A blind man could see that you want to. But you're too inept to make a move. Li sighed. She had been forced to witness so many clumsy attempts at intimacy since men and women had started serving together in the navy. It was always so obvious. Tedious and vulgar. Sooner or later everyone wanted to jump into bed with each other. Surely they could have come up with something better to do than trying to get inside Johanson's head?

'We're going to have to get used to the idea that Rubin's cover could be blown,' she said to Vanderbilt.

The CIA boss was standing behind her, mug of coffee in hand. They were alone in the room. Peak was on the well deck, trying to chivvy along the clean-up operation and vet the state of the equipment.

'Then what?'

'There'll be an obvious decision to take.'

'We're not ready to do anything of the kind. Rubin's still busy. Besides, it would be nice not to have to.'

'What's wrong, Jack? Don't tell me you've got scruples.'

'Take it easy, honey. This is your damn plan, but it's my responsibility to make certain it works. My scruples won't get in the way. You can depend on that.' He chuckled. 'After all, I've got my reputation to think of.'

Li turned to face him. 'You have?'

Vanderbilt slurped his coffee noisily. 'You know what I like about you, Jude? You're so darned nasty. You make me feel like a nice guy – and that's really saying something.'

Combat Information Center

Crowe and Shankar couldn't make sense of it. The computer screen was covered in labyrinthine images. Parallel lines suddenly diverged, moving outwards, arching into curves, then uniting into one. Large empty spaces of varying sizes yawned between them. A series of similar images made up the Scratch signal. They looked as though they should fit together in one big picture, yet somehow they didn't. The lines didn't match. And, so far, Crowe didn't have a clue as to what they might mean.

'Water is the baseline information,' pondered Shankar, 'and each of the water molecules is coupled with ancillary data. But what could they be describing? Something to do with water?'

'Such as?'

'Temperature.'

'I guess, or salinity.'

'Or it might have nothing to do with physical or chemical properties. The data might be describing the yrr. The lines could be population densities.'

'You mean they'd be telling us where they live?'

Shankar rubbed his chin. 'Doesn't seem likely, does it?'

'I don't know, Murray. Would we tell them where our cities are?'

'No, but the yrr don't think like us.'

'Thanks for reminding me.' Crowe produced a wreath of smoke. 'OK, let's start again. Water. That part of the message is straightforward enough. *Water is our world.*'

'Which corresponds exactly to the message we sent them.'

'True. We told them that we live on land. Then we described our DNA and our body shape.'

'Supposing they've responded point by point,' said Shankar. 'Could the lines represent their shape?'

Crowe pursed her lips. 'They don't have one – I mean, it hardly characterises them. They've got more of a definable shape when they're a collective, but that makes it even harder to pin them down: yrr-jelly has thousand of shapes, and none to call its own.'

'So shape's out. What other pieces of information might be of interest. Size of population?'

'Murray! There'd be so many zeros behind that number you could scrawl it all over this ship and still run out of space. Besides, they're continually dividing or dying . . . I bet even *they* don't know how many of them there are.' Crowe waggled the cigarette between her teeth. 'Individual amoebas don't matter. What counts is the whole. The idea of the yrr, if you like. The essence of yrr. The yrr genome.'

Shankar peered at her over the rim of his glasses. 'We only told them that our biochemistry was based on DNA. You'd expect them to tell us, "Ours too". Surely they wouldn't have sequenced their genome for us?'

'They might have done.'

'But why?'

'Because it's pretty much the only defining statement they could

744

make. DNA and aggregation are at the heart of their existence. Everything else is based round that.'

'Fine, but how could they describe it, if it's constantly changing?'

Crowe was back to staring helplessly at the lines. 'What about the map idea again, then?'

'A map of what?'

'Who knows?' She sighed. 'Let's take it from the beginning again. H_2O. We live in water . . .'

Behind Closed Doors

Li had set the treadmill to maximum speed. Under normal circumstances she would have done her bit for team spirit and worked out in the gym. On this occasion, though, she didn't want to be disturbed. It was time for her daily satellite consultation with Offutt Air Force Base.

'How's morale, then, Jude?'

'Excellent, sir. The attack was a serious blow, but we're in control of the situation.'

'And everyone's still motivated?'

'More than ever before.'

'Well, I'm concerned.' The President was sitting all on his own in the war room at the air-force base. 'Boston's been fully evacuated. We've had to write off New York and Washington. And there's a new wave of horror stories from Philadelphia and Norfolk.'

'I know.'

'This country's going to hell, Jude. There isn't a single person in the world who doesn't seem to know about the creatures in the sea. Someone couldn't keep their mouth shut, and I'd like to know who.'

'What does it matter, sir?'

'What does it matter?' The President slammed his hand on the desk. 'The United States of America has agreed to lead this operation. I'm not about to tolerate some asshole from the UN taking matters into his own hands. They're all so busy trying to push their ridiculous little countries to the forefront. Have you seen what's going on out there? Things are escalating beyond our control.'

'I know exactly what's going on.'

'It could be that one of your guys has talked.'

'With all due respect, sir, there's no reason why other people shouldn't have arrived at the yrr hypothesis on their own. Besides, from what I've heard, the bulk of speculation still centres around natural disasters and international terrorism. Only this morning some scientist from Pyongyang said—'

'I know what he said.' The President brushed aside her point. 'He said *we* were the bad guys. Apparently we're skulking round in silent submarines attacking our own cities so we can pin it on the Commies.' He leaned forward. 'Well, they can say what they like. I don't give a damn about being popular. I just want to see this problem solved. I need some options, Jude. There isn't a single country left with the strength to help anyone else. Even the United States of America has been forced to beg for aid. We're being invaded and poisoned. The population is fleeing inland. I'm having to shelter in this goddamn security bunker like some kind of mole. We've got anarchy and looting on the streets, the military and security forces are hopelessly overstretched, and all we can offer our citizens is contaminated food supplies and drugs that don't work.'

'Sir . . .'

'God's still holding his protective hand over the West, but if you stick your feet in the water you're bound to lose your toes. The worm colonies off the coasts of America and Asia are growing, and La Palma's on the point of collapse. Regimes are crumbling. Heaven knows who's going to inherit their armaments. We're not in a position to intervene.'

'In your last speech, sir—'

'Don't get me started. I spend all my waking hours coming up with impassioned statements. But do you think the speechwriters use them? I don't believe they even understand what I'm trying to communicate to this country and to the rest of the world. Make the people feel confident, I keep telling them. The American people need to see the determination of their leader, to know he'll do whatever it takes to win this war, no matter how many faces the devil might show. I want the world to take heart. I'm not saying we should give them false hope – we have to prepare for the worst – but people should know that *we're going to get through this*. I keep explaining that to the speechwriters, but when they try to sound reassuring it comes across as insincere and overblown. You can even *hear* that they're afraid. Do any of them listen to me?'

'The people are listening,' Li said firmly. 'The world's stopped listening to everyone else. It's just you and the Germans.'

'Which reminds me, the Germans . . .' The President's eyes narrowed. 'Is it true what I'm hearing, that the Germans have their own mission planned?'

Li almost fell off the treadmill. That was ridiculous. 'Of course not. We're in charge. The UN has handed us the reins. Sure, the Germans are co-ordinating the European effort, but we're working together. Take La Palma.'

'So why's the CIA been telling me this stuff?'

'Because Vanderbilt's been peddling lies.'

'Come on, Jude.'

'He's a game player, always has been.'

'My dear Jude, when the time comes for you to take your rightful place, Vanderbilt won't be anywhere in sight.'

Li exhaled slowly. She'd allowed herself to get emotional. For a moment her guard had slipped and she'd given too much away. That wasn't good. In future she'd have to watch herself. She couldn't afford to be drawn.

'Although,' she said, with a smile, 'I don't really see Jack as a problem. He's a partner.'

The President nodded. 'The Russians have sent us a team. They've been helping the CIA with detailed information from the Black Sea region. We're in close contact with the Chinese, and the stuff about Germany is probably nothing. I don't get the impression that they're trying to go it alone, but you know how rumours start at times like this. We should be thankful, really. It's a wonderful thing to see so many people from different nations uniting in God to drive the devil from the sea.' He passed his hands over his eyes. 'So how are we *really* doing, Jude? I didn't want to ask you in front of the others in case you had to put a gloss on things. I wanted to spare you that embarrassment. I need you to be frank with me. *How much longer?*

'Not long. We're on the verge of a breakthrough.'

'How long is not long?'

'Rubin says that if all goes to plan, he can be ready in a day or two. We got lucky in the lab. The yrr are using a pheromone to communicate. We already know how to synthesise it and we—'

'Skip the details. So, Rubin says he can handle it?'

'He's certain of it, sir,' said Li. 'And so am I.'

The President pursed his lips. 'I'm relying on you, Jude. Any problems with your scientists?'

'No,' she lied. 'Things couldn't be better.'

Why all the questions? Had Vanderbilt . . .

Get a grip, she told herself. He was only enquiring. It wasn't in Vanderbilt's interest to tell tales. The fat bastard had a malicious tongue, but he'd never say anything to make himself look bad. 'I can assure you, sir,' she said, 'that we're making good progress. I gave you my word that I'd settle this problem in all our interests, and I'm going to do just that. The United States will save the world. *You* will save the world.'

'Just like in the movies, huh?'

'Better than that.'

The President nodded bleakly. Then he flashed her a smile. It wasn't the broad grin of old, but there was still a hint of his indomitable spirit, for which she admired him. 'God be with you, Jude,' he said.

He hung up. Li stayed on her treadmill. All of a sudden she doubted that she could pull it off.

Combat Information Center

Whatever the message had to say about the creatures in the sea, Shankar's stomach was communicating his need of food so loudly that Crowe couldn't bear to listen to the rumbling any longer. She sent him to get something to eat.

'But I'm fine,' he insisted.

'You'll be doing me a favour,' said Crowe.

'We don't have time to eat.'

'I know. But a couple of skeletons aren't going to solve the problem. At least I've got my Lucky Strikes to keep me going. Go on, Murray. Come back fortified and see if you can belch out a few good ideas.'

Shankar left, and she was alone.

A bit of space was what she needed. It was nothing against Shankar – he was a brilliant scientist and a great help – but he specialised in acoustics. Second-guessing non-human thought patterns didn't come easily to him and, anyway, Crowe always had her best ideas when she was surrounded by nothing but smoke.

She lit a cigarette, and went through the problem again. H_2O. We live in water.

The message looked like a woven design on a rug. A repeating pattern of H_2O. The same motif again and again, yet each molecule of H_2O was linked to an ancillary piece of data. Millions of pairs of data, one after the next. In graphic form, they appeared as lines. The obvious assumption was that the ancillary data described a characteristic of water or of something that lived in the water.

What would a yrr have to say about itself?

Water. But what else?

Crowe turned it over in her mind. Suddenly she thought of an analogy. Two statements. First statement: *this is a bucket*. Second statement: *this is water*. When you add them together: *this is a bucket of water*. The water molecules would all look identical, but the same wasn't true of the data on the bucket. The data describing the bucket would differ according to its form, texture and markings. A description of a bucket, broken down into thousands of individual statements, would be anything but uniform. Stating that the bucket was full of water would be easy. You just took each of the individual bucket statements and attached an ancillary statement: *water*.

Or, to put it another way, the statement H_2O could be coupled with data describing something with no intrinsic connection to water. Like a bucket, for instance.

We live in water.

But where in the water? How could you describe the location of something that was devoid of fixed shape?

By describing what delimited it.

Coastlines and seabeds.

The empty spaces were the continents, bordered by coastlines.

Crowe's cigarette almost fell to the floor. She started punching commands into the keyboard. Suddenly she knew why the lines didn't make a picture: they weren't describing two dimensions, but three. You had to bend them to make them fit. Bend them until they turned into something three-dimensional.

A globe.

Planet Earth.

Johanson was still working on the tissue samples they'd taken from the yrr. After twelve hours of intensive work Oliviera had given up – she couldn't keep her eyes open, let alone look down a microscope. Over the past few nights she'd only had a few hours' sleep. Slowly but surely the mission was taking its toll. Their work was advancing in leaps and bounds, but the pressure was getting to them. Everyone responded differently. Greywolf had retreated to the well deck, where he took care of the three remaining dolphins, monitored the data from their sensors and kept himself to himself. Some of the team were visibly tetchy, while others reacted more stoically. In Rubin's case, the stress seemed to take the form of migraines – which meant that once Oliviera had withdrawn for some hard-earned sleep, Johanson was left on his own in the half-light of the lab.

He'd switched off the main lights, leaving just the desk lamps and computer screens to brighten the gloom. The chamber hummed softly, generating a barely perceptible blue glow. The layer of jelly lay motionless at the bottom. The organism looked dead, but Johanson knew better.

If the jelly was glowing, the yrr were alive.

Footsteps rang out on the ramp. Anawak poked his head round the door. Johanson looked up from his work. 'Leon, good to see you.'

Anawak pulled up a chair, and sat down on it back to front. He rested his arms on the top. 'It's three in the morning,' he said. 'What the hell are you doing?'

'Working. You?'

'Can't sleep.'

'I think we've earned ourselves a drink. A glass of Bordeaux?'

'Oh, um . . .' Anawak looked embarrassed. 'Thanks for offering, but I don't touch alcohol.'

'Never?'

'Never.'

'That's funny.' Johanson frowned. 'I usually notice stuff like that. I guess we're all pretty distracted at the moment.'

'You could say that.' Anawak paused. 'How's it shaping up?'

'Fine. I solved your problem.' He said it almost casually.

'Problem?'

'The one you and Karen were working on. Memory via mutating DNA. Well, you were right. It's possible, and I've found out how.'

Anawak stared at him incredulously. 'I can't believe you're not jumping up and down.'

'I'd turn a few cartwheels if I had enough energy. But you're right: we should celebrate.'

'Well, aren't you going to tell me how it works?'

'You remember those hypervariable segments? They're clusters. The genome is covered with clusters that code different proteins. They're . . . Does this mean anything to you?'

'You'll have to help me out a little.'

'Clusters are a sub-class of gene. They're genes that take care of a particular function, like producing certain substances or coding receptors. If a section of DNA contains a high concentration of genes that serve the same function, you get a cluster. The yrr-genome has masses of them. And this is where it gets interesting: the yrr-cells *are* repairing themselves, but the repair process *doesn't* occur globally across the whole genome. The enzymes don't scan the DNA from top to bottom for mistakes, they react to specific signals. They're a bit like trains. If the signal tells them to go, they start the repair mechanism. But if the signal says stop, they don't go any further because otherwise they'd run into—'

'The clusters.'

'Right. And the clusters are protected.'

'You mean the yrr are able to shield part of their genome to stop it being repaired?'

'Exactly. They've got repair inhibitors – biological bouncers, if you like – which protect the clusters from repair enzymes. So, in the course of the repairs, the core genetic information is preserved, while other sequences are free to mutate continuously. Impressive, eh? Each yrr is an ever-evolving brain.'

'But how do they communicate?'

'Like Sue said, from cell to cell. Via ligands and receptors. The ligand – the signal transmitted from the other cells – reaches a receptor and sets off a chemical cascade towards the nucleus. The genome then mutates and passes on the signal to the surrounding cells. It happens almost instantaneously. That pile of jelly is thinking at the speed of a superconductor.'

Anawak gave a low whistle. 'So it's a brand new biochemical set-up.'

'Or a very old one. It may be new to us, but it's probably been around for millions of years. Maybe as long as life itself. It's a different evolutionary system running parallel to our own.' Johanson gave a short laugh. 'And it's highly effective.'

Anawak rested his chin on his hands. 'So, what now?'

'Good question. I don't think I've ever felt so directionless. I've got all this information and I don't know what to do with it. Right now it just confirms our fears – we've got almost nothing in common with the yrr.' He stretched and yawned. 'Who knows whether Crowe's attempts at communication will pay off? Seems to me that they're happy to chat to us while merrily plotting our doom. Maybe they don't see that as a contradiction. Either way, it's not my idea of conversation.'

'We've got no choice. We have to find a way of making ourselves understood.' Anawak sucked in his cheeks. 'And while we're on the subject – do you think we're all pulling together?'

Johanson stiffened. 'Why do you ask?'

'Well . . .' Anawak frowned. 'OK, don't be mad at her, but Karen told me what you saw – or what you thought you saw – the night of your mysterious accident.'

Johanson gave him a hard look. 'And what does she think?'

'That you did see Rubin.'

'I thought so. And you?'

'I don't know.' Anawak shrugged. 'You're Norwegian. You guys believe in trolls.'

Johanson sighed. 'If it hadn't been for Sue, none of this would ever have come back to me,' he said. 'She jogged my memory. That night when we were sitting on the hangar deck, I thought I saw Rubin, even though he was supposed to be in bed with a migraine. Just like he's supposed to have a migraine now. Ever since then, bits and pieces have been coming back to me. I'm starting to remember things – things I can't have made up. Sometimes it feels as though I'm on the verge of seeing everything, and then . . . I'm standing in front of an open door, looking into the light. I step inside – and it all goes black.'

'What makes you think you didn't dream it?'

'Sue.'

'But she didn't see anything.'

'And Li.'

'Why Li?'

752

'We were chatting at the party and she was a bit too concerned about the state of my memory. I got the feeling she was trying to gauge how much I knew.' Johanson looked at Anawak. 'You wanted my opinion. Well, I don't think we're pulling together. I never have done, not even in Whistler. There's always been something funny about Li, but now there's Rubin and his migraines too. I don't know what to make of it, but something tells me it doesn't add up.'

'Male intuition . . .' Anawak grinned nervously. 'So, what does Li want from us?'

Johanson glanced at the ceiling. 'You'd have to ask her.'

Control Room

At that moment Johanson was looking straight into Vanderbilt's eyes through one of the hidden cameras, although he didn't know it. The CIA agent had taken over from Li at the desk. He heard Johanson say, 'You'd have to ask her.'

'Smart bastard,' Vanderbilt murmured. Li was in her cabin. He called her on a secure line.

She appeared on the screen.

'I told you those drugs were a risk,' said Vanderbilt. 'Johanson's recovering his memory.'

'So what?'

'Aren't you worried?'

Li gave a thin smile. 'Rubin's been working very hard. He was here just now.'

'And?'

'It's brilliant!' There was a glint in her eyes. 'I know we're not particularly fond of the shit, but I have to say he's excelled himself.'

'Has he trialled the stuff?'

'On a small scale. But the scale doesn't matter: it works. In a few hours I'm going to call the President. Then I'll take Rubin for a dive.'

'You want to do it in person?' exclaimed Vanderbilt.

'Well, there's no way *you*'re going to fit inside a boat like that,' said Li, and hung up.

Well Deck

The electrical systems filled the *Independence*'s empty hangars and decks with an eerie buzz, causing the bulkheads to quiver imperceptibly. They could be heard in the hospital and the deserted officers' mess, and anyone pressing their fingertips to the lockers in the troop-berthing area could feel their faint vibration.

They even penetrated into the bowels of the vessel, where Greywolf was lying near the edge of the embankment, staring at the steel girders on the ceiling. He felt overwhelmed with grief and the conviction that he had done everything wrong. He hadn't even been able to save Licia. He'd tried to protect her and failed.

The only time when he'd ever been truly proud of himself was when he'd rescued that kid. He'd done a good job on the *Lady Wexham*. He'd helped a crowd of people, and he'd won back Leon as a friend. A photographer had taken a picture, and the next day the newspaper had immortalised the moment.

But the whales were still rampaging, the dolphins were suffering, nature was in agony – and Licia was dead.

Greywolf felt empty and useless. He wasn't going to talk to anyone about it: he was just going to do his job until the nightmare was over. And then . . .

Tears welled in his eyes.

The Big Picture

'See this sphere?' said Crowe. 'That's planet Earth.' She'd blown up some printouts and pinned them to the wall. She walked slowly down the line. 'These markings baffled us at first, but now we think they're the Earth's magnetic field. The blank spaces are definitely continents. Once we'd worked that out, we'd basically cracked it.'

Li frowned. 'Are you sure? Those so-called continents don't look much like the continents I know.'

Crowe smiled. 'They're not supposed to. They're the continents a hundred and eighty million years ago. Just one big land mass – Pangaea, the supercontinent. The lines probably correspond to the magnetic field back then.'

'Have you checked that out?'

'It's difficult to reconstruct the field lines, but the configuration of the continents is easily verified. At first we didn't know what they'd sent us, but once we realised it was a map of the world it all fell into place. It's actually quite straightforward. They used water as the baseline for the message, and paired each water molecule with geographical data.'

'But how would they know what the Earth looked like all that time ago?' Vanderbilt said.

'They remember it,' said Johanson.

'But no one can remember the prehistoric era. Only single-cell organisms—' Vanderbilt broke off.

'Exactly,' said Johanson. 'Only single-cell organisms and the first multicellular life-forms. Last night the final piece of the jigsaw fell into place. The yrr have hypermutating DNA. Let's say they gained consciousness at the beginning of the Jurassic era. That's two hundred million years ago, and they've been storing knowledge ever since. You know the classic lines you get in sci-fi? *Whatever it is, it's coming our way,* or *Get me the President on the line?* Well, there's always the one about the enemy being superior, though by the end of the story you mostly feel cheated. This time you won't. The yrr *are* superior.'

'Because their DNA stores knowledge?' asked Li.

'Right. That's the crucial difference. Humans aren't endowed with genetic memory. For our culture to survive, we need words, written accounts and pictures. We can't transmit experience directly. When our body dies, our mind goes with it. We talk about not forgetting the lessons of the past but we're kidding ourselves. To forget something you have to be able to remember it. None of us can remember the experience of earlier generations. We can record and refer to other people's memories, but it doesn't alter the fact that *we weren't there*. Every newborn baby starts from scratch. Each of us has to touch the stove to find out that it's hot. Things are very different for the yrr. One cell absorbs information, then divides into two – it duplicates its genome, complete with all the information stored on it. It's like us being able to duplicate our brain and all our memories with it. New cells don't inherit abstract knowledge – they get real experience, as though they'd been there themselves. Ever since the very first yrr came into being, they've had collective memory.' Johanson turned to Li. 'So, do you see what we're up against?'

Li nodded slowly. 'The only way we could rob the yrr of their knowledge is by destroying entire collectives.'

'Entire collectives probably wouldn't be enough: you'd have to kill every last one of them,' said Johanson. 'And there are plenty of reasons why you can't do that. For one thing, we don't know how dense their networks are. Their cellular chains might stretch hundreds of kilometres. We're outnumbered. And they're not like humans – they don't just live in the present. They don't need statistics, averages or any other intellectual crutch. Taken together they're their own statistics, the sum of all parts, their own history. They're able to survey developments spanning thousands of years. We don't even manage to act for the good of our children and grandchildren. We repress memory. The yrr compare, analyse, diagnose, predict and act on the strength of their ever-present memory. Nothing ever gets lost, not even the smallest innovation. Everything feeds into the development of new strategies and ideas. It's an infinite process of selection towards the perfect solution. They compare back, modify, refine, learn from their mistakes, adapt, make their projections – and act.'

'Cold-blooded little beasts,' said Vanderbilt.

'Do you think so?' Li shook her head. 'I admire them. Within minutes they produce strategies that would keep us busy for years. Even just knowing exactly what *won't* work! Then knowing it because it's part of your memory, because you were the one who messed up in the first place – even though you weren't physically present . . .'

'And that's why the yrr probably get along better in their habitat than we do in ours,' said Johanson. 'For the yrr every thought process is collective and embedded in the genes. They inhabit every era simultaneously. Humans don't have a clear view of the past and they don't pay attention to the future. Our whole existence centres on the individual, the here and now. We're too busy pursuing our own personal goals to worry about higher knowledge. We know we can't exist beyond death, so we try to leave our legacy in manifestos, books and music. We're intent on making sure our names aren't forgotten. We try to leave a record of ourselves to be passed on, misinterpreted, falsified and used for ideological purposes long after we're dead. We're so obsessed with assuring our own perpetuity that our goals seldom coincide with what would be good for humankind. Our minds champion the aesthetic, the individual, the intellectual and the abstract. We're determined not to be animals. On the one hand our body is our temple, but on the other we despise it for being mere machinery. We've become accustomed to valuing mind over body. We feel nothing but contempt for the factors relating to our physical survival.'

'But for the yrr this division doesn't exist,' Li mused. For some reason the thought seemed to please her. 'Body *is* mind, and mind *is* body. No yrr would ever do anything that runs counter to the interests of the collective. Survival matters for the species, not the individual, and action is always a collective decision. Fantastic! The yrr don't give prizes for good ideas. Being able to take part in their implementation is all the fame a yrr could wish for. The question is, do the individual amoebas have an individual consciousness?'

'Not in the way we know it,' said Anawak. 'I'm not sure you can talk about individual consciousness in relation to single cells. But the amoebas are certainly creative on an individual basis. They're sensors that turn experience into something they can use, before feeding it into the collective. A thought is probably only taken into consideration if the impulse behind it is strong enough, that's to say if enough yrr are trying to introduce it into the collective at the same time. Each thought is weighed up against a range of others, and the fittest survives.'

'Just like evolution,' nodded Weaver. 'Thinking by natural selection.'

'That's some enemy!' Li seemed full of admiration. 'Zero loss of information and no pointless vanities. We never see more than part of the whole, while they see everything throughout time and space.'

'And that's why we're destroying our planet,' said Crowe. 'We can't see what we're doing. They must know that – which means they know we don't have genetic memory.'

'Right. It all adds up. No wonder they don't want to negotiate. They could make a deal with you or me, but what if we die tomorrow? Then who would they deal with? Having genetic memory would save us from our own stupidity, but it's not the way we're made. Trying to get along with humans is a pipedream. The yrr have seen that. It's part of their collective knowledge and it's the reason they've decided to mobilise against us.'

'Once they learn something, no one can take it away from them,' said Oliviera. 'In a yrr-collective everyone knows everything. They don't need think tanks, scientists, generals or leaders. You can kill as many yrr as you like – but so long as some survive, their collective knowledge lives on too.'

'Just a minute.' Li turned to her. 'Didn't you say that there might be some queen-yrr?'

'Yes. Even if collective knowledge is part of each yrr, collective action might be initiated centrally. My guess is that queen-yrr exist.'

'As single cells?'

'Well, they'd have to share the same biochemistry as the aggregated jelly, so it's likely that they're single cells. But they're highly organised. The only way we're ever going to get close to them is through communication.'

'But all they send us are cryptic messages!' said Vanderbilt. 'They sent us a picture of prehistoric Earth. Why? What are they trying to tell us?'

'Everything,' said Crowe.

'Could you be a little more specific?'

'They're telling us is that this is their planet – which they've been ruling for a hundred and eighty million years, maybe more. They're telling us they've got genetic memory, the magnetic field is their compass, and they're everywhere where there's water. They want us to know that we're in the here and now, whereas they're everywhere and for ever. Those are the facts. It's all in the message, and it says a lot.'

Vanderbilt scratched his belly. 'So what do we tell them?'

'They've decided they want to destroy us. We're not going to defeat that logic by arguing that we want to survive. Our only chance lies in trying to show them that we acknowledge their primacy . . .'

'The primacy of amoebas?'

'. . . and in persuading them that we no longer pose a threat.'

'But we are a threat,' said Weaver.

'She's right,' said Johanson. 'Empty promises won't help. We need to give them a signal that we're withdrawing from their world. We need to stop contaminating the seas with chemical and noise pollution, and we need to do it fast enough to make them wonder whether they could live with us, after all.'

'It's up to you now, Jude,' said Crowe. 'You know what we think, but it's for you to pass that on. Or to put it into action.'

All eyes were fixed on Li.

She nodded. 'I think you're right,' she said. 'But we shouldn't rush into anything. If we want to pull out of the seas, we need to send them a message to convey that exactly and convincingly.' She looked at the faces turned towards her. 'I want you all working on this together. And I don't want anyone rushing or panicking. We mustn't be too hasty. A few days here or there won't make any difference. What really matters is that you get the tone right. The yrr are more alien to us than anything we'd ever imagined. If there's the smallest chance of coming to a peaceful solution, we have to seize it. So, do your best.'

'Thanks, Jude,' smiled Crowe. 'Wise words from the American military.'

Li left the room, followed by Peak and Vanderbilt. 'Has Rubin been able to synthesise enough of that stuff?' she muttered.

'Yep,' said Vanderbilt.

'Good. I want him to get one of the Deepflights ready. In two or three hours we can start to get this over with.'

'Why the hurry?' asked Peak.

'Johanson. He looks as though he's about to have a revelation. I'm not in the mood for discussion.'

'And we're one hundred per cent ready to go?'

Li looked at him. 'Sal, I've told the President we're ready. And if the President thinks we're ready, we're ready.'

Well Deck

'Hey, Jack.'

Anawak headed towards the dolphin tank. Greywolf glanced up, then turned back to the miniature video camera he was disassembling. As the newcomer drew closer, two dolphins stuck their heads out of the water and greeted him with whistles and chatter. They swam over to claim their share of affection. 'I'm not interrupting anything, am I?' asked Anawak, as he patted the dolphins.

'Uh-uh.'

It wasn't the first time that Anawak had been down to the well deck since the attack. On each occasion he'd tried to get Greywolf to talk to him, but to no avail. His friend seemed to have retreated inside himself. He hadn't attended any of the meetings and had taken to merely summarising the dolphin footage in handwritten notes. The pictures didn't show much anyway. The images of the jelly approaching the ship were disappointing: a blue glow that faded into the depths, then shadowy glimpses of orcas. After that the dolphins had taken fright and huddled under the keel, filming the expanse of steel. Greywolf had put forward the case for the remainder of the fleet to keep up their role as the vessel's early-warning system and resume their patrol of the boat. Anawak no longer believed that the dolphins could help them, but he was careful not to voice his doubts. Secretly he suspected that all Greywolf wanted was to carry on as usual.

They stood in silence for a while. A group of soldiers and technicians emerged from the bottom of the basin, where they'd finished dismantling the shattered glass hatch. One of the technicians went up to the control desk on the jetty. The pumps kicked into action.

'Time for us to leave,' said Greywolf.

They made their way up the embankment. Anawak watched as the basin filled with water. 'They're flooding it again,' he said.

'Yeah, well, it's easier to release the dolphins when the basin's full.'

'You're letting them out?'

Greywolf nodded.

'I'll help,' said Anawak. 'If you like.'

'Sure.' Greywolf opened the back of the camera and inserted a miniature screwdriver.

'Right away?'

'I've got to get this working first.'

'Why don't you take a break? We could get something to drink. We all need a rest from time to time.'

'It's not like I'm busy, Leon. All I do is mess around with the equipment and make sure the dolphins are OK. I'm on one perpetual break already.'

'You should come to the meetings, then.'

Greywolf carried on working in silence. The conversation dried up.

'Jack,' said Anawak, 'you can't hide yourself away for ever.'

'Who said anything about for ever?'

'What do you call this, then?'

'I'm just doing my job.' Greywolf shrugged. 'I listen to what the dolphins report, monitor the video footage, and if anyone needs me, I'm here.'

'But you're not here, really. You don't know anything about what's happened over the past twenty-four hours.'

'I do.'

'How?'

'Sue's been to see me a few times. Even Peak was down here earlier to check things out. They all tell me stuff. I don't even have to ask.'

Anawak stared straight ahead. Suddenly he was furious. 'Well, I guess you don't need me, then,' he snapped.

Greywolf didn't respond.

'You've decided to rot down here by yourself?'

'I prefer the company of animals.'

Licia was killed by one, Anawak felt like saying. He stopped himself just in time.

'I lost Licia too, you know,' he said finally.

Briefly Greywolf froze. Then he carried on poking the screwdriver inside the camera. 'That's not what this is about.'

'Then what is it about?'

'What do you want from me, Leon?'

'You know what, Jack? I don't know. To be honest, I'm beginning to wonder.'

He'd almost reached the tunnel when he heard Greywolf say in a low voice, 'Leon! Don't go.'

Memories

Johanson couldn't keep his eyes open. The late-night session in the lab had taken its toll. He was stationed in front of the monitors at the control desk, while Oliviera synthesised batches of yrr-pheromone in the containment facility. They were planning to release some of the chemical into the tank. There wasn't much sign of the collective, just swarms of amoebas clouding the water. The jelly seemed to have disaggregated and the glow had gone. By adding the synthesised pheromone, they were hoping to induce the yrr to aggregate so that they could carry out more tests.

Maybe, thought Johanson, we should experiment with one of Crowe's messages to see if the collective responds.

His head was throbbing and he knew what was causing it. It wasn't a question of working too hard or sleeping too little. His brain was aching from the memories trapped inside.

Ever since the meeting that morning the pain had got worse. His internal slide projector was back in action, triggered by a remark Li had made. The short sequence of words had expanded to occupy his mind and prevent him focusing. Johanson's head lolled back as he slipped into a doze, caught in a perpetual loop of Li's words.

We mustn't be too hasty. Mustn't be too hasty. Mustn't . . .

He heard noises and woke briefly, blinked in the lights of the lab, then closed his eyes again.

Mustn't be too hasty.

Darkness.

The hangar deck.

A sound like grating metal. He jolts awake. For a fleeting moment he can't remember where he is. Then he feels the steel side of the vessel in the small of his back. The sky is brightening above the sea. He sits up, and glances at the bulkhead.

A door stands wide open, luminous in the gloom, spilling light into the hangar. Johanson stands up. He must have been sitting there for hours – or so his aching joints tell him. He moves slowly towards the rectangle of light. He can see now that it's a passageway with plain walls on either side and neon lights above. It extends a few metres, then stops and turns right.

Johanson peers through the door and listens.

Voices and noises. He takes a step back.

Indecision.

Mustn't be too hasty. Don't be hasty.

He hesitates.

Then a barrier bursts open.

He enters. Nothing but plain walls, then the change in direction. He follows the passageway round to the right. It turns again, this time to the left. It's spacious in here – wide enough to drive a car. The voices and noises return, this time more loudly. They must be close, just round the second bend. He draws nearer, then a sharp left turn, and . . .

The lab.

No, not *the* lab. *A* lab. Smaller, with a lower ceiling. But it's above the converted vehicle deck, where the deep-sea chamber is located. This lab has a chamber too, a much smaller one. And there's something glowing inside it; a blue thing with tentacles.

He looks around in disbelief.

The whole room is a small but perfect copy of the one beneath it. Rows of benches, pieces of equipment, barrels of liquid nitrogen. A control desk and monitors. An electron microscope. Across the room, a biohazard symbol marks a reinforced door, and at the back of the lab a narrow passageway leads inside the ship.

Three people are standing next to the chamber. They're talking, unaware of the intruder. The two men have their backs to him, but the woman is standing in profile, scribbling something on a pad. Her gaze shifts between the two men, then round the room and settles on Johanson.

Her jaw drops, and the men spin round. He recognises a guy from Vanderbilt's team. No one knows what he does – the usual CIA story.

The second is Rubin.

Johanson is too bewildered to do anything but stare. He sees the shock in Rubin's eyes, sees him searching for a way to save the situation. And it's that look that rouses Johanson from his paralysis as it dawns on him that his work is a charade. He's being used. He, Oliviera, Anawak, Weaver, Crowe . . .

Unless Rubin isn't the only one acting more than one part.

Why?

Rubin approaches slowly. His lips are tensed into a smile. 'Sigur! Goodness me, can't you sleep either?'

Johanson's eyes are wandering round the room, taking in the other faces. One look into their eyes confirms that he doesn't belong here. 'What's all this about, Mick?'

'Oh, nothing, it's just . . .'

'What is this place? What's going on?'

Rubin draws himself up to his full height. 'I can explain everything, Sigur. You see, we weren't really planning to use the extra lab. It's only here for emergencies – in case anything . . . Well, in case anything happens to the main one. We've just been inspecting the systems to make sure it's ready, so—'

Johanson points to the organism in the chamber. 'But you've got *that* in there.'

'Oh, you mean the jelly.' Rubin's head swivels round and then back. 'That's, er, well, we had to check it out. Just to be certain. We didn't mention it because, well, there was really no need, I mean . . .'

Nothing but lies.

Johanson may not be totally sober, but that doesn't prevent him noticing that Rubin is trying to talk himself out of a hole.

He turns and strides towards the exit.

'Sigur! Dr Johanson!' He hears footsteps behind him. Rubin comes alongside him. His fingers tug at Johanson's sleeve. 'Slow down, Sigur.'

'*What's going on here?*'

'It's not like you think. I—'

'How would you know what I think?'

'It's just a precaution.'

'A what?'

'A precaution. The lab is just a precaution.'

Johanson jerks himself free. 'Perhaps I should talk to Li about it.'

'No, I—'

'Or maybe I should tell Oliviera. Actually, maybe I should tell the whole damn team. What do you think, Mick? Is this some kind of game?'

'Of course not.'

'Then perhaps you should tell me what the hell you're up to!'

Rubin's eyes are filled with panic. 'Sigur, I don't think that's wise. You mustn't be too hasty. Do you hear me, Sigur? Don't do anything hasty.'

Johanson gives an indignant snort and marches off. He can hear Rubin hurrying after him. He feels the other man's fear on his back.

Mustn't be too hasty.

White light.

Something explodes in his eyes, and pain washes over his mind. The walls, the passageway, everything blurs. He sees the ground rush towards him.

The ceiling of the lab. It had all fallen into place.

Johanson jumped up. Oliviera was still busy in the containment facility. Breathing deeply, he glanced at the control desk, the benches, the chamber. He looked up at the ceiling.

Above him there was a second laboratory. And no one was meant to know. Rubin must have knocked him out, and they'd drugged him to make him forget.

But why?

Johanson clenched his fists. He felt helpless and furious. Then he was outside, running up the ramp.

'You don't need me at the meetings,' said Greywolf. 'It's not like I can help.'

Anawak's fury ebbed away. He turned and walked back. The basin was still filling with water. 'That's not true, Jack.'

'It is.' He said it in a neutral, almost absent voice. 'I couldn't stop the navy torturing dolphins. I tried to stick up for the whales, but now no one can save them. In my mind I'd decided that animals were better than people. It was stupid, I know, but it was one way of coping. And now I've lost Licia to an orca. I can't help anyone.'

'Stop beating yourself up, Jack.'

'Those are the facts.'

Anawak sat down next to him. 'Leaving the navy was the right decision, and you stuck to it,' he said. 'You were the best handler they had, and it was your decision to quit, not theirs. You didn't have to go, but you did.'

'Sure, but my leaving didn't change anything.'

'For you it did. You took a stand.'

'Achieving what, exactly?'

Anawak was silent.

'You know,' said Greywolf, 'the worst thing is feeling you don't belong. You love someone and lose them. You love animals, and they're responsible. I'm beginning to feel like I hate those orcas.'

'We all feel like that. You—'

'Licia died in the jaws of an orca. I watched and there was nothing I could do. Don't try to tell me that that's anyone's problem but mine. If I were to keel over and die right now, it wouldn't make any difference to the survival of the planet. Who would care? I haven't achieved anything to make anyone think that my presence on this planet was worthwhile.'

'I'd care,' said Anawak. He expected a cutting reply, but he heard a soft sound, a kind of hiccup, like a muffled sigh, in Greywolf's throat.

'And in case you'd forgotten,' said Anawak, 'Licia cared too.'

He felt so livid that he could have grabbed Rubin, hauled him up to the flight deck and tossed him overboard. He might even have done so, had the biologist crossed his path. But Rubin was nowhere to be seen. Instead he bumped into Weaver, who was going the other way.

For a moment he wasn't sure how to react, then he pulled himself together. 'Karen!' He smiled at her. 'Coming to join us in the lab?'

'Actually, I'm off to the well deck – to see Leon and Jack.'

'Oh, right. Hmm, Jack . . .' Johanson had to force himself to stay calm. 'He's in a bad way, isn't he?'

'He and Licia meant more to each other than he was willing to admit. It's hard to get through to him.'

'Leon's a good friend. He'll manage.'

Weaver nodded and looked at him enquiringly. She'd realised that this was a non-conversation. 'Are you all right?' she asked.

'Fine.' Johanson took her by the arm. 'I've just had the most amazing idea about what we're going to say in this big new message. Fancy a stroll on the roof?'

'Well, actually, I was—'

'It'll only take ten minutes. I just want to hear what you think. Seems like I've been shut inside for days. I need some fresh air.'

'Are you sure you'll be warm enough?'

Johanson glanced down. He was wearing a sweater and jeans. His thick down jacket was in the lab. 'I'm toughening myself up,' he said.

'Any particular reason?'

'Stops you getting flu. Keeps you young. Helps you deal with stupid questions.' He was raising his voice. Go easy, he told himself. 'Listen, I have to talk to someone about it. It was your computer program that made me think of it. But it doesn't seem right to discuss it on the ramp. Won't you come outside?'

'Well, in that case, sure.'

They walked up through the tunnel and into the island. Johanson had to make a real effort not to keep checking for hidden cameras and bugs. He knew he wouldn't spot them anyway. Instead he said brightly, 'Jude's right, of course. We mustn't be overhasty. I reckon we'll need at least a couple of days to figure it out, but what I was thinking was . . .'

And so he went on. He kept producing intelligent-sounding nonsense, all the while pushing Weaver gently out of the island and into the open. Gesticulating expansively, he strode out in front of her until he came to one of the helicopter landing points on the starboard side of the vessel. It was colder and windier than usual. A veil of mist had descended on the ocean, and the swell had increased. The waves rolled beneath them like primitive mammals, grey and sluggish, exhaling a dank salty vapour into the air. Johanson was cold, but an inner fury seemed to warm him.

'Sigur,' said Weaver, 'I don't know what you mean.'

Johanson turned his face into the wind. 'That makes two of us. Look, I don't suppose they can hear us out here – you'd have to go to extraordinary lengths to eavesdrop on the flight deck.'

Weaver peered at him in confusion. 'What are you talking about?'

'I've got my memory back, Karen. I know what happened the night before last.'

'Have you found the door?'

'No. But I can guarantee it's there.'

He outlined what had happened. Weaver listened to him intently. Her expression didn't flicker. 'So you're saying we've got a fifth column on board.'

'Yes.'

'But what would be the point?'

'Remember what Jude said? We mustn't be too hasty. Think about it! You, Leon, Sam, Murray, me, Sue – and Mick, I suppose – we've all been working flat out to furnish them with a description of the yrr. OK, maybe we're kidding ourselves, maybe we've got it wrong – but on balance it doesn't seem likely. In fact, all the evidence suggests that we're right in our assumptions about what kind of intelligence we're dealing with and how it works. So why, after we've worked day and night are we supposed to slow down?'

'Because they don't need us any more,' Weaver said flatly. 'Because Mick's already working on it with another bunch of people in a different lab.'

'We're only here to supply the information.' Johanson nodded. 'We've served our purpose.'

'But I don't get it.' What project could Mick be working on that doesn't fit with ours? I mean, we don't have much choice – our only option is to try to make peace with the yrr. What else could he be aiming for?'

'Evidently there's a rival initiative, and Mick's playing a double game. But you can bet he's not in charge.'

'Who is, then?'

'Jude.'

'You were suspicious of her from the start, huh?'

'The feeling was mutual. I think we both realised early on that we're not the sort to be taken for a ride. There was always something not quite right about her – but I couldn't think of a single good reason for not believing what she said.'

'So what now?' asked Weaver.

'I've had time to clear my mind,' said Johanson, hugging his chest to keep warm. 'Jude's going to see us standing here. She's bound to be keeping tabs on me. She won't know for sure what we're talking about, but she'll be aware of the possibility that my memory might return. She's running out of time. That speech this morning was to get us off her back. If she's got her own plan of action, she's got to strike now.'

'In other words, we need to find out what they're up to as soon as we can.' Weaver thought for a second. 'Why don't we mobilise the others?'

'It's too risky. She'd notice straight away. The whole ship is bound to be crawling with bugs. They'd lock us up and throw away the key. No, if there's a way of pushing her into a corner, I intend to find it. I want to know what's going on here, and for that I'll need your help.'

'What do you want me to do?'

'Find Rubin and get him to talk, while I deal with Jude.'

'Any idea where he might be?'

'I expect he's in that shady lab of his. At least I know where it is now, but don't ask me how you get there. We'll have to hope he's kicking around somewhere else on the boat.' Johanson sighed. 'It all sounds like something out of a bad film, doesn't it? Most likely I'm the one who's cracking up. If it turns out that I'm paranoid, I'll have plenty of time later to eat my words. Right now, I mean to find out what's going on.'

'You're not paranoid, Sigur.'

Johanson gave her a grateful smile. 'Let's go back in.'

Walking through the island and down the ramp, they kept up a steady stream of soundbites about message encryption and peaceful dialogue.

'Well, I'm off to see Leon,' said Weaver. 'I can't wait to hear what he says. After lunch we'll get started on that program. Who knows? We may even have it running by this afternoon.'

'Excellent,' said Johanson. 'I'll catch you later.' He watched Weaver disappear, then climbed down a companionway to 02 LEVEL and went into the CIC, where Crowe and Shankar were sitting at their computers. 'What are you two up to?' he asked.

'Thinking,' said Crowe, from inside her usual cloud of smoke. 'Any progress with the pheromone?'

'Sue's in the process of synthesising the next batch. We must have about two dozen ampoules by now.'

'Then you're doing better than we are. We're starting to lose our faith in math. Maybe it isn't the path to salvation.' Shankar gave a wry grin. 'Besides, their arithmetic seems better than ours.'

'Any other ideas?'

'Emotion.' Crowe expelled the smoke through her nostrils. 'Weird, huh? Trying to appeal to the yrr's feelings – after all we know about them. But if yrr-emotion is based on biochemistry . . .'

'Like human emotion,' Shankar chipped in.

'. . . then the pheromone might be able to help us. Thank you, Murray. I don't need to be told that love is merely chemistry.'

'Felt any chemical attraction lately, Sigur?' said Shankar, idly.

'Right now I've got enough sparks flying of my own. You haven't seen Jude, have you?'

'She was in the LFOC just now,' said Crowe.

'Thanks.'

'Oh, and Mick was looking for you.'

'Mick?'

'He and Li were chatting, and then he said something about heading down to the lab. He left a few minutes ago.'

'Oh, good,' he said. 'He can help us synthesise the pheromone, provided he doesn't get any more migraines, poor guy.'

'He should take up smoking,' said Crowe. 'It's great for headaches.'

Johanson grinned and walked over to the LFOC. Most of the electronic data had been diverted there so that Crowe and Shankar were not distracted in the CIC. Low rustling noises, then the occasional click or whistle came from the speakers. The silhouette of a dolphin passed over one of the screens. Greywolf had evidently released the fleet again.

No sign of Li, Peak or Vanderbilt. Johanson checked out the JIC. It was empty, as were the other control and command rooms. He debated whether to look in the officers' mess, but he'd probably only find soldiers or some of Vanderbilt's agents. Li might be in the gym or her cabin. He didn't have time to search the whole vessel.

If Rubin was on his way to the lab, Weaver would flush him out. He had to speak to Li first.

Fine, he thought. If I can't find you, you'll have to find me. He made his way unhurriedly to his cabin, went in and positioned himself in the middle of the room.

'Hello, Jude,' he said.

He wondered where the cameras and mikes were hidden.

'You'll never guess what I just remembered. There's an extra lab above the main one. Rubin likes to go there when he's suffering from his migraines. Maybe you could tell me what he does there. Apart from beating up his colleagues.'

His eyes swept over the furniture, the lamps, the TV set . . .

'I guessed you weren't going to volunteer the information, so I took a few precautions. If you're not careful, I'll tell the rest of the team what I've remembered, and there'll be nothing you can do.' That was laying it on a bit thick, but he needed to grab her attention. 'Is that what you want, Jude? Or how about you, Sal? Oh, sorry, Jack, I'd almost forgotten you were there. Any views?'

He took slow, deliberate paces round the room. 'I can wait, you know. The question is, can you? I doubt it.' He shrugged. 'Of course, we could always keep the whole thing quiet. Maybe your intentions are honourable and that's why you've got Rubin working in a ghost lab. I'd love to know that it's all in the interests of international security. But I don't take too kindly to being knocked out. You understand that, don't you, Jude?'

What if Li couldn't care less? She might not even be listening.

Oh, she was listening to him, all right. He knew she was.

'Jude, you treated Mick to his very own deep-sea simulation chamber. I know it's smaller than the main one, but I can't help wondering what he's doing with it that he couldn't do with ours. I hope you haven't joined forces with the yrr behind our backs. I'm sorry, but you're going to have to help me make sense of this, because to tell you the truth I—'

'Dr Johanson.'

He spun around. Peak's tall frame filled the open door.

'Well, what a surprise,' Johanson said softly. 'Good old Sal. Can I offer you a cup of tea?'

'Jude wants to speak to you.'

'Oh, really?' The corners of Johanson's mouth twitched. 'I wonder what she wants.'

Weaver

Oliviera was leaving the containment facility with a metal carry-case in her hand when Weaver walked in. 'Have you seen Mick?'

'Nope, just pheromones.' Oliviera lifted the case for her to see. It was an open-sided wire cage with racks for samples. Row upon row of glass tubes containing a colourless fluid were lined up inside. 'He called here earlier, though, and threatened to come down. I should think he'll be here any moment.'

'Yrr-scent?' asked Weaver, indicating the test-tubes.

'Yes – we'll be sprinkling a few drops of it into the tank this afternoon. Who knows? Maybe we'll persuade those cells to aggregate. If so, our theory will be gospel, so to speak.' Oliviera glanced around the lab. 'You haven't seen Sigur, have you?'

'I was just chatting to him on the flight deck. He's had some interesting ideas about the next message. It should make life easier for Sam. Anyway, I'll come back later.'

'No problem.'

Weaver considered. She could take a look round the hangar deck, but if Johanson's suspicions were right, she would only draw attention to herself. Besides, the forbidden door was scarcely going to open while she was snooping around outside.

She continued down the tunnel to the well deck.

The basin was almost full, the remaining technicians from Roscovitz's team supervising the process. She spotted Greywolf and Anawak in the water.

'Have you let the dolphins out?' she called.

Anawak hauled himself out. 'Yes.' He walked over to her. 'What've you been up to?'

'Not much. I think we're all trying to gather our thoughts.'

'We could do that together, if you like,' he said softly.

She met his gaze and realised just how much she wanted to throw her arms round him. To forget the whole awful business and do what should have been done a long time ago.

But none of them could escape the situation. And there was Greywolf, who'd lost Licia . . .

She gave a fleeting smile.

03 LEVEL

Peak and Johanson made their way up through the vessel, cut across part of the hospital and went down a passageway. They turned off to the side, and came to a door.

'What do you call this place, anyway?' asked Johanson, as Peak's fingers darted over the keypad. It made an electronic beeping noise, then the door swung open. The passageway continued on the other side.

'That's the CIC overhead,' said Peak.

Johanson tried to get his bearings. It was difficult to picture the layout of the vessel. If the CIC was above them, the secret lab was probably underneath.

They stopped in front of a second door. This time Peak had to scan his retina before they were allowed in. Johanson stepped into a room almost identical to the CIC, even down to its electronic hum. There was a low murmur of voices. At least a dozen people were at work. Monitors lined the walls, showing satellite images and footage from cameras – sections of the vehicle ramp, Buchanan and Anderson in the bridge, the flight and hangar decks. Johanson also spotted Crowe and Shankar in the CIC, Weaver talking to Anawak and Greywolf in the well deck, and Oliviera working in the lab. Additional monitors showed the insides of all the cabins, including his, the camera mounted above the door. He must have given them some great footage, delivering his monologue from the centre of the room.

Li and Vanderbilt were sitting at a large table lit from below. The commander-in-chief stood up.

'Hello, Jude,' Johanson said cheerily. 'Nice place you've got here.'

'Sigur.' She smiled back. 'We owe you an apology.'

'Oh, don't mention it.' Johanson marvelled at his surroundings. 'I must say, I'm impressed. I guess all good things come in twos.'

'I can show you the schematics if you like.'

'I'd settle for an explanation.'

'And you shall have one.' Li did her best to look sheepish. 'But, first, let me assure you of how deeply sorry I am about the incident that led you here. Rubin should never have hit you.'

'I'm not interested in what he did. What's he doing *now*? What's he up to in that lab?'

'He's looking for a toxin,' said Vanderbilt.

'For a . . .' Johanson swallowed. 'A toxin?'

'Come on, Sigur.' Li wrung her hands. 'We couldn't rely on resolving this peacefully. I know how terrible this must sound – as if we've been operating behind your back and abusing your trust, but . . . well, we didn't want to push you in the wrong direction. To learn more about the yrr, it was imperative to get you working on a peaceful solution. And you've all done well. But you'd never have made such headway if we'd told you we were developing a weapon.'

'What weapon?'

'War and peace are two different ballgames. If you're working towards peace, it doesn't do to be thinking of war. Mick's exploring the alternative to peace – with the help of your research, of course.'

'He's developing a toxin to kill them?'

'Would you rather we'd commissioned *you* to do it?' said Vanderbilt.

'Now, look here,' said Johanson, 'our brief was to make *contact*. To *persuade* them to halt the attack. Not to destroy them.'

'You're a dreamer,' Vanderbilt said contemptuously.

'But we can do it, Jack. For God's sake, we can . . .' Johanson was dismayed.

'You can, can you? How?'

'We've learned so much in so little time. There's bound to be a way.'

'And if there isn't?'

'We could have discussed it together. I thought we were a team.'

'Sigur.' Li looked serious. 'There's no clear provision for what we're doing in the UN resolution. I'm well aware that we're supposed to be making contact – and that's what we're trying to do. On the other hand, I don't think we'd cause anyone much heartache if we wiped out the enemy. Don't you think it's an option we need to consider?'

Johanson stared at her. 'Well, yes – but why the charade?'

'Because high command doesn't trust you,' said Li. 'You might make a fuss. People get their ideas about scientists from the movies. They think scientists are intent on protecting and studying other life-forms, even if they turn out to be evil and dangerous . . .'

'The movies? The kind where the army blows up everything in sight?'

'That proves our point,' said Vanderbilt. He ran his hand over his belly.

'Please be reasonable, Sigur . . .'

'You're telling me that you went to all this trouble just because you thought we'd react like characters in a film?'

'No,' said Li, firmly. 'Of course not. It was a question of focusing your attention on finding out about the yrr and making contact.'

Johanson's hand swept round the room, taking in the banks of monitors.

'So why are you spying on us?'

'Rubin made a mistake that night,' Li said insistently. 'He had no right to hit you. Our surveillance systems are here for your safety. We kept the military side of the mission secret because we didn't want to unsettle the rest of the team and distract you from your work.'

'And what exactly is the purpose of our work?' Johanson was almost touching Li, staring into her eyes. 'To make peace – or be duped into providing you with all the necessary information to launch a military offensive that you've been planning from the start?'

'We had to keep both options open.'

'How far has Mick got with the military one?'

'He's had a few ideas that seem promising, but nothing concrete.' Li took a deep breath. 'I'd like to ask you in the interests of international security not to tell any of the others what you've heard. Give us time to tell them ourselves. It would be wrong to jeopardise their work when billions of people are depending on it. Soon we'll be able to co-operate as one team on both options. You've achieved the seemingly impossible – you've given our enemy a face. Once the message is ready, there'll be no more need for secrecy. And when we start working together on a weapon, we'll do so in the hope that we'll never have to—'

'Do you know what, Jude?' hissed Johanson. He was so close now that there wasn't room to pass a hand between their faces. 'I don't believe you. As soon as you've got your bloody weapons, you're going to use them. Don't you see what will happen? They're *amoebas*, Jude! *Millions and billions of single-cell organisms.* They've been around since the beginning of time. We haven't even begun to understand their role in our ecosystem. There's no way of knowing what will happen to the oceans if you kill them. There's no way of knowing what will happen to *us* if you kill them. But quite apart from anything else: *we won't be able to stop what they've started.* Are you too blinkered to see that? How do you think you're going to get the Gulf Stream flowing without the yrr? What are you going to do about the worms?'

'When we've finished with the yrr,' said Li, 'we'll start on the worms and bacteria.'

'What? You want to pick a fight with bacteria? This whole planet is made of bacteria! You can't seriously intend to exterminate microbes. Exactly how deluded are you? You might think you rule the world, but if you were to go around exterminating microbes, you'd kill this planet. You'd be the ones destroying the Earth, not the yrr. You'd wipe out all the marine life and then—'

'So darned what?' Vanderbilt erupted. 'You pathetic, ignorant, stupid, know-it-all asshole of a scientist. Who gives a toss if a few fish die, so long as we survive—'

'But we won't!' Johanson was yelling now. 'Don't you get it? Life is interconnected. And we can't fight the yrr – they're superior to us. Fighting microbes is futile. Even normal viral infections defeat us – but that's not the point. Humans only survive on this planet because Earth is ruled by microbes.'

'Sigur . . .' Li implored him.

He turned round. 'Open the door,' he said. 'As far as I'm concerned, this conversation is over.'

'Fine.' Li nodded, tight-lipped. 'Show Dr Johanson out, Sal.'

Peak hesitated.

'Is there something wrong with your ears, Sal? Dr Johanson has expressed his wish to leave.'

'Are you sure we can't change your mind?' said Peak, sounding helpless and strained. 'Then maybe you'd see that it is the right decision.'

'Just open the door, Sal,' said Johanson.

Peak stepped forward reluctantly and pushed a switch on the wall. The door slid open.

'And the other door, if you don't mind.'

'Of course.'

Johanson walked out.

'Sigur!'

He stopped. 'What now, Jude?'

'You've accused me of failing to see the consequences of my actions. Who knows? Perhaps you're right. But make sure you face up to the consequences of yours. If you tell the others, you'll endanger their efforts to make contact. Maybe we didn't have the right to lie to you in the first place – but you need to consider whether you've got the right to tell the truth.'

Johanson turned round slowly. Li was standing in the door of the control room. 'I'll certainly give it my careful consideration,' he said.

'Then let's strike a deal. If you hold off until I've had time to find a solution, we can talk it through this evening. And, in the meantime, neither of us will do anything that might cause problems for the other. Can you see a way of co-operating with my proposal?'

Johanson's jaw was grinding. What would happen if he dropped the bombshell? What would happen *to him* if he turned her down point-blank?

'Done,' he said.

Li smiled. 'Thank you, Sigur.'

Weaver

All things considered, she would have preferred to stay on the well deck. Anawak was still doing his best to lift Greywolf's spirits, which made her feel doubly disinclined to go. Her feelings for one man made her want to stay with him; the grief of the other made her reluctant to leave. She couldn't bear to see Greywolf so overwhelmed with sorrow. Yet what Johanson had told her was even more disturbing. The more she thought about it, the more ominous his memories seemed. Deep down she felt that they were all in grave danger.

And by now Rubin would be back at the lab.

'I'll see you later,' she said. 'Stuff to do.'

As soon as the words were out of her mouth, she knew they sounded false. Too casual.

Anawak's brow furrowed. 'Stuff?'

'Oh, you know, bits and pieces.'

She was rubbish at this kind of thing. She hurried up the ramp and into the passageway. The door to the lab was open. As she walked in, she caught sight of Rubin talking to Oliviera. They were standing by one of the benches. Rubin turned to her. 'Hi. You wanted to ask me something?'

Weaver pushed the switch on the wall, so that the door closed behind her. 'I wondered if you could explain something.'

'You picked the right man.' Rubin grinned.

'That's good to know.' She joined them. Her eyes scanned the bench. All manner of equipment was littered over it, including an upright holder filled with scalpels of varying sizes. She said, 'I don't suppose you'll have any trouble telling me why there's a hidden lab up there, what you're doing in it, and why you knocked out Sigur?'

Hangar Deck

Johanson was seething with rage. He was too furious to know what to do with himself, so he ran to the hangar deck and inspected the wall. In his memory he knew exactly where the door was, but there was still no trace of a camouflaged passageway. It was a waste of time looking for it: Li had already admitted that the lab existed. But he wasn't prepared to let it lie.

Suddenly he noticed long streaks of rust in the grey paint of the bulkhead. Or, rather, he'd always known that they were there, but he'd never paid any attention to them because peeling paint and corrosion were not unusual on a vessel. Now it dawned on him that rust had no business on a new warship – and the *Independence* was brand new.

He took a few steps back. The pipes on the left stretched up along the bulkhead, leading to a long streak of rust. Above that was a fuse box, surrounded by flaking paint.

He'd found the door.

It was incredibly well concealed. He would never have spotted it if he hadn't been looking so determinedly. Even when he and Weaver had searched for it earlier, they'd fallen for the artful disguise. He still couldn't make out the contours, just an apparently random collection of details that in combination hid a door.

Weaver!

Would she have got to Rubin? Should he call her off, in line with what he'd said to Li?

Breathing heavily, he paced up and down the empty deck, unsure what to do. Suddenly the ship took on the aspect of a prison. Even the gloomy hangar with its yellow lights seemed oppressive.

He had to think.

Striding towards the starboard side of the vessel, he stepped on to the elevator. Gusts of wind tugged at his clothes and hair. The swell was still rising. Within seconds his face was covered with spray. He walked to the edge and gazed down at the turbulent lunar landscape of the Greenland Sea.

What was he to do?

Control Room

Li was standing in front of the monitors. She watched as Johanson inspected the bulkhead and strode across the hangar deck in frustration.

'What was all that crap about an agreement?' growled Vanderbilt. 'You don't really think he'll keep his mouth shut until tonight?'

'It wouldn't surprise me,' said Li.

'And what if he doesn't?'

Johanson disappeared out of the hangar bay on to the elevator. Li turned. 'You should know better than to ask. You're going to solve the problem, Jack. Right away.'

'Hang on a minute,' Peak objected. 'That's not what we'd agreed.'

'How do you mean, *solve*?' Vanderbilt asked warily.

'Solve,' said Li. 'I mean *solve*. A storm's getting up out there. You'd think people would know better than to wander outside. A gust of wind . . .'

'No,' said Peak. 'No one said anything about—'

'That's enough, Sal.'

'Jude, we could lock him up for a few hours. That's all we need.'

Li didn't bother to acknowledge him. 'Do your job, Jack,' she said to Vanderbilt. 'And make sure you do it *personally*.'

Vanderbilt grinned. 'With pleasure, baby.'

Lab

Oliviera's long face was now even longer. She stared at Weaver, then at Rubin.

'Well?' said Weaver.

Rubin blanched. 'I don't know what you're talking about.'

'Mick, listen to me.' Weaver moved between him and the table and laid an arm across his shoulders in a gesture that seemed almost friendly. 'I'm not a great talker. I like short, snappy conversations. So why don't we start again? This time, don't wind me up with excuses. There's a lab directly above us. You can get there from the hangar deck. Sure, the door's well camouflaged, but Sigur saw you going in and out. And you socked him one. Isn't that right?'

'I might have guessed.' Oliviera looked at Rubin contemptuously.

The biologist tried to free himself from Weaver's grip, and failed. 'I've never heard such utter—No! Stop!'

Weaver's free hand was wielding a scalpel. She pressed the tip against his artery. Rubin flinched. She pushed the blade a little further into his skin and tightened her grip. The biologist was locked in her embrace. 'Are you out of your mind?' he croaked. 'What right do you have to—'

'Mick, I'm not squeamish. And I'm stronger than you'd think. When I was little, I cuddled a cat and accidentally crushed it. Isn't that awful? I only wanted to stroke it, and then, crunch . . . So, you'd do well to think over carefully what you're about to tell me . . .'

Vanderbilt

Vanderbilt had no real desire to kill Johanson, but neither was he interested in keeping him alive. In a funny way he liked the guy, but that was beside the point: he'd been given the assignment, and his instructions were clear. Johanson wouldn't pose a security risk for much longer.

Floyd Anderson accompanied him. Like most of the men on the *Independence*, the first officer was there to serve a dual role. His training was with the navy, true, but his loyalties lay with the CIA. Almost everyone on board, with the exception of Buchanan and a few crew men, was on the CIA's books. Anderson had already taken part in covert operations in Pakistan and the Gulf. He was a good agent.

And a killer.

Vanderbilt pondered the turn of events. He'd maintained his belief that they were fighting terrorists until the bitter end, but now he had to concede that Johanson had been right all along. It seemed a shame to kill him, particularly as it was Li's idea. Vanderbilt couldn't stand that blue-eyed witch. Li was paranoid, conniving and twisted. He hated her, and yet he couldn't fault the perfidious logic of her ruthlessness. She might be crazy, but she was right. And she was right about this.

Suddenly he thought of how he'd warned Johanson about Li in Nanaimo.

She's nuts. Capisce?

Clearly Johanson hadn't understood.

No one understood at first. They didn't get what was wrong with Li: her tendency to see conspiracies everywhere and her obsessive ambition meant that she overreacted. She lied, deceived and was willing to sacrifice anyone and anything to achieve her goals. That was the real Judith Li. She was the President's darling, and even he didn't see her for who she really was. The most powerful man in the world had no idea who he was fostering.

We should all watch out, thought Vanderbilt. Unless someone grabs a gun and solves the problem – when the time comes.

They hurried along the passageways. In loitering on the external platform, Johanson was doing them a big favour. How had that mad bitch put it? A gust of wind . . .

Control Room

Vanderbilt was barely out of the room when Li was summoned to one of the consoles. The man at the desk pointed to the monitor. 'Looks like funny business in the lab,' he said.

Li watched the action on the screen. Weaver, Oliviera and Rubin were standing in a huddle. Weaver had an arm round Rubin's shoulders and was pressing him to her chest. Since when had those two been such good friends?

'More sound,' said Li.

They heard Weaver talking. Her voice was faint, but clear. She was interrogating Rubin about the hidden lab. On closer inspection, Rubin's eyes were filled with fear, and Weaver was holding something that glinted in the light. It was uncomfortably close to Rubin's throat.

Li had seen and heard enough. 'Sal, I need you and three men with machine guns – at the double. We're going in.'

'What do you intend to do?' asked Peak.

'Restore order.' She turned away from the screen and went to the door. 'That question just cost us two seconds. Waste any more time, Sal, and I'll shoot you myself. Get your men. You've got one minute. Then we're going to straighten out a thing or two with Weaver. The closed season for scientists is over.'

Lab

'You worthless bastard,' said Oliviera. 'You knocked Sigur unconscious. What the hell were you thinking?'

There was blind panic in Rubin's eyes. He scanned the ceiling.

'That's not true, I—'

'Don't bother looking for cameras, Mick,' Weaver said softly. 'You'll be dead before anyone gets here.'

Rubin started to shake.

'I'm going to ask you again, Mick, *what's going on up there?*'

'We've developed a toxin,' he stuttered.

'A toxin?' echoed Oliviera.

'We used your work, Sue. I mean, yours and Sigur's, of course. Once you'd worked out the formula for the pheromone, there was nothing to stop us manufacturing as much of it as we liked and . . . Well, we coupled it to a radioactive isotope.'

'You did what?'

'We contaminated the pheromone – the yrr-cells can't tell the difference. We ran some trials and—'

'Do you mean you've got a deep-sea chamber up there too?'

'Only a small one . . . Karen, please. Put the knife away. It's futile. They can hear and see everything—'

'Stick to the point,' said Weaver. 'And then what?'

'Well, the pheromone kills defective yrr-cells. They die because they don't have special receptors – it's just like Sue said. Once it was obvious that programmed cell death is part of yrr-biochemistry, we had to find a way of inducing it in healthy yrr as well.'

'Via the pheromone?'

'It's the only way. We can't mess with the DNA directly because we haven't fully decoded the genome, and that would take years. We coupled the scent to a radioactive isotope that the yrr can't detect.'

'And what does it do?'

'It shuts down the special receptor. It means the pheromone is deadly. It can kill healthy cells too.'

'Why didn't you tell us?' said Oliviera. 'None of us actually likes these creatures. We could have come up with a solution together.'

'Li's got her own plans,' squawked Rubin.

'But it won't work.'

'It has worked. We trialled it.'

'It's madness, Mick. You don't know what you're unleashing. What if you wipe out the yrr? They control seventy per cent of our planet. They're the force behind a sophisticated form of biotechnology that's been around since the year dot. They live in other creatures too. I mean, for all we know, they could be present in every single marine organism. And what if they're breaking down methane or carbon dioxide? God knows what will happen to the planet if you destroy them.'

'But why should it kill *all* of them?' asked Weaver. 'Doesn't the toxin just kill individual cells? Or collectives?'

'No, it starts a chain reaction.' Rubin was wheezing now. 'Programmed cell death. As soon as they start to aggregate, they all destroy themselves. Once the pheromone docks on to them, it's too late. There's nothing they can do to stop it. We're recoding the yrr. It's like a deadly virus. They all infect each other.'

Oliviera grabbed Rubin by the collar. 'You've got to stop these trials,' she said urgently. 'You can't go down that route. For God's sake, Mick, don't you see that they're the ones in charge? It's their planet. They *are* the planet. They're a superorganism. Thanks to them, the oceans are intelligent. You've got no idea what you're doing.'

'And if we don't use the toxin?' Rubin gave a croaky laugh. 'Don't give me all that self-righteous crap about ecosystems. We're going to die, that's what. Do you think we should wait for the next tsunami? I suppose there's always the methane build-up or the ice age to look forward to.'

'We haven't been here a week yet, and we've already made contact,' said Weaver. 'Why can't we keep trying for an agreement?'

'It's too late,' rasped Rubin.

Weaver's eyes darted over the ceiling and walls. She didn't know how much time she had left before Li or Peak showed up. Maybe Vanderbilt would come running. It couldn't be long. 'What do you mean, too late?'

'It's too late!' screamed Rubin. 'We're releasing the toxin in less than two hours.'

'You're crazy,' Oliviera whispered.

'Mick,' Weaver said, 'I need you to tell me exactly how you're going to do it. Otherwise my hand might slip.'

'I'm not authorised—'

'I mean it.'

Rubin was trembling all over. 'We're using two torpedoes on Deepflight 3. We've packed the radioactive pheromone into projectiles.'

'Are they on the sub already?'

'No, it's my job to load them and—'

'Who's taking them down?'

'I'm going with Li.'

'She's going herself?'

'Well, it was her idea. She doesn't leave anything to chance.' Rubin managed a smile. 'You won't be able to stop her, Karen. There's nothing you can do. We're the ones who're going to save this planet. Our names are the ones that people will remember—'

'Shut up, Mick.' Weaver began to push him towards the door. 'You're going to take me to your lab. That toxin isn't going anywhere. The script's just changed.'

'So is anything going on between you and Karen?' asked Greywolf, stowing equipment in crates.

Anawak was taken aback. 'Er, no. Not really.'

'Not really?'

'As far as I know, we're just good friends.'

Greywolf gave him a look. 'It's about time one of us started to do things right,' he said.

'What if she's not interested?' As soon as he'd said it, Anawak realised what he'd confessed. 'I'm hopeless at that kind of thing, Jack.'

'Evidently,' said Greywolf, sarcastically. 'You didn't join the world of the living until your old man died.'

'Hey . . .'

'Calm down, buddy, you know I'm right. Why don't you chase after her? She obviously wants you to.'

'I came down here to see you, not because of Karen.'

'I appreciate it. Now, go.'

'For God's sake, Jack. Stop shutting yourself away. Let's take a walk before your feet turn into fins.'

'Fins would suit me fine.'

Anawak glanced at the tunnel, unsure what to do. Of course he was impatient to go after Weaver – and not only because he had feelings for her, as he'd just admitted to Greywolf and himself. No, he was sure that something was bothering her. She'd seemed agitated and tense. He couldn't help thinking of what she'd told him about Johanson.

'OK, you moulder away by yourself, then,' he said to Greywolf, 'but feel free to come and find me if you change your mind.'

He left the well deck and walked past the lab. The door was closed. He thought about popping in. Maybe Johanson would be there. Then he decided against it and carried on up the ramp towards the hangar deck to look at the mysterious wall.

As he entered the bay he caught sight of Vanderbilt and Anderson disappearing on to the elevator platform.

Suddenly he felt uneasy. What were they doing there?

And where had Weaver got to?

A strong westerly howled through the air. It was blowing in from the polar ice caps, sending white-crested waves crashing into the *Independence*'s hull and drawing what was left of the warmth from the sea.

Beneath its turbulent surface the ocean was swirling and raging, but as the depth increased, the storm died down. It was here that, only a few months previously, icy cascades of salt-laden water had poured into the depths. It was still bitterly cold, but now the salt was being diluted as fresh water streamed in from the ice caps, which were melting rapidly because of an influx of warmth. The North Atlantic pump, which drew oxygen-rich water into the depths like an underwater lung, was slowly coming to a halt. The ocean conveyor slowed, and the warmth-giving current from the tropics dried up.

But it hadn't stopped yet. Even though the chimneys could no longer be detected, small quantities of cold water were still trickling into the depths. Through the lightless calm of the ocean they fell towards the bottom of the Greenland basin, metre by metre, till they were hundreds, then thousands of metres down.

At a depth of 3.5 kilometres, just above the silty seabed, the darkness gave way to a blue glow.

It covered a vast expanse, not as a cloud of light, but as a long tube of jelly with thin walls. It was anchored to the seabed by countless tiny feet. Inside the tube millions of tentacular protuberances were rising and falling in rhythmical waves, a meadow of feelers moving in synchrony. They were conveying big lumps of a whitish substance towards a large object. The blue glow was barely strong enough to illuminate its contours, so all that was visible were two open pods. The Deepflight stuck out of the silt at an angle, but most of the submersible was hidden in the gloom.

For some time now, the organism had been loading it with frozen white lumps, and the boat was nearly full. The supply chain ceased. One section of the tube separated off, sank towards the boat and began to encase it. The transparent substance around the hull contracted, closing the pods as it compressed. Shimmering layers of blue spread out and merged until the vessel was sealed with jelly. A long thin tube moved towards it and began to pulsate. Water was being pumped through it. Water that didn't belong there. The delicate tube of jelly was drawing it from an enormous organic balloon suspended over the boat and filled with warm water originating from the mud volcano near the Norwegian continental shelf. By all rights, the balloon should have risen to the surface, propelled by the warmer – and lighter – water inside, but its weight kept it stable.

Warmth streamed into the sac of jelly that was wrapped round the boat.

The white lumps reacted immediately. In a matter of seconds the frozen cages trapping the gas had melted. The compressed methane expanded to 164 times its former volume, filling the Deepflight with gas and inflating the sack of jelly until it was taut and swollen. It detached from the tube and sealed itself off. Unable to escape, the gas rose upwards, slowly at first, but then, as the pressure around it decreased, picking up speed. The gas, the cocoon, and the submersible shot towards the surface.

Lab

With one arm clamped round Rubin and the other hand holding the scalpel to his throat, Weaver shuffled forward. She didn't get far. The door to the lab slid open. Three heavily armed soldiers stormed inside and took aim. She heard Oliviera cry out in horror. Weaver stopped in her tracks, but held on to Rubin.

Li walked into the lab, followed by Peak. 'You're not going anywhere, Karen.'

'Jude,' croaked Rubin, 'about time too. Get this lunatic off me.'

'Quiet,' Peak barked at him. 'We wouldn't be in this situation if it weren't for you.'

Li smiled. 'Karen,' she said, 'don't you think you're taking this a little too far?'

'Given what Mick has been saying . . . No.'

'And what *has* he been saying?'

'Oh, he was very helpful. Weren't you, Mick? Told us everything we need to know.'

'She's lying,' hissed Rubin.

'Hmm . . . Chain reactions, torpedoes full of toxins and Deepflight 3. Oh, and he mentioned that the two of you were planning an excursion – in the next few hours.'

'Tsk.' Li took a step forward. Weaver grabbed Rubin and pulled him back towards Oliviera, who was standing motionless beside the bench. She still had the test-tube rack containing the pheromone samples in her hand.

'Mick Rubin is probably one of the best biologists in the world,' said Li. 'The trouble is, he always has to prove himself. He'd give anything to be famous. That's why he finds it so hard to keep his mouth shut. You'll have to excuse him. Mick would sell his own grandmother for a taste of fame.' She came to a halt. 'But no matter. You know what we're planning so you'll understand our reasons. I've done my best to stop the situation escalating, but now everyone seems to know the secret, so you've left me no choice.'

'Don't do anything stupid, Karen,' Peak implored her. 'Let him go.'

'I'll do no such thing.'

'He's still got work to do. If you let him go, we'll talk later.'

'There's been more than enough talking already.' Li pulled out her pistol and took aim at Weaver. 'Let go of him, Karen. or I'll shoot. I'm not going to warn you again.'

Weaver looked into the small round barrel of the gun. 'You wouldn't,' she said.

'Really?'

'There's no need.'

'You're making a mistake, Jude,' Oliviera said hoarscly. 'You can't use the toxin. I was just telling Mick how . . .'

Li wheeled around, took aim at Oliviera and pulled the trigger. The scientist was tossed back against the bench and slid slowly to the floor. The case of test-tubes dropped from her hand. For a second she looked, surprised, at the fist-sized hole in her chest, then her eyes glazed.

'*What the hell are you playing at?*' shrieked Peak.

The gun was pointing at Weaver. 'Now let him go,' said Li.

Deck Elevator

'Dr Johanson!'

Johanson swivelled. Vanderbilt and Anderson were heading towards him across the platform. Anderson looked impassive and detached. His black button eyes were fixed on something in the distance.

Vanderbilt was beaming. 'I guess you're pretty pissed at us,' he said.

There was something chummy and casual about his demeanour. Johanson frowned as he watched them approach. He was standing at the far end of the platform, only metres from the edge. Hefty gusts of wind buffeted his face. The waves were crashing beneath him. He'd been thinking about going inside. 'What brings you here, Jack?'

'Nothing in particular.' Vanderbilt made an apologetic gesture. 'I just wanted to say I'm sorry. It's all so unnecessary. We shouldn't be arguing. The whole darned thing is ridiculous.'

Johanson didn't reply. Vanderbilt and Anderson were getting closer. He took a step to the side. They stopped.

'Is there something you wanted to discuss?' asked Johanson.

'I was rude to you earlier,' said Vanderbilt. 'I apologise.'

Johanson raised his eyebrows.

'That's very noble of you, Jack. Apology accepted. Can I help you with anything else?'

Vanderbilt faced into the gale. His thinning pale blond hair quivered in the wind like beach grass. 'Pretty darned cold out here,' he said, moving forward. Anderson followed his lead. A distance opened between them. It looked as though they were trying to close in on Johanson. There was no longer any room for him to slip between them or dodge to either side.

What they were intending was so obvious that he didn't even feel surprised. He was gripped by fear – fear, mixed with desperate fury. Without thinking he took a step backwards, and knew he had made a mistake. He was very close to the edge now. Their job was almost done for them. A sudden gust could knock him into the nets or over the top and into the water. 'Jack,' he said slowly, 'you wouldn't be planning to kill me, would you?'

'Whatever gave you that idea?' Vanderbilt assumed a look of mock-amazement. 'I only want to talk.'

'Then why bring Anderson?'

'Oh, he was just passing. Pure coincidence. We thought—'

Johanson rushed towards Vanderbilt, ducked and darted to the right. He was away from the edge. Anderson leaped towards him. For a moment it looked as though the improvised tactic had worked, then Johanson felt himself grabbed and dragged backwards. Anderson's fist flew towards him and landed in his face.

He fell and skidded across the platform.

The first officer moved towards him without any urgency. His powerful hands disappeared beneath Johanson's armpits and hauled him up. Johanson tried to prise his fingers under Anderson's grip and loosen it, but it was like grappling with concrete. His feet left the ground. He kicked out wildly as Anderson carried him towards the edge where Vanderbilt was waiting, peering down at the sea.

'Quite a swell today,' said the CIA agent. 'I hope you won't mind if we cast you off now, Dr Johanson. I'm afraid you'll have to swim.' His teeth flashed. 'But don't worry, you won't be going any great distance. The water's pretty chilly – two degrees at most. It will be quite relaxing. The body just slows down, the senses go numb, the heart packs up, and—'

Johanson started to shout. 'Help!' he screamed. 'Help!'

His feet were dangling over the side. The net was beneath him. It only extended two metres beyond the platform. Not far enough. Anderson could easily throw him over the top.

Help!

He heard Anderson groan as suddenly he was yanked towards the safety of the platform. The sky came into view as Anderson thudded on to his back, pulling Johanson with him, then letting go. Johanson rolled to the side and jumped up. 'Leon!' he gasped.

A grotesque scene was unfolding before him. Anderson was trying to clamber to his feet. Anawak had fastened himself on to him from behind and was clutching his jacket. They'd fallen to the ground together. Now Anawak was attempting to free himself from the man's weight without releasing his grip.

Johanson was about to intervene.

'Stop!'

Vanderbilt barred his path. He was holding a gun. Slowly he walked round the bodies on the floor until he was standing with his back to the exit.

'Nice try,' he said. 'But that's enough now. Dr Anawak, please be so kind as to allow Mr Anderson here to get up. He's only doing his job.'

Reluctantly Anawak let go of Anderson's hood. The first officer shot up. He didn't wait until his adversary was on his feet, but hoisted him into the air like a sack of coal. The next instant Anawak's body was flying towards the edge.

'No!' roared Johanson.

Anawak slammed down on to the deck then slid to the edge of the platform.

Anderson's head turned towards Johanson. One arm shot out, grabbed him, and a fist rammed into his stomach. Johanson gasped for air. A wave of pain spread through his guts. He folded like a penknife and fell to his knees.

The pain was almost unbearable.

He crouched there, retching, as the wind whipped through his hair, waiting for Anderson to punch him again.

PART FOUR

SINKING

Research shows that human beings are incapable of discerning intelligence beyond a certain micro- or meta-threshold. For us to perceive intelligence, it has to fit within our behavioural framework. If we were to encounter intelligence operating outside that framework – on a micro-level, for instance – we would fail to see it. Similarly, if we were to come into contact with a far higher intelligence, a mind vastly superior to our own, we would see only chaos, as its reasoning would elude us. Decisions taken by a higher instance of intelligence would prove inscrutable to our intellect, having been made within parameters beyond the reach of human understanding. Imagine a dog's view of us. To the dog, a person appears not as a mind, but as a force to be obeyed. From its perspective, human behaviour is arbitrary: our actions are based on considerations that canine perception fails to grasp. It follows therefore that, should God exist, we would be incapable of recognising him or her as an intelligent being, since divine thought would encompass a totality of factors too complex for us to comprehend. Consequently, God would appear as a force of chaos, and therefore scarcely the entity that we would like to see governing the outcome of a football match, let alone a war. A being of that kind would exist beyond the limits of human perception. And that in turn prompts the question as to whether the meta-being God would be capable of perceiving intelligence on the sub-level of the human. Maybe we are an experiment in a petri-dish after all . . .

Samantha Crowe, *Diaries*

Deepflight

Anderson's punch never came.

A few seconds earlier the crew of the *Independence* had been thrown into a state of red alert: the dolphins had reported an unknown object. Now the sonar systems detected it too. Something of unspecified size and shape was approaching at speed. It didn't sound like a torpedo, and there was nothing on the sonar to show what could have launched it. What made the crew on the bridge and at the consoles particularly nervous wasn't merely its silent and rapid ascent, but that it was coming at them vertically. They stared at the monitors and watched as a round, bluish patch emerged from the darkness. A rippling orb was rushing towards them, at least ten metres in diameter, gaining in size and detail on their screens.

By the time Buchanan had given the order to shoot it down, it was already too late.

The sphere exploded directly beneath the hull. Over the last few minutes of its journey, the gas inside it had continued to expand, accelerating its ascent. As it raced upwards, the cocoon's thin skin of jelly had stretched to bursting point, then ripped open from top to bottom. The scraps hung in the water. The gas continued upwards, surging towards the surface, carrying a large rectangular object.

Spinning on its axis, the lost Deepflight raced towards the *Independence*, striking it bow-first and ramming its torpedoes through the hull.

An eternity elapsed.

And then the explosion.

The enormous vessel quaked.

Buchanan, who had seen the disaster coming, narrowly succeeded in staying upright by clinging to the chart table. Others weren't so lucky and crashed to the floor. In the control rooms beneath the island the vessel shook so violently that the monitors cracked and pieces of equipment flew through the air. In the CIC Crowe and Shankar were thrown from their chairs. In a matter of seconds chaos had broken out all over the ship. The harsh buzz of the alarm had kicked in, mixed with shouting, running footsteps, and jangling, droning, clunking noises, as the rumblings spread through the passageways, along the compartments and from level to level.

Seconds after impact the majority of the engine- and boiler-room technicians were dead. A vast crater had been torn in the hull amidships, where the ammunition magazines and the engine room, with its two LM 2500 gas turbines, were located. The gaping tear was twenty metres long. Water blasted in with the force of a sledge-hammer, killing everyone who had survived the explosion. Anyone trying to escape was confronted by locked doors. The only way to save the *Independence* was to sacrifice those in the catacombs of the vessel, locking them in with the raging water to prevent the torrent swamping the vessel.

Deck Elevator

The platform shuddered violently, then catapulted Floyd Anderson over Johanson's head. The first officer flung out his arms, fingers clutching at the air, then fell face down, flipped over and lay motionless, eyes open and empty.

Vanderbilt was almost knocked off his feet. He let go of the gun, which slid across the platform, stopping centimetres from the edge. He caught sight of Johanson trying to drag himself upright, darted over and kicked him in the ribs. The scientist toppled sideways with a muffled cry. Vanderbilt had no idea what had happened to the vessel, only that it must have been disastrous. But his brief was to eliminate Johanson and he intended to fulfil it. He was bending down to drag the groaning, bleeding man across the platform, intending to throw him over the nets, when someone cannoned into him from the side.

'Vanderbilt, you bastard!' screamed Anawak.

Suddenly he found himself under attack. Anawak's fists were battering him with frenzied violence. Vanderbilt retreated. He raised his arms to shield his head, ducked to the side and kicked his assailant in the kneecap.

Anawak swayed and his legs gave way. Vanderbilt transferred his weight to the other foot. Most people who met Jack Vanderbilt misjudged his strength and agility. They saw only his girth. But he was fully trained in self-defence and martial arts and, despite his hundred or so kilos, could still perform some serious moves. He ran forward, threw himself into the air and rammed his boot against Anawak's sternum. Anawak thumped on to his back. His mouth opened in an O, but no sound came out. Good, thought Vanderbilt. He'd winded him. Bending down, he pulled Anawak up by the hair and shoved his elbow into the man's solar plexus.

That should do it. Now back to Johanson. Once he'd got the Norwegian into the water, Anawak could follow.

As he straightened up, he saw Greywolf bearing down on him. Vanderbilt went on the attack. He spun round, kicked out his right leg, made contact with his opponent – and rebounded.

That's not right, he thought, confused. The kick had been enough to make anyone slump to the floor or double up with pain. But the man continued towards him. There was no mistaking the look in his eyes. Suddenly Vanderbilt realised that he had no choice but to win this fight if he wanted to survive. His arms whirled above his head as he prepared to land the next blow. He lunged forward and felt his arm brushed away casually. Then Greywolf's left hand had buried itself in his double chin. Vanderbilt kicked out. Without breaking stride Greywolf shoved him towards the edge, raised his fist and punched.

Vanderbilt's field of vision exploded. Everything went red. There was a crunch as his nose broke. The next blow shattered his cheekbone. A gurgled scream rose from his throat. The fist rammed into his mouth. His teeth splintered. Vanderbilt was delirious with pain and rage. The giant's other hand prevented him moving. His face was being pulped.

Greywolf let go and Vanderbilt toppled backwards. He couldn't see much, just a bit of sky, grey asphalt and the yellow markings of the platform, all through a veil of blood. His gun was lying next to him. He reached for it, grasped it, jerked up his arm and fired.

For a moment it was quiet.

Had he hit him? He fired again. His arm sagged backwards. He caught a glimpse of Anawak looming above him, then the gun was knocked from his hand and he was looking into Greywolf's eyes.

Pain rushed through him.

He wasn't on his back any more, he was standing upright. Or was he hanging upside-down? He couldn't tell. He seemed to be floating. No, he was flying backwards. Through a mist of blood he saw the platform, then the edge of the platform, moving away from him, disappearing into the sky with the nets.

The cold hit him like a blow. Foaming water washed the blood from Vanderbilt's eyes, as his body dropped into the depths. There was no sign of the vessel, just featureless green, a darkening expanse from which a shadow emerged.

It was moving quickly. Its mouth opened as it approached.

Then there was nothing.

Lab

'*What the hell are you playing at?*'

'Let him go.'

The words were still echoing in Weaver's head: Peak's horrified question, followed by Li's brutal order. Then the lab shook and heeled. The rumble of the blast was drowned by a cacophony of noises as everything around them toppled and smashed. Weaver was hurled across the room with Rubin. They landed behind a bench in a hail of instruments and receptacles. A thunderous noise swept round the lab. Everything was vibrating. Then they heard glass shattering. Weaver's first thought was for the containment facility. She hoped to God that its hermetically sealed chambers and armoured glass would hold. On her butt, she shuffled away from Rubin.

She spotted the metal case of test-tubes. It had slid across the floor towards her feet. She and Rubin stared at it.

There was a brief pause while they weighed up their chances. Then Weaver lunged forward, but Rubin was quicker. He grabbed the case, jumped up and ran towards the back of the lab. Weaver swore, knowing she'd have to leave the shelter of the bench. Whatever was going on around them, no matter what Li was up to, she had to have that case.

Two soldiers were slumped on the floor. One lay still, but the other was clambering to his feet. The third had kept his balance and was holding his gun at the ready. Li bent down to take the weapon from the motionless body. At the next second it was pointing at Weaver. Peak was leaning stiffly against the locked door. 'Karen,' he shouted, 'don't move. We won't hurt you. For Christ's sake, Karen, don't move.'

His voice was drowned by the rattle of the gun. Weaver sprang, cat-like, behind a nearby cluster of benches. She had no idea what Li was firing, but the ammunition shredded the benches as though they were cardboard. Splinters of glass flew past her head and a hundred kilograms of microscope crashed to the floor. Amid the chaos the alarm buzzed steadily. Suddenly Rubin was running towards her, eyes wide with panic.

'Mick!' yelled Li. 'Mick, you moron, get over here.'

Weaver dived out of her hiding-place. She flung herself on top of Rubin and seized the case. Just then the vessel shook again, and the room tilted further. Rubin slid across the floor and crashed into a shelving unit, which toppled over, bombarding him with test-tubes and trapping him on his back. He howled, his arms and legs waving in the air. Out of the corner of her eye Weaver saw Li turn the weapon towards her. The third soldier was leaping over the ruins of the benches. He had one of the enormous black weapons too, and raised it.

There was nowhere for her to run. She dropped down beside Rubin.

'Don't shoot,' she heard Li shout. 'It's too—'

The soldier fired. He missed her. The shots thudded against the deep-sea simulator, making a gong-like sound on the glass. They ploughed straight through the oval window in a single line from left to right.

Suddenly there was an eerie silence, except for the alarm, which continued to buzz at regular intervals. They all froze and stared transfixed at the tank. Weaver heard a single loud crack. She turned her head and saw fissures spreading through the enormous sheet of glass.

'Oh, God,' groaned Rubin.

'Mick,' yelled Li. 'Get the hell over here!'

'I can't,' he whimpered, 'It's my leg. I can't move.'

'Too bad,' said Li. 'He's expendable. Let's go.'

'You can't just—' Peak was cut off before he could finish.

'Open the door, Sal.'

If Peak said anything, no one heard it. There was a deafening bang as the glass shattered. Tonnes of seawater spurted towards them. Weaver ran. Behind her a torrent of water raged through the laboratory, knocking down everything in its path.

'Karen,' she heard Rubin cry out. 'Don't leave—'

The room was full of spray. She saw Peak limping through the door, followed by Li. As the commander walked out her hand hit a switch on the wall beside the door. Weaver knew what that meant.

Li intended to lock them inside.

Water rushed up her back, pitching her forward. She crashed to her knees and scrambled up. She was drenched, but her arms were still wrapped round the case. Panting and trying not to be dragged back by the tide, she fought her way to the door as it started to close. She covered the last few metres in a single bound, glanced off the doorframe and tumbled on to the ramp.

Deck Elevator

Greywolf and Anawak helped Johanson to his feet. The biologist was in a bad way, but still conscious. 'Where's Vanderbilt?' he murmured.

'Gone fishing,' said Greywolf.

Anawak felt as though he'd been run over by a train. His belly was hurting so much that he could barely keep upright.

'Jack,' he kept saying, 'Jeez, Jack.' Greywolf had saved him again. It was becoming a tradition. 'How did you get here?'

'I was a bit short with you earlier,' said Greywolf. 'I wanted to apologise.'

'Are you crazy? You shouldn't be apologising for anything.'

'Thank goodness he didn't see it that way,' said Johanson, between groans.

Greywolf's face was waxen beneath the copper-coloured skin. What's wrong with him? thought Anawak. Then his friend's shoulders slumped and his eyelids fluttered . . .

Suddenly he noticed that Greywolf's T-shirt was covered with blood. For a moment he allowed himself to believe it was Vanderbilt's. Then he saw that the stain was growing bigger – blood was spilling from his stomach. The ship was rocked by another blast and Johanson stumbled into him. Greywolf tipped forwards and disappeared over the edge.

'Jack!' Anawak dropped to his knees and slid over to where Greywolf had been standing. He was caught in one of the nets, gazing up at him. The waves crashed below. 'Jack, give me your hand.'

Greywolf didn't move. He stared up at Anawak, pressing his hands to his belly. Blood welled through his fingers.

Vanderbilt. The bastard had shot him.

'It's going to be OK, Jack.' Words from a movie. 'Give me your hand. I'll pull you out of there. We can do it.'

Johanson crawled to the edge. Lying flat on his belly, he tried to reach down into the net, but his arms weren't long enough.

'You need to pick yourself up,' Anawak said. Then: 'Stay there, Jack. I'm coming down. I'll push you up, and Sigur can drag you from above.'

'No,' said Greywolf.

'Jack . . .'

'It's better this way.'

'Don't talk like that!' Anawak snapped at him. 'I don't want to hear any of that Hollywood shit about not worrying about you and leaving you to—'

'Leon, buddy.'

'Jack! I said no!'

A thin ribbon of blood trickled out of Greywolf's mouth. 'Leon . . .' He smiled. All of a sudden he seemed to relax. He sat up with a jerk, rolled towards the edge of the net and splashed into the waves.

Lab

Rubin couldn't see or hear. Water from the tank swirled over him. He wondered what on earth had happened in the last few seconds. Then he felt the raging mass of water lift the shelving unit off his leg. He rose, spluttering, to the surface.

Thank God for that, he thought. At least the worst is over.

The tank held a hell of a lot of water, but not enough to flood the lab. Once it had spread out, it wouldn't come higher than a metre.

Where was Li?

The body of a soldier was drifting alongside him. Another picked himself up from the water in stunned confusion.

Li was gone.

She'd abandoned them.

Rubin looked at the water, then at the door. His mind cleared. He had to get out of there. There'd been an explosion on the vessel, and they were probably sinking.

He was about to stand up, when the laboratory started to glow.

Light flashed.

It wasn't only water escaping from the tank. He tried to get up, but skidded and fell backwards. His head disappeared under water. He paddled with his hands to steady himself, and met with resistance. Something smooth. It was moving.

Lightning flashed in his eyes, then his mouth was sealed as a film of jelly spread over his face. Rubin tore at it, but his fingers kept sliding off. As soon as he touched it, it morphed or dissociated. New tissue formed in its place.

This can't be happening, he thought. No!

He opened his mouth and felt the substance glide inside. He was crazy with fear. A thin feeler snaked down his throat, while other tendrils invaded his nostrils. He retched, flailing wildly and rearing up in the water. The pain was unbearable, as though instruments of torture were being inserted inside his skull. In a final moment of clarity he realised that the jelly was inside his brain.

Ever since the incident on the well deck, Rubin had been wondering whether it was strategic intention, mere curiosity or a primeval drive to crawl inside whatever looked interesting that led the yrr to explore the human brain.

Now he would wonder no more.

Greywolf

He felt peace. Utter calm. That probably wasn't what Vanderbilt had felt. Vanderbilt had been afraid. His death had been brutal, and rightly so, but it was different without fear.

Greywolf sank into the depths. He held his breath. Despite the terrible pain in his guts he was determined not to breathe out. Not because he thought he could lengthen his life. It was a last exertion of will-power, a final act of self-control. He would determine when the water should enter his lungs.

Licia was down there. Everything he'd ever wanted, everything he'd valued, was under water. It was only logical that he was on his way there too. It was time for him to go.

Live a good life, and one day you'll come back as an orca.

He saw a dark shadow flit through the water above him. Then another. The whales paid him no attention. That's right, thought Greywolf, I'm your friend. You won't hurt me. He knew, of course, that the real explanation was more prosaic. They hadn't noticed him. Orcas like those had no friends. They weren't even orcas any more. They had been subjugated by a species that was as ruthless as mankind.

But some day it would be OK again. The time would come. And the Grey Wolf would become an orca.

He breathed out.

Peak

'Are you completely insane?' Peak's voice reverberated in the tunnel. Li sped ahead of him. He tried to ignore the throbbing in his ankle and keep pace with her. She'd abandoned the machine-gun and was carrying her pistol.

'You're starting to get on my nerves, Sal.' Li headed for the nearest companionway. They climbed in single file to the level above, where a passageway took them to the restricted area. From the bowels of the vessel came the sounds of destruction. There was another explosion. The floor shook and tilted, forcing them to pause. The bulkheads must be giving way to the pressure. Now the *Independence* was at a noticeable angle. The passageway became an uphill slope. Men and women streamed out of the control room, running towards them. They looked at Li expectantly, awaiting her orders. Their commander strode past.

'On your nerves?' Peak blocked her path. His horror was turning into blind rage. 'You can't just go around shooting people or having them killed. For Christ's sake, Li, *it's uncalled for*. We never planned it this way. No one agreed to this.'

Li's face was calm, but her blue eyes were flicking back and forth. Peak had never noticed that before. Suddenly he knew that this highly intelligent, well-educated, distinguished general was mad.

'Vanderbilt knows,' she said.

'You cleared it with the CIA?'

'With Vanderbilt *of* the CIA.'

'So you and that scumbag agreed to this lunacy?' Peak's lips curled in disgust. 'Well, it makes me sick. Right now we should be helping to evacuate this vessel.'

'We've got presidential approval,' Li added.

'Yeah, right.'

'Or as good as.'

'Not for this. I don't believe you.'

'Well, I *know* he'd approve it.' She pushed past him. 'Now, get out of my way. We're running out of time.'

Peak rushed after her. 'But these people have done nothing wrong. They risked their lives by joining this mission. They're our allies. Arrest them if you have to, but don't kill them.'

'They're either with me or against me. Can't you see that, Sal?'

'Johanson wasn't against you.'

'He was against me from the start.' She spun round, glaring up at him. 'Are you blind or just stupid? Don't you understand what will happen if America doesn't win this war? Another state's victory is America's defeat.'

'But this isn't about America! It's about the world.'

'America *is* the world.'

Peak stared at her. 'You're crazy,' he whispered.

'No, just realistic. And it's about time you did as you were told. You're under my command.' Li walked off. 'Come on. We've got a job to do. I need to be in that submersible before this ship is blown to pieces. Help me find Rubin's radioactive torpedoes. Then you can do as you like.'

Vehicle Ramp

Weaver couldn't make up her mind which way to run until she heard voices coming from the ramp. Li and Peak had vanished. They were probably on their way to Rubin's lab to fetch the contaminated pheromone. She ran to the next bend in the tunnel and saw Anawak and Johanson at the entrance to the hangar deck, each propping up the other, about to head down.

'Leon!' she cried. 'Sigur!'

She ran forward and threw her arms round them. It meant a pretty big stretch but she needed to hold them both. One especially. Johanson grunted in pain. She jerked away. 'Oh, I'm sorry, I—'

'It's OK.' He wiped the blood off his beard. 'The spirit is willing but . . . Anyway, what's going on?'

'Whatever happened to *you*?'

The deck rumbled beneath their feet. The *Independence*'s hull gave a drawn-out squeal. The hangar bay tilted another degree towards the bow.

Hurriedly they swapped accounts, Anawak still in shock from Grey-wolf's death. 'Does either of you know what's happening to the ship?' he asked.

'No, but I don't think we've time to worry about it.' Weaver glanced round. 'I'd say we've got two urgent jobs to deal with: stopping Li getting into that sub, and somehow getting out of here alive.'

'You think she'll stick to her plan?'

'Of course she will,' Johanson growled.

Noises were coming from the flight deck above them. They heard the thump of rotors. 'Do you hear that? The rats are deserting the ship.'

'But what's come over her?' Anawak shook his head uncomprehend-ingly. 'Why would Li kill Sue?'

'She did her best to kill me too. She'd shoot anyone who stands in her way. She never intended to negotiate peacefully.'

'But what's she trying to achieve?'

'It doesn't matter now,' said Johanson. 'Her schedule will have moved forward dramatically. Someone's got to stop her. We can't let her take that stuff down there.'

'No,' said Weaver. 'We need to take *this* stuff down there instead.'

For the first time Johanson noticed the case in Weaver's hand. His eyes widened. 'Is that the new batch of pheromone?'

'Sue's legacy.'

'But how's that going to help us?'

'I've had an idea.' She hesitated. 'God knows if it'll work, though. I thought of it yesterday, but somehow it didn't seem viable. I guess things have changed.' She summarised.

803

'Sounds promising,' said Anawak. 'But we must act fast. We may have only minutes. We need to be out of here before the ship sinks.'

'But I don't know how we can do it in practice.'

'Well, I do.' Anawak pointed down the ramp. 'We need a dozen hypodermic syringes. I'll fetch them. You two go down and take care of the submersible.' He thought for a moment. 'And we'll need . . . Do you think you'll find someone in the lab?'

'Sure. No problem. But where are you going to get syringes?'

'The infirmary.'

Above them the noise intensified. Through the opening to the port-side elevator they saw a helicopter rise up and wheel round, flying close to the waves. The steel girders of the hangar deck groaned. The ship was warping.

'Be quick,' said Weaver.

Anawak met her gaze. Their eyes lingered. 'You can depend on it,' he said.

Evacuation

Unlike most people on the *Independence*, Crowe knew almost exactly what had happened. Footage of the glowing sphere had been relayed via the cameras on the hull to the monitors above. From what she could tell, the ball had been made of jelly, and there'd been gas inside, which had expanded when it burst. Probably methane, thought Crowe. Amid the swirling bubbles she'd caught sight of something familiar: the outline of a submersible racing towards the ship.

A Deepflight armed with torpedoes.

In the seconds that followed the explosion all hell had broken loose. Shankar's head had cracked down on the desk and was bleeding profusely. Crowe had helped him to his feet, before soldiers and technicians stormed into the CIC and hustled them outside. The repeated buzz of the alarm kept them moving. People were crowding into the companionways, but the crew seemed on top of the situation. An officer was there to help them out. He guided them aft to a companion-way that led upwards.

'Straight through the island and on to the flight deck,' he said. 'Don't stop for anything. You'll get further instructions at the top.'

Crowe pushed the dazed Shankar up the ladder. She was small and dainty, and Shankar was big and heavy. She had to summon all her strength. 'Come on, Murray,' she gasped.

Shankar's hands trembled as he reached for the rungs. He pulled himself up with difficulty. 'I never thought making contact would end like this,' he gasped.

'You must have seen the wrong movies.'

Ruefully she thought of the cigarette she'd lit only seconds before the explosion. It was still smouldering in the CIC. What a waste. She'd have given anything for a cigarette now. Just one before she died. Instinct told her that no one on the ship was likely to survive.

But no, she thought suddenly. Of course. They weren't reliant on lifeboats. They had helicopters.

Relief flooded through her. Shankar had reached the top of the companionway. Hands stretched down to haul him out. As Crowe followed, it struck her that what they were experiencing might be the kind of contact humans knew best – aggressive, ruthless and murderous.

Soldiers pulled her into the island.

Well, Ms Alien, she thought, what do you think now about finding intelligent life in space?

'You wouldn't happen to have a cigarette, would you?' she asked a soldier.

He stared at her. 'You've got to be kidding, lady. Just get the hell out of here.'

Buchanan

Buchanan was on the bridge with the second officer and the helmsman, keeping himself informed of developments and giving orders. He stayed calm. As far as he could tell, the blast had destroyed some of the ammunition magazines and the engine room. They could have lived with the loss of the magazines, but the damage to the engine room had sparked a chain reaction in the hydraulic system and the fuel-pumping stations, triggering more explosions. One by one the vessel's systems failed. The ship drew her electricity from a series of motor-driven power plants. In addition to the two gas turbines, the *Independence* had six diesel generators, which now broke down in quick succession. The main priority now was to evacuate. The explosion had occurred amidships, but some of the forward cargo compartments had already flooded, causing the *Independence* to sink bow-first.

There was too much water in the hull. As the pressure built, it would force its way towards the far end of the bow, then blast through the bulkheads and on to the level above. If the bulkheads at the stern gave way too, the ship would fill with water.

Buchanan had no illusions: he knew that the vessel would sink. It was merely a question of when. Whether or not they survived depended on him and his ability to assess what was happening. Right now he estimated that the water was about to break into the vehicle stowage compartments located below the lab. It would probably flood some of the troop berthing too. The one small comfort was that there were no marines aboard. During a normal operation he would have had to evacuate three thousand men. Now he had only a hundred and eighty, and they were mainly on the upper levels.

Some of the monitors that usually displayed the information from the integrated main screen in the CIC had stopped working. Directly above Buchanan's head was the sealed case containing the red phone: his hotline to the Pentagon. His gaze wandered over the chart tables, communication devices and navigational aids, all arranged in neat, logical order. None of that could help him now.

Useless clutter.

On the roof, the landing crew were keeping everyone moving. People were being led out of the island and over to where the helicopters were waiting, rotors whirring. Everything happened quickly. Buchanan spoke briefly to Flight Control and looked out through the green-tinted windows of the bridge. A helicopter had just taken off and was disappearing from the vessel. They had no time to lose. If the bow dipped any further, the flight deck would turn into a chute. The helicopters were securely tethered, but soon the situation would become critical.

03 LEVEL

Anawak didn't encounter many people. He was afraid he might run into Li or Peak, but they must have headed in the other direction. Out of breath, with a constant pain in his chest, he raced along the passageway towards the infirmary.

It was deserted. There was no sign of Angeli or his staff. He had to pass through a series of rooms lined with beds before he came to the one that held equipment. Cupboard doors gaped open, and the floor was littered with shards of glass that crunched as he walked. One after another he yanked open all the drawers and rummaged through the debris on the shelves, but failed to find a syringe.

Where the hell did they keep them?

He tried to think where they were usually kept at the doctor's surgery. In little drawers. He could picture it. Shiny white cabinets with lots of little drawers.

There was a rumble beneath him. Groaning noises rose through the ship. The steel was buckling.

Anawak hurried into the compartment across the way. Much of the equipment had been smashed, but the room contained several white cabinets, which seemed to have been bolted into place. He opened them, searched inside and finally found what he was looking for. He grabbed a dozen syringes in sterile packaging and shoved them into his jacket.

Their plan was crazy.

Either Karen was right, and it was a stroke of genius, or they had no idea of the reality of the situation. On the one hand it seemed plausible, but on the other impracticable and naïve, especially compared to the sophisticated messages that Crowe had been sending into the depths . . .

Where was Crowe?

There was a deafening clanging noise as though a bell had exploded. The deck tilted further. He could hear a muffled sloshing.

Anawak wondered whether he had time to get out. Then he stopped wondering and started running.

Lab

Weaver didn't know what lay ahead. Just the thought of opening the door to the laboratory made her stomach churn. But if they were to go through with the plan, it was their only hope.

The floor shook. From under the deck they heard gurgling. Johanson leaned against her, breathing heavily. 'Well, go on, then,' he said.

The red light was flashing above the keypad. The lab was sealed. Weaver tapped in the code and the door slid open. Water rushed towards them, swirling round their feet, but instead of flowing down the ramp, it collected round their ankles. The level rose. In a flash Weaver saw why: the ship was tilting at such an angle that it couldn't run down to the well deck. This section of the ramp wasn't a ramp any more: it was level.

She took a step back. 'Careful,' she said. 'The jelly might have got out.'

Johanson looked inside. Two lifeless bodies floated next to the wreckage of the chamber. He waded into the streaming water, and advanced through the door. Weaver followed. Her eyes shot over to the two large containers that made up the biohazard lab. They appeared intact, and she felt a wave of relief. This wasn't the time to be poisoned by *Pfiesteria*.

Aft, the deck sloped out of the water, most of which had formed a deep pool at the opposite end of the lab. 'They're all dead,' she whispered.

Johanson squinted over the water. 'Look!'

There was a third body – Rubin's.

Weaver fought back revulsion and fear. 'We're going to have to take one,' she said. 'It doesn't matter which.'

'That means wading in deeper.'

'It can't be helped.' She set off.

'Karen, watch out!'

She tried to turn, but something collided with her from behind and her feet skidded out from under her. Yelping, she landed in the water, and rose, spluttering, to the surface. She struggled on to her back.

A soldier was standing in front of her, training an enormous black weapon on them both.

'Oh, no,' he said slowly. 'Ooooh, no.'

In his eyes she could see panic and incipient madness. She got up slowly and raised her hands, showing her palms.

'Oh, no,' he repeated.

He was very young, no more than nineteen, and the weapon trembled in his hands. He took a step back and glanced from Weaver to Johanson, then back again.

'It's OK,' said Johanson. 'We're trying to help you.'

'You locked us in,' said the soldier. His voice sounded whiny, as though he were about to scream.

'That wasn't us,' said Weaver.

'You locked us in with that — that — You left us alone with it.'

This was all they needed — the *Independence* was sinking, they were racing against time to stop Li, they still had to get hold of a corpse and now they had to deal with a hysterical boy.

'What's your name?' Johanson asked abruptly.

'What?' The soldier's gaze wobbled. Then he raised his gun and pointed it at Johanson.

'No!' screamed Weaver.

Johanson looked into the barrel of the gun and spoke softly: 'Could you tell us your name, please?'

The soldier hesitated.

'We need to know your name,' said Johanson, in the tone of a friendly parish priest.

'MacMillan. I'm . . . My name is MacMillan.'

Weaver realised what Johanson was up to. The best way to bring someone back to normality was to remind them of who they were.

'Thank you, MacMillan. Good. Now, listen, we need your help. This vessel is sinking. It's imperative that we go through with our last experiment. It could save us all.'

'All of us?'

'Do you have family, MacMillan?'

'Why do you need to know?'

'Tell me where they live, MacMillan.'

'Boston.' The boy's face crumpled. He started to cry. 'But Boston's—'

'I know,' Johanson said urgently. 'Listen, there's something we can do to stop all this. To stop everything — even in Boston. But we need your help. And we need it now. Your family's lives could be hanging in the balance with every second we waste.'

'Please help us,' said Weaver. 'Please.'

The soldier looked from one to the other. He snuffled and lowered his gun. 'Will you get us out of here?' he asked.

'Yes.' Weaver nodded. 'I promise.' What the hell are you talking about? she thought. You can't promise anything. Not a thing.

The secret laboratory seemed unscathed. The floor was covered with broken glass, but otherwise everything seemed to be in its rightful place. A few monitors flickered in the background.

'Now, where would he have put those cylinders?' Li wondered aloud.

She slid her gun back into its holster. The room was deserted. She'd expected to see a blue glow emanating from the miniature tank, but then she remembered that Rubin had tested the toxin – very successfully, as he'd assured her. She peered through one of the portholes. Nothing. No organism. No glow.

Peak wandered among the benches and cabinets. 'Over here,' he called.

Li hurried over. A stand had toppled over, leaving a collection of slim, torpedo-shaped cylinders in a heap, each just under a metre long. They picked them up one by one. Two were noticeably heavier than the others, and Li spotted the markings on their sides. Rubin had drawn on them in permanent ink. 'Look, Sal,' she said, mesmerised. 'I'm holding the new world order in my hands.'

'I see.' A test-tube rolled off the side of one of the benches and shattered with a tinkle. 'In that case let's get the new world order out of here.'

Li let out a peal of laughter. She passed a cylinder to Peak and walked out of the lab with the other. 'In five minutes' time I'm going to send the yrr into the underworld for ever, you can depend on it.'

'Who're you going to take down with you? Is Mick still alive, do you think?'

'I don't give a shit about Mick.'

'I could come.'

'Well, that's incredibly generous of you, Sal, but exactly *how* were you planning to help? The last thing I need is you bawling your eyes out because you can't stand the thought of me killing a lump of blue slime.'

'That's different and you know it. There's a hell of a difference between—'

They were almost at the companionway. Someone was approaching from the opposite direction, running with his head down.

'Leon!'

Anawak stopped abruptly. They were very close. Only the entrance to the companionway lay between them.

'Jude, Sal . . .' Anawak stared at them. 'What a surprise.'

What a surprise. It was pathetic. The man couldn't act even though his life depended on it. From the moment Li had looked into his eyes she'd known that Anawak knew everything.

'Where've you been?' she asked.

'I'm . . . Well, I can't find the others so . . .'

She was running out of time. Maybe he was looking for his friends, or maybe he was up to something. It didn't matter. Anawak was in the way.

Li drew her gun.

Flight Deck

Crowe had been behind Shankar as they walked out on to the roof, but then she'd been stopped. 'Wait there,' said a man in uniform.

'But I've got to—'

'You'll be in the next group.'

Two Super Stallions had left the deck already and two more were waiting beside the island, one parked in front of the other. Shankar turned to her as he ran with the group of soldiers and civilians towards a chopper. The enormous flight deck was sloping more dramatically than ever, but it was so big that it looked as though the foaming, raging sea was tilting, rather than the ship.

'I'll see you later,' shouted Shankar. 'You'll be on the next flight.'

Crowe watched as he hurried up the ramp that rose under the tail and into the belly of the Super Stallion. A glacial wind lashed her face. The evacuation was going pretty much to plan. So she'd just have to be patient. But where were the others? Leon, Sigur, Karen . . .

Maybe they'd left already.

It was a reassuring thought. The hatch closed behind Shankar. The rotors spun faster.

Hull

Barely thirty metres below the flight deck the flood of seawater was pushing up against the bulkheads of the forward cargo compartments and the lower troop berthing. A single torpedo floated in the water. It had been released when the submersible exploded but its charge hadn't detonated. That was unusual, but by no means unheard of. After being propelled by the water into one of the munitions magazines, it had sunk into a metal storage cage that had been partially wrenched out of position and now was shifting up and down in the darkness. It rolled gently from side to side, advancing centimetre by centimetre, in line with the vessel's inclination.

The bulkheads stood firm, but the cage screeched and groaned with the pressure. The struts to which it was still attached began to buckle under the strain. Fine fracture lines opened in the steel of the magazine's wall. One of the sturdy attachment bolts was being dragged out of its fixing, its thread stripping under the strain . . .

With an almighty bang it was free.

The tension that had been building was instantaneously released. The cage jerked up, as the bolts shot out and the partition collapsed. In the turmoil, the torpedo was catapulted towards a spot that bordered on the cargo holds at the bow, the vast living quarters for the marines and the empty vehicle deck below the lab.

It was one of the most sensitive intersection points on the ship.

This time the explosive didn't fail.

03 LEVEL

'No,' said Peak. He dropped the cylinder and turned his gun on Li. 'You can't do that.'

Li's pistol was still trained on Anawak. 'Sal, I've had enough of your insubordination,' she hissed.

'Put the gun down.'

'For Christ's sake, Sal! I'll have you court-martialled, I'll—'

'On the count of three I'm going to shoot. I'm serious, Jude. I'm not going to stand by and let you keep killing people. Now, put the gun down. One . . . Two . . .'

Li exhaled noisily and lowered it. 'Are you happy now?'

'Drop it.'

'Why don't we just talk this over and—'

'Drop it!'

An expression of pure hatred filled Li's eyes. The weapon clattered to the deck.

Anawak glanced at Peak. 'Thanks,' he said, and bounded to the companionway. He disappeared down it and his footsteps faded. Li swore.

'General Commander Judith Li,' Peak said solemnly, 'I'm relieving you of your command on the grounds of insanity. From now on you will follow my orders. You may—'

The ship gave a terrible lurch and plunged forward. Peak thudded down, rolled over and scrambled up. Where was his gun? Where was Li?

'Sal!' Li was kneeling in front of him. She raised the gun.

Peak froze. 'Jude.' He shook his head. 'Listen, Jude . . .'

'Moron,' said Li, and pulled the trigger.

Flight Deck

Crowe swayed. The deck tipped even further. Rotors thudding, the Super Stallion carrying Shankar and the others skidded into the helicopter parked in front of it. Its engine roared as it lifted up and tried to pull away.

Crowe caught her breath. No, she thought. This can't be happening. Not now. Not when they were so close to being saved.

There were screams as people crashed to the ground or started running. She was pulled along by the crowd, then lost her balance. Sprawled on the deck, she saw the Super Stallion lift away from the stationary chopper. One of the window-mounted machine-guns struck its tail. It started to heel.

The Stallion was out of control.

She leaped to her feet. Gripped with panic she ran.

Bridge

Buchanan couldn't believe what he was seeing. He'd been hurled without warning against his captain's chair, with its comfortable arm- and footrests. Everyone envied him that chair: it was a cross between Captain Kirk's command chair and a bar stool. Equipment flew across the room. Buchanan dragged himself up and dived towards the side window, in time to see one of the Super Stallions pitch slowly to one side. It was stuck.

'Everyone out of here!' he yelled.

People were fleeing the bridge now, but he watched as the trapped helicopter kept tipping.

Suddenly it broke free and rose into the air.

Buchanan gulped. For a moment it seemed that the pilot was back in control. But the chopper was at an impossible tilt, the tail sticking vertically into the air. The engine screamed louder, then the Super Stallion hurtled towards him, rotors first.

With a total loaded weight of over thirty-three tonnes, and carrying nine thousand litres of fuel, the aircraft crashed into the bridge and transformed the front of the island into a blazing inferno. A ball of flame shot through the superstructure, charring the furniture, causing monitors to blow out and bulkheads to tear open. It bore down on the fleeing figures, incinerating them as it swept down the passageways into the heart of the island.

Flight Deck

Crowe was running for dear life. Burning debris rained from above. She raced towards the stern. The *Independence* was at such an angle now that she had to run uphill, which induced a fit of wheezing. Over the last few years her lungs had taken in more cigarette smoke than fresh air. And she'd always thought she'd die of lung cancer.

She stumbled and skidded over the asphalt. As she picked herself up she saw that the entire front section of the island had disappeared in flames. The second helicopter was burning too. People were running across the deck, human torches crashing to the ground. It was a horrific sight, but more horrifying was the certainty that she no longer stood a chance of escaping from the sinking ship.

Balls of fire rose over the vessel as violent explosions shook it. Then there was a deafening bang, followed by a shower of sparks only metres from her feet.

Shankar had died in the inferno.

That wasn't what she wanted for herself.

She darted towards the stern, without the faintest idea of what she would do when she got there.

Li swore. She still had a torpedo under her arm, but the second had rolled out of sight. It had either fallen down the companionway or was sliding down the corridor towards the bow. And all because of that asshole Peak.

She stepped over the body, still trying to decide whether to make do with just one torpedo. But what if it didn't eject the toxin?

Straining her eyes, she peered down the passageway.

Suddenly she heard an incredible roar above her. This time the vessel shook even more violently. She was flung backwards, and slid down the passageway on her back. She had to get out. This was no longer just about seeing through the mission – to survive she needed the Deepflight.

The torpedo slipped out of her grip.

'Shit!'

She made a grab for it, but it clattered away. If it had been packed with explosive, it would have detonated by now. Instead it was full of liquid – enough to wipe out an entire intelligent race.

She braced her arms and legs, and a few seconds later she stopped sliding, aching as though she'd been bludgeoned with an iron rod. She used the wall to push herself up and looked around.

The second torpedo had vanished too.

She could have screamed.

The noises from the flood waters sounded alarmingly close and she could hear cracking and banging from above. There wasn't much time.

She stood still. There was no mistaking it. It was getting warmer.

She had to find those torpedoes.

Lab

The young soldier had been right behind them, gun at the ready, when the blast rocked the lab. They all splashed into the water. As Weaver surfaced, there was another almighty bang overhead. Then the lights went out and she was staring into darkness.

'Sigur?' she called.

No answer.

'MacMillan?'

'Over here.'

Her feet touched the deck. She was up to her chest in water. Why now? She'd almost got hold of one of the bodies . . . Something prodded her shoulder and her hand whipped up. A boot – and inside it a leg.

'Karen?'

Johanson was somewhere close by. Little by little her eyes adjusted to the darkness. Without warning the emergency lighting flashed on, illuminating the laboratory with a red glow. She saw the outline of Johanson's head protruding from the water. 'This way!' she called. 'I need a hand.'

A dull roar came from above as well as below. The lab was getting warmer. Johanson appeared beside her.

'Who is it?'

'No idea. Just help me shift it.'

'We've got to get out,' MacMillan said breathlessly. 'Hurry.'

'We're just coming, we're—'

'Hurry!'

Weaver's eyes were drawn to the far end of the lab.

A faint blue glow.

Then a flash.

She tightened her grip on the body and fought through the water to the door. Johanson had the dead man's arm. Or was it a woman? Weaver prayed that it wasn't poor Sue. She trod on something that slid away to one side. Her head disappeared under water.

Eyes wide she stared into the darkness. Something was snaking towards her. It bore down on her rapidly like a long, glittering eel. No, not an eel. More like an enormous headless worm. And it wasn't alone.

Her head shot up. 'Let's get out of here.'

Johanson yanked at the corpse. Below the surface a tangle of swarming tentacles had appeared. MacMillan raised his gun. Weaver felt something slide past her ankle.

In a flash, feelers were winding themselves round her body, crawling upwards. She tore at them, trying to prise them off. Then Johanson was beside her, digging his fingers under the tentacles, but he might as well have been trying to free her from an anaconda.

The creature was pulling her backwards.

Creature? It wasn't one creature she was fighting but billions. Billions and billions of amoebas.

'It's no good!' Johanson gasped.

The jelly slid over her chest, and she was pushed back under the water. The glow was brighter now. At the far end of the tentacles a large mass was approaching. The main body of the organism.

She fought to the surface. 'MacMillan,' she gurgled.

The soldier raised his gun.

'It's no use shooting,' screamed Johanson. 'It won't help.'

All of a sudden MacMillan seemed calm. He took aim, keeping his sights on the mass of jelly as it moved through the water. 'Oh, this'll help, all right,' he said.

There was a dry staccato sound as he fired.

'This *always* helps.'

The volley pierced the organism. Water sprayed in all directions. MacMillan fired a second round, and the creature was blasted to shreds. Clumps of jelly whirled through the air. Suddenly Weaver was free. Johanson grasped the body, and together they pulled it frantically through the water, picking up speed as the water level sank. The ship was tilting more drastically than ever now, prompting most of the water to collect at the bow end of the lab. The area around the door was almost dry. They hurried up the slope, careful not to slip, until suddenly the water was only ankle deep.

They heaved the body out on to the ramp. Weaver was almost sure she'd heard a muffled cry.

'MacMillan?'

She stuck her head back around the door. 'MacMillan? Where are you?'

The glowing organism was aggregating again. There was no sign of tentacles. The creature was now a flat sheet.

'Close the door,' Johanson shouted. 'It could still get out. There's water everywhere.'

'MacMillan?'

Weaver gripped the doorframe and stared into the room, but the soldier was gone. He hadn't made it.

A thin, glowing tendril approached. She leaped back and hit the switch for the door. The tendril rushed forward, but the door snapped shut.

Anawak had been climbing down a companionway when the blast rocked the boat. Now his breath was coming in gasps and his knee hurt. He swore. He'd had trouble with that knee ever since the crash in the seaplane, and then Vanderbilt had kicked it.

The only way to the well deck now was via the vehicle ramp leading down from the hangar bay. He turned and went up until he was on the right level to get to the ramp. It got steadily warmer as he ascended. What was happening up there? He stumbled on to the hangar deck and saw thick black smoke pouring through the gateways from the elevators.

Suddenly he heard someone calling for help.

He took a few steps into the hangar. 'Is anyone there?' he shouted.

It was hard to see anything: the pale yellow lights weren't strong enough to penetrate the dark smoke. But he could hear the voice clearly now.

It was Crowe.

'Sam?' Anawak ran part-way through the sooty cloud. He stopped to listen. 'Sam? Where are you?'

No answer.

He waited for a moment, then turned and ran towards the ramp. He didn't notice until too late that it was now as steep as a chute. His legs gave way and he thudded downwards, praying that at least some of the syringes would survive. At the bottom, he splashed into a pool of water that cushioned his fall. He shook himself, crawled out on all fours and saw Weaver and Johanson walking away from the lab, dragging a body in the direction of the well deck.

Ahead, the floor was covered with a thin film of water.

Of course! The basin had been full of water, which was now streaming into the passageway. If the ship tilted any further this whole compartment would flood.

They had to hurry.

'I've got the syringes,' he shouted after them.

Johanson glanced round. 'About time.'

'Who've you got?' Anawak ran to catch up with them, and looked down at the body.

Rubin.

Crouched at the far end of the roof Crowe watched the island go up in smoke.

A man with Pakistani features was lying next to her, shaking all over and dressed in a cook's uniform. Either they were the only ones to have run in this direction, or no one else had made it. The man coughed and sat up.

'This is what happens when intelligent species disagree,' Crowe told him.

He stared at her as though she had three heads.

Crowe sighed. She'd run to a spot directly above the starboard-side elevator. Below them was the opening to the hangar deck. She'd called over the side a few times, but no one had answered.

The boat was burning, and they were going to sink.

Maybe there were lifeboats somewhere on board, but they wouldn't be much use. Everything on a helicopter carrier was set up for people to be evacuated by air. And, anyway, even if they did find the lifeboats, they'd still need someone to lower them, and everyone who knew how to do so had vanished in the blaze.

Tarry black smoke drifted towards them. 'Have you got any cigarettes?' she asked.

She expected him to pronounce her completely insane, but instead he dug out a packet of Marlboros. 'They're Lights,' he explained.

'Oh, the healthy option . . .' Crowe smiled and inhaled as the cook put his lighter to the tip. 'Very sensible.'

Pheromones

'We'll squirt it into his tongue, his nose, his eyes and his ears,' said Weaver.

'Why?' asked Anawak.

'To give it a better chance of escaping.'

'In that case we should get some into his fingertips and toes. The more the better.'

The well deck was deserted. The technicians had fled. They undressed Rubin to his underpants, working as swiftly as they could, while

Johanson filled Anawak's syringes with the pheromone. Rubin was laid out above the embankment. The water was only a few centimetres deep, but it was rising all the time. They'd removed the layers of jelly clinging to his head and flung them out of reach of the water. There was more inside his ears, which Anawak fished out.

'You could inject some into his arse,' said Johanson. 'We've got plenty.'

'Do you think it will work?' Weaver asked doubtfully.

'The few yrr that are still trapped inside him won't be able to make nearly as much of the pheromone as we're giving him. So *if* they fall for the ruse, they'll think it's all coming from him.' Johanson crouched and held out a bunch of syringes. 'who's going first?'

Weaver felt a wave of revulsion.

'Well, don't all shout at once,' said Johanson. 'Leon?'

In the end they did it together. Hastily they pumped Rubin with nearly two litres of the pheromone solution. Half of that probably ran straight back out.

'The water's rising,' said Anawak.

Weaver listened. Screeching and whining noises were still coming from all over the boat. 'It's getting warmer.'

'Because the roof's on fire.'

'Come on.' Weaver put her hands under Rubin's armpits and pulled him up. 'Let's get this over with before Li shows up.'

'I thought Peak had put her out of action,' said Johanson.

'I wouldn't count on it,' said Anawak, as they dragged Rubin's body to the basin. 'You know Li. She's not that easy to get rid of.'

03 LEVEL

Li was beside herself with rage. She raced down the passageway, stopping at every open door, then sprinting onwards. That damn torpedo had to be somewhere. It was probably right in front of her. 'Look harder,' she scolded herself. 'They're torpedoes, for Christ's sake. You can't be that stupid, you pathetic half-witted . . .'

The deck shuddered. She lost her balance and clung to the side. The water had evidently torn down more bulkheads. The passageway tilted further. The *Independence* was so bow-heavy that it wouldn't be long before waves were washing the flight deck.

She was running out of time.

All of a sudden she spotted the torpedo. It had rolled out from an open passageway. Li whooped in triumph. She darted forwards, grabbed it and ran back towards the companionway. Peak's body had slumped through the entrance. She pulled away the heavy corpse, then climbed down the ladder and jumped the final two metres.

The second torpedo was lying at the bottom.

From now on it would be child's play. She hurried on. Maybe it wouldn't be so easy after all – fallen objects blocked several of the companionways. It would take too long to clear them. She had to go back. Up and on to the hangar deck, then down the ramp.

Hugging the torpedoes, she made her way up as fast as she could.

Anawak

Rubin weighed a tonne. Once they'd pulled on their wetsuits – to Johanson's groans of pain – they combined forces to drag the body up the starboard jetty, which was sticking out into the air like a ski-jump. The water had drained away from the stern gate now, exposing the planked floor. The four moored Zodiacs had risen steadily as the contents of the basin flowed into the tunnel towards the lab. Anawak listened to the creaking steel and wondered how much longer the vessel could bear the strain.

The three submersibles were hanging obliquely from the ceiling. Deepflight 2 had taken the place of the missing Deepflight 1. The other two boats had each moved up a position.

'Which one was Li intending to take?' asked Anawak.

'Deepflight 3,' said Weaver.

They inspected the control panel and flipped various switches. Nothing happened.

Anawak's eyes scanned the console. 'Roscovitz said that the well deck had its own power supply.' He bent closer to the desk and read the labels. 'OK, this is the one. It lowers the submersibles. Let's have Deepflight 3, so Li can't cause any trouble if she shows up here.'

Weaver activated the mechanism. A submersible descended from the rail, but it was the first, not the second.

'Um, can't you get Deepflight 3 for me?'

'Well, I expect I could, if I knew how the bloody thing worked. They're going to have to come down one by one.'

'Never mind,' Johanson said. 'We don't have time to worry about it. Take Deepflight 2 instead.'

They waited until the boat was hovering alongside the jetty. Weaver bounded over and opened the pods. Rubin's body was unbelievably heavy, saturated with water and pheromone fluid. His head jerked back and forth, eyes glazed and staring emptily into space. Together they pushed and pulled until it plopped into the co-pilot's pod.

They were ready.

Anawak thought of the iceberg in his dream. He'd known that the time would come when he'd be called under water. The iceberg would melt and he'd sink to the bottom of an unknown sea . . .

But who or what would he meet there?

Weaver

'You're not going, Leon.'

'What do you mean?'

'What I say.' One of Rubin's feet was sticking out of the pod. Weaver kicked it back in. 'I'm going.'

'Why?'

'Because that's how it should be, that's why.'

'You can't.' He took her by the shoulders. 'Karen, you might not come back alive, it's—'

'I know the risks,' she said softly, 'but none of our chances are good. You two take the other subs and wish me luck.'

'Karen! Why?'

'Do you really need to hear reasons?'

'Forgive me for interrupting,' said Johanson, 'but we're rather pushed for time. Why don't you both stay, and I'll go?'

'No.' Weaver hadn't taken her eyes off Anawak. 'Leon knows I'm right. I can steer a Deepflight in my sleep. I've got the edge over you both there. I've been down thousands of metres in *Alvin*, exploring the Mid-Atlantic Ridge. I know more about submersibles than the two of you put together and —'

'Nonsense,' cried Anawak. 'I can fly it as well as you can.'

'It's my world down there. It's the deep blue sea, Leon. That's been my world since I was ten.'

He opened his mouth but Weaver pressed her finger to his lips and shook her head. 'I'm going.' She looked around. 'Once I'm in, you can open the sluice and lower me. God knows what will happen once the flaps are open. We may find ourselves under attack, or maybe nothing will happen. Let's hope for the best. Once I've released the boat from the chain, wait a minute or so if you can, then take the second sub. Don't try to follow me. Stay close to the surface and get away from the ship. I may have to dive pretty deep. And afterwards . . .' She paused. 'Well, hopefully someone will fish us out. At least these things have satellite transmitters.'

'At a rate of twelve knots it would take two days to get to Greenland or Svalbard,' said Johanson. 'There's not enough fuel.'

Her heart felt heavier all the time. She gave Johanson a hug – and remembered their escape from the tsunami in the Shetlands. They'd see each other again.

'Brave girl,' he said.

Then she took Anawak's face in both hands and pressed her lips firmly to his. They'd never really talked, never done any of the things that would have been so right . . . Then she leaped into the pilot's pod. The submersible rocked gently. Lying on her belly, Weaver got into position and activated the locks. Slowly the pods closed. She scanned the instruments and gave the thumbs-up.

The World of the Living

Johanson stepped up to the control desk, opened the sluice and lowered the boat. They watched as the Deepflight dropped down and the steel flaps swung open beneath it. Dark water. This time nothing tried to force its way inside the vessel. Weaver used the controls to uncouple the submersible from its chain. It splashed down and sank through the water. Trapped air shimmered inside the clear domes. The craft's colours paled, its contours blurred, and it became a shadow.

It vanished.

Anawak felt a twinge.

The heroes' roles were handed out long ago, and they're only for dead men. You belong in the world of the living.

Greywolf!

Perhaps you'll need someone to tell you what the bird spirit sees.

Akesuk had been talking about Greywolf. His friend had been able to interpret his dream. The iceberg had melted, but Anawak's path didn't lead into the depths: it took him up to the light.

Into the world of the living.

To Crowe.

Anawak's mind jerked back to the present. Of course. How could he have allowed himself to be sidetracked? There was work to be done on board the *Independence*.

'What now?' asked Johanson.

'Plan B.'

'Which is?'

'I've got to go back up.'

'Are you crazy? Whatever for?'

'I need to find Sam – Sam and Murray.'

'They've all gone,' said Johanson. 'The ship must have been evacuated by now. They were in the CIC last time I saw them. They were probably on the first helicopter out.'

'No.' Anawak shook his head. 'They can't have been. Or, at least, Sam wasn't – I'm sure I heard her shouting for help. Look, I don't want to bore you with my problems, Sigur, but I've spent too long avoiding things in life. I'm not like that any more, and I can't just look away. Do you see?'

Johanson smiled.

'I'm going to give it one last try. In the meantime, you can lower Deepflight 3 and get her ready to go. If I don't find Sam in the next few minutes, I'll come back and we'll get the hell out of here.'

'And if you do find her?'

'Then we've always got Deepflight 4.'

'OK.'

'Do you mean that?'

'Of course.' Johanson spread his hands. 'What are you waiting for?'

Anawak bit his lip. 'If I'm not back in five minutes you're to leave without me.'

'I'll wait.'

'Five minutes. No longer.'

Anawak ran down the jetty. The opening of the tunnel was flooded, but the ship hadn't tilted any further during the last few minutes.

Water swirled round his ankles. He waded in, swam a few strokes and walked a couple of metres until it got deeper. As he approached the start of the ramp leading up to the hangar, the ceiling seemed to tilt towards the water. There were still a few metres of air left overhead. He swam past the locked door to the lab, turned the corner and looked up. While parts of the ramp had become almost level, others were precipitously steep. The section leading up to the hangar deck now formed a gloomy peak. A dark cloud of smoke hung above it. He'd have to crawl up on all fours. In spite of the wetsuit he was cold. Even if they escaped in the submersible, there was no guarantee that they'd come out of this alive.

They had to: he had to see Karen again.

He set about trying to clamber up.

It was easier than he'd expected: the steel ramp was ridged to provide grip for military vehicles and troops. Little by little Anawak pulled himself up. The temperature rose as he ascended, and he felt warmer. Now he was plagued by thick, sticky smoke, which settled in his lungs. The higher he climbed, the denser it became. Now the roaring noise from the flight deck was audible again.

The fire had already been blazing when he'd heard Crowe's shouts for help. If she'd survived the start of it, she might still be alive.

Coughing, he hauled himself up the final few metres and was surprised to find that visibility on the hangar deck was better than it was on the ramp. The tunnel had trapped the smoke, while up here it could circulate, entering through one gateway and escaping through the other. The air in the bay was as hot and oppressive as a furnace. Anawak covered his nose and mouth with his forearm and ran across the deck.

'Sam?' he shouted.

No answer.

'Sam Crowe? Samantha Crowe?'

He had to be mad.

But it was better than living like a dead man. Greywolf had been right: he'd been no better than a corpse.

'Sam!'

Johanson was alone.

He had no doubt that several of his ribs were broken, thanks to Floyd Anderson. Every little movement hurt like hell. During their efforts to retrieve Rubin's body and load it into the Deepflight, there'd been several occasions when he could have screamed, but he'd gritted his teeth.

His strength was running out.

He thought of the Bordeaux in his cabin. What a waste! He could have used a glass of it now. So what if he had to drink it by himself? He was the only *bon vivant* left on board. In fact, among all the people he'd met over the last few months not one had shared his taste for the finer things in life.

He was probably a dinosaur.

A *Saurus exquisitus*, he thought, as he lowered Deepflight 3 until it was level with the jetty.

The idea appealed to him. *Saurus exquisitus*. It described him exactly. A fossil who was happy to be just that . . . exhilarated by the future and the past, which filled his dreams, squeezing out the present.

Gerhard Bohrmann would have known how to appreciate a glass of Bordeaux, but otherwise there was no one. Sure, Sue Oliviera had enjoyed it, but she would have enjoyed a supermarket bottle just as much. Among all the people who'd worked together in the Chateau, there was no one whose tastes were sufficiently cultivated to appreciate a fine vintage Pomerol. Except perhaps . . .

Judith Li.

He tried to block out the pain in his chest as he jumped on to the Deepflight. Landing upright, he groaned, knees quaking. Then he crouched, opened the control flap and activated the mechanism to unlock the pods.

The domed tops rose slowly into the vertical position. The pods lay open at his feet. 'All aboard,' he trumpeted.

It was odd. There he was, balancing on top of a submersible, left alone in a well deck that was tilting out of the sea. You never could tell where life would take you next.

And as for Li . . .

He'd rather pour his wine into the Greenland Sea than give a drop of it to her. Sometimes the only way to do justice to the finer things in life was to make sure certain people couldn't have them.

Li

She ran up to the hangar deck, panting for breath The bay was shrouded in smoke. She stared at the sooty clouds, trying to discern what lay beyond them.

Then she heard the voice: 'Sam? Samantha Crowe?'

Was that Anawak shouting?

There didn't seem much point in killing him now. Besides, the bow's remaining bulkheads might give way at any moment. The vessel was in danger of splitting, and when that happened, the *Independence* would go down in seconds.

She ran to the ramp and peered into a smoke-filled cavern. Her stomach turned. Li wasn't easily scared, she wasn't cowed by the need to go down there, but if she let go of the torpedoes, they'd end up in the water.

She edged down the ramp, feet turned sideways, taking one small step at a time. It was dark and oppressive and the smoke was smothering her The soles of her boots made empty clunking noises on the metal.

All of a sudden she lost her balance and sat down with a thud, legs stretched out in front of her. Still clutching the torpedoes, she slid painfully over the uneven surface of the ramp. The ridges hammered against her spine and the water rushed towards her.

The ramp fell away and she splashed down, then surfaced, gasping for air.

She still had the torpedoes.

A muffled groan shook the tunnel walls. She pushed off and swam through the passageway, round the corner and towards the well deck. The water wasn't as cold as she'd expected. It must have come from the basin. The lights had gone out in the tunnel, but the well deck had its own power supply. She could see it getting brighter ahead. As she got closer she could make out the outlines of the jetties sticking up into the air, then the stern gate looming menacingly over the basin, and two submersibles, one of which was dangling at the height of the jetty.

Two submersibles?

Deepflight 2 had vanished.

And someone in a wetsuit was balanced on Deepflight 3. Johanson.

Flight Deck

Apart from supplying Crowe with cigarettes, the Pakistani cook wasn't proving very helpful. Huddled wretchedly at the far end of the stern, he was in no fit state to make plans. Her own attempt had been no more successful. She stared helplessly at the raging flames. Everything inside her rebelled at the idea of giving up. As someone who'd spent decades listening for signals from space, the idea of resigning herself to death seemed absurd. It just wasn't an option.

All of a sudden there was a thunderous bang. A fiery cloud spread over the island, crackling and bursting like a firework display. Powerful vibrations shook the deck, then plumes of flames shot out of the inferno, stretching towards them.

The cook screamed. He jumped up, took a step backwards, stumbled, and toppled over the side. Crowe tried to grab his outstretched hands. For a split second he steadied himself, face twisted with fear, then fell. He hit the rising stern gate, then disappeared. Crowe heard a splash, drew back from the edge in horror, and glanced around.

She was surrounded by flames. Everywhere around her the asphalt was burning. It was unbearably hot. Only the starboard quarter had escaped the shower of fire. For the first time she was seized with real despair.

The heat forced her to retreat. She ran to the starboard quarter and continued along the side.

Past the equipment for the elevator.

What now?

'Sam?'

Great, now she was hearing things too. Or had someone just called her name? Impossible.

'Sam Crowe?'

Someone was calling her name.

'I'm over here,' she yelled.

Where was the voice coming from? There was no sign of anyone on the flight deck.

Then it dawned on her.

She leaned cautiously over the edge and saw the outline of the platform, tilting towards the sea.

'Sam?'

'I'm here! Up here!'

She was screaming her heart out. All of a sudden someone ran on to the platform, looking up at the deck.

It was Anawak.

'Leon!' she called. 'Leon, I'm up here!'

'Jesus, Sam.' He stared up at her. 'I'll come and get you.'

'How?'

'I'll run up.'

'There's nowhere left to run,' she shouted. 'It's a mass of flames; the island, the flight deck, everything.'

'Where's Murray?'

'Dead.'

'We've got to get out of here, Sam.'

'Thanks for pointing it out.'

'Can you jump?'

Crowe stared down. 'I don't know.'

'Do you have a better idea that might work in the next ten seconds?'

'No.'

'We'll escape in a Deepflight.' Anawak stretched out his arms. 'Just jump. I'll catch you.'

'Forget it, Leon. You'd be better off standing to one side.'

'Come on, Sam. Stop talking, start jumping.'

Crowe cast a final look over her shoulder. The flames were licking towards her. 'OK, Leon, here goes.'

Well Deck

Where the hell had Anawak got to? The submersible rocked gently on the water. Johanson crouched on top of it. There was nothing in the darkness to indicate the presence of the yrr. Why would there be? It wasn't as though an attack would be necessary. All they had to do was bide their time and wait for the vessel to sink. In the end they'd humbled even the mighty *Independence*.

The five minutes were up.

Strictly speaking, he could go. There'd still be a submersible left for Anawak and Crowe.

But if Anawak returned with Crowe *and* Shankar, they'd have to use both boats. He couldn't leave.

Under his breath he started humming Mahler's Symphony No. 1.

'Sigur!'

Johanson spun round. Pain stabbed through his upper body, preventing him breathing. Li was standing behind him, level with the boat. Two slim cylinders lay beside her on the jetty. She was pointing a gun at him.

'Come down from the boat, Sigur. Don't force me to shoot.'

Johanson grabbed the chain attaching the Deepflight to the rack.

'Move!' Li barked.

'Are you threatening me, Jude?' He gave a dry laugh as he tried to think. He had to delay her. He needed to improvise – to stall her, keep her talking until Anawak arrived. 'Well, I wouldn't shoot if I were you. Not if you're planning on using this sub.'

'What's that supposed to mean?'

'You'll see soon enough.'

'Explain yourself.'

'All these explanations are tedious, don't you think? Come on, General Commander Li, don't be shy – shoot me now and find out later.'

Li hesitated. 'What have you done to the boat, you goddamn jerk?'

'You'll never believe this,' Johanson struggled to his feet, 'but I'm actually going to tell you. In fact, I'll even help you fix it – providing *you* explain yourself to *me*.'

'There's no time.'

'Uh-huh. That's awkward.'

Li glared at him. She lowered the gun. 'Ask away.'

'Oh, surely you know the question already. Why?'

'Do you really have to ask?' Li snorted. 'Why don't you use that high-powered brain of yours? What do you think the world would do without America? There's only one enduring model of national and international order that works for every individual in every single society, and that's the American one. We can't allow the world to solve this problem. We can't allow the UN to solve it. The yrr have inflicted untold damage on humanity, but their stock of knowledge and understanding could be even more deadly. Who would you like to see inherit that knowledge, Sigur?'

'Those most competent to deal with it.'

'Exactly.'

'But that's what we were working towards, Jude. Don't we want the same things? We could reach an agreement with the yrr. We could—'

'Don't you get it? We don't have that option. It's against the interests of my country. That knowledge belongs to the United States of America, and we're obliged to do everything in our power to prevent others attaining it. It leaves us with no choice: we have to liberate the planet from the yrr. Even agreeing to coexist would be an admission of failure – a sign of our defeat, the defeat of humanity, of our faith in God and the world's faith in American supremacy. But the worst thing about coexisting with the yrr would be the new world order that would follow. We'd all be equal in the eyes of the yrr. Any state with the requisite technology would be able to communicate with them. They'd all try to forge alliances, try to seize the yrr's knowledge — who knows? In the end the yrr might even be conquered. And whoever conquers the yrr will rule the planet.' She took a step towards him. 'Don't you see what that would mean? There's a species down there that uses biotechnology of a kind we'd never even dreamed of. The only way of communicating with them is by biological means. The whole world will start experimenting with microbes, and there'll be nothing we can do. We can't let that happen. There's no alternative but to destroy the yrr. America has to take charge. We can't afford to cede power to anyone else – and especially not to that joke of a UN assembly, where every last scumbag gets a vote.'

'You must be out of your mind,' said Johanson. He was racked with coughing. 'What kind of a person are you, Li?'

'The kind who's devoted to God and to—'

'The only thing you're devoted to is your career. You're power-crazy.'

'I believe in God and my country,' Li yelled. 'I believe that the United States has a calling to save humanity and to—'

'Put everyone else in their place once and for all.'

'So what? Everyone always wants America to do all the dirty work, and now we're doing it. It's only right. We can't allow the world to share in the yrr's knowledge, so we have to destroy them and preserve that knowledge for ourselves. Then there'll be no doubt who controls the fate of the planet. Hostile regimes or dictators won't stand a chance. No one will be capable of contesting our supremacy.'

'What you're planning is the destruction of mankind.'

Li flashed her teeth in a grin. 'You scientists are always so quick to come up with these tired old objections. None of you ever had the courage to think we could defeat our enemy – it didn't even occur to you that annihilating the yrr would solve all our problems. You just keep whining away about how eliminating amoebas could destroy the planet's ecosystem. Well, the yrr are destroying the ecosystem already. *They're wiping us out!* Don't you think a little short-term environmental damage is a fair price to pay for restoring us to our position as the dominant race?'

'You're the only one who's interested in domination, you poor fool. How are you going to deal with the worms and stop the—'

'We'll poison them all. Once the yrr are out of the way, we'll be able to do what we like down there.'

'You'll be poisoning humans.'

'Well, here's a thing, Sigur. Destroying humans is an opportunity in itself. It would do the planet a favour if there was a little more air to go round.' Li's eyes narrowed. 'And now get out of my way.'

Johanson didn't move. He clung to the chain, and shook his head slowly. 'I've sabotaged the boat,' he said.

'I don't believe you.'

'Then you'll have to take your chances.'

Li nodded. 'I will.'

Her arm jerked up and she fired. Johanson tried to dodge sideways. He felt the bullet perforate his sternum and a wave of pain washed through him.

She'd shot him, the bitch.

His fingers let go of the chain. He wobbled, tried to say something, then fell belly first into the pilot's pod.

Deck Elevator

The instant he saw Crowe leaping towards him Anawak was seized with doubt. Arms flailing, Crowe had launched herself too far to the left. He ran sideways, arms outstretched, hoping that the impact wouldn't pitch them into the sea.

For all her daintiness, Crowe still hit him like a speeding bus.

Anawak toppled backwards, Crowe on top of him. They were sliding down the slope. He heard her screaming and his own voice joined in. The back of his head banged on the asphalt, as he tried to brace his heels against the surface. It was the second time in one day that he'd had a bad experience on the elevator, and he hoped it would be the last – whatever the outcome.

They stopped just short of the edge.

Crowe stared at him. 'Are you OK?' she asked hoarsely.

'Never better.'

She rolled off him, tried to stand up, then pulled a face and slumped down.

'No go,' she said.

Anawak jumped up. 'What's wrong?'

'My right foot.'

He knelt down next to her and felt her ankle.

Crowe groaned. 'I think it's broken.'

Anawak paused. Had he imagined it or was the ship tipping forward? The platform squealed.

'Put your arm round my neck.'

He helped Crowe to her feet. She could hobble along beside him at least. They made their way awkwardly into the hangar. They could barely see what was in front of them. And the deck was even steeper than before.

How the hell are we going to get down the ramp? thought Anawak. It must be like a precipice now.

Suddenly he was filled with rage.

They were in the Greenland Sea, in the Arctic, his territory. He was an Inuk through and through. He'd been born in the Arctic, and he belonged there. But he wasn't going to die there, and neither was Crowe.

'Come on,' he said. 'Let's get moving.'

Deepflight 3

Li ran to the control desk. She'd wasted too much time. She should never have allowed herself to be dragged into such a ridiculous discussion.

She raised the Deepflight, then swung it over the jetty until it was hanging directly above her. She immediately spotted the two empty tubes. The larger torpedoes were in their usual position, but the smaller ones had been dismounted to make way for the radioactive cylinders. Excellent. With weapons like these, the Deepflight was handsomely armed.

Quickly she pushed the cylinders into the tubes and locked them into place. The system was foolproof. As soon as they were fired, a detonator would ensure that the contaminated pheromone sprayed out at high pressure, ideally over the blue cloud. The sea would disperse it, and the yrr would take care of the rest. That was the best thing about the plan: Rubin's use of programmed cell death. Once the yrr had been contaminated, the collective would destroy itself in an incredible chain reaction.

He had done well.

She double-checked that the cylinders were firmly in place, manoeuvred the Deepflight back over the sluice, and lowered it until it was bobbing on the water. There was no time to put on a wetsuit. She'd just have to be careful. She raced down the ladder to the boat and clambered on board. The Deepflight rocked. Her gaze fell on the open pilot's pod, where Johanson was lying prone and inert.

That stubborn old fool. Why couldn't he have toppled to the side and fallen into the sluice? Now she had to dispose of a body too.

Suddenly she felt almost sorry. In a way she'd liked and admired the guy.

Under different circumstances she might . . .

The vessel rumbled.

It was too late to dispose of him. And, besides, it made no difference. The boat could be steered just as well from the co-pilot's pod. It simply meant transferring the controls. And she could always get rid of Johanson later, once the boat was under water.

There was a loud sound of breaking steel. Li crawled inside hastily and closed the pods. Her fingers sped over the controls. A low hum filled the air, as rows of lights and two small screens lit up. All the systems were ready. The Deepflight lay calmly on the dark green sea, ready to drop through the three-metre sluice into the depths. Li felt euphoric.

She'd done it.

Johanson was sitting by the lake. The water lay still before him, covered with stars. He'd been longing to return there. He looked at the landscape of his soul and was filled with joy and awe. He felt strangely disembodied, with no sensation of warmth or cold. Something had changed. He felt as though *he* were the lake, the small house beside it, the silent dark forest all around him, the noises in the undergrowth, the dappled moon . . . He was everything, and everything was in him.

Tina Lund.

It was a pity that she couldn't be here too. He would have liked to grant her this restfulness, this peace. But she was dead, killed by nature's violent protest against the rot of civilisation that had spread along the coasts. Wiped away, like everything else, leaving nothing but the image in front of his eyes. The lake was eternal. This night would never end. And the solitude would give way to soothing nothingness, the final pleasure of the egotist.

Was that what he wanted?

Solitude had undeniable advantages. Time was precious, and being alone meant that you could spend it with yourself. If you listened, you could hear the most extraordinary things.

But when did solitude become loneliness?

Suddenly he felt fear.

Fear, like a pain spreading through him, eating at his chest and stealing his breath. A chill crept over him and he shivered. The stars in the lake expanded into red and green lights and buzzed with electricity. The landscape blurred, becoming shiny and rectangular. He was lying in a tunnel, a pipe or a tube.

In a flash he was conscious.

You're dead, he told himself.

No, he wasn't quite dead. But he knew he had only seconds. He was lying in a submersible bound for the depths, laden with radioactive pheromone to repay the yrr's crimes, if that was what they were, with an even worse transgression.

There were no stars in front of him; just the control panel of the Deeplight. The lights were on. He raised his eyes in time to see the well deck disappear.

They were in the sluice.

In a tremendous act of will-power he swivelled his head to the side. In the body pod next to him he saw the beautiful profile of Judith Li.

Li.

She had killed him.

Almost.

The boat sank. Steel plates and rivets flashed past. Soon the submersible would be out of the vessel. Then nothing and no one would be able to prevent Li emptying her murderous cargo into the sea.

He couldn't let it happen.

Sweating with effort he pushed his hands from under his body and stretched out his fingers. He nearly blacked out. The instruments were in front of him. He was lying in the pilot's pod. Li had transferred the controls, and was steering with the co-pilot's instruments – but that could be changed.

One push of a button and the controls would switch to him.

Which one?

Roscovitz's chief technician, Kate Ann Browning, had shown him how to use the boat. She'd been thorough, and he'd listened attentively. He was interested in that kind of thing. The invention of the Deepflight heralded a new era of deep-sea exploration, and Johanson had always been fascinated by the future. He knew where the button was. And he knew how to use the other instruments and how to achieve what he intended. All he had to do was retrieve it from his memory.

Think.

Like dying spiders his fingers crawled over the control panel, smearing it with blood. His blood.

Think.

There it was. And next to it . . .

He couldn't do much now. The life was ebbing from his body, but he still had a last reserve of strength. And that would suffice.

Go to hell, Judith Li.

Li

Judith Li stared out of the view dome. A few metres in front of her she could see the steel wall of the sluice. The boat was sinking leisurely towards the depths. One more metre, and she'd start up the propeller.

Then a steep course downwards and to the side. If the *Independence* was going to sink within the next few minutes, she wanted to be as far away from it as possible.

When would she encounter the first collective? A large one might pose a problem, she was aware of that, and she had no idea how large a collective could be. There was also the danger of running into orcas, but whatever happened she could blast her way free. She had nothing to fear.

She had to wait for the blue cloud. The right moment to release the pheromone was when the yrr-cells were on the point of aggregation.

Those goddamn amoebas were about to get the shock of their lives. Such an odd thought. Did amoebas feel shock?

She did a double-take. A change had taken place on the control panel. One of the display lights had gone out, telling her that the controls had been . . .

The controls!

She was no longer in charge of the submersible. The controls had been switched to the pilot. A display screen appeared on the monitor, showing a diagram of four torpedoes; two slim ones and two larger ones.

One of the heavyweight torpedoes lit up.

Li gasped in horror. She banged on the control panel, trying to regain the use of the instruments, but the command to launch the missile couldn't be reversed. The figures on the display reflected in her deep blue eyes, running backwards in an inexorable countdown:

00.03 . . . 00.02 . . . 00.01 . . .

'No!'

00.00

Her face froze.

Torpedo

The torpedo that Johanson had launched left its tube and shot forwards. It got less than three metres through the water before it hit a steel wall and exploded.

An enormous pressure wave took hold of the Deepflight. It slammed backwards into the sluice. A fountain of water shot out. While it was still spinning through the water, the second torpedo launched. With a deafening bang the well deck exploded. The Deepflight, its two passengers and its deadly cargo went up in a ferocious ball of flames that consumed all evidence that they'd ever existed. Flying debris bored its way through the decks and bulkheads, piercing the ballast tanks at the stern, allowing water to gush in. Thousands of tonnes of seawater poured into the crater that had once been the basin.

The stern plunged.

The vessel was sinking at an incredible speed.

Exit

Anawak and Crowe had just reached the top of the ramp when the shockwave from the explosion shook the vessel. Anawak was flung through the air. He saw the smoke-wreathed walls of the tunnel spinning round him, then plummeted head first inside the black maw. Crowe tumbled through the air beside him, then disappeared. The ridged steel scraped his shoulders, back, chest and butt, tearing at his skin. He sat up, flipped over and was seized by another shockwave, which catapulted him so violently that he seemed to fly back into the hangar. There was an incredible din all around him, as though the whole ship had been blown to smithereens. Plummeting downwards, he curved through the air towards the water, and vanished beneath the surface.

He kicked out with his arms and legs, fighting the current, with no idea which way was up or down. Hadn't the *Independence* been sinking bow first? Why was the stern full of water?

The well deck had exploded.

Johanson!

Something smacked him in the face. An arm. He seized it, gripping it tightly as he pushed off with his feet. He didn't seem to be getting anywhere. He was thrown on to his side and pushed back, as the water tugged him in all directions. His lungs felt as though he were breathing liquid fire. He needed to cough and felt nausea rising as the watery rollercoaster plunged him down again.

Suddenly he surfaced.

Dim light.

Crowe bobbed up next to him. He was still gripping her arm. Eyes closed, she retched and spat, then her head disappeared below the surface. Anawak pulled her up. The water was foaming around them. He realised that they were at the bottom of the tunnel. In place of the lab and the well deck he was in a fearsome flood tide.

The water was rising, and it was bitterly cold. Icy water straight from the ocean. His neoprene wetsuit would protect him for a while, but Crowe didn't have one.

We're going to drown, he thought. Or freeze to death. Either way, it's over. We're trapped in the bowels of this nightmarish ship, and it's filling with water. We're going down with the *Independence*.

We're going to die.

I'm going to die.

He was overwhelmed with fear. He didn't want to die. He didn't want it all to be over. He loved life, and there was too much to catch up on. He couldn't die now. He didn't have time. This wasn't the moment.

Agonising fear.

He was dunked under water. Something had pushed itself over his head. It hadn't knocked him very hard, but it was heavy enough to force him under. Anawak kicked out and freed himself. Gasping, he surfaced and saw what had hit him. His heart leaped.

One of the Zodiacs had been swept up by the current. The pressure wave from the explosion must have wrenched it from its mooring on the well deck. It was drifting, spinning on the foaming water, as it climbed up through the tunnel. A perfectly good inflatable with an outboard motor and a cabin. It was built for eight, so it was certainly big enough for two, and it was filled with emergency equipment.

'Sam!' he shouted.

He couldn't see her. Just dark water. No, he thought. She was here just a second ago. 'Sam!'

The water was still rising. Half of the tunnel was already submerged. He stretched up, grabbed the Zodiac, pulled himself out of the water and looked around. Crowe had disappeared. 'No,' he howled. 'No, for Christ's sake, no!'

Crawling on all fours he dragged himself to the other side of the boat and looked down into the water.

There she was! She was drifting, eyes half closed, beside the boat. Water flowed over her face. Her hands paddled weakly. Anawak leaned out, grabbed her wrists and pulled.

'Sam!' he screamed.

Crowe's eyelids fluttered. Then she coughed, releasing a fountain of water. Anawak dug his feet against the side and pulled. The pain in his arms was so excruciating that he was sure he would let go, but he had to save her. Abandon her, and you may as well stay behind too, he thought.

Groaning and whimpering, he pulled and tugged until all of a sudden she was with him in the boat.

Anawak's legs folded.

His strength was gone.

Don't stop now, his inner voice told him. Sitting in a Zodiac won't get you anywhere. You've got to get out of the *Independence* before she pulls you into the depths.

The Zodiac was dancing on top of the rising column of water as it surged towards the hangar bay. There was only a short distance to go before they were swept on to the deck. Anawak stood up and fell down again. Fine, he thought. I'll crawl. On his hands and knees he went to the cabin and hauled himself up. He cast his eye over the instruments. They were distributed around the wheel in a pattern he knew from the *Blue Shark*. He could handle that.

They were shooting up the last few metres of the ramp now. He waited until the time was right.

Suddenly they were out of the tunnel. The wave washed them into the hangar bay, which had started to fill with water.

Anawak tried to start the outboard motor.

Nothing.

Come on, he thought. Don't play around, you piece of shit. Start, goddamn it!

Still nothing.

Start, goddamn it!

All of a sudden the motor roared and the Zodiac sped away. Anawak closed his hands around the wheel. Speeding through the hangar, they veered around and shot towards the starboard elevator.

The gateway was shrinking before his eyes.

Its height was decreasing even as they raced towards it. It was unbelievable how quickly the deck was filling. Water streamed in from the sides in jagged grey waves. Within seconds the eight-metre-high gateway was just four metres high.

Less than four.

Three.

The outboard motor screamed.

Less than three.
Now!

Like a cannonball they shot into the open. The roof of the cabin scraped against the top of the gateway, then the Zodiac flew along the crest of a wave, hovered momentarily in the air, and splashed down hard.

The swell was high. Watery grey monsters rose towards them. Anawak was clinging so tightly to the wheel that his knuckles blanched. He raced up the next wave, fell into the trough, rose again and plummeted. Then he cut the speed. It was safer to go slower. Now he could see that the waves were big, but not steep. He turned the Zodiac by 180 degrees, allowed the boat to be lifted on the next wave, pulled back on the throttle and looked around.

It was an eerie sight.

The *Independence*'s island towered out of the slate-grey sea in a cloud of dark smoke. It looked as though a volcano had erupted in the middle of the ocean. The flight deck was almost totally submerged, with only a few burning ruins defying their fate. He'd managed to get a fair distance away from the sinking ship, but the noise of the flames was still clearly audible.

He stared out breathlessly.

'Intelligent life-forms.' Crowe appeared next to him, deathly pale, with blue lips, and shaking all over. She clung to his jacket, keeping the weight off her injured leg. 'They cause nothing but trouble.'

Anawak was silent.

Together they watched the *Independence* go down.

PART FIVE

CONTACT

The search for extraterrestrial intelligence is a search for our-selves.

Carl Sagan

Dreams

Wake up!

I am awake.

How can you tell? There's nothing but darkness around you. You're flying to the bottom of the world. What can you see?

Nothing.

What can you see?

I see the red and green lights of the flight controls in front of me. I see the gauges that tell me about the pressure inside and outside the boat. I see how much oxygen I'm using, how much fuel I have left, how fast I'm travelling and how steeply the Deepflight is diving. It tests the water composition, and I see the results in statistics and charts. The temperature is monitored by sensors, and I see a number.

What else can you see?

I see particles swirling in the water, flurries of snow in the floodlights, tiny scraps of organic matter sinking to the depths. The water is saturated with organic compounds. It looks murky. No – wait. It looks very murky.

You still see too much. Don't you want to see everything?

Everything?

Nearly one kilometre stretches between Weaver and the surface. Nothing has tried to attack her. Her path has been clear of orcas and yrr. Everything in the Deepflight is in perfect working order. The submersible winds its way down in a sweeping ellipsoidal spiral. Every now and then small fish swim into the lights, then dart away. Detritus tumbles through the water. Krill are caught in the beam, each tiny crustacean a speck of white matter. The shower of particles reflects the light back to its source.

For ten minutes she has been peering into the dirty-grey cocoon of light that the Deepflight casts before it. Artificially lit darkness: light that illuminates nothing. Ten minutes in which she has lost all sense of up and down. Every few seconds she checks the display for information that can't be gleaned from the view: how fast she's travelling, how steeply she's diving, how much time has elapsed . . .

She can depend on the computer.

Of course she knows that it's her own voice she's beginning to converse with. It's the quintessence of all experience, of knowledge that comes from learning and observation, of nascent understanding. Yet at the same time something is talking from inside her, talking to her; something of which she was previously unaware. It is asking questions, making suggestions, bewildering her.

What can you see?

Not much.

Even that is an exaggeration. Only humans would come up with the absurd idea of sticking with a sensory organ when the external conditions mean it inevitably fails. No disrespect to your gadgets, Karen, but a beam of light won't help you. Your lights are just a narrow tunnel. A prison. Free your mind. Do you want to see everything?

Yes.

Then turn out the lights.

Weaver hesitates. She knows she'll have to switch them off to see the blue glow. When? It surprises her how dependent she has become on a pathetic beam of light. She has been clinging to it for too long. Using it like a torch under the bedclothes. One by one she turns off the powerful floodlights. Now only the control panel is still glowing. The shower of particles has disappeared.

Perfect darkness surrounds her.

Polar waters are blue. In the Arctic, the north Pacific and parts of the Antarctic, there isn't enough chlorophyll-containing life to colour the water green. A few metres below the surface, the blue takes on the aspect of a sky. Just as an astronaut in a spaceship sees the familiar sky darken as he travels away from the Earth until the blackness of outer space engulfs him, so the submersible travels in the opposite direction through an *inner space*, the unknown reaches of a lightless universe. Up or down, the direction makes no difference: in either case, the passing of familiar landscapes is accompanied by a loss of familiar perceptions, of the feelings derived from human senses – of sight, and then gravity. The laws of gravity may still apply in the oceans, but a thousand metres below the surface there is no way of telling whether you're rising or falling. You have to put your trust in the depth gauge. Neither your inner ear nor your vision is of any use.

Weaver is now travelling at the maximum rate of descent. It took no time for the Deepflight to pass through the topsy-turvy polar sky, and the light faded quickly. When the depth gauge showed sixty metres, the sensors could still detect four per cent of the light that was shining on the surface – but by then she had already turned on the floodlights, an astronaut trying to illuminate the universe with the help of a torch.

Wake up, Karen.

I am awake.

Sure, you're awake and your mind is focused, but you're dreaming the wrong dream. All mankind is trapped within a waking dream of a world that doesn't exist. We live in an imaginary cosmos of taxonomic tables and norms, incapable of perceiving nature as it really is. Unable to comprehend how everything is interwoven, interlinked and irretrievably connected, we grade it and rank it, and set ourselves at the head. To make sense of things, we need symbols and idols, and we pronounce them real. We invent hierarchies and gradations that distort time and place. We have to see things in order to comprehend them, but in the act of picturing them we fail to understand. Our eyes are wide open, and yet we are blind. Look into the darkness, Karen. Look at what lies at the heart of the Earth. It's dark.

The darkness is threatening.

Why should it be? It deprives us of the co-ordinates of visible existence, but is that so terrible? Nature exists independent of our eyes, and it's bursting with variety. It's only through the lens of prejudice that it appears impoverished – because we judge it in terms of what we find pleasing. We always see ourselves, even in the flickering of a screen. Do any of the pictures on our computers and televisions show the world as it is? Can our perceptions allow us to see variety, when we always need prototypes – 'the cat' or 'the colour yellow' – to grasp anything? Oh, it's amazing how the human brain wrests these norms from such infinite variety. It allows us to comprehend the incomprehensible through an ingenious trick, but it comes at a price. Life becomes abstract. The end result is an idealised world, in which ten supermodels provide the templates for millions of women, families produce 1.2 children, Chinese men are five foot seven and live until the age of sixty-three. We're so obsessed with norms that we forget that normality is born of abnormality, of divergence. The history of statistics is a history of misunderstandings. They provide us with an overview, but they blot out variation. They've estranged us from the world.

Yet they bring us closer together.

Is that what you think?

Well, we tried to communicate with the yrr, didn't we? We even succeeded. We had mathematics as our common ground.

Hold on. That's different. There's no room for variation in Pythagoras' theorem. The speed of light is always the same. Within a defined environment, mathematical formulae are unerringly valid. Maths doesn't ascribe values. A mathematical formula can't live in a burrow or in a tree. It's not something that can be stroked or that bares its teeth when threatened. You can't have an average law of gravity: there's only one law that applies. Sure, maths allowed us to communicate with the yrr, but do we understand each other any better for it? Has maths ever brought humanity closer? The way we label the world is determined by the evolution of our cultures. Different cultural groups see the world differently. The Inuit have no word for snow, only hundreds of words for all of its different kinds. The Dani people of Papua New Guinea have none for different colours.

What can you see?

Weaver stares into the darkness. The submersible continues its silent descent, travelling at an angle of sixty degrees and a rate of twelve knots. She is 1500 metres from the surface already. The submersible moves noiselessly, without so much as a creak or a groan from the hull. Mick Rubin is lying in the neighbouring pod. She tries not to think about him. It's a funny feeling, flying through the night in the company of a corpse.

A dead messenger, the bearer of their hopes.

Lights flare.

Yrr?

No, she's flying through a shoal of cuttlefish. From one moment to the next she finds herself in an underwater Las Vegas. In the eternal night of the depths, neither garish clothes nor funky dancing will help attract a mate, so single males in search of a companion do all their showing off with lights. Their photophores, small transparent pouches, open and close to reveal luminescing bacteria, allowing the cuttlefish's organs to pulse with light in a ballet of winks, a noiseless deep-sea clamour. But they're not trying to court Weaver's boat: the flashes are designed to frighten it. Back off, they tell it. When that doesn't work, they throw open their photophores, surrounding the submersible and shimmering with light. Among them are smaller organisms, pale creatures with red and blue cores: jellyfish.

Weaver can't see it, but something has joined them; her sonar tells her so. A large dense mass. Weaver's initial thought is that it must be a collective, but yrr-collectives glow, and this thing is as dark as the water round it. Its form is elongated, bulky at one end, tapering off at the other. Weaver's flight path takes her straight towards it. Adjusting the angle, she soars through the water above it. As she passes overhead, it dawns on her what it might be.

Whales have to drink water to survive. It seems incredible, given their habitat, but a whale runs the same risk of dehydration as a human abandoned on a raft. Jellyfish are made of almost nothing but water – fresh water. Cuttlefish are another source of life-sustaining fluid, so the quest for drinking water draws sperm whales to the depths. Plunging vertically they descend a thousand, two thousand, sometimes even three thousand metres below the surface, linger for more than an hour, then come up to breathe for ten minutes, and dive again.

Weaver has encountered a sperm whale. A motionless predator, equipped with good eyes. In the realm of darkness, the creatures have good eyes. At this depth, they all have good vision.

What can you see? What can't you?

You're walking along the street. Some distance ahead, a man is coming towards you. A few steps in front of him is a woman with a dog. Click, you take a picture. How many living organisms are there in the street? How far away is each creature from the other?

There are four.

No, wait . . . There are three birds in the trees, so that makes seven. The man is eighteen metres away. There are fifteen metres from me to the woman. Her dog is only thirteen metres away – it's scampering in front of her, straining at the leash. The birds are ten metres above the ground, each sitting fifty centimetres from the next. Wrong! What you don't see is that billions of organisms are swarming all over the street. Only three are human. One is a dog. In addition to the three birds you counted, there are fifty-seven that you haven't seen. The trees are living organisms, and in their bark and foliage live hordes of tiny insects. Mites infest the birds' plumage and the pores of your skin. Fifty or so fleas, fourteen ticks and two flies are buried in the dog's coat, while thousands of tiny worms inhabit its stomach. Its saliva is full of bacteria. The three human bodies are covered with microbes, and the distance between all these organisms is practically nil. Floating above the street are spores, bacteria and viruses that form chains of organic matter – chains of which humans are a part – knitting us together in one super-organism. In the sea it's no different.

What are you, Karen Weaver?

I'm the only human life-form for miles around – unless you count Rubin, who's not a life-form any more.

You're a particle.

One among countless different particles. In the same way as no cell is identical to another, no other human is identical to you. There is always a difference somewhere. That's how you should see the world. As a spectrum of diverging similarities. It's comforting to see yourself as a particle, isn't it, once you know you're unique?

A particle moving in space and time.

The depth gauge flashes.

2000 metres.

I've been diving for seventeen minutes.

Is that what your display is telling you?

Yes.

To understand the world, you need to find a different way of seeing time. You need to be able to remember – but you can't. Mankind has been short-sighted for two million years now. Most of *Homo sapiens'* evolution has been spent hunting and gathering, and that's what shaped our brains. For our forefathers the future was never more than the next moment in time. Anything beyond that seemed as vague and hazy as the distant past. We used to live for the moment, driven by an urge to reproduce. Disasters were forgotten or laid down in myth. Forgetting was once a gift of evolution, but now it's a curse. Our minds are still bounded by a temporal horizon that prevents us seeing any further than a few years in either direction. Generations pass, and we forget, repress and ignore. Unable to remember and learn from the past, we're incapable of considering the future. Humans aren't designed to see the whole and the role they play within it. We don't share the world's memory.

Rubbish! The world has no memory. People have memories, but not the world. All that stuff about the planet's memory is esoteric crap.

Do you think so? The yrr remember everything. The yrr *are* memory.

Weaver feels dizzy.

She checks the oxygen supply. Ideas are tumbling through her mind. The dive seems to be turning into a hallucinogenic trip. Her thoughts disperse in all directions through the darkness of the Greenland Sea.

Where have the yrr got to?

They're here.

Where?

You'll see them.

You're a particle moving through time.

You sink through the silent depths with countless others of your kind, a cold salt-laden particle of water, heavy and weary from the heat-draining journey north from the tropics to the inhospitable Arctic reaches. You've gathered in the Greenland Basin, forming an enormous pool of incredibly cold and heavy water. From there you flow over the submarine ridges that lie between Greenland, Iceland and Scotland, and into the Atlantic Basin. On and on you go, over the mounds of lava and deposits of sediment, into the abyss. You're a powerful current, you and the other particles, and near the coast of Newfoundland you're joined by water from the Labrador Sea. It isn't as cold or as heavy as you are. You continue towards Bermuda, and circular UFOs spin across the ocean to meet you, warm, salty Mediterranean eddies from the Strait of Gibraltar. The Greenland Sea, the Labrador Sea, the Mediterranean – all the waters mingle, and you push southwards, flowing through the depths.

You watch as the Earth brings itself into being.

Your path takes you along the Atlantic Ridge, one in a chain of mid-ocean ridges that extend across the oceans. With a mass as large as all the continents put together, they form a network covering sixty thousand kilometres, tipped with peak upon peak of periodically erupting volcanoes. Towering three thousand metres above the seabed, and sometimes separated from the surface by just as much water again, the ridges are evidence of cracks in the Earth. Where their crest is riven, magma rises from underground reservoirs. In the high pressure of the deep-sea, the molten rock doesn't shoot out explosively, but oozes in leisurely bulges. The pillows of lava push their way through the middle of the ridge, forcing it apart with the persistence and impertinence of chubby children, newly born seabed that has yet to find its form. Slowly, incredibly slowly, the ridge moves apart. The seabed is hot where the lava meanders through the darkness of the depths. Earthquakes shake the chasm and the crests on either side. Towards the edges of the rift, the lava cools. Beyond the crests, the topography consists of older stone; the further away from the ridge-crest, the older, colder and denser the rock, until the old, cold, heavy seabed slopes into the abyss. Creeping over the deep-sea plains, studded with mountains and covered with layers of loose sediment, it moves west towards America and east towards Europe and Africa, a conveyor-belt of past ages, until one day it pushes itself under the continents and plunges deep into the mantle of the Earth to melt in the furnaces of the asthenosphere, reappearing millions of years later as red-hot magma in oceanic rifts.

It's an extraordinary cycle. The sea floor moves tirelessly round the globe, fractured by pressure from within and pulled by the weight of its sinking boundaries. A continual straining, pulling and tugging of geo-lithic labour pains and burial rites shapes the face of the Earth. In time, Africa will unite with Europe. Will *reunite* with Europe. The continents are moving, not like icebreakers ploughing through brittle crust, but being dragged impassively on top of it, kept in constant motion ever since Rodinia, the first supercontinent, was torn apart in the Precambrian. Even now her fragments still strive to reassemble, as they did when they formed Pannotia and finally Pangaea, before they, too, broke apart. A divided family with a 165-million-year memory of the last complete landmass with a single ocean round it, now dependent on the flow rate of viscous mantle rock, and consigned to wandering the surface of the planet until they reunite.

You're a particle.

You only experience a heartbeat of all that. The Atlantic seabed shifts by five centimetres, and you've already been flowing for a year. Your journey takes you to places where there is life without sunlight. The lava cools rapidly, forming faults and cracks. Seawater pours into the porous new seabed. It streams down for kilometres, stopping just before it reaches the hot magma chambers inside the Earth, then returns, rich with life-giving minerals and warmth. Blackened with sulphide, the water spurts out of chimney-like rock formations as tall as houses, boiling hot, yet never boiling. At that depth, water heated to 350 degrees doesn't boil, it just flows up, dispersing its wealth of nutrients, supplying a hundred-fold of what the surrounding waters have to offer. You voyage through the unknown universe has led you to the first outpost of an alien world in which living creatures survive without light. It is home to bushy clumps of metre-long tubeworms, mussels the length of a human arm, hordes of blind white crabs, fish and, most important of all, bacteria. They're primary producers, equivalent to the green plants on the Earth's surface that nourish themselves from sunlight and provide all living creatures with the energy to survive. But these bacteria don't need sunlight: they oxidise hydrogen sulphide. Their source of life comes from deep inside the Earth. They cover the seabed in vast bacterial mats, living in symbiosis with worms, mussels and crabs, while other crabs and fish live in symbiosis with mussels and worms – and all without the need for a ray of sunshine.

Perhaps the oldest life-forms didn't come into being on the surface but here, in the lightless depths. Perhaps, Karen, you're seeing the real Garden of Eden as you travel along the bottom of the Atlantic. There can be no doubting that the yrr are the more ancient of the two intelligent species, one of which inherited firm ground and forfeited its cradle.

Imagine if the yrr were the privileged species.

God's creatures.

Time to check the display.

Weaver retrieves her thoughts from their journey past Africa. She has to focus on the present. It feels as though she's been travelling for a century already. A ghostly glow sweeps through the water some distance from the boat, but it's not the yrr, just a swarm of tiny krill, although there's no real way of telling – they might be cuttlefish instead.

2500 metres.

Another thousand metres to the seabed. All around her there is nothing but open water, yet the sonar is making frenzied clicks. Something large is approaching. No – not just approaching. It's heading straight for her, and it's vast. A solid expanse sinking down from above. Weaver's latent fear turns to panic. She flies through the water, banking at 180 degrees, as the thing draws closer. The microphones pipe an empty, unearthly din inside the boat, an eerie wailing and droning that's getting louder all the time. Weaver is tempted to flee, but curiosity prevails. She is far enough away from it and there's no sign that it's pursuing her.

Perhaps it's not a creature.

Banking again, she glides back towards it. They're at the same depth now, and the unknown thing is straight ahead. The Deepflight is rocked by turbulence.

Turbulence?

What could possibly be that big? A whale? But this thing is the size of ten whales, of a hundred whales, or even more . . .

She turns on the floodlights.

And at that moment she realises that she's closer than she thought. At the very edge of the beam, the thing comes into view. For a second Weaver is thrown, incapable of identifying the smooth surface in front of her or what it might belong to. It drops past her, then something catches in the floodlights. Bold lines, metre-long uprights, followed by curves. They seem horribly familiar, morphing into letters that read: USS *Inde* . . .

She cries out in shock.

The sound dies without an echo, reminding her that she's sealed inside her pod. On her own. With the sinking ship before her, she feels more alone than ever. Her thoughts turn to Anawak, Johanson, Crowe, Shankar and all the others.

Leon!

She is staring in disbelief.

The side of the flight deck appears briefly, then vanishes. The rest is hidden in the darkness, leaving nothing but a furious flurry of escaping air.

Then she feels the pull, and the Deepflight is tugged under.

No!

Feverishly she tries to stabilise the boat. It's her own fault for being so nosy. Why couldn't she have kept her distance? The boat's in trouble, she can see that from the controls. Weaver fights against the pull, using maximum propulsion to get it to rise. The submersible struggles and spins, following the *Independence* to its grave. Suddenly the Deepflight demonstrates the true brilliance of her design: she escapes from the vessel's wake and soars upwards.

The next second it's as though it never happened.

Weaver can hear her heart pounding. It thunders in her ears. Like a piston, it pumps the blood into her head. She turns off the floodlights, lowers the nose of the Deepflight, and continues her flight to the bottom of the Greenland Sea.

Time passes – maybe minutes or just seconds – and she sobs. She'd known that the *Independence* would sink – they all had – but so fast?

Yes, they'd known it would be fast.

But she doesn't know if Leon is alive. Or whether Sigur has made it. She feels terribly alone.

I want to turn back.

I want to turn back.

'I want to turn back!'

Face awash with tears, lips quivering, she questions the sense of her mission. She's nearing the ocean bottom, and there's still no sign of the yrr. She checks the display. The onboard computer reassures her. She's been travelling for thirty minutes, it tells her, and she's 2700 metres deep.

Thirty minutes. How long should she stay down?

Do you want to see everything?

What?

Do you want to see everything, little particle?

Weaver snuffles, an earthly snuffle in the night-time wonderland of thoughts. 'Dad?' she whimpers.

Calm. You've got to stay calm.

A particle doesn't ask how long things take. A particle simply moves or stays still. It follows the rhythm of creation, an obedient servant to the whole. The obsession with duration is peculiar to humans, a doomed attempt to defy our own nature, to separate out the moments of our lives. The yrr aren't interested in time. They carry time in their genome, from the very beginnings of cellular life. It's all there: 200 million years ago, when oceanic plates joined with the land mass that is now North America; sixty-five million years ago, when Greenland began to detach itself from Europe; thirty-six million years ago, when the topographical features of the Atlantic were formed, and when Spain was still far away from Africa; then twenty million years ago, when the submarine ridges separating the Arctic from the Atlantic sank low enough for the waters to circulate, allowing you to make your journey from the Greenland Basin, leading onwards past Africa and further south towards Antarctica.

You're travelling towards the Circumpolar Current, the marshalling yard for ocean currents, towards the never-ending loop of water.

You head out of the cold into the cold.

You may only be a particle, but you're part of a mass of water that's eighty times bigger than the Amazon. You flow across the seabed, over the equator, crossing the southern Atlantic Basin towards the south-ernmost tip of South America. Until now you've been flowing evenly and calmly. But once you've passed Cape Horn you run into turbu-lence. Reeling and tumbling you're pulled into a commotion resem-bling the lunch-time traffic around the Arc de Triomphe, but infinitely more violent. The Antarctic Circumpolar Current flows from west to east around the White Continent like a vast mixer, transporting and redistributing all the waters of the world. The circular current never stops, never hits land. It chases its tail, carrying enough water for eight hundred Amazons, pulling the planet's water inside it, tearing currents apart and mixing them together, expunging all trace of their identity and origin. Near the Antarctic coast it washes you towards the surface, where you shiver with cold. Foaming breakers sweep you onwards, until you sink back slowly into the vast circumpolar carousel.

It carries you for a while, then ejects you.

You travel northwards again at a depth of 800 metres. All the world's seas are fed by this circular Antarctic current. Some of the water flows into the subsurface South Atlantic current, some into the Indian Ocean, but most of it flows into the Pacific, and so do you. Hugging the western flank of South Africa you course towards the equator, where trade winds part the waters, and tropical heat warms you. You rise to the surface and are pulled to the west, right through the chaos of Indonesia with its islands and islets, currents, eddies, shallows and whirlpools. It seems impossible to pick your way through. Further south you're driven past the Philippines and through the Makassar Strait between Borneo and Sulawesi. Rather than squeeze through the Lombok Strait, you bypass it, flowing eastwards round Timor, a better route that takes you to the open waters of the Indian Ocean.

Now you head towards Africa.

The warm shallows of the Arabian Sea charge you with salt. Passing Mozambique, you travel south. You're in the Agulhas Current now, hurrying in anticipation of returning to the ocean of your origin, throwing yourself into an adventure that has cost so many sailors their lives. You reach the Cape of Good Hope, and it pitches you back. Too many currents collide here. The Antarctic Place de L'Étoile with its Friday-afternoon traffic is all too close. No matter how hard you try, you fail to make headway. Eventually you pinch off from the main current to form an eddy, and at last you're in the South Atlantic. You flow westwards with the Equatorial Current, spinning in vast eddies past Brazil and Venezuela, until you reach Florida and the ring of water tears apart.

You're in the Caribbean, the birthplace of the Gulf Stream. Fuelled by tropical sunshine you begin your passage up towards Newfoundland and on towards Iceland, drifting proudly on the surface and spreading your warmth magnanimously throughout Europe as though you could never run out. You barely notice that you're getting colder. At the same time, the waters of the North Atlantic are evaporating, saddling you with a burden of salt that weighs ever heavier. All of a sudden you find yourself back in the Greenland Basin where your journey began.

You've been travelling for a thousand years.

Ever since the Pacific was divided from the Atlantic by the Isthmus of Panama three million years ago, particles of water have been taking this route. Only another shift in the continents could interfere with the great ocean conveyor belt – or so we used to think. Now the equilibrium of the climate has been disrupted by mankind. And while the opposing factions continue to argue over whether global warming will lead to the icecaps melting and the Gulf Stream stopping, the current has stopped already. The yrr have put a stop to it. They've stopped the journey of the particles, put an end to Europe's warmth, called time on the future of the self-appointed chosen species. Yes, they know very well what will happen when the Gulf Stream stops, unlike their foes, who never see the consequences of their actions, unable to imagine the future because they lack genetic memory, incapable of seeing that in the logic of creation an end is a beginning and a beginning is also an end.

*   *   *

One thousand years, little particle. More than ten generations of humans, and you've circumnavigated the world.

One thousand trips like that, and the seabed will have renewed itself.

Hundreds of new seabeds and seas will have disappeared, continents will have grown together or pulled apart, new oceans will have been created, and the face of the world will have changed.

During one single second of your voyage, simple forms of life came into being and died. In nanoseconds, atoms vibrated. In a fraction of a nanosecond, chemical reactions took place.

And somewhere amid all this is man.

And above all this is the yrr.

The conscious ocean.

You've circumnavigated the world, seen how it was and how it is, becoming part of the eternal cycle that knows no beginning and no end, only variation and continuation. From the moment it was born, this planet has been changing. Every single organism is part of its web, a web that covers its surface, inextricably linking all forms of life in a network of food chains. Simple beings exist alongside complex life-forms, many organisms have vanished for ever, while others evolve, and some have always been here and will inhabit the Earth until it is swallowed by the sun.

Somewhere amid all this is man.

Somewhere within all this are the yrr.

What can you see?

What can you see?

Weaver feels unbearably tired, as though she's been travelling for years. A tired little particle, sad and alone.

'Mum? Dad?'

She has to force herself to look at the display.

Cabin pressure: OK. Oxygen: OK.

Dive angle: O.

Zero?

The Deepflight is horizontal. Weaver stares. Suddenly she's wide awake again. The speedometer is showing zero too.

Depth: 3466 metres.

Darkness all around.

The boat's not sinking any more. It's reached the bottom of the Greenland Basin.

She hardly dares look at the clock for fear of what she might see – perhaps evidence that she's been there for hours already and is too low on oxygen to fly back. But the figures glow calmly on the digital display, announcing that her dive began only thirty-five minutes earlier. So she can't have blacked out. She just can't remember landing, although she seems to have followed procedure. The propellers have stopped, the systems are working. She could fly home now . . .

And then it starts.

Collective

At first Weaver thinks she is hallucinating. She sees a faint blue glow in the distance. The apparition rises, swirling up like a scattering of dark-blue dust blown from an enormous palm, then fading into nothing.

The glow reappears, this time closer and more spread out. It doesn't vanish, but arches upwards, passing over the boat, obliging Weaver to crane her neck. What she sees reminds her of a cosmic cloud. It's impossible to say how far away or big it is, but it gives her the feeling of having reached the edge of a distant galaxy, not the bottom of the sea.

The blue light starts to blur. For a moment she thinks it's getting fainter, then she realises that it's an illusion: the glow isn't fading, it's becoming part of a far larger cloud that's sinking gently towards her boat.

Suddenly it dawns on her that she can't stay on the seabed if she wants to get rid of Rubin.

She angles the wings and starts the propeller. The Deepflight scrapes over the seabed, stirring up sediment, then lifts off. Lightning flashes in the vast night sky, and Weaver sees that the yrr are aggregating.

The collective is enormous.

From all sides the blue and white light is closing in. The Deepflight is caught in the middle of an aggregating cloud. Weaver knows that the jelly can contract into strong elastic tissue. She tries not to think what will happen if the muscle of amoebas closes round her boat. For a split second she pictures an egg being crushed by a fist.

She's ten metres above the seabed.

That should be enough.

It's time.

A push of a button on which everything depends. It would only take a moment of inattentiveness, a clumsy finger quivering with nerves or fear, and the wrong pod would open. She'd be dead within an instant. 3500 metres below the surface, the pressure is equivalent to 385 atmospheres. Her body might retain its shape, but she wouldn't be alive to see it.

She hits the right button.

The domed lid of the co-pilot's pod rises upright. Air shoots out explosively, lifting Rubin's body and dragging him partway out of the pod. With the lid open, the submersible is almost impossible to steer, but Weaver speeds forward, then plunges abruptly, ejecting Rubin from the boat. His dark silhouette hovers in front of the approaching storm of flashing light. The hostile environment squashes his organs and his flesh, crushing his skull, snapping his bones, and squeezing the fluid from his body.

The light is everywhere.

Rubin's reeling body is seized by the jelly and thrust against the submersible as Weaver tries to flee. The organism is coming at her from both sides, from all directions simultaneously, above and below. It pushes up to the boat, wrapping itself round Rubin, solidifying, and Weaver screams—

The boat has been released.

The jelly withdraws as fast as it approached. It backs right off. If any human emotion could be used to approximate the collective's reaction, it would be dismay.

Weaver realises that she's whimpering.

The blue glow still surrounds her. Blurred lightning scuds through the mass of jelly, which walls in the boat like an enormous rampart, stretching up as far as she can see. She turns her head and looks into Rubin's crushed face, faintly illuminated by the lights on the control panel. The contracting jelly has squashed him against the side of the view dome, and he stares at her through two dark holes. Hydrostatic pressure has forced out his eyeballs. Dark fluid seeps out of the cavities, then the body detaches itself slowly from the boat and falls into the night. Now he is just a shadow against the illuminated backdrop, body spinning in curious movements as though he were dancing slowly and awkwardly in honour of some heathen God.

Weaver is hyperventilating. She has to force herself to stay calm. Under any other circumstances she would have felt sick, but she can't afford feelings now.

The ring continues to retreat, bulging upwards at the edges. Darkness emerges beneath it. Ripples run through its sides, as the organism gathers itself in rising waves of jelly. The biologist's corpse disappears into the night. Almost immediately tentacles stretch down from above; long tapering feelers, slender like jungle lianas. Moving in concert and with evident purpose, they find Rubin and sweep over his corpse. Weaver can't see the body, but it shows up on the sonar. The careful groping movements of the feelers trace the outlines of a human form.

From the tips of the tentacles grow delicate tendrils that home in on individual body parts before feeling their way onwards. Sometimes they hover without moving or branch off. Every now and then they glide under and over each other as though conferring without sound. Until now Weaver has only ever seen blue yrr, but these feelers are an iridescent white. It would be easy to believe that their movements were choreographed, like a ballet unfolding in the silence. Suddenly in the distance Weaver hears music from her childhood: Debussy's 'La plus que lente', the slower-than-slow waltz that her father loved. It surprises and delights her, and her fear falls away. Of course there is no one in the ocean to play 'La plus que lente', but it is wonderfully appropriate. The rising and falling music is almost unbearably exquisite, and all that Weaver can discern at this moment is . . .

Beauty.

She finds her parents in a vision of beauty.

Weaver looks up. Above her is a shimmering blue bell of enormous proportions, high above her like a heavenly vault.

Weaver doesn't believe in God, but she has to stop herself lapsing into prayer. She remembers Crowe's warning about the temptation to humanise aliens, about representations of otherness that are really mirror images, about the need to make room for bolder visions of alien life. Perhaps Crowe would have resented the purity of the light; perhaps she would have wished for something less symbolically charged than the sacred white of the feelers, but the light doesn't stand for anything but itself. White is a common bioluminescent colour, like blue, red and green. The glow isn't a manifestation of the divine, just a host of stimulated yrr-cells. Besides, what God with any human affinity would choose to reveal itself in tentacular form?

What overwhelms her is the knowledge that things have changed for ever. The debate about whether a single-cell organism could develop intelligence. The question as to whether the ability of cells to organise themselves was evidence of conscious life or just an unusually well-developed form of mimicry. In the end the yrr had raised the stakes by breaking through the hull of the *Independence* as a tentacle-wielding monster of jelly, making H. G. Wells's Martians look harmless, and earning their place in the cabinet of horrors. But none of that is important in the face of this strange, yet sublime display. Weaver watches, and needs no further proof that she is seeing highly developed, unmistakably non-human intelligence.

Her gaze wanders up the blue dome, climbing until she sees its apex, from which something is descending, the source of the tentacles, which hang down from beneath. It is almost perfectly round and big like the moon. Grey shadows flit beneath its white surface, casting complex patterns that vanish in a trice, shades of white upon white, symmetrical configurations of light, flashing combinations of lines and dots, a cryptic code – a semiotician's feast. To Weaver's eyes it looks like a living computer, whose innards and surface are processing calculations of staggering complexity. She watches as the being thinks. Then it occurs to her that it's thinking for everything around it, for the enormous mass of jelly, for the whole blue firmament, and finally she realises what it is.

She has found the queen.

The queen makes contact.

Weaver hardly dares to breathe. The immense pressure of the water has compressed the fluids in Rubin's body, at the same time causing them to spill out of the wreckage and disperse. From the site of the pheromonal injections, a chemical seeps out of the corpse, a chemical to which the yrr reacted immediately and instinctively. For one brief moment aggregation took place and ended abruptly. Weaver isn't certain that the plan will work, but if her reasoning turns out to be right, the encounter with Rubin will have thrown the collective into Babylonian confusion – although in Babel there was recognition without under-standing. Now the opposite is true. Never before has the pheromone-based message been sent or received by anything other than the yrr. The collective tries in vain to identify Rubin. His body tells them that he is the enemy, the species they have decided to wipe out, yet the enemy is saying, *Aggregate!*

Rubin is saying: *I am the yrr.*

What can the queen be thinking? Has she seen through the ruse? Does she know that Rubin is nothing like a yrr-collective, that his cells are locked together, that he doesn't have receptors? He is by no means the first human that the yrr have examined. Everything about him tells them that he is their enemy. According to yrr-logic, non-yrr should be disregarded or attacked. The question is: have yrr ever turned against yrr?

Can she be sure?

At least this is one point about which Weaver feels certain, and she knows that Johanson, Anawak and all the others would agree. The yrr don't kill each other. Of course, diseased and defective cells are expelled from the collective, triggering their death, but the process is no different from a human body shedding dead skin, and no one could describe that as a battle of cells, since they all form one being. It's the same with the yrr – there are millions and billions of them, yet they're all one. Even individual collectives with individual queens belong to one vast being with one vast memory, a brain that encompasses the world, capable of making wrong decisions, yet never knowing moral blame, permitting space for individual ideas, without allowing any one cell to gain preference. There can be no punishments and no wars within that single being. There are only normal and diseased cells, and the diseased cells die.

A dead yrr could never emit a pheromonal signal like the one coming from this piece of flesh in human form. The message from the dead enemy tells the yrr that the corpse isn't hostile, that the corpse is alive.

Karen, leave the spider alone.

Karen is only little. She has picked up a book, and is about to kill a spider. The spider is only little too, but it has committed the terrible sin of being born a spider.

Why kill it?

The spider is ugly.

Ugliness is in the eye of the beholder. Why do you find the spider ugly?

Stupid question. Why is a spider ugly? Because it is. It doesn't gaze up imploringly with puppy-dog eyes, it's not sweet, you can't love it, you can't even stroke it. It looks strange, and evil – as though it should be killed.

The book swishes down, splatting the spider.

It isn't long before she regrets it. She sits down to watch *The Adventures of Maya the Bee*, of which previous episodes have taught her that honeybees are fine. This time there's a spider too, eight legs and a fixed stare, just demanding to be squished. Then the spider's lipless mouth opens and a squeaky childish voice comes out – not to utter terrifying threats of the kind that little girls expect to hear. Oh, no. This spider is as sweet as can be, a dear little thing.

All of a sudden she can't imagine how she could ever kill a spider. Already she knows that the one she has murdered will haunt her in her dreams, reproaching her in its high-pitched voice. Just the thought of it is too horrible for her to bear, and Karen sobs.

That was when she learned respect.

Back then she learned something that years later, on board the *Independence*, gave rise to an idea. An idea as to how one highly intelligent species could outsmart another while bypassing its intellect. An idea that could buy them time, or maybe even mutual understanding. An idea that requires man, who is accustomed to seeing himself as the template for earthly intelligence, to humble himself and be yrr-like.

What a comedown for creatures created in God's image.

Whichever species that might be.

Hovering above her is an intelligent white moon.

It's descending.

Rubin is reeled in by its tentacles, drawn into the light as a mummified torso swathed in jelly. They pull him inside. The queen is still sinking, descending towards the Deepflight, a mighty presence many times bigger than the boat. All of a sudden the depths are dark no longer. The moon starts to close round the submersible. There is nothing but light. White light pulsates round Weaver as the queen engulfs the boat, absorbing it into her thoughts.

Weaver feels fear returning. She gasps for breath. She has to resist the impulse to start the propeller, even though she's desperate to escape. The enchantment has vanished, leaving her to face the threat. But she knows that a propeller can do nothing against the jelly. It's too resilient and strong. The movement might vex it, tickle it or leave it indifferent, but it certainly won't cause it to retreat. It's pointless to think of escaping.

She feels the boat being lifted.

Can the creature *see* her?

How could it? Weaver doesn't have the least idea. The yrr-collective doesn't have eyes, but who's to say that it doesn't see?

They hadn't had nearly enough time on board the *Independence*.

She hopes with all her heart that the jelly can somehow perceive her through the dome. What if it succumbs to the temptation of opening the pod in an effort to touch her? The approach, no matter how well intentioned, would bring things to a deadly end.

The queen won't do that. She's intelligent.

She?

The human mindset takes over so quickly.

Weaver bursts out laughing. It's as though she's issued a signal, and the light around her thins. It seems to be retreating on all sides, and then it dawns on Weaver that the queen, as she's been calling her, is disbanding. The light melts away, billowing around her for the duration of one incredible second, as though showering her with stardust from the universe when it was young. Small white dots dance in front of the view dome. If each one is a single amoeba, then they're big – almost the size of a pea.

The Deepflight is set free, and the moon coalesces, hovering just beneath her, borne on a disc of blue light extending endlessly in all directions. The boat must have been lifted quite some distance through the water. Weaver looks down at the surface of the disc and can think of only one way to describe what she sees: a confusion of traffic. Multitudes of shimmering creatures swarm over the surface. Chimerical fish emerge from the jelly, bodies aglitter with intricate patterns. Swimming together, they slump back into the mass. Fireworks sparkle in the distance, then cascades of red dots flare up, appearing in ever-changing formations right in front of the submersible, too fast for the eye to keep up. As they sink back towards the white orb they slowly begin to take shape, but it's not until they reach the queen that the truth of their nature is revealed. Weaver gasps. They're not tiny fish, as she'd assumed, but one enormous being with ten arms and a long, slender body.

A squid. A squid the size of a bus.

The queen sends out a glowing tendril and touches the middle of the creature, and the dots of light come to rest.

What's happening?

Weaver can't stop staring. As she watches, swarms of plankton light up like glowing snow, falling upwards through the water. A squadron of gaudy green cuttlefish shoots past, eyes bulging on sticks. The infinite expanse of blue is shot through with flashes of light that fade into the distance where Weaver can't follow their glow.

She stares and stares.

Until suddenly it's too much.

She can't bear it any longer. She notices that the submersible has started to sink again, dropping towards the glowing moon, and she fears that the next time she approaches this agonisingly beautiful, agonisingly alien world she may never be allowed to leave.

No. No!

Frantically she closes the open pod, pumping pressurised air inside it. The sonar tells her that she is a hundred metres above the seabed and sinking. Weaver checks the pod pressure, oxygen supply and fuel. She gets the all-clear. The systems are ready. She tilts the side wings and starts the propeller. Her underwater aeroplane starts to rise, slowly at first, then faster, escaping from the alien world at the bottom of the Greenland Sea and heading towards a more familiar sky.

Soaring back to earth.

Never in her life has Weaver experienced so many emotions in such a short time. Suddenly a thousand questions are racing through her mind. Do the yrr have cities? Where do they create their biotechnology? How is Scratch produced? What has she seen of their alien civilisation? How much have they *allowed* her to see? Everything? Or nothing? Has she seen a mobile town?

Or just an outpost?

What can you see? What have you seen?

I don't know.

Ghosts

Rising and falling, up and down.

Dreariness.

866

The waves lift the Deepflight and let it fall. The submersible drifts on the surface. It's a long time since Weaver set off from the bottom of the sea. Now she feels as though she's trapped inside a schizophrenic elevator. Up and down, up and down. The waves are high, but evenly spaced. Their crests seldom break, like monotonous grey cliffs in constant motion.

Opening the pods would be too risky. The Deepflight would fill within seconds. So she stays inside, staring out in the hope that the water will calm. She still has some fuel; not enough to get to Greenland or Svalbard, but at least to get her closer. Once the swell drops, she'll be able to resume her trip – wherever it might lead her.

She still isn't sure what she's seen. Could she have convinced the creature at the bottom of the ocean that humans and yrr have something in common, even if that something is only a scent? If so, feeling will have triumphed over logic, and humanity will have been granted extra time – a loan to be repaid in goodwill, circumspection and action. One day the yrr will reach a new consensus, because their origin, evolution and survival demand it. And by then mankind will have played its part in determining what that consensus will be.

Weaver doesn't want to think about any of the rest of it. Not about Sigur Johanson, or Sam Crowe and Murray Shankar, or any of those who have died – Sue Oliviera, Alicia Delaware, Jack Greywolf. She doesn't want to think about Salomon Peak, Jack Vanderbilt, Luther Roscovitz. She doesn't want to think about anyone, not even Judith Li.

She doesn't want to think about Leon, because thinking means fear.

It happens all the same. One by one they join her, as though they were coming to a party, making themselves at home in her mind.

'Well, our hostess is utterly charming,' says Johanson. 'It's just a shame she didn't think to buy some decent wine.'

'What do you expect on a submersible?' Oliviera answers. 'It doesn't have a wine cellar.'

'It's won't be much of a party without wine.'

'Oh, Sigur.' Anawak smiles. 'You should be grateful. She's been saving the world.'

'Very commendable.'

'Uh-huh?' asks Crowe. 'The world, you say?'

They fall silent as no one knows how to respond.

'Well, if you ask me,' says Delaware, shifting her chewing-gum from one cheek to the other, 'I'd say the world couldn't care less. Mankind or no mankind, it carries on spinning through the universe. We can only save or destroy *our* world.'

'Harrumph.' Greywolf clears his throat.

Anawak joins in: 'It doesn't make the blindest bit of difference to the atmosphere whether the air is safe for us to breathe. If we humans were to disappear, we'd take our messed-up system of values with us. Then Tofino on a sunny day would be no more beautiful or ugly than a pool of boiling sulphur.'

'Well said, Leon,' Johanson proclaims. 'Let's drink the wine of humility. It's plain to see that humanity is going down the drain. We used to be at the centre of the universe until Copernicus moved it. We were at the pinnacle of creation until Darwin pushed us off. Then Freud claimed that our reason is in thrall to the unconscious. At least we were still the only civilised species on the planet – but now the yrr are trying to kill us.'

'God has abandoned us,' Oliviera says fiercely.

'Well, not entirely,' Anawak protests. 'Thanks to Karen's efforts, we've been granted an extension.'

'But at what cost?' Johanson's face fell. 'Some of us had to die.'

'Oh, no one's going to miss a little chaff,' Delaware teases.

'Don't pretend you didn't mind.'

'Well, what do you expect me to do? I thought I was brave. When you see that kind of thing in the movies, it's the old guys who die. The young survive.'

'That's because we're just apes,' Oliviera says drily. 'Old genes have to make way for younger, healthier ones so that reproduction can be optimised. It wouldn't work the other way round.'

'Not even in movies.' Crowe nods. 'There's always an uproar if the old survive and the young die. To most people, that's not a happy ending. Unbelievable, isn't it? Even all that romantic stuff about happy endings is just biological necessity. Who said anything about free will? Has anyone got a cigarette?'

'Sorry. No wine, no cigarettes,' Johanson says maliciously.

'You've got to look at it positively,' Shankar's gentle voice chimes in. 'The yrr are a wonder of nature, and that wonder has outlasted us. I mean, think of King Kong, Jaws and the rest of them. The mythical monsters always die. Humans get on their trail. They gaze at them in admiration and amazement, captivated by their strangeness, and promptly shoot them dead. Is that what we want?' We were captivated by Scratch. The yrr's strangeness and mystery fascinated us – but what were we aiming for? To wipe them from the planet? Why should we be allowed to keep killing the world's wonders?'

'So that the hero and heroine can fall into each other's arms and produce a pack of screaming kids,' growls Greywolf.

'That's right!' Johanson thumps his chest. 'Even the wise old scientist has to die in favour of unthinking conformists whose only virtue is to be young.'

'Gee, thanks,' says Delaware.

'I didn't mean you.'

'Calm down, children.' Oliviera quells them with a gesture. 'Amoebas, apes, monsters, humans, wonders of nature – it makes no odds. They're all the same. Organic matter – nothing to get excited about. To see our species in a different light you only have to put us under the microscope or describe us in the language of biology. Men and women are just males and females, the individual's goal in life is to eat, we don't look after our kids, we rear them . . .'

'Sex is merely reproduction,' Delaware says enthusiastically.

'Precisely. Armed conflict decimates the biological population and – depending on the weaponry – can threaten the survival of the species. In short, we're all conveniently excused from taking responsibility for our moronic behaviour. We can blame it all on natural drives.'

'Drives?' Greywolf puts his arm around Delaware. 'I've got nothing against drives.'

There's a ripple of laughter, shared conspiratorially, then stowed away.

Anawak hesitates. 'Well, to come back to that business about happy endings . . .'

Everyone looks at him.

'You could ask whether humanity deserves to stay alive. But there is no humanity, only people. Individuals. And there are plenty of individuals who could give you a stack of good reasons as to why they should live.'

'Why do you want to live, Leon?' asks Crowe.

'Because . . .' Anawak shrugs. 'That's easy, really. There's someone I'd like to live for.'

'A happy ending.' Johanson sighs. 'I knew it.'

Crowe smiles at Anawak. 'Don't tell me it all ends up with you falling in love?'

'Ends up?' Anawak thinks. 'Yes. I guess in the end that I've fallen in love.'

The conversation continues, voices echoing in Weaver's head until they fade in the noise of the waves.

You dreamer, she tells herself. You hopeless dreamer.

She's alone again.

Weaver is crying.

After an hour or so the sea starts to calm. After another hour the wind has dropped sufficiently for the towering peaks to flatten into rolling hills.

Three hours later she dares to open the pod.

The lock releases with a click, lid humming as it rises. She is wrapped in freezing air. She stares out and sees a hump lift in the distance and disappear beneath the waves. It's not an orca: it's bigger than that. The next time it surfaces, it's already much closer, and a powerful fluke lifts out of the water.

A humpback.

For a moment she thinks about closing the pods. But what good will that do against the immense weight of a humpback? She can lie prone in the pod or sit up – if the whale doesn't want her to survive beyond the next few minutes, she won't.

The hump rises again through the ruffled grey water. It's enormous. It lingers on the surface, close to the boat. It swims so close that Weaver would only have to stretch out a hand to touch the barnacle-encrusted head. The whale turns on its side, and for a few seconds its left eye watches the small frame of the woman in the machine.

Weaver returns its gaze.

It discharges its blow with a bang, then dives down without creating a wave.

Weaver clings to the side of the pod.

It hasn't attacked her.

She can scarcely believe it. Her whole head is throbbing. There's a buzzing in her ears. As she stares into the water, the buzzing and throbbing get louder, and they're not inside her head. The noise is coming from above, deafeningly loud and directly overhead. Weaver looks up.

The helicopter is hovering just above the water.

People are crowded in the open doorway. Soldiers in uniform and one person who's waving at her with both arms. His mouth is wide open in a forlorn attempt to drown the rattling rotors.

Eventually he'll manage it, but for now the helicopter wins.

Weaver is crying and laughing.

It's Leon Anawak.

FROM THE DIARIES
OF SAMANTHA CROWE

15 August

Nothing is the way it used to be.

A year to this day the *Independence* sank. I've decided to keep a diary, one year on. It seems we humans need the symbolism of dates to start something new or end it. Sure, the events of the past few months will be chronicled by a host of other people, but they won't be recording *my* thoughts. I'd like to be able to look back some day and reassure myself that I haven't misremembered.

I called Leon in the early hours of this morning. Back then we had the choice of burning, drowning or freezing. He saved my life twice. After the *Independence* went down, I was as close to death as ever: drenched to the bone in Arctic water, with a broken ankle and no real prospect of being fished out of the sea. The Zodiac had a survival kit on board, but I would never have managed to use it on my own. To add to our problems, I blacked out almost as soon as we escaped. My brain still refuses to replay that final sequence. I remember tumbling down the ramp and the last thing I see is water. I woke up in hospital, with hypothermia, pneumonia, concussion and a craving for nicotine.

Leon's doing well. He and Karen are in London at present. We talked about the dead: Sigur Johanson, who never made it back to Norway and his house by the lake, Sue Oliviera, Murray Shankar, Alicia Delaware and Greywolf. Leon misses his friends, especially on a day like today. That's humans for you. Even in our mourning we rely on fixed dates, temporal anchors where we can deposit our grief. When it's time to unlock our pain, it seems smaller than we remembered. Death is best left to the dead. The talk soon turned to the living. I met Gerhard Bohrmann recently. A nice man, affable and relaxed. After his experience, I'm not sure I'd ever want to go near the water again, but he takes the view that nothing could top La Palma. He's making lots of dive trips in an effort to assess the damage to the continental slopes. Yes, humans can venture under water again.

The attacks came to a halt soon after the *Independence* sank. At around that time the SOSUS arrays picked up some Scratch signals that were audible from one end of the ocean to the other. A few hours later, a rescue squad arrived at the seamount to liberate Bohrmann from his underwater cave, only to find that the sharks had disappeared. Overnight the whales returned to their normal routine. The worms vanished, as did the armies of jellies and all the other toxic creatures: crabs stopped invading the coast. Little by little the oceanic pump has eased back into action, in time to save us from an ice age. Even the hydrates are stabilising, or so Bohrmann tells me. To this day Karen doesn't know what she saw at the bottom of the Greenland Sea, but her idea must have worked. The Scratch signals coincide with her encounter with the queen. The Deepflight's computer logged the time at which she opened the pod to release Rubin's body, and not long afterwards the terror ceased.

Or was it merely suspended?

Are we using our reprieve?

I don't know. Europe is slowly recovering from the chaos left by the tsunami. Epidemics still plague the east coast of America, though the devastation is decreasing, and the serums have started to work. That's the good news. On the downside, the world is still reeling in confusion. How can mankind begin to heal its wounds when its identity is in pieces? The established religions can't offer any answers. Christianity is a case in point. Adam and Eve had long since handed over to the building blocks of evolution. The Church had no choice but to accept that mankind was born of proteins and amino acids, and not the archetypal human couple. Christianity could cope with that. What counted was God's *intention* to create us. It didn't especially matter *how* He did it, provided it happened in accordance with His plan. God does not play dice, as Einstein put it. Plans devised by God were inherently guaranteed to succeed. His infallibility was by definition *a priori*!

Even when speculation started about intelligence on other

planets, Christianity managed to keep pace. After all, wasn't God at liberty to replicate creation as often as He liked? There was nothing to say that alien life-forms had to resemble humans to be part of God's plan. Mankind was called into being as the perfect species for the specific environment created on God's Earth. Other planets had different environments, so it was reasonable to expect that alien life-forms wouldn't be the same. In any event, God created each different life-form in His image, which wasn't a contradiction, but a metaphorical turn of phrase. God's creatures didn't literally conform to His appearance, but to the vision in His mind's eye when He called them into being.

Yet there was a hitch. If it were true that the cosmos was populated with intelligent life-forms created by God, wouldn't the Son of God have come down to every planet? Wouldn't each of those alien races have sinned and been saved by the Messiah?

Naturally you could argue that a race created by God wouldn't necessarily sin. It might develop differently. An alien species on some faraway planet might adhere to God's laws and never need to be redeemed. But that was precisely the problem. In the eyes of the Lord, wouldn't a species living in accordance with His precepts be fundamentally *better* than humanity? Such a species would prove itself worthier of His love, and God would have to give it preference. With its history of misbehaviour, mankind would be relegated to the rank of a second-rate creation, having been flooded once already for its sins. Put more bluntly: mankind was no masterpiece. God had messed up. Having failed to prevent humans succumbing to sin, he had been forced to sacrifice His only son to expiate their guilt. Mankind gained free credit, which God paid for with Christ's blood. That wasn't the sort of decision a father would take lightly. God must have arrived at the conclusion that humanity was a mistake.

Soon scientists were postulating the existence of tens of thousands of civilisations in space. On balance, it seemed unlikely that all of those species would be paragons of virtue. Surely at least some would have fallen from grace and required a redeemer. When it came to the question of sin, Christianity knew no shades of grey, just dogma and principles. What mattered wasn't *how much* an individual had sinned, but that they had sinned in the first place.

877

God didn't strike deals, so to speak. A transgression of whatever kind was always a transgression. Punishment was punishment, and redemption, redemption.

It seemed reasonable to suppose that the story of deliverance wasn't a one-off. But what if God had found alternative means for redeeming the sins of creation? Could He have developed a new method of atonement that bypassed the death of His Son? Christian doctrine was faced with a problem. Christ's death had been agonising, but necessary, because God had chosen it as the only viable path. But what if there were other paths elsewhere? What did it say about God's infallibility if He sacrificed his son to wash away the sins of creation in one world and not in all the rest? Had He regretted the Passion and sought to avoid a recurrence? Why would anyone worship a God who didn't appear to be entirely on the ball?

The fact was, Christianity could only contemplate the existence of alien civilisations if every single one experienced the Passion. Any other scenario made either God or humanity look bad. But even the guardians of Christian orthodoxy could scarcely postulate the existence of a universe bursting with innumerable Passions of Christ. What other options remained?

Mankind's singularity on Earth.

God created this planet for humans, for God's own people, whom He entrusted with the task of subduing the Earth. Even if the universe were riddled with civilisations, and other intelligent beings came down to Earth, it wouldn't change a thing. Earth belonged to mankind, and the alien species had their dominion elsewhere. At home on their planet, each of God's species was God's chosen race.

But now the last bastion has fallen. The yrr have destroyed Christianity's last remaining big claim. It's not just the supremacy of mankind that's in question: it's the nature of God's plan. But suppose we were to resign ourselves to the idea that God created two equal races on Earth: the yrr would either have had to experience the Passion or live according to God's laws. Failing that, they must have sinned without redemption – but then they should have felt the fury of God's wrath.

Needless to say, the yrr don't live within God's tenets. For reasons of biology, they break the Fifth Commandment all the time. That leaves three possible explanations: (a.) God doesn't exist: (b.) He's not in control; or (c.) He approves of the yrr – which would mean that we've been labouring under a delusion that's as ancient as mankind. We weren't the ones who were chosen after all.

These are the kind of paroxysms that are shaking Christianity – not to mention Judaism and Islam. Each religion is trying to define, analyse and interpret what has happened, yet at the same time their very basis is collapsing, taking with it our crumbling economies, which relied on God's capital more heavily than we thought. At the same time, Buddhism and Hinduism, whose teachings have always accepted man's co-existence with other life-forms, are attracting people in their droves. Esoteric practices are booming, new religious movements are emerging, and traditional tribal religions are flourishing. Of all the old sects Mormonism is proving the most resilient, for the Mormon God provides for many different worlds. But even the Mormons can't explain why God raised two children within the same nursery.

In one recent development, a Catholic bishop has set sail with a delegation from Rome, sprinkling the waves with holy water and ordering the devil to depart. It's extraordinary: the very species that has systematically scorned God's principles and defiled His creation sends a so-called representative of the faith to take the enemy to task. We've got the cheek to cast ourselves as the prosecuting counsel for a Creator whose instructions we ignored. It's as though we're trying to preach the Gospel to our Maker in the hope that He might spare us.

The world is collapsing.

The UN has revoked the United States of America's leadership mandate. A futile gesture. Anarchy has broken out in many states. Wherever you turn, marauding masses are roaming the Earth. Armed conflicts are spreading. The weak are attacking the weaker. As creatures of animal instinct, it's not in our nature to take pity on others. Those who stumble are preyed on, and the plunder continues unchecked. The yrr didn't merely destroy our cities: they laid waste to us internally. We roam the Earth with nothing to believe in, abandoned savage children in search of a new beginning, but regressing all the time.

879

Yet there is also hope, the first signs that we're starting to re-evaluate the role of mankind on this planet. People are learning to grasp the diversity of nature, to understand its unifying principles and to sweep away the hierarchies and see the real connections. After all, the connections are what are keeping us alive. Has mankind ever considered the psychological impact of an impoverished planet on future generations? For all we know, the health of our psyche may depend on the existence of other animal species. Our minds yearn for forests, coral reefs, seas full of fish, fresh air, clean rivers and oceans. If we continue to damage the Earth and destroy the diversity of nature, we'll be destroying a complex system that we can't explain, let alone replace. What mankind separates can never be rejoined. Is there any part of the vast web of nature that we could live without? Who can tell? The secret of nature's connections depends on them staying intact. Humanity has overstepped the mark once already, and was almost excluded from the web of life. For the moment there's a truce. Whatever conclusions the yrr may be coming to, we'd do well to make their decision as straightforward as possible. They won't fall for Karen's trick a second time.

Today, a year after the vessel sank, I open the newspaper and read: 'The yrr have changed the world for ever.'

Have they?

They played a decisive role in our fate, yet we know virtually nothing about them. We think that we understand their biochemical make-up, but is that really knowledge? We haven't seen them since. Their signals still echo through the oceans, although we can't understand them as they're not meant for human ears. How does a mass of jelly create noise? How does it receive it? Just two among millions of futile questions. Only we can provide the answers. The onus lies with us.

Perhaps it's time for humanity to enter a new phase of evolution and finally reconcile our primordial genetic inheritance with our development as a civilised race. If we want to prove ourselves worthy of the gift that is the Earth, it isn't the yrr we should be studying but ourselves. Amid our skyscrapers and computers we've learned to disavow our nature, but the path to a better future lies in knowing our origins.

No, the yrr haven't changed the world. They've shown us how it really is.

Nothing is as it was. Although, come to think of it, I haven't stopped smoking.

We all need continuity of some kind, don't you think?